PENGUIN

BARNABY RUDGE

CHARLES DICKENS was born in Portsmouth on 7 February 1812, the second of eight children. Dickens's childhood experiences were similar to those depicted in *David Copperfield*. His father, who was a government clerk, was imprisoned for debt and Dickens was briefly sent to work in a blacking warehouse at the age of twelve. He received little formal education, but taught himself shorthand and became a reporter of parliamentary debates for the *Morning Chronicle*. He began to publish sketches in various periodicals, which were subsequently republished as *Sketches by Boz*. The *Pickwick Papers* was published in 1836–7 and after a slow start became a publishing phenomenon and Dickens's characters the centre of a popular cult. Part of the secret of his success was the method of cheap serial publication he adopted; thereafter, all Dickens's novels were first published in serial form. He began *Oliver Twist* in 1837, followed by *Nicholas Nickleby* (1838) and *The Old Curiosity Shop* (1840–41). After finishing *Barnaby Rudge* (1841) Dickens set off for America; he went full of enthusiasm for the young republic but, in spite of a triumphant reception, he returned disillusioned. His experiences are recorded in *American Notes* (1842). *A Christmas Carol*, the first of the hugely popular *Christmas Books*, appeared in 1843, while *Martin Chuzzlewit*, which included a fictionalized account of his American travels, was first published over the period 1843–4. During 1844–6 Dickens travelled abroad and he began *Dombey and Son* while in Switzerland. This and *David Copperfield* (1849–50) were more serious in theme and more carefully planned than his early novels. In later works, such as *Bleak House* (1853) and *Little Dorrit* (1857), Dickens's social criticism became more radical and his comedy more savage. In 1850 Dickens started the weekly periodical *Household Words*, succeeded in 1859 by *All the Year Round*; in these he published *Hard Times* (1854), *A Tale of Two Cities* (1859) and *Great Expectations* (1860–61). Dickens's health was failing during the 1860s and the physical strain of the public readings which he began in 1858 hastened his decline, although *Our Mutual Friend* (1865) retained some of his best comedy. His last novel, *The Mystery of Edwin Drood*, was never completed and he died on 9 June 1870. Public grief at his death was considerable and he was buried in the Poets' Corner of Westminster Abbey.

JOHN BOWEN was educated at Trinity Hall, Cambridge, and the Centre for Contemporary Cultural Studies, Birmingham, and is now a Reader in the Department of English, at Keele University. He is the author of *Other Dickens: Pickwick to Chuzzlewit* (Oxford University Press, 2000), a Trustee of the Dickens Society and a member of the faculty of the Dickens Project of the University of California.

CHARLES DICKENS

Barnaby Rudge

A Tale of the Riots of 'Eighty

Edited with an Introduction and Notes by
JOHN BOWEN

PENGUIN BOOKS

PENGUIN BOOKS

Published by the Penguin Group
Penguin Books Ltd, 80 Strand, London WC2R ORL, England
Penguin Putnam Inc., 375 Hudson Street, New York, New York 10014, USA
Penguin Books Australia Ltd, 250 Camberwell Road, Camberwell, Victoria 3124, Australia
Penguin Books Canada Ltd, 10 Alcorn Avenue, Toronto, Ontario, Canada M4V 3B2
Penguin Books India (P) Ltd, 11, Community Centre, Panchsheel Park, New Delhi – 110 017, India
Penguin Books (NZ) Ltd, Cnr Rosedale and Airborne Roads, Albany, Auckland, New Zealand
Penguin Books (South Africa) (Pty) Ltd, 24 Sturdee Avenue, Rosebank 2196, South Africa

Penguin Books Ltd, Registered Offices: 80 Strand, London WC2R ORL, England

www.penguin.com

First published in *Master Humphrey's Clock* in 1841
Published in Penguin Classics 2003

028

Editorial material copyright © John Bowen, 2003
A Dickens Chronology copyright © Stephen Wall, 1995
All rights reserved

The moral right of the editor has been asserted

Set in 9.75/11.75 pt PostScript Adobe Sabon
Typeset by Rowland Phototypesetting Ltd, Bury St Edmunds, Suffolk
Printed and bound in Great Britain by Clays Ltd, Elcograf S.p.A.

ISBN-13: 978-0-140-43728-7

www.greenpenguin.co.uk

Contents

Acknowledgements

I should like to thank Robert Mighall, who commissioned this edition; Gordon Spence, the editor of the previous Penguin edition of *Barnaby Rudge*, for generously responding to my queries; the British Library for supplying a microfilm of the first edition; Kath Begley at the Bank of England and the librarians at the Universities of Keele and Birmingham for their assistance. Michael Allen, Gill Ballinger, Hannah Barker, Malcolm Crook, Brian Harding, Colin Jones, Dick Leith, Fred Levit, Patrick McCarthy, David Parker, Roger Pooley, Michael Slater, Grahame Smith, Carolyn Steedman, Charles Swann, Andrew Xavier and Jack Zipes have also been most helpful. Lindeth Vasey has been the most scrupulous of copy-editors. Jim McLaverty has patiently answered questions on matters textual, and Sally Gray and Flora Bowen have given invaluable assistance throughout. I was lucky enough to have been invited to the annual Dickens Universe at the University of California, Santa Cruz in August 1999 when its proceedings were devoted to the study and discussion of *Barnaby Rudge*. I am particularly grateful to my fellow lecturers Patrick Brantlinger, John Glavin, David Parker, Hilary Schor, Jeff Spear, Robert Tracy and Judith Wilt, from whom I learned so much about a novel I had thought I knew well. To faculty members Murray Baumgarten, Florence Boos, Janice Carlisle, Maria Teresa Chialant, Joe Childers, Bill Daleski, Ed Eigner, Kathleen Hulley, Gerhard Joseph, Carol Mackay, Helena Michie, Goldie Morgentaler, George Newlin, Bob Newsom, Angelique Richardson, Catherine Robson and Michael Timko, to John Romano, JoAnna Rottke, Pat Vinci and all participants in that week, my warmest thanks. I owe a particular debt of gratitude to Catherine Gallagher, Martin Jay, John Jordan and Joss Marsh for their many kindnesses. The Dickens Universe at Santa Cruz and the work of the Dickens Project are models of intellectual collaboration and pleasure; for me the fires of Newgate will be forever mingled with the scent of redwoods on that beautiful campus.

A Dickens Chronology

1812 *7 February* Charles John Huffam Dickens born at Portsmouth, where his father is a clerk in the Navy Pay Office. The eldest son in a family of eight, two of whom die in childhood.

1817 After previous postings to London and Sheerness and frequent changes of address, John Dickens settles his family in Chatham.

1821 Dickens attends local school kept by a Baptist minister.

1822 Family returns to London.

1824 Dickens's father in Marshalsea Debtors' Prison for three months. During this time and afterwards Dickens employed in a blacking warehouse, labelling bottles. Resumes education at Wellington House Academy, Hampstead Road, London, 1825–7.

1827 Becomes a solicitor's clerk.

1830 Admitted as a reader to the British Museum.

1832 Becomes a parliamentary reporter after mastering shorthand. In love with Maria Beadnell, 1830–33. Misses audition as an actor at Covent Garden because of illness.

1833 First published story, 'A Dinner at Poplar Walk', in the *Monthly Magazine*. Further stories and sketches in this and other periodicals, 1834–5.

1834 Becomes reporter on the *Morning Chronicle*.

1835 Engaged to Catherine Hogarth, daughter of editor of the *Evening Chronicle*.

1836 *Sketches by Boz*, First and Second Series, published. Marries Catherine Hogarth. Meets John Forster, his literary adviser and future biographer. *The Strange Gentleman*, a farce, and *The Village Coquettes*, a pastoral operetta, professionally performed in London.

1837 *The Pickwick Papers* published in one volume (issued in monthly parts, 1836–7). Birth of a son, the first of ten children.

Death of Mary Hogarth, Dickens's sister-in-law. Edits *Bentley's Miscellany*, 1837–9.

1838 *Oliver Twist* published in three volumes (serialized monthly in *Bentley's Miscellany*, 1837–9). Visits Yorkshire schools of the Dotheboys type.

1839 *Nicholas Nickleby* published in one volume (issued in monthly parts, 1838–9). Moves to 1 Devonshire Terrace, Regents Park, London.

1841 Declines invitation to stand for Parliament. *The Old Curiosity Shop* and *Barnaby Rudge* published in separate volumes after appearing in weekly numbers in *Master Humphrey's Clock*, 1840–41. Public dinner in his honour at Edinburgh.

1842 *January–June* First visit to North America, described in *American Notes*, two volumes. Georgina Hogarth, Dickens's sister-in-law, becomes permanent member of the household.

1843 Speech on the Press to Printer's Pension Society, followed by others on behalf of various causes throughout Dickens's career. *A Christmas Carol* published in December.

1844 *Martin Chuzzlewit* published in one volume (issued in monthly parts, 1843–4). Dickens and family leave for Italy, Switzerland and France. Dickens returns to London briefly to read *The Chimes* to friends before its publication in December.

1845 Dickens and family return from Italy. *The Cricket on the Hearth* published at Christmas. Writes autobiographical fragment, ?1845–6, not published until included in Forster's *Life* (three volumes, 1872–4).

1846 Becomes first editor of the *Daily News* but resigns after seventeen issues. *Pictures from Italy* published. Dickens and family in Switzerland and Paris. *The Battle of Life* published at Christmas.

1847 Returns to London. Helps Miss Burdett Coutts to set up, and later to run, a 'Home for Homeless Women'.

1848 *Dombey and Son* published in one volume (issued in monthly parts, 1846–8). Organizes and acts in charity performances of *The Merry Wives of Windsor* and *Every Man in His Humour* in London and elsewhere. *The Haunted Man* published at Christmas.

1850 *Household Words*, a weekly journal 'Conducted by Charles Dickens', begins in March and continues until 1859. Dickens makes a speech at first meeting of Metropolitan Sanitary Association. *David Copperfield* published in one volume (issued in monthly parts, 1849–50).

1851 Death of Dickens's father and of infant daughter. Further theatrical activities in aid of the Guild of Literature and Art, including a performance before Queen Victoria. *A Child's History of England* appears at intervals in *Household Words*, published in three volumes (1852, 1853, 1854). Moves to Tavistock House, Tavistock Square, London.

1853 *Bleak House* published in one volume (issued in monthly parts, 1852–3). Dickens gives first public readings for charity (from *A Christmas Carol*).

1854 Visits Preston, Lancashire, to observe industrial unrest. *Hard Times* appears weekly in *Household Words* and is published in book form.

1855 Speech in support of the Administrative Reform Association. Disappointing meeting with now married Maria Beadnell.

1856 Dickens buys Gad's Hill Place, near Rochester.

1857 *Little Dorrit* published in one volume (issued in monthly parts, 1855–7). Dickens acts in Wilkie Collins's melodrama *The Frozen Deep* and falls in love with the young actress Ellen Ternan. *The Lazy Tour of Two Idle Apprentices*, written jointly with Wilkie Collins about a holiday in Cumberland, appears in *Household Words*.

1858 Publishes *Reprinted Pieces* (articles from *Household Words*). Separation from his wife followed by statement in *Household Words*. First public readings for his own profit in London, followed by provincial tour. Dickens's household now largely run by his sister-in-law Georgina.

1859 *All the Year Round*, a weekly journal again 'Conducted by Charles Dickens', begins. *A Tale of Two Cities*, serialized both in *All the Year Round* and in monthly parts, appears in one volume.

1860 Dickens sells London house and moves family to Gad's Hill.

1861 *Great Expectations* published in three volumes after appearing weekly in *All the Year Round* (1860–61). *The Uncommercial Traveller* (papers from *All the Year Round*) appears; expanded edition, 1868. Further public readings, 1861–3.

1863 Death of Dickens's mother, and of his son Walter (in India). Reconciled with Thackeray, with whom he had quarrelled, shortly before the latter's death. Publishes 'Mrs Lirriper's Lodgings' in Christmas number of *All the Year Round*.

1865 *Our Mutual Friend* published in two volumes (issued in monthly parts, 1864–5). Dickens severely shocked after a serious train accident at Staplehurst, Kent, when returning from France with Ellen Ternan and her mother.

1866 Begins another series of readings. Takes a house for Ellen at Slough. 'Mugby Junction' appears in Christmas number of *All the Year Round*.

1867 Moves Ellen to Peckham. Second journey to America. Gives readings in Boston, New York, Washington and elsewhere, despite increasing ill-health. 'George Silverman's Explanation' appears in *Atlantic Monthly* (then in *All the Year Round*, 1868).

1868 Returns to England. Readings now include the sensational 'Sikes and Nancy' from *Oliver Twist*; Dickens's health further undermined.

1870 Farewell readings in London. *The Mystery of Edwin Drood* issued in six monthly parts, intended to be completed in twelve.

9 June Dies, after stroke, at Gad's Hill, aged fifty-eight. Buried in Westminster Abbey.

Stephen Wall, 2002

Introduction

Barnaby Rudge is a novel full of mystery, and it is almost impossible to discuss the book without revealing some of its secrets. Readers new to the novel may prefer to read the story first and treat this introduction as a postscript.

I

Barnaby Rudge is the most untimely of historical novels. It was untimely in its birth, its publishers, its subject matter, its title and its initial reception. It is untimely still. Dickens's fifth novel was first published in his short-lived weekly magazine *Master Humphrey's Clock* in 1841, immediately following the triumphant success of *The Old Curiosity Shop*. Dickens was then at the top of the tree, at twenty-nine the most successful of all English novelists, with a popular following which had recently reached another peak with the heart-wringing (to contemporary readers at least) death of Little Nell. *Barnaby Rudge*, however, failed to repeat the success of its precursor, and the magazine's circulation fell steadily from an initial 70,000 to 30,000 by the end: a more than respectable number by most standards, but not those of Dickens, who had become used to an ever-rising reputation and readership. Unlike some of his critically less successful later novels, such as *Hard Times* or *Little Dorrit*, *Barnaby Rudge* has, so far, not been rescued by later generations and, despite some vigorous defences of its achievement, it has remained probably the least-liked and most neglected of his novels. Yet passages, particularly the scenes of the storming of Newgate, have long been among the most admired in his work, and have a continuing dramatic force and power. In part because of its comparative neglect, *Barnaby Rudge* still retains the power to shock and surprise its readers; it can still take our breath away.

Uniquely among Dickens's novels, the composition of *Barnaby Rudge* was repeatedly delayed. Dickens had first mooted a tale about the anti-Catholic Gordon Riots of 1780 (to be called 'Gabriel Vardon: The Locksmith of London') in 1836, seizing on one of the most dramatic episodes of popular unrest in London's history as the basis for his first attempt at an historical novel. He did not begin writing the book, however, until January 1839, but this was to be a false start, to be followed by another in October of that year; turning back to his manuscript once more in 1841, he succeeded in completing what was now called *Barnaby Rudge; A Tale of the Riots of 'Eighty*. The novel of Dickens most concerned with time and what appears in time consistently refused to appear on time. There were several reasons for this, not least his troubled relations with the three different publishers to whom at various points he had promised the book, but perhaps the most important was the quite unprecedented success of his first novel, *Pickwick Papers* (1836–7), which made his reputation as a novelist of contemporary life. Its successors – *Oliver Twist, Nicholas Nickleby, The Old Curiosity Shop* – built on this, and added a campaigning radicalism against social injustice. *Barnaby Rudge* was a departure in both subject matter and tone, with none of the vivid life of contemporary England that had made Dickens famous, and a more complex sense of political motivation and action. It was closer to the ideas and terrain of his great predecessor Sir Walter Scott, or of friends and rivals such as Edward Bulwer-Lytton and William Harrison Ainsworth, whose own novel about a great conflagration in London, *Old Saint Paul's*, was serialized in the *Sunday Times* at the same time as *Barnaby Rudge* was appearing. When Dickens first thought of writing an historical novel five years before as a struggling hack author, it had seemed to promise the chance of literary respectability as well as popular success. When it finally appeared, it did so within a literary culture that had been transformed by his own work.

Historical fiction was 'the most successful form of the century'[1] and one that almost every major figure of the age attempted at some stage in his or her career: not only Dickens with *A Tale of Two Cities* and *Barnaby Rudge*, but also William Makepeace Thackeray, Anthony Trollope, Elizabeth Gaskell, Wilkie Collins, George Eliot and Thomas Hardy. The historical novel had great appeal, both to readers and authors, from its emergence in the late eighteenth century with the novels of Scott; an appeal that continued throughout the nineteenth century. Yet today, as John Sutherland puts it, it is the 'least-honoured of Victorian fictional genres',[2] and there are miles of mouldering library shelves to confirm it. Nothing seems to date more quickly than a previous era's

view of the past, and even those novels by the masters of Victorian
prose are only marginal to our sense of their creators' achievement:
no one now would see *Romola* (1863) as George Eliot's greatest
work, admire Collins's *Antonina, or The Fall of Rome* (1850) over
The Woman in White (1860), or read Trollope's tedious *La Vendée*
(1850) in preference to the Barchester chronicles. Fiction's attempt
to master history leads, more often than not, to being made redun-
dant by it. Yet it was a persistent desire of Victorian novelists to
repeat the success of Scott and to raise the novel to the seriousness
and dignity that history was thought to offer, and to animate their
stories with a newly expanded historical knowledge, a desire too
often undercut by the wish for novelty and simple wish-fulfilment,
for stories of heroic apprentices, distressed virgins and villainous
barons.

Barnaby Rudge shares many characteristics with both 'serious'
historical novels and the more popular romances of Ainsworth and
G. P. R. James: it follows the progress of a number of characters,
from a range of social classes, and shows how their interlinked
fates develop through the course of a great historical action; it
contains, like so many novels of Scott and Ainsworth, a pair of
love stories that are hindered by social and religious barriers and
difficulties but which end triumphantly; it has a fast-paced and
gripping action, with a complex plot and highly dramatic encounters of competing individuals and social forces; it places 'real'
historical figures side by side with imaginary characters; it provides
a detailed topography of the places in which it is set, and takes
pains to be historically and geographically accurate. Like many
other historical novels of the period, it climaxes in a dramatic public
event – the storming of Newgate prison – which also decides the
fate of the individuals whose story we have followed. Like other
historical romances, it has conflicts of love and belief that cross
class boundaries, and a plot furnished with an upstart apprentice,
a scheming aristocrat, an heroic working man, a banished son,
a double murderer and no less than three abducted virgins.

Yet in many ways, *Barnaby Rudge* is an unusual and deviant
example of the form. It is only for example in Chapter the Thirty-
fourth, more than a third of the way through the book, that anything
remotely like an historical event takes place. Until then, the story
seems to be a romance or mystery tale concerning a double murder
and a strange disappearance twenty-two years before. Nor is

Barnaby Rudge a typical hero: he is a sort of idiot, and in the central action of the novel he is joined by other socially marginal and unheroic figures such as Dennis, the public hangman, and Hugh, the semi-human ostler. Indeed, at one point Dickens's intention was to have the Riots led by three escapees from Bedlam.[3] The plotting seems more to resemble that of a Gothic novel, full of ruins, secrets and ghostly reappearances. Gothic fiction, with stories often set in exotic and mysterious landscapes and buildings, and with plots which were nightmarish explorations of irrational fear and unearthly deeds, had flourished since the latter decades of the eighteenth century, although, by the 1840s, Gothic effects were increasingly confined to ephemeral and popular fiction. In *Barnaby Rudge*, alongside the normal causal mechanisms and events that we find in historical fiction, we constantly encounter uncanny effects and ghostly mysteries. Although there were precedents for this in Ainsworth's work in particular, Dickens uses the interplay of 'Gothic' and 'historical' elements in much more innovative and complex ways, which entangle the historical plot within the stranger, temporally dislocating, forces of Gothic. Modern history rests on our sense that the past is safely over and can become the subject of disinterested knowledge; the Gothic elements of *Barnaby Rudge* ensure that this novel carries no such reassurance.

For in this novel, history is a repetitive and strangely doubled business.[4] Instead of safely progressing, here things repeat and repeat. Characters, names, events, all return or are in danger of returning. This repetition is of various sorts: psychic repetition; repetition within families, particularly in the relation between fathers and sons; historical repetition where the present repeats the past; and traumatic repetition, where suffering and pain seem able to arrest and disorder time itself. The events of the latter part of the book, set in 1780, repeat those of the earlier chapters, set five years earlier, and both periods are haunted by the murder which occurred more than twenty years before as Rudge Senior, the man thought to be dead, comes back alive. For Lord George Gordon, the leader of the riots that bear his name and which come to dominate the book, the period he is living through is a repetition of the events of both the sixteenth century and the political settlement that debarred Roman Catholics from the throne, the 'Glorious Revolution' of 1688. Dickens's presentation of events, particularly the climactic burning of Newgate, is self-consciously a repetition

or echoing of scenes from the French Revolution, which began in
1789, only a few years later. The scenes also repeat or echo another
French Revolution, Thomas Carlyle's celebrated 1837 history, a
book which Dickens admired and which was later to colour deeply
his only other historical novel, *A Tale of Two Cities* (1859), which
resembles *Barnaby Rudge* in its subject matter and mode of writing,
but which it also differs from in substantial ways. Both books centre
on spectacular popular upheavals in the late eighteenth century and
the terror of mob rule, both climax with an escape from prison and
both move to redemptive and optimistic endings. *A Tale of Two
Cities* is, as its title hints, as fascinated and troubled as *Barnaby
Rudge* is by the power of doubling and repetition in history. But
the differences between the two books are equally striking, for *A
Tale of Two Cities* is a shorter and more tightly focused work which
subordinates Dickens's usual rich characterization and linguistic
inventiveness to the needs of a fast-paced and dramatic plot. Its
emphasis on incident over character, and dialogue over description,
has made *A Tale of Two Cities* successful and popular on a scale
that *Rudge* has never been – although *Tale*'s ability to win a
large readership has never really been matched by a corresponding
critical acclaim. Its promise is that revolutionary upheavals, however violent and distressing, can be transfigured by one man's
self-sacrificing love, while *Barnaby Rudge* has a more complex
sense of the strangeness of historical events and the inability of
human intentions and actions to influence them.

   Barnaby Rudge repeats in other ways too. It echoes the kind of
novels that had made Scott famous, for example, as well as certain
celebrated scenes within them, like the storming of the Tollbooth
in *The Heart of Mid-Lothian* (1818). It also represents (which is
itself a form of repetition) certain real persons, such as Gordon and
Edward Dennis, the public hangman from 1771 to 1786, who was
imprisoned for riot, and whose name Dickens borrows for his
fictional rioting hangman. The consequence is that there seem to
be many different competing times and temporalities imposed on
top of each other in the book: from Varden's secular and progressive
time and Rudge's haunted and repetitive life outside time to
Gordon's sacred and prophetic time. They are inextricably bound
together but difficult to reconcile to a single story or coherent
development. This historical doubling is seen as both necessary –
no historical understanding is possible without it – and a potentially

tragic error, for those, like Gordon, condemned to the misrecognitions it inevitably engenders.

In his influential study of the historical novel, George Lukács argued that the French Revolution marked an epoch in literary as well as political history.[5] The experience of the mass armies of the Napoleonic wars radically changed people's conception of themselves and their place in society, creating a qualitatively new and *historical* understanding of the world, as an apparently unchanging social order suddenly gave way to a much more unstable and openly conflictual society. But the French Revolution also saw the birth of an equally powerful and influential form, to which *Barnaby Rudge* has a strong affinity: melodrama. For Peter Brooks, in his classic account, the loss of the sacred and its institutions of Church and Monarchy at this period, and the eclipse of literary forms such as tragedy and the comedy of manners, led to a distinctively new *melodramatic* way of depicting and understanding the world.[6] Melodrama, both on stage and in fiction, he argues, stages a confrontation of absolute and contending moral forces, which through a procession of heightened and often implausible events leads to a purging of the social order and the triumphant display of moral purity and goodness. The language of melodrama moves to forms of absolute expression, to a perfect externalization of primordial and excessive emotion, to static and polarized oppositions. This leads not to an historical understanding but to the revelation of an essentially unhistorical 'moral occult' of dramatically opposed moral qualities, which entails 'a reassertion of magic and taboo, a recognition of the diabolical forces which inhabit our world and our inner being'.[7] This is true of much of *Barnaby Rudge*, a novel constantly drawn to vivid contrasts, implausible coincidences and heightened emotions: Barnaby's father, Rudge, for example, is described in characteristic passages as 'a spectre at . . . licentious feasts' (ch. 16) and 'a ghost upon the earth' (ch. 17), and his wife fears that the walls will drip blood at the mention of her name.

Historical fiction is drawn to the battlefield, to the confrontation of public choices and destinies; melodrama to the confines of castles and vaults. History is either the bearer and realizer of human progress through the struggle of classes; or, as in melodrama, a mere backdrop against which the more essential psychic conflicts of generations and families are played out. Perhaps all historical fiction, perhaps all fiction, partakes of both these modes of understanding, but *Barnaby Rudge* is peculiarly torn by the conflicting claims of popular mass action and public conflict on the one hand, and psychic terror and the conflict of generations on the other. Indeed, it could almost be said that *Barnaby Rudge* stages the war of these two forces, these two understandings, these two world views – the historical and the melodramatic. In that conflict we find the book's continuing and disturbing power.

2

It is often thought that Dickens's decision to use the Gordon Riots as the subject of his novel was an eccentric one and that they were an historically marginal event, chosen simply for the sake of a vivid climax in the burning down of Newgate at the end.[8] Although the Riots create little resonance today, this was far from the case when Dickens was writing, for they were 'the largest, deadliest and most protracted urban riots in British history' and took place a mere two generations before the book's publication.[9] Nor were they a throwback to an earlier, more intolerant age or simply an excuse for thuggish violence, for they articulated an essential component of British national identity, its Protestantism, and one which was a continuing and living force in Dickens's day. In 1828–9, for example, in the build-up to the legislation that released Catholics from most legal disabilities, there were hundreds of anti-Catholic petitions to Parliament and in Dickens's county of Kent a meeting of 60,000 anti-Catholic protesters and the widespread circulation of anti-Catholic tracts that would have warmed the cockles of Mrs Varden and her fellow-proselytes.[10] For the British throughout the eighteenth and well into the nineteenth century, as Linda Colley has written, 'the struggles of the Protestant reformation had not ended, but were to be fought over and over again'.[11]

Dickens thus chose an event that encapsulated a central part of the political history of both the previous century and his own, in which two of the major forces that shaped the national polity were at work: the fear of insurrection and popular anti-Catholicism. Lukács in *The Historical Novel* dismissed Dickens's historical fiction on the grounds that their historical settings were used simply as a background to provide 'purely accidental circumstances for "purely human" tragedies'.[12] This is a misleading judgement, because Dickens here brilliantly seized on a significant moment in national history, which since at least the time of Edmund Burke's *Reflections on the Revolution in France* (1790) had been seen 'not as an isolated eruption of disorder but as a failed revolution' with Gordon himself an 'archetypal revolutionary figure' who embodied some of the most threatening and unstable forces of the age.[13] Dickens was personally sympathetic to Gordon, describing him as 'at heart a kind man, and a lover of the despised and rejected, after his fashion',[14] but could see in the riots that bear his name a set of events both exceptional in their scale and representative of a vital strain in national self-formation. His dramatization of these riots reveals a complex tangle of forces and motives underpinning a profoundly ambiguous set of events, which are simultaneously an attempted *coup d'état*, a popular uprising and a religious pogrom.

Identity, whether national or personal, constitutes itself largely through what it desires and what it rejects or expels, and British identity in this period drew on 'a vast superstructure of prejudice' to attack and scapegoat the many 'men and women who were not allowed to be British so that others could be'.[15] Dickens is deeply sympathetic to the victimized Catholics of the story: Geoffrey Haredale is consummately virtuous, and it is his enemy, the sinister Protestant conspirator Sir John Chester, who has the classically 'Jesuitical' qualities of deceit and guile. The Protestant Association is brutal and bigoted, and it is Dennis the public hangman who describes his job as 'sound, Protestant, constitutional, English work' (ch. 37). As so often in Walter Scott's novels, romantic love – here that of Emma Haredale and Edward Chester – has to overcome religious difference as well as family enmity in its passage to happiness. But Dickens looks forward as well as back, for, as the nineteenth century progressed, encounters with the Catholic 'other' of British identity were increasingly supplanted by similarly polarized and complex encounters with Colonial 'others', who were equally desired and feared. In this novel full of doubles, the meetings and conflicts of Protestant and Catholic which dominate the action are doubled by offstage colonial confrontations and exchanges: Edward goes to the West Indies to free himself from his father's sway, and Joe Willet finds his self by losing his arm in the American War of Independence.[16]

In the main action, political questions, as so often in Dickens's novels, are entangled with those of justice and the law. When the novel opens, this appears to be an essentially private matter: the unsolved mystery of Reuben Haredale's murder. As the book develops, it becomes a matter of public policy and struggle, as Gordon's mob besieges the Houses of Parliament in an attempt to force it to repeal the Catholic Relief Act, and the Riots culminate in the burning of the house of the Lord Chief Justice, Lord Mansfield. Dickens's relationship to the law throughout his career is a complex one, in which he is drawn to the enforcement of the law in his fiction while taking an often disturbing delight in its transgression. While planning the novel he wrote in a letter to John Cay, an Edinburgh lawyer, to say that 'I think I can make a better riot than Lord George Gordon did',[17] and nearing its completion gleefully wrote to his friend and future biographer, John Forster, that he had 'let all the prisoners out of Newgate, burnt down Lord Mansfield's, and played the very devil. Another number will finish the fires, and help us on towards the end. I feel quite smoky when I am at work.'[18] Often savagely critical of the existing legal apparatus, Dickens is rarely simply an exponent or enactor of the law, nor is he an anarchic opponent of it. It is probably best to think of him as what we could call a *paranomian*, a figure who simulates and disorders the law, and yet also holds out the hope and possibility of a better justice.

Many of the most important scenes in Dickens's fiction take place in prison, and *Barnaby Rudge* is no exception. His father had been imprisoned for debt when Dickens was a boy, and it is only in prison that Barnaby can meet his own errant father. More darkly, in one of the more grotesque scenes in a novel full of grotesquerie, Dennis the hangman breaks into Newgate in company with the rioters in order to gloat over the deaths of the men in the condemned cells, trapped by the fire that is supposed to liberate them. Dickens here takes one of the most important images of Romantic literature and culture, that of liberation from a prison, and turns it into something more sinister. For many nineteenth-century writers, history was the history of human beings gradually learning to choose the form of their society and culture and in the process liberating themselves from the tyranny of superstition. Although there are occasions when men and women make their own history in this book, as when Gabriel Varden heroically resists the mob, more often characters find themselves trapped in actions or patterns of behaviour without apparent sense or reason. This is often an

uncanny matter, as when Haredale, for all his virtue, is finally led
or driven to the Warren where he meets, fatally, the phantom that
has haunted him so long. Much of the time, the characters seem
to move without foreknowledge, their actions contradictory and
self-defeating: some of the anti-Catholic rioters, Dickens tells us at
the end, 'owned themselves to be catholics' (ch. 77).

The psychic life of the novel is thus as strange as the events it
depicts. There is a repeated emphasis on the violence of history and
the mental disturbance and disorder that both precedes and is
caused by it. In Dickens's account, Gordon is a sort of political
hysteric, who suffers from a compulsive need to remember and
re-enact the past, projecting his psychic disorder on to public life,
just as Sim Tappertit directs his adolescent resentment into the
fantasies of the Apprentice Knights. Perhaps the most remarkable
is the character of Barnaby himself, who must be one of the most
unusual heroes of any Victorian novel. Dickens had pioneered in
Oliver Twist and *The Old Curiosity Shop* the use of children as
the moral and emotional centres of the books. Here, he attempts
something even more difficult and surprising: naming a novel after
someone as socially marginal and intellectually weak as Barnaby is
a remarkable act of confidence in his own dramatic powers. The
nature of Barnaby's condition has been disputed over the years.
Dickens clearly draws on the tradition of the 'holy fool' who is wise
as well as foolish, and on figures from Romantic literature such as
Wordsworth's 'The Idiot Boy' and Scott's Madge Wildfire in *The
Heart of Mid-Lothian*, but there is also something dangerous about
him: the narrator at one point describes the state of his mind as
'ghastly' and 'cunning' (ch. 25).[19] It is in Hugh, the ostler at the
Maypole, however, who we later learn is the illegitimate son of Sir
John Chester, where desire and violence unconstrained by rational
thought are most deeply explored by Dickens. Like Barnaby, his
mental affliction seems deeply, if obscurely, linked to the evil and
neglect he suffers from his father; unlike Barnaby he is dangerous
both sexually and politically. Mental disorder is not just the property of these characters however, and the novel moves towards a
number of climactic events – the sacking of the Maypole, the
burning of the Warren, the fall of Newgate – all of which have
psychically devastating consequences for those who experience or
witness them. Indeed, the whole novel is built around traumatic
events, as when John Willet watches the total destruction of his

world in the sacking of the Maypole or Rudge Senior in prison is 'fearful alike, of those within the prison and of those without; of noise and silence; light and darkness; of being released, and being left there to die' (ch. 65). It is almost as if to witness or experience any historical event in this book is to suffer trauma: a single glimpse of the condemned men escaping from Newgate, writes the narrator, is 'an image of force enough to dim the whole concourse; to find itself an all-absorbing place, and hold it ever after' (ch. 65).

As we witness these historical convulsions, we recognize the difficulty of expressing them in language. When Gordon first enters public political life, he does so 'as suddenly as he appears in these pages' (ch. 37), without cause, precedent or reason. The most significant events in the book, both private and public, seem to stand outside time: Reuben Haredale appears to his murderer, even twenty-eight years after his death, 'never changed . . . never grown older, nor altered in the least degree' (ch. 62), just as for John Willet, 'old Time lay snoring, and the world stood still' (ch. 55) from the moment his beloved sanctuary at the Maypole is violated. The novel constantly emphasizes the impossibility of relying on one's senses to understand the world – many things in the Riots, comments the narrator, are 'like nothing that we know of, even in our dreams' (ch. 65) – and repeatedly takes the reader to paradoxical and contradictory states of mind and feeling. The 'monstrous and improbable' events of the Riots, 'but that we know them to be matter of history', comments the narrator, would be 'rejected . . . as wholly fabulous and absurd' (ch. 54). The book, which begins by taking its place within a dominant strand of early Victorian representations of the past, that of picturesque history, increasingly comes to figure history not as picturesque, but sublime, exceeding and defeating expression in language.[20]

3

Barnaby Rudge was written as the political unrest of one decade – the 'Angry Thirties' – turned into the suffering of the 'Hungry Forties', and a long trade depression threw millions of men and women out of work, with enormous consequent social distress and popular anger. Working people had no formal political representation, and there was little regulation of the often appalling conditions under which they worked. The Chartist agitation for political rights and enfranchisement was moving to its height, and there was widespread fear of bloody social upheaval as mass meetings, riots and uprisings regularly erupted within the political landscape. Dickens was sympathetic to many of the goals of the Chartist movement and consistently identified himself as radical at this period, as he did for much of his life: *Oliver Twist* had campaigned against the new Poor Law, *Nicholas Nickleby* against the abuses of the Yorkshire schools, and *The Old Curiosity Shop*, *Barnaby Rudge*'s immediate precursor, had contained some particularly moving encounters between Nell and the unemployed, starving poor of the Black Country. After the victory of the conservative Robert Peel in the election of June–July 1841, Dickens wrote a set of anti-Tory verses, of which the best is 'The Fine Old English Gentleman'; it satirizes nostalgia for an England of the past, which Dickens saw as oppressive and tyrannical, a time of 'gibbets, whips and chains'.[21] Writing to Forster in the middle of *Barnaby Rudge*, he exclaimed: 'By Jove how radical I am getting! I wax stronger and stronger in the true principles every day.'[22]

Barnaby Rudge at first seems to share Dickens's characteristic impatience with political conservatism and reaction. It is, for example, the absurd fantasizing apprentice Tappertit, not the heroic and admirable Varden, who wants to recapture the past through the secret organizations of the Apprentice Knights and United Bulldogs. One of the most savagely critical scenes Dickens ever wrote is the meeting in Chapter the Forty-seventh between the Tory country magistrate and the homeless and pathetic Barnaby and his mother. The magistrate is an illiterate drunkard and a bully who uses his power to oppress both his wife and the poor. In the two novels written immediately before this, the central protagonists leave London and become performers – Nicholas Nickleby at Crummles's theatre and Little Nell at Mrs Jarley's waxworks – where they find havens of friendship and security from the evil forces that pursue them. Here, the opposite occurs: Barnaby and his pet raven, Grip, are forced to perform for the magistrate, which brings them in danger of imprisonment or worse. Whereas the earlier novels had created counter-worlds of theatre and entertainment, which embodied values excluded by the dominant world of the novel, here performance is foolish and potentially deadly, both in Grip's performance and Sim's theatrical and preposterous Apprentice Knights. One of the most highly valued things in Dickens's work becomes nightmarish and oppressive, so that even the traumatic destruction of the Maypole Inn seems like a 'queer play or entertainment' (ch. 54).

Although *Barnaby Rudge* is clearly hostile to such authority figures such as Sir John Chester, John Willet and the Tory country magistrate, it is often seen, with good reason, as one of the more conservative of Dickens's works, as is clear in its treatment of popular insurrection. Dickens was troubled by the possibility that events of the early 1840s were repeating those of the 1780s, in particular the alliance the Gordon Riots epitomized between ultra-conservative forces (represented by the manipulative Sir John Chester) and the explosive force of the radical mob, led by Barnaby, Hugh and Sim.[23] Not surprisingly therefore, Dickens's treatment of the Riots is singularly ambivalent. They are political in one sense – Gordon wished to change the law through petitioning Parliament – but the motives that lead people to participate in them are any-thing but. Although Gordon himself is sympathetically treated, Dickens clearly did not think of him as being in his right mind, and he is egged on throughout the book by his sinister and malevolent secretary, Gashford. His followers whom we see most clearly are Hugh, Dennis and Barnaby: none is heroic, two are utterly amoral and one (Barnaby) pathetic and misled. Although the Riots them-selves are a popular uprising, they do not have radical aims but reactionary ones in Dickens's telling: to attack and persecute a religious minority. Political violence is seen as essentially pathologi-cal, its motivations either trivial or capricious.

More surprisingly, perhaps, the political activity of the book is deeply enmeshed in Gothic and melodramatic material. Political activity in Gordon's case is seen as a strange kind of haunting or echo chamber, on the edge of insanity. For Gashford the threat of Catholic emancipation means that 'Queen Elizabeth . . . weeps within her tomb, and Bloody Mary, with a brow of gloom and shadow, stalks triumphant' (ch. 35). Tappertit can become an historical agent only by wearing a three-cornered hat and wav-ing a thigh-bone about in a grotesque parody of contemporary trades union ceremonies.[24] Gordon and the Apprentice Knights resemble nothing so much as Karl Marx's description of the later, more successful, conservative revolutionaries who brought Louis

Napoleon Bonaparte to the throne of France: 'they timidly conjure up the spirits of the past to help them; they borrow their names, slogans and costumes so as to stage the new world-historical scene in this venerable disguise and borrowed language'.[25] At times, the historical novel itself becomes a strange or ghostly doubling of history – both of the historical events themselves and of their narration in later sources. All writing has a ghostly quality, conjuring up the presence of things when there is nothing there, but historical novels, particularly one as haunted as *Barnaby Rudge*, provide a peculiarly intense version of this experience, a story of ghosts of ghosts of ghosts.

A ghost is an anomalous and repetitious presence in the human world which brings something from the past that is simultaneously an inheritance and an obligation. *Barnaby Rudge* is very concerned with the nature of inheritance, in particular what we inherit from our parents. Although there are important relationships between mothers and their children in the book, in particular that of Barnaby and Mary Rudge, who show a deep mutual devotion, they are dwarfed in significance by the conflicts of fathers and sons. Indeed, Steven Marcus has gone so far as to say that the novel only 'contemplates one kind of relation – that of fathers and sons'.[26] Apart from Gabriel Varden, who is a much more sympathetic character than his wife Martha, fathers in the book are deeply oppressive and tyrannical figures. The most striking example of this is John Willet's treatment of his son Joe, whom he constantly humiliates, diminishing his stature, treating him as a child, refusing him recognition of his adult masculinity, castrating him, in short. Sir John Chester unites the personal and political forms of oppression in the book, a desperately bad father to his two sons and a wholly immoral Member of Parliament and public figure. Rudge, Barnaby's father, is an even more disturbing figure, closer to what Slavov Zizek describes as the 'obscene father', and Patrick Brantlinger calls a terrifying 'undead, unholy figure ... embodiment of everyone's worst nightmares, the demon-father whose own demon-father is, according to Gothic convention, the Devil'.[27] Radically evil, Rudge is said to have sold his soul to the devil, existing in a strange half-life, haunting, but also human enough to be haunted. Mrs Rudge, pregnant with Barnaby, sees her husband after his murder of Reuben Haredale, and her child is marked for ever by the physical scar, and perhaps also the mental affliction, that is the result of this encounter. Like Hamlet, Barnaby is haunted by the ghost of his father.

In the end, however, Dickens wants to have nothing to do with ghosts, or at least is determined to lay them to rest. At the beginning of Chapter the Thirty-seventh, in an important passage about a recurrent interest, Dickens had written:

To surround anything, however monstrous or ridiculous, with an air of mystery, is to invest it with a secret charm, and power of attraction which to the crowd is irresistible. False priests, false prophets, false doctors, false patriots, false prodigies of every kind, veiling their proceedings in mystery, have always addressed themselves at an immense advantage to the popular credulity, and have been, perhaps, more indebted to that resource in gaining and keeping for a time the upper hand of Truth and Common Sense, than to any half-dozen items in the whole catalogue of imposture.

This novel is, of course, constructed through just such forces. Airs of mystery, monstrous and ridiculous events and characters, prodigies, secret powers and things veiled in mystery drive forward its plot and action. But the novel promises that 'Truth and Common Sense' will prevail and the ghosts, who so trouble the boundaries between public life and private hallucination, between the living and the dead and the virtuous and the evil, will all be exorcized. The strange forces embodied by the rioters are expunged through the deaths of Hugh and Dennis, just as Sir John Chester and Geoffrey Haredale's relationship comes to a poetically just end and a second Maypole Inn arises from the ashes of the old. There is a return at the end of the book to property, possession and inheritance, to a wholesale restoration of patriarchal order, as Gabriel Varden is superlatively restored as 'the centre of the system: the source of light, heat, life, and frank enjoyment' (ch. 80) of his household.

However, one aspect of the ghostly and uncanny forces is not so easily exorcized. Early on in the writing of the novel, Dickens told Forster of his plans to have Barnaby accompanied by 'a pet raven who is immeasurably more knowing than himself. To this end, I have been studying my bird, and think I could make a very queer character of him.'[28] John Ruskin described the book as 'an entirely profitless and monstrous story, in which the principal characters are a coxcomb, an idiot, a madman, a savage blackguard, a foolish tavern-keeper, a mean old maid and a conceited apprentice', the whole thing 'a filthy mass', but nevertheless found Grip delightful.[29] The bird resembles the trickster figure in Native American folklore (often embodied as ravens or crows) who 'continually violates the boundary between nature and culture' and is not guided by moral conceptions of good and evil.[30] A spirit of disorder, an enemy of boundaries, he is inassimilable to rational or coherent explanation, a figure for what is the evil or waste of historical understanding. In a novel deeply interested in and committed to the binary logics both of historical conflict – Protestant versus Catholic; order opposed to disorder – and of melodrama – good against evil; innocence confronting guilt – Grip and his inhumanly human speech are the remainder of the system, what cannot be thought of or narrated within such polarities. It is impossible to decide who or what he is – harmless pet or an evil spirit – or to domesticate him within the homes of the novel or history. He is also, of course, much more intelligent than his master, Barnaby. In his *Twilight of the Idols or How to Philosophize with a Hammer*, Friedrich Nietzsche wondered if wisdom 'would perhaps appear on earth as a raven'.[31] It was a question Charles Dickens had asked himself half a century before.

4

Barnaby Rudge first appeared in Dickens's weekly magazine, *Master Humphrey's Clock*, which was originally intended as a miscellany to which other authors could contribute.[32] This would have taken some of the pressure off him always to be writing new full-length novels, but, for better or worse, it was not successful with the public, and Dickens rapidly changed his original plan by extending one of his early stories, 'The Old Curiosity Shop', into a full-length novel, and then immediately following this with *Barnaby Rudge*. The opening numbers of the magazine, however, had created an elaborate framework of narrators and narrative scenes within which both novels appeared. The main narrator is Master Humphrey, an elderly gentleman, in company with his equally eccentric and solitary friends, who tell each other stories, usually historical or Gothic, which they discover in Master Humphrey's clock-case. Although these are anonymous, the writer of *Barnaby*

Rudge, according to Humphrey, is Jack Redburn, 'something of a musician, something of an author, something of an actor, something of a painter, very much of a carpenter, and an extraordinary gardener'.[33] Moreover, this 'whimsical jumble' of a man, it is hinted, has mingled with the story 'something of his own endurance and experience'. At the end of the novel, which was also the end of the magazine, Humphrey's friend, the Deaf Gentleman, makes this hint more explicit by telling us that Redburn's story 'may possibly be shadowed out in the history of Mr Chester and his son'.[34] It is a surprising, disturbing thought that the upright and upstanding young man who we have just seen in the novel some fifty years before happily married to Emma Haredale with a large family has become this impoverished eccentric. It is, by any standards, an unlikely and tenuous link between the novel and the magazine, but it is of a piece with the story's consistent wish to trouble the boundaries between inside and outside, and past and present, and our sense of what it is to have a human identity. Jack Redburn and Master Humphrey will not let us believe either that we know for sure where *Barnaby Rudge* comes from or that we are now finished with the story and can safely let it go. Edward Chester, like Barnaby's father, has come back, much later, in a most unexpected and disturbing place and form.

Dickens never wrote at length about his aesthetic ideas and beliefs, and published relatively little criticism of other people's writing. The great span of his letters, however, now published in full, provides a very rich self-portrait and some revealing remarks on his creative life. Reporting himself 'fearfully hard at work, morning, noon, and night' during the composition of *Barnaby Rudge*, he told Forster near its end with typical confidence: 'I was always sure I could make a good thing of *Barnaby*, and I think you'll find that it comes out strong to the last word.'[35] In a letter to John Landseer, the distinguished painter, who had dared to proffer him advice about his depiction of the riots, Dickens wrote:

in the description of such scenes, a broad, bold, hurried effect must be produced, or the reader instead of being forced and driven along by imaginary crowds will find himself dawdling very uncomfortably through the town, and greatly wondering what may be the matter. In this kind of work, the object is, – not to tell everything, but to select the striking points and beat them into the page with a sledge-hammer . . . my object has been to convey an idea of multitudes, violence, and fury; and even to lose my own dramatis personae in the throng, or only to see them dimly, through the fire and smoke.[36]

They are important and revealing remarks, emphasizing the *power* of writing, a power strong enough to force and drive its readers as if in a mighty crowd, and for the writer himself to lose sight of his own characters. It is also a deeply cinematic vision of narrative and of the urban crowd as the novel's greatest subject.

Part of this power comes from the very close relationship between Dickens's text and the many illustrations of the book. Harrison Ainsworth, Dickens's friend and rival, had already changed the nature of the historical novel both by 'fusing . . . violent history with Gothic accessories and characters' and by working in collaborative ways with his illustrators, in particular the brilliant George Cruik-shank.[37] Dickens also took great care with the illustrations to *Barnaby Rudge* and asked George Cattermole, a well-known painter and illustrator who specialized in architectural and antiquarian topics, to join Hablot Browne ('Phiz'), the artist most closely associated with his work, who had already illustrated *Pickwick Papers*, *Nicholas Nickleby* and *The Old Curiosity Shop*, in illustrating the book. Cattermole ('Kittenmoles' to Dickens) contributed seventeen beautifully detailed cuts, mainly of buildings and settings, to the book and Browne another fifty-nine. As for *The Old Curiosity Shop*, the illustrations were not the steel engravings on separate pages which Dickens used in the majority of his works, but woodcuts which could be placed with great accuracy in the text, able not only to illustrate but also to punctuate, interrupt or emphasize points in the narrative. Dickens was delighted with the result and wrote enthusiastically to Cattermole 'this is the *very first time* any designs for what I have written have touched and moved me and caused me to feel that they expressed the idea I had in my mind'.[38]

This confidence in the power of the book and its illustrations was unfortunately not echoed by contemporary readers and reviewers, one of whom renamed it *Barnaby Rubbish*. Although Dickens had basked in public acclaim since *Pickwick Papers* had made him a celebrity at 25, and had recently triumphantly liquefied the hearts of the nation with the death of Little Nell, *Barnaby Rudge* was never a popular book. Perhaps surprisingly, many nineteenth-century readers found Dolly Varden the novel's most interesting character. Indeed, Dolly has a rich cultural history in her own right, inspiring songs, paintings and fashions, and giving her name to a buffer on a railway tender,[39] as well as a species of trout and a kind of horse. Despite her popularity, however, contemporary reviews, which were far fewer than for his earlier works, 'ranged from the negative to the severe'.[40] Many of his contemporaries doubtless felt that Dickens had become over-familiar, writing as he had done so much at such speed, others that the historical subject matter did not really suit his gifts. A trade depression when the novel was published cannot have helped either. Others felt that the problem lay with the structure of the story, in particular the strange narrative break or hiatus that occurs with the arrival of Gordon in Chapter the Thirty-fourth. Even Forster felt constrained to say that 'The interest with which the tale begins, has ceased to be its interest before the close.'[41] But the problem may be a deeper one, lying in the view of history the novel implies. *Barnaby Rudge*, it is clear, belongs to the genre and history of the historical novel, but does not safely or easily find a home there. Its relationship to its fictional antecedents – to Scott in particular – seems to be that of a wicked and not a good son. Public history and family life alike are crossed in the novel by uncanny forces, by the power of ghosts, dreams and prophecy, by hauntings that trouble the boundary between the human and inhuman. Its most important character is an immortal talking bird. In its attempt to write a narrative equal to the convulsions of history, the book is drawn to figures – the living dead, ghosts, shadows, monsters – which are usually at the very margins of historical understanding. What are often seen as failures or flaws in the novel may simply be its resistance to our common assumptions about history, causality and narration.

NOTES

1. Franco Moretti, *An Atlas of the European Novel 1800–1900* (London: Verso, 1999), p. 33.
2. John Sutherland, *Longman Companion to Victorian Fiction* (London: Longman, 1988), p. 297.
3. John Forster, *The Life of Charles Dickens* (London: Chapman and Hall, 1872–4), Bk 2, ch. 9; ed. A. J. Hoppé (London: Dent, 1966), Vol. I, p. 142.

4. On repetition in historical fiction, see J. Hillis Miller, '*Henry Esmond*: Repetition and Irony', in *Fiction and Repetition* (Cambridge: Harvard University Press, 1982), pp. 73–115.

5. George Lukács, *The Historical Novel* (Harmondsworth: Penguin, 1969), pp. 20–24.

6. Peter Brooks, *The Melodramatic Imagination: Balzac, Henry James, Melodrama and the Mode of Excess* (New Haven: Yale University Press, 1976), pp. 11–15.

7. Ibid., pp. 18–19.

8. On the history of the riots, see Appendix VI and Further Reading.

9. Linda Colley, *Britons: Forging the Nation 1707–1837* (London: Vintage, 1996), p. 352.

10. Ibid., p. 351. A possible source for Dickens's depiction of Gordon and the rioters is the Kent uprising, which was widely reported in the press in June 1838, of 'Sir William Percy Honeywood Courtenay'. Courtenay, or John Thom, led what E. P. Thompson called 'the last peasants' revolt' (*The Making of the English Working Class* (Harmondsworth: Penguin, 1968), p. 881), which was eventually put down by troops with the loss of several lives. There are a number of parallels between contemporary accounts of these events and Dickens's portrayal of Gordon and his followers. For an excellent account of the significance of Courtenay, see Richard Stein, *Victoria's Year: English Literature and Culture 1837–8* (New York: Oxford University Press, 1987), pp. 169–76.

11. Colley, *Britons*, p. 351.

12. Lukács, *The Historical Novel*, pp. 292–3.

13. Ian McAlman, 'Prophesying Revolution: "Mad Lord George", Edmund Burke and Madame La Motte', in *Living and Learning: Essays in Honour of J. F. C. Harrison*, ed. Malcolm Chase and Ian Dyck (Aldershot: Scolar, 1996), p. 53.

14. 3 June 1841, *The Letters of Charles Dickens, Volume 2, 1840–1*, ed. Madeline House and Graham Storey (Oxford: Clarendon Press, 1969), pp. 294–5.

15. Colley, *Britons*, pp. 38, 57.

16. '[T]he younger (masculine) generation achieves its identity and masculinity in America and the West Indies, while the older generation . . . plays out the final act of the Roman and the English, the Jesuit and the Virgin', Judith Wilt, 'Masques of the English in *Barnaby Rudge*', *Dickens Studies Annual* 30 (2001), 78.

17. 21 July 1841, *Letters of Charles Dickens*, p. 337.

18. 18 September 1841, ibid., p. 385.

19. Sally Shuttleworth, '"So childish and so dreadfully un-childlike": Cultural Constructions of Idiocy in the Mid-Nineteenth Century', in *Crossing Boundaries: Thinking through Literature*, ed. Julie Scanlon and Amy Waste (Sheffield: Sheffield Academic Press, 2001).

20. On 'picturesque history' in this period, see Rosemary Mitchell, *Picturing the Past: English History in Text and Image* (Oxford: Clarendon, 2000). Asking George Cattermole, one of the book's illustrators, to depict the ruins of the Warren, Dickens writes 'I think it would make a queer picturesque thing in your hands' (*Letters of Charles Dickens*, p. 352).

21. *Examiner*, 7 August 1841, reprinted in Forster, *The Life of Charles Dickens*, Bk 2, ch. 12; Hoppé, Vol. I, pp. 164–5.

22. 6 August 1841, *Letters of Charles Dickens*, p. 357.

23. See Thomas Jackson Rice, 'The Politics of *Barnaby Rudge*', in *The Changing World of Charles Dickens*, ed. Robert Giddings (London: Vision, 1986), pp. 51–74.

24. See E. P. Thompson, *The Making of the English Working Class* (Harmondsworth: Penguin, 1968), p. 559.

25. Karl Marx, 'The Eighteenth Brumaire of Louis Napoleon Bonaparte', in *Surveys from Exile: Political Writings*, Vol. 2, ed. David Fernbach (Harmondsworth: Penguin, 1973), p. 146.

26. Steven Marcus, 'Sons and Fathers', *Dickens: From Pickwick to Dombey* (London: Chatto and Windus, 1963), p. 184.

27. Slavov Zizek, *Enjoy Your Symptom!: Jacques Lacan In Hollywood and Out* (London: Routledge, 1992), pp. 124–5; Patrick Brantlinger, *The Reading Lesson: The Threat of Mass Literacy in Nineteenth-Century British Fiction* (Bloomington: Indiana University Press, 1998), p. 31.

28. *Letters of Charles Dickens*, pp. 197–8.

29. John Ruskin, *The Complete Works of John Ruskin*, ed. E. T. Cook and Alexander Wedderburn, Vol. XXII (London: George Allen, 1906), p. 467. In 'Fiction, Fair and Foul' Ruskin describes the novel as a product of 'brain disease' which 'runs entirely wild'. Ruskin, *The Complete Works*, Vol. XXIV, pp. 278–9.

30. Paul Radin, *The Trickster* (New York: Schrocken, 1972), p. 155.

31. Friedrich Nietzsche, 'The Problem of Socrates', in *Twilight of the Idols or How to Philosophize with a Hammer*, trans. Duncan Large (Oxford: Oxford University Press, 1998), p. 11.

32. See Appendix II.

33. Charles Dickens, *Master Humphrey's Clock and Other Stories*, ed. Peter Mudford (London: Everyman, 1997), p. 64.

34. Ibid., pp. 65, 146.

35. *Letters of Charles Dickens*, pp. 304, 356.

36. Ibid., p. 418.

37. Robert L. Patten, 'William Harrison Ainsworth', in Paul Schlicke (ed.), *The Oxford Reader's Companion to Dickens* (Oxford: Oxford University Press, 1999), p. 7. See also Martin Meisel, *Realizations: Narrative, Pictorial, and Theatrical Arts in Nineteenth-Century England* (Princeton: Princeton University Press, 1983), pp. 261–5.

38. *Letters of Charles Dickens*, p. 199.

39. Paul Schlicke, '*Barnaby Rudge*', in Schlicke (ed.), *The Oxford Reader's Companion to Dickens*, p. 33.

40. Ibid. According to Kathryn Chittick, the novel 'went almost totally unnoticed' on its first appearance: Kathryn Chittick, *Dickens and the 1830s* (Cambridge: Cambridge University Press, 1990), p. ix.

41. Forster, *Life of Charles Dickens*, Bk 2, ch. 9; Hoppé, Vol. I, p. 144.

Further Reading

LETTERS

The Letters of Charles Dickens, Volumes 1 and 2: 1820–1839 and 1840–1, ed. Madeline House and Graham Storey (Oxford: Clarendon Press, 1965, 1969). Referred to as the Pilgrim Edition. This edition enables the reader to trace in detail Dickens's changing conception of the novel.

BIOGRAPHIES

Ackroyd, Peter, *Dickens* (London: Sinclair-Stevenson, 1990). The most vivid and illuminating modern biography.

Forster, John, *The Life of Charles Dickens* (London: Chapman and Hall, 1872–4); ed. A. J. Hoppé (London: Dent, 1966). The classic Victorian life of Dickens, by his closest friend.

Smith, Grahame, *Charles Dickens: A Literary Life* (London: Macmillan, 1996). A very useful study of Dickens's professional life as a writer.

CRITICISM

Bowen, John, 'The Historical Novel', in *A Companion to the Victorian Novel*, ed. Patrick Brantlinger and W. B. Thesing (Oxford: Blackwell, 2002), pp. 244–59. Places Dickens's work in the wider context of the Victorian historical novel.

——, 'History's Grip: *Barnaby Rudge*', in *Other Dickens: Pickwick to Chuzzlewit* (Oxford: Oxford University Press, 2000), pp. 157–182. Examines the relation between the historical and the Gothic and melodramatic aspects of the novel.

Brantlinger, Patrick, 'Did Dickens have a Philosophy of History? The Case of *Barnaby Rudge*', *Dickens Studies Annual* 30 (2001), 59–74.

——, *The Spirit of Reform: British Literature and Politics 1832–1867* (Cambridge: Harvard University Press, 1977), pp. 81–96. Influential study of the social and political conflicts of the 1830s and 40s.

Butt, John and Kathleen Tillotson, '*Barnaby Rudge*: The First Projected Novel', in *Dickens at Work* (London: Methuen, 1957), pp. 76–89. A path-breaking analysis of the novel's evolution.

Chesterton, G. K., '*Barnaby Rudge*', in *Chesterton on Dickens*, ed. Michael Slater (London: Everyman, 1992), pp. 65–75. A characteristically witty study of the 'picaresque' elements in the novel.

Chittick, Kathryn, 'The Historical Novelist: *Jack Sheppard* and *Barnaby Rudge*', in *Dickens and the 1830s* (Cambridge: Cambridge University Press, 1990), pp. 152–77. A useful comparison of Ainsworth's novel and Dickens's.

Collins, Philip, *Dickens and Crime* (London: Macmillan, 1962), pp. 44–51.

Connor, Steven, 'Space, Place and the Body of Riot in *Barnaby Rudge*', in *Charles Dickens: Longman Critical Readers*, ed. Steven Connor (London: Longman, 1996), pp. 211–29. An illuminating discussion of the depiction of space in the book.

Dickens Quarterly 8 (March 1991). Special number on *Barnaby Rudge*.

Dransfield, Scott, 'Reading the Gordon Riots in 1841: Social Violence and Moral Management in *Barnaby Rudge*', *Dickens Studies Annual* 27 (1998), 69–95. Discusses the depiction of insanity in the novel.

Duncan, Ian, *Modern Romance and Transformations of the Novel: The Gothic, Scott, Dickens* (Cambridge: Cambridge University Press, 1992), pp. 220–37. Important study of Dickens's debt to Sir Walter Scott and Gothic fiction.

Fleishman, Avrom, 'Dickens: Visions of Revolution', in *The English Historical Novel: Walter Scott to Virginia Woolf* (Baltimore: Johns Hopkins University Press, 1971), pp. 102–26.

Glavin, John, 'Politics and *Barnaby Rudge*: Surrogation, Restoration, and Revival', *Dickens Studies Annual* 30 (2001), 95–112.

Gottshall, James K., 'Devils Abroad: The Unity and Significance of *Barnaby Rudge*', *Nineteenth Century Fiction* 16 (1961), 133–46. Makes an eloquent case for the coherence of the novel.

John, Juliet, *Dickens's Villains: Melodrama, Character, Popular Culture* (Oxford: Oxford University Press, 2001), pp. 103–21. An important defence of Dickens's use of melodramatic techniques in his fiction.

Kincaid, James, '*Barnaby Rudge*: Laughter and Structure', in *Dickens and the Rhetoric of Laughter* (Oxford: Clarendon Press, 1971), pp. 105–31. Entertainingly argues that the second half of the novel undercuts the values of the first half.

Lucas, John, 'Barnaby Rudge', in *The Melancholy Man: A Study of Dickens's Novels* (London: Methuen, 1970), pp. 92–112. A sympathetic and intelligent reading of the novel.

Lukács, George, *The Historical Novel* (Harmondsworth: Penguin, 1969). The classic study of the historical novel in Europe.

McKnight, Natalie, 'The Conventional Idiot: Surfaces and Signs in *Barnaby Rudge*', in *Idiots, Madmen and Other Prisoners in Dickens* (New York: St Martin's Press, 1993), pp. 81–93. Argues that Dickens's 'conservative impulses' silence the radical potential inherent in Barnaby's character.

McMaster, Juliet, ' "Better to be Silly": From Vision to Reality in *Barnaby Rudge*', *Dickens Studies Annual* 13 (1984), 1–17.

Magnet, Myron, '*Barnaby Rudge*', in *Dickens and the Social Order* (Philadelphia: University of Pennsylvania Press, 1985), pp. 49–171. Argues at length that Dickens is a more conservative author than is often thought.

Marcus, Steven, 'Sons and Fathers', in *Dickens: From Pickwick to Dombey* (London: Chatto, 1963), pp. 169–212. A brilliant study of the significance of father–son relationships in the novel.

Michasiw, Kim Ian, '*Barnaby Rudge*: "The Since of the Fathers" ', *ELH* 56 (1989), 571–92. A rich study of the novel's complex relationship to the works of Carlyle and Scott.

Morgentaler, Goldie, *Dickens and Heredity: When Like Begets Like* (London: Macmillan, 2000), pp. 111–22.

Newman, S. J., 'Art and Anarchy in *Barnaby Rudge*', in *Dickens at Play* (London: Macmillan, 1981), pp. 88–98. Argues that the novel is 'the nearest Dickens comes to turning art into psychosis'.

——, '*Barnaby Rudge*: Dickens and Scott', in *Literature of the*

Romantic Period 1750–1850, ed. R. T. Davies and B. G. Beatty (Liverpool: Liverpool University Press, 1976), pp. 171–88.

Parker, David, 'Barnaby Rudge: Narrative Games', in *The Doughty Street Novels: Pickwick Papers, Oliver Twist, Nicholas Nickleby, Barnaby Rudge* (New York: AMS Press, 2002), pp. 181–212.

Patten, Robert L., *Charles Dickens and his Publishers* (Oxford: Clarendon Press, 1978). The definitive study of this topic.

Rice, Thomas Jackson, 'The End of Dickens's Apprenticeship: Variable Focus in *Barnaby Rudge*', *Nineteenth-Century Fiction* 30 (1975), 172–84. Sees the novel as the first work of Dickens's maturity, made coherent through its sophisticated use of variable narrative focus.

——, 'The Politics of *Barnaby Rudge*', in *The Changing World of Charles Dickens*, ed. Robert Giddings (London: Vision, 1986), pp. 51–74. Makes a thorough case for the presence of detailed similarities between the political situation of the late 1830s and early 40s and that depicted in the novel.

Sanders, Andrew, 'The Track of a Storm: Charles Dickens's Historical Novels', in *The English Historical Novel 1840–1880* (London: Macmillan, 1978), pp. 68–96. A lucid and intelligent account of Dickens's two historical novels.

Stevens, Joan, ' "Woodcuts Dropped into the Text": The Illustrations in *The Old Curiosity Shop* and *Barnaby Rudge*', *Studies in Bibliography* 20 (1967), 113–33. An excellent account of the significance of the illustrations to Dickens's conception of the novel.

Tracy, Robert, 'Clock Work: *The Old Curiosity Shop* and *Barnaby Rudge*', *Dickens Studies Annual* 30 (2001), 23–44. Discusses the relationship of the novel to its framing material in *Master Humphrey's Clock*.

Viswanathan, Gauri, *Outside the Fold: Conversion, Modernity, and Belief* (Princeton: Princeton University Press, 1998), pp. 22–6. Insightful discussion of ideas of religious toleration and Englishness in the novel.

Walder, Dennis, *Dickens and Religion* (London: Allen and Unwin, 1981), pp. 91–104.

Wilt, Judith, 'Masques of the English in *Barnaby Rudge*', *Dickens Studies Annual* 30 (2001), 75–94. The best account of Dickens's portrayal of religious conflict.

For a full bibliography up to 1987, see Thomas Jackson Rice, *Barnaby Rudge: An Annotated Bibliography* (New York: Garland, 1987).

For early reviews, see Philip Collins, *Dickens: The Critical Heritage* (London: Routledge and Kegan Paul, 1971), pp. 101–11, and *New Cambridge Bibliography of English Literature Volume 4: 1800–1900*, ed. Joanne Shattock, 3rd edn (Cambridge: Cambridge University Press, 1999), pp. 1206–7.

THE GORDON RIOTS

Ackroyd, Peter, *London: The Biography* (London: Vintage, 2000), pp. 484–95. A dramatic account of London's 'most violent and widespread riot of its last thousand years'.

de Castro, J. P., *The Gordon Riots* (London: Oxford University Press, 1926). Dated but still useful study of the Riots.

Hibbert, Christopher, *King Mob: The Story of Lord George Gordon and the London Riots of 1780* (London: Longman, 1958). A lucid, popular account of Gordon and the Riots.

Linebaugh, Peter, 'The Delivery of Newgate, 6 June 1780', in *The London Hanged: Crime and Civil Society in the Eighteenth Century* (London: Allen Lane, 1991), pp. 333–70. A vivid account of the central event of the Riots.

McAlman, Ian, 'Prophesying Revolution: "Mad Lord George", Edmund Burke and Madame La Motte', in *Living and Learning: Essays in Honour of J. F. C. Harrison*, ed. Malcolm Chase and Ian Dyck (Aldershot: Scolar, 1996), pp. 52–65. Discusses the symbolic significance of Gordon as a figure of revolution.

Rogers, Nicholas, 'Crowd and Power in the Gordon Riots', in *The Transformation of Political Culture: England and Germany in the Late Eighteenth Century*, ed. Eckhart Hellmuth (Oxford: Oxford University Press, 1990), pp. 39–55.

Stevenson, John, *Popular Disturbances in England 1700–1832*, 2nd edn (London: Longman, 1992), pp. 94–113. Clear, modern account of the Riots in the wider context of popular disturbances in the period.

A Note on the Text and Illustrations

The complete holograph manuscript, written between January and November 1841, of *Barnaby Rudge* is in the Forster Collection of the Victoria and Albert Museum, London. The first forty-eight pages (substantially chapters 1–3) were probably recopied from an earlier manuscript of 1839. No proofs, working notes or number plans survive, other than proofs for chapters 17 and 18, also in the Forster Collection. John Butt and Kathleen Tillotson conclude that 'the considerable differences between manuscript and printed text show that much revision must have taken place in proof'.[1] Dickens left much of this work to John Forster, as is clear from various letters, such as those of 5 April 1841, in which he tells Forster to 'erase anything that seems to you too strong', and of 29 April 1841, in which he apologizes for asking him to cut the preceding number.[2] Butt and Tillotson reproduce several passages cut in proof; Joel J. Brattin, in ' "Secrets Inside . . . to Strike to your Heart": New Readings from Dickens's manuscript of *Barnaby Rudge*, Chapter 75' (*Dickens Quarterly* 8 (March 1991), 15–28), examines in detail the manuscript of chapter 75; and Sylvère Monod reproduces a deleted manuscript passage from chapter 43 (*Dickens the Novelist* (Norman: University of Oklahoma Press, 1968), p. 202).

Barnaby Rudge was first published in Dickens's weekly journal *Master Humphrey's Clock*, nos. 46–88, 13 February–27 November 1841. As Robert Patten notes, '*Master Humphrey's Clock* appeared in a bewildering variety of formats. There were eighty-eight weekly threepenny numbers in white paper covers . . . The four or five numbers per month were also collated and sold in twenty monthly parts, stitched in a green wrapper, for 1s or 1s 3d. At half-yearly intervals, the *Clock* numbers were collected into volumes . . . On the same day as Volume III appeared, the *Shop* and *Barnaby* were issued separate from the *Clock*, as the original edition, bound in

cloth for 13s each.'[3] Three later editions published within Dickens's
lifetime are significant: the Cheap Edition of 1849, which contains
a large number of slight alterations of phrasing and punctuation,
the Library Edition of 1858 and the Charles Dickens Edition of
1867–8, which contains further slight alterations. The Charles
Dickens edition also has new running headlines by Dickens (see
Appendix IV). In the case of these collected editions, however,
Dickens 'rarely consulted his manuscript, almost never restored
passages omitted from it, and sometimes left in errors introduced
by the compositor'.[4] I have therefore chosen the first volume edition
of 1841, reprinted from the stereotype plates of *Master Humphrey's
Clock*, as my copy-text and have corrected only those errors that
are obvious and interfere with sense. Otherwise I have retained
the spelling, punctuation and inconsistencies of the original. Elizabeth M. Brennan in her Clarendon edition of *The Old Curiosity
Shop* ((Oxford: Clarendon Press, 1997), p. lxxxi), the novel closest
to *Barnaby Rudge* in its publication history, points out that Dickens
was inconsistent in spelling and punctuation; in a single manuscript chapter, for example, he wrote 'waxwork', 'wax work' and
'wax-work' and closed reported speech, within little more than a
dozen lines of manuscript, in three different ways: with and without
a comma, and with a short dash. As he allowed his punctuation to
be altered by both the printer and Forster and did not insist on
adherence to the majority of his idiosyncratic spellings, she con-
cludes that 'it is not an editor's job to do so on his behalf'. In this
edition, full stops have been added on some half-dozen occasions
where there was no closing punctuation to a sentence, a score or
more quotation marks have been completed or moved to their
correct position where they were missing or misplaced, and a similar
number of commas have been added before the closing quotation
marks in passages of dialogue. I have not, though, attempted to
regularize such variant forms as 'up stairs' and 'up-stairs' or 'lantern' and 'lanthorn' or make consistent the various ways in which
the names of streets and other locations are given in the text. In
accordance with the Penguin house style, I have used single quotation marks first, en rules for dashes and em rules where Dickens
uses double dashes, and deleted the point after titles, including Dr,
Mrs and Mr (and in Appendices II and III). An asterisk indicates
where the weekly parts ended; an asterisk set in a rule the end of
monthly parts. I have also made the following emendations:

p. 42 beating MS; heaving 1841
p. 47 apron on, was quite MS; apron on quite 1841
p. 87 waltz MS; walk 1841
p. 442 witness policy MS; witness' policy 1841
p. 541 cells, who were certain MS; cells, certain 1841
p. 554 and seemed mightily MS; and seem mightily 1841
p. 554 remained closed Spence;[5] remained unclosed 1841

In letter to Forster of 25 March 1841, Dickens declared that he wished to restore some of Joe's references to Dolly in chapter 14 (no. 53, published 3 April), which had been cut in proof, but he did not do so, and I have not made any change to the published text, but as the *Letters* editors note, they add little.[5]

Barnaby Rudge is a copiously illustrated novel. As Michael Steig has shown,[6] although it is only about three-quarters the length of one of Dickens's long novels, such as *David Copperfield*, it has seventy-six illustrations compared with *Copperfield*'s forty, so the frequency of illustration is two to three times greater than the majority of Dickens's works. Rather than the engraved plates printed on separate pages which illustrate the majority of Dickens's works, the illustrations to *Barnaby Rudge* are woodcuts which are less than a full page in size and were printed with the text, at the top or bottom of a page or with text above and below. This enabled a very precise placing of the illustration and thus a close integration of text and image. Two illustrators were employed: fifty-nine cuts by Hablot K. Browne and seventeen by George Cattermole (see Appendix I). Dickens took great care to direct them: as Joan Stevens points out: 'The letters pour out a torrent of detail for Cattermole and Browne.'[7] Because the text page of this edition is much smaller than that of *Master Humphrey's Clock* it is not possible to match the placement of the illustrations as Dickens had them. They are printed on separate pages. It has unfortunately not been possible to reproduce the eleven ornamental capitals of the first edition within the text, but they are gathered in Appendix I. The illustrations at the beginning of each volume of *Master Humphrey's Clock* and between novels were not reproduced in the volume editions of *Barnaby Rudge*. A number of illustrations were inappropriately placed at the beginning of the monthly numbers of *Master Humphrey's Clock* and subsequent editions have followed this placing. For example, an illustration of the Warren was placed at the beginning

of chapter 13, to provide a picturesque opening to Volume III of
Master Humphrey's Clock; the Warren features later in the chapter,
which begins at the Maypole.

NOTES

1. John Butt and Kathleen Tillotson, *Dickens at Work* (London: Methuen,
1957), p. 80.

2. *The Letters of Charles Dickens, Volume 2, 1840–1*, ed. Madeline House
and Graham Storey (Oxford: Clarendon Press, 1969), pp. 253, 275.

3. Robert L. Patten, *Charles Dickens and his Publishers* (Oxford: Oxford
University Press, 1978), p. 117.

4. J. Donn Vann, 'Editions', in Paul Schlicke (ed.), *The Oxford Reader's
Companion to Dickens* (Oxford: Oxford University Press, 1999), p. 208.

5. Charles Dickens, *Barnaby Rudge*, ed. Gordon Spence (Harmondsworth:
Penguin, 1973), p. 36.

6. *Letters of Charles Dickens*, p. 243 and note.

7. Michael Steig, *Dickens and Phiz* (Bloomington: Indiana University Press,
1978), p. 52.

8. Joan Stevens, ' "Woodcuts Dropped into the Text": The Illustrations in
The Old Curiosity Shop and *Barnaby Rudge*', *Studies in Bibliography* 20
(1967), 125.

Barnaby Rudge;

A Tale of the Riots of 'Eighty

If the object an author has had, in writing a book, cannot be discovered from its perusal, the probability is that it is either very deep, or very shallow. Hoping that mine may lie somewhere between these two extremes, I shall say very little about it, and that, only in reference to one point.

No account of the Gordon Riots, having been to my knowledge introduced into any Work of Fiction,[1] and the subject presenting very extraordinary and remarkable features, I was led to project this Tale.

It is unnecessary to say, that those shameful tumults, while they reflect indelible disgrace upon the time in which they occurred, and all who had act or part in them, teach a good lesson. That what we falsely call a religious cry is easily raised by men who have no religion, and who in their daily practice set at nought the commonest principles of right and wrong; that it is begotten of intolerance and persecution; that it is senseless, besotted, inveterate, and unmerciful; all History teaches us. But perhaps we do not know it in our hearts too well, to profit by even so humble and familiar an example as the 'No Popery' riots of Seventeen Hundred and Eighty.

However imperfectly those disturbances are set forth in the following pages, they are impartially painted by one who has no sympathy with the Romish Church, although he acknowledges, as most men do, some esteemed friends among the followers of its creed.

It may be observed that, in the description of the principal outrages, reference has been had to the best authorities of that time, such as they are; and that the account given in this Tale, of all the main features of the Riots, is substantially correct.

It may be further remarked, that Mr Dennis's allusions to the flourishing condition of his trade in those days, have their foundation in Truth, not in the Author's fancy. Any file of old Newspapers, or odd volume of the Annual Register,[2] will prove this with terrible ease.

Even the case of Mary Jones,[3] dwelt upon with so much pleasure by the same character, is no effort of invention. The facts were stated exactly as they are stated here, in the House of Commons.

Whether they afforded as much entertainment to the merry gentle-men assembled there, as some other most affecting circumstances of a similar nature mentioned by Sir Samuel Romilly,[4] is not recorded.

It is a great pleasure to me to add in this place – for which I have reserved the acknowledgment – that for a beautiful thought, in the last chapter but one of 'The Old Curiosity Shop,' I am indebted to Mr Rogers. It is taken from his charming Tale, 'Ginevra:'

> 'And long might'st thou have seen
> An old man wandering *as in quest of something*,
> Something he could not find – he knew not what.'[5]

DEVONSHIRE TERRACE, YORK GATE,
November 1841.

In the year 1775, there stood upon the borders of Epping Forest, at a distance of about twelve miles from London – measuring from the Standard in Cornhill or rather from the spot on or near to which the Standard used to be in days of yore – a house of public entertainment called the Maypole;[1] which fact was demonstrated to all such travellers as could neither read nor write (and sixty-six years ago[2] a vast number both of travellers and stay-at-homes were in this condition) by the emblem reared on the roadside over against the house, which, if not of those goodly proportions that Maypoles were wont to present in olden times, was a fair young ash, thirty feet in height, and straight as any arrow that ever English yeoman drew.

The Maypole – by which term from henceforth is meant the house, and not its sign – the Maypole was an old building, with more gable ends than a lazy man would care to count on a sunny day; huge zig-zag chimneys, out of which it seemed as though even smoke could not choose but come in more than naturally fantastic shapes, imparted to it in its tortuous progress; and vast stables, gloomy, ruinous and empty. The place was said to have been built in the days of King Henry the Eighth; and there was a legend, not only that Queen Elizabeth[3] had slept there one night while upon a hunting excursion, to wit in a certain oak-panneled room with a deep bay window, but that next morning, while standing on a mounting block before the door with one foot in the stirrup, the virgin monarch had then and there boxed and cuffed an unlucky page for some neglect of duty. The matter-of-fact and doubtful folks, of whom there were a few among the Maypole customers, as unluckily there always are in every little community, were inclined to look upon this tradition as rather apocryphal; but whenever the landlord of that ancient hostelry appealed to the mounting block itself as evidence, and triumphantly pointed out that there it stood in the same place to that very day, the doubters never failed to be put down by a large majority, and all true believers exulted as in a victory.

Whether these, and many other stories of the like nature, were true or untrue, the Maypole was really an old house, a very old house, perhaps as old as it claimed to be, and perhaps older, which

will sometimes happen with houses of an uncertain, as with ladies of a certain age. Its windows were old diamond pane lattices, its floors were sunken and uneven, its ceilings blackened by the hand of time and heavy with massive beams. Over the doorway was an ancient porch, quaintly and grotesquely carved; and here on summer evenings the more favoured customers smoked and drank – ay, and sang many a good song too, sometimes – reposing on two grim-looking high backed settles, which, like the twin dragons of some fairy tale, guarded the entrance to the mansion.

In the chimneys of the disused rooms, swallows had built their nests for many a long year, and from earliest spring to latest autumn whole colonies of sparrows chirped and twittered in the eaves. There were more pigeons about the dreary stable yard and outbuildings than anybody but the landlord could reckon up. The wheeling and circling flights of runts, fantails, tumblers, and pouters, were perhaps not quite consistent with the grave and sober character of the building, but the monotonous cooing, which never ceased to be raised by some among them all day long, suited it exactly, and seemed to lull it to rest. With its overhanging stories, drowsy little panes of glass, and front bulging out and projecting over the pathway, the old house looked as if it were nodding in its sleep. Indeed it needed no very great stretch of fancy to detect in it other resemblances to humanity. The bricks of which it was built had originally been a deep dark red, but had grown yellow and discoloured like an old man's skin; the sturdy timbers had decayed like teeth; and here and there the ivy, like a warm garment to comfort it in its age, wrapt its green leaves closely round the time-worn walls.

It was a hale and hearty age though, still: and in the summer or autumn evenings, when the glow of the setting sun fell upon the oak and chestnut trees of the adjacent forest, the old house, partaking of its lustre, seemed their fit companion, and to have many good years of life in him yet.

The evening with which we have to do, was neither a summer nor an autumn one, but the twilight of a day in March, when the wind howled dismally among the bare branches of the trees, and rumbling in the wide chimneys and driving the rain against the windows of the Maypole Inn, gave such of its frequenters as chanced to be there at the moment, an undeniable reason for prolonging their stay, and caused the landlord to prophesy that the night

would certainly clear at eleven o'clock precisely, – which by a
remarkable coincidence was the hour at which he always closed
his house.

The name of him upon whom the spirit of prophecy thus descended was John Willet, a burly, large-headed man with a fat
face, which betokened profound obstinacy and slowness of apprehension, combined with a very strong reliance upon his own merits.
It was John Willet's ordinary boast in his more placid moods that
if he was slow he was sure; which assertion could in one sense at
least be by no means gainsaid, seeing that he was in everything
unquestionably the reverse of fast, and withal one of the most
dogged and positive fellows in existence – always sure that what he
thought or said or did was right, and holding it as a thing quite
settled and ordained by the laws of nature and Providence, that
anybody who said or did or thought otherwise must be inevitably
and of necessity wrong.

Mr Willet walked slowly up to the window, flattened his fat nose
against the cold glass, and shading his eyes that his sight might not
be affected by the ruddy glow of the fire, looked abroad. Then he
walked slowly back to his old seat in the chimney-corner, and,
composing himself in it with a slight shiver, such as a man might
give way to and so acquire an additional relish for the warm blaze,
said, looking round upon his guests:

'It'll clear at eleven o'clock. No sooner and no later. Not before
and not arterwards.'

'How do you make out that?' said a little man in the opposite
corner. 'The moon is past the full, and she rises at nine.'

John looked sedately and solemnly at his questioner until he had
brought his mind to bear upon the whole of his observation, and
then made answer, in a tone which seemed to imply that the moon
was peculiarly his business and nobody else's:

'Never you mind about the moon. Don't you trouble yourself
about her. You let the moon alone, and I'll let you alone.'

'No offence I hope?' said the little man.

Again John waited leisurely until the observation had thoroughly
penetrated to his brain, and then replying, 'No offence *as yet,*'
applied a light to his pipe and smoked in placid silence; now and
then casting a sidelong look at a man wrapped in a loose riding-coat
with huge cuffs ornamented with tarnished silver lace and large

metal buttons, who sat apart from the regular frequenters of the house, and wearing a hat flapped over his face, which was still further shaded by the hand on which his forehead rested, looked unsociable enough.

There was another guest, who sat, booted and spurred, at some distance from the fire also, and whose thoughts – to judge from his folded arms and knitted brows, and from the untasted liquor before him – were occupied with other matters than the topics under discussion or the persons who discussed them. This was a young man of about eight-and-twenty, rather above the middle height, and though of a somewhat slight figure, gracefully and strongly made. He wore his own dark hair, and was accoutred in a riding-dress, which, together with his large boots (resembling in shape and fashion those worn by our Life Guardsmen at the present day), showed indisputable traces of the bad condition of the roads. But travel-stained though he was, he was well and even richly attired, and without being over-dressed looked a gallant gentleman.

Lying upon the table beside him, as he had carelessly thrown them down, were a heavy riding-whip and a slouched hat, the latter worn no doubt as being best suited to the inclemency of the weather. There, too, were a pair of pistols in a holster-case, and a short riding-cloak. Little of his face was visible, except the long dark lashes which concealed his downcast eyes, but an air of careless ease and natural gracefulness of demeanour pervaded the figure, and seemed to comprehend even these slight accessories, which were all handsome, and in good keeping.

Towards this young gentleman the eyes of Mr Willet wandered but once, and then as if in mute inquiry whether he had observed his silent neighbour. It was plain that John and the young gentleman had often met before. Finding that his look was not returned, or indeed observed by the person to whom it was addressed, John gradually concentrated the whole power of his eyes into one focus, and brought it to bear upon the man in the flapped hat, at whom he came to stare in course of time with an intensity so remarkable, that it affected his fireside cronies, who all, as with one accord, took their pipes from their lips, and stared with open mouths at the stranger likewise.

The sturdy landlord had a large pair of dull fish-like eyes, and the little man who had hazarded the remark about the moon (and who was the parish clerk and bell-ringer of Chigwell;[4] a village hard by,) had little round black shiny eyes like beads; moreover this little man wore at the knees of his rusty black breeches, and on his rusty black coat, and all down his long flapped waistcoat, little queer buttons like nothing except his eyes; but so like them, that as they twinkled and glistened in the light of the fire, which shone too in his bright shoe-buckles, he seemed all eyes from head to foot, and to be gazing with every one of them at the unknown customer. No wonder that a man should grow restless under such an inspection as this, to say nothing of the eyes belonging to short Tom Cobb the general chandler and post-office keeper, and long Phil Parkes the ranger, both of whom, infected by the example of their companions, regarded him of the flapped hat no less attentively.

The stranger became restless; perhaps from being exposed to this raking fire of eyes, perhaps from the nature of his previous meditations – most probably from the latter cause, for as he changed his position and looked hastily round, he started to find himself the object of such keen regard, and darted an angry and suspicious glance at the fireside group. It had the effect of immediately diverting all eyes to the chimney, except those of John Willet, who finding himself, as it were, caught in the fact, and not being (as has been already observed) of a very ready nature, remained staring at his guest in a particularly awkward and disconcerted manner.

'Well?' said the stranger.

Well. There was not much in well. It was not a long speech. 'I thought you gave an order,' said the landlord, after a pause of two or three minutes for consideration.

The stranger took off his hat, and disclosed the hard features of a man of sixty or thereabouts, much weather-beaten and worn by time, and the naturally harsh expression of which was not improved by a dark handkerchief which was bound tightly round his head, and, while it served the purpose of a wig, shaded his forehead, and almost hid his eyebrows. If it were intended to conceal or divert attention from a deep gash, now healed into an ugly seam, which when it was first inflicted must have laid bare his cheekbone, the object was but indifferently attained, for it could scarcely fail to be noted at a glance. His complexion was of a cadaverous hue, and he had a grizzly jagged beard of some three weeks' date. Such was the figure (very meanly and poorly clad) that now rose from the seat, and stalking across the room sat down in a corner of the chimney,

which the politeness or fears of the little clerk very readily assigned to him.

'A highwayman!' whispered Tom Cobb to Parkes the ranger.

'Do you suppose highwaymen don't dress handsomer than that?' replied Parkes. 'It's a better business than you think for, Tom, and highwaymen don't need or use to be shabby, take my word for it.'

Meanwhile, the subject of their speculations had done due honour to the house by calling for some drink, which was promptly supplied by the landlord's son Joe, a broad-shouldered strapping young fellow of twenty, whom it pleased his father still to consider a little boy, and to treat accordingly. Stretching out his hands to warm them by the blazing fire, the man turned his head towards the company, and after running his eye sharply over them, said in a voice well suited to his appearance:

'What house is that which stands a mile or so from here?'

'Public-house?' said the landlord, with his usual deliberation.

'Public-house, father!' exclaimed Joe, 'where's the public-house within a mile or so of the Maypole? He means the great house – the Warren[5] – naturally and of course. The old red brick house, sir, that stands in its own grounds – ?'

'Ay,' said the stranger.

'And that fifteen or twenty years ago stood in a park five times as broad, which with other and richer property has bit by bit changed hands and dwindled away – more's the pity!' pursued the young man.

'Maybe,' was the reply. 'But my question related to the owner. What it has been I don't care to know, and what it is I can see for myself.'

The heir-apparent to the Maypole pressed his finger on his lips, and glancing at the young gentleman already noticed, who had changed his attitude when the house was first mentioned, replied in a lower tone,

'The owner's name is Haredale, Mr Geoffrey Haredale, and' – again he glanced in the same direction as before – 'and a worthy gentleman too – hem!'

Paying as little regard to this admonitory cough, as to the significant gesture that had preceded it, the stranger pursued his questioning.

'I turned out of my way coming here, and took the footpath that crosses the grounds. Who was the young lady that I saw entering a carriage? His daughter?'

'Why, how should I know, honest man?' replied Joe, contriving in the course of some arrangements about the hearth, to advance close to his questioner and pluck him by the sleeve, '*I* didn't see the young lady you know. Whew! There's the wind again – *and* rain – well it *is* a night!'

'Rough weather indeed!' observed the strange man.

'You're used to it?' said Joe, catching at anything which seemed to promise a diversion of the subject.

'Pretty well,' returned the other. 'About the young lady – has Mr Haredale a daughter?'

'No, no,' said the young fellow fretfully, 'he's a single gentleman – he's – be quiet, can't you man? Don't you see this talk is not relished yonder?'

Regardless of this whispered remonstrance and affecting not to hear it, his tormentor provokingly continued:

'Single men have had daughters before now. Perhaps she may be his daughter, though he is not married.'

'What do you mean?' said Joe, adding in an under tone as he approached him again, 'You'll come in for it presently, I know you will!'

'I mean no harm' – returned the traveller boldly, 'and have said none that I know of. I ask a few questions – as any stranger may, and not unnaturally – about the inmates of a remarkable house in a neighbourhood which is new to me, and you are as aghast and disturbed as if I were talking treason against King George.[6] Perhaps you can tell me why, sir, for (as I say) I am a stranger, and this is Greek to me?'

The latter observation was addressed to the obvious cause of Joe Willet's discomposure, who had risen and was adjusting his riding-cloak preparatory to sallying abroad. Briefly replying that he could give him no information, the young man beckoned to Joe, and handing him a piece of money in payment of his reckoning, hurried out attended by young Willet himself, who taking up a candle followed to light him to the house door.

While Joe was absent on this errand, the elder Willet and his three companions continued to smoke with profound gravity, and in a deep silence, each having his eyes fixed on a huge copper boiler that was suspended over the fire. After some time Joe Willet slowly shook his head, and thereupon his friends slowly shook theirs; but no man withdrew his eyes from the boiler, or altered the solemn expression of his countenance in the slightest degree.

At length Joe returned – very talkative and conciliatory, as though with a strong presentiment that he was going to be found fault with.

'Such a thing as love is!' he said, drawing a chair near the fire, and looking round for sympathy. 'He has set off to walk to London, – all the way to London. His nag gone lame in riding out here this blessed afternoon, and comfortably littered down in our stable at this minute; and he giving up a good hot supper and our best bed, because Miss Haredale has gone to a masquerade up in town, and he has set his heart upon seeing her! I don't think I could persuade myself to do that, beautiful as she is, – but then I'm not in love, (at least I don't think I am,) and that's the whole difference.'

'He is in love then?' said the stranger.

'Rather,' replied Joe. 'He'll never be more in love, and may very easily be less.'

'Silence sir!' cried his father.

'What a chap you are Joe!' said Long Parkes.

'Such a inconsiderate lad!' murmured Tom Cobb.

'Putting himself forward and wringing the very nose off his own father's face!' exclaimed the parish clerk, metaphorically.

'What *have* I done?' reasoned poor Joe.

'Silence sir!' returned his father, 'what do you mean by talking, when you see people that are more than two or three times your age, sitting still and silent and not dreaming of saying a word?'

'Why that's the proper time for me to talk, isn't it?' said Joe rebelliously.

'The proper time sir!' retorted his father, 'the proper time's no time.'

'Ah to be sure!' muttered Parkes, nodding gravely to the other two who nodded likewise, observing under their breaths that that was the point.

'The proper time's no time sir,' repeated John Willet; 'when I was your age I never talked, I never wanted to talk, I listened and improved myself, that's what *I* did.'

'And you'd find your father rather a tough customer in argeyment, Joe, if anybody was to try and tackle him' – said Parkes.

'For the matter o' that Phil!' observed Mr Willet, blowing a long, thin, spiral cloud of smoke out of the corner of his mouth, and staring at it abstractedly as it floated away; 'For the matter o' that, Phil, argeyment is a gift of Natur. If Natur has gifted a man with powers of argeyment, a man has a right to make the best of 'em, and has not a right to stand on false delicacy, and deny that he is so gifted; for that is a turning of his back on Natur, a flouting of her, a slighting of her precious caskets, and a proving of one's self to be a swine that isn't worth her scattering pearls before.'[7]

The landlord pausing here for a very long time, Mr Parkes naturally concluded that he had brought his discourse to an end; and therefore, turning to the young man with some austerity, exclaimed:

'You hear what your father says, Joe? You wouldn't much like to tackle him in argeyment, I'm thinking sir.'

'– IF,' said John Willet, turning his eyes from the ceiling to the face of his interrupter, and uttering the monosyllable in capitals, to apprise him that he had put in his oar, as the vulgar say, with unbecoming and irreverent haste; 'IF, sir, Natur has fixed upon me the gift of argeyment, why should I not own to it, and rather glory in the same? Yes sir, I *am* a tough customer that way. You are right sir. My toughness has been proved, sir, in this room many and many a time, as I think you know; and if you don't know,' added John, putting his pipe in his mouth again, 'so much the better, for I an't proud and am not a going to tell you.'

A general murmur from his three cronies, and a general shaking of heads at the copper boiler, assured John Willet that they had had good experience of his powers and needed no further evidence to assure them of his superiority. John smoked with a little more dignity and surveyed them in silence.

'It's all very fine talking,' muttered Joe, who had been fidgeting in his chair with divers uneasy gestures. 'But if you mean to tell me that I'm never to open my lips –'

'Silence sir!' roared his father. 'No, you never are. When your opinion's wanted, you give it. When you're spoke to, you speak. When your opinion's not wanted and you're not spoke to, don't you give an opinion and don't you speak. The world's undergone a nice alteration since my time, certainly. My belief is that there an't any boys left – that there isn't such a thing as a boy – that there's nothing now between a male baby and a man – and that all the boys went out with his blessed Majesty King George the Second.'[8]

'That's a very true observation, always excepting the young princes,'[9] said the parish-clerk, who, as the representative of church and state in that company, held himself bound to the nicest loyalty. 'If it's godly and righteous for boys, being of the ages of boys, to behave themselves like boys, then the young princes must be boys and cannot be otherwise.'

'Did you ever hear tell of mermaids, sir?' said Mr Willet.

'Certainly I have,' replied the clerk.

'Very good,' said Mr Willet. 'According to the constitution of mermaids, so much of a mermaid as is not a woman must be a fish. According to the constitution of young princes, so much of a young prince (if anything) as is not actually an angel, must be godly and righteous. Therefore if it's becoming and godly and righteous in the young princes (as it is at their ages) that they should be boys, they are and must be boys, and cannot by possibility be anything else.'

This elucidation of a knotty point being received with such marks of approval as to put John Willet into a good humour, he contented himself with repeating to his son his command of silence, and addressing the stranger, said:

'If you had asked your questions of a grown-up person – of me or any of these gentlemen – you'd have had some satisfaction, and wouldn't have wasted breath. Miss Haredale is Mr Geoffrey Haredale's niece.'

'Is her father alive?' said the man carelessly.

'No,' rejoined the landlord, 'he is not alive, and he is not dead –'

'Not dead!' cried the other.

'Not dead in a common sort of way,' said the landlord.

The cronies nodded to each other, and Mr Parkes remarked in an under tone, shaking his head meanwhile as who should say, 'let no man contradict me, for I won't believe him,' that John Willet was in amazing force to-night, and fit to tackle a Chief Justice.

The stranger suffered a short pause to elapse, and then asked abruptly, 'What do you mean?'

'More than you think for, friend,' returned John Willet. 'Perhaps there's more meaning in them words than you suspect.'

'Perhaps there is,' said the strange man, gruffly; 'but what the devil do you speak in such mysteries for? You tell me first that a man is not alive, nor yet dead – then that he's not dead in a common sort of way – then, that you mean a great deal more than I think for. To tell you the truth, you may do that easily; for so far as I can make out, you mean nothing. What *do* you mean, I ask again?'

'That,' returned the landlord, a little brought down from his dignity by the stranger's surliness, 'is a Maypole story, and has been any time these four-and-twenty years. That story is Solomon Daisy's story. It belongs to the house; and nobody but Solomon Daisy has ever told it under this roof, or ever shall – that's more.'

The man glanced at the parish-clerk, whose air of consciousness and importance plainly betokened him to be the person referred to, and, observing that he had taken his pipe from his lips, after a very long whiff to keep it alight, and was evidently about to tell his story without further solicitation, gathered his large coat about him, and shrinking further back was almost lost in the gloom of the spacious chimney corner, except when the flame, struggling from under a great faggot whose weight almost crushed it for the time, shot upward with a strong and sudden glare, and illumining his figure for a moment, seemed afterwards to cast it into deeper obscurity than before.

By this flickering light, which made the old room, with its heavy timbers and panneled walls, look as if it were built of polished ebony – the wind roaring and howling without, now rattling the latch and creaking the hinges of the stout oaken door, and now driving at the casement as though it would beat it in – by this light, and under circumstances so auspicious, Solomon Daisy began his tale:

'It was Mr Reuben Haredale, Mr Geoffrey's elder brother –'

Here he came to a dead stop, and made so long a pause that even John Willet grew impatient and asked why he did not proceed.

'Cob,' said Solomon Daisy, dropping his voice and appealing to the post-office keeper; 'what day of the month is this?'

'The nineteenth.'

'Of March,' said the clerk, bending forward, 'the nineteenth of March; that's very strange.'

In a low voice they all acquiesced, and Solomon went on:

'It was Mr Reuben Haredale, Mr Geoffrey's elder brother, that twenty-two years ago was the owner of the Warren, which, as Joe has said – not that you remember it, Joe, for a boy like you can't do that, but because you have often heard me say so – was then a much larger and better place, and a much more valuable property than it is now. His lady was lately dead, and he was left with one child – the Miss Haredale you have been inquiring about – who was then scarcely a year old.'

Although the speaker addressed himself to the man who had shown so much curiosity about this same family, and made a pause here as if expecting some exclamation of surprise or encouragement, the latter made no remark, nor gave any indication that he heard or was interested in what was said. Solomon therefore turned to his old companions, whose noses were brightly illuminated by the deep red glow from the bowls of their pipes; assured, by long experience, of their attention, and resolved to show his sense of such indecent behaviour.

'Mr Haredale,' said Solomon, turning his back upon the strange man, 'left this place when his lady died, feeling it lonely like, and went up to London, where he stopped some months; but finding that place as lonely as this – as I suppose and have always heard say – he suddenly came back again with his little girl to the Warren, bringing with him besides, that day, only two women servants, and his steward, and a gardener.'

Mr Daisy stopped to take a whiff at his pipe, which was going out, and then proceeded – at first in a snuffling tone, occasioned by keen enjoyment of the tobacco and strong pulling at the pipe, and afterwards with increasing distinctness:

' – Bringing with him two women servants, and his steward and a gardener. The rest stopped behind up in London, and were to follow next day. It happened that that night, an old gentleman who lived at Chigwell-row, and had long been poorly, deceased, and an order came to me at half after twelve o'clock at night to go and toll the passing-bell.'

There was a movement in the little group of listeners, sufficiently indicative of the strong repugnance any one of them would have felt to have turned out at such a time upon such an errand. The clerk felt and understood it, and pursued his theme accordingly.

'It *was* a dreary thing, especially as the grave-digger was laid up in his bed, from long working in a damp soil and sitting down to take his dinner on cold tombstones, and I was consequently under obligation to go alone, for it was too late to hope to get any other companion. However, I wasn't unprepared for it; as the old gentleman had often made it a request that the bell should be tolled as soon as possible after the breath was out of his body, and he had been expected to go for some days. I put as good a face upon it as I could, and muffling myself up (for it was mortal cold), started out with a lighted lantern in one hand and the key of the church in the other.'

At this point of the narrative, the dress of the strange man rustled as if he had turned himself to hear more distinctly. Slightly pointing over his shoulder, Solomon elevated his eyebrows and nodded a silent inquiry to Joe whether this was the case. Joe shaded his eyes with his hand and peered into the corner, but could make out nothing, and so shook his head.

'It was just such a night as this; blowing a hurricane, raining heavily, and very dark – I often think now, darker than I ever saw it before or since; that may be my fancy, but the houses were all close shut and the folks in-doors, and perhaps there is only one other man who knows how dark it really was. I got into the church, chained the door back so that it should keep ajar – for to tell the truth, I didn't like to be shut in there alone – and putting my lantern on the stone seat in the little corner where the bell-rope is, sat down beside it to trim the candle.

'I sat down to trim the candle, and when I had done so, I could not persuade myself to get up again and go about my work. I don't know how it was, but I thought of all the ghost stories I had ever heard, even those that I had heard when I was a boy at school, and had forgotten long ago; and they didn't come into my mind one after another, but all crowding at once, like. I recollected one story there was in the village, how that on a certain night in the year (it might be that very night for anything I knew), all the dead people came out of the ground and sat at the heads of their own graves till morning. This made me think how many people I had known were buried between the church door and the churchyard gate, and what a dreadful thing it would be to have to pass among them and know them again, so earthy and unlike themselves. I had known all the niches and arches in the church from a child; still I couldn't persuade myself that those were their natural shadows which I saw on the pavement, but felt sure there were some ugly figures hiding among 'em and peeping out. Thinking on in this way, I began to think of the old gentleman who was just dead, and I could have sworn, as I looked up the dark chancel, that I saw him in his usual place, wrapping his shroud about him and shivering as if he felt it cold. All this time I sat listening and listening, and hardly dared to breathe. At length I started up and took the bell-rope in my hands.

At that minute there rang – not that bell, for I had hardly touched the rope – but another.

'I heard the ringing of another bell, and a deep bell too, plainly. It was only for an instant, and even then the wind carried the sound away, but I heard it. I listened for a long time, but it rang no more. I had heard of corpse candles, and at last I persuaded myself that this must be a corpse bell tolling of itself at midnight for the dead. I tolled my bell – how, or how long, I don't know – and ran home to bed as fast as I could touch the ground.

'I was up early next morning after a restless night, and told the story to my neighbours. Some were serious and some made light of it: I don't think anybody believed it real. But that morning, Mr Reuben Haredale was found murdered in his bedchamber, and in his hand was a piece of the cord attached to an alarm-bell outside the roof, which hung in his room and had been cut asunder, no doubt by the murderer when he seized it.

'That was the bell I heard.

'A bureau was found opened, and a cash-box, which Mr Haredale had brought down that day, and was supposed to contain a large sum of money, was gone. The steward and gardener were both missing and both suspected for a long time, but they were never found, though hunted far and wide. And far enough they might have looked for poor Mr Rudge the steward, whose body – scarcely to be recognized but by his clothes and the watch and ring he wore – was found, months afterwards, at the bottom of a piece of water in the grounds, with a deep gash in the breast where he had been stabbed with a knife. He was only partly dressed; and people all agreed that he had been sitting up reading in his own room, where there were many traces of blood, and was suddenly fallen upon and killed before his master.

'Everybody now knew that the gardener must be the murderer, and though he has never been heard of from that time to this, he will be, mark my words. The crime was committed this day two-and-twenty years – on the nineteenth of March, one thousand seven hundred and fifty three. On the nineteenth of March in some year, no matter when – I know it, I am sure of it, for we have always, in some strange way or other, been brought back to the subject on that day ever since – on the nineteenth of March in some year, sooner or later, that man will be discovered.'

*

CHAPTER THE SECOND

'A strange story!' said the man who had been the cause of the narration. – 'Stranger still if it comes about as you predict. Is that all?'

A question so unexpected nettled Solomon Daisy not a little. By dint of relating the story very often, and ornamenting it (according to village report) with a few flourishes suggested by the various hearers from time to time, he had come by degrees to tell it with great effect; and 'is that all?' after the climax, was not what he was accustomed to.

'Is that all!' he repeated, 'yes, that's all sir. And enough too, I think.'

'I think so too. My horse, young man. He is but a hack hired from a roadside posting house, but he must carry me to London to-night.'

'To-night!' said Joe.

'To-night,' returned the other. 'What do you stare at? This tavern would seem to be a house of call for all the gaping idlers of the neighbourhood!'

At this remark, which evidently had reference to the scrutiny he had undergone, as mentioned in the foregoing chapter, the eyes of John Willet and his friends were diverted with marvellous rapidity to the copper boiler again. Not so with Joe, who, being a mettlesome fellow, returned the stranger's angry glance with a steady look, and rejoined:

'It's not a very bold thing to wonder at your going on to-night. Surely you have been asked such a harmless question in an inn before, and in better weather than this. I thought you mightn't know the way, as you seem strange to this part.'

'The way –' repeated the other, irritably.

'Yes. *Do* you know it?'

'I'll – humph! – I'll find it,' replied the man, waving his hand and turning on his heel. 'Landlord, take the reckoning here.'

John Willet did as he was desired; for on that point he was seldom slow, except in the particulars of giving change, and testing the goodness of any piece of coin that was proffered to him, by the application of his teeth or his tongue, or some other test, or, in doubtful cases, by a long series of tests terminating in its rejection.

The guest then wrapt his garments about him so as to shelter himself as effectually as he could from the rough weather, and without any word or sign of farewell betook himself to the stable-yard. Here Joe (who had left the room on the conclusion of their short dialogue) was protecting himself and the horse from the rain under the shelter of an old pent-house roof.

'He's pretty much of my opinion,' said Joe, patting the horse upon the neck; 'I'll wager that your stopping here to-night would please him better than it would please me.'

'He and I are of different opinions, as we have been more than once on our way here,' was the short reply.

'So I was thinking before you came out, for he has felt your spurs, poor beast.'

The stranger adjusted his coat-collar about his face, and made no answer.

'You'll know me again, I see,' he said, marking the young fellow's earnest gaze, when he had sprung into the saddle.

'The man's worth knowing, master, who travels a road he don't know, mounted on a jaded horse, and leaves good quarters to do it on such a night as this.'

'You have sharp eyes and a sharp tongue I find.'

'Both I hope by nature, but the last grows rusty sometimes for want of using.'

'Use the first less too, and keep their sharpness for your sweethearts, boy,' said the man.

So saying he shook his hand from the bridle, struck him roughly on the head with the butt end of his whip, and galloped away; dashing through the mud and darkness with a headlong speed, which few badly mounted horsemen would have cared to venture, even had they been thoroughly acquainted with the country; and which, to one who knew nothing of the way he rode, was attended at every step with great hazard and danger.

The roads even within twelve miles of London were at that time ill paved, seldom repaired, and very badly made. The way this rider traversed had been ploughed up by the wheels of heavy wagons, and rendered rotten by the frosts and thaws of the preceding winter, or possibly of many winters. Great holes and gaps had worn into the soil, which, being now filled with water from the late rains, were not easily distinguishable even by day; and a plunge into any one of them might have brought down a surer-footed horse than

the poor beast now urged forward to the utmost extent of his powers. Sharp flints and stones rolled from under his hoofs continually; the rider could scarcely see beyond the animal's head, or further on either side than his own arm would have extended. At that time, too, all the roads in the neighbourhood of the metropolis were infested by footpads or highwaymen, and it was a night, of all others, in which any evil-disposed person of this class might have pursued his unlawful calling with little fear of detection.

Still, the traveller dashed forward at the same reckless pace, regardless alike of the dirt and wet which flew about his head, the profound darkness of the night, and the probability of encountering some desperate characters abroad. At every turn and angle, even where a deviation from the direct course might have been least expected, and could not possibly be seen until he was close upon it, he guided the bridle with an unerring hand and kept the middle of the road. Thus he sped onward, raising himself in the stirrups, leaning his body forward until it almost touched the horse's neck, and flourishing his heavy whip above his head with the fervour of a madman.

There are times when, the elements being in unusual commotion, those who are bent on daring enterprises, or agitated by great thoughts whether of good or evil, feel a mysterious sympathy with the tumult of nature and are roused into corresponding violence. In the midst of thunder, lightning, and storm, many tremendous deeds have been committed; men self-possessed before, have given a sudden loose to passions they could no longer control. The demons of wrath and despair have striven to emulate those who ride the whirlwind and direct the storm;[1] and man, lashed into madness with the roaring winds and boiling waters, has become for the time as wild and merciless as the elements themselves.

Whether the traveller was possessed by thoughts which the fury of the night had heated and stimulated into a quicker current, or was merely impelled by some strong motive to reach his journey's end, on he swept more like a hunted phantom than a man, nor checked his pace until, arriving at some cross roads one of which led by a longer route to the place whence he had lately started, he bore down so suddenly upon a vehicle which was coming towards him, that in the effort to avoid it he well nigh pulled his horse upon his haunches, and narrowly escaped being thrown.

'Yoho!' cried the voice of a man. 'What's that? who goes there?'

'A friend!' replied the traveller.

'A friend!' repeated the voice. 'Who calls himself a friend and rides like that, abusing Heaven's gifts in the shape of horseflesh, and endangering, not only his own neck, which might be no great matter, but the necks of other people?'

'You have a lantern there, I see,' said the traveller dismounting, 'lend it me for a moment. You have wounded my horse, I think, with your shaft or wheel.'

'Wounded him!' cried the other, 'if I haven't killed him, it's no fault of yours. What do you mean by galloping along the king's highway like that, eh?'

'Give me the light,' returned the traveller, snatching it from his hand, 'and don't ask idle questions of a man who is in no mood for talking.'

'If you had said you were in no mood for talking before, I should perhaps have been in no mood for lighting,' said the voice. 'Hows'ever as it's the poor horse that's damaged and not you, one of you is welcome to the light at all events – but it's not the crusty one.'

The traveller returned no answer to this speech, but holding the light near to his panting and reeking beast, examined him in limb and carcase. Meanwhile the other man sat very composedly in his vehicle, which was a kind of chaise with a depository for a large bag of tools, and watched his proceedings with a careful eye.

The looker-on was a round, red-faced, sturdy yeoman, with a double chin, and a voice husky with good living, good sleeping, good humour, and good health. He was past the prime of life, but Father Time is not always a hard parent, and, though he tarries for none of his children, often lays his hand lightly upon those who have used him well; making them old men and women inexorably enough, but leaving their hearts and spirits young and in full vigour. With such people the grey head is but the impression of the old fellow's hand in giving them his blessing, and every wrinkle but a notch in the quiet calendar of a well-spent life.

The person whom the traveller had so abruptly encountered was of this kind, bluff, hale, hearty, and in a green old age: at peace with himself, and evidently disposed to be so with all the world. Although muffled up in divers coats and handkerchiefs – one of which, passed over his crown and tied in a convenient crease of his double chin, secured his three-cornered hat and bob-wig from blowing off his head – there was no disguising his plump and comfortable figure; neither did certain dirty finger-marks upon his face give it any other than an odd and comical expression, through which its natural good humour shone with undiminished lustre.

'He is not hurt,' – said the traveller at length, raising his head and the lantern together.

'You have found that out at last, have you?' rejoined the old man. 'My eyes have seen more light than yours, but I wouldn't change with you.'

'What do you mean?'

'Mean! I could have told you he wasn't hurt, five minutes ago. Give me the light, friend; ride forward at a gentler pace; and good night.'

In handing up the lantern, the man necessarily cast its rays full on the speaker's face. Their eyes met at the instant. He suddenly dropped it and crushed it with his foot.

'Saw you never a locksmith before, that you start as if you had come upon a ghost?' cried the old man in the chaise, 'or is this,' he added hastily, thrusting his hand into the tool basket and drawing out a hammer, 'a scheme for robbing me? I know these roads, friend. When I travel them, I carry nothing but a few shillings, and not a crown's worth of them. I tell you plainly, to save us both trouble, that there's nothing to be got from me but a pretty stout arm considering my years, and this tool, which mayhap from long acquaintance with I can use pretty briskly. You shall not have it all your own way, I promise you, if you play at that game.' With these words he stood upon the defensive.

'I am not what you take me for, Gabriel Varden,' replied the other.

'Then what and who are you?' returned the locksmith. 'You know my name it seems. Let me know yours.'

'I have not gained the information from any confidence of yours, but from the inscription on your cart which tells it to all the town,' replied the traveller.

'You have better eyes for that than you had for your horse then,' said Varden, descending nimbly from his chaise; 'who are you? Let me see your face.'

While the locksmith alighted, the traveller had regained his saddle, from which he now confronted the old man, who, moving as the horse moved in chafing under the tightened rein, kept close beside him.

'Let me see your face, I say.'

'Stand off!'

'No masquerading tricks,' said the locksmith, 'and tales at the club to-morrow how Gabriel Varden was frightened by a surly voice and a dark night. Stand – let me see your face.'

Finding that further resistance would only involve him in a personal struggle with an antagonist by no means to be despised, the traveller threw back his coat, and stooping down looked steadily at the locksmith.

Perhaps two men more powerfully contrasted, never opposed each other face to face. The ruddy features of the locksmith so set off and heightened the excessive paleness of the man on horseback, that he looked like a bloodless ghost, while the moisture, which hard riding had brought out upon his skin, hung there in dark and heavy drops, like dews of agony and death. The countenance of the old locksmith was lighted up with the smile of one expecting to detect in this unpromising stranger some latent roguery of eye or lip, which should reveal a familiar person in that arch disguise, and spoil his jest. The face of the other, sullen and fierce, but shrinking too, was that of a man who stood at bay; while his firmly closed jaws, his puckered mouth, and more than all a certain stealthy motion of the hand within his breast, seemed to announce a desperate purpose very foreign to acting, or child's play.

Thus they regarded each other for some time, in silence.

'Humph!' he said when he had scanned his features; 'I don't know you.'

'Don't desire to?' – returned the other, muffling himself as before.

'I don't,' said Gabriel; 'to be plain with you, friend, you don't carry in your countenance a letter of recommendation.'

'It's not my wish,' said the traveller. 'My humour is to be avoided.'

'Well,' said the locksmith bluntly, 'I think you'll have your humour.'

'I will, at any cost,' rejoined the traveller. 'In proof of it, lay this to heart – that you were never in such peril of your life as you have been within these few moments; when you are within five minutes of breathing your last, you will not be nearer death than you have been to-night!'

'Aye!' said the sturdy locksmith.

'Aye! and a violent death.'

'From whose hand?'

'From mine,' replied the traveller.

With that he put spurs to his horse, and rode away; at first plashing heavily through the mire at a smart trot, but gradually increasing in speed until the last sound of his horse's hoofs died away upon the wind; when he was again hurrying on at the same furious gallop, which had been his pace when the locksmith first encountered him.

Gabriel Varden remained standing in the road with the broken lantern in his hand, listening in stupified silence until no sound reached his ear but the moaning of the wind, and the fast-falling rain; when he struck himself one or two smart blows in the breast by way of rousing himself, and broke into an exclamation of surprise.

'What in the name of wonder can this fellow be! a madman? a highwayman? a cut-throat? If he had not scoured off so fast, we'd have seen who was in most danger, he or I. I never nearer death than I have been to-night! I hope I may be no nearer to it for a score of years to come – if so, I'll be content to be no further from it. My stars! – a pretty brag this to a stout man – pooh, pooh!'

Gabriel resumed his seat, and looked wistfully up the road by which the traveller had come; murmuring in a half whisper:

'The Maypole – two miles to the Maypole. I came the other road from the Warren after a long day's work at locks and bells, on purpose that I should not come by the Maypole and break my promise to Martha by looking in – there's resolution! It would be dangerous to go on to London without a light; and it's four miles, and a good half-mile besides, to the Halfway-House; and between this and that is the very place where one needs a light most. Two miles to the Maypole! I told Martha I wouldn't; I said I wouldn't, and I didn't – there's resolution!'

Repeating these two last words very often, as if to compensate for the little resolution he was going to show by piquing himself on the great resolution he had shown, Gabriel Varden quietly turned back, determining to get a light at the Maypole, and to take nothing but a light.

When he got to the Maypole, however, and Joe, responding to his well-known hail, came running out to the horse's head, leaving the door open behind him, and disclosing a delicious perspective of warmth and brightness – when the ruddy gleam of the fire, streaming through the old red curtains of the common room, seemed to bring with it, as part of itself, a pleasant hum of voices, and a fragrant odour of steaming grog and rare tobacco, all steeped as it were in the cheerful glow – when the shadows, flitting across the curtain, showed that those inside had risen from their snug seats, and were making room in the snuggest corner (how well he knew that corner!) for the honest locksmith, and a broad glare, suddenly streaming up, bespoke the goodness of the crackling log from which a brilliant train of sparks was doubtless at that moment whirling up the chimney in honour of his coming – when, super-added to these enticements, there stole upon him from the distant kitchen a gentle sound of frying, with a musical clatter of plates and dishes, and a savoury smell that made even the boisterous wind a perfume – Gabriel felt his firmness oozing rapidly away. He tried to look stoically at the tavern, but his features would relax into a look of fondness. He turned his head the other way, and the cold black country seemed to frown him off, and to drive him for a refuge into its hospitable arms.

'The merciful man, Joe,' said the locksmith, 'is merciful to his beast. I'll get out for a little while.'

And how natural it was to get out. And how unnatural it seemed for a sober man to be plodding wearily along through miry roads, encountering the rude buffets of the wind and pelting of the rain, when there was a clean floor covered with crisp white sand, a well swept hearth, a blazing fire, a table decorated with white cloth, bright pewter flagons, and other tempting preparations for a well-cooked meal – when there were these things, and company disposed to make the most of them, all ready to his hand, and entreating him to enjoyment!

CHAPTER THE THIRD

Such were the locksmith's thoughts when first seated in the snug
corner, and slowly recovering from a pleasant defect of vision –
pleasant, because occasioned by the wind blowing in his eyes; which
made it a matter of sound policy and duty to himself, that he should
take refuge from the weather, and tempted him, for the same
reason, to aggravate a slight cough, and declare he felt but poorly.
Such were still his thoughts more than a full hour afterwards, when
supper over, he still sat with shining jovial face in the same warm
nook, listening to the cricket-like chirrup of little Solomon Daisy,
and bearing no unimportant or slightly respected part in the social
gossip round the Maypole fire.

'I wish he may be an honest man, that's all,' said Solomon,
winding up a variety of speculations relative to the stranger, concerning whom Gabriel had compared notes with the company, and
so raised a grave discussion; '*I* wish he may be an honest man.'

'So we all do, I suppose, don't we?' observed the locksmith.

'I don't,' said Joe.

'No!' cried Gabriel.

'No. He struck me with his whip, the coward, when he was
mounted and I afoot, and I should be better pleased that he turned
out what I think him.'

'And what may that be, Joe?'

'No good, Mr Varden. You may shake your head father, but I
say no good, and will say no good, and I would say no good a
hundred times over, if that would bring him back to have the
drubbing he deserves.'

'Hold your tongue sir,' said John Willet.

'I won't, father. It's all along of you that he dared to do what he
did. Seeing me treated like a child, and put down like a fool, *he*
plucks up a heart and has a fling at a fellow that he thinks – and
may well think too – hasn't a grain of spirit. But he's mistaken, as
I'll show him, and as I'll show all of you before long.'

'Does the boy know what he's a saying of!' cried the astonished
John Willet.

'Father,' returned Joe, 'I know what I say and mean, well – better
than you do when you hear me. I can bear with you, but I cannot
bear the contempt that your treating me in the way you do, brings

upon me from others every day. Look at other young men of my
age. Have they no liberty, no will, no right to speak? Are they
obliged to sit mumchance, and to be ordered about till they are the
laughing-stock of young and old? I am a bye-word all over Chigwell,
and I say – and it's fairer my saying so now, than waiting till you
are dead, and I have got your money – I say that before long I shall
be driven to break such bounds, and that when I do, it won't be me
that you'll have to blame, but your own self, and no other.'

John Willet was so amazed by the exasperation and boldness of
his hopeful son, that he sat as one bewildered, staring in a ludicrous
manner at the boiler, and endeavouring, but quite ineffectually, to
collect his tardy thoughts, and invent an answer. The guests,
scarcely less disturbed, were equally at a loss; and at length, with
a variety of muttered, half-expressed condolences, and pieces of
advice, rose to depart; being at the same time slightly muddled
with liquor.

The honest locksmith alone addressed a few words of coherent
and sensible advice to both parties, urging John Willet to remember
that Joe was nearly arrived at man's estate, and should not be ruled
with too tight a hand, and exhorting Joe himself to bear with
his father's caprices, and rather endeavour to turn them aside by
temperate remonstrance than by ill-timed rebellion. This advice
was received as such advice usually is. On John Willet it made
almost as much impression as on the sign outside the door, while
Joe, who took it in the best part, avowed himself more obliged
than he could well express, but politely intimated his intention
nevertheless of taking his own course uninfluenced by anybody.

'You have always been a very good friend to me, Mr Varden,' he
said, as they stood without the porch, and the locksmith was
equipping himself for his journey home; 'I take it very kind of you
to say all this, but the time's nearly come when the Maypole and I
must part company.'

'Roving stones gather no moss, Joe,' said Gabriel.

'Nor mile-stones much,' replied Joe. 'I'm little better than one
here, and see as much of the world.'

'Then what would you do, Joe,' pursued the locksmith, stroking
his chin reflectively. 'What could you be? where could you go, you
see?'

'I must trust to chance, Mr Varden.'

'A bad thing to trust to, Joe. I don't like it. I always tell my girl when we talk about a husband for her, never to trust to chance, but to make sure beforehand that she has a good man and true, and then chance will neither make her nor break her. What are you fidgeting about there, Joe? Nothing gone in the harness I hope?'

'No no,' said Joe – finding, however, something very engrossing to do in the way of strapping and buckling – 'Miss Dolly quite well?'

'Hearty, thankye. She looks pretty enough to be well, and good too.'

'She's always both sir'–

'So she is, thank God!'

'I hope' – said Joe after some hesitation, 'that you won't tell this story against me – this of my having been beat like the boy they'd make of me – at all events, till I have met this man again and settled the account. It'll be a better story then.'

'Why who should I tell it to?' returned Gabriel. 'They know it here, and I'm not likely to come across anybody else who would care about it.'

'That's true enough' – said the young fellow with a sigh. 'I quite forgot that. Yes, that's true!'

So saying, he raised his face, which was very red, – no doubt from the exertion of strapping and buckling as aforesaid, – and giving the reins to the old man, who had by this time taken his seat, sighed again and bade him good night.

'Good night!' cried Gabriel. 'Now think better of what we have just been speaking of, and don't be rash, there's a good fellow; I have an interest in you, and wouldn't have you cast yourself away. Good night!'

Returning his cheery farewell with cordial good will, Joe Willet lingered until the sound of wheels ceased to vibrate in his ears, and then, shaking his head mournfully, re-entered the house.

Gabriel Varden wended his way towards London, thinking of a great many things, and most of all of flaming terms in which to relate his adventure, and so account satisfactorily to Mrs Varden for visiting the Maypole, despite certain solemn covenants between himself and that lady. Thinking begets, not only thought, but drowsiness occasionally, and the more the locksmith thought, the more sleepy he became.

A man may be very sober – or at least firmly set upon his legs on that neutral ground which lies between the confines of perfect sobriety and slight tipsiness – and yet feel a strong tendency to mingle up present circumstances with others which have no manner of connexion with them; to confound all consideration of persons, things, times, and places; and to jumble his disjointed thoughts together in a kind of mental kaleidoscope, producing combinations as unexpected as they are transitory. This was Gabriel Varden's state, as, nodding in his dog sleep, and leaving his horse to pursue a road with which he was well acquainted, he got over the ground unconsciously, and drew nearer and nearer home. He had roused himself once, when the horse stopped until the turnpike gate was opened, and had cried a lusty 'good night' to the toll-keeper, but then he woke out of a dream about picking a lock in the stomach of the Great Mogul,[1] and even when he did wake, mixed up the turnpike man with his mother-in-law who had been dead twenty years. It is not surprising, therefore, that he soon relapsed, and jogged heavily along, quite insensible to his progress.

And now he approached the great city, which lay outstretched before him like a dark shadow on the ground, reddening the sluggish air with a deep dull light, that told of labyrinths of public ways and shops, and swarms of busy people. Approaching nearer and nearer yet, this halo began to fade, and the causes which produced it slowly to develop themselves. Long lines of poorly lighted streets might be faintly traced, with here and there a lighter spot, where lamps were clustered about a square or market, or round some great building; after a time these grew more distinct, and the lamps themselves were visible; slight yellow specks, that seemed to be rapidly snuffed out one by one as intervening obstacles hid them from the sight. Then sounds arose – the striking of church clocks, the distant bark of dogs, the hum of traffic in the streets; then outlines might be traced – tall steeples looming in the air, and piles of unequal roofs oppressed by chimneys: then the noise swelled into a louder sound, and forms grew more distinct and numerous still, and London – visible in the darkness by its own faint light, and not by that of Heaven – was at hand.

The locksmith, however, all unconscious of its near vicinity, still jogged on, half sleeping and half waking, when a loud cry at no great distance ahead, roused him with a start.

For a moment or two he looked about him like a man who had been transported to some strange country in his sleep, but soon recognizing familiar objects, rubbed his eyes lazily and might have relapsed again, but that the cry was repeated – not once or twice or thrice, but many times, and each time, if possible, with increased vehemence. Thoroughly aroused, Gabriel, who was a bold man and not easily daunted, made straight to the spot, urging on his stout little horse as if for life or death.

The matter indeed looked sufficiently serious, for, coming to the place whence the cries had proceeded, he descried the figure of a man extended in an apparently lifeless state upon the pathway, and hovering round him another person with a torch in his hand, which he waved in the air with a wild impatience, redoubling meanwhile those cries for help which had brought the locksmith to the spot.

'What's here to do?' said the old man, alighting. 'How's this – what – Barnaby?'

The bearer of the torch shook his long loose hair back from his eyes, and thrusting his face eagerly into that of the locksmith, fixed upon him a look which told his history at once.

'You know me, Barnaby?' said Varden.

He nodded – not once or twice, but a score of times, and that with a fantastic exaggeration which would have kept his head in motion for an hour, but that the locksmith held up his finger, and fixing his eye sternly upon him caused him to desist; then pointed to the body with an inquiring look.

'There's blood upon him,' said Barnaby with a shudder. 'It makes me sick.'

'How came it there?' demanded Varden.

'Steel, steel, steel!' he replied fiercely, imitating with his hand the thrust of a sword.

'Is he robbed?' said the locksmith.

Barnaby caught him by the arm, and nodded 'Yes;' then pointed towards the city.

'Oh!' said the old man, bending over the body and looking round as he spoke into Barnaby's pale face, strangely lighted up by something which was *not* intellect. 'The robber made off that way, did he? Well well, never mind that just now. Hold your torch this way – a little further off – so. Now stand quiet while I try to see what harm is done.'

With these words, he applied himself to a closer examination of the prostrate form, while Barnaby, holding the torch as he had been directed, looked on in silence, fascinated by interest or curiosity, but repelled nevertheless by some strong and secret horror which convulsed him in every nerve.

As he stood at that moment, half shrinking back and half bending forward, both his face and figure were full in the strong glare of the link, and as distinctly revealed as though it had been broad day. He was about three-and-twenty years old, and though rather spare, of a fair height and strong make. His hair, of which he had a great profusion, was red, and hanging in disorder about his face and shoulders, gave to his restless looks an expression quite unearthly – enhanced by the paleness of his complexion, and the glassy lustre of his large protruding eyes. Startling as his aspect was, the features were good, and there was something even plaintive in his wan and haggard aspect. But the absence of the soul is far more terrible in a living man than in a dead one; and in this unfortunate being its noblest powers were wanting.

His dress was of green, clumsily trimmed here and there – apparently by his own hands – with gaudy lace; brightest where the cloth was most worn and soiled, and poorest where it was at the best. A pair of tawdry ruffles dangled at his wrists, while his throat was nearly bare. He had ornamented his hat with a cluster of peacock's feathers, but they were limp and broken, and now trailed negligently down his back. Girded to his side was the steel hilt of an old sword without blade or scabbard; and some parti-coloured ends of ribands and poor glass toys completed the ornamental portion of his attire. The fluttered and confused disposition of all the motley scraps that formed his dress, bespoke, in a scarcely less degree than his eager and unsettled manner, the disorder of his mind, and by a grotesque contrast set off and heightened the more impressive wildness of his face.

'Barnaby,' said the locksmith, after a hasty but careful inspection, 'this man is not dead, but he has a wound in his side, and is in a fainting-fit.'

'I know him, I know him!' cried Barnaby, clapping his hands.

'Know him?' repeated the locksmith.

'Hush!' said Barnaby, laying his fingers on his lips. 'He went out to-day a wooing. I wouldn't for a light guinea that he should never go a wooing again, for if he did some eyes would grow dim that are now as bright as – see, when I talk of eyes, the stars come out. Whose eyes are they? If they are angels' eyes, why do they look

down here and see good men hurt, and only wink and sparkle all the night?'

'Now Heaven help this silly fellow,' murmured the perplexed locksmith, 'can he know this gentleman? His mother's house is not far off; I had better see if she can tell me who he is. Barnaby my man, help me to put him in the chaise, and we'll ride home together.'

'I can't touch him!' cried the idiot falling back, and shuddering as with a strong spasm; 'he's bloody.'

'It's in his nature I know,' muttered the locksmith, 'it's cruel to ask him, but I must have help. Barnaby – good Barnaby – dear Barnaby – if you know this gentleman, for the sake of his life and everybody's life that loves him, help me to raise him and lay him down.'

'Cover him then, wrap him close – don't let me see it – smell it – hear the word. Don't speak the word – don't!'

'No, no, I'll not. There, you see he's covered now. Gently. Well done, well done!'

They placed him in the carriage with great ease, for Barnaby was strong and active, but all the time they were so occupied he shivered from head to foot, and evidently experienced such an ecstacy of terror that the locksmith could scarcely endure to witness his suffering.

This accomplished, and the wounded man being covered with Varden's own great-coat which he took off for the purpose, they proceeded onwards at a brisk pace: Barnaby gaily counting the stars upon his fingers, and Gabriel inwardly congratulating himself upon having an adventure now, which would silence Mrs Varden on the subject of the Maypole for that night, or there was no faith in woman.

*

CHAPTER THE FOURTH

In the venerable suburb – it was a suburb once – of Clerkenwell, towards that part of its confines which is nearest to the Charter House,[1] and in one of those cool, shady streets, of which a few, widely scattered and dispersed, yet remain in such old parts of the metropolis, – each tenement quietly vegetating like an ancient

citizen who long ago retired from business, and dozing on in its
infirmity until in course of time it tumbles down, and is replaced
by some extravagant young heir, flaunting in stucco and ornamental
work, and all the vanities of modern days, – in this quarter, and in
a street of this description, the business of the present chapter
lies.

At the time of which it treats, though only six-and-sixty years
ago, a very large part of what is London now had no existence.
Even in the brains of the wildest speculators, there had sprung up
no long rows of streets connecting Highgate with Whitechapel,[2] no
assemblages of palaces in the swampy levels, nor little cities in the
open fields. Although this part of town was then, as now, parcelled
out in streets and plentifully peopled, it wore a different aspect.
There were gardens to many of the houses, and trees by the pavement side; with an air of freshness breathing up and down, which
in these days would be sought in vain. Fields were nigh at hand,
through which the New River[3] took its winding course, and where
there was merry hay-making in the summer time. Nature was not
so far removed or hard to get at, as in these days; and although
there were busy trades in Clerkenwell, and working jewellers by
scores, it was a purer place, with farm-houses nearer to it than
many modern Londoners would readily believe; and lovers' walks
at no great distance, which turned into squalid courts, long before
the lovers of this age were born, or, as the phrase goes, thought of.

In one of these streets, the cleanest of them all, and on the shady
side of the way – for good housewives know that sunlight damages
their cherished furniture, and so choose the shade rather than its
intrusive glare – there stood the house with which we have to
deal. It was a modest building, not over-newly fashioned, not very
straight, not large, not tall; not bold-faced, with great staring
windows, but a shy, blinking house, with a conical roof going up
into a peak over its garret window of four small panes of glass, like
a cocked hat on the head of an elderly gentleman with one eye. It
was not built of brick or lofty stone, but of wood and plaster; it
was not planned with a dull and wearisome regard to regularity,
for no one window matched the other, or seemed to have the
slightest reference to anything besides itself.

The shop – for it had a shop – was, with reference to the first
floor, where shops usually are; and there all resemblance between
it and any other shop stopped short and ceased. People who went

in and out didn't go up a flight of steps to it, or walk easily in upon a level with the street, but dived down three steep stairs, as into a cellar. Its floor was paved with stone and brick, as that of any other cellar might be; and in lieu of window framed and glazed it had a great black wooden flap or shutter, nearly breast high from the ground, which turned back in the day-time, admitting as much cold air as light, and very often more. Behind this shop was a wainscoted parlour, looking first into a paved yard, and beyond that again into a little terrace garden, raised some few feet above it. Any stranger would have supposed that this wainscoted parlour, saving for the door of communication by which he had entered, was cut off and detached from all the world; and indeed most strangers on their first entrance were observed to grow extremely thoughtful, as weighing and pondering in their minds whether the upper rooms were only approachable by ladders from without; never suspecting that two of the most unassuming and unlikely doors in existence, which the most ingenious mechanician on earth must of necessity have supposed to be the doors of closets, opened out of this room – each without the smallest preparation, or so much as a quarter of an inch of passage – upon two dark winding flights of stairs, the one upward, the other downward; which were the sole means of communication between that chamber and the other portions of the house.

With all these oddities, there was not a neater, more scrupulously tidy, or more punctiliously ordered house, in Clerkenwell, in London, in all England. There were not cleaner windows, or whiter floors, or brighter stoves, or more highly shining articles of furniture in old mahogany; there was not more rubbing, scrubbing, burnishing and polishing, in the whole street put together. Nor was this excellence attained without some cost and trouble and great expenditure of voice, as the neighbours were frequently reminded when the good lady of the house overlooked and assisted in its being put to rights on cleaning days; which were usually from Monday morning till Saturday night, both days inclusive.

Leaning against the door-post of this, his dwelling, the locksmith stood early on the morning after he had met with the wounded man, gazing disconsolately at a great wooden emblem of a key, painted in vivid yellow to resemble gold, which dangled from the house-front, and swung to and fro with a mournful creaking noise, as if complaining that it had nothing to unlock. Sometimes he looked over his shoulder into the shop, which was so dark and dingy with numerous tokens of his trade, and so blackened by the smoke of a little forge, near which his 'prentice was at work, that it would have been difficult for one unused to such espials to have distinguished anything but various tools of uncouth make and shape, great bunches of rusty keys, fragments of iron, half-finished locks, and such-like things, which garnished the walls and hung in clusters from the ceiling.

After a long and patient contemplation of the golden key, and many such backward glances, Gabriel stepped into the road, and stole a look at the upper windows. One of them chanced to be thrown open at the moment, and a roguish face met his; a face lighted up by the loveliest pair of sparkling eyes that ever locksmith looked upon; the face of a pretty, laughing, girl; dimpled and fresh, and healthful – the very impersonation of good-humour and blooming beauty.

'Hush!' she whispered, bending forward, and pointing archly to the window underneath. 'Mother is still asleep.'

'Still, my dear,' returned the locksmith in the same tone. 'You talk as if she had been asleep all night, instead of little more than half an hour. But I'm very thankful. Sleep's a blessing – no doubt about it.' The last few words he muttered to himself.

'How cruel of you to keep us up so late this morning, and never tell us where you were, or send us word!' said the girl.

'Ah Dolly, Dolly!' returned the locksmith, shaking his head, and smiling, 'how cruel of you to run up stairs to bed! Come down to breakfast, madcap, and come down lightly, or you'll wake your mother. She must be tired, I am sure – *I* am!'

Keeping these latter words to himself, and returning his daughter's nod, he was passing into the workshop, with the smile she had awakened still beaming on his face, when he just caught sight of his 'prentice's brown paper cap ducking down to avoid observation, and shrinking from the window back to its former place, which the wearer no sooner reached than he began to hammer lustily.

'Listening again, Simon!' said Gabriel to himself. 'That's bad. What in the name of wonder does he expect the girl to say, that I always catch him listening when *she* speaks, and never at any other time! A bad habit, Sim, a sneaking, underhanded way. Ah! you may hammer, but you won't beat that out of me, if you work at it till your time's up!'

So saying, and shaking his head gravely, he re-entered the work-shop, and confronted the subject of these remarks.

'There's enough of that just now,' said the locksmith. 'You needn't make any more of that confounded clatter. Breakfast's ready.'

'Sir,' said Sim, looking up with amazing politeness, and a peculiar little bow cut short off at the neck, 'I shall attend you immediately.'

'I suppose,' muttered Gabriel, 'that's out of the 'Prentice's Garland, or the 'Prentice's Delight, or the 'Prentice's Warbler, or the 'Prentice's Guide to the Gallows,[4] or some such improving text-book. Now he's going to beautify himself – here's a precious locksmith!'

Quite unconscious that his master was looking on from the dark corner by the parlour door, Sim threw off the paper cap, sprang from his seat, and in two extraordinary steps, something between skating and minuet dancing, bounded to a washing place at the other end of the shop, and there removed from his face and hands all traces of his previous work – practising the same step all the time with the utmost gravity. This done, he drew from some concealed place a little scrap of looking-glass, and with its assistance arranged his hair, and ascertained the exact state of a little carbuncle on his nose. Having now completed his toilet, he placed the fragment of mirror on a low bench, and looked over his shoulder at so much of his legs as could be reflected in that small compass, with the greatest possible complacency and satisfaction.

Sim, as he was called in the locksmith's family, or Mr Simon Tappertit, as he called himself, and required all men to style him out of doors, on holidays, and Sundays out, – was an old-fashioned, thin-faced, sleek-haired, sharp-nosed, small-eyed little fellow, very little more than five feet high, and thoroughly convinced in his own mind that he was above the middle size; rather tall, in fact, than otherwise. Of his figure, which was well enough formed, though somewhat of the leanest, he entertained the highest admiration; and with his legs, which, in knee-breeches, were perfect curiosities of littleness, he was enraptured to a degree amounting to enthusiasm. He also had some majestic, shadowy ideas, which had never been quite fathomed by his most intimate friends, concerning the power of his eye. Indeed he had been known to go so far as to boast that he could utterly quell and subdue the haughtiest beauty by a

simple process, which he termed 'eyeing her over;' but it must be
added, that neither of this faculty, nor of the power he claimed to
have, through the same gift, of vanquishing and beating down
dumb animals, even in a rabid state, had he ever furnished evidence
which could be deemed quite satisfactory and conclusive.

It may be inferred from these premises, that in the small body
of Mr Tappertit there was locked up an ambitious and aspiring
soul. As certain liquors, confined in casks too cramped in their
dimensions, will ferment, and fret, and chafe in their imprisonment, so the spiritual essence or soul of Mr Tappertit would sometimes fume within that precious cask, his body, until, with great
foam and froth and splutter, it would force a vent, and carry all
before it. It was his custom to remark, in reference to any one of
these occasions, that his soul had got into his head; and in this
novel kind of intoxication many scraps and mishaps befel him,
which he had frequently concealed with no small difficulty from his
worthy master.

Sim Tappertit, among the other fancies upon which his before-
mentioned soul was for ever feasting and regaling itself (and which
fancies, like the liver of Prometheus,[5] grew as they were fed upon),
had a mighty notion of his order; and had been heard by the
servant-maid openly expressing his regret that the 'prentices no
longer carried clubs wherewith to mace the citizens: that was his
strong expression. He was likewise reported to have said that in
former times a stigma had been cast upon the body by the execution
of George Barnwell,[6] to which they should not have basely submitted, but should have demanded him of the legislature – temperately
at first; then by an appeal to arms, if necessary – to be dealt with
as they in their wisdom might think fit. These thoughts always led
him to consider what a glorious engine the 'prentices might yet
become if they had but a master spirit at their head; and then he
would darkly, and to the terror of his hearers, hint at certain
reckless fellows that he knew of, and at a certain Lion Heart[7] ready
to become their captain, who, once afoot, would make the Lord
Mayor tremble on his throne.

In respect of dress and personal decoration, Sim Tappertit was
no less of an adventurous and enterprising character. He had been
seen, beyond dispute, to pull off ruffles of the finest quality at the
corner of the street on Sunday nights, and to put them carefully in
his pocket before returning home; and it was quite notorious that

on all great holiday occasions it was his habit to exchange his plain steel knee-buckles for a pair of glittering paste, under cover of a friendly post, planted most conveniently in that same spot. Add to this that he was in years just twenty, in his looks much older, and in conceit at least two hundred; that he had no objection to be jested with touching his admiration of his master's daughter; and had even, when called upon at a certain obscure tavern to pledge the lady whom he honoured with his love, toasted, with many winks and leers, a fair creature whose Christian name, he said, began with a D –; – and as much is known of Sim Tappertit, who has by this time followed the locksmith in to breakfast, as is necessary to be known in making his acquaintance.

It was a substantial meal; for over and above the ordinary tea equipage, the board creaked beneath the weight of a jolly round of beef, a ham of the first magnitude, and sundry towers of buttered Yorkshire cake, piled slice upon slice in most alluring order. There was also a goodly jug of well-browned clay, fashioned into the form of an old gentleman, not by any means unlike the locksmith, atop of whose bald head was a fine white froth answering to his wig, indicative, beyond dispute, of sparkling home-brewed ale. But better far than fair home-brewed, or Yorkshire cake, or ham, or beef, or anything to eat or drink that earth or air or water can supply, there sat, presiding over all, the locksmith's rosy daughter, before whose dark eyes even beef grew insignificant, and malt became as nothing.

Fathers should never kiss their daughters when young men are by. It's too much. There are bounds to human endurance. So thought Sim Tappertit when Gabriel drew those rosy lips to his – those lips within Sim's reach from day to day, and yet so far off. He had a respect for his master, but he wished the Yorkshire cake might choke him.

'Father,' said the locksmith's daughter, when this salute was over, and they took their seats at table, 'what is this I hear about last night?'

'All true, my dear; true as the Gospel, Doll.'

'Young Mr Chester robbed, and lying wounded in the road, when you came up?'

'Ay – Mr Edward. And beside him, Barnaby, calling for help with all his might. It was well it happened as it did; for the road's a lonely one, the hour was late, and, the night being cold, and poor

Barnaby even less sensible than usual from surprise and fright, the young gentleman might have met his death in a very short time.'

'I dread to think of it!' cried his daughter with a shudder. 'How did you know him?'

'Know him!' returned the locksmith. 'I didn't know him – how could I? I had never seen him, often as I had heard and spoken of him. I took him to Mrs Rudge's; and she no sooner saw him than the truth came out.'

'Miss Emma, father – If this news should reach her, enlarged upon as it is sure to be, she will go distracted.'

'Why, lookye there again, how a man suffers for being good-natured,' said the locksmith. 'Miss Emma was with her uncle at the masquerade at Carlisle House,[8] where she had gone, as the people at the Warren told me, sorely against her will. What does your blockhead father when he and Mrs Rudge have laid their heads together, but goes there when he ought to be abed, makes interest with his friend the doorkeeper, slips him on a mask and domino, and mixes with the masquers.'

'And like himself to do so!' cried the girl, putting her fair arm round his neck, and giving him a most enthusiastic kiss.

'Like himself!' repeated Gabriel, affecting to grumble, but evidently delighted with the part he had taken, and with her praise. 'Very like himself – so your mother said. However, he mingled with the crowd, and prettily worried and badgered he was, I warrant you, with people squeaking, "Don't you know me?" and "I've found you out," and all that kind of nonsense in his ears. He might have wandered on till now, but in a little room there was a young lady who had taken off her mask, on account of the place being very warm, and was sitting there alone.'

'And that was she?' said his daughter hastily.

'And that was she,' replied the locksmith; 'and I no sooner whispered to her what the matter was – as softly, Doll, and with nearly as much art as you could have used yourself – than she gives a kind of scream and faints away.'

'What did you do – what happened next?' asked his daughter.

'Why, the masks came flocking round, with a general noise and hubbub, and I thought myself in luck to get clear off, that's all,' rejoined the locksmith. 'What happened when I reached home you may guess, if you didn't hear it. Ah! Well, it's a poor heart that never rejoices. – Put Toby this way, my dear.'

This Toby was the brown jug of which previous mention has been made. Applying his lips to the worthy old gentleman's benevolent forehead, the locksmith, who had all this time been ravaging among the eatables, kept them there so long, at the same time raising the vessel slowly in the air, that at length Toby stood on his head upon his nose, when he smacked his lips, and set him on the table again with fond reluctance.

Although Sim Tappertit had taken no share in this conversation, no part of it being addressed to him, he had not been wanting in such silent manifestations of astonishment, as he deemed most compatible with the favourable display of his eyes. Regarding the pause which now ensued, as a particularly advantageous opportunity for doing great execution with them upon the locksmith's daughter (who he had no doubt was looking at him in mute admiration), he began to screw and twist his face, and especially those features, into such extraordinary, hideous, and unparalleled contortions, that Gabriel, who happened to look towards him, was stricken with amazement.

'Why, what the devil's the matter with the lad!' cried the locksmith. 'Is he choking?'

'Who?' demanded Sim, with some disdain.

'Who? why, you,' returned his master. 'What do you mean by making those horrible faces over your breakfast?'

'Faces are matters of taste, sir,' said Mr Tappertit, rather discomfited; not the less so because he saw the locksmith's daughter smiling.

'Sim,' rejoined Gabriel, laughing heartily. 'Don't be a fool, for I'd rather see you in your senses. These young fellows,' he added, turning to his daughter, 'are always committing some folly or another. There was a quarrel between Joe Willet and old John last night – though I can't say Joe was much in fault either. He'll be missing one of these mornings, and will have gone away upon some wild-goose errand, seeking his fortune. – Why, what's the matter, Doll? *You* are making faces now. The girls are as bad as the boys every bit!'

'It's the tea,' said Dolly, turning alternately very red and very white, which is no doubt the effect of a slight scald – 'so very hot.'

Mr Tappertit looked immensely big at a quartern loaf on the table and breathed hard.

'Is that all?' returned the locksmith. 'Put some more milk in it.

Yes, I am sorry for Joe, because he is a likely young fellow, and gains upon one every time one sees him. But he'll start off you'll find. Indeed he told me as much himself!'

'Indeed!' cried Dolly in a faint voice. 'In—deed!'

'Is the tea tickling your throat still, my dear?' said the locksmith.

But before his daughter could make him any answer, she was taken with a troublesome cough, and it was such a very unpleasant cough, that when she left off the tears were starting in her bright eyes. The good-natured locksmith was still patting her on the back and applying such gentle restoratives, when a message arrived from Mrs Varden, making known to all whom it might concern, that she felt too much indisposed to rise after her great agitation and anxiety of the previous night; and therefore desired to be immediately accommodated with the little black tea-pot of strong mixed tea, a couple of rounds of buttered toast, a middling-sized dish of beef and ham cut thin, and the Protestant Manual[9] in two volumes post octavo. Like some other ladies who in remote ages flourished upon this globe, Mrs Varden was most devout when most ill-tempered. Whenever she and her husband were at unusual variance, then the Protestant Manual was in high feather.

Knowing from experience what these requests portended, the triumvirate broke up: Dolly to see the orders executed with all despatch; Gabriel to some out-of-door work in his little chaise; and Sim to his daily duty in the workshop, to which retreat he carried the big look, although the loaf remained behind.

Indeed the big look increased immensely, and when he had tied his apron on, was quite gigantic. It was not until he had several times walked up and down with folded arms, and the longest strides he could take, and had kicked a great many small articles out of his way, that his lip began to curl. At length a gloomy derision came upon his features, and he smiled; uttering meanwhile with supreme contempt the monosyllable 'Joe!'

'I eyed her over while he talked about the fellow,' he said, 'and that was of course the reason of her being confused. Joe!'

He walked up and down again much quicker than before, and if possible with longer strides; sometimes stopping to take a glance at his legs, and sometimes to jerk out as it were, and cast from him, another 'Joe!' In the course of quarter an hour or so he again assumed the paper cap and tried to work. No. It could not be done.

'I'll do nothing to-day,' said Mr Tappertit, dashing it down again, 'but grind. I'll grind up all the tools. Grinding will suit my present humour well. Joe!'

Whirr-r-r-r. The grindstone was soon in motion; the sparks were flying off in showers. This was the occupation for his heated spirit.

Whirr-r-r-r-r-r.

'Something will come of this!' said Mr Tappertit, pausing as if in triumph, and wiping his heated face upon his sleeve. 'Something will come of this. I hope it mayn't be human gore.'

Whirr-r-r-r-r-r-r.

CHAPTER THE FIFTH

As soon as the business of the day was over, the locksmith sallied forth alone to visit the wounded gentleman and ascertain the progress of his recovery. The house where he had left him was in a by-street in Southwark, not far from London Bridge;[1] and thither he hied with all speed, bent upon returning with as little delay as might be, and getting to bed betimes.

The evening was boisterous – scarcely better than the previous night had been. It was not easy for a stout man like Gabriel to keep his legs at the street corners, or to make head against the high wind; which often fairly got the better of him, and drove him back some paces, or, in defiance of all his energy, forced him to take shelter in an arch or doorway until the fury of the gust was spent. Occasionally a hat or wig, or both, came spinning and trundling past him, like a mad thing; while the more serious spectacle of falling tiles and slates, or of masses of brick and mortar or fragments of stone-coping rattling upon the pavement near at hand, and splitting into fragments, did not increase the pleasure of the journey, or make the way less dreary.

'A trying night for a man like me to walk in!' said the locksmith, as he knocked softly at the widow's door. 'I'd rather be in old John's chimney-corner, faith!'

'Who's there?' demanded a woman's voice from within. Being answered, it added a hasty word of welcome, and the door was quickly opened.

She was about forty – perhaps two or three years older – with a cheerful aspect, and a face that had once been pretty. It bore traces of affliction and care, but they were of an old date, and Time had smoothed them. Any one who had bestowed but a casual glance on Barnaby might have known that this was his mother, from the strong resemblance between them; but where in his face there was wildness and vacancy, in hers there was the patient composure of long effort and quiet resignation.[2]

One thing about this face was very strange and startling. You could not look upon it in its most cheerful mood without feeling that it had some extraordinary capacity of expressing terror. It was not on the surface. It was in no one feature that it lingered. You could not take the eyes, or mouth, or lines upon the cheek, and say, if this or that were otherwise, it would not be so. Yet there it always lurked – something for ever dimly seen, but ever there, and never absent for a moment. It was the faintest, palest shadow of some look, to which an instant of intense and most unutterable horror only could have given birth; but indistinct and feeble as it was, it did suggest what that look must have been, and fixed it in the mind as if it had had existence in a dream.

More faintly imaged, and wanting force and purpose, as it were, because of his darkened intellect, there was this same stamp upon the son. Seen in a picture, it must have had some legend with it, and would have haunted those who looked upon the canvas. They who knew the Maypole story, and could remember what the widow was, before her husband's and his master's murder, understood it well. They recollected how the change had come, and could call to mind that when her son was born, upon the very day the deed was known, he bore upon his wrist what seemed a smear of blood[3] but half washed out.

'God save you, neighbour,' said the locksmith, as he followed her with the air of an old friend into a little parlour where a cheerful fire was burning.

'And you,' she answered, smiling. 'Your kind heart has brought you here again. Nothing will keep you at home, I know of old, if there are friends to serve or comfort, out of doors.'

'Tut, tut,' returned the locksmith, rubbing his hands and warming them. 'You women are such talkers. What of the patient, neighbour?'

'He is sleeping now. He was very restless towards daylight, and for some hours tossed and tumbled sadly. But the fever has left him, and the doctor says he will soon mend. He must not be removed until to-morrow.'

'He has had visitors to-day – humph?' said Gabriel, slyly.

'Yes. Old Mr Chester has been here ever since we sent for him, and had not been gone many minutes when you knocked.'

'No ladies?' said Gabriel, elevating his eyebrows and looking disappointed.

'A letter,' replied the widow.

'Come. That's better than nothing!' cried the locksmith. 'Who was the bearer?'

'Barnaby, of course.'

'Barnaby's a jewel!' said Varden; 'and comes and goes with ease where we who think ourselves much wiser would make but a poor hand of it. He is not out wandering, again, I hope?'

'Thank Heaven he is in his bed; having been up all night, as you know, and on his feet all day. He was quite tired out. Ah, neighbour, if I could but see him oftener so – if I could but tame down that terrible restlessness –'

'In good time,' said the locksmith kindly, 'in good time – don't be down-hearted. To my mind he grows wiser every day.'

The widow shook her head. And yet, though she knew the locksmith sought to cheer her, and spoke from no conviction of his own, she was glad to hear even this praise of her poor benighted son.

'He will be a 'cute man yet,' resumed the locksmith. 'Take care, when we are growing old and foolish, Barnaby doesn't put us to the blush, that's all. But our other friend,' he added, looking under the table and about the floor – 'sharpest and cunningest of all the sharp and cunning ones – where's he?'

'In Barnaby's room,' rejoined the widow, with a faint smile.

'Ah! He's a knowing blade!' said Varden, shaking his head. 'I should be sorry to talk secrets before him. Oh! He's a deep customer. I've no doubt he can read and write and cast accounts if he chooses. What was that – him tapping at the door?'

'No,' returned the widow. 'It was in the street, I think. Hark! Yes. There again! 'Tis some one knocking softly at the shutter. Who can it be!'

They had been speaking in a low tone, for the invalid lay overhead, and the walls and ceilings being thin and poorly built, the sound of their voices might otherwise have disturbed his slumber.

The party without, whoever it was, could have stood close to the
shutter without hearing anything spoken; and, seeing the light
through the chinks and finding all so quiet, might have been persuaded that only one person was there.

'Some thief or ruffian, maybe,' said the locksmith. 'Give me the
light.'

'No, no,' she returned hastily. 'Such visitors have never come to
this poor dwelling. Do you stay here. You're within call, at the
worst. I would rather go myself – alone.'

'Why?' said the locksmith, unwillingly relinquishing the candle
he had caught up from the table.

'Because – I don't know why – because the wish is strong upon
me,' she rejoined. 'There again – do not detain me, I beg of
you!'

Gabriel looked at her, in great surprise to see one who was
usually so mild and quiet thus agitated, and with so little cause.
She left the room and closed the door behind her. She stood for a
moment as if hesitating, with her hand upon the lock. In this short
interval the knocking came again, and a voice close to the window
– a voice the locksmith seemed to recollect, and to have some
disagreeable association with – whispered 'Make haste.'

The words were uttered in that low distinct voice which finds its
way so readily to sleepers' ears, and wakes them in a fright. For a
moment it startled even the locksmith; who involuntarily drew
back from the window, and listened.

The wind rumbling in the chimney made it difficult to hear what
passed, but he could tell that the door was opened, that there was
the tread of a man upon the creaking boards, and then a moment's
silence – broken by a suppressed something which was not a shriek,
or groan, or cry for help, and yet might have been either or all
three; and the words 'My God!' uttered in a voice it chilled him
to hear.

He rushed out upon the instant. There, at last, was that dreadful
look – the very one he seemed to know so well and yet had never
seen before – upon her face. There she stood, frozen to the ground,
gazing with starting eyes, and livid cheeks, and every feature fixed
and ghastly, upon the man he had encountered in the dark last
night. His eyes met those of the locksmith. It was but a flash, an
instant, a breath upon a polished glass, and he was gone.

The locksmith was upon him – had the skirts of his streaming garment almost in his grasp – when his arms were tightly clutched, and the widow flung herself upon the ground before him.

'The other way – the other way,' she cried. 'He went the other way. Turn – turn.'

'The other way! I see him now,' rejoined the locksmith, pointing – 'yonder – there – there is his shadow passing by that light. What – who is this? Let me go.'

'Come back, come back!' exclaimed the woman, wrestling with and clasping him; 'Do not touch him on your life. I charge you, come back. He carries other lives besides his own. Come back!'

'What does this mean?' cried the locksmith.

'No matter what it means, don't ask, don't speak, don't think about it. He is not to be followed, checked, or stopped. Come back!'

The old man looked at her in wonder, as she writhed and clung about him; and, borne down by her passion, suffered her to drag him into the house. It was not until she had chained and double-locked the door, fastened every bolt and bar with the heat and fury of a maniac, and drawn him back into the room, that she turned upon him once again that stony look of horror, and, sinking down into a chair, covered her face, and shuddered, as though the hand of death were on her.

—— * ——

CHAPTER THE SIXTH

Beyond all measure astonished by the strange occurrences which had passed with so much violence and rapidity, the locksmith gazed upon the shuddering figure in the chair like one half stupified, and would have gazed much longer, had not his tongue been loosened by compassion and humanity.

'You are ill,' said Gabriel. 'Let me call some neighbour in.'

'Not for the world,' she rejoined, motioning to him with her trembling hand, and still holding her face averted. 'It is enough that you have been by, to see this.'

'Nay, more than enough – or less,' said Gabriel.

'Be it so,' she returned. 'As you like. Ask me no questions, I entreat you.'

'Neighbour,' said the locksmith, after a pause. 'Is this fair, or reasonable, or just to yourself? Is it like you, who have known me so long and sought my advice in all matters – like you, who from a girl have had a strong mind and a staunch heart?'

'I have had need of them,' she replied. 'I am growing old, both in years and care. Perhaps that, and too much trial, have made them weaker than they used to be. Do not speak to me.'

'How can I see what I have seen, and hold my peace!' returned the locksmith. 'Who was that man, and why has his coming made this change in you?'

She was silent, but clung to the chair as though to save herself from falling on the ground.

'I take the license of an old acquaintance, Mary,' said the locksmith, 'who has ever had a warm regard for you, and maybe has tried to prove it when he could. Who is this ill-favoured man, and what has he to do with you? Who is this ghost, that is only seen in the black nights and bad weather? How does he know and why does he haunt this house, whispering through chinks and crevices, as if there was that between him and you, which neither durst so much as speak aloud of? Who is he?'

'You do well to say he haunts this house,' returned the widow, faintly. 'His shadow has been upon it and me, in light and darkness, at noonday and midnight. And now, at last, he has come in the body!'

'But he wouldn't have gone in the body,' returned the locksmith with some irritation, 'if you had left my arms and legs at liberty. What riddle is this?'

'It is one,' she answered, rising as she spoke, 'that must remain for ever as it is. I dare not say more than that.'

'Dare not!' repeated the wondering locksmith.

'Do not press me,' she replied. 'I am sick and faint, and every faculty of life seems dead within me. – No! – Do not touch me, either.'

Gabriel, who had stepped forward to render her assistance, fell back as she made this hasty exclamation, and regarded her in silent wonder.

'Let me go my way alone,' she said in a low voice, 'and let the hands of no honest man touch mine to-night.' When she had tottered to the door, she turned, and added with a stronger effort. 'This is a secret, which, of necessity, I trust to you. You are a true man. As you have ever been good and kind to me, – keep it. If any noise was heard above, make some excuse – say anything but what you really saw, and never let a word or look between us, recal this circumstance. I trust to you. Mind, I trust to you. How much I trust, you never can conceive.'

Fixing her eyes upon him for an instant, she withdrew, and left him there alone.

Gabriel, not knowing what to think, stood staring at the door with a countenance full of surprise and dismay. The more he pondered on what had passed, the less able he was to give it any favourable interpretation. To find this widow woman, whose life for so many years had been supposed to be one of solitude and retirement, and who, in her quiet suffering character, had gained the good opinion and respect of all who knew her – to find her linked mysteriously with an ill-omened man, alarmed at his appearance, and yet favouring his escape, was a discovery that pained as much as it startled him. Her reliance on his secrecy, and his tacit acquiescence, increased his distress of mind. If he had spoken boldly, persisted in questioning her, detained her when she rose to leave the room, made any kind of protest, instead of silently compromising himself, as he felt he had done, he would have been more at ease.

'Why did I let her say it was a secret, and she trusted it to me!' said Gabriel, putting his wig on one side to scratch his head with greater ease, and looking ruefully at the fire. 'I have no more readiness than old John himself. Why didn't I say firmly, "You have no right to such secrets, and I demand of you to tell me what this means," instead of standing gaping at her, like an old mooncalf as I am! But there's my weakness. I can be obstinate enough with men if need be, but women may twist me round their fingers at their pleasure.'

He took his wig off outright as he made this reflection, and warming his handkerchief at the fire began to rub and polish his bald head with it, until it glistened again.

'And yet,' said the locksmith, softening under this soothing process, and stopping to smile, 'it *may* be nothing. Any drunken brawler trying to make his way into the house, would have alarmed a quiet soul like her. But then' – and here was the vexation – 'how came it to be that man; how comes he to have this influence over her; how came she to favour his getting away from me; and more

than all, how came she not to say it was a sudden fright, and
nothing more? It's a sad thing to have, in one minute, reason to
mistrust a person I have known so long, and an old sweetheart into
the bargain; but what else can I do, with all this upon my mind! –
Is that Barnaby outside there?'

'Ay!' he cried, looking in and nodding. 'Sure enough it's Barnaby
– how did you guess?'

'By your shadow,' said the locksmith.

'Oho!' cried Barnaby, glancing over his shoulder, 'He's a merry
fellow, that shadow, and keeps close to me, though I *am* silly. We
have such pranks, such walks, such runs, such gambols on the
grass. Sometimes he'll be half as tall as a church steeple, and
sometimes no bigger than a dwarf. Now he goes on before, and
now behind, and anon he'll be stealing slyly on, on this side, or on
that, stopping whenever I stop, and thinking I can't see him, though
I have my eye on him sharp enough. Oh! he's a merry fellow. Tell
me – is he silly too? I think he is.'

'Why?' asked Gabriel.

'Because he never tires of mocking me, but does it all day long.
– Why don't you come?'

'Where?'

'Up stairs. He wants you. Stay – where's his shadow? Come.
You're a wise man; tell me that.'

'Beside him, Barnaby; beside him, I suppose,' returned the
locksmith.

'No!' he replied, shaking his head. 'Guess again.'

'Gone out a walking, maybe?'

'He has changed shadows with a woman,' the idiot whispered in
his ear, and then fell back with a look of triumph. 'Her shadow's
always with him, and his with her. That's sport I think, eh?'

'Barnaby,' said the locksmith, with a grave look; 'come hither,
lad.'

'I know what you want to say. I know!' he replied, keeping away
from him. 'But I'm cunning, I'm silent. I only say so much to you –
are you ready?' As he spoke, he caught up the light, and waved it
with a wild laugh above his head.

'Softly – gently,' said the locksmith, exerting all his influence to
keep him calm and quiet. 'I thought you had been asleep.'

'So I *have* been asleep,' he rejoined, with widely-opened eyes.
'There have been great faces coming and going – close to my face,

and then a mile away – low places to creep through, whether I would or no – high churches to fall down from – strange creatures crowded up together neck and heels, to sit upon the bed – that's sleep, eh?'

'Dreams, Barnaby, dreams,' said the locksmith.

'Dreams!' he echoed softly, drawing closer to him. 'Those are not dreams.'

'What are,' replied the locksmith, 'if they are not?'

'I dreamed,' said Barnaby, passing his arm through Varden's, and peering close into his face as he answered in a whisper, 'I dreamed just now that something – it was in the shape of a man – followed me – came softly after me – wouldn't let me be – but was always hiding and crouching, like a cat in dark corners, waiting till I should pass; when it crept out and came softly after me. – Did you ever see me run?'

'Many a time, you know.'

'You never saw me run as I did in this dream. Still it came creeping on to worry me. Nearer, nearer, nearer – I ran faster – leaped – sprung out of bed, and to the window – and there, in the street below – but he is waiting for us. Are you coming?'

'What in the street below, dear Barnaby?' said Varden, imagining that he traced some connexion between this vision and what had actually occurred.

Barnaby looked into his face, muttered incoherently, waved the light above his head again, laughed, and drawing the locksmith's arm more tightly through his own, led him up the stairs in silence.

They entered a homely bedchamber, garnished in a scanty way with chairs whose spindle-shanks bespoke their age, and other furniture of very little worth; but clean and neatly kept. Reclining in an easy chair before the fire, pale and weak from waste of blood, was Edward Chester, the young gentleman that had been the first to quit the Maypole on the previous night, who, extending his hand to the locksmith, welcomed him as his preserver and friend.

'Say no more, sir, say no more,' said Gabriel. 'I hope I would have done at least as much for any man in such a strait, and most of all for you, sir. A certain young lady,' he added, with some hesitation, 'has done us many a kind turn, and we naturally feel – I hope I give you no offence in saying this, sir?'

The young man smiled and shook his head; at the same time moving in his chair as if in pain.

'It's no great matter,' he said, in answer to the locksmith's sympathising look, 'a mere uneasiness arising at least as much from being cooped up here, as from the slight wound I have, or from the loss of blood. Be seated, Mr Varden.'

'If I may make so bold, Mr Edward, as to lean upon your chair,' returned the locksmith, accommodating his action to his speech,[1] and bending over him, 'I'll stand here, for the convenience of speaking low. Barnaby is not in his quietest humour to-night, and at such times talking never does him good.'

They both glanced at the subject of this remark, who had taken a seat on the other side of the fire, and, smiling vacantly, was making puzzles on his fingers with a skein of string.

'Pray, tell me, sir,' said Varden, dropping his voice still lower, 'exactly what happened last night. I have my reason for inquiring. You left the Maypole, alone?'

'And walked homeward alone until I had nearly reached the place where you found me, when I heard the gallop of a horse.'

'– Behind you?' said the locksmith.

'Indeed, yes – behind me. It was a single rider, who soon overtook me, and checking his horse, inquired the way to London.'

'You were on the alert, sir, knowing how many highwaymen there are, scouring the roads in all directions?' said Varden.

'I was, but I had only a stick, having imprudently left my pistols in their holster-case with the landlord's son. I directed him as he desired. Before the words had passed my lips, he rode upon me furiously, as if bent on trampling me down beneath his horse's hoofs. In starting aside I slipped and fell. You found me with this stab and an ugly bruise or two, and without my purse – in which he found little enough for his pains. And now, Mr Varden,' he added, shaking the locksmith by the hand, 'saving the extent of my gratitude to you, you know as much as I.'

'Except,' said Gabriel, bending down yet more, and looking cautiously towards their silent neighbour, 'except in respect of the robber himself. What like was he, sir? Speak low, if you please. Barnaby means no harm, but I have watched him oftener than you, and I know, little as you would think it, that he's listening now.'

It required a strong confidence in the locksmith's veracity to lead any one to this belief, for every sense and faculty that Barnaby possessed, seemed to be fixed upon his game, to the exclusion of all other things. Something in the young man's face expressed this

opinion, for Gabriel repeated what he had just said, more earnestly than before, and with another glance towards Barnaby, again asked what like the man was.

'The night was so dark,' said Edward, 'the attack so sudden, and he so wrapped and muffled up, that I can hardly say. It seems that – '

'Don't mention his name, sir,' returned the locksmith, following his look towards Barnaby; 'I know *he* saw him. I want to know what *you* saw.'

'All I remember is,' said Edward, 'that as he checked his horse his hat was blown off. He caught it and replaced it on his head, which I observed was bound with a dark handkerchief. A stranger entered the Maypole while I was there, whom I had not seen, for I sat apart for reasons of my own, and when I rose to leave the room and glanced round, he was in the shadow of the chimney and hidden from my sight. But if he and the robber were two different persons, their voices were strangely and most remarkably alike; for directly the man addressed me in the road, I recognised his speech again.'

'It is as I feared. The very man was here to-night,' thought the locksmith, changing colour. 'What dark history is this!'

'Halloa!' cried a hoarse voice in his ear. 'Halloa, halloa, halloa! Bow wow wow. What's the matter here! Hal-loa!'

The speaker – who made the locksmith start, as if he had been some supernatural agent – was a large raven;[2] who had perched upon the top of the easy-chair, unseen by him and Edward, and listened with a polite attention and a most extraordinary appearance of comprehending every word, to all they had said up to this point; turning his head from one to the other, as if his office were to judge between them, and it were of the very last importance that he should not lose a word.

'Look at him!' said Varden, divided between admiration of the bird and a kind of fear of him. 'Was there ever such a knowing imp as that! Oh he's a dreadful fellow!'

The raven, with his head very much on one side, and his bright eye shining like a diamond, preserved a thoughtful silence for a few seconds, and then replied in a voice so hoarse and distant, that it seemed to come through his thick feathers rather than out of his mouth.

'Halloa, halloa, halloa! What's the matter here! Keep up your spirits. Never say die. Bow wow wow. I'm a devil, I'm a devil, I'm a devil. Hurrah!' – And then, as if exulting in his infernal character, he began to whistle.

'I more than half believe he speaks the truth. Upon my word I do,' said Varden. 'Do you see how he looks at me, as if he knew what I was saying?'

To which the bird, balancing himself on tiptoe, as it were, and moving his body up and down in a sort of grave dance, rejoined, 'I'm a devil, I'm a devil, I'm a devil,' and flapped his wings against his sides as if he were bursting with laughter. Barnaby clapped his hands, and fairly rolled upon the ground in an ecstacy of delight.

'Strange companions, sir,' said the locksmith, shaking his head and looking from one to the other. 'The bird has all the wit.'

'Strange indeed!' said Edward, holding out his forefinger to the raven, who, in acknowledgement of the attention, made a dive at it immediately with his iron bill. 'Is he old?'

'A mere boy, sir,' replied the locksmith. 'A hundred and twenty, or thereabouts. Call him down, Barnaby my man.'

'Call him!' echoed Barnaby, sitting upright upon the floor, and staring vacantly at Gabriel, as he thrust his hair back from his face. 'But who can make him come! He calls me, and makes me go where he will. He goes on before, and I follow. He's the master, and I'm the man. Is that the truth, Grip?'

The raven gave a short, comfortable, confidential kind of croak; – a most expressive croak, which seemed to say 'You needn't let these fellows into our secrets. We understand each other. It's all right.'

'I make *him* come!' cried Barnaby, pointing to the bird. 'Him, who never goes to sleep, or so much as winks! – Why, any time of night, you may see his eyes in my dark room, shining like two sparks. And every night, and all night too, he's broad awake, talking to himself, thinking what he shall do to-morrow, where we shall go, and what he shall steal, and hide, and bury. I make *him* come! Ha, ha, ha!'

On second thoughts, the bird appeared disposed to come of himself. After a short survey of the ground, and a few sidelong looks at the ceiling and at everybody present in turn, he fluttered to the floor, and went to Barnaby – not in a hop, or walk, or run, but in a pace like that of a very particular gentleman with exceedingly tight boots on, trying to walk fast over loose pebbles.

Then, stepping into his extended hand, and condescending to be held out at arm's length, he gave vent to a succession of sounds, not unlike the drawing of some eight or ten dozen of long corks, and again asserted his brimstone birth and parentage with great distinctness.

The locksmith shook his head – perhaps in some doubt of the creature's being really nothing but a bird – perhaps in pity for Barnaby, who by this time had him in his arms, and was rolling about with him on the ground. As he raised his eyes from the poor fellow he encountered those of his mother, who had entered the room, and was looking on in silence.

She was quite white in the face, even to her lips, but had wholly subdued her emotion, and wore her usual quiet look. Varden fancied as he glanced at her that she shrunk from his eye; and that she busied herself about the wounded gentleman to avoid him the better.

It was time he went to bed, she said. He was to be removed to his own home on the morrow, and he had already exceeded his time for sitting up, by a full hour. Acting on this hint, the locksmith prepared to take his leave.

'By the bye,' said Edward, as he shook him by the hand, and looked from him to Mrs Rudge and back again, 'what noise was that below? I heard your voice in the midst of it, and should have inquired before, but our other conversation drove it from my memory. What was it?'

The locksmith looked towards her, and bit his lip. She leant against the chair, and bent her eyes upon the ground. Barnaby too – he was listening.

– 'Some mad or drunken fellow, sir,' Varden at length made answer, looking steadily at the widow as he spoke. 'He mistook the house, and tried to force an entrance.'

She breathed more freely, but stood quite motionless. As the locksmith said 'Good night,' and Barnaby caught up the candle to light him down the stairs, she took it from him, and charged him – with more haste and earnestness than so slight an occasion appeared to warrant – not to stir. The raven followed them to satisfy himself that all was right below, and when they reached the street-door, stood on the bottom stair, drawing corks out of number.

With a trembling hand she unfastened the chain and bolts, and turned the key. As she had her hand upon the latch, the locksmith said in a low voice,

'I have told a lie to-night, for your sake, Mary, and for the sake of bygone times and old acquaintances, when I would scorn to do so for my own. I hope I may have done no harm, or led to none. I can't help the suspicions you have forced upon me, and I am loath, I tell you plainly, to leave Mr Edward here. Take care he comes to no hurt. I doubt the safety of this roof, and am glad he leaves it so soon. Now, let me go.'

For a moment she hid her face in her hands and wept; but resisting the strong impulse which evidently moved her to reply, opened the door – no wider than was sufficient for the passage of his body – and motioned him away. As the locksmith stood upon the step, it was chained and locked behind him, and the raven, in furtherance of these precautions, barked like a lusty house-dog.

'In league with that ill-looking figure that might have fallen from a gibbet – he listening and hiding here – Barnaby first upon the spot last night – can she who has always borne so fair a name be guilty of such crimes in secret!' said the locksmith, musing. 'Heaven forgive me if I am wrong, and send me just thoughts; but she is poor, the temptation may be great, and we daily hear of things as strange. – Ay, bark away, my friend. If there's any wickedness going on, that raven's in it, I'll be sworn.'

CHAPTER THE SEVENTH

Mrs Varden was a lady of what is commonly called an uncertain temper – a phrase which being interpreted signifies a temper tolerably certain to make every body more or less uncomfortable. Thus it generally happened, that when other people were merry, Mrs Varden was dull; and that when other people were dull, Mrs Varden was disposed to be amazingly cheerful. Indeed the worthy house-wife was of such a capricious nature, that she not only attained a higher pitch of genius than Macbeth, in respect of her ability to be wise, amazed, temperate and furious, loyal and neutral[1] in an instant, but would sometimes ring the changes backwards and forwards on all possible moods and flights in one short quarter of an hour; performing, as it were, a kind of triple bob major on the

peal of instruments in the female belfry, with a skilfulness and
rapidity of execution that astonished all who heard her.

It had been observed in this good lady (who did not want for
personal attractions, being plump and buxom to look at, though
like her fair daughter, somewhat short in stature) that this uncertainty of disposition strengthened and increased with her temporal
prosperity; and divers wise men and matrons, on friendly terms
with the locksmith and his family, even went so far as to assert,
that a tumble down some half-dozen rounds in the world's ladder
– such as the breaking of the bank in which her husband kept his
money, or some little fall of that kind – would be the making of
her, and could hardly fail to render her one of the most agreeable
companions in existence. Whether they were right or wrong in this
conjecture, certain it is that minds, like bodies, will often fall into
a pimpled ill-conditioned state from mere excess of comfort, and
like them, are often successfully cured by remedies in themselves
very nauseous and unpalatable.

Mrs Varden's chief aider and abettor, and at the same time her
principal victim and object of wrath, was her single domestic servant,
one Miss Miggs; or as she was called, in conformity with those prejudices of society which lop and top from poor handmaidens all such
genteel excrescences – Miggs. This Miggs was a tall young lady,
very much addicted to pattens in private life; slender and shrewish,
of a rather uncomfortable figure, and though not absolutely ill-
looking, of a sharp and acid visage. As a general principle and
abstract proposition, Miggs held the male sex to be utterly con-
temptible and unworthy of notice; to be fickle, false, base, sottish,
inclined to perjury, and wholly undeserving. When particularly
exasperated against them (which, scandal said, was when Sim
Tappertit slighted her most) she was accustomed to wish with great
emphasis that the whole race of women could but die off, in order
that the men might be brought to know the real value of the
blessings by which they set so little store; nay, her feeling for her
order ran so high, that she sometimes declared, if she could only
have good security for a fair, round number – say ten thousand – of
young virgins following her example, she would, to spite mankind,
hang, drown, stab, or poison herself, with a joy past all expression.

It was the voice of Miggs that greeted the locksmith, when he
knocked at his own house, with a shrill cry of 'Who's there?'

'Me, girl, me,' returned Gabriel.

'What, already, sir!' said Miggs, opening the door with a look of surprise. 'We was just getting on our nightcaps to sit up, – me and mistress. Oh, she has been *so* bad!'

Miggs said this with an air of uncommon candour and concern; but the parlour-door was standing open, and as Gabriel very well knew for whose ears it was designed, he regarded her with anything but an approving look as he passed in.

'Master's come home, mim,' cried Miggs, running before him into the parlour. 'You was wrong, mim, and I was right. I thought he wouldn't keep us up so late, two nights running, mim. Master's always considerate so far. I'm so glad, mim, on your account. I'm a little' – here Miggs simpered – 'a little sleepy myself; I'll own it now, mim, though I said I wasn't when you asked me. It an't of no consequence, mim, of course.'

'You had better,' said the locksmith, who most devoutly wished that Barnaby's raven was at Miggs' ancles, 'you had better get to bed at once then.'

'Thanking you kindly, sir,' returned Miggs, 'I couldn't take my rest in peace, nor fix my thoughts upon my prayers, otherways than that I knew mistress was comfortable in her bed this night; by rights she should have been there, hours ago.'

'You're talkative, mistress,' said Varden, pulling off his greatcoat, and looking at her askew.

'Taking the hint, sir,' cried Miggs, with a flushed face, 'and thanking you for it most kindly, I will make bold to say, that if I give offence by having consideration for my mistress, I do not ask your pardon, but am content to get myself into trouble and to be in suffering.'

Here Mrs Varden, who, with her countenance shrouded in a large nightcap, had been all this time intent upon the Protestant Manual, looked round, and acknowledged Miggs' championship by commanding her to hold her tongue.

Every little bone in Miggs' throat and neck developed itself with a spitefulness quite alarming, as she replied, 'Yes, mim, I will.'

'How do you find yourself now, my dear?' said the locksmith, taking a chair near his wife (who had resumed her book), and rubbing his knees hard as he made the inquiry.

'You're very anxious to know, an't you?' returned Mrs Varden, with her eyes upon the print. 'You, that have not been near me all day, and wouldn't have been if I was dying!'

'My dear Martha –' said Gabriel.

Mrs Varden turned over to the next page; then went back again to the bottom line over leaf to be quite sure of the last words; and then went on reading with an appearance of the deepest interest and study.

'My dear Martha,' said the locksmith, 'how can you say such things, when you know you don't mean them? If you were dying! Why, if there was anything serious the matter with you, Martha, shouldn't I be in constant attendance upon you?'

'Yes!' cried Mrs Varden, bursting into tears, 'yes, you would. I don't doubt it, Varden. Certainly you would. That's as much as to tell me that you would be hovering round me like a vulture, waiting till the breath was out of my body, that you might go and marry somebody else.'

Miggs groaned in sympathy – a little short groan, checked in its birth, and changed into a cough. It seemed to say, 'I can't help it. It's wrung from me by the dreadful brutality of that monster master.'

'But you'll break my heart one of these days,' added Mrs Varden, with more resignation, 'and then we shall both be happy. My only desire is to see Dolly comfortably settled, and when she is, you may settle *me* as soon as you like.'

'Ah!' cried Miggs – and coughed again.

Poor Gabriel twisted his wig about in silence for a long time, and then said mildly, 'Has Dolly gone to bed?'

'Your master speaks to you,' said Mrs Varden, looking sternly over her shoulder at Miss Miggs in waiting.

'No, my dear, I spoke to you,' suggested the locksmith.

'Did you hear me, Miggs?' cried the obdurate lady, stamping her foot upon the ground. '*You* are beginning to despise me now, are you? But this is example!'

At this cruel rebuke, Miggs, whose tears were always ready, for large or small parties, on the shortest notice and the most unreasonable terms, fell a crying violently; holding both her hands tight upon her heart meanwhile, as if nothing less would prevent its splitting into small fragments. Mrs Varden, who likewise possessed that faculty in high perfection, wept too, against Miggs; and with such effect that Miggs gave in after a time, and, except for an occasional sob, which seemed to threaten some remote intention of breaking out again, left her mistress in possession of the field.

Her superiority being thoroughly asserted, that lady soon desisted likewise, and fell into a quiet melancholy.

The relief was so great, and the fatiguing occurrences of last night so completely overpowered the locksmith, that he nodded in his chair, and would doubtless have slept there all night, but for the voice of Mrs Varden, which, after a pause of some five minutes, awoke him with a start.

'If I am ever,' said Mrs V. – not scolding, but in a sort of monotonous remonstrance – 'in spirits, if I am ever cheerful, if I am ever more than usually disposed to be talkative and comfortable, this is the way I am treated.'

'Such spirits as you was in too, mim, but half an hour ago!' cried Miggs. 'I never see such company!'

'Because,' said Mrs Varden, 'because I never interfere or interrupt; because I never question where anybody comes or goes; because my whole mind and soul is bent on saving where I can save, and labouring in this house; – therefore, they try me as they do.'

'Martha,' urged the locksmith, endeavouring to look as wakeful as possible, 'what is it you complain of? I really came home with every wish and desire to be happy. I did, indeed.'

'What do I complain of!' retorted his wife. 'Is it a chilling thing to have one's husband sulking and falling asleep directly he comes home – to have him freezing all one's warm-heartedness, and throwing cold water over the fireside? Is it natural, when I know he went out upon a matter in which I am as much interested as anybody can be, that I should wish to know all that has happened, or that he should tell me without my begging and praying him to do it? Is that natural, or is it not?'

'I am very sorry, Martha,' said the good-natured locksmith. 'I was really afraid you were not disposed to talk pleasantly: I'll tell you everything; I shall only be too glad, my dear.'

'No, Varden,' returned his wife, rising with dignity. 'I dare say – thank you. I'm not a child to be corrected one minute and petted the next – I'm a little too old for that, Varden. Miggs, carry the light. *You* can be cheerful, Miggs, at least.'

Miggs, who, to this moment, had been in the very depths of compassionate despondency, passed instantly into the liveliest state conceivable, and tossing her head as she glanced towards the locksmith, bore off her mistress and the light together.

'Now, who would think,' thought Varden, shrugging his shoulders and drawing his chair nearer to the fire, 'that that woman could ever be pleasant and agreeable? And yet she can be. Well, well, all of us have our faults. I'll not be hard upon hers. We have been man and wife too long for that.'

He dozed again – not the less pleasantly, perhaps, for his hearty temper. While his eyes were closed, the door leading to the upper stairs was partially opened; and a head appeared, which, at sight of him, hastily drew back again.

'I wish,' murmured Gabriel, waking at the noise, and looking round the room, 'I wish somebody would marry Miggs. But that's impossible! I wonder whether there's any madman alive, who would marry Miggs!'

This was such a vast speculation that he fell into a doze again, and slept until the fire was quite burnt out. At last he roused himself; and having double-locked the street-door according to custom, and put the key in his pocket, went off to bed.

He had not left the room in darkness many minutes, when the head again appeared, and Sim Tappertit entered, bearing in his hand a little lamp.

'What the devil business has he to stop up so late!' muttered Sim, passing into the workshop, and setting it down upon the forge. 'Here's half the night gone already. There's only one good that has ever come to me, out of this cursed old rusty mechanical trade, and that's this piece of ironmongery, upon my soul!'

As he spoke, he drew from the right hand, or rather right leg pocket of his smalls, a clumsy large-sized key, which he inserted cautiously in the lock his master had secured, and softly opened the door. That done, he replaced his piece of secret workmanship in his pocket; and leaving the lamp burning, and closing the door carefully and without noise, stole out into the street – as little suspected by the locksmith in his sound deep sleep, as by Barnaby himself in his phantom-haunted dreams.

*

CHAPTER THE EIGHTH

Clear of the locksmith's house, Sim Tappertit laid aside his cautious manner, and assuming in its stead that of a ruffling, swaggering, roving blade, who would rather kill a man than otherwise, and eat him too if needful, made the best of his way along the darkened streets.

Half pausing for an instant now and then to smite his pocket and assure himself of the safety of his master key, he hurried on to Barbican,[1] and turning into one of the narrowest of the narrow streets which diverged from that centre, slackened his pace and wiped his heated brow, as if the termination of his walk were near at hand.

It was not a very choice spot for midnight expeditions, being in truth one of more than questionable character, and of an appearance by no means inviting. From the main street he had entered, itself little better than an alley, a low-browed doorway led into a blind court, or yard, profoundly dark, unpaved, and reeking with stagnant odours. Into this ill-favoured pit, the locksmith's vagrant 'prentice groped his way; and stopping at a house from whose defaced and rotten front the rude effigy of a bottle swung to and fro like some gibbeted malefactor, struck thrice upon an iron grating with his foot. After listening in vain for some response to his signal, Mr Tappertit became impatient, and struck the grating thrice again.

A further delay ensued, but it was not of long duration. The ground seemed to open at his feet, and a ragged head appeared.

'Is that the captain?' said a voice as ragged as the head.

'Yes,' replied Mr Tappertit haughtily, descending as he spoke, 'who should it be?'

'It's so late, we gave you up,' returned the voice, as its owner stopped to shut and fasten the grating. 'You're late, sir.'

'Lead on,' said Mr Tappertit, with a gloomy majesty, 'and make remarks when I require you. Forward!'

This latter word of command was perhaps somewhat theatrical and unnecessary, inasmuch as the descent was by a very narrow, steep, and slippery flight of steps, and any rashness or departure from the beaten track must have ended in a yawning water-butt. But Mr Tappertit being, like some other great commanders, favourable to strong effects, and personal display, cried 'Forward!' again, in the hoarsest voice he could assume; and led the way, with folded arms and knitted brows, to the cellar down below, where there was a small copper fixed in one corner, a chair or two, a form and table, a glimmering fire, and a truckle-bed, covered with a ragged patchwork rug.

'Welcome, noble captain!' cried a lanky figure, rising as from a nap.

The captain nodded. Then, throwing off his outer coat, he stood composed in all his dignity, and eyed his follower over.

'What news to-night?' he asked, when he had looked into his very soul.

'Nothing particular,' replied the other, stretching himself – and he was so long already that it was quite alarming to see him do it – 'how come you to be so late?'

'No matter,' was all the captain deigned to say in answer. 'Is the room prepared?'

'It is,' replied his follower.

'The comrade – is he here?'

'Yes. And a sprinkling of the others – you hear 'em?'

'Playing skittles!' said the captain moodily. 'Light-hearted revellers!'

There was no doubt respecting the particular amusement in which these heedless spirits were indulging, for even in the close and stifling atmosphere of the vault, the noise sounded like distant thunder. It certainly appeared, at first sight, a singular spot to choose, for that or any other purpose of relaxation, if the other cellars answered to the one in which this brief colloquy took place; for the floors were of sodden earth, the walls and roof of damp bare brick tapestried with the tracks of snails and slugs; the air was sickening, tainted, and offensive. It seemed, from one strong flavour which was uppermost among the various odours of the place, that it had, at no very distant period, been used as a storehouse for cheeses; a circumstance which, while it accounted for the greasy moisture that hung about it, was agreeably suggestive of rats. It was naturally damp besides, and little trees of fungus sprung from every mouldering corner.

The proprietor of this charming retreat, and owner of the ragged head before mentioned – for he wore an old tie-wig as bare and frouzy as a stunted hearth-broom – had by this time joined them;

and stood a little apart, rubbing his hands, wagging his hoary bristled chin, and smiling in silence. His eyes were closed; but had they been wide open, it would have been easy to tell, from the attentive expression of the face he turned towards them – pale and unwholesome as might be expected in one of his underground existence – and from a certain anxious raising and quivering of the lids, that he was blind.

'Even Stagg hath been asleep,' said the long comrade, nodding towards this person.

'Sound, captain, sound!' cried the blind man; 'what does my noble captain drink – is it brandy, rum, usquebaugh? Is it soaked gunpowder, or blazing oil? Give it a name, heart of oak, and we'd get it for you, if it was wine from a bishop's cellar, or melted gold from King George's mint.'

'See,' said Mr Tappertit haughtily, 'that it's something strong, and comes quick; and so long as you take care of that, you may bring it from the devil's cellar, if you like.'

'Boldly said, noble captain!' rejoined the blind man. 'Spoken like the 'Prentices' Glory. Ha, ha! From the devil's cellar! A brave joke! The captain joketh. Ha, ha, ha!'

'I'll tell you what, my fine feller,' said Mr Tappertit, eyeing the host over as he walked to a closet, and took out a bottle and glass as carelessly as if he had been in full possession of his sight, 'if you make that row, you'll find that the captain's very far from joking, and so I tell you.'

'He's got his eyes on me!' cried Stagg, stopping short on his way back, and affecting to screen his face with the bottle. 'I feel 'em though I can't see 'em. Take 'em off, noble captain. Remove 'em, for they pierce like gimlets.'

Mr Tappertit smiled grimly at his comrade; and twisting out one more look – a kind of ocular screw – under the influence of which the blind man feigned to undergo great anguish and torture, bade him, in a softened tone, approach, and hold his peace.

'I obey you, captain,' cried Stagg, drawing close to him and filling out a bumper without spilling a drop, by reason that he held his little finger at the brim of the glass, and stopped at the instant the liquor touched it, 'drink, noble governor. Death to all masters, life to all 'prentices, and love to all fair damsels. Drink, brave general, and warm your gallant heart!'

Mr Tappertit condescended to take the glass from his outstretched hand. Stagg then dropped on one knee, and gently smoothed the calves of his legs, with an air of humble admiration.

'That I had but eyes!' he cried, 'to behold my captain's symmetrical proportions! That I had but eyes, to look upon these twin invaders of domestic peace!'

'Get out!' said Mr Tappertit, glancing downward at his favourite limbs. 'Go along, will you, Stagg!'

'When I touch my own afterwards,' cried the host, smiting them reproachfully, 'I hate 'em. Comparatively speaking, they've no more shape than wooden legs, beside these models of my noble captain's.'

'Yours!' exclaimed Mr Tappertit. 'No, I should think not. Don't talk about those precious old toothpicks in the same breath with mine; that's rather too much. Here. Take the glass. Benjamin. Lead on. To business!'

With these words, he folded his arms again; and frowning with a sullen majesty, passed with his companion through a little door at the upper end of the cellar, and disappeared; leaving Stagg to his private meditations.

The vault they entered, strewn with sawdust and dimly lighted, was between the outer one from which they had just come, and that in which the skittle-players were diverting themselves; as was manifested by the increased noise and clamour of tongues, which was suddenly stopped, however, and replaced by a dead silence, at a signal from the long comrade. Then, this young gentleman, going to a little cupboard, returned with a thigh-bone, which in former times must have been part and parcel of some individual at least as long as himself, and placed the same in the hands of Mr Tappertit; who, receiving it as a sceptre and staff of authority, cocked his three-cornered hat fiercely on the top of his head, and mounted a large table, whereon a chair of state, cheerfully ornamented with a couple of skulls, was placed ready for his reception.[2]

He had no sooner assumed this position, than another young gentleman appeared, bearing in his arms a huge clasped book, who made him a profound obeisance, and delivering it to the long comrade, advanced to the table, and turning his back upon it, stood there Atlas-wise.[3] Then, the long comrade got upon the table too; and seating himself in a lower chair than Mr Tappertit's, with much state and ceremony, placed the large book on the shoulders of their mute companion as deliberately as if he had been a wooden desk, and prepared to make entries therein with a pen of corresponding size.

When the long comrade had made these preparations, he looked towards Mr Tappertit; and Mr Tappertit, flourishing the bone, knocked nine times therewith upon one of the skulls. At the ninth stroke, a third young gentleman emerged from the door leading to the skittle ground, and bowing low, awaited his commands.

' 'Prentice!' said the mighty captain, 'who waits without?'

The 'prentice made answer that a stranger was in attendance, who claimed admission into that secret society of 'Prentice Knights, and a free participation in their rights, privileges, and immunities. Thereupon Mr Tappertit flourished the bone again, and giving the other skull a prodigious rap on the nose, exclaimed 'Admit him!' At these dread words the 'prentice bowed once more, and so withdrew as he had come.

There soon appeared at the same door, two other 'prentices, having between them a third, whose eyes were bandaged, and who was attired in a bag-wig, and a broad-skirted coat, trimmed with tarnished lace; and who was girded with a sword, in compliance with the laws of the Institution regulating the introduction of candidates, which required them to assume this courtly dress, and kept it constantly in lavender, for their convenience. One of the conductors of this novice held a rusty blunderbuss pointed towards his ear, and the other a very ancient sabre, with which he carved imaginary offenders as he came along in a sanguinary and anatomical manner.

As this silent group advanced, Mr Tappertit fixed his hat upon his head. The novice then laid his hand upon his breast and bent before him. When he had humbled himself sufficiently, the captain ordered the bandage to be removed, and proceeded to eye him over.

'Ha!' said the captain, thoughtfully, when he had concluded this ordeal. 'Proceed.'

The long comrade read aloud as follows: – 'Mark Gilbert. Age, nineteen. Bound to Thomas Curzon, hosier, Golden Fleece, Aldgate. Loves Curzon's daughter. Cannot say that Curzon's daughter loves him. Should think it probable. Curzon pulled his ears last Tuesday week.'

'How!' cried the captain, starting.

'For looking at his daughter, please you,' said the novice.

'Write Curzon down, Denounced,' said the captain. 'Put a black cross against the name of Curzon.'

'So please you,' said the novice, 'that's not the worst – he calls his 'prentice idle dog, and stops his beer unless he works to his liking. He gives Dutch cheese, too, eating Cheshire sir, himself;[4] and Sundays out, are only once a month.'

'This,' said Mr Tappertit gravely, 'is a flagrant case. Put two black crosses to the name of Curzon.'

'If the society,' said the novice, who was an ill-looking, one-sided, shambling lad, with sunken eyes set close together in his head – 'if the society would burn his house down – for he's not insured – or beat him as he comes home from his club at night, or help me to carry off his daughter, and marry her at the Fleet,[5] whether she gave consent or no –'

Mr Tappertit waved his grizzly truncheon as an admonition to him not to interrupt, and ordered three black crosses to the name of Curzon.

'Which means,' he said in gracious explanation, 'vengeance, complete and terrible. 'Prentice, do you love the Constitution?'

To which the novice (being to that end instructed by his attendant sponsors) replied 'I do!'

'The Church, the State, and everything established – but the masters?' quoth the captain.

Again the novice said 'I do.'

Having said it, he listened meekly to the captain, who, in an address prepared for such occasions, told him how that under that same Constitution (which was kept in a strong-box somewhere, but where exactly he could not find out, or he would have endeavoured to procure a copy of it), the 'prentices had, in times gone by, had frequent holidays of right, broken people's heads by scores, defied their masters, nay, even achieved some glorious murders in the streets, which privileges had gradually been wrested from them, and in all which noble aspirations they were now restrained; how the degrading checks imposed upon them were unquestionably attributable to the innovating spirit of the times, and how they united therefore to resist all change, except such change as would restore those good old English customs, by which they would stand or fall. After illustrating the wisdom of going backward, by reference to that sagacious fish, the crab, and the not unfrequent practice of the mule and donkey, he described their general objects;

which were briefly vengeance on their Tyrant Masters (of whose grievous and insupportable oppression no 'prentice could entertain a moment's doubt) and the restoration, as aforesaid, of their ancient rights and holidays; for neither of which objects were they now quite ripe, being barely twenty strong, but which they pledged themselves to pursue with fire and sword when needful. Then he described the oath which every member of that small remnant of a noble body took, and which was of a dreadful and impressive kind; binding him, at the bidding of his chief, to resist and obstruct the Lord Mayor, sword-bearer, and chaplain; to despise the authority of the sheriffs; and to hold the court of aldermen[6] as nought; but not on any account, in case the fullness of time should bring a general rising of 'prentices, to damage or in any way disfigure Temple Bar,[7] which was strictly constitutional and always to be approached with reverence. Having gone over these several heads with great eloquence and force, and having further informed the novice that this society had had its origin in his own teeming brain, stimulated by a swelling sense of wrong and outrage, Mr Tappertit demanded whether he had strength of heart to take the mighty pledge required, or whether he would withdraw while retreat was yet within his power.

To this, the novice made rejoinder that he would take the vow, though it should choke him; and it was accordingly administered with many impressive circumstances, among which the lighting up of the two skulls with a candle-end inside of each, and a great many flourishes with the bone, were chiefly conspicuous; not to mention a variety of grave exercises with the blunderbuss and sabre, and some dismal groaning by unseen 'prentices without. All these dark and direful ceremonies being at length completed, the table was put aside, the chair of state removed, the sceptre locked up in its usual cupboard, the doors of communication between the three cellars thrown freely open, and the 'Prentice Knights resigned themselves to merriment.

But Mr Tappertit, who had a soul above the vulgar herd, and who, on account of his greatness, could only afford to be merry now and then, threw himself on a bench with the air of a man who was faint with dignity. He looked with an indifferent eye, alike on skittles, cards, and dice, thinking only of the locksmith's daughter, and the base degenerate days on which he had fallen.

'My noble captain neither games, nor sings, nor dances,' said his host, taking a seat beside him. 'Drink, gallant general!'

Mr Tappertit drained the proffered goblet to the dregs; then thrust his hands into his pockets, and with a lowering visage walked among the skittles, while his followers (such is the influence of superior genius) restrained the ardent ball, and held his little shins in dumb respect.

'If I had been born a corsair or a pirate, a brigand, gen-teel highwayman or patriot – and they're the same thing,' thought Mr Tappertit, musing among the nine-pins, 'I should have been all right. But to drag out a ignoble existence unbeknown to mankind in general – patience! I will be famous yet. A voice within me keeps on whispering Greatness. I shall burst out one of these days, and when I do, what power can keep me down? I feel my soul getting into my head at the idea. More drink there!'

'The novice,' pursued Mr Tappertit, not exactly in a voice of thunder, for his tones, to say the truth, were rather cracked and shrill, – but very impressively, notwithstanding – 'where is he?'

'Here, noble captain!' cried Stagg. 'One stands beside me who I feel is a stranger.'

'Have you,' said Mr Tappertit, letting his gaze fall on the party indicated, who was indeed the new knight, by this time restored to his own apparel; 'Have you the impression of your street-door key in wax?'

The long comrade anticipated the reply, by producing it from the shelf on which it had been deposited.

'Good,' said Mr Tappertit, scrutinising it attentively, while a breathless silence reigned around; for he had constructed secret door-keys for the whole society, and perhaps owed something of his influence to that mean and trivial circumstance – on such slight accidents do even men of mind depend! – 'This is easily made. Come hither, friend.'

With that, he beckoned the new knight apart, and putting the pattern in his pocket, motioned to him to walk by his side.

'And so,' he said, when they had taken a few turns up and down, 'you – you love your master's daughter?'

'I do,' said the 'prentice. 'Honour bright. No chaff, you know.'

'Have you,' rejoined Mr Tappertit, catching him by the wrist, and giving him a look which would have been expressive of the most deadly malevolence, but for an accidental hiccup that rather interfered with it; 'have you a – a rival?'

'Not as I know on,' replied the 'prentice.

'If you had now –' said Mr Tappertit – 'what would you – eh – ?'
The 'prentice looked fierce and clenched his fists.

'It is enough,' cried Mr Tappertit hastily, 'we understand each other. We are observed. I thank you.'

So saying, he cast him off again; and calling the long comrade aside after taking a few hasty turns by himself, bade him immediately write and post against the wall, a notice, proscribing one Joseph Willet (commonly known as Joe) of Chigwell; forbidding all 'Prentice Knights to succour, comfort, or hold communion with him; and requiring them, on pain of excommunication, to molest, hurt, wrong, annoy, and pick quarrels with the said Joseph, whensoever and wheresoever they, or any of them, should happen to encounter him.

Having relieved his mind by this energetic proceeding, he condescended to approach the festive board, and warming by degrees, at length deigned to preside, and even to enchant the company with a song. After this, he rose to such a pitch as to consent to regale the society with a hornpipe, which he actually performed to the music of a fiddle (played by an ingenious member) with such surpassing agility and brilliancy of execution, that the spectators could not be sufficiently enthusiastic in their admiration; and their host protested, with tears in his eyes, that he had never truly felt his blindness until that moment.

But the host withdrawing – probably to weep in secret – soon returned with the information that it wanted little more than an hour of day, and that all the cocks in Barbican had already begun to crow, as if their lives depended on it. At this intelligence, the 'Prentice Knights arose in haste, and marshalling into a line, filed off one by one and dispersed with all speed to their several homes, leaving their leader to pass the grating last.

'Good night, noble captain,' whispered the blind man as he held it open for his passage out; 'Farewell brave general. Bye, bye, illustrious commander. Good luck go with you for a – conceited, bragging, empty-headed, duck-legged idiot.'

With which parting words, coolly added as he listened to his receding footsteps and locked the grate upon himself, he descended the steps, and lighting the fire below the little copper, prepared, without any assistance, for his daily occupation; which was to retail at the area-head above pennyworths of broth and soup, and savoury puddings, compounded of such scraps as were to be bought in the

heap for the least money at Fleet Market[8] in the evening time; and
for the sale of which he had need to have depended chiefly on his
private connexion, for the court had no thoroughfare, and was not
that kind of place in which many people were likely to take the air,
or to frequent as an agreeable promenade.

CHAPTER THE NINTH

Chroniclers are privileged to enter where they list, to come and go
through keyholes, to ride upon the wind, to overcome, in their
soarings up and down, all obstacles of distance, time, and place.
Thrice blessed be this last consideration, since it enables us to
follow the disdainful Miggs even into the sanctity of her chamber,
and to hold her in sweet companionship through the dreary watches
of the night!

Miss Miggs, having undone[1] her mistress, as she phrased it
(which means, assisted to undress her), and having seen her
comfortably to bed in the back room on the first floor, withdrew
to her own apartment, in the attic story. Notwithstanding her
declaration in the locksmith's presence, she was in no mood for
sleep; so, putting her light upon the table and withdrawing the
little window curtain, she gazed out pensively at the wild night
sky.

Perhaps she wondered what star was destined for her habitation
when she had run her little course below; perhaps speculated which
of those glimmering spheres might be the natal orb of Mr Tappertit;
perhaps marvelled how they could gaze down on that perfidious
creature, man, and not sicken and turn green as chemists' lamps;[2]
perhaps thought of nothing in particular. Whatever she thought
about, there she sat, until her attention, alive to anything connected
with the insinuating 'prentice, was attracted by a noise in the next
room to her own – his room; the room in which he slept, and
dreamed – it might be, sometimes dreamed of her.

That he was not dreaming now, unless he was taking a walk in
his sleep, was clear, for every now and then there came a shuffling
noise, as though he were engaged in polishing the whitewashed
wall; then a gentle creaking of his door; then the faintest indication
of his stealthy footsteps on the landing-place outside. Noting this

latter circumstance, Miss Miggs turned pale and shuddered, as mistrusting his intentions; and more than once exclaimed, below her breath, 'Oh! what a Providence it is as I am bolted in!' – which, owing doubtless to her alarm, was a confusion of ideas on her part between a bolt and its use; for though there was one on the door, it was not fastened.

Miss Miggs' sense of hearing, however, having as sharp an edge as her temper, and being of the same snappish and suspicious kind, very soon informed her that the footsteps passed her door, and appeared to have some object quite separate and disconnected from herself. At this discovery she became more alarmed than ever, and was about to give utterance to those cries of 'Thieves!' and 'Murder!' which she had hitherto restrained, when it occurred to her to look softly out, and see that her fears had some good palpable foundation.

Looking out accordingly, and stretching her neck over the hand-rail, she descried, to her great amazement, Mr Tappertit completely dressed, stealing down stairs, one step at a time, with his shoes in one hand and a lamp in the other. Following him with her eyes, and going down a little way herself to get the better of an intervening angle, she beheld him thrust his head in at the parlour door, draw it back again with great swiftness, and immediately begin a retreat up stairs with all possible expedition.

'Here's mysteries!' said the damsel, when she was safe in her own room again, quite out of breath. 'Oh gracious, here's mysteries!'

The prospect of finding anybody out in anything, would have kept Miss Miggs awake under the influence of henbane. Presently she heard the step again, as she would have done if it had been that of a feather endowed with motion and walking down on tip-toe. Then gliding out as before, she again beheld the retreating figure of the 'prentice; again he looked cautiously in at the parlour door, but this time, instead of retreating, he passed in and disappeared.

Miggs was back in her room, and had her head out of the window, before an elderly gentleman could have winked and recovered from it. Out he came at the street door, shut it carefully behind him, tried it with his knee, and swaggered off, putting something in his pocket as he went along. At this spectacle Miggs cried 'Gracious!' again, and then 'Goodness gracious!' and then, 'Goodness gracious me!' and then, candle in hand, went down stairs as he had done. Coming to the workshop, she saw the lamp burning on the forge, and everything as Sim had left it.

'Why I wish I may only have a walking funeral, and never be buried decent with a mourning-coach and feathers,[3] if the boy hasn't been and made a key for his own self!' cried Miggs. 'Oh the little villain!'

This conclusion was not arrived at without consideration, and much peeping and peering about; nor was it unassisted by the recollection that she had on several occasions come upon the 'prentice suddenly, and found him busy at some mysterious occupation. Lest the fact of Miss Miggs calling him, on whom she stooped to cast a favourable eye, a boy, should create surprise in any breast, it may be observed that she invariably affected to regard all male bipeds under thirty as mere chits and infants; which phenomenon is not unusual in ladies of Miss Miggs's temper, and is indeed generally found to be the associate of such indomitable and savage virtue.

Miss Miggs deliberated within herself for some little time, looking hard at the shop door while she did so, as though her eyes and thoughts were both upon it; and then, taking a sheet of paper from a drawer, twisted it into a long thin spiral tube. Having filled this instrument with a quantity of small coal dust from the forge, she approached the door, and dropping on one knee before it, dexterously blew into the keyhole as much of these fine ashes as the lock would hold. When she had filled it to the brim in a very workmanlike and skilful manner, she crept up stairs again, and chuckled as she went.

'There!' cried Miggs, rubbing her hands, 'now let's see whether you won't be glad to take some notice of me, mister. He, he, he! You'll have eyes for somebody besides Miss Dolly now, I think. A fat-faced puss she is, as ever I come across!'

As she uttered this criticism, she glanced approvingly at her small mirror, as who should say, I thank my stars that can't be said of me! – as it certainly could not; for Miss Miggs' style of beauty was of that kind which Mr Tappertit himself had not inaptly termed, in private, 'scraggy.'

'I don't go to bed this night!' said Miggs, wrapping herself in a shawl, drawing a couple of chairs near the window, flouncing down upon one, and putting her feet upon the other, 'till you come home,

my lad. I wouldn't,' said Miggs viciously, 'no, not for five-and-forty pound!'

With that, and with an expression of face in which a great number of opposite ingredients, such as mischief, cunning, malice, triumph, and patient expectation, were all mixed up together in a kind of physiognomical punch, Miss Miggs composed herself to wait and listen, like some fair ogress who had set a trap and was watching for a nibble from a plump young traveller.

She sat there, with perfect composure, all night. At length, just upon break of day, there was a footstep in the street, and presently she could hear Mr Tappertit stop at the door. Then she could make out that he tried his key – that he was blowing into it – that he knocked it on the nearest post to beat the dust out – that he took it under a lamp to look at it – that he poked bits of stick into the lock to clear it – that he peeped into the keyhole, first with one eye, and then with the other – that he tried the key again – that he couldn't turn it, and what was worse couldn't get it out – that he bent it – that then it was much less disposed to come out than before – that he gave it a mighty twist and a great pull, and then it came out so suddenly that he staggered backwards – that he kicked the door – that he shook it – finally, that he smote his forehead, and sat down on the step in despair.

When this crisis had arrived, Miss Miggs, affecting to be exhausted with terror, and to cling to the window-sill for support, put out her nightcap, and demanded in a faint voice who was there.

Mr Tappertit cried 'Hush!' and, backing into the road, exhorted her in frenzied pantomime to secrecy and silence.

'Tell me one thing,' said Miggs. 'Is it thieves?'

'No – no – no!' cried Mr Tappertit.

'Then,' said Miggs, more faintly than before, 'it's fire. Where is it, sir? It's near this room, I know. I've a good conscience, sir, and would much rather die than go down a ladder. All I wish is, respecting my love to my married sister, Golden Lion Court, number twenty-sivin, second bell-handle on the right hand door-post.'

'Miggs!' cried Mr Tappertit, 'don't you know me? Sim, you know – Sim –'

'Oh! what about him!' cried Miggs, clasping her hands. 'Is he in any danger? Is he in the midst of flames and blazes? Oh gracious, gracious!'

'Why I'm here, an't I?' rejoined Mr Tappertit, knocking himself on the breast. 'Don't you see me? What a fool you are, Miggs!'

'There!' cried Miggs, unmindful of this compliment. 'Why – so it – Goodness, what is the meaning of – If you please Mim here's – '

'No, no!' cried Mr Tappertit, standing on tiptoe, as if by that means he, in the street, were any nearer being able to stop the mouth of Miggs in the garret. 'Don't! – I've been out without leave, and something or another's the matter with the lock. Come down, and undo the shop window, that I may get in that way.'

'I durstn't do it, Simmun,' cried Miggs – for that was her pronunciation of his christian name. 'I durstn't do it, indeed. You know as well as anybody, how particular I am. And to come down in the dead of night, when the house is wrapped in slumbers and weiled in obscurity.' And there she stopped and shivered, for her modesty caught cold at the very thought.

'But Miggs,' cried Mr Tappertit, getting under the lamp, that she might see his eyes. 'My darling Miggs – '

Miggs screamed slightly.

' – That I love so much, and never can help thinking of,' – and it is impossible to describe the use he made of his eyes when he said this – 'do – for my sake, do.'

'Oh Simmun,' cried Miggs, 'this is worse than all. I know if I come down, you'll go, and – '

'And what, my precious?' said Mr Tappertit.

'And try,' said Miggs, hysterically, 'to kiss me, or some such dreadfulness; I know you will!'

'I swear I won't,' said Mr Tappertit, with remarkable earnestness. 'Upon my soul I won't. It's getting broad day and the watchman's waking up. Angelic Miggs! If you'll only come and let me in, I promise you faithfully and truly I won't.'

Miss Miggs, whose gentle heart was touched, did not wait for the oath (knowing how strong the temptation was, and fearing he might forswear himself), but tripped lightly down the stairs, and with her own fair hands drew back the rough fastenings of the workshop window. Having helped the wayward 'prentice in, she faintly articulated the words 'Simmun is safe!' and yielding to her woman's nature, immediately became insensible.

'I knew I should quench her,' said Sim, rather embarrassed by this circumstance. 'Of course I was certain it would come to this, but there was nothing else to be done – if I hadn't eyed her over, she wouldn't have come down. Here. Keep up a minute, Miggs. What a slippery figure she is! There's no holding her, comfortably. Do keep up a minute, Miggs, will you?'

As Miggs, however, was deaf to all entreaties, Mr Tappertit leant her against the wall as one might dispose of a walking-stick or umbrella, until he had secured the window, when he took her in his arms again, and, in short stages and with great difficulty – arising mainly from her being tall and his being short, and perhaps in some degree from that peculiar physical conformation on which he had already remarked – carried her up stairs, and planting her, in the same umbrella or walking-stick fashion, just inside her own door, left her to her repose.

'He may be as cool as he likes,' said Miss Miggs, recovering as soon as she was left alone; 'but I'm in his confidence and he can't help himself, nor couldn't if he was twenty Simmunses!'

*

CHAPTER THE TENTH

It was on one of those mornings, common in early spring, when the year, fickle and changeable in its youth like all other created things, is undecided whether to step backward into winter or forward into summer, and in its uncertainty inclines now to the one and now to the other, and now to both at once – wooing summer in the sunshine, and lingering still with winter in the shade – it was, in short, on one of those mornings, when it is hot and cold, wet and dry, bright and lowering, sad and cheerful, withering and genial, in the compass of one short hour, that old John Willet, who was dropping asleep over the copper boiler, was roused by the sound of a horse's feet, and glancing out at window, beheld a traveller of goodly promise checking his bridle at the Maypole door.

He was none of your flippant young fellows, who would call for a tankard of mulled ale, and make themselves as much at home as if they had ordered a hogshead of wine; none of your audacious young swaggerers, who would even penetrate into the bar – that solemn sanctuary – and, smiting old John upon the back, inquire if there was never a pretty girl in the house, and where he hid his little chambermaids, with a hundred other impertinencies of that nature; none of your free-and-easy companions, who would scrape their boots upon the fire-dogs in the common room, and be not at all particular on the subject of spittoons; none of your unconscionable blades, requiring impossible chops, and taking unheard-of pickles for granted. He was a staid, grave, placid gentleman, something past the prime of life, yet upright in his carriage, for all that, and slim as a greyhound. He was well-mounted upon a sturdy chesnut cob, and had the graceful seat of an experienced horseman; while his riding gear, though free from such fopperies as were then in vogue, was handsome and well chosen. He wore a riding-coat of a somewhat brighter green than might have been expected to suit the taste of a gentleman of his years, with a short black velvet cape, laced pocket-holes and cuffs, all of a jaunty fashion; his linen, too, was of the finest kind, worked in a rich pattern at the wrists and throat, and scrupulously white. Although he seemed, judging from the mud he had picked up on the way, to have come from London, his horse was as smooth and cool as his own iron-grey periwig and pig-tail. Neither man nor beast had turned a single hair; and, saving for his soiled skirts and spatterdashes, this gentleman, with his blooming face, white teeth, exactly-ordered dress, and perfect calmness, might have come from making an elaborate and leisurely toilet, to sit for an equestrian portrait at old John Willet's gate.

It must not be supposed that John observed these several characteristics by other than very slow degrees, or that he took in more than half a one at a time, or that he even made up his mind upon that, without a great deal of very serious consideration. Indeed, if he had been distracted in the first instance by questionings and orders, it would have taken him at the least a fortnight to have noted what is here set down; but it happened that the gentleman, being struck with the old house, or with the plump pigeons which were skimming and curtseying about it, or with the tall maypole, on the top of which a weathercock, which had been out of order for fifteen years, performed a perpetual waltz to the music of its own creaking, sat for some little time looking round in silence. Hence John, standing with his hand upon the horse's bridle, and his great eyes on the rider, and with nothing passing to divert his thoughts, had really got some of these little circumstances into his brain, by the time he was called upon to speak.

'A quaint place this,' said the gentleman – and his voice was as rich as his dress. 'Are you the landlord?'

'At your service, sir,' replied John Willet.

'You can give my horse good stabling, can you, and me an early dinner (I am not particular what, so that it be cleanly served), and a decent room – of which there seems to be no lack in this great mansion,' said the stranger, again running his eyes over the exterior.

'You can have, sir,' returned John, with a readiness quite surprising, 'anything you please.'

'It's well I am easily satisfied,' returned the other with a smile, 'or that might prove a hardy pledge, my friend.' And saying so, he dismounted, with the aid of the block before the door, in a twinkling.

'Halloa there! Hugh!' roared John. 'I ask your pardon, sir, for keeping you standing in the porch; but my son has gone to town on business, and the boy being, as I may say, of a kind of use to me, I'm rather put out when he's away. Hugh! – a dreadful idle vagrant fellow, sir – half a gipsy as I think – always sleeping in the sun in summer, and in the straw in winter time sir – Hugh! Dear Lord, to keep a gentleman a waiting here, through him! – Hugh! I wish that chap was dead, I do indeed.'

'Possibly he is,' returned the other. 'I should think if he were living he would have heard you by this time.'

'In his fits of laziness, he sleeps so desperate hard,' said the distracted host, 'if you were to fire off cannon-balls into his ears, it wouldn't wake him, sir.'

The guest made no remark upon this novel cure for drowsiness, and recipe for making people lively, but with his hands clasped behind him stood in the porch, apparently very much amused to see old John, with the bridle in his hand, wavering between a strong impulse to abandon the animal to his fate, and a half disposition to lead him into the house, and shut him up in the parlour, while he waited on his master.

'Pillory the fellow, here he is at last,' cried John, in the very height and zenith of his distress. 'Did you hear me a calling, villain?'

The figure he addressed made no answer, but putting his hand upon the saddle, sprung into it at a bound, turned the horse's head towards the stable, and was gone in an instant.

'Brisk enough when he is awake,' said the guest.

'Brisk enough, sir!' replied John, looking at the place where the horse had been, as if not yet understanding quite, what had become of him. 'He melts, I think. He goes like a drop of froth. You look at him, and there he is. You look at him again, and – there he isn't.'

Having, in the absence of any more words, put this sudden climax to what he had faintly intended should be a long explanation of the whole life and character of his man, the oracular John Willet led the gentleman up his wide dismantled staircase into the Maypole's best apartment.

It was spacious enough in all conscience, occupying the whole depth of the house, and having at either end a great bay window, as large as many modern rooms; in which some few panes of stained glass, emblazoned with fragments of armorial bearings, though cracked, and patched, and shattered, yet remained; attesting, by their presence, that the former owner had made the very light subservient to his state, and pressed the sun itself into his list of flatterers; bidding it, when it shone into his chamber, reflect the badges of his ancient family, and take new hues and colours from their pride.

But those were old days, and now every little ray came and went as it would; telling the plain, bare, searching truth. Although the best room of the inn, it had the melancholy aspect of grandeur in decay, and was much too vast for comfort. Rich rustling hangings, waving on the walls; and, better far, the rustling of youth and beauty's dress; the light of women's eyes, outshining the tapers and their own rich jewels; the sound of gentle tongues, and music, and the tread of maiden feet, had once been there, and filled it with delight. But they were gone, and with them all its gladness. It was no longer a home; children were never born and bred there; the fireside had become mercenary – a something to be bought and sold – a very courtezan: let who would die, or sit beside, or leave it, it was still the same – it missed nobody, cared for nobody, had equal warmth and smiles for all. God help the man whose heart ever changes with the world, as an old mansion when it becomes an inn!

No effort had been made to furnish this chilly waste, but before the broad chimney a colony of chairs and tables had been planted on a square of carpet, flanked by a ghostly screen, enriched with figures, grinning and grotesque. After lighting with his own hands the faggots which were heaped upon the hearth, old John withdrew to hold grave council with his cook, touching the stranger's

entertainment; while the guest himself, seeing small comfort in the yet unkindled wood, opened a lattice in the distant window, and basked in a sickly gleam of cold March sun.

Leaving the window now and then, to rake the crackling logs together, or pace the echoing room from end to end, he closed it when the fire was quite burnt up, and having wheeled the easiest chair into the warmest corner, summoned John Willet.

'Sir,' said John.

He wanted pen, ink, and paper. There was an old standish on the high mantel-shelf containing a dusty apology for all three. Having set this before him, the landlord was retiring, when he motioned him to stay.

'There's a house not far from here,' said the guest when he had written a few lines, 'which you call the Warren, I believe?'

As this was said in the tone of one who knew the fact, and asked the question as a thing of course, John contented himself with nodding his head in the affirmative; at the same time taking one hand out of his pockets to cough behind, and then putting it in again.

'I want this note' – said the guest, glancing on what he had written, and folding it, 'conveyed there without loss of time, and an answer brought back here. Have you a messenger at hand?'

John was thoughtful for a minute or thereabouts, and then said Yes.

'Let me see him,' said the guest.

This was disconcerting; for Joe being out, and Hugh engaged in rubbing down the chestnut cob, he designed sending on the errand, Barnaby, who had just then arrived in one of his rambles, and who, so that he thought himself employed on grave and serious business, would go anywhere.

'Why, the truth is,' said John after a long pause, 'that the person who'd go quickest, is a sort of natural, as one may say, sir; and though quick of foot, and as much to be trusted as the post itself, he's not good at talking, being touched and flighty, sir.'

'You don't,' said the guest, raising his eyes to John's fat face, 'you don't mean – what's the fellow's name – you don't mean Barnaby?'

'Yes I do,' returned the landlord, his features turning quite expressive with surprise.

'How comes he to be here?' inquired the guest, leaning back in his chair; speaking in the bland, even tone, from which he never varied; and with the same soft, courteous, never-changing smile upon his face. 'I saw him in London last night.'

'He's for ever here one hour, and there the next,' returned old John, after the usual pause to get the question in his mind. 'Sometimes he walks, and sometimes runs. He's known along the road by everybody, and sometimes comes here in a cart or chaise, and sometimes riding double. He comes and goes, through wind, rain, snow, and hail, and on the darkest nights. Nothing hurts *him*.'

'He goes often to this Warren, does he not?' said the guest carelessly. 'I seem to remember his mother telling me something to that effect yesterday. But I was not attending to the good woman much.'

'You're right sir,' John made answer, 'he does. His father, sir, was murdered in that house.'

'So I have heard,' returned the guest, taking a gold toothpick from his pocket with the same sweet smile. 'A very disagreeable circumstance for the family.'

'Very,' said John with a puzzled look, as if it occurred to him, dimly and afar off, that this might by possibility be a cool way of treating the subject.

'All the circumstances after a murder,' said the guest soliloquising, 'must be dreadfully unpleasant – so much bustle and disturbance – no repose – a constant dwelling upon one subject – and the running in and out, and up and down stairs, intolerable. I wouldn't have such a thing happen to anybody I was nearly interested in, on any account. 'T would be enough to wear one's life out. – You were going to say, friend –' he added, turning to John again.

'Only that Mrs Rudge lives on a little pension from the family, and that Barnaby's as free of the house as any cat or dog about it,' answered John. 'Shall he do your errand sir?'

'Oh yes,' replied the guest. 'Oh certainly. Let him do it by all means. Please to bring him here that I may charge him to be quick. If he objects to come you may tell him it's Mr Chester. He will remember my name, I dare say.'

John was so very much astonished to find who his visitor was, that he could express no astonishment at all, by looks or otherwise, but left the room as if he were in the most placid and imperturbable of all possible conditions. It has been reported that when he got down stairs, he looked steadily at the boiler for ten minutes by the clock, and all that time never once left off shaking his head; for which statement there would seem to be some ground of truth and feasibility, inasmuch as that interval of time did certainly elapse, before he returned with Barnaby to the guest's apartment.

'Come hither, lad,' said Mr Chester. 'You know Mr Geoffrey Haredale?'

Barnaby laughed, and looked at the landlord as though he would say, 'You hear him?' John, who was greatly shocked at this breach of decorum, clapped his finger to his nose, and shook his head, in mute remonstrance.

'He knows him sir,' said John, frowning aside at Barnaby, 'as well as you or I do.'

'I haven't the pleasure of much acquaintance with the gentleman,' returned his guest. '*You* may have. Limit the comparison to yourself, my friend.'

Although this was said with the same easy affability, and the same smile, John felt himself put down, and laying the indignity at Barnaby's door, determined to kick his raven, on the very first opportunity.

'Give that,' said the guest, who had by this time sealed the note, and who beckoned his messenger towards him as he spoke, 'into Mr Haredale's own hands. Wait for an answer, and bring it back to me – here. If you should find that Mr Haredale is engaged just now, tell him – can he remember a message, landlord?'

'When he chooses sir,' replied John. 'He won't forget this one.'

'How are you sure of that?'

John merely pointed to him as he stood with his head bent forward, and his earnest gaze fixed closely on his questioner's face; and nodded sagely.

'Tell him then, Barnaby, should he be engaged,' said Mr Chester, 'that I shall be glad to wait his convenience here, and to see him (if he will call) at any time this evening. – At the worst I can have a bed here, Willet, I suppose?'

Old John, immensely flattered by the personal notoriety implied in this familiar form of address, answered, with something like a knowing look, 'I should believe you could sir,' and was turning over in his mind various forms of eulogium, with the view of selecting one appropriate to the qualities of his best bed, when his ideas were put to flight by Mr Chester giving Barnaby the letter, and bidding him make all speed away.

'Speed!' said Barnaby, folding the little packet in his breast, 'Speed! If you want to see hurry and mystery, come here. Here!'

With that, he put his hand, very much to John Willet's horror, on the guest's fine broadcloth sleeve, and led him stealthily to the back window.

'Look down there,' he said softly; 'do you mark how they whisper in each other's ears; then dance and leap, to make believe they are in sport? Do you see how they stop for a moment, when they think there is no one looking, and mutter among themselves again; and then how they roll and gambol, delighted with the mischief they've been plotting? Look at 'em now. See how they whirl and plunge. And now they stop again, and whisper, cautiously together – little thinking, mind, how often I have lain upon the grass and watched them. I say – what is it that they plot and hatch? Do you know?'

'They are only clothes,' returned the guest, 'such as we wear; hanging on those lines to dry, and fluttering in the wind.'

'Clothes!' echoed Barnaby, looking close into his face, and falling quickly back. 'Ha ha! Why, how much better to be silly, than as wise as you! You don't see shadowy people there, like those that live in sleep – not you. Nor eyes in the knotted panes of glass, nor swift ghosts when it blows hard, nor do you hear voices in the air, nor see men stalking in the sky – not you! I lead a merrier life than you, with all your cleverness. You're the dull men. We're the bright ones. Ha! ha! I'll not change with you, clever as you are, – not I!'

With that, he waved his hat above his head, and darted off.

'A strange creature, upon my word!' said the guest, pulling out a handsome box, and taking a pinch of snuff.

'He wants imagination,' said Mr Willet, very slowly, and after a long silence; 'that's what he wants. I've tried to instil it into him, many and many's the time; but' – John added this, in confidence – 'he an't made for it; that's the fact.'

To record that Mr Chester smiled at John's remark would be little to the purpose, for he preserved the same conciliatory and pleasant look at all times. He drew his chair nearer to the fire though, as a kind of hint that he would prefer to be alone, and John, having no reasonable excuse for remaining, left him to himself.

Very thoughtful old John Willet was, while the dinner was preparing; and if his brain were ever less clear at one time than another, it is but reasonable to suppose that he addled it in no slight degree by shaking his head so much that day. That Mr Chester, between whom and Mr Haredale, it was notorious to all the neighbourhood, a deep and bitter animosity existed, should come down there for the sole purpose, as it seemed, of seeing him, and should choose the Maypole for their place of meeting, and should send to him express, were stumbling blocks John could not overcome. The only resource he had, was to consult the boiler, and wait impatiently for Barnaby's return.

But Barnaby delayed beyond all precedent. The visitor's dinner was served, removed, his wine was set, the fire replenished, the hearth clean swept; the light waned without, it grew dusk, became quite dark, and still no Barnaby appeared. Yet, though John Willet was full of wonder and misgiving, his guest sat cross-legged in the easy chair, to all appearance as little ruffled in his thoughts as in his dress – the same calm, easy, cool gentleman, without a care or thought beyond his golden toothpick.

'Barnaby's late,' John ventured to observe, as he placed a pair of tarnished candlesticks, some three feet high, upon the table, and snuffed the lights they held.

'He is rather so,' replied the guest, sipping his wine. 'He will not be much longer, I dare say.'

John coughed and raked the fire together.

'As your roads bear no very good character, if I may judge from my son's mishap, though,' said Mr Chester, 'and as I have no fancy to be knocked on the head – which is not only disconcerting at the moment, but places one, besides, in a ridiculous position with respect to the people who chance to pick one up – I shall stop here to-night. I think you said you had a bed to spare?'

'Such a bed, sir,' returned John Willet; 'ay, such a bed as few, even of the gentry's houses, own. A fixter here, sir. I've heard say that bedstead is nigh two hundred years of age. Your noble son – a fine young gentleman – slept in it last, sir, half a year ago.'

'Upon my life, a recommendation!' said the guest, shrugging his shoulders and wheeling his chair nearer to the fire. 'See that it be well aired, Mr Willet, and let a blazing fire be lighted there at once. This house is something damp and chilly.'

John raked the faggots up again, more from habit than presence of mind, or any reference to this remark, and was about to withdraw, when a bounding step was heard upon the stair, and Barnaby came panting in.

'He'll have his foot in the stirrup in an hour's time,' he cried, advancing. 'He has been riding hard all day – has just come home – but will be in the saddle again as soon as he has eat and drank, to meet his loving friend.'

'Was that his message?' asked the visitor, looking up, but without the smallest discomposure – or at least without the smallest show of any.

'All but the last words,' Barnaby rejoined. 'He meant those. I saw that, in his face.'

'This for your pains,' said the other, putting money in his hand, and glancing at him stedfastly. 'This for your pains, sharp Barnaby.'

'For Grip, and me, and Hugh, to share among us,' he rejoined, putting it up, and nodding, as he counted it on his fingers. 'Grip one, me two, Hugh three; the dog, the goat, the cats – well, we shall spend it pretty soon, I warn you. Stay. – Look. Do you wise men see nothing there, now?'

He bent eagerly down on one knee, and gazed intently at the smoke, which was rolling up the chimney in a thick black cloud. John Willet, who appeared to consider himself particularly and chiefly referred to under the term wise men, looked that way likewise, and with great solidity of feature.

'Now, where do they go to, when they spring so fast up there,' asked Barnaby; 'eh? Why do they tread so closely on each other's heels, and why are they always in a hurry – which is what you blame me for, when I only take pattern by these busy folk about me. More of 'em! catching to each other's skirts; and as fast as they go, others come! What a merry dance it is! I would that Grip and I could frisk like that!'

'What has he in that basket at his back?' asked the guest after a few moments, during which Barnaby was still bending down to look higher up the chimney, and earnestly watching the smoke.

'In this?' he answered, jumping up, before John Willet could reply – shaking it as he spoke, and stooping his head to listen. 'In this? What is there here? Tell him!'

'A devil, a devil, a devil,' cried a hoarse voice.

'Here's money!' said Barnaby, chinking it in his hand, 'money for a treat, Grip!'

'Hurrah! Hurrah! Hurrah!' replied the raven, 'keep up your spirits. Never say die. Bow, wow, wow!'

Mr Willet, who appeared to entertain strong doubts whether a customer in a laced coat and fine linen could be supposed to have any acquaintance even with the existence of such unpolite gentry as the bird claimed to belong to, took Barnaby off at this juncture, with the view of preventing any other improper declarations, and quitted the room with his very best bow.

CHAPTER THE ELEVENTH

There was great news that night for the regular Maypole customers, to each of whom, as he straggled in to occupy his allotted seat in the chimney corner, John, with a most impressive slowness of delivery, and in an apoplectic whisper, communicated the fact that Mr Chester was alone in the large room up-stairs, and was waiting the arrival of Mr Geoffrey Haredale, to whom he had sent a letter (doubtless of a threatening nature) by the hands of Barnaby, then and there present.

For a little knot of smokers and solemn gossips, who had seldom any new topics of discussion, this was a perfect Godsend. Here was a good, dark-looking, mystery progressing under that very roof – brought home to the fireside as it were, and enjoyable without the smallest pains or trouble. It is extraordinary what a zest and relish it gave to the drink, and how it heightened the flavour of the tobacco. Every man smoked his pipe with a face of grave and serious delight, and looked at his neighbour with a sort of quiet congratulation. Nay, it was felt to be such a holiday and special night, that, on the motion of little Solomon Daisy, every man (including John himself) put down his sixpence for a can of flip, which grateful beverage was brewed with all despatch, and set down in the midst of them on the brick floor; both that it might simmer and stew before the fire, and that its fragrant steam, rising up among them and mixing with the wreaths of vapour from their pipes, might shroud them in a delicious atmosphere of their own, and shut out all the world. The very furniture of the room seemed to mellow and deepen in its tone; the ceiling and walls looked blacker and more highly polished, the curtains of a ruddier red; the fire burnt clear and high, and the crickets in the hearth-stone chirped with a more than wonted satisfaction.

There were present, two, however, who showed but little interest in the general contentment. Of these, one was Barnaby himself, who slept, or, to avoid being beset with questions, feigned to sleep, in the chimney-corner; the other, Hugh, who, sleeping too, lay stretched upon the bench on the opposite side, in the full glare of the blazing fire.

The light that fell upon this slumbering form, showed it in all its muscular and handsome proportions. It was that of a young man, of a hale athletic figure, and a giant's strength, whose sunburnt face and swarthy throat, overgrown with jet black hair, might have served a painter for a model. Loosely attired, in the coarsest and roughest garb, with scraps of straw and hay – his usual bed – clinging here and there, and mingling with his uncombed locks, he had fallen asleep in a posture as careless as his dress. The negligence and disorder of the whole man, with something fierce and sullen in his features, gave him a picturesque appearance, that attracted the regards even of the Maypole customers who knew him well, and caused Long Parkes to say that Hugh looked more like a poaching rascal to-night than ever he had seen him yet.

'He's waiting here, I suppose,' said Solomon, 'to take Mr Haredale's horse.'

'That's it, sir,' replied John Willet. 'He's not often in the house, you know. He's more at his ease among horses than men. I look upon him as a animal himself.'

Following up this opinion with a shrug that seemed meant to say, 'we can't expect everybody to be like us,' John put his pipe into his mouth again, and smoked like one who felt his superiority over the general run of mankind.

'That chap, sir,' said John, taking it out again after a time, and pointing at him with the stem, 'though he's got all his faculties about him – bottled up and corked down, if I may say so, somewheres or another –'

'Very good!' said Parkes, nodding his head. 'A very good expression, Johnny. You'll be a tackling somebody presently. You're in twig to-night, I see.'

'Take care,' said Mr Willet, not at all grateful for the compliment, 'that I don't tackle you, sir, which I shall certainly endeavour to do, if you interrupt me when I'm making observations. – That chap, I was a saying, though he has all his faculties about him, somewheres

or another, bottled up and corked down, has no more imagination than Barnaby has. And why hasn't he?'

The three friends shook their heads at each other; saying by that action, without the trouble of opening their lips, 'Do you observe what a philosophical mind our friend has?'

'Why hasn't he?' said John, gently striking the table with his open hand. 'Because they was never drawed out of him when he was a boy. That's why. What would any of us have been, if our fathers hadn't drawed our faculties out of us? What would my boy Joe have been, if I hadn't drawed his faculties out of him? – Do you mind what I'm a saying of, gentlemen?'

'Ah! we mind you,' cried Parkes. 'Go on improving of us, Johnny.'

'Consequently, then,' said Mr Willet, 'that chap, whose mother was hung when he was a little boy, along with six others, for passing bad Notes[1] – and it's a blessed thing to think how many people are hung in batches every six weeks for that, and such like offences, as showing how wide awake our government is – that chap that was then turned loose, and had to mind cows, and frighten birds away, and what not, for a few pence to live on, and so got on by degrees to mind horses, and to sleep in course of time in lofts and litter, instead of under haystacks and hedges, till at last he come to be hostler at the Maypole for his board and lodging and a annual trifle – that chap that can't read nor write, and has never had much to do with anything but animals, and has never lived in any way but like the animals he has lived among, *is* a animal. And,' said Mr Willet, arriving at his logical conclusion, 'is to be treated accordingly.'

'Willet,' said Solomon Daisy, who had exhibited some impatience at the intrusion of so unworthy a subject on their more interesting theme, 'when Mr Chester come this morning, did he order the large room?'

'He signified, sir,' said John, 'that he wanted a large apartment. Yes. Certainly.'

'Why then, I'll tell you what,' said Solomon, speaking softly and with an earnest look. 'He and Mr Haredale are going to fight a duel in it.'

Everybody looked at Mr Willet, after this alarming suggestion. Mr Willet looked at the fire, weighing in his own mind the effect which such an occurrence would be likely to have, on the establishment.

'Well,' said John, 'I don't know – I am sure – I remember that when I went up last, he *had* put the lights upon the mantel-shelf.'

'It's as plain,' returned Solomon, 'as the nose on Parkes's face' – Mr Parkes, who had a large nose, rubbed it, and looked as if he considered this a personal allusion – 'they'll fight in that room. You know by the newspapers what a common thing it is for gentlemen to fight in coffee-houses without seconds. One of 'em will be wounded or perhaps killed in this house.'

'That was a challenge that Barnaby took then, eh?' said John.

'– Inclosing a slip of paper with the measure of his sword upon it, I'll bet a guinea,' answered the little man. 'We know what sort of gentleman Mr Haredale is. You have told us what Barnaby said about his looks, when he came back. Depend upon it, I'm right. Now, mind.'

The flip had had no flavour till now. The tobacco had been of mere English growth, compared with its present taste. A duel in that great old rambling room up stairs, and the best bed ordered already for the wounded man!

'Would it be swords or pistols now?' said John.

'Heaven knows. Perhaps both,' returned Solomon. 'The gentlemen wear swords, and may easily have pistols in their pockets – most likely have, indeed. If they fire at each other without effect, then they'll draw, and go to work in earnest.'

A shade passed over Mr Willet's face as he thought of broken windows and disabled furniture, but bethinking himself that one of the parties would probably be left alive to pay the damage, he brightened up again.

'And then,' said Solomon, looking from face to face, 'then we shall have one of those stains upon the floor that never come out. If Mr Haredale wins, depend upon it, it'll be a deep one; or if he loses, it will perhaps be deeper still, for he'll never give in unless he's beaten down. We know him better, eh?'

'Better indeed!' they whispered all together.

'As to it's ever being got out again,' said Solomon, 'I tell you it never will, or can be. Why, do you know that it has been tried, at a certain house we are acquainted with?'

'The Warren!' cried John. 'No, sure!'

'Yes, sure – yes. It's only known by very few. It has been whispered about though, for all that. They planed the board away, but there it was. They went deep, but it went deeper. They put new boards down, but there was one great spot that came through still, and showed itself in the old place. And – harkye – draw nearer – Mr Geoffrey made that room his study, and sits there, always, with his foot (as I have heard) upon it; and he believes, through thinking of it long and very much, that it will never fade until he finds the man who did the deed.'

As this recital ended, and they all drew closer round the fire, the tramp of a horse was heard without.

'The very man!' cried John, starting up, 'Hugh! Hugh!'

The sleeper staggered to his feet, and hurried after him. John quickly returned, ushering in with great attention and deference (for Mr Haredale was his landlord) the long expected visitor, who strode into the room clanking his heavy boots upon the floor; and looking keenly round upon the bowing group, raised his hat in acknowledgement of their profound respect.

'You have a stranger here, Willet, who sent to me,' he said, in a voice which sounded naturally stern and deep. 'Where is he?'

'In the great room up-stairs, sir,' answered John.

'Show the way. Your staircase is dark, I know. Gentlemen, good night.'

With that, he signed to the landlord to go on before; and went clanking out, and up the stairs; old John, in his agitation, ingeniously lighting everything but the way, and making a stumble at every second step.

'Stop!' he said, when they reached the landing. 'I can announce myself. Don't wait.'

He laid his hand upon the door, entered, and shut it heavily. Mr Willet was by no means disposed to stand there listening by himself, especially as the walls were very thick; so descended, with much greater alacrity than he had come up, and joined his friends below.

*

CHAPTER THE TWELFTH

There was a brief pause in the state-room of the Maypole, as Mr Haredale tried the lock to satisfy himself that he had shut the door securely, and, striding up the dark chamber to where the screen inclosed a little patch of light and warmth, presented himself, abruptly and in silence, before the smiling guest.

If the two had no greater sympathy in their inward thoughts than in their outward bearing and appearance, the meeting did not seem likely to prove a very calm or pleasant one. With no great disparity between them in point of years, they were, in every other respect, as unlike and far removed from each other as two men could well be. The one was soft-spoken, delicately made, precise, and elegant; the other, a burly square-built man, negligently dressed, rough and abrupt in manner, stern, and, in his present mood, forbidding both in look and speech. The one preserved a calm and placid smile; the other, a distrustful frown. The new-comer, indeed, appeared bent on showing by his every tone and gesture his determined opposition and hostility to the man he had come to meet. The guest who received him, on the other hand, seemed to feel that the contrast between them was all in his favour, and to derive a quiet exultation from it which put him more at his ease than ever.

'Haredale,' said this gentleman, without the least appearance of embarrassment or reserve, 'I am very glad to see you.'

'Let us dispense with compliments. They are misplaced between us,' returned the other, waving his hand, 'and say plainly what we have to say. You have asked me to meet you. I am here. Why do we stand face to face again?'

'Still the same frank and sturdy character I see!'

'Good or bad, sir, I am,' returned the other, leaning his arm upon the chimney-piece, and turning a haughty look upon the occupant of the easy-chair, 'the man I used to be. I have lost no old likings or dislikings; my memory has not failed me by a hair's-breadth. You ask me to give you a meeting. I say, I am here.'

'Our meeting, Haredale,' said Mr Chester, tapping his snuff-box, and following with a smile the impatient gesture he had made – perhaps unconsciously – towards his sword, 'is one of conference and peace, I hope?'

'I have come here,' returned the other, 'at your desire, holding myself bound to meet you, when and where you would. I have not come to bandy pleasant speeches, or hollow professions. You are a smooth man of the world, sir, and at such play have me at a disadvantage. The very last man on this earth with whom I would enter the lists to combat with gentle compliments and masked faces, is Mr Chester, I do assure you. I am not his match at such weapons, and have reason to believe that few men are.'

'You do me a great deal of honour, Haredale,' returned the other, most composedly, 'and I thank you. I will be frank with you – '

'I beg your pardon – will be what?'

'Frank – open – perfectly candid.'

'Hah!' cried Mr Haredale, drawing in his breath with a sarcastic smile. 'But don't let me interrupt you.'

'So resolved am I to hold this course,' returned the other, tasting his wine with great deliberation, 'that I have determined not to quarrel with you, and not to be betrayed into a warm expression or a hasty word.'

'There again,' said Mr Haredale, 'you will have me at a great advantage. Your self-command – '

'Is not to be disturbed, when it will serve my purpose, you would say' – rejoined the other, interrupting him with the same complacency. 'Granted. I allow it. And I have a purpose to serve now. So have you. I am sure our object is the same. Let us attain it like sensible men, who have ceased to be boys some time. – Do you drink?'

'With my friends,' returned the other.

'At least,' said Mr Chester, 'you will be seated?'

'I will stand,' returned Mr Haredale impatiently, 'on this dismantled, beggared hearth, and not pollute it, fallen as it is, with mockeries. Go on!'

'You are wrong, Haredale,' said the other, crossing his legs, and smiling as he held his glass up in the bright glow of the fire. 'You are really very wrong. The world is a lively place enough, in which we must accommodate ourselves to circumstances, sail with the stream as glibly as we can, be content to take froth for substance, the surface for the depth, the counterfeit for the real coin. I wonder no philosopher has ever established that our globe itself is hollow. It should be, if Nature is consistent in her works.'

'*You* think it is, perhaps?'

'I should say,' he returned, sipping his wine, 'there could be no doubt about it. Well; we, in our trifling with this jingling toy, have had the ill luck to jostle and fall out. We are not what the world calls friends; but we are as good and true and loving friends for all that, as nine out of every ten of those on whom it bestows the title. You have a niece, and I a son – a fine lad, Haredale, but foolish. They fall in love with each other, and form what this same world calls an attachment; meaning a something fanciful and false like all the rest, which, if it took its own free time, would break like any other bubble. But it may not have its own free time – will not, if they are left alone – and the question is, shall we two, because society calls us enemies, stand aloof, and let them rush into each other's arms, when, by approaching each other sensibly, as we do now, we can prevent it, and part them?'

'I love my niece,' said Mr Haredale, after a short silence. 'It may sound strangely in your ears; but I love her.'

'Strangely, my good fellow!' cried Mr Chester, lazily filling his glass again, and pulling out his toothpick. 'Not at all. I like Ned too – or, as you say, love him – that's the word among such near relations. I'm very fond of Ned. He's an amazingly good fellow, and a handsome fellow – foolish and weak as yet; that's all. But the thing is, Haredale – for I'll be very frank, as I told you I would at first – independently of any dislike that you and I might have to being related to each other, and independently of the religious differences between us – and damn it, that's important – I couldn't afford a match of this description. Ned and I couldn't do it. It's impossible.'

'Curb your tongue, in God's name, if this conversation is to last,' retorted Mr Haredale fiercely. 'I have said I love my niece. Do you think that, loving her, I would have her fling her heart away on any man who had your blood in his veins?'

'You see,' said the other, not at all disturbed, 'the advantage of being so frank and open. Just what I was about to add, upon my honour! I am amazingly attached to Ned – quite doat upon him, indeed – and even if we could afford to throw ourselves away, that very objection would be quite insuperable. – I wish you'd take some wine.'

'Mark me,' said Mr Haredale, striding to the table, and laying his hand upon it heavily. 'If any man believes – presumes to think

– that I, in word, or deed, or in the wildest dream, ever entertained remotely the idea of Emma Haredale's favouring the suit of one who was akin to you – in any way – I care not what – he lies. He lies, and does me grievous wrong, in the mere thought.'

'Haredale,' returned the other, rocking himself to and fro as in assent, and nodding at the fire, 'it's extremely manly, and really very generous in you, to meet me in this unreserved and handsome way. Upon my word, those are exactly my sentiments, only expressed with much more force and power than I could use – you know my sluggish nature, and will forgive me, I am sure.'

'While I would restrain her from all correspondence with your son, and sever their intercourse here, though it should cause her death,' said Mr Haredale, who had been pacing to and fro, 'I would do it kindly and tenderly if I can. I have a trust to discharge which my nature is not formed to understand, and, for this reason, the bare fact of there being any love between them comes upon me to-night, almost for the first time.'

'I am more delighted than I can possibly tell you,' rejoined Mr Chester with the utmost blandness, 'to find my own impression so confirmed. You see the advantage of our having met. We understand each other. We quite agree. We have a most complete and thorough explanation, and we know what course to take. – Why don't you taste your tenant's wine? It's really very good.'

'Pray who,' said Mr Haredale, 'have aided Emma, or your son? Who are their go-betweens, and agents – do you know?'

'All the good people hereabouts – the neighbourhood in general, I think,' returned the other, with his most affable smile. 'The messenger I sent to you to-day, foremost among them all.'

'The idiot? Barnaby?'

'You are surprised? I am glad of that, for I was rather so myself. Yes. I wrung that from his mother – a very decent sort of woman – from whom, indeed, I chiefly learnt how serious the matter had become, and so determined to ride out here to-day, and hold a parley with you on this neutral ground. – You're stouter than you used to be, Haredale, but you look extremely well.'

'Our business, I presume, is nearly at an end,' said Mr Haredale, with an expression of impatience he was at no pains to conceal. 'Trust me, Mr Chester, my niece shall change from this time. I will appeal,' he added in a lower tone, 'to her woman's heart, her dignity, her pride, her duty' –

'I shall do the same by Ned,' said Mr Chester, restoring some errant faggots to their places in the grate with the toe of his boot. 'If there is anything real in the world, it is those amazingly fine feelings and those natural obligations which must subsist between father and son. I shall put it to him on every ground of moral and religious feeling. I shall represent to him that we cannot possibly afford it – that I have always looked forward to his marrying well, for a genteel provision for myself in the autumn of life – that there are a great many clamorous dogs to pay, whose claims are perfectly just and right, and who must be paid out of his wife's fortune. In short, that the very highest and most honourable feelings of our nature, with every consideration of filial duty and affection, and all that sort of thing, imperatively demand that he should run away with an heiress.'

'And break her heart as speedily as possible?' said Mr Haredale, drawing on his glove.

'There Ned will act exactly as he pleases,' returned the other, sipping his wine; 'that's entirely his affair. I wouldn't for the world interfere with my son, Haredale, beyond a certain point. The relationship between father and son, you know, is positively quite a holy kind of bond. – *Won't* you let me persuade you to take one glass of wine? Well! as you please, as you please,' he added, helping himself again.

'Chester,' said Mr Haredale, after a short silence, during which he had eyed his smiling face from time to time intently, 'you have the head and heart of an evil spirit in all matters of deception.'

'Your health!' said the other, with a nod. 'But I have interrupted you – '

'If now,' pursued Mr Haredale, 'we should find it difficult to separate these young people, and break off their intercourse – if, for instance, you find it difficult on your side, what course do you intend to take?'

'Nothing plainer, my good fellow, nothing easier,' returned the other, shrugging his shoulders and stretching himself more comfortably before the fire. 'I shall then exert those powers on which you flatter me so highly – though, upon my word, I don't deserve your compliments to their full extent – and resort to a few little trivial subterfuges for rousing jealousy and resentment. You see?'

'In short, justifying the means by the end, we are, as a last resource for tearing them asunder, to resort to treachery and – and lying,' said Mr Haredale.

'Oh dear no. Fie, fie!' returned the other, relishing a pinch of snuff extremely. 'Not lying. Only a little management, a little diplomacy, a little – intriguing, that's the word.'

'I wish,' said Mr Haredale, moving to and fro, and stopping, and moving on again, like one who was ill at ease, 'that this could have been foreseen or prevented. But as it has gone so far, and it is necessary for us to act, it is of no use shrinking or regretting. Well! I shall second your endeavours to the utmost of my power. There is one topic in the whole wide range of human thoughts on which we both agree. We shall act in concert, but apart. There will be no need, I hope, for us to meet again.'

'Are you going?' said Mr Chester, rising with a graceful indolence. 'Let me light you down the stairs.'

'Pray keep your seat,' returned the other dryly, 'I know the way.' So, waving his hand slightly, and putting on his hat as he turned upon his heel, he went clanking out as he had come, shut the door behind him, and tramped down the echoing stairs.

'Pah! A very coarse animal, indeed!' said Mr Chester, composing himself in the easy chair again. 'A rough brute. Quite a human badger!'

John Willet and his friends, who had been listening intently for the clash of swords, or firing of pistols in the great room, and had indeed settled the order in which they should rush in when summoned – in which procession old John had carefully arranged that he should bring up the rear – were very much astonished to see Mr Haredale come down without a scratch, call for his horse, and ride away thoughtfully at a footpace. After some consideration, it was decided that he had left the gentleman above, for dead, and had adopted this stratagem to divert suspicion or pursuit.

As this conclusion involved the necessity of their going up stairs forthwith, they were about to ascend in the order they had agreed upon, when a smart ringing at the guest's bell, as if he had pulled it vigorously, overthrew all their speculations, and involved them in great uncertainty and doubt. At length Mr Willet agreed to go up stairs himself, escorted by Hugh and Barnaby, as the strongest and stoutest fellows on the premises, who were to make their appearance under pretence of clearing away the glasses.

Under this protection, the brave and broad-faced John boldly entered the room, half a foot in advance, and received an order for a boot-jack without trembling. But when it was brought, and he leant his sturdy shoulder to the guest, Mr Willet was observed to look very hard into his boots as he pulled them off, and, by opening his eyes much wider than usual, to appear to express some surprise and disappointment at not finding them full of blood. He took occasion too, to examine the gentleman as closely as he could, expecting to discover sundry loop-holes in his person, pierced by his adversary's sword. Finding none, however, and observing in course of time that his guest was as cool and unruffled, both in his dress and temper, as he had been all day, old John at last heaved a deep sigh, and began to think no duel had been fought that night.

'And now, Willet,' said Mr Chester, 'if the room's well aired, I'll try the merits of that famous bed.'

'The room, sir,' returned John, taking up a candle, and nudging Barnaby and Hugh to accompany them, in case the gentleman should unexpectedly drop down faint or dead, from some internal wound, 'the room's as warm as any toast in a tankard. Barnaby, take you that other candle, and go on before. Hugh! Follow up, sir, with the easy-chair.'

In this order – and still, in his earnest inspection, holding his candle very close to the guest; now making him feel extremely warm about the legs, now threatening to set his wig on fire, and constantly begging his pardon with great awkwardness and embarrassment – John led the party to the best bed-room, which was nearly as large as the chamber from which they had come, and held, drawn out near the fire for warmth, a great old spectral bedstead, hung with faded brocade, and ornamented, at the top of each carved post, with a plume of feathers that had once been white, but with dust and age had now grown hearse-like and funereal.

'Good night, my friends,' said Mr Chester with a sweet smile, seating himself, when he had surveyed the room from end to end, in the easy-chair which his attendants wheeled before the fire. 'Good night! Barnaby, my good fellow, you say some prayers before you go to bed, I hope?'

Barnaby nodded. 'He has some nonsense that he calls his prayers, sir,' returned old John, officiously. 'I'm afraid there a'nt much good in 'em.'

'And Hugh?' said Mr Chester, turning to him.

'Not I,' he answered. 'I know his' – pointing to Barnaby – 'they're well enough. He sings 'em sometimes in the straw. I listen.'

'He's quite a animal, sir,' John whispered in his ear with dignity. 'You'll excuse him, I'm sure. If he has any soul at all, sir, it must be such a very small one, that it don't signify what he does or doesn't in that way. Good night, sir!'

The guest rejoined 'God bless you!' with a fervour that was quite affecting; and John, beckoning his guards to go before, bowed himself out of the room, and left him to his rest in the Maypole's ancient bed.

—— * ——

CHAPTER THE THIRTEENTH

If Joseph Willet, the denounced and proscribed of 'prentices, had happened to be at home when his father's courtly guest presented himself before the Maypole door – that is, if it had not perversely chanced to be one of the half-dozen days in the whole year on which he was at liberty to absent himself for as many hours without question or reproach – he would have contrived, by hook or crook, to dive to the very bottom of Mr Chester's mystery, and to come at his purpose with as much certainty as though he had been his confidential adviser. In that fortunate case, the lovers would have had quick warning of the ills that threatened them, and the aid of various timely and wise suggestions to boot; for all Joe's readiness of thought and action, and all his sympathies and good wishes, were enlisted in favour of the young people, and were staunch in devotion to their cause. Whether this disposition arose out of his old prepossessions in favour of the young lady, whose history had surrounded her in his mind, almost from his cradle, with circumstances of unusual interest; or from his attachment towards the young gentleman, into whose confidence he had, through his shrewdness and alacrity, and the rendering of sundry important services as a spy and messenger, almost imperceptibly glided; whether they had their origin in either of these sources, or in the habit natural to youth, or in the constant badgering and worrying of his venerable parent, or in any hidden little love affair of his own which gave him something of a fellow-feeling in the matter; it is needless to inquire – especially as Joe was out of the way, and had no opportunity on that particular occasion of testifying to his sentiments either on one side or the other.

It was, in fact, the twenty-fifth of March, which, as most people know to their cost, is, and has been time out of mind, one of those unpleasant epochs termed quarter-days. On this twenty-fifth of March, it was John Willet's pride annually to settle, in hard cash, his account with a certain vintner and distiller in the city of London; to give into whose hands a canvas bag containing its exact amount, and not a penny more or less, was the end and object of a journey for Joe, so surely as the year and day came round.

This journey was performed upon an old grey mare, concerning whom John had an indistinct set of ideas hovering about him, to the effect that she could win a plate or cup if she tried. She never had tried, and probably never would now, being some fourteen or fifteen years of age, short in wind, long in body, and rather the worse for wear in respect of her mane and tail. Notwithstanding these slight defects, John perfectly gloried in the animal; and when she was brought round to the door by Hugh, actually retired into the bar, and there, in a secret grove of lemons, laughed with pride.

'There's a bit of horseflesh, Hugh!' said John, when he had recovered enough self-command to appear at the door again. 'There's a comely creatur! There's high mettle! There's bone!'

There was bone enough beyond all doubt; and so Hugh seemed to think, as he sat sideways in the saddle, lazily doubled up with his chin nearly touching his knees; and heedless of the dangling stirrups and loose bridle-rein, sauntered up and down on the little green before the door.

'Mind you take good care of her, sir,' said John, appealing from this insensible person to his son and heir, who now appeared, fully equipped and ready. 'Don't you ride hard.'

'I should be puzzled to do that, I think, father,' Joe replied, casting a disconsolate look at the animal.

'None of your impudence, sir, if you please,' retorted old John. 'What would you ride, sir? A wild ass or zebra would be too tame for you, wouldn't he, eh sir? You'd like to ride a roaring lion, wouldn't you sir, eh sir? Hold your tongue, sir.' When Mr Willet, in his differences with his son, had exhausted all the questions that occurred to him, and Joe had said nothing at all in answer, he generally wound up by bidding him hold his tongue.

'And what does the boy mean,' added Mr Willet, after he had stared at him for a little time, in a species of stupefaction, 'by cocking his hat, to such an extent! Are you a going to kill the wintner, sir?'

'No,' said Joe, tartly; 'I'm not. Now your mind's at ease, father.'

'With a milintary air, too!' said Mr Willet, surveying him from top to toe; 'with a swaggering, fire-eating, biling-water drinking sort of way with him! And what do you mean by pulling up the crocuses and snowdrops, eh sir?'

'It's only a little nosegay,' said Joe, reddening. 'There's no harm in that, I hope?'

'You're a boy of business, you are, sir!' said Mr Willet, disdainfully, 'to go supposing that wintners care for nosegays.'

'I don't suppose anything of the kind,' returned Joe. 'Let them keep their red noses for bottles and tankards. These are going to Mr Varden's house.'

'And do you suppose *he* minds such things as crocuses?' demanded John.

'I don't know, and to say the truth, I don't care,' said Joe. 'Come father, give me the money, and in the name of patience let me go.'

'There it is, sir,' replied John; 'and take care of it; and mind you don't make too much haste back, but give the mare a long rest. – Do you mind?'

'Ay, I mind,' returned Joe. 'She'll need it, Heaven knows.'

'And don't you score up too much at the Black Lion,'[1] said John. 'Mind that too.'

'Then why don't you let me have some money of my own?' retorted Joe, sorrowfully; 'why don't you, father? What do you send me into London for, giving me only the right to call for my dinner at the Black Lion, which you're to pay for next time you go, as if I was not to be trusted with a few shillings? Why do you use me like this? It's not right of you. You can't expect me to be quiet under it.'

'Let him have money!' cried John, in a drowsy reverie. 'What does he call money – guineas? Hasn't he got money? Over and above the tolls, hasn't he one and sixpence?'

'One and sixpence!' repeated his son contemptuously.

'Yes, sir,' returned John, 'one and sixpence. When I was your age, I had never seen so much money, in a heap. A shilling of it is in case of accidents – the mare casting a shoe, or the like of that.

The other sixpence is to spend in the diversions of London; and the diversion I recommend is going to the top of the Monument,[2] and sitting there. There's no temptation there, sir – no drink – no young women – no bad characters of any sort – nothing but imagination. That's the way I enjoyed myself when I was your age, sir.'

To this, Joe made no answer, but beckoning Hugh, leaped into the saddle and rode away; and a very stalwart manly horseman he looked, deserving a better charger than it was his fortune to bestride. John stood staring after him, or rather after the grey mare, (for he had no eyes for her rider) until man and beast had been out of sight some twenty minutes, when he began to think they were gone, and slowly re-entering the house, fell into a gentle doze.

The unfortunate grey mare, who was the agony of Joe's life, floundered along at her own will and pleasure until the Maypole was no longer visible, and then, contracting her legs into what in a puppet would have been looked upon as a clumsy and awkward imitation of a canter, mended her pace all at once, and did it of her own accord. The acquaintance with her rider's usual mode of proceeding, which suggested this improvement in hers, impelled her likewise to turn up a bye-way, leading – not to London, but through lanes running parallel with the road they had come, and passing within a few hundred yards of the Maypole, which led finally to an inclosure surrounding a large, old, red-brick mansion – the same of which mention was made as the Warren in the first chapter of this history. Coming to a dead stop in a little copse thereabout, she suffered her rider to dismount with right good-will, and to tie her to the trunk of a tree.

'Stay there, old girl,' said Joe, 'and let us see whether there's any little commission for me to-day.' So saying, he left her to browse upon such stunted grass and weeds as happened to grow within the length of her tether, and passing through a wicket gate, entered the grounds on foot.

The pathway, after a very few minutes' walking, brought him close to the house, towards which, and especially towards one particular window, he directed many covert glances. It was a dreary, silent building, with echoing courtyards, desolated turret-chambers, and whole suites of rooms shut up and mouldering to ruin.

The terrace-garden, dark with the shade of overhanging trees, had an air of melancholy that was quite oppressive. Great iron

gates, disused for many years, and red with rust, drooping on their hinges and overgrown with long rank grass, seemed as though they tried to sink into the ground, and hide their fallen state among the friendly weeds. The fantastic monsters on the walls, green with age and damp, and covered here and there with moss, looked grim and desolate. There was a sombre aspect even on that part of the mansion which was inhabited and kept in good repair, that struck the beholder with a sense of sadness; of something forlorn and failing, whence cheerfulness was banished. It would have been difficult to imagine a bright fire blazing in the dull and darkened rooms, or to picture any gaiety of heart or revelry that the frowning walls shut in. It seemed a place where such things had been, but could be no more – the very ghost of a house, haunting the old spot in its old outward form, and that was all.

Much of this decayed and sombre look was attributable, no doubt, to the death of its former master, and the temper of its present occupant; but remembering the tale connected with the mansion, it seemed the very place for such a deed, and one that might have been its predestined theatre years upon years ago. Viewed with reference to this legend, the sheet of water where the steward's body had been found appeared to wear a black and sullen character, such as no other pool might own; the bell upon the roof that had told the tale of murder to the midnight wind, became a very phantom whose voice would raise the listener's hair on end; and every leafless bough that nodded to another, had its stealthy whispering of the crime.

Joe paced up and down the path, sometimes stopping in affected contemplation of the building or the prospect, sometimes leaning against a tree with an assumed air of idleness and indifference, but always keeping an eye upon the window he had singled out at first. After some quarter of an hour's delay, a small white hand was waved to him for an instant from this casement, and the young man, with a respectful bow, departed; saying under his breath as he crossed his horse again, 'No errand for me to-day!'

But the air of smartness, the cock of the hat to which John Willet had objected, and the spring nosegay, all betokened some little errand of his own, having a more interesting object than a vintner or even a locksmith. So, indeed, it turned out; for when he had settled with the vintner – whose place of business was down in some deep cellars hard by Thames-street, and who was as purple-faced an old gentleman as if he had all his life supported their arched roof on his head – when he had settled the account, and taken the receipt, and declined tasting more than three glasses of old sherry, to the unbounded astonishment of the purple-faced vinter, who, gimlet in hand, had projected an attack upon at least a score of dusty casks, and who stood transfixed, or morally gimleted as it were, to his own wall – when he had done all this, and disposed besides of a frugal dinner at the Black Lion in Whitechapel; spurning the Monument and John's advice, he turned his steps towards the locksmith's house, attracted by the eyes of blooming Dolly Varden.

Joe was by no means a sheepish fellow, but, for all that, when he got to the corner of the street in which the locksmith lived, he could by no means make up his mind to walk straight to the house. First, he resolved to stroll up another street for five minutes, then up another street for five minutes more, and so on until he had lost full half an hour, when he made a bold plunge and found himself with a red face and a beating heart in the smoky workshop.

'Joe Willet, or his ghost!' said Varden, rising from the desk at which he was busy with his books, and looking at him under his spectacles. 'Which is it? Joe in the flesh, eh? That's hearty. And how are all the Chigwell company, Joe?'

'Much as usual, sir – they and I agree as well as ever.'

'Well, well!' said the locksmith. 'We must be patient, Joe, and bear with old folks' foibles. How's the mare, Joe? Does she do the four miles an hour as easily as ever? Ha, ha, ha! Does she, Joe? Eh? – What have we there, Joe – a nosegay?'

'A very poor one, sir – I thought Miss Dolly –'

'No, no,' said Gabriel, dropping his voice and shaking his head, 'not Dolly. Give 'em to her mother, Joe. A great deal better give 'em to her mother. Would you mind giving 'em to Mrs Varden, Joe?'

'Oh no, sir,' Joe replied, and endeavouring, but not with the greatest possible success, to hide his disappointment. 'I shall be very glad, I'm sure.'

'That's right,' said the locksmith, patting him on the back. 'It don't matter who has 'em, Joe?'

'Not a bit, sir.' – Dear heart, how the words stuck in his throat!

'Come in,' said Gabriel. 'I have just been called to tea. She's in the parlour.'

'She,' thought Joe. 'Which of 'em I wonder – Mrs or Miss?' The locksmith settled the doubt as neatly as if it had been expressed aloud, by leading him to the door, and saying, 'Martha, my dear, here's young Mr Willet.'

Now, Mrs Varden, regarding the Maypole as a sort of humane man-trap, or decoy for husbands; viewing its proprietor, and all who aided and abetted him, in the light of so many poachers among Christian men; and believing, moreover, that the publicans coupled with sinners[3] in Holy Writ were veritable licensed victuallers; was far from being favourably disposed towards her visitor. Wherefore she was taken faint directly; and being duly presented with the crocuses and snowdrops, divined on further consideration that they were the occasion of the languor which had seized upon her spirits. 'I'm afraid I couldn't bear the room another minute,' said the good lady, 'if they remained here. *Would* you excuse my putting them out of window?'

Joe begged she wouldn't mention it on any account, and smiled feebly as he saw them deposited on the sill outside. If anybody could have known the pains he had taken to make up that despised and misused bunch of flowers! –

'I feel it quite a relief to get rid of them, I assure you,' said Mrs Varden. 'I'm better already.' And indeed she did appear to have plucked up her spirits.

Joe expressed his gratitude to Providence for this favourable dispensation, and tried to look as if he didn't wonder where Dolly was.

'You're sad people at Chigwell, Mr Joseph,' said Mrs V.

'I hope not, ma'am,' returned Joe.

'You're the cruellest and most inconsiderate people in the world,' said Mrs Varden, bridling. 'I wonder old Mr Willet, having been a married man himself, doesn't know better than to conduct himself as he does. His doing it for profit is no excuse. I would rather pay the money twenty times over, and have Varden come home like a respectable and sober tradesman. If there is one character,' said Mrs Varden with great emphasis, 'that offends and disgusts me more than another, it is a sot.'

'Come, Martha, my dear,' said the locksmith cheerily, 'let us have tea, and don't let us talk about sots. There are none here, and Joe don't want to hear about them, I dare say.'

At this crisis, Miggs appeared with toast.

'I dare say he does not,' said Mrs Varden; 'and I dare say you do not, Varden. It's a very unpleasant subject I have no doubt, though I won't say it's personal' – Miggs coughed – 'whatever I may be forced to think' – Miggs sneezed expressively. 'You never will know, Varden, and nobody at young Mr Willet's age – you'll excuse me, sir – can be expected to know, what a woman suffers when she is waiting at home under such circumstances. If you don't believe me, as I know you don't, here's Miggs, who is only too often a witness of it – ask her.'

'Oh! she were very bad the other night, sir, indeed she were,' said Miggs. 'If you hadn't the sweetness of an angel in you, mim, I don't think you could abear it, I raly don't.'

'Miggs,' said Mrs Varden, 'you're profane.'

'Begging your pardon, mim,' returned Miggs, with shrill rapidity, 'such was not my intentions, and such I hope is not my character, though I am but a servant.'

'Answering me, Miggs, and providing yourself,' retorted her mistress, looking round with dignity, 'is one and the same thing. How dare you speak of angels in connection with your sinful fellow-beings – mere' – said Mrs Varden, glancing at herself in a neighbouring mirror, and arranging the ribbon of her cap in a more becoming fashion – 'mere worms and grovellers as we are!'

'I did not intend, mim, if you please, to give offence,' said Miggs, confident in the strength of her compliment, and developing strongly in the throat as usual, 'and I did not expect it would be took as such. I hope I know my own unworthiness, and that I hate and despise myself and all my fellow-creatures as every practicable Christian should.'

'You'll have the goodness, if you please,' said Mrs Varden loftily, 'to step up stairs and see if Dolly has finished dressing, and to tell her that the chair that was ordered for her will be here in a minute, and that if she keeps it waiting, I shall send it away that instant. – I'm sorry to see that you don't take your tea, Varden, and that you don't take yours, Mr Joseph; though of course it would be foolish of me to expect that anything that can be had at home, and in the company of females, would please *you.*'

This pronoun was understood in the plural sense, and included both gentlemen, upon both of whom it was rather hard and unde-served, for Gabriel had applied himself to the meal with a very promising appetite, until it was spoilt by Mrs Varden herself, and Joe had as great a liking for the female society of the locksmith's house – or for a part of it at all events – as man could well entertain.

But he had no opportunity to say anything in his own defence, for at that moment Dolly herself appeared, and struck him quite dumb with her beauty. Never had Dolly looked so handsome as she did then, in all the glow and grace of youth, with all her charms increased a hundred fold by a most becoming dress, by a thousand little coquettish ways which nobody could assume with a better grace, and all the sparkling expectation of that accursed party. It is impossible to tell how Joe hated that party wherever it was, and all the other people who were going to it, whoever they were.

And she hardly looked at him – no, hardly looked at him. And when the chair was seen through the open door coming blundering into the workshop, she actually clapped her hands and seemed glad to go. But Joe gave her his arm – there was some comfort in that – and handed her into it. To see her seat herself inside, with her laughing eyes brighter than diamonds, and her hand – surely she had the prettiest hand in the world – on the ledge of the open window, and her little finger provokingly and pertly tilted up, as if it wondered why Joe didn't squeeze or kiss it! To think how well one or two of the modest snowdrops would have become that delicate boddice, and how they were lying neglected outside the parlour window! To see how Miggs looked on, with a face express-ive of knowing how all this loveliness was got up, and of being in the secret of every string and pin and hook and eye, and of saying it ain't half as real as you think, and I could look quite as well myself if I took the pains! To hear that provoking precious little scream when the chair was hoisted on its poles, and to catch that transient but not-to-be-forgotten vision of the happy face within – what torments and aggravations, and yet what delights were these! The very chairmen seemed favoured rivals as they bore her down the street.

There never was such an alteration in a small room in a small time as in that parlour when they went back to finish tea. So dark, so deserted, so perfectly disenchanted. It seemed such sheer nonsense to be sitting tamely there, when she was at a dance with more lovers than man could calculate fluttering about her – with the whole party doting on and adoring her, and wanting to marry her. Miggs was hovering about too; and the fact of her existence, the mere circumstance of her ever having been born, appeared, after Dolly, such an unaccountable practical joke. It was impossible to talk. It couldn't be done. He had nothing left for it but to stir his tea round, and round, and round, and ruminate on all the fascinations of the locksmith's lovely daughter.

Gabriel was dull too. It was a part of the certain uncertainty of Mrs Varden's temper, that when they were in this condition, she should be gay and sprightly.

'I need have a cheerful disposition, I am sure,' said the smiling housewife, 'to preserve any spirits at all; and how I do it I can scarcely tell.'

'Ah, mim,' sighed Miggs, 'begging your pardon for the interruption, there an't a many like you.'

'Take away, Miggs,' said Mrs Varden, rising, 'take away, pray. I know I'm a restraint here, and as I wish everybody to enjoy themselves as they best can, I feel I had better go.'

'No, no, Martha,' cried the locksmith. 'Stop here. I'm sure we shall be very sorry to lose you, eh Joe?' Joe started, and said 'Certainly.'

'Thank you, Varden, my dear,' returned his wife; 'but I know your wishes better. Tobacco, and beer, or spirits, have much greater attractions than any *I* can boast of, and therefore I shall go and sit up stairs and look out of window, my love. Good night, Mr Joseph. I'm very glad to have seen you, and only wish I could have provided something more suitable to your taste. Remember me very kindly if you please to old Mr Willet, and tell him that whenever he comes here I have a crow to pluck with him. Good night!'

Having uttered these words with great sweetness of manner, the good lady dropped a curtsey remarkable for its condescension, and serenely withdrew.

And it was for this Joe had looked forward to the twenty-fifth of March for weeks and weeks, and had gathered the flowers with so much care, and had cocked his hat, and made himself so smart! This was the end of all his bold determination, resolved upon for the hundredth time, to speak out to Dolly and tell her how he loved her! To see her for a minute – for but a minute – to find her going out to a party and glad to go; to be looked upon as a common pipe-smoker, beer-bibber, spirit-guzzler, and tosspot! He bade farewell to his friend the locksmith, and hastened to take horse at the Black Lion, thinking as he turned towards home, as many another Joe has thought before and since, that here was an end to all his hopes – that the thing was impossible and never could be – that she didn't care for him – that he was wretched for life – and that the only congenial prospect left him, was to go for a soldier or a sailor, and get some obliging enemy to knock his brains out as soon as possible.

CHAPTER THE FOURTEENTH

Joe Willet rode leisurely along in his desponding mood, picturing the locksmith's daughter going down long country-dances, and poussetting dreadfully with bold strangers – which was almost too much to bear – when he heard the tramp of a horse's feet behind him, and looking back, saw a well-mounted gentleman advancing at a smart canter. As this rider passed, he checked his steed, and called him of the Maypole by his name. Joe set spurs to the grey mare, and was at his side directly.

'I thought it was you, sir,' he said, touching his hat. 'A fair evening, sir. Glad to see you out of doors again.'

The gentleman smiled and nodded. 'What gay doings have been going on to-day, Joe? Is she as pretty as ever? Nay, don't blush, man.'

'If I coloured at all, Mr Edward,' said Joe, 'which I didn't know I did, it was to think I should have been such a fool as ever to have any hope of her. She's as far out of my reach as – as Heaven is.'

'Well, Joe, I hope that's not altogether beyond it,' said Edward good-humouredly. 'Eh?'

'Ah!' sighed Joe. 'It's all very fine talking, sir. Proverbs are easily made in cold blood. But it can't be helped. Are you bound for our house, sir?'

'Yes. As I am not quite strong yet, I shall stay there to-night, and ride home coolly in the morning.'

'If you're in no particular hurry,' said Joe after a short silence, 'and will bear with the pace of this poor jade, I shall be glad to ride on with you to the Warren, sir, and hold your horse when you dismount. It'll save you having to walk from the Maypole, there and back again. I can spare the time well, sir, for I am too soon.'

'And so am I,' returned Edward, 'though I was unconsciously riding fast just now, in compliment I suppose to the pace of my thoughts, which were travelling post. We will keep together, Joe, willingly, and be as good company as may be. And cheer up, cheer up, think of the locksmith's daughter with a stout heart, and you shall win her yet.'

Joe shook his head; but there was something so cheery in the buoyant hopeful manner of this speech, that his spirits rose under its influence, and communicated as it would seem some new impulse even to the grey mare, who, breaking from her sober amble into a gentle trot, emulated the pace of Edward Chester's horse, and appeared to flatter herself that he was doing his very best.

It was a fine dry night, and the light of a young moon, which was then just rising, shed around that peace and tranquillity which gives to evening time its most delicious charm. The lengthened shadows of the trees, softened as if reflected in still water, threw their carpet on the path the travellers pursued, and the light wind stirred yet more softly than before, as though it were soothing Nature in her sleep. By little and little they ceased talking, and rode on side by side in a pleasant silence.

'The Maypole lights are brilliant to-night,' said Edward, as they rode along the lane from which, while the intervening trees were bare of leaves, that hostelry was visible.

'Brilliant indeed, sir,' returned Joe, rising in his stirrups to get a better view. 'Lights in the large room, and a fire glimmering in the best bed-chamber? Why, what company can this be for, I wonder!'

'Some benighted horseman wending towards London, and deterred from going on to-night by the marvellous tales of my friend the highwayman, I suppose,' said Edward.

'He must be a horseman of good quality to have such accommodations. Your bed too, sir – !'

'No matter, Joe. Any other room will do for me. But come – there's nine striking. We may push on.'

They cantered forward at as brisk a pace as Joe's charger could attain, and presently stopped in the little copse where he had left her in the morning. Edward dismounted, gave his bridle to his companion, and walked with a light step towards the house.

A female servant was waiting at a side gate in the garden-wall, and admitted him without delay. He hurried along the terrace-walk, and darted up a flight of broad steps leading into an old and gloomy hall, whose walls were ornamented with rusty suits of armour, antlers, weapons of the chase, and suchlike garniture. Here he paused, but not long; for as he looked round, as if expecting the attendant to have followed, and wondering she had not done so, a lovely girl appeared, whose dark hair next moment rested on his breast. Almost at the same instant a heavy hand was laid upon her arm, Edward felt himself thrust away, and Mr Haredale stood between them.

He regarded the young man sternly without removing his hat; with one hand clasped his niece, and with the other, in which he held his riding-whip, motioned him towards the door. The young man drew himself up, and returned his gaze.

'This is well done of you, sir, to corrupt my servants, and enter my house unbidden and in secret, like a thief!' said Mr Haredale. 'Leave it, sir, and return no more.'

'Miss Haredale's presence,' returned the young man, 'and your relationship to her, give you a license which, if you are a brave man, you will not abuse. You have compelled me to this course, and the fault is yours – not mine.'

'It is neither generous, nor honourable, nor the act of a true man, sir,' retorted the other, 'to tamper with the affections of a weak, trusting girl, while you shrink, in your unworthiness, from her guardian and protector, and dare not meet the light of day. More than this I will not say to you, save that I forbid you this house, and require you to be gone.'

'It is neither generous, nor honourable, nor the act of a true man to play the spy,' said Edward. 'Your words imply dishonour, and I reject them with the scorn they merit.'

'You will find,' said Mr Haredale, calmly, 'your trusty go-between in waiting at the gate by which you entered. I have played no spy's part, sir. I chanced to see you pass the gate, and followed. You might have heard me knocking for admission, had you been less swift of foot, or lingered in the garden. Please to withdraw. Your presence here is offensive to me and distressful to my niece.' As he said these words, he passed his arm about the waist of the terrified and weeping girl, and drew her closer to him; and though the habitual severity of his manner was scarcely changed, there was yet apparent in the action an air of kindness and sympathy for her distress.

'Mr Haredale,' said Edward, 'your arm encircles her on whom I have set my every hope and thought, and to purchase one minute's happiness for whom I would gladly lay down my life; this house is

the casket that holds the precious jewel of my existence. Your niece has plighted her faith to me, and I have plighted mine to her. What have I done that you should hold me in this light esteem, and give me these discourteous words?'

'You have done that, sir,' answered Mr Haredale, 'which must be undone. You have tied a lover's-knot here which must be cut asunder. Take good heed of what I say. Must. I cancel the bond between ye. I reject you, and all of your kith and kin – all the false, hollow, heartless stock.'

'High words, sir,' said Edward scornfully.

'Words of purpose and meaning, as you will find,' replied the other. 'Lay them to heart.'

'Lay you then, these,' said Edward. 'Your cold and sullen temper, which chills every breast about you, which turns affection into fear, and changes duty into dread, has forced us on this secret course, repugnant to our nature and our wish, and far more foreign, sir, to us than you. I am not a false, a hollow, or a heartless man; the character is yours, who poorly venture on these injurious terms, against the truth, and under the shelter whereof I reminded you just now. You shall not cancel the bond between us. I will not abandon this pursuit. I rely upon your niece's truth and honour, and set your influence at nought. I leave her with a confidence in her pure faith, which you will never weaken, and with no concern but that I do not leave her in some gentler care.'

With that, he pressed her cold hand to his lips, and once more encountering and returning Mr Haredale's steady look, withdrew.

A few words to Joe as he mounted his horse sufficiently explained what had passed, and renewed all that young gentleman's despondency with tenfold aggravation. They rode back to the Maypole without exchanging a syllable, and arrived at the door with heavy hearts.

Old John, who had peeped from behind the red curtain as they rode up shouting for Hugh, was out directly, and said with great importance as he held the young man's stirrup,

'He's comfortable in bed – the best bed. A thorough gentleman; the smilingest, affablest gentleman I ever had to do with.'

'Who, Willet?' said Edward carelessly, as he dismounted.

'Your worthy father, sir,' replied John. 'Your honourable, venerable father.'

'What does he mean?' said Edward, looking with a mixture of alarm and doubt at Joe.

'What *do* you mean?' said Joe. 'Don't you see Mr Edward doesn't understand, father?'

'Why, didn't you know of it, sir?' said John, opening his eyes wide. 'How very singular! Bless you, he's been here ever since noon to-day, and Mr Haredale has been having a long talk with him, and hasn't been gone an hour.'

'My father, Willet!'

'Yes, sir, he told me so – a handsome, slim, upright gentleman, in green-and-gold. In your old room up yonder, sir. No doubt you can go in, sir,' said John, walking backwards into the road and looking up at the window. 'He hasn't put out his candles yet, I see.'

Edward glanced at the window also, and hastily murmuring that he had changed his mind – forgotten something – and must return to London, mounted his horse again and rode away; leaving the Willets, father and son, looking at each other in mute astonishment.

*

CHAPTER THE FIFTEENTH

At noon next day, John Willet's guest sat lingering over his breakfast in his own home, surrounded by a variety of comforts, which left the Maypole's highest flight and utmost stretch of accommodation at an infinite distance behind, and suggested comparisons very much to the disadvantage and disfavour of that venerable tavern.

In the broad old-fashioned window-seat – as capacious as many modern sofas, and cushioned to serve the purpose of a luxurious settee – in the broad old-fashioned window-seat of a roomy chamber, Mr Chester lounged, very much at his ease, over a well-furnished breakfast-table. He had exchanged his riding-coat for a handsome morning-gown, his boots for slippers; had been at great pains to atone for the having been obliged to make his toilet when he rose without the aid of dressing-case and tiring equipage; and, having gradually forgotten through these means the discomforts of an indifferent night and an early ride, was in a state of perfect complacency, indolence, and satisfaction.

The situation in which he found himself, indeed, was particularly favourable to the growth of these feelings; for, not to mention the lazy influence of a late and lonely breakfast, with the additional sedative of a newspaper, there was an air of repose about his place of residence peculiar to itself, and which hangs about it, even in these times, when it is more bustling and busy than it was in days of yore.

There are, still, worse places than the Temple, on a sultry day, for basking in the sun, or resting idly in the shade. There is yet a drowsiness in its courts, and a dreamy dulness in its trees and gardens; those who pace its lanes and squares may yet hear the echoes of their footsteps on the sounding stones, and read upon its gates, in passing from the tumult of the Strand or Fleet Street, 'Who enters here leaves noise behind.'[1] There is still the plash of falling water in fair Fountain Court,[2] and there are yet nooks and corners where dun-haunted students may look down from their dusty garrets, on a vagrant ray of sunlight patching the shade of the tall houses, and seldom troubled to reflect a passing stranger's form. There is yet, in the Temple, something of a clerkly monkish atmosphere, which public offices of law have not disturbed, and even legal firms have failed to scare away. In summer time, its pumps suggest to thirsty idlers, springs cooler, and more sparkling, and deeper than other wells; and as they trace the spillings of full pitchers on the heated ground, they snuff the freshness, and, sighing, cast sad looks towards the Thames, and think of baths and boats, and saunter on, despondent.

It was in a room in Paper Buildings[3] – a row of goodly tenements, shaded in front by ancient trees, and looking, at the back, upon the Temple Gardens – that this, our idler, lounged; now taking up again the paper he had laid down a hundred times; now trifling with the fragments of his meal; now pulling forth his golden tooth-pick, and glancing leisurely about the room, or out at window into the trim garden walks, where a few early loiterers were already pacing to and fro. Here a pair of lovers met to quarrel and make up; there a dark-eyed nursery-maid had better eyes for Templars than her charge; on this hand an ancient spinster, with her lapdog in a string, regarded both enormities with scornful sidelong looks; on that a weazen old gentleman, ogling the nursery-maid, looked with like scorn upon the spinster, and wondered she didn't know she was no longer young. Apart from all these, on the river's margin, two or three couple of business-talkers walked slowly up and down in earnest conversation; and one young man sat thoughtfully on a bench, alone.

'Ned is amazingly patient!' said Mr Chester, glancing at this last-named person as he set down his teacup and plied the golden toothpick, 'immensely patient! He was sitting yonder when I began to dress, and has scarcely changed his posture since. A most eccentric dog!'

As he spoke, the figure rose, and came towards him with a rapid pace.

'Really, as if he had heard me,' said the father, resuming his newspaper with a yawn. 'Dear Ned!'

Presently the room-door opened, and the young man entered; to whom his father gently waved his hand, and smiled.

'Are you at leisure for a little conversation, sir?' said Edward.

'Surely, Ned. I am always at leisure. You know my constitution. – Have you breakfasted?'

'Three hours ago.'

'What a very early dog!' cried his father, contemplating him from behind the toothpick, with a languid smile.

'The truth is,' said Edward, bringing a chair forward, and seating himself near the table, 'that I slept but ill last night, and was glad to rise. The cause of my uneasiness cannot but be known to you, sir; and it is upon that, I wish to speak.'

'My dear boy,' returned his father, 'confide in me, I beg. But you know my constitution – don't be prosy, Ned.'

'I will be plain, and brief,' said Edward.

'Don't say you will, my good fellow,' returned his father, crossing his legs, 'or you certainly will not. You are going to tell me —'

'Plainly this, then,' said the son, with an air of great concern, 'that I know where you were last night – from being on the spot, indeed – and whom you saw, and what your purpose was.'

'You don't say so!' cried his father. 'I am delighted to hear it. It saves us the worry, and terrible wear and tear of a long explanation, and is a great relief for both. At the very house! Why didn't you come up? I should have been charmed to see you.'

'I knew that what I had to say would be better said after a night's reflection, when both of us were cool,' returned the son.

' 'Fore Gad, Ned,' rejoined the father, 'I was cool enough last night. That detestable Maypole! By some infernal contrivance of the builder, it holds the wind, and keeps it fresh. You remember

the sharp east wind that blew so hard five weeks ago? I give you my honour it was rampant in that old house last night, though out of doors there was a dead calm. But you were saying—'

'I was about to say, Heaven knows how seriously and earnestly, that you have made me wretched, sir. Will you hear me gravely for a moment?'

'My dear Ned,' said his father, 'I will hear you with the patience of an anchorite. Oblige me with the milk.'

'I saw Miss Haredale last night,' Edward resumed, when he had complied with this request; 'her uncle, in her presence, immediately after your interview, and, as of course I know, in consequence of it, forbade me the house, and, with circumstances of indignity which are of your creation I am sure, commanded me to leave it on the instant.'

'For his manner of doing so, I give you my honour, Ned, I am not accountable,' said his father. 'That you must excuse. He is a mere boor, a log, a brute, with no address in life. – Positively a fly in the jug. The first I have seen this year.'

Edward rose, and paced the room. His imperturbable parent sipped his tea.

'Father,' said the young man, stopping at length before him, 'we must not trifle in this matter. We must not deceive each other, or ourselves. Let me pursue the manly open part I wish to take, and do not repel me by this unkind indifference.'

'Whether I am indifferent or no,' returned the other, 'I leave you, my dear boy, to judge. A ride of twenty-five or thirty miles, through miry roads – a Maypole dinner – a tête-à-tête with Haredale, which, vanity apart, was quite a Valentine and Orson[4] business – a Maypole bed – a Maypole landlord, and a Maypole retinue of idiots and centaurs;[5] – whether the voluntary endurance of these things looks like indifference, dear Ned, or like the excessive anxiety, and devotion, and all that sort of thing, of a parent, you shall determine for yourself.'

'I wish you to consider, sir,' said Edward, 'in what a cruel situation I am placed. Loving Miss Haredale as I do —'

'My dear fellow,' interrupted his father with a compassionate smile, 'you do nothing of the kind. You don't know anything about it. There's no such thing, I assure you. Now, do take my word for it. You have good sense, Ned, – great good sense. I wonder you should be guilty of such amazing absurdities. You really surprise me.'

'I repeat,' said his son firmly, 'that I love her. You have interposed to part us, and have, to the extent I have just now told you of, succeeded. May I induce you, sir, in time, to think more favourably of our attachment, or is it your intention and your fixed design to hold us asunder if you can?'

'My dear Ned,' returned his father, taking a pinch of snuff and pushing his box towards him, 'that *is* my purpose most undoubtedly.'

'The time that has elapsed,' rejoined his son, 'since I began to know her worth, has flown in such a dream that until now I have hardly once paused to reflect upon my true position. What is it? From my childhood I have been accustomed to luxury and idleness, and have been bred as though my fortune were large, and my expectations almost without a limit. The idea of wealth has been familiarised to me from my cradle. I have been taught to look upon those means, by which men raise themselves to riches and distinction, as being beyond my heeding, and beneath my care. I have been, as the phrase is, liberally educated, and am fit for nothing. I find myself at last wholly dependent upon you, with no resource but in your favour. In this momentous question of my life we do not, and it would seem we never can, agree. I have shrunk instinctively alike from those to whom you have urged me to pay court, and from the motives of interest and gain which have rendered them in your eyes visible objects for my suit. If there never has been thus much plain-speaking between us before, sir, the fault has not been mine, indeed. If I seem to speak too plainly now, it is, believe me father, in the hope that there may be a franker spirit, a worthier reliance, and a kinder confidence between us in time to come.'

'My good fellow,' said his smiling father, 'you quite affect me. Go on, my dear Edward, I beg. But remember your promise. There is great earnestness, vast candour, a manifest sincerity in all you say, but I fear I observe the faintest indications of a tendency to prose.'

'I am very sorry, sir.'

'I am very sorry too, Ned, but you know that I cannot fix my mind for any long period upon one subject. If you'll come to the point at once, I'll imagine all that ought to go before, and conclude it said. Oblige me with the milk again. Listening, invariably makes me feverish.'

'What I would say then, tends to this,' said Edward. 'I cannot bear this absolute dependence, sir, even upon you. Time has been lost and opportunity thrown away, but I am yet a young man, and may retrieve it. Will you give me the means of devoting such abilities and energies as I possess, to some worthy pursuit? Will you let me try to make for myself an honourable path in life? For any term you please to name – say for five years if you will – I will pledge myself to move no further in the matter of our difference without your full concurrence. During that period, I will endeavour earnestly and patiently, if ever man did, to open some prospect for myself, and free you from the burden you fear I should become if I married one whose worth and beauty are her chief endowments. Will you do this, sir? At the expiration of the term we agree upon, let us discuss this subject again. Till then, unless it is revived by you, let it never be renewed between us.'

'My dear Ned,' returned his father, laying down the newspaper at which he had been glancing carelessly, and throwing himself back in the window-seat, 'I believe you know how very much I dislike what are called family affairs, which are only fit for plebeian Christmas days, and have no manner of business with people of our condition. But as you are proceeding upon a mistake, Ned – altogether upon a mistake – I will conquer my repugnance to entering on such matters, and give you a perfectly plain and candid answer, if you will do me the favour to shut the door.'

Edward having obeyed him, he took an elegant little knife from his pocket, and paring his nails, continued:

'You have to thank me, Ned, for being of good family; for your mother, charming person as she was, and almost broken-hearted, and so forth, as she left me, when she was prematurely compelled to become immortal – had nothing to boast of in that respect.'

'Her father was at least an eminent lawyer, sir,' said Edward.

'Quite right, Ned; perfectly so. He stood high at the bar, had a great name and great wealth, but having risen from nothing – I have always closed my eyes to the circumstance and steadily resisted its contemplation, but I fear his father dealt in pork, and that his business did once involve cow-heel and sausages – he wished to marry his daughter into a good family. He had his heart's desire, Ned. I was a younger son's younger son, and I married her. We each had our object, and gained it. She stepped at once into the politest and best circles, and I stepped into a fortune which I assure you was very necessary to my comfort – quite indispensable. Now, my good fellow, that fortune is among the things that have been. It is gone, Ned, and has been gone – how old are you? I always forget.'

'Seven-and-twenty, sir.'

'Are you indeed?' cried his father, raising his eyelids in a languishing surprise. 'So much! Then I should say, Ned, that as nearly as I remember, its skirts vanished from human knowledge, about eighteen or nineteen years ago. It was about that time when I came to live in these chambers (once your grandfather's, and bequeathed by that extremely respectable person to me), and commenced to live upon an inconsiderable annuity and my past reputation.'

'You are jesting with me, sir,' said Edward.

'Not in the slightest degree, I assure you,' returned his father with great composure. 'These family topics are so extremely dry, that I am sorry to say they don't admit of any such relief. It is for that reason, and because they have an appearance of business, that I dislike them so very much. Well! You know the rest. A son, Ned, unless he is old enough to be a companion – that is to say, unless he is some two or three and twenty – is not the kind of thing to have about one. He is a restraint upon his father, his father is a restraint upon him, and they make each other mutually uncomfortable. Therefore, until within the last four years or so – I have a poor memory for dates, and if I mistake, you will correct me in your own mind – you pursued your studies at a distance, and picked up a great variety of accomplishments. Occasionally we passed a week or two together here, and disconcerted each other as only such near relations can. At last you came home. I candidly tell you, my dear boy, that if you had been awkward and overgrown, I should have exported you to some distant part of the world.'

'I wish with all my soul you had, sir,' said Edward.

'No you don't, Ned,' rejoined his father coolly; 'you are mistaken, I assure you. I found you a handsome, prepossessing, elegant fellow, and I threw you into the society I can still command. Having done that, my dear fellow, I consider that I have provided for you in life, and rely on your doing something to provide for me in return.'

'I do not understand your meaning, sir.'

'My meaning, Ned, is obvious – I observe another fly in the

cream-jug, but have the goodness not to take it out as you did the first, for their walk when their legs are milky, is extremely ungraceful and disagreeable – my meaning is, that you must do as I did; that you must marry well and make the most of yourself.'

'A mere fortune-hunter!' cried the son, indignantly.

'What in the devil's name, Ned, would you be!' returned the father. 'All men are fortune-hunters, are they not? The law, the church, the court, the camp – see how they are all crowded with fortune-hunters, jostling each other in the pursuit. The Stock-exchange, the pulpit, the counting-house, the royal drawing-room, the senate, – what but fortune-hunters are they filled with? A fortune-hunter! Yes. You *are* one; and you would be nothing else, my dear Ned, if you were the greatest courtier, lawyer, legislator, prelate, or merchant, in existence. If you are squeamish and moral, Ned, console yourself with the reflection that at the worst your fortune-hunting can make but one person miserable or unhappy. How many people do you suppose these other kinds of huntsmen crush in following their sport – hundreds at a step? Or thousands?'

The young man leant his head upon his hand, and made no answer.

'I am quite charmed,' said the father rising, and walking slowly to and fro – stopping now and then to glance at himself in a mirror, or survey a picture through his glass, with the air of a connoisseur, 'that we have had this conversation, Ned, unpromising as it was. It establishes a confidence between us which is quite delightful; and was certainly necessary, though how you can ever have mistaken our position and designs, I confess I cannot understand. I conceived, until I found your fancy for this girl, that all these points were tacitly agreed upon between us.'

'I knew you were embarrassed, sir,' returned the son, raising his head for a moment, and then falling into his former attitude, 'but I had no idea we were the beggared wretches you describe. How could I suppose it, bred as I have been; witnessing the life you have always led; and the appearance you have always made?'

'My dear child,' said the father – 'for you really talk so like a child that I must call you one – you were bred upon a careful principle; the very manner of your education, I assure you, maintained my credit surprisingly. As to the life I lead, I must lead it, Ned. I must have these little refinements about me. I have always been used to them, and I cannot exist without them. They must surround me, you observe, and therefore they are here. With regard to our circumstances, Ned, you may set your mind at rest upon that score. They are desperate. Your own appearance is by no means despicable, and our joint pocket-money alone devours our income. That's the truth.'

'Why have I never known this before? Why have you encouraged me, sir, to an expenditure and mode of life to which we have no right or title?'

'My good fellow,' returned his father more compassionately than ever, 'if you made no appearance how could you possibly succeed in the pursuit for which I destined you? As to our mode of life, every man has a right to live in the best way he can; and to make himself as comfortable as he can, or he is an unnatural scoundrel. Our debts, I grant, are very great, and therefore it the more behoves you, as a young man of principle and honour, to pay them off as speedily as possible.'

'The villain's part,' muttered Edward, 'that I have unconsciously played! I to win the heart of Emma Haredale! I would, for her sake, I had died first!'

'I am glad you see, Ned,' returned his father, 'how perfectly self-evident it is, that nothing can be done in that quarter. But apart from this, and the necessity of your speedily bestowing yourself in another (as you know you could to-morrow, if you chose), I wish you'd look upon it pleasantly. In a religious point of view alone, how could you ever think of uniting yourself to a catholic, unless she was amazingly rich? You who ought to be so very Protestant, coming of such a Protestant family as you do. Let us be moral, Ned, or we are nothing. Even if one could set that objection aside, which is impossible, we come to another which is quite conclusive. The very idea of marrying a girl whose father was killed, like meat! Good God, Ned, how disagreeable! Consider the impossibility of having any respect for your father-in-law under such unpleasant circumstances – think of his having been "viewed" by jurors, and "sat upon" by coroners, and of his very doubtful position in the family ever afterwards. It seems to me such an indelicate sort of thing that I really think the girl ought to have been put to death by the state to prevent its happening. But I tease you perhaps. You would rather be alone? My dear Ned, most willingly. God bless you. I shall be going out presently, but we shall meet to-night, or if not to-night, certainly to-morrow. Take care of yourself in the mean time, for both our sakes. You are a person of great consequence to me, Ned – of vast consequence indeed. God bless you!'

With these words, the father, who had been arranging his cravat in the glass, while he uttered them in a disconnected careless manner, withdrew, humming a tune as he went. The son, who had appeared so lost in thought as not to hear or understand them, remained quite still and silent. After the lapse of half an hour or so, the elder Chester, gaily dressed, went out. The younger still sat with his head resting on his hands, in what appeared to be a kind of stupor.

CHAPTER THE SIXTEENTH

A series of pictures representing the streets of London in the night, even at the comparatively recent date of this tale, would present to the eye something so very different in character from the reality which is witnessed in these times, that it would be difficult for the beholder to recognise his most familiar walks in the altered aspect of little more than half a century ago.

They were, one and all, from the broadest and best to the narrowest and least frequented, very dark. The oil and cotton lamps, though regularly trimmed twice or thrice in the long winter nights, burnt feebly at the best; and at a late hour, when they were unassisted by the lamps and candles in the shops, cast but a narrow track of doubtful light upon the footway, leaving the projecting doors and house-fronts in the deepest gloom. Many of the courts and lanes were left in total darkness; those of the meaner sort, where one glimmering light twinkled for a score of houses, being favoured in no slight degree. Even in these places, the inhabitants had often good reason for extinguishing their lamp as soon as it was lighted; and the watch[1] being utterly inefficient and powerless to prevent them, they did so at their pleasure. Thus, in the lightest thoroughfares, there was at every turn some obscure and dangerous spot whither a thief might fly for shelter, and few would care to follow; and the city being belted round by fields, green lanes, waste grounds, and lonely roads, dividing it at that time from the suburbs that have joined it since, escape, even where the pursuit was hot, was rendered easy.

It is no wonder that with these favouring circumstances in full and constant operation, street robberies, often accompanied by cruel wounds, and not unfrequently by loss of life, should have been of nightly occurrence in the very heart of London, or that quiet folks should have had great dread of traversing its streets after the shops were closed. It was not unusual for those who wended home alone at midnight, to keep the middle of the road, the better to guard against surprise from lurking footpads; few would venture to repair at a late hour to Kentish Town or Hampstead, or even to Kensington or Chelsea, unarmed and unattended; while he who had been loudest and most valiant at the supper-table or the tavern, and had but a mile or so to go, was glad to fee a link-boy to escort him home.

There were many other characteristics – not quite so disagreeable – about the thoroughfares of London then, with which they had been long familiar. Some of the shops, especially those to the eastward of Temple Bar, still adhered to the old practice of hanging out a sign; and the creaking and swinging of these boards in their iron frames on windy nights, formed a strange and mournful concert for the ears of those who lay awake in bed or hurried through the streets. Long stands of hackney-chairs and groups of chairmen, compared with whom the coachmen of our day are gentle and polite, obstructed the way and filled the air with clamour; night-cellars, indicated by a little stream of light crossing the pavement, and stretching out half way into the road, and by the stifled roar of voices from below, yawned for the reception and entertainment of the most abandoned of both sexes; under every shed and bulk small groups of link-boys gamed away the earnings of the day; or one more weary than the rest, gave way to sleep, and let the fragment of his torch fall hissing on the puddled ground.

Then there was the watch with staff and lanthorn crying the hour, and the kind of weather; and those who woke up at his voice and turned them round in bed, were glad to hear it rained, or snowed, or blew, or froze, for very comfort's sake. The solitary passenger was startled by the chairmen's cry of 'By your leave there!' as two came trotting past him with their empty vehicle – carried backwards to show its being disengaged – and hurried to the nearest stand. Many a private chair too, inclosing some fine

lady, monstrously hooped and furbelowed, and preceded by running-footmen bearing flambeaux – for which extinguishers are yet suspended before the doors of a few houses of the better sort – made the way gay and light as it danced along, and darker and more dismal when it had passed. It was not unusual for these running gentry, who carried it with a very high hand, to quarrel in the servants' hall while waiting for their masters and mistresses; and, falling to blows either there or in the street without, to strew the place of skirmish with hair-powder, fragments of bag-wigs, and scattered nosegays. Gaming, the vice which ran so high among all classes (the fashion being of course set by the upper), was generally the cause of these disputes; for cards and dice were as openly used, and worked as much mischief, and yielded as much excitement below stairs, as above. While incidents like these, arising out of drums and masquerades and parties at quadrille, were passing at the west end of the town, heavy stage-coaches and scarce heavier waggons were lumbering slowly towards the city, the coachmen, guard, and passengers, armed to the teeth, and the coach – a day or so, perhaps, behind its time, but that was nothing – despoiled by highwaymen; who made no scruple to attack, alone and single-handed, a whole caravan of goods and men, and sometimes shot a passenger or two and were sometimes shot themselves, just as the case might be. On the morrow, rumours of this new act of daring on the road yielded matter for a few hours' conversation through the town, and a Public Progress of some fine gentleman (half drunk) to Tyburn,[2] dressed in the newest fashion and damning the ordinary with unspeakable gallantry and grace, furnished to the populace, at once a pleasant excitement and a wholesome and profound example.

Among all the dangerous characters who, in such a state of society, prowled and skulked in the metropolis at night, there was one man, from whom many as uncouth and fierce as he, shrunk with an involuntary dread. Who he was, or whence he came, was a question often asked, but which none could answer. His name was unknown, he had never been seen until within eight days or thereabouts, and was equally a stranger to the old ruffians, upon whose haunts he ventured fearlessly, as to the young. He could be no spy, for he never removed his slouched hat to look about him, entered into conversation with no man, heeded nothing that passed, listened to no discourse, regarded nobody that came or went. But so surely as the dead of night set in, so surely this man was in the midst of the loose concourse in the night-cellar where outcasts of every grade resorted; and there he sat till morning.

He was not only a spectre at their licentious feasts; a something in the midst of their revelry and riot that chilled and haunted them; but out of doors he was the same. Directly it was dark, he was abroad – never in company with any one, but always alone; never lingering or loitering, but always walking swiftly; and looking (so they said who had seen him) over his shoulder from time to time, and as he did so quickening his pace. In the fields, the lanes, the roads, in all quarters of the town – east, west, north, and south – that man was seen gliding on, like a shadow. He was always hurrying away. Those who encountered him, saw him steal past, caught sight of the backward glance, and so lost him in the darkness.

This constant restlessness and flitting to and fro, gave rise to strange stories. He was seen in such distant and remote places, at times so nearly tallying with each other, that some doubted whether there were not two of them, or more – some, whether he had not unearthly means of travelling from spot to spot. The footpad hiding in a ditch had marked him passing like a ghost along its brink; the vagrant had met him on the dark high-road; the beggar had seen him pause upon the bridge to look down at the water, and then sweep on again; they who dealt in bodies with the surgeons[3] could swear he slept in churchyards, and that they had beheld him glide away among the tombs, on their approach. And as they told these stories to each other, one who had looked about him would pull his neighbour by the sleeve, and there he would be among them.

At last, one man – he was of those whose commerce lay among the graves – resolved to question this strange companion. Next night, when he had eat his poor meal voraciously (he was accustomed to do that, they had observed, as though he had no other in the day), this fellow sat down at his elbow.

'A black night, master!'

'It is a black night.'

'Blacker than last, though that was pitchy too. Didn't I pass you near the turnpike[4] in the Oxford-road?'

'It's like you may. I don't know.'

'Come, come, master,' cried the fellow, urged on by the looks of his comrades, and slapping him on the shoulder; 'be more companionable and communicative. Be more the gentleman in this

good company. There are tales among us that you have sold yourself
to the devil, and I know not what.'

'We all have, have we not?' returned the stranger, looking up. 'If
we were fewer in number, perhaps he would give better wages.'

'It goes rather hard with you, indeed,' said the fellow, as the
stranger disclosed his haggard unwashed face, and torn clothes.
'What of that? Be merry, master. A stave of a roaring song now –'

'Sing you, if you desire to hear one,' replied the other, shaking
him roughly off; 'and don't touch me, if you're a prudent man; I
carry arms which go off easily – they have done so, before now –
and make it dangerous for strangers who don't know the trick of
them, to lay hands upon me.'

'Do you threaten?' said the fellow.

'Yes,' returned the other, rising and turning upon him, and
looking fiercely round as if in apprehension of a general attack.

His voice, and look, and bearing – all expressive of the wildest
recklessness and desperation – daunted while they repelled the
bystanders. Although in a very different sphere of action now, they
were not without much of the effect they had wrought at the
Maypole Inn.

'I am what you all are, and live as you all do,' said the man
sternly, after a short silence. 'I am in hiding here like the rest, and
if we were surprised would perhaps do my part with the best of ye.
If it's my humour to be left to myself, let me have it. Otherwise,' –
and here he swore a tremendous oath – 'there'll be mischief done
in this place, though there *are* odds of a score against me.'

A low murmur, having its origin perhaps in a dread of the man
and the mystery that surrounded him, or perhaps in a sincere
opinion on the part of some of those present, that it would be an
inconvenient precedent to meddle too curiously with a gentleman's
private affairs if he saw reason to conceal them, warned the fellow
who had occasioned this discussion that he had best pursue it no
further. After a short time, the strange man lay down upon a bench
to sleep, and when they thought of him again, they found that he
was gone.

Next night, as soon as it was dark, he was abroad again and
traversing the streets; he was before the locksmith's house more
than once, but the family were out, and it was close shut. This night
he crossed London bridge and passed into Southwark. As he glided
down a bye street, a woman with a little basket on her arm, turned

into it at the other end. Directly he observed her, he sought the shelter of an archway, and stood aside until she had passed. Then he emerged cautiously from his hiding-place, and followed.

She went into several shops to purchase various kinds of household necessaries, and round every place at which she stopped he hovered like her evil spirit; following her when she reappeared. It was nigh eleven o'clock, and the passengers in the streets were thinning fast, when she turned, doubtless to go home. The phantom still followed her.

She turned into the same bye street in which he had seen her first, which, being free from shops, and narrow, was extremely dark. She quickened her pace here, as though distrustful of being stopped, and robbed of such trifling property as she carried with her. He crept along on the other side of the road. Had she been gifted with the speed of wind, it seemed as if his terrible shadow would have tracked her down.

At length the widow – for she it was – reached her own door, and, panting for breath, paused to take the key from her basket. In a flush and glow, with the haste she had made, and the pleasure of being safe at home, she stooped to draw it out, when, raising her head, she saw him standing silently beside her; the apparition of a dream.

His hand was on her mouth, but that was needless, for her tongue clove to its roof, and her power of utterance was gone. 'I have been looking for you many nights. Is the house empty? Answer me. Is any one inside?'

She could only answer by a rattle in her throat.

'Make me a sign.'

She seemed to indicate that there was no one there. He took the key, unlocked the door, carried her in, and secured it carefully behind them.

*

CHAPTER THE SEVENTEENTH

It was a chilly night, and the fire in the widow's parlour had burnt low. Her strange companion placed her in a chair, and stooping down before the half-extinguished ashes, raked them together and fanned them with his hat. From time to time he glanced at her over his shoulder, as though to assure himself of her remaining quiet and making no effort to depart; and that done, busied himself about the fire again.

It was not without reason that he took these pains, for his dress was dank and drenched with wet, his jaws rattled with cold, and he shivered from head to foot. It had rained hard during the previous night and for some hours in the morning, but since noon it had been fine. Wheresoever he had passed the hours of darkness, his condition sufficiently betokened that many of them had been spent beneath the open sky. Besmeared with mire; his saturated clothes clinging with a damp embrace about his limbs; his beard unshaven, his face unwashed, his meagre cheeks worn into deep hollows, – a more miserable wretch could hardly be, than this man who now cowered down upon the widow's hearth, and watched the struggling flame with bloodshot eyes.

She had covered her face with her hands, fearing, as it seemed, to look towards him. So they remained for some short time in silence. Glancing round again, he asked at length:

'Is this your house?'

'It is. Why, in the name of Heaven, do you darken it?'

'Give me meat and drink,' he answered sullenly, 'or I dare do more than that. The very marrow in my bones is cold, with wet and hunger. I must have warmth and food, and I will have them here.'

'You were the robber on the Chigwell road.'

'I was.'

'And nearly a murderer then.'

'The will was not wanting. There was one came upon me and raised the hue-and-cry, that it would have gone hard with, but for his nimbleness. I made a thrust at him.'

'You thrust your sword at *him!*' cried the widow, looking upwards. 'You hear this man! you hear and saw!'

He looked at her, as, with her head thrown back, and her hands tight clenched together, she uttered these words in an agony of appeal. Then, starting to his feet as she had done, he advanced towards her.

'Beware!' she cried in a suppressed voice, whose firmness stopped him midway. 'Do not so much as touch me with a finger, or you are lost; body and soul, you are lost.'

'Hear me,' he replied, menacing her with his hand. 'I, that in the form of a man live the life of a hunted beast; that in the body am a spirit, a ghost upon the earth, a thing from which all creatures shrink, save those curst beings of another world, who will not leave me; – I am, in my desperation of this night, past all fear but that of the hell in which I exist from day to day. Give the alarm, cry out, refuse to shelter me. I will not hurt you. But I will not be taken alive; and so surely as you threaten me above your breath, I fall a dead man on this floor. The blood with which I sprinkle it, be on you and yours, in the name of the Evil Spirit that tempts men to their ruin!'

As he spoke, he took a pistol from his breast, and firmly clutched it in his hand.

'Remove this man from me, good Heaven!' cried the widow. 'In thy grace and mercy, give him one minute's penitence, and strike him dead!'

'It has no such purpose,' he said, confronting her. 'It is deaf. Give me to eat and drink, lest I do that, it cannot help my doing, and will not do for you.'

'Will you leave me, if I do thus much? Will you leave me and return no more?'

'I will promise nothing,' he rejoined, seating himself at the table, 'nothing but this – I will execute my threat if you betray me.'

She rose at length, and going to a closet or pantry in the room, brought out some fragments of cold meat and bread and put them on the table. He asked for brandy, and for water. These she produced likewise; and he ate and drank with the voracity of a famished hound. All the time he was so engaged she kept at the uttermost distance of the chamber, and sat there shuddering, but with her face towards him. She never turned her back upon him once; and although when she passed him (as she was obliged to do in going to and from the cupboard) she gathered the skirts of her garment about her, as if even its touching his by chance were horrible to think of, still, in the midst of all this dread and terror, she kept her face directed to his own, and watched his every movement.

His repast ended – if that can be called one, which was a mere ravenous satisfying of the calls of hunger – he moved his chair towards the fire again, and warming himself before the blaze which had now sprung brightly up, accosted her once more.

'I am an outcast, to whom a roof above his head is often an uncommon luxury, and the food a beggar would reject is delicate fare. You live here at your ease. Do you live alone?'

'I do not,' she made answer with an effort.

'Who dwells here besides?'

'One – it is no matter who. You had best begone, or he may find you here. Why do you linger?'

'For warmth,' he replied, spreading out his hands before the fire. 'For warmth. You are rich, perhaps?'

'Very,' she said faintly. 'Very rich. No doubt I am very rich.'

'At least you are not penniless. You have some money. You were making purchases to-night.'

'I have a little left. It is but a few shillings.'

'Give me your purse. You had it in your hand at the door. Give it to me.'

She stepped to the table and laid it down. He reached across, took it up, and told the contents into his hand. As he was counting them, she listened for a moment, and sprung towards him.

'Take what there is, take all, take more if more were there, but go before it is too late. I have heard a wayward step without, I know full well. It will return directly. Begone.'

'What do you mean?'

'Do not stop to ask. I will not answer. Much as I dread to touch you, I would drag you to the door if I possessed the strength, rather than you should lose an instant. Miserable wretch! fly from this place.'

'If there are spies without, I am safer here,' replied the man, standing aghast. 'I will remain here, and will not fly till the danger is past.'

'It is too late!' cried the widow, who had listened for the step, and not to him. 'Hark to that foot upon the ground. Do you tremble to hear it! It is my son, my idiot son!'

As she said this wildly, there came a heavy knocking at the door. He looked at her, and she at him.

'Let him come in,' said the man, hoarsely. 'I fear him less than the dark, houseless night. He knocks again. Let him come in!'

'The dread of this hour,' returned the widow, 'has been upon me all my life, and I will not. Evil will fall upon him, if you stand eye to eye. My blighted boy! Oh! all good angels who know the truth

– hear a poor mother's prayer, and spare my boy from knowledge of this man!'

'He rattles at the shutters!' cried the man. 'He calls you. That voice and cry! It was he who grappled with me in the road. Was it he?'

She had sunk upon her knees, and so knelt down, moving her lips, but uttering no sound. As he gazed upon her, uncertain what to do or where to turn, the shutters flew open. He had barely time to catch a knife from the table, sheathe it in the loose sleeve of his coat, hide in the closet, and do all with the lightning's speed, when Barnaby tapped at the bare glass, and raised the sash exultingly.

'Why, who can keep out Grip and me!' he cried, thrusting in his head, and staring round the room. 'Are you there, mother? How long you keep us from the fire and light.'

She stammered some excuse and tendered him her hand. But Barnaby sprung lightly in without assistance, and putting his arms about her neck, kissed her a hundred times.

'We have been afield, mother – leaping ditches, scrambling through hedges, running down steep banks, up and away, and hurrying on. The wind has been blowing, and the rushes and young plants bowing and bending to it, lest it should do them harm, the cowards – and Grip – ha ha ha! – brave Grip, who cares for nothing, and when the wind rolls him over in the dust, turns manfully to bite it – Grip, bold Grip, has quarrelled with every little bowing twig – thinking, he told me, that it mocked him – and has worried it like a bull-dog. Ha ha ha!'

The raven, in his little basket at his master's back, hearing this frequent mention of his name in a tone of exultation, expressed his sympathy by crowing like a cock, and afterwards running over his various phrases of speech with such rapidity, and in so many varieties of hoarseness, that they sounded like the murmurs of a crowd of people.

'He takes such care of me besides!' said Barnaby. 'Such care, mother! He watches all the time I sleep, and when I shut my eyes, and make-believe to slumber, he practises new learning softly; but he keeps his eye on me the while, and if he sees me laugh, though never so little, stops directly. He won't surprise me till he's perfect.'

The raven crowed again in a rapturous manner which plainly said, 'Those are certainly some of my characteristics, and I glory in

them.' In the meantime, Barnaby closed the window and secured
it, and coming to the fire-place, prepared to sit down with his face
to the closet. But his mother prevented this, by hastily taking that
side herself, and motioning him towards the other.

'How pale you are to-night!' said Barnaby, leaning on his stick.
'We have been cruel, Grip, and made her anxious!'

Anxious in good truth, and sick at heart! The listener held the
door of his hiding-place open with his hand, and closely watched
her son. Grip – alive to everything his master was unconscious of –
had his head out of the basket, and in return was watching him
intently with his glistening eye.

'He flaps his wings,' said Barnaby, turning almost quickly
enough to catch the retreating form and closing door, 'as if there
were strangers here; but Grip is wiser than to fancy that. Jump
then!'

Accepting this invitation with a dignity peculiar to himself, the
bird hopped up on his master's shoulder, from that to his extended
hand, and so to the ground. Barnaby unstrapping the basket and
putting it down in a corner with the lid open, Grip's first care was
to shut it down with all possible despatch, and then to stand
upon it. Believing, no doubt, that he had now rendered it utterly
impossible, and beyond the power of mortal man, to shut him up
in it any more, he drew a great many corks in triumph, and uttered
a corresponding number of hurrahs.

'Mother!' said Barnaby, laying aside his hat and stick, and
returning to the chair from which he had risen, 'I'll tell you where
we have been to-day, and what we have been doing, – shall I?'

She took his hand in hers, and holding it, nodded the word she
could not speak.

'You mustn't tell,' said Barnaby, holding up his finger, 'for it's a
secret, mind, and only known to me, and Grip, and Hugh. We had
the dog with us, but he's not like Grip, clever as he is, and doesn't
guess it yet, I'll wager. – Why do you look behind me so?'

'Did I!' she answered faintly. 'I didn't know I did. Come nearer
me.'

'You are frightened!' said Barnaby, changing colour. 'Mother –
you don't see –'

'See what?'

'There's – there's none of this about, is there?' he answered in a
whisper, drawing closer to her and clasping the mark upon his

wrist. 'I am afraid there is, somewhere. You make my hair stand
on end, and my flesh creep. Why do you look like that? Is it in the
room as I have seen it in my dreams, dashing the ceiling and the
walls with red? Tell me. Is it?'

He fell into a shivering fit as he put the question, and shutting
out the light with his hands, sat shaking in every limb until it had
passed away. After a time, he raised his head and looked about
him.

'Is it gone?'

'There has been nothing here,' rejoined his mother, soothing him.
'Nothing indeed, dear Barnaby. Look! You see there are but you
and me.'

He gazed at her vacantly, and, becoming reassured by degrees,
burst into a wild laugh.

'But let us see,' he said, thoughtfully. 'Were we talking? Was it
you and me? Where have we been?'

'Nowhere but here.'

'Aye, but Hugh, and I,' said Barnaby, ' – that's it. Maypole Hugh,
and I, you know, and Grip – we have been lying in the forest, and
among the trees by the road side, with a dark-lanthorn after night
came on, and the dog in a noose ready to slip him when the man
came by.'

'What man?'

'The robber; him that the stars winked at. We have waited for
him after dark these many nights, and we shall have him. I'd know
him in a thousand. Mother, see here! This is the man. Look!'

He twisted his handkerchief round his head, pulled his hat upon
his brow, wrapped his coat about him, and stood up before her: so
like the original he counterfeited, that the dark figure peering out
behind him might have passed for his own shadow.

'Ha ha ha! We shall have him,' he cried, ridding himself of the
semblance as hastily as he had assumed it. 'You shall see him,
mother, bound hand and foot, and brought to London at a saddle-
girth; and you shall hear of him at Tyburn Tree if we have luck. So
Hugh says. You're pale again, and trembling. And why *do* you look
behind me so?'

'It is nothing,' she answered. 'I am not quite well. Go you to bed,
dear, and leave me here.'

'To bed!' he answered. 'I don't like bed. I like to lie before the
fire, watching the prospects in the burning coals – the rivers, hills,

and dells, in the deep, red sunset, and the wild faces. I am hungry too, and Grip has eaten nothing since broad noon. Let us to supper. Grip! To supper, lad!'

The raven flapped his wings, and, croaking his satisfaction, hopped to the feet of his master, and there held his bill open, ready for snapping up such lumps of meat as he should throw him. Of these he received about a score in rapid succession, without the smallest discomposure.

'That's all,' said Barnaby.

'More!' cried Grip. 'More!'

But it appearing for a certainty that no more was to be had, he retreated with his store; and disgorging the morsels one by one from his pouch, hid them in various corners – taking particular care, however, to avoid the closet, as being doubtful of the hidden man's propensities and power of resisting temptation. When he had concluded these arrangements, he took a turn or two across the room with an elaborate assumption of having nothing on his mind (but with one eye hard upon his treasure all the time), and then, and not till then, began to drag it out, piece by piece, and eat it with the utmost relish.

Barnaby, for his part, having pressed his mother to eat, in vain, made a hearty supper too. Once, during the progress of his meal, he wanted more bread from the closet and rose to get it. She hurriedly interposed to prevent him, and, summoning her utmost fortitude, passed into the recess, and brought it out herself.

'Mother,' said Barnaby, looking at her stedfastly as she sat down beside him after doing so; 'is to-day my birthday?'

'To-day!' she answered. 'Don't you recollect it was but a week or so ago, and that summer, autumn, and winter have to pass before it comes again?'

'I remember that it has been so till now,' said Barnaby. 'But I think to-day must be my birthday too, for all that.'

She asked him why? 'I'll tell you why,' he said. 'I have always seen you – I didn't let you know it, but I have – on the evening of that day grow very sad. I have seen you cry when Grip and I were most glad; and look frightened with no reason; and I have touched your hand, and felt that it was cold – as it is now. Once, mother (on a birthday that was, also) Grip and I thought of this after we went up stairs to bed, and when it was midnight, striking one o'clock, we came down to your door to see if you were well. You

were on your knees. I forget what it was you said. Grip, what was
it we heard her say that night?'

'I'm a devil!' rejoined the raven promptly.

'No, no,' said Barnaby. 'But you said something in a prayer; and
when you rose and walked about, you looked (as you have done
ever since, mother, towards night on my birthday) just as you do
now. I have found that out, you see, though I am silly. So I say
you're wrong; and this must be my birthday – my birthday, Grip!'

The bird received this information with a crow of such duration
as a cock, gifted with intelligence beyond all others of his kind,
might usher in the longest day with. Then, as if he had well considered the sentiment, and regarded it as apposite to birthdays, he
cried, 'Never say die!' a great many times, and flapped his wings
for emphasis.

The widow tried to make light of Barnaby's remark, and endeavoured to divert his attention to some new subject; too easy a task
at all times, as she knew. His supper done, Barnaby, regardless of
her entreaties, stretched himself on the mat before the fire; Grip
perched upon his leg, and divided his time between dozing in the
grateful warmth, and endeavouring (as it presently appeared) to
recal a new accomplishment he had been studying all day.

A long and profound silence ensued, broken only by some change
of position on the part of Barnaby, whose eyes were still wide open
and intently fixed upon the fire; or by an effort of recollection on
the part of Grip, who would cry in a low voice from time to time,
'Polly put the ket – '[1] and there stop short, forgetting the remainder,
and go off in a doze again.

After a long interval, Barnaby's breathing grew more deep and
regular, and his eyes were closed. But even then the unquiet spirit
of the raven interposed. 'Polly put the ket – ' cried Grip, and his
master was broad awake again.

At length Barnaby slept soundly; and the bird with his bill sunk
upon his breast, his breast itself puffed out into a comfortable
alderman-like form, and his bright eye growing smaller and smaller,
really seemed to be subsiding into a state of repose. Now and then
he muttered in a sepulchral voice, 'Polly put the ket – ' but very
drowsily, and more like a drunken man than a reflecting raven.

The widow, scarcely venturing to breathe, rose from her seat.
The man glided from the closet, and extinguished the candle.

'– tle on,' cried Grip, suddenly struck with an idea and very much excited. '– tle on. Hurrah! Polly put the ket-tle on, we'll all have tea; Polly put the ket-tle on, we'll all have tea. Hurrah, hurrah, hurrah! I'm a devil, I'm a devil, I'm a ket-tle on, Keep up your spirits, Never say die, Bow wow wow, I'm a devil, I'm a ket-tle, I'm a – Polly put the ket-tle on we'll all have tea.'

They stood rooted to the ground, as though it had been a voice from the grave.

But even this failed to awaken the sleeper. He turned over towards the fire, his arm fell to the ground, and his head drooped heavily upon it. The widow and her unwelcome visitor gazed at him and at each other for a moment, and then she motioned him towards the door.

'Stay,' he whispered. 'You teach your son well.'

'I have taught him nothing that you heard to-night. Depart instantly, or I will rouse him.'

'You are free to do so. Shall *I* rouse him?'

'You dare not do that.'

'I dare do anything, I have told you. He knows me well, it seems. At least I will know him.'

'Would you kill him in his sleep?' cried the widow, throwing herself between them.

'Woman,' he returned between his teeth, as he motioned her aside, 'I would see him nearer, and I will. If you want one of us to kill the other, wake him.'

With that he advanced, and bending down over the prostrate form, softly turned back the head and looked into the face. The light of the fire was upon it, and its every lineament was revealed distinctly. He contemplated it for a brief space, and hastily uprose.

'Observe,' he whispered in the widow's ear: 'In him, of whose existence I was ignorant until to-night, I have you in my power. Be careful how you use me. Be careful how you use me. I am destitute and starving, and a wanderer upon the earth. I may take a sure and slow revenge.'

'There is some dreadful meaning in your words. I do not fathom it.'

'There is a meaning in them, and I see you fathom it to its very depth. You have anticipated it for years; you have told me as much. I leave you to digest it. Do not forget my warning.'

He pointed, as he left her, to the slumbering form, and stealthily withdrawing, made his way into the street. She fell on her knees beside the sleeper, and remained like one stricken into stone, until the tears which fear had frozen so long, came tenderly to her relief.

'Oh Thou,' she cried, 'who hast taught me such deep love for this one remnant of the promise of a happy life, out of whose affliction, even, perhaps the comfort springs that he is ever a relying, loving child to me – never growing old or cold at heart, but needing my care and duty in his manly strength as in his cradle-time – help him, in his darkened walk through this sad world, or he is doomed, and my poor heart is broken!'

CHAPTER THE EIGHTEENTH

Gliding along the silent streets, and holding his course where they were darkest and most gloomy, the man who had left the widow's house crossed London Bridge, and arriving in the City, plunged into the back ways, lanes, and courts, between Cornhill and Smithfield;[1] with no more fixedness of purpose than to lose himself among their windings, and baffle pursuit, if any one were dogging his steps.

It was the dead time of the night, and all was quiet. Now and then a drowsy watchman's footsteps sounded on the pavement, or the lamp-lighter on his rounds went flashing past, leaving behind a little track of smoke mingled with glowing morsels of his hot red link. He hid himself even from these partakers of his lonely walk, and, shrinking in some arch or doorway while they passed, issued forth again when they were gone and so pursued his solitary way.

To be shelterless and alone in the open country, hearing the wind moan and watching for day through the whole long weary night; to listen to the falling rain, and crouch for warmth beneath the lee of some old barn or rick, or in the hollow of a tree; are dismal things – but not so dismal as the wandering up and down where shelter is, and beds and sleepers are by thousands; a houseless rejected creature. To pace the echoing stones from hour to hour, counting the dull chimes of the clocks; to watch the lights twinkling in chamber windows, to think what happy forgetfulness each house shuts in; that here are children coiled together in their beds, here youth, here age, here poverty, here wealth, all equal in their sleep, and all at rest; to have nothing in common with the slumbering world around, not even sleep, Heaven's gift to all its creatures, and be akin to nothing but despair; to feel, by the wretched contrast with everything on every hand, more utterly alone and cast away than in a trackless desert; – this is a kind of suffering, on which the rivers of great cities close full many a time, and which the solitude in crowds alone awakens.

The miserable man paced up and down the streets – so long, so wearisome, so like each other – and often cast a wistful look towards the east, hoping to see the first faint streaks of day. But obdurate night had yet possession of the sky, and his disturbed and restless walk found no relief.

One house in a back street was bright with the cheerful glare of lights; there was the sound of music in it too, and the tread of dancers, and there were cheerful voices, and many a burst of laughter. To this place – to be near something that was awake and glad – he returned again and again; and more than one of those who left it when the merriment was at its height, felt it a check upon their mirthful mood to see him flitting to and fro like an uneasy ghost. At last the guests departed, one and all; and then the house was close shut up, and became as dull and silent as the rest.

His wanderings brought him at one time to the city jail.[2] Instead of hastening from it as a place of ill omen, and one he had cause to shun, he sat down on some steps hard by, and, resting his chin upon his hand, gazed upon its rough and frowning walls as though even they became a refuge in his jaded eyes. He paced it round and round, came back to the same spot, and sat down again. He did this often, and once, with a hasty movement, crossed to where some men were watching in the prison lodge, and had his foot upon the steps as though determined to accost them. But looking round, he saw that the day began to break, and failing in his purpose, turned and fled.

He was soon in the quarter he had lately traversed, and pacing to and fro again as he had done before. He was passing down a mean street, when from an alley close at hand some shouts of revelry arose, and there came straggling forth a dozen madcaps, whooping and calling to each other, who, parting noisily, took different ways and dispersed in smaller groups.

Hoping that some low place of entertainment which would afford him a safe refuge might be near at hand, he turned into this court when they were all gone, and looked about for a half-opened door, or lighted window, or other indication of the place whence they had come. It was so profoundly dark, however, and so ill-favoured, that he concluded they had but turned up there, missing their way, and were pouring out again when he observed them. With this impression, and finding there was no outlet but that by which he had entered, he was about to turn, when from a grating near his feet a sudden stream of light appeared, and the sound of talking came. He retreated into a doorway to see who these talkers were, and to listen to them.

The light came to the level of the pavement as he did this, and a man ascended, bearing in his hand a torch. This figure unlocked and held open the grating as for the passage of another, who presently appeared, in the form of a young man of small stature and uncommon self-importance, dressed in an obsolete and very gaudy fashion.

'Good night, noble captain,' said he with the torch. 'Farewell, commander. Good luck, illustrious general!'

In return to these compliments, the other bade him hold his tongue, and keep his noise to himself; and laid upon him many similar injunctions, with great fluency of speech and sternness of manner.

'Commend me, captain, to the stricken Miggs,' returned the torch-bearer in a lower voice. 'My captain flies at higher game than Miggses. Ha, ha, ha! My captain is an eagle, both as respects his eye and soaring wings. My captain breaketh hearts as other bachelors break eggs at breakfast.'

'What a fool you are, Stagg!' said Mr Tappertit, stepping on the pavement of the court, and brushing from his legs the dust he had contracted in his passage upward.

'His precious limbs!' cried Stagg, clasping one of his ancles. 'Shall a Miggs aspire to these proportions! No, no, my captain. We will inveigle ladies fair, and wed them in our secret cavern. We will unite ourselves with blooming beauties, captain.'

'I'll tell you what, my buck,' said Mr Tappertit, releasing his leg, 'I'll trouble you not to take liberties, and not to broach certain questions unless certain questions are broached to you. Speak when you're spoke to on particular subjects, and not otherways. Hold the torch up till I've got to the end of the court, and then kennel yourself, do you hear?'

'I hear you, noble captain.'

'Obey then,' said Mr Tappertit haughtily. 'Gentlemen, lead on!'
With which word of command (addressed to an imaginary staff or
retinue) he folded his arms, and walked with surpassing dignity
down the court.

His obsequious follower stood holding the torch above his head,
and then the observer saw for the first time, from his place of
concealment, that he was blind. Some involuntary motion on his
part caught the quick ear of the blind man, before he was conscious
of having moved an inch towards him, for he turned suddenly and
cried, 'Who's there?'

'A man,' said the other, advancing. 'A friend.'

'A stranger!' rejoined the blind man. 'Strangers are not my
friends. What do you do there?'

'I saw your company come out, and waited here till they were
gone. I want a lodging.'

'A lodging at this time!' returned Stagg, pointing towards the
dawn as though he saw it. 'Do you know the day is breaking?'

'I know it,' rejoined the other, 'to my cost. I have been traversing
this iron-hearted town all night.'

'You had better traverse it again,' said the blind man, preparing
to descend, 'till you find some lodgings suitable to your taste. I
don't let any.'

'Stay!' cried the other, holding him by the arm.

'I'll beat this light about that hangdog face of yours (for hangdog
it is, if it answers to your voice), and rouse the neighbourhood
besides, if you detain me,' said the blind man. 'Let me go. Do you
hear?'

'Do *you* hear!' returned the other, chinking a few shillings
together, and hurriedly pressing them into his hand. 'I beg nothing
of you. I will pay for the shelter you give me. Death! Is it much to
ask of such as you! I have come from the country, and desire to rest
where there are none to question me. I am faint, exhausted, worn
out, almost dead. Let me lie down, like a dog, before your fire. I
ask no more than that. If you would be rid of me, I will depart
to-morrow.'

'If a gentleman has been unfortunate on the road,' muttered
Stagg, yielding to the other, who, pressing on him, had already
gained a footing on the steps – 'and can pay for his accommodation –'

'I will pay you with all I have. I am just now past the want of

food, God knows, and wish but to purchase shelter. What companion have you below?'

'None.'

'Then fasten your grate there, and show me the way. Quick!'

The blind man complied after a moment's hesitation, and they
descended together. The dialogue had passed as hurriedly as the
words could be spoken, and they stood in his wretched room before
he had had time to recover from his first surprise.

'May I see where that door leads to, and what is beyond?' said
the man, glancing keenly round. 'You will not mind that?'

'I will show you myself. Follow me, or go before. Take your
choice.'

He bade him lead the way, and, by the light of the torch which
his conductor held up for the purpose, inspected all three cellars,
narrowly. Assured that the blind man had spoken truth, and that
he lived there alone, the visitor returned with him to the first, in
which a fire was burning, and flung himself with a deep groan upon
the ground before it.

His host pursued his usual occupation without seeming to heed
him any further. But directly he fell asleep – and he noted his falling
into a slumber, as readily as the keenest-sighted man could have
done – he knelt down beside him, and passed his hand lightly but
carefully over his face and person.

His sleep was checkered with starts and moans, and sometimes
with a muttered word or two. His hands were clenched, his brow
bent, and his mouth firmly set. All this, the blind man accurately
marked; and as if his curiosity were strongly awakened, and he had
already some inkling of his mystery, he sat watching him, if the
expression may be used, and listening, until it was broad day.

*

CHAPTER THE NINETEENTH

Dolly Varden's pretty little head was yet bewildered by various
recollections of the party, and her bright eyes were yet dazzled by
a crowd of images, dancing before them like motes in the sunbeams,
among which the effigy of one partner in particular did especially
figure, the same being a young coachmaker (a master in his own

right) who had given her to understand, when he handed her into
the chair at parting, that it was his fixed resolve to neglect his
business from that time, and die slowly for the love of her – Dolly's
head, and eyes, and thoughts, and seven senses, were all in a state
of flutter and confusion for which the party was accountable,
although it was now three days old, when, as she was sitting listlessly at breakfast, reading all manner of fortunes (that is to say, of
married and flourishing fortunes) in the grounds of her teacup, a
step was heard in the workshop, and Mr Edward Chester was
descried through the glass door, standing among the rusty locks
and keys, like love among the roses[1] – for which apt comparison
the historian may by no means take any credit to himself, the same
being the invention, in a sentimental mood, of the chaste and
modest Miggs, who, beholding him from the doorsteps she was
then cleaning, did, in her maiden meditation,[2] give utterance to
the simile.

The locksmith, who happened at the moment to have his eyes
thrown upward and his head backward, in an intense communing
with Toby, did not see his visitor, until Mrs Varden, more watchful
than the rest, had desired Sim Tappertit to open the glass door and
give him admission – from which untoward circumstance the good
lady argued (for she could deduce a precious moral from the most
trifling event) that to take a draught of small ale in the morning
was to observe a pernicious, irreligious, and Pagan custom, the
relish whereof should be left to swine, and Satan, or at least to
Popish persons, and should be shunned by the righteous as a work
of sin and evil. She would no doubt have pursued her admonition
much further, and would have founded on it a long list of precious
precepts of inestimable value, but that the young gentleman standing by in a somewhat uncomfortable and discomfited manner while
she read her spouse this lecture, occasioned her to bring it to a
premature conclusion.

'I'm sure you'll excuse me sir,' said Mrs Varden, rising and
curtseying. 'Varden is so very thoughtless, and needs so much
reminding – Sim, bring a chair here.'

Mr Tappertit obeyed, with a flourish implying that he did so,
under protest.

'And you can go, Sim,' said the locksmith.

Mr Tappertit obeyed again, still under protest; and betaking himself to the workshop, began seriously to fear that he might find it necessary to poison his master, before his time was out.

In the meantime, Edward returned suitable replies to Mrs Varden's courtesies, and that lady brightened up very much; so that when he accepted a dish of tea from the fair hands of Dolly, she was perfectly agreeable.

'I am sure if there's anything we can do, – Varden, or I, or Dolly either, – to serve you, sir, at any time, you have only to say it, and it shall be done,' said Mrs V.

'I am much obliged to you, I am sure,' returned Edward. 'You encourage me to say that I have come here now, to beg your good offices.'

Mrs Varden was delighted beyond measure.

'It occurred to me that probably your fair daughter might be going to the Warren, either to-day or to-morrow,' said Edward, glancing at Dolly; 'and if so, and you will allow her to take charge of this letter, Ma'am, you will oblige me more than I can tell you. The truth is, that while I am very anxious it should reach its destination, I have particular reasons for not trusting it to any other conveyance; so that without your help, I am wholly at a loss.'

'She was not going that way sir, either to-day, or to-morrow, nor indeed all next week,' the lady graciously rejoined, 'but we shall be very glad to put ourselves out of the way on your account, and if you wish it, you may depend upon its going to-day. You might suppose,' said Mrs Varden, frowning at her husband, 'from Varden's sitting there so glum and silent, that he objected to this arrangement; but you must not mind that, sir, if you please. It's his way at home. Out of doors, he can be cheerful and talkative enough.'

Now, the fact was, that the unfortunate locksmith, blessing his stars to find his helpmate in such good humour, had been sitting with a beaming face, hearing this discourse with a joy past all expression. Wherefore this sudden attack quite took him by surprise.

'My dear Martha –' he said.

'Oh yes, I dare say,' interrupted Mrs Varden, with a smile of mingled scorn and pleasantry. 'Very dear! We all know that.'

'No, but my good soul,' said Gabriel, 'you are quite mistaken. You are indeed. I was delighted to find you so kind and ready. I waited, my dear, anxiously, I assure you, to hear what you would say.'

'You waited anxiously,' repeated Mrs V. 'Yes! Thank you, Varden. You waited, as you always do, that I might bear the blame, if any came of it. But I am used to it,' said the lady with a kind of solemn titter, 'and that's my comfort!'

'I give you my word, Martha –' said Gabriel.

'Let me give you *my* word, my dear,' interposed his wife with a christian smile, 'that such discussions as these between married people, are much better left alone. Therefore, if you please Varden, we'll drop the subject. I have no wish to pursue it. I could. I might say a great deal. But I would rather not. Pray don't say any more.'

'I don't want to say any more,' rejoined the goaded locksmith.

'Well then, don't,' said Mrs Varden.

'Nor did I begin it Martha,' added the locksmith, good humouredly, 'I must say that.'

'You did not begin it, Varden!' exclaimed his wife, opening her eyes very wide and looking round upon the company, as though she would say, You hear this man! 'You did not begin it, Varden! But you shall not say I was out of temper. No, you did not begin it, oh dear no, not you, my dear!'

'Well, well,' said the locksmith. 'That's settled then.'

'Oh yes,' rejoined his wife, 'quite. If you like to say Dolly began it, my dear, I shall not contradict you. I know my duty. I need know it, I am sure. I am often obliged to bear it in mind, when my inclination perhaps would be for the moment to forget it. Thank you, Varden.' And so, with a mighty show of humility and forgiveness, she folded her hands, and looked round again, with a smile which plainly said 'If you desire to see the first and foremost among female martyrs, here she is, on view!'

This little incident, illustrative though it was of Mrs Varden's extraordinary sweetness and amiability, had so strong a tendency to check the conversation and to disconcert all parties but that excellent lady, that only a few monosyllables were uttered until Edward withdrew; which he presently did, thanking the lady of the house a great many times for her condescension, and whispering in Dolly's ear that he would call on the morrow, in case there should happen to be an answer to the note – which, indeed, she knew without his telling, as Barnaby and his friend Grip had dropped in on the previous night to prepare her for the visit which was then terminating.

Gabriel, who had attended Edward to the door, came back with his hands in his pockets; and, after fidgeting about the room in a very uneasy manner, and casting a great many sidelong looks at Mrs Varden (who with the calmest countenance in the world was five fathoms deep in the Protestant Manual), inquired of Dolly how she meant to go. Dolly supposed by the stage-coach, and looked at her lady mother, who finding herself silently appealed to, dived down at least another fathom into the Manual, and became unconscious of all earthly things.

'Martha –' said the locksmith.

'I hear you, Varden,' said his wife, without rising to the surface.

'I am sorry, my dear, you have such an objection to the Maypole and old John, for otherways as it's a very fine morning, and Saturday's not a busy day with us, we might have all three gone to Chigwell in the chaise, and had quite a happy day of it.'

Mrs Varden immediately closed the Manual, and bursting into tears, requested to be led up-stairs.

'What is the matter now Martha?' inquired the locksmith.

To which Martha rejoined 'Oh! don't speak to me,' and protested in agony that if anybody had told her so, she wouldn't have believed it.

'But Martha,' said Gabriel, putting himself in the way as she was moving off with the aid of Dolly's shoulder, 'wouldn't have believed what? Tell me what's wrong now. Do tell me. Upon my soul I don't know. Do *you* know child? Damme!' cried the locksmith, plucking at his wig in a kind of frenzy, 'nobody does know, I verily believe, but Miggs!'

'Miggs,' said Mrs Varden faintly, and with symptoms of approaching incoherence, 'is attached to me, and that is sufficient to draw down hatred upon her in this house. She is a comfort to me, whatever she may be to others.'

'She's no comfort to me,' cried Gabriel, made bold by despair. 'She's the misery of my life. She's all the plagues of Egypt[3] in one.'

'She's considered so, I have no doubt,' said Mrs Varden. 'I was prepared for that; it's natural; it's of a piece with the rest. When you taunt me as you do to my face, how can I wonder that you taunt her behind her back!' And here the incoherence coming on very strong, Mrs Varden wept, and laughed, and sobbed, and shivered, and hiccoughed, and choaked; and said she knew it was very foolish but she couldn't help it; and that when she was dead and gone, perhaps they would be sorry for it – which really under the circumstances did not appear quite so probable as she seemed to think – with a great deal more to the same effect. In a word, she passed with great decency through all the ceremonies incidental to such occasions; and being supported up-stairs, was deposited in a highly spasmodic state on her own bed, where Miss Miggs shortly afterwards flung herself upon the body.

The philosophy of all this was, that Mrs Varden wanted to go to Chigwell; that she did not want to make any concession or explanation; that she would only go on being implored and entreated so to do; and that she would accept no other terms. Accordingly, after a vast amount of moaning and crying up-stairs, and much damping of foreheads, and vinegaring of temples, and hartshorning of noses, and so forth; and after most pathetic adjurations from Miggs, assisted by warm brandy-and-water not over-weak, and divers other cordials, also of a stimulating quality, administered at first in teaspoonsful and afterwards in increasing doses, and of which Miss Miggs herself partook as a preventive measure (for fainting is infectious); after all these remedies, and many more too numerous to mention, but not to take, had been applied; and many verbal consolations, moral, religious, and miscellaneous, had been superadded thereto; the locksmith humbled himself, and the end was gained.

'If it's only for the sake of peace and quietness, father,' said Dolly, urging him to go up-stairs.

'Oh, Doll, Doll,' said her good-natured father. 'If you ever have a husband of your own –'

Dolly glanced at the glass.

'– Well, *when* you have,' said the locksmith, 'never faint, my darling. More domestic unhappiness has come of easy fainting, Doll, than from all the greater passions put together. Remember that, my dear, if you would be really happy, which you never can be, if your husband isn't. And a word in your ear, my precious. Never have a Miggs about you!'

With this advice he kissed his blooming daughter on the cheek, and slowly repaired to Mrs Varden's room; where that lady, lying all pale and languid on her couch, was refreshing herself with a

sight of her last new bonnet, which Miggs, as a means of calming
her scattered spirits, displayed to the best advantage at her bedside.

'Here's master, mim,' said Miggs. 'Oh, what a happiness it is
when man and wife come round again! Oh gracious, to think that
him and her should ever have a word together!' In the energy of
these sentiments, which were uttered as an apostrophe to the
Heavens in general, Miss Miggs perched the bonnet on the top of
her own head, and folding her hands, turned on her tears.

'I can't help it,' cried Miggs. 'I couldn't, if I was to be drownded
in 'em. She has such a forgiving spirit! She'll forget all that has
passed, and go along with you, sir – Oh, if it was to the world's
end, she'd go along with you.'

Mrs Varden with a faint smile gently reproved her attendant for
this enthusiasm, and reminded her at the same time that she was
far too unwell to venture out that day.

'Oh no, you're not, mim, indeed you're not,' said Miggs; 'I repeal
to master; master knows you're not, mim. The hair, and motion of
the shay, will do you good, mim, and you must not give way, you
must not raly. She must keep up mustn't she, sir, for all our sakes?
I was a telling her that, just now. She must remember us, even if
she forgets herself. Master will persuade you, mim, I'm sure. There's
Miss Dolly's a going you know, and master, and you, and all so
happy and so comfortable. Oh!' cried Miggs, turning on the tears
again, previous to quitting the room in great emotion, 'I never see
such a blessed one as she is for the forgiveness of her spirit, I never,
never, never did. Nor more did master neither; no, nor no one –
never!'

For five minutes or thereabouts, Mrs Varden remained mildly
opposed to all her husband's prayers that she would oblige him by
taking a day's pleasure, but relenting at length, she suffered herself
to be persuaded, and granting him her free forgiveness (the merit
whereof, she meekly said, rested with the Manual and not with her),
desired that Miggs might come and help her dress. The handmaid
attended promptly, and it is but justice to their joint exertions to
record that, when the good lady came down-stairs in course of
time, completely decked out for the journey, she really looked as
if nothing had happened, and appeared in the very best health
imaginable.

As to Dolly, there she was again, the very pink and pattern of
good looks, in a smart little cherry-coloured mantle, with a hood

of the same drawn over her head, and upon the top of that hood, a little straw hat trimmed with cherry-coloured ribbons, and worn the merest trifle on one side – just enough in short to make it the wickedest and most provoking head-dress that ever malicious milliner devised. And not to speak of the manner in which these cherry-coloured decorations brightened her eyes, or vied with her lips, or shed a new bloom on her face, she wore such a cruel little muff, and such a heart-rending pair of shoes, and was so surrounded and hemmed in, as it were, by aggravations of all kinds, that when Mr Tappertit, holding the horse's head, saw her come out of the house alone, such impulses came over him to decoy her into the chaise and drive off like mad, that he would unquestionably have done it, but for certain uneasy doubts besetting him as to the shortest way to Gretna Green;[4] whether it was up the street or down, or up the right-hand turning or the left; and whether, supposing all the turnpikes to be carried by storm, the blacksmith in the end would marry them on credit; which by reason of his clerical office appeared, even to his excited imagination, so unlikely, that he hesitated. And while he stood hesitating, and looking post-chaises-and-six at Dolly, out came his master and his mistress, and the constant Miggs, and the opportunity was gone for ever. For now the chaise creaked upon its springs, and Mrs Varden was inside; and now it creaked again, and more than ever, and the locksmith was inside; and now it bounded once, as if its heart beat lightly, and Dolly was inside; and now it was gone and its place was empty, and he and that dreary Miggs were standing in the street together.

The hearty locksmith was in as good a humour as if nothing had occurred for the last twelve months to put him out of his way, Dolly was all smiles and graces, and Mrs Varden was agreeable beyond all precedent. As they jogged through the streets talking of this thing and of that, who should be descried upon the pavement but that very coachmaker, looking so genteel that nobody would have believed he had ever had anything to do with a coach but riding in it, and bowing like any nobleman. To be sure Dolly was confused when she bowed again, and to be sure the cherry-coloured ribbons trembled a little when she met his mournful eye, which seemed to say, 'I have kept my word, I have begun, the business is going to the devil, and you're the cause of it.' There he stood, rooted to the ground: as Dolly said, like a statue; and as Mrs Varden said, like a pump; till they turned the corner: and when her father thought it was like his impudence, and her mother wondered what he meant by it, Dolly blushed again till her very hood was pale.

But on they went, not the less merrily for this, and there was the locksmith in the incautious fulness of his heart 'pulling-up' at all manner of places, and evincing a most intimate acquaintance with all the taverns on the road, and all the landlords and all the landladies, with whom, indeed, the little horse was on equally friendly terms, for he kept on stopping of his own accord. Never were people so glad to see other people as these landlords and landladies were to behold Mr Varden and Mrs Varden and Miss Varden; and wouldn't they get out, said one; and they really must walk up-stairs, said another; and she would take it ill and be quite certain they were proud if they wouldn't have a little taste of something, said a third; and so on, that it really was quite a Progress rather than a ride, and one continued scene of hospitality from beginning to end. It was pleasant enough to be held in such esteem, not to mention the refreshments; so Mrs Varden said nothing at the time, and was all affability and delight – but such a body of evidence as she collected against the unfortunate locksmith that day, to be used thereafter as occasion might require, never was got together for matrimonial purposes.

In course of time – and in course of a pretty long time too, for these agreeable interruptions delayed them not a little, – they arrived upon the skirts of the Forest, and riding pleasantly on among the trees, came at last to the Maypole, where the locksmith's cheerful 'Yoho!' speedily brought to the porch old John, and after him young Joe, both of whom were so transfixed at sight of the ladies, that for a moment they were perfectly unable to give them any welcome, and could do nothing but stare.

It was only for a moment, however, that Joe forgot himself, for speedily reviving he thrust his drowsy father aside – to Mr Willet's mighty and inexpressible indignation – and darting out, stood ready to help them to alight. It was necessary for Dolly to get out first. Joe had her in his arms; – yes, though for a space of time no longer than you could count one in, Joe had her in his arms. Here was a glimpse of happiness!

It would be difficult to describe what a flat and common-place affair the helping Mrs Varden out afterwards was, but Joe did it, and did it too with the best grace in the world. Then old John, who, entertaining a dull and foggy sort of idea that Mrs Varden wasn't fond of him, had been in some doubt whether she might not have come for purposes of assault and battery, took courage, hoped she was well, and offered to conduct her into the house. This tender being amicably received, they marched in together; Joe and Dolly followed, arm-in-arm, (happiness again!) and Varden brought up the rear.

Old John would have it that they must sit in the bar, and nobody objecting, into the bar they went. All bars are snug places, but the Maypole's was the very snuggest, cosiest, and completest bar, that ever the wit of man devised. Such amazing bottles in old oaken pigeon-holes; such gleaming tankards dangling from pegs at about the same inclination as thirsty men would hold them to their lips; such sturdy little Dutch kegs ranged in rows on shelves; so many lemons hanging in separate nets, and forming the fragrant grove already mentioned in this chronicle, suggestive, with goodly loaves of snowy sugar stowed away hard by, of punch, idealised beyond all mortal knowledge; such closets, such presses, such drawers full of pipes, such places for putting things away in hollow window-seats, all crammed to the throat with eatables, drinkables, or savoury condiments; lastly, and to crown all, as typical of the immense resources of the establishment, and its defiances to all visitors to cut and come again, such a stupendous cheese!

It is a poor heart that never rejoices – it must have been the poorest, weakest, and most watery heart that ever beat, which would not have warmed towards the Maypole bar. Mrs Varden's did directly. She could no more have reproached John Willet among those household gods, the kegs and bottles, lemons, pipes, and cheese, than she could have stabbed him with his own bright carving-knife. The order for dinner too – it might have soothed a savage. 'A bit of fish,' said John to the cook, 'and some lamb chops (breaded, with plenty of ketchup), and a good salad, and a roast spring chicken, with a dish of sausages and mashed potatoes, or something of that sort.' Something of that sort! The resources of these inns! To talk carelessly about dishes, which in themselves were a first-rate holiday kind of dinner, suitable to one's wedding day, as something of that sort: meaning, if you can't get a spring chicken, any other trifle in the way of poultry will do – such as a Peacock, perhaps! The kitchen too, with its great broad cavernous chimney; the kitchen, where nothing in the way of cookery seemed impossible; where you could believe in anything to eat, they chose to tell you of. Mrs Varden returned from the contemplation of these wonders to the bar again, with a head quite dizzy and bewildered. Her housekeeping capacity was not large enough to comprehend them. She was obliged to go to sleep. Waking was pain, in the midst of such immensity.

Dolly in the meanwhile, whose gay heart and head ran upon other matters, passed out at the garden door, and glancing back now and then (but of course not wondering whether Joe saw her), tripped away by a path across the fields with which she was well acquainted, to discharge her mission at the Warren; and this deponent hath been informed and verily believes,[5] that you might have seen many less pleasant objects than the cherry-coloured mantle and ribbons, as they went fluttering along the green meadows in the bright light of the day, like giddy things as they were.

CHAPTER THE TWENTIETH

The proud consciousness of her trust, and the great importance she derived from it, might have advertised it to all the house if she had had to run the gauntlet of its inhabitants; but as Dolly had played in every dull room and passage many and many a time, when a child, and had ever since been the humble friend of Miss Haredale, whose foster-sister she was, she was as free of the building as the young lady herself. So, using no greater precaution than holding her breath and walking on tiptoe as she passed the library door, she went straight to Emma's room as a privileged visitor.

It was the liveliest room in the building. The chamber was sombre like the rest for the matter of that, but the presence of youth and beauty would make a prison cheerful (saving alas! that confinement withers them), and lend some charms of their own to the gloomiest scene. Birds, flowers, books, drawing, music, and a hundred such graceful tokens of feminine loves and cares, filled it with more of life and human sympathy than the whole house besides seemed made to hold. There was heart in the room; and who that has a heart, ever fails to recognize the silent presence of another!

Dolly had one undoubtedly, and it was not a tough one either,

though there was a little mist of coquettishness about it, such as
sometimes surrounds that sun of life in its morning, and slightly
dims its lustre. Thus, when Emma rose to greet her, and kissing her
affectionately on the cheek, told her in her quiet way, that she had
been very unhappy, the tears stood in Dolly's eyes, and she felt
more sorry than she could tell; but next moment she happened
to raise them to the glass, and really there was something there
so exceedingly agreeable, that as she sighed, she smiled, and felt
surprisingly consoled.

'I have heard about it Miss,' said Dolly, 'and it's very sad indeed,
but when things are at the worst they are sure to mend.'

'But are you sure they are at the worst?' asked Emma with a
smile.

'Why, I don't see how they can very well be more unpromising
than they are; I really don't,' said Dolly. 'And I bring something to
begin with.'

'Not from Edward?'

Dolly nodded and smiled, and feeling in her pockets (there were
pockets in those days) with an affectation of not being able to find
what she wanted, which greatly enhanced her importance, at length
produced the letter. As Emma hastily broke the seal and became
absorbed in its contents, Dolly's eyes, by one of those strange
accidents for which there is no accounting, wandered to the glass
again. She could not help wondering whether the coachmaker
suffered very much, and quite pitied the poor man.

It was a long letter – a very long letter, written close on all four
sides of the sheet of paper, and crossed afterwards;[1] but it was not
a consolatory letter, for as Emma read it she stopped from time to
time to put her handkerchief to her eyes. To be sure Dolly marvelled
greatly to see her in so much distress, for to her thinking a love
affair ought to be one of the best jokes, and the slyest, merriest
kind of thing in life. But she set it down in her own mind that all
this came from Miss Haredale's being so constant, and that if she
would only take on with some other young gentleman – just in the
most innocent way possible, to keep her first lover up to the mark
– she would find herself inexpressibly comforted.

'I am sure that's what I should do if it was me,' thought Dolly.
'To make one's sweethearts miserable is well enough and quite
right, but to be made miserable one's self is a little too much!'

However it wouldn't do to say so, and therefore she sat looking

on in silence. She needed a pretty considerable stretch of patience, for when the long letter had been read once all through it was read again, and when it had been read twice all through it was read again. During this tedious process, Dolly beguiled the time in the most improving manner that occurred to her, by curling her hair on her fingers, with the aid of the looking-glass before mentioned, and giving it some killing twists.

Everything has an end. Even young ladies in love cannot read their letters for ever. In course of time the packet was folded up, and it only remained to write the answer.

But as this promised to be a work of time likewise, Emma said she would put it off until after dinner, and that Dolly must dine with her. As Dolly had made up her mind to do so beforehand, she required very little pressing; and when they had settled this point, they went to walk in the garden.

They strolled up and down the terrace walks, talking incessantly – at least, Dolly never left off once – and making that quarter of the sad and mournful house quite gay. Not that they talked loudly or laughed much, but they were both so very handsome, and it was such a breezy day, and their light dresses and dark curls appeared so free and joyous in their abandonment, and Emma was so fair, and Dolly so rosy, and Emma so delicately shaped, and Dolly so plump, and – in short, there are no flowers for any garden like such flowers, let horticulturists say what they may, and both house and garden seemed to know it, and to brighten up sensibly.

After this, came the dinner and the letter writing, and some more talking, in the course of which Miss Haredale took occasion to charge upon Dolly certain flirtish and inconstant propensities, which accusations Dolly seemed to think very complimentary indeed, and to be mightily amused with. Finding her quite incorrigible in this respect, Emma suffered her to depart; but not before she had confided to her that important and never-sufficiently-to-be-taken-care-of answer, and endowed her moreover with a pretty little bracelet as a keepsake. Having clasped it on her arm, and again advised her half in jest and half in earnest to amend her roguish ways, for she knew she was fond of Joe at heart (which Dolly stoutly denied, with a great many haughty protestations that she hoped she could do better than that indeed! and so forth), she bade her farewell; and after calling her back to give her more supplementary messages for Edward, than anybody with tenfold the gravity of Dolly Varden could be reasonably expected to remember, at length dismissed her.

Dolly bade her good bye, and tripping lightly down the stairs arrived at the dreaded library door, and was about to pass it again on tiptoe, when it opened, and behold! there stood Mr Haredale. Now, Dolly had from her childhood associated with this gentleman the idea of something grim and ghostly, and being at the moment conscience-stricken besides, the sight of him threw her into such a flurry that she could neither acknowledge his presence nor run away, so she gave a great start, and then with downcast eyes stood still and trembled.

'Come here, girl,' said Mr Haredale, taking her by the hand. 'I want to speak to you.'

'If you please sir, I'm in a hurry,' faltered Dolly, 'and – and you have frightened me by coming so suddenly upon me sir – I would rather go sir, if you'll be so good as to let me.'

'Immediately,' said Mr Haredale, who had by this time led her into the room and closed the door. 'You shall go directly. You have just left Emma?'

'Yes sir, just this minute. – Father's waiting for me sir, if you'll please to have the goodness —'

'I know. I know,' said Mr Haredale. 'Answer me a question. What did you bring here to-day?'

'Bring here, sir?' faltered Dolly.

'You will tell me the truth, I am sure. Yes.'

Dolly hesitated for a little while, and somewhat emboldened by his manner, said at last, 'Well then sir. It was a letter.'

'From Mr Edward Chester, of course. And you are the bearer of the answer?'

Dolly hesitated again, and not being able to decide upon any other course of action, burst into tears.

'You alarm yourself without cause,' said Mr Haredale. 'Why are you so foolish? Surely you can answer me. You know that I have but to put the question to Emma and learn the truth directly. Have you the answer with you?'

Dolly had what is popularly called a spirit of her own, and being now fairly at bay, made the best of it.

'Yes sir,' she rejoined, trembling and frightened as she was. 'Yes sir, I have. You may kill me if you please sir, but I won't give it up. I'm very sorry, – but I won't. There sir.'

'I commend your firmness, and your plain-speaking,' said Mr Haredale. 'Rest assured that I have as little desire to take your letter as your life. You are a very discreet messenger and a good girl.'

Not feeling quite certain, as she afterwards said, whether he might not be 'coming over her' with these compliments, Dolly kept as far from him as she could, cried again, and resolved to defend her pocket (for the letter was there) to the last extremity.

'I have some design,' said Mr Haredale after a short silence, during which a smile, as he regarded her, had struggled through the gloom and melancholy that was natural to his face, 'of providing a companion for my niece; for her life is a very lonely one. Would you like the office? You are the oldest friend she has, and the best entitled to it.'

'I don't know sir,' answered Dolly, not sure but he was bantering her; 'I can't say. I don't know what they might wish at home. I couldn't give an opinion sir.'

'If your friends had no objection, would you have any?' said Mr Haredale. 'Come. There's a plain question; and easy to answer.'

'None at all that I know of sir,' replied Dolly. 'I should be very glad to be near Miss Emma of course, and always am.'

'That's well,' said Mr Haredale. 'That is all I had to say. You are anxious to go. Don't let me detain you.'

Dolly didn't let him, nor did she wait for him to try, for the words had no sooner passed his lips than she was out of the room, out of the house, and in the fields again.

The first thing to be done, of course, when she came to herself and considered what a flurry she had been in, was to cry afresh; and the next thing, when she reflected how well she had got over it, was to laugh heartily. The tears once banished gave place to the smiles, and at last Dolly laughed so much that she was fain to lean against a tree, and give vent to her exultation. When she could laugh no longer, and was quite tired, she put her head-dress to rights, dried her eyes, looked back very merrily and triumphantly at the Warren chimneys, which were just visible, and resumed her walk.

The twilight had come on, and it was quickly growing dusk, but the path was so familiar to her from frequent traversing that she hardly thought of this, and certainly felt no uneasiness at being alone. Moreover, there was the bracelet to admire; and when she had given it a good rub, and held it out at arm's length, it sparkled and glittered so beautifully on her wrist, that to look at it in every point of view and with every possible turn of the arm, was quite an absorbing business. There was the letter, too, and it looked so mysterious and knowing, when she took it out of her pocket, and it held, as she knew, so much inside, that to turn it over and over, and think about it, and wonder how it began, and how it ended, and what it said all through, was another matter of constant occupation. Between the bracelet and the letter, there was quite enough to do without thinking of anything else; and admiring each by turns, Dolly went on gaily.

As she passed through a wicket gate to where the path was narrow, and lay between two hedges garnished here and there with trees, she heard a rustling close at hand, which brought her to a sudden stop. She listened. All was very quiet, and she went on again – not absolutely frightened, but a little quicker than before perhaps, and possibly not quite so much at her ease, for a check of that kind is startling.

She had no sooner moved on again, than she was conscious of the same sound, which was like that of a person tramping stealthily among bushes and brushwood. Looking towards the spot whence it appeared to come, she almost fancied she could make out a crouching figure. She stopped again. All was quiet as before. On she went once more – decidedly faster now – and tried to sing softly to herself. It must be the wind.

But how came the wind to blow only when she walked, and cease when she stood still? She stopped involuntarily as she made the reflection, and the rustling noise stopped likewise. She was really frightened now, and was yet hesitating what to do, when the bushes crackled and snapped, and a man came plunging through them, close before her.

*

CHAPTER THE TWENTY-FIRST

It was for the moment an inexpressible relief to Dolly, to recognize in the person who forced himself into the path so abruptly, and now stood directly in her way, Hugh of the Maypole, whose name she uttered in a tone of delighted surprise that came from her heart.

'Was it you?' she said, 'how glad I am to see you! and how could you terrify me so!'

In answer to which, he said nothing at all, but stood quite still, looking at her.

'Did you come to meet me?' asked Dolly.

Hugh nodded, and muttered something to the effect that he had been waiting for her, and had expected her sooner.

'I thought it likely they would send,' said Dolly, greatly re-assured by this.

'Nobody sent me,' was his sullen answer. 'I came of my own accord.'

The rough bearing of this fellow, and his wild, uncouth appearance, had often filled the girl with a vague apprehension even when other people were by, and had occasioned her to shrink from him involuntarily. The having him for an unbidden companion in so solitary a place, with the darkness fast gathering about them, renewed and even increased the alarm she had felt at first.

If his manner had been merely dogged and passively fierce, as usual, she would have had no greater dislike to his company than she always felt – perhaps, indeed, would have been rather glad to have had him at hand. But there was something of coarse bold admiration in his look, which terrified her very much. She glanced timidly towards him, uncertain whether to go forward or retreat, and he stood gazing at her like a handsome satyr; and so they remained for some short time without stirring or breaking silence. At length Dolly took courage, shot past him, and hurried on.

'Why do you spend so much breath in avoiding me?' said Hugh, accommodating his pace to hers, and keeping close at her side.

'I wish to get back as quickly as I can, and you walk too near me,' answered Dolly.

'Too near!' said Hugh, stooping over her so that she could feel his breath upon her forehead. 'Why too near? You're always proud to *me*, mistress.'

'I am proud to no one. You mistake me,' answered Dolly. 'Fall back, if you please, or go on.'

'Nay, mistress,' he rejoined, endeavouring to draw her arm through his. 'I'll walk with you.'

She released herself, and clenching her little hand, struck him with right good will. At this, Maypole Hugh burst into a roar of

laughter, and passing his arm about her waist, held her in his strong grasp as easily as if she had been a bird.

'Ha ha ha! Well done mistress! Strike again. You shall beat my face, and tear my hair, and pluck my beard up by the roots, and welcome, for the sake of your bright eyes. Strike again mistress. Do. Ha ha ha! I like it.'

'Let me go,' she cried, endeavouring with both her hands to push him off. 'Let me go this moment.'

'You had as good be kinder to me, Sweetlips,' said Hugh. 'You had, indeed. Come. Tell me now. Why are you always so proud? I don't quarrel with you for it. I love you when you're proud. Ha ha ha! You can't hide your beauty from a poor fellow; that's a comfort!'

She gave him no answer, but as he had not yet checked her progress, continued to press forward as rapidly as she could. At length, between the hurry she had made, her terror, and the tightness of his embrace, her strength failed her, and she could go no further.

'Hugh,' cried the panting girl, 'good Hugh; if you will leave me I will give you anything – everything I have – and never tell one word of this to any living creature.'

'You had best not,' he answered. 'Harkye, little dove, you had best not. All about here know me, and what I dare do if I have a mind. If ever you are going to tell, stop when the words are on your lips, and think of the mischief you'll bring, if you do, upon some innocent heads that you wouldn't wish to hurt a hair of. Bring trouble on me, and I'll bring trouble and something more on them in return. I care no more for them than for so many dogs; not so much – why should I? I'd sooner kill a man than a dog any day. I've never been sorry for a man's death in all my life, and I have for a dog's.'

There was something so thoroughly savage in the manner of these expressions, and the looks and gestures by which they were accompanied, that her great fear of him gave her new strength, and enabled her by a sudden effort to extricate herself and run fleetly from him. But Hugh was as nimble, strong, and swift of foot, as any man in broad England, and it was but a fruitless expenditure of energy, for he had her in his encircling arms again before she had gone a hundred yards.

'Softly, darling – gently – would you fly from rough Hugh, that loves you as well as any drawing-room gallant?'

'I would,' she answered, struggling to free herself again. 'I will. Help!'

'A fine for crying out,' said Hugh. 'Ha ha ha! A fine, pretty one, from your lips. I pay myself! Ha ha ha!'

'Help! Help! Help!' As she shrieked with the utmost violence she could exert, a shout was heard in answer, and another, and another.

'Thank Heaven!' cried the girl in an ecstacy. 'Joe, dear Joe, this way. Help!'

Her assailant paused, and stood irresolute for a moment, but the shouts drawing nearer and coming quick upon them, forced him to a speedy decision. He released her, whispered with a menacing look, 'Tell *him;* and see what follows!' and leaping the hedge, was gone in an instant. Dolly darted off, and fairly ran into Joe Willet's open arms.

'What is the matter? are you hurt? what was it? who was it? where is he? what was he like?' with a great many encouraging expressions and assurances of safety, were the first words Joe poured forth. But poor little Dolly was so breathless and terrified, that for some time she was quite unable to answer him, and hung upon his shoulder, sobbing and crying as if her heart would break.

Joe had not the smallest objection to have her hanging on his shoulder; no, not the least, though it crushed the cherry-coloured ribbons sadly, and put the smart little hat out of all shape. But he couldn't bear to see her cry; it went to his very heart. He tried to console her, bent over her, whispered to her – some say kissed her, but that's a fable. At any rate he said all the kind and tender things he could think of, and Dolly let him go on and didn't interrupt him once, and it was a good ten minutes before she was able to raise her head and thank him.

'What was it that frightened you?' said Joe.

A man whose person was unknown to her had followed her, she answered; he began by begging, and went on to threats of robbery, which he was on the point of carrying into execution, and would have executed, but for Joe's timely aid. The hesitation and confusion with which she said this, Joe attributed to the fright she had sustained, and no suspicion of the truth occurred to him for a moment.

'Stop when the words are on your lips.' A hundred times that night, and very often afterwards, when the disclosure was rising to her tongue, Dolly thought of that, and repressed it. A deeply rooted dread of the man; the conviction that his ferocious nature, once roused, would stop at nothing; and the strong assurance that if she impeached him, the full measure of his wrath and vengeance would be wreaked on Joe, who had preserved her; these were considerations she had not the courage to overcome, and inducements to secrecy too powerful for her to surmount.

Joe, for his part, was a great deal too happy to inquire very curiously into the matter; and Dolly being yet too tremulous to walk without assistance, they went forward very slowly, and in his mind very pleasantly, until the Maypole lights were near at hand, twinkling their cheerful welcome, when Dolly stopped suddenly and with a half scream exclaimed,

'The letter!'

'What letter?' cried Joe.

'That I was carrying – I had it in my hand. My bracelet too,' she said, clasping her wrist. 'I have lost them both.'

'Do you mean just now?' said Joe.

'Either I dropped them then, or they were taken from me,' answered Dolly, vainly searching her pocket and rustling her dress. 'They are gone, both gone. What an unhappy girl I am!' With these words poor Dolly, who to do her justice was quite as sorry for the loss of the letter as for her bracelet, fell a crying again, and bemoaned her fate most movingly.

Joe tried to comfort her with the assurance that directly he had housed her safely in the Maypole, he would return to the spot with a lantern (for it was now quite dark) and make strict search for the missing articles, which there was great probability of his finding, as it was not likely that anybody had passed that way since, and she was not conscious of their having been forcibly taken from her. Dolly thanked him very heartily for this offer, though with no great hope of his quest being successful; and so, with many lamentations on her side, and many hopeful words on his, and much weakness on the part of Dolly and much tender supporting on the part of Joe, they reached the Maypole bar at last, where the locksmith and his wife and old John were yet keeping high festival.

Mr Willet received the intelligence of Dolly's trouble with that surprising presence of mind and readiness of speech for which he was so eminently distinguished above all other men. Mrs Varden expressed her sympathy for her daughter's distress by scolding her roundly for being so late; and the honest locksmith divided himself between condoling with and kissing Dolly, and shaking hands heartily with Joe, whom he could not sufficiently praise or thank.

In reference to this latter point, old John was far from agreeing with his friend; for besides that he by no means approved of an adventurous spirit in the abstract, it occurred to him that if his son and heir had been seriously damaged in a scuffle, the consequences would assuredly have been expensive and inconvenient, and might perhaps have proved detrimental to the Maypole business. Wherefore, and because he looked with no favourable eye upon young girls, but rather considered that they and the whole female sex were a kind of nonsensical mistake on the part of Nature, he took occasion to retire and shake his head in private at the boiler; inspired by which silent oracle, he was moved to give Joe various stealthy nudges with his elbow, as a parental reproof and gentle admonition to mind his own business and not make a fool of himself.

Joe, however, took down the lantern and lighted it; and arming himself with a stout stick, asked whether Hugh was in the stable.

'He's lying asleep before the kitchen fire, sir,' said Mr Willet. 'What do you want with him?'

'I want him to come with me to look after this bracelet and letter,' answered Joe. 'Halloa there! Hugh!'

Dolly turned pale as death, and felt as if she must faint forthwith. After a few moments, Hugh came staggering in, stretching himself and yawning according to custom, and presenting every appearance of having been roused from a sound nap.

'Here, sleepy-head,' said Joe, giving him the lantern. 'Carry this, and bring the dog, and that small cudgel of yours. And woe betide the fellow if we come upon him.'

'What fellow?' growled Hugh, rubbing his eyes and shaking himself.

'What fellow!' returned Joe, who was in a state of a great valour and bustle; 'a fellow you ought to know of, and be more alive about. It's well for the like of you, lazy giant that you are, to be snoring your time away in chimney-corners, when honest men's daughters can't cross even our quiet meadows at nightfall without being set upon by footpads, and frightened out of their precious lives.'

'They never rob me,' cried Hugh with a laugh. 'I have got nothing to lose. But I'd as lief knock them at head as any other men. How many are there?'

'Only one,' said Dolly faintly, for everybody looked at her.

'And what was he like, mistress?' said Hugh with a glance at young Willet, so slight and momentary that the scowl it conveyed was lost on all but her. 'About my height?'

'Not – not so tall,' Dolly replied, scarce knowing what she said.

'His dress,' said Hugh, looking at her keenly, 'like – like any of ours now? I know all the people hereabouts, and maybe could give a guess at the man, if I had anything to guide me.'

Dolly faltered and turned paler yet; then answered that he was wrapped in a loose coat and had his face hidden by a handkerchief, and that she could give no other description of him.

'You wouldn't know him if you saw him then, belike?' said Hugh with a malicious grin.

'I should not,' answered Dolly, bursting into tears again. 'I don't wish to see him. I can't bear to think of him. I can't talk about him any more. Don't go to look for these things, Mr Joe, pray don't. I entreat you not to go with that man.'

'Not to go with me!' cried Hugh. 'I'm too rough for them all. They're all afraid of me. Why, bless you mistress, I've the tenderest heart alive. I love all the ladies ma'am,' said Hugh, turning to the locksmith's wife.

Mrs Varden opined that if he did, he ought to be ashamed of himself; such sentiments being more consistent (so she argued) with a benighted Mussulman or wild Islander than with a stanch Protestant. Arguing from this imperfect state of his morals, Mrs Varden further opined that he had never studied the Manual. Hugh admitting that he never had, and moreover that he couldn't read, Mrs Varden declared with much severity, that he ought to be even more ashamed of himself than before, and strongly recommended him to save up his pocket-money for the purchase of one, and further to teach himself the contents with all convenient diligence. She was still pursuing this train of discourse, when Hugh, somewhat unceremoniously and irreverently, followed his young master out, and left her to edify the rest of the company. This she proceeded to do, and finding that Mr Willet's eyes were fixed upon her with an appearance of deep attention, gradually addressed the whole of her discourse to him, whom she entertained with a moral and theological lecture of considerable length, in the conviction that great workings were taking place in his spirit. The simple truth was, however, that Mr Willet, although his eyes were wide open and he saw a woman before him whose head by long and steady looking at seemed to grow bigger and bigger until it filled the whole bar, was to all other intents and purposes fast asleep; and so sat leaning back in his chair with his hands in his pockets until his son's return caused him to wake up with a deep sigh, and a faint impression that he had been dreaming about pickled pork and greens – a vision of his slumbers which was no doubt referable to the circumstance of Mrs Varden's having frequently pronounced the word 'Grace' with much emphasis; which word, entering the portals of Mr Willet's brain as they stood ajar, and coupling itself with the words 'before meat,' which were there ranging about, did in time suggest a particular kind of meat together with that description of vegetable which is usually its companion.

The search was wholly unsuccessful. Joe had groped along the path a dozen times, and among the grass, and in the dry ditch, and in the hedge, but all in vain. Dolly, who was quite inconsolable for her loss, wrote a note to Miss Haredale giving her the same account of it that she had given at the Maypole, which Joe undertook to deliver as soon as the family were stirring next day. That done, they sat down to tea in the bar, where there was an uncommon display of buttered toast, and – in order that they might not grow faint for want of sustenance, and might have a decent halting-place or half-way house between dinner and supper – a few savoury trifles in the shape of great rashers of broiled ham, which being well cured, done to a turn, and smoking hot, sent forth a tempting and delicious fragrance.

Mrs Varden was seldom very Protestant at meals, unless it happened that they were under-done, or over-done, or indeed that anything occurred to put her out of humour. Her spirits rose considerably on beholding these goodly preparations, and from the nothingness of good works,[1] she passed to the somethingness of ham and toast with great cheerfulness. Nay, under the influence of these wholesome stimulants, she sharply reproved her daughter for being low and despondent (which she considered an unacceptable frame of mind) and remarked, as she held her own plate for a fresh supply, that it would be well for Dolly who pined over the loss of a toy and a sheet of paper, if she would reflect upon the voluntary sacrifices of the missionaries in foreign parts who lived chiefly on salads.

The proceedings of such a day occasion various fluctuations in the human thermometer, and especially in instruments so sensitively and delicately constructed as Mrs Varden. Thus, at dinner Mrs V. stood at summer heat; genial, smiling, and delightful. After dinner, in the sunshine of the wine, she went up at least half-a-dozen degrees, and was perfectly enchanting. As its effect subsided, she fell rapidly, went to sleep for an hour or so at temperate, and woke at something below freezing. Now she was at summer heat again, in the shade; and when tea was over, and old John, producing a bottle of cordial from one of the oaken cases, insisted on her sipping two glasses thereof in slow succession, she stood steadily at ninety for one hour and a quarter. Profiting by experience, the locksmith took advantage of this genial weather to smoke his pipe in the porch, and in consequence of this prudent management, he was fully prepared, when the glass went down again, to start homewards directly.

The horse was accordingly put in, and the chaise brought round to the door. Joe, who would on no account be dissuaded from escorting them until they had passed the most dreary and solitary part of the road, led out the grey mare at the same time; and having helped Dolly into her seat (more happiness!) sprung gaily into the saddle. Then, after many good nights, and admonitions to wrap up, and glancing of lights, and handing in of cloaks and shawls, the chaise rolled away, and Joe trotted beside it – on Dolly's side, no doubt, and pretty close to the wheel too.

CHAPTER THE TWENTY-SECOND

It was a fine bright night, and for all her lowness of spirits Dolly kept looking up at the stars in a manner so bewitching (and *she* knew it!) that Joe was clean out of his senses, and plainly showed that if ever a man were – not to say over head and ears, but over the Monument and the top of Saint Paul's[1] in love, that man was himself. The road was a very good one; not at all a jolting road, or an uneven one; and yet Dolly held the side of the chaise with one little hand, all the way. If there had been an executioner behind him with an uplifted axe ready to chop off his head if he touched that hand, Joe couldn't have helped doing it. From putting his own hand upon it as if by chance, and taking it away again after a minute or so, he got to riding along without taking it off at all; as if he, the escort, were bound to do that as an important part of his duty, and had come out for the purpose. The most curious circumstance about this little incident was, that Dolly didn't seem to know of it. She looked so innocent and unconscious when she turned her eyes on Joe, that it was quite provoking.

She talked though; talked about her fright, and about Joe's coming up to rescue her, and about her gratitude, and about her fear that she might not have thanked him enough, and about their always being friends from that time forth – and about all that sort of thing. And when Joe said, not friends he hoped, Dolly was quite surprised, and said not enemies she hoped; and when Joe said, couldn't they be something much better than either, Dolly all of a sudden found out a star which was brighter than all the other stars, and begged to call his attention to the same, and was ten thousand times more innocent and unconscious than ever.

In this manner they travelled along, talking very little above a whisper, and wishing the road could be stretched out to some dozen times its natural length – at least that was Joe's desire – when, as they were getting clear of the forest and emerging on the more frequented road, they heard behind them the sound of a horse's feet at a round trot, which growing rapidly louder as it drew nearer, elicited a scream from Mrs Varden, and the cry 'a friend!' from the rider, who now came panting up, and checked his horse beside them.

'This man again!' cried Dolly, shuddering.

'Hugh!' said Joe. 'What errand are you upon?'

'I come to ride back with you,' he answered, glancing covertly at the locksmith's daughter. '*He* sent me.'

'My father!' said poor Joe; adding under his breath, with a very unfilial apostrophe, 'Will he never think me man enough to take care of myself!'

'Ay!' returned Hugh to the first part of the inquiry. 'The roads are not safe just now he says, and you'd better have a companion.'

'Ride on then,' said Joe. 'I'm not going to turn yet.'

Hugh complied, and they went on again. It was his whim or humour to ride immediately before the chaise, and from this position he constantly turned his head, and looked back. Dolly felt that he looked at her, but she averted her eyes and feared to raise them once, so great was the dread with which he had inspired her.

This interruption, and the consequent wakefulness of Mrs Varden, who had been nodding in her sleep up to this point, except for a minute or two at a time, when she roused herself to scold the locksmith for audaciously taking hold of her to prevent her nodding herself out of the chaise, put a restraint upon the whispered conversation, and made it difficult of resumption. Indeed, before they had gone another mile, Gabriel stopped at his wife's desire, and that good lady protested she would not hear of Joe's going a step further on any account whatever. It was in vain for Joe to protest on the other hand that he was by no means tired, and would turn back presently, and would see them safely past such and such a point, and so forth. Mrs Varden was obdurate, and being so was not to be overcome by mortal agency.

'Good night – if I must say it,' said Joe, sorrowfully.

'Good night,' said Dolly. She would have added, 'Take care of that man, and pray don't trust him,' but he had turned his horse's head, and was standing close to them. She had therefore nothing for it but to suffer Joe to give her hand a gentle squeeze, and when the chaise had gone on for some distance, to look back and wave it, as he still lingered on the spot where they had parted, with the tall dark figure of Hugh beside him.

What she thought about, going home; and whether the coachmaker held as favourable a place in her meditations as he had occupied in the morning, is unknown. They reached home at last – at last, for it was a long way, made none the shorter by Mrs Varden's grumbling. Miggs hearing the sound of wheels was at the door immediately.

'Here they are, Simmun! Here they are!' cried Miggs, clapping her hands, and issuing forth to help her mistress to alight. 'Bring a chair, Simmun. Now, an't you the better for it, mim? Don't you feel more yourself than you would have done if you'd have stopped at home? Oh, gracious! how cold you are! Goodness me, sir, she's a perfect heap of ice.'

'I can't help it, my good girl. You had better take her in to the fire,' said the locksmith.

'Master sounds unfeeling, mim,' said Miggs, in a tone of commiseration, 'but such is not his intentions, I'm sure. After what he has seen of you this day, I never will believe but that he has a deal more affection in his heart than to speak unkind. Come in and sit yourself down by the fire; there's a good dear – do.'

Mrs Varden complied. The locksmith followed with his hands in his pockets, and Mr Tappertit trundled off with the chaise to a neighbouring stable.

'Martha, my dear,' said the locksmith, when they reached the parlour, 'if you'll look to Dolly yourself, or let somebody else do it, perhaps it will be only kind and reasonable. She has been frightened, you know, and is not at all well to-night.'

In fact, Dolly had thrown herself upon the sofa, quite regardless of all the little finery of which she had been so proud in the morning, and with her face buried in her hands was crying very much.

At first sight of this phenomenon (for Dolly was by no means accustomed to displays of this sort, rather learning from her mother's example to avoid them as much as possible) Mrs Varden expressed her belief that never was any woman so beset as she; that her life was a continued scene of trial; that whenever she was disposed to be well and cheerful, so sure were the people around her to throw, by some means or other, a damp upon her spirits; and that, as she had enjoyed herself that day, and Heaven knew it was very seldom she did enjoy herself, so she was now to pay the penalty. To all such propositions Miggs assented freely. Poor Dolly, however, grew none the better for these restoratives, but rather worse, indeed; and seeing that she was really ill, both Mrs Varden and Miggs were moved to compassion, and tended her in earnest.

But even then, their very kindness shaped itself into their usual course of policy, and though Dolly was in a swoon, it was rendered clear to the meanest capacity, that Mrs Varden was the sufferer. Thus when Dolly began to get a little better, and passed into that stage in which matrons hold that remonstrance and argument may be successfully applied, her mother represented to her, with tears in her eyes, that if she had been flurried and worried that day, she must remember it was the common lot of humanity, and in especial of womankind, who through the whole of their existence must expect no less, and were bound to make up their minds to meek endurance and patient resignation. Mrs Varden entreated her to remember that one of these days she would, in all probability, have to do violence to her feelings so far as to be married; and that marriage, as she might see every day of her life (and truly she did) was a state requiring great fortitude and forbearance. She represented to her in lively colours, that if she (Mrs V.) had not, in steering her course through this vale of tears, been supported by a strong principle of duty which alone upheld and prevented her from drooping, she must have been in her grave many years ago; in which case she desired to know what would have become of that errant spirit (meaning the locksmith), of whose eye she was the very apple, and in whose path she was, as it were, a shining light[2] and guiding star?

Miss Miggs also put in her word to the same effect. She said that indeed and indeed Miss Dolly might take pattern by her blessed mother, who, she always had said, and always would say, though she were to be hanged, drawn, and quartered for it next minute, was the mildest, amiablest, forgivingest-spirited, longest-sufferingest female as ever she could have believed; the mere narration of whose excellencies had worked such a wholesome change in the mind of her own sister-in-law, that, whereas, before, she and her husband lived like cat and dog, and were in the habit of exchanging brass candlesticks, pot-lids, flat-irons, and other such strong resentments, they were now the happiest and affectionatest couple upon earth; as could be proved any day on application at Golden Lion Court, number twenty-sivin, second bell-handle on the right-hand door-post. After glancing at herself as a comparatively worthless vessel, but still as one of some desert, she besought her to bear in mind that her aforesaid dear and only mother was of a weakly consti-tution and excitable temperament, who had constantly to sustain afflictions in domestic life, compared with which thieves and robbers were as nothing, and yet never sunk down or gave way to despair or wrath, but, in prize-fighting phraseology, always came up to time with a cheerful countenance, and went in to win as if nothing had happened. When Miggs had finished her solo, her mistress struck in again, and the two together performed a duet to the same purpose; the burden being, that Mrs Varden was per-secuted perfection, and Mr Varden, as the representative of man-kind in that apartment, a creature of vicious and brutal habits, utterly insensible to the blessings he enjoyed. Of so refined a charac-ter, indeed, was their talent of assault under the mask of sympathy, that when Dolly, recovering, embraced her father tenderly, as in vindication of his goodness, Mrs Varden expressed her solemn hope that this would be a lesson to him for the remainder of his life, and that he would do some little justice to a woman's nature ever afterwards – in which aspiration Miss Miggs, by divers sniffs and coughs, more significant than the longest oration, expressed her entire concurrence.

But the great joy of Miggs's heart was, that she not only picked up a full account of what had happened, but had the exquisite delight of conveying it to Mr Tappertit for his jealousy and torture. For that gentleman, on account of Dolly's indisposition, had been requested to take his supper in the workshop, and it was conveyed thither by Miss Miggs's own fair hands.

'Oh, Simmun!' said the young lady, 'such goings on to-day! Oh, gracious me, Simmun!'

Mr Tappertit, who was not in the best of humours, and who disliked Miss Miggs more when she laid her hand on her heart and panted for breath than at any other time, as her deficiency of outline was most apparent under such circumstances, eyed her over in his loftiest style, and deigned to express no curiosity whatever.

'I never heard the like, nor nobody else,' pursued Miggs. 'The idea of interfering with *her*. What people can see in her to make it worth their while to do so, that's the joke – he, he, he!'

Finding there was a lady in the case, Mr Tappertit haughtily requested his fair friend to be more explicit, and demanded to know what she meant by 'her.'

'Why, that Dolly,' said Miggs, with an extremely sharp emphasis on the name. 'But, oh upon my word and honour, young Joseph Willet is a brave one; and he do deserve her, that he do.'

'Woman!' said Mr Tappertit, jumping off the counter on which he was seated; 'beware!'

'My stars, Simmun!' cried Miggs, in affected astonishment. 'You frighten me to death! What's the matter?'

'There are strings,' said Mr Tappertit, flourishing his bread-and-cheese knife in the air, 'in the human heart that had better not be wibrated. That's what's the matter.'

'Oh, very well – if you're in a huff,' cried Miggs, turning away.

'Huff or no huff,' said Mr Tappertit, detaining her by the wrist. 'What do you mean, Jezebel?[3] What were you going to say? Answer me!'

Notwithstanding this uncivil exhortation, Miggs gladly did as she was required; and told him how that their young mistress, being

alone in the meadows after dark, had been attacked by three or
four tall men, who would have certainly borne her away and
perhaps murdered her, but for the timely arrival of Joseph Willet,
who with his own single hand put them all to flight, and rescued
her; to the lasting admiration of his fellow-creatures generally, and
to the eternal love and gratitude of Dolly Varden.

'Very good,' said Mr Tappertit, fetching a long breath when the
tale was told, and rubbing his hair up till it stood stiff and straight
on end all over his head. 'His days are numbered.'

'Oh, Simmun!'

'I tell you,' said the 'prentice, 'his days are numbered. Leave me.
Get along with you.'

Miggs departed at his bidding, but less because of his bidding
than because she desired to chuckle in secret. When she had given
vent to her satisfaction, she returned to the parlour; where the
locksmith, stimulated by quietness and Toby, had become talkative,
and was disposed to take a cheerful review of the occurrences
of the day. But Mrs Varden, whose practical religion (as is not
uncommon) was usually of the retrospective order, cut him short
by declaiming on the sinfulness of such junkettings, and holding
that it was high time to go to bed. To bed therefore she withdrew,
with an aspect as grim and gloomy as that of the Maypole's own
state couch; and to bed the rest of the establishment soon afterwards
repaired.

—— * ——

CHAPTER THE TWENTY-THIRD

Twilight had given place to night some hours, and it was high noon
in those quarters of the town in which 'the world' condescended to
dwell – the world being then, as now, of very limited dimensions
and easily lodged – when Mr Chester reclined upon a sofa in his
dressing-room in the Temple, entertaining himself with a book.

He was dressing, as it seemed, by easy stages, and having performed half the journey was taking a long rest. Completely attired
as to his legs and feet in the trimmest fashion of the day, he had yet
the remainder of his toilet to perform. The coat was stretched,
like a refined scarecrow, on its separate horse; the waistcoat was

displayed to the best advantage; the various ornamental articles of dress were severally set out in most alluring order; and yet he lay dangling his legs between the sofa and the ground, as intent upon his book as if there were nothing but bed before him.

'Upon my honour,' he said, at length raising his eyes to the ceiling with the air of a man who was reflecting seriously on what he had read; 'upon my honour, the most masterly composition, the most delicate thoughts, the finest code of morality, and the most gentlemanly sentiments in the universe! Ah Ned, Ned, if you would but form your mind by such precepts, we should have but one common feeling on every subject that could possibly arise between us!'

This apostrophe was addressed, like the rest of his remarks, to empty air: for Edward was not present, and the father was quite alone.

'My Lord Chesterfield,'[1] he said, pressing his hand tenderly upon the book as he laid it down, 'if I could but have profited by your genius soon enough to have formed my son on the model you have left to all wise fathers, both he and I would have been rich men. Shakspeare was undoubtedly very fine in his way; Milton good, though prosy; Lord Bacon deep, and decidedly knowing; but the writer who should be his country's pride, is my Lord Chesterfield.'

He became thoughtful again, and the toothpick was in requisition.

'I thought I was tolerably accomplished as a man of the world,' he continued, 'I flattered myself that I was pretty well versed in all those little arts and graces which distinguish men of the world from boors and peasants, and separate their character from those intensely vulgar sentiments which are called the national character. Apart from any natural prepossession in my own favour, I believed I was. Still, in every page of this enlightened writer, I find some captivating hypocrisy which has never occurred to me before, or some superlative piece of selfishness to which I was utterly a stranger. I should quite blush for myself before this stupendous creature, if, remembering his precepts, one might blush at anything. An amazing man! a nobleman indeed! any King or Queen may make a Lord, but only the Devil himself – and the Graces[2] – can make a Chesterfield.'

Men who are thoroughly false and hollow, seldom try to hide those vices from themselves; and yet in the very act of avowing them, they lay claim to the virtues they feign most to despise. 'For,' say they, 'this is honesty, this is truth. All mankind are like us, but they have not the candour to avow it.' The more they affect to deny the existence of any sincerity in the world, the more they would be thought to possess it in its boldest shape; and this is an unconscious compliment to Truth on the part of these philosophers, which will turn the laugh against them to the Day of Judgment.[3]

Mr Chester, having extolled his favourite author as above recited, took up the book again in the excess of his admiration and was composing himself for a further perusal of its sublime morality, when he was disturbed by a noise at the outer door; occasioned as it seemed by the endeavours of his servant to obstruct the entrance of some unwelcome visitor.

'A late hour for an importunate creditor,' he said, raising his eyebrows with as indolent an expression of wonder as if the noise were in the street, and one with which he had not the smallest personal concern. 'Much after their accustomed time. The usual pretence I suppose. No doubt a heavy payment to make up to-morrow. Poor fellow, he loses time, and time is money as the good proverb says – I never found it out though. Well. What now? You know I am not at home.'

'A man, Sir,' replied the servant, who was to the full as cool and negligent in his way as his master, 'has brought home the riding-whip you lost the other day. I told him you were out, but he said he was to wait while I brought it in, and wouldn't go till I did.'

'He was quite right,' returned his master, 'and you're a block-head, possessing no judgment or discretion whatever. Tell him to come in, and see that he rubs his shoes for exactly five minutes first.'

The man laid the whip on a chair, and withdrew. The master, who had only heard his foot upon the ground and had not taken the trouble to turn round and look at him, shut his book, and pursued the train of ideas his entrance had disturbed.

'If time were money,' he said, handling his snuff-box, 'I would compound with my creditors, and give them – let me see – how much a day? There's my nap after dinner – an hour – they're extremely welcome to that, and to make the most of it. In the morning, between my breakfast and the paper, I could spare them another hour; in the evening before dinner, say another. Three hours a day. They might pay themselves in calls, with interest, in twelve months. I think I shall propose it to them. Ah, my centaur, are you there?'

'Here I am,' replied Hugh, striding in, followed by a dog, as rough and sullen as himself; 'and trouble enough I've had to get here. What do you ask me to come for, and keep me out when I *do* come?'

'My good fellow,' returned the other, raising his head a little from the cushion and carelessly surveying him from top to toe, 'I am delighted to see you, and to have, in your being here, the very best proof that you are not kept out. How are you?'

'I'm well enough,' said Hugh impatiently.

'You look a perfect marvel of health. Sit down.'

'I'd rather stand,' said Hugh.

'Please yourself, my good fellow,' returned Mr Chester rising, slowly pulling off the loose robe he wore, and sitting down before the dressing-glass. 'Please yourself by all means.'

Having said this in the politest and blandest tone possible, he went on dressing, and took no further notice of his guest, who stood in the same spot as uncertain what to do next, eyeing him sulkily from time to time.

'Are you going to speak to me, master?' he said, after a long silence.

'My worthy creature,' returned Mr Chester, 'you are a little ruffled and out of humour. I'll wait till you're quite yourself again. I am in no hurry.'

This behaviour had its intended effect. It humbled and abashed the man, and made him still more irresolute and uncertain. Hard words he could have returned, violence he would have repaid with interest; but this cool, complacent, contemptuous, self-possessed reception, caused him to feel his inferiority more completely than the most elaborate arguments. Everything contributed to this effect. His own rough speech, contrasted with the soft persuasive accents of the other; his rude bearing, and Mr Chester's polished manner; the disorder and negligence of his ragged dress, and the elegant attire he saw before him; with all the unaccustomed luxuries and comforts of the room, and the silence that gave him leisure to observe these things, and feel how ill at ease they made him; all these influences, which have too often some effect on tutored minds and become of almost resistless power when brought to bear on such a mind as his, quelled Hugh completely. He moved by little and little nearer to Mr Chester's chair, and glancing over his shoulder at the reflection of his face in the glass, as if seeking for some encouragement in its expression, said at length, with a rough attempt at conciliation,

'*Are* you going to speak to me, master, or am I to go away?'

'Speak you,' said Mr Chester, 'speak you, good fellow. I have spoken, have I not? I am waiting for you.'

'Why, look'ee sir,' returned Hugh with increased embarrassment, 'am I the man that you privately left your whip with before you rode away from the Maypole, and told to bring it back whenever he might want to see you on a certain subject?'

'No doubt the same, or you have a twin brother,' said Mr Chester, glancing at the reflection of his anxious face; 'which is not probable, I should say.'

'Then I have come sir,' said Hugh, 'and I have brought it back, and something else along with it. A letter sir, it is, that I took from the person who had charge of it.' As he spoke, he laid upon the dressing-table, Dolly's lost epistle. The very letter that had cost her so much trouble.

'Did you obtain this by force, my good fellow?' said Mr Chester, casting his eye upon it without the least perceptible surprise or pleasure.

'Not quite,' said Hugh. 'Partly.'

'Who was the messenger from whom you took it?'

'A woman. One Varden's daughter.'

'Oh indeed!' said Mr Chester, gaily. 'What else did you take from her?'

'What else?'

'Yes,' said the other, in a drawling manner, for he was fixing a very small patch of sticking-plaster on a very small pimple near the corner of his mouth. 'What else?'

'Well – a kiss,' replied Hugh, after some hesitation.

'And what else?'

'Nothing.'

'I think,' said Mr Chester, in the same easy tone, and smiling twice or thrice to try if the patch adhered – 'I think there was something else. I have heard a trifle of jewellery spoken of – a mere trifle – a thing of such little value, indeed, that you may have forgotten it. Do you remember anything of the kind – such as a bracelet now, for instance?'

Hugh with a muttered oath thrust his hand into his breast, and drawing the bracelet forth, wrapped in a scrap of hay, was about to lay it on the table likewise, when his patron stopped his hand and bade him put it up again.

'You took that for yourself, my excellent friend,' he said, 'and may keep it. I am neither a thief, nor a receiver. Don't show it to me. You had better hide it again, and lose no time. Don't let me see where you put it either,' he added, turning away his head.

'You're not a receiver!' said Hugh bluntly, despite the increasing awe in which he held him. 'What do you call *that*, master?' striking the letter with his heavy hand.

'I call that quite another thing,' said Mr Chester coolly. 'I shall prove it presently, as you will see. You are thirsty, I suppose?'

Hugh drew his sleeve across his lips, and gruffly answered yes.

'Step to that closet, and bring me a bottle you will see there, and a glass.'

He obeyed. His patron followed him with his eyes, and when his back was turned, smiled as he had never done when he stood beside the mirror. On his return he filled the glass, and bade him drink. That dram despatched, he poured him out another, and another.

'How many can you bear?' he said, filling the glass again.

'As many as you like to give me. Pour on. Fill high. A bumper with a bead in the middle! Give me enough of this,' he added, as he tossed it down his hairy throat, 'and I'll do murder if you ask me!'

'As I don't mean to ask you, and you might possibly do it without being invited if you went on much further,' said Mr Chester with great composure, 'we will stop, if agreeable to you my good friend, at the next glass. – You were drinking before you came here.'

'I always am when I can get it,' cried Hugh boisterously, waving the empty glass above his head, and throwing himself into a rude dancing attitude. 'I always am. Why not? Ha ha ha! What's so good to me as this? What ever has been? What else has kept away the cold on bitter nights, and driven hunger off in starving times? What else has given me the strength and courage of a man, when men would have left me to die, a puny child? I should never have had a man's heart but for this. I should have died in a ditch. Where's he who when I was a weak and sickly wretch, with trembling legs and fading sight, bade me cheer up, as this did? I never knew him; not I. I drink to the drink, master. Ha ha ha!'

'You are an exceedingly cheerful young man,' said Mr Chester, putting on his cravat with great deliberation, and slightly moving his head from side to side to settle his chin in its proper place. 'Quite a boon companion.'

'Do you see this hand, master,' said Hugh, 'and this arm?' baring the brawny limb to the elbow. 'It was once mere skin and bone, and would have been dust in some poor church-yard by this time, but for the drink.'

'You may cover it,' said Mr Chester, 'it's sufficiently real in your sleeve.'

'I should never have been spirited up to take a kiss from the proud little beauty, master, but for the drink,' cried Hugh. 'Ha ha ha! It was a good one. As sweet as honey-suckle I warrant you. I thank the drink for it. I'll drink to the drink again, master. Fill me one more. Come. One more!'

'You are such a promising fellow,' said his patron, putting on his waistcoat with great nicety, and taking no heed of this request, 'that I must caution you against having too many impulses from the drink, and getting hung before your time. What's your age?'

'I don't know.'

'At any rate,' said Mr Chester, 'you are young enough to escape what I may call a natural death for some years to come. How can you trust yourself in my hands on so short an acquaintance, with a halter round your neck. What a confiding nature yours must be!'

Hugh fell back a pace or two and surveyed him with a look of mingled terror, indignation, and surprise. Regarding himself in the glass with the same complacency as before, and speaking as smoothly as if he were discussing some pleasant chit-chat of the town, his patron went on:

'Robbery on the king's highway, my young friend, is a very dangerous and ticklish occupation. It is pleasant, I have no doubt, while it lasts; but like many other pleasures in this transitory world, it seldom lasts long. And really if, in the ingenuousness of youth, you open your heart so readily on the subject, I am afraid your career will be an extremely short one.'

'How's this?' said Hugh, 'What do you talk of, master? Who was it set me on?'

'Who?' said Mr Chester, wheeling sharply round, and looking full at him for the first time. 'I didn't hear you. Who was it?'

Hugh faltered, and muttered something which was not audible.

'Who was it? I am curious to know,' said Mr Chester, with surpassing affability. 'Some rustic beauty perhaps? But be cautious, my good friend. They are not always to be trusted. Do take my advice now, and be careful of yourself.' With these words he turned to the glass again, and went on with his toilet.

Hugh would have answered him that he, the questioner himself, had set him on, but the words stuck in his throat. The consummate art with which his patron had led him to this point, and managed the whole conversation, perfectly baffled him. He did not doubt that if he had made the retort which was on his lips when Mr Chester turned round and questioned him so keenly, he would straightway have given him into custody and had him dragged before a justice with the stolen property upon him; in which case it was as certain he would have been hung as it was that he had been born. The ascendancy which it was the purpose of the man of the world to establish over this savage instrument, was gained from that time. Hugh's submission was complete. He dreaded him beyond description; and felt that accident and artifice had spun a web about him, which at a touch from such a master-hand as his, would bind him to the gallows.

With these thoughts passing through his mind, and yet wondering at the very same time how he who came there rioting in the confidence of this man (as he thought), should be so soon and so thoroughly subdued, Hugh stood cowering before him, regarding him uneasily from time to time, while he finished dressing. When he had done so, he took up the letter, broke the seal, and throwing himself back in his chair, read it leisurely through.

'Very neatly worded upon my life! Quite a woman's letter, full of what people call tenderness, and disinterestedness, and heart, and all that sort of thing!'

As he spoke, he twisted it up, and glancing lazily round at Hugh as though he would say 'You see this?' held it in the flame of the candle. When it was in a full blaze, he tossed it into the grate, and there it smouldered away.

'It was directed to my son,' he said, turning to Hugh, 'and you did quite right to bring it here. I opened it on my own responsibility, and you see what I have done with it. Take this, for your trouble.'

Hugh stepped forward to receive the piece of money he held out to him. As he put it in his hand, he added:

'If you should happen to find anything else of this sort, or to pick up any kind of information you may think I would like to have, bring it here will you, my good fellow?'

This was said with a smile which implied – or Hugh thought it did – 'fail to do so at your peril!' He answered that he would.

'And don't,' said his patron, with an air of the very kindest patronage, 'don't be at all downcast or uneasy respecting that little rashness we have been speaking of. Your neck is as safe in my hands, my good fellow, as though a baby's fingers clasped it, I assure you. – Take another glass. You are quieter now.'

Hugh accepted it from his hand, and looking stealthily at his smiling face, drank the contents in silence.

'Don't you, – ha ha! – don't you drink to the drink any more?' said Mr Chester, in his most winning manner.

'To you, sir,' was the sullen answer, with something approaching to a bow. 'I drink to you.'

'Thank you. God bless you. By the bye, what is your name, my good soul? You are called Hugh, I know, of course – your other name?'

'I have no other name.'

'A very strange fellow! Do you mean that you never knew one, or that you don't choose to tell it? Which?'

'I'd tell it if I could,' said Hugh, quickly. 'I can't. I have been always called Hugh; nothing more. I never knew, nor saw, nor thought about a father; and I was a boy of six – that's not very old – when they hung my mother up at Tyburn for a couple of thousand men to stare at. They might have let her live. She was poor enough.'

'How very sad!' exclaimed his patron, with a condescending smile. 'I have no doubt she was an exceedingly fine woman.'

'You see that dog of mine?' said Hugh, abruptly.

'Faithful, I dare say?' rejoined his patron, looking at him through his glass; 'and immensely clever? Virtuous and gifted animals, whether man or beast, always are so very hideous.'

'Such a dog as that, and one of the same breed, was the only living thing except me that howled that day,' said Hugh. 'Out of the two thousand odd – there was a larger crowd for its being a woman – the dog and I alone had any pity. If he'd have been a man, he'd have been glad to be quit of her, for she had been forced to keep him lean and half-starved; but being a dog, and not having a man's sense, he was sorry.'

'It was dull of the brute, certainly,' said Mr Chester, 'and very like a brute.'

Hugh made no rejoinder, but whistling to his dog, who sprung up at the sound and came jumping and sporting about him, bade his sympathising friend good night.

'Good night,' he returned. 'Remember; you're safe with me – quite safe. So long as you deserve it, my good fellow, as I hope you always will, you have a friend in me, on whose silence you may rely. Now do be careful of yourself, pray do, and consider what jeopardy you might have stood in. Good night! bless you!'

Hugh truckled before the hidden meaning of these words as much as such a being could, and crept out of the door so submissively and subserviently – with an air, in short, so different from that with which he had entered – that his patron on being left alone, smiled more than ever.

'And yet,' he said, as he took a pinch of snuff, 'I do not like their having hanged his mother. The fellow has a fine eye, and I am sure she was handsome. But very probably she was coarse – red-nosed perhaps, and had clumsy feet. Aye. It was all for the best, no doubt.'

With this comforting reflection, he put on his coat, took a farewell glance at the glass, and summoned his man, who promptly attended, followed by a chair and its two bearers.

'Foh!' said Mr Chester. 'The very atmosphere that centaur has breathed, seems tainted with the cart and ladder.⁴ Here, Peak. Bring some scent and sprinkle the floor; and take away the chair he sat upon, and air it; and dash a little of that mixture upon me. I am stifled!'

The man obeyed; and the room and its master being both purified, nothing remained for Mr Chester but to demand his hat, to fold it jauntily under his arm, to take his seat in the chair and be carried off; humming a fashionable tune.

CHAPTER THE TWENTY-FOURTH

How the accomplished gentleman spent the evening in the midst of a dazzling and brilliant circle; how he enchanted all those with whom he mingled by the grace of his deportment, the politeness of his manner, the vivacity of his conversation, and the sweetness of his voice; how it was observed in every corner, that Chester was a man of that happy disposition that nothing ruffled him, that he was one on whom the world's cares and errors sat lightly as his dress, and in whose smiling face a calm and tranquil mind was constantly reflected; how honest men, who by instinct knew him better, bowed down before him nevertheless, deferred to his every word, and courted his favourable notice; how people, who really had good in them, went with the stream, and fawned and flattered, and approved, and despised themselves while they did so, and yet had not the courage to resist; how, in short, he was one of those who are received and cherished in society (as the phrase is) by scores who individually would shrink from and be repelled by the object of their lavish regard; are things of course, which will suggest themselves. Matter so common-place needs but a passing glance, and there an end.

The despisers of mankind – apart from the mere fools and mimics, of that creed – are of two sorts. They who believe their merit neglected and unappreciated, make up one class; they who receive adulation and flattery, knowing their own worthlessness, compose the other. Be sure that the coldest-hearted misanthropes are ever of this last order.

Mr Chester sat up in bed next morning, sipping his coffee, and remembering with a kind of contemptuous satisfaction how he had shone last night, and how he had been caressed and courted, when his servant brought in a very small scrap of dirty paper, tightly sealed in two places, on the inside whereof was inscribed in pretty large text these words. 'A friend. Desiring of a conference. Immediate. Private. Burn it when you've read it.'

'Where in the name of the Gunpowder Plot[1] did you pick up this?' said his master.

It was given him by a person then waiting at the door, the man replied.

'With a cloak and dagger?' said Mr Chester.

With nothing more threatening about him, it appeared, than a leather apron and a dirty face. 'Let him come in.' In he came – Mr Tappertit; with his hair still on end, and a great lock in his hand, which he put down on the floor in the middle of the chamber as if he were about to go through some performances in which it was a necessary agent.

'Sir,' said Mr Tappertit with a low bow, 'I thank you for this condescension, and am glad to see you. Pardon the menial office in which I am engaged sir, and extend your sympathies to one, who, humble as his appearance is, has inn'ard workings far above his station.'

Mr Chester held the bed-curtain farther back, and looked at him with a vague impression that he was some maniac, who had not only broken open the door of his place of confinement, but had brought away the lock. Mr Tappertit bowed again, and displayed his legs to the best advantage.

'You have heard sir,' said Mr Tappertit, laying his hand upon his breast, 'of G. Varden Locksmith and bell-hanger and repairs neatly executed in town and country, Clerkenwell, London?'

'What then?' asked Mr Chester.

'I am his 'prentice, sir.'

'What *then*?'

'Ahem!' said Mr Tappertit. 'Would you permit me to shut the door sir, and will you further, sir, give me your honour bright, that what passes between us is in the strictest confidence?'

Mr Chester laid himself calmly down in bed again, and turning a perfectly undisturbed face towards the strange apparition, which had by this time closed the door, begged him to speak out, and to be as rational as he could, without putting himself to any very great personal inconvenience.

'In the first place sir,' said Mr Tappertit, producing a small pocket-handkerchief, and shaking it out of the folds, 'as I have not a card about me (for the envy of masters debases us below that level) allow me to offer the best substitute that circumstances will admit of. If you will take that in your own hand, sir, and cast your eye on the right-hand corner,' said Mr Tappertit, offering it with a graceful air, 'you will meet with my credentials.'

'Thank you,' answered Mr Chester, politely accepting it, and turning to some blood-red characters at one end. ' "Four. Simon Tappertit. One." Is that the —'

'Without the numbers, sir, that is my name,' replied the 'prentice. 'They are merely intended as directions to the washerwoman, and have no connection with myself or family. *Your* name, sir,' said Mr Tappertit, looking very hard at his nightcap, 'is Chester, I suppose? You needn't pull it off, sir, thank you. I observe E. C.² from here. We will take the rest for granted.'

'Pray, Mr Tappertit,' said Mr Chester, 'has that complicated piece of ironmongery which you have done me the favour to bring with you, any immediate connexion with the business we are to discuss?'

'It has not, sir,' rejoined the 'prentice. 'It's going to be fitted on a ware'us door in Thames Street.'

'Perhaps, as that is the case,' said Mr Chester, 'and as it has a stronger flavour of oil than I usually refresh my bedroom with, you will oblige me so far as to put it outside the door?'

'By all means, sir,' said Mr Tappertit, suiting the action to the word.

'You'll excuse my mentioning it, I hope?'

'Don't apologise, sir, I beg. And now, if you please, to business.'

During the whole of this dialogue, Mr Chester had suffered nothing but his smile of unvarying serenity and politeness to appear upon his face. Sim Tappertit, who had far too good an opinion of himself to suspect that anybody could be playing upon him,[3] thought within himself that this was something like the respect to which he was entitled, and drew a comparison from this courteous demeanour of a stranger, by no means favourable to the worthy locksmith.

'From what passes in our house,' said Mr Tappertit, 'I am aware, sir, that your son keeps company with a young lady against your inclinations. Sir, your son has not used me well.'

'Mr Tappertit,' said the other, 'you grieve me beyond description.'

'Thank you, sir,' replied the 'prentice. 'I'm glad to hear you say so. He's very proud, sir, is your son; very haughty.'

'I am afraid he *is* haughty,' said Mr Chester. 'Do you know I was really afraid of that before; and you confirm me?'

'To recount the menial offices I've had to do for your son, sir,' said Mr Tappertit; 'the chairs I've had to hand him, the coaches I've had to call for him, the numerous degrading duties, wholly unconnected with my indenters, that I've had to do for him, would fill a family Bible. Besides which, sir, he is but a young man himself, and I do not consider "thank'ee Sim," a proper form of address on those occasions.'

'Mr Tappertit, your wisdom is beyond your years. Pray go on.'

'I thank you for your good opinion, sir,' said Sim, much gratified, 'and will endeavour so to do. Now sir, on this account (and perhaps for another reason or two which I needn't go into) I am on your side. And what I tell you is this – that as long as our people go backwards and forwards, to and fro, up and down, to that there jolly old Maypole, lettering, and messaging, and fetching and carrying, you couldn't help your son keeping company with that young lady by deputy, – not if he was minded night and day by all the Horse Guards,[4] and every man of 'em in the very fullest uniform.'

Mr Tappertit stopped to take breath after this, and then started fresh again.

'Now, sir, I am a coming to the point. You will inquire of me, "how is this to be prevented?" I'll tell you how. If an honest, civil, smiling gentleman like you –'

'Mr Tappertit – really –'

'No, no, I'm serious,' rejoined the 'prentice, 'I am, upon my soul. If an honest, civil, smiling gentleman like you, was to talk but ten minutes to our old woman – that's Mrs Varden – and flatter her up a bit, you'd gain her over for ever. Then there's this point got – that her daughter Dolly,' – here a flush came over Mr Tappertit's face – 'wouldn't be allowed to be a go-between from that time forward; and till that point's got, there's nothing ever will prevent her. Mind that.'

'Mr Tappertit, your knowledge of human nature –'

'Wait a minute,' said Sim, folding his arms with a dreadful calmness. 'Now I come to THE point. Sir, there is a villain at that Maypole, a monster in human shape, a vagabond of the deepest dye, that unless you get rid of, and have kidnapped and carried off at the very least – nothing less will do – will marry your son to that young woman, as certainly and surely as if he was the Archbishop of Canterbury himself. He will, sir, for the hatred and malice that he bears to you; let alone the pleasure of doing a bad action, which to him is its own reward. If you knew how this chap, this Joseph Willet – that's his name – comes backwards and forwards to our house, libelling, and denouncing, and threatening you, and how I shudder when I hear him, you'd hate him worse than I do, – worse than I do sir,' said Mr Tappertit wildly, putting his hair up straighter, and making a crunching noise with his teeth; 'if sich a thing is possible.'

'A little private vengeance in this, Mr Tappertit?'

'Private vengeance, sir, or public sentiment, or both combined – destroy him,' said Mr Tappertit. 'Miggs says so too. Miggs and me both say so. We can't bear the plotting and undermining that takes place. Our souls recoil from it. Barnaby Rudge and Mrs Rudge are in it likewise; but the villain, Joseph Willet, is the ringleader. Their plottings and schemes are known to me and Miggs. If you want information of 'em, apply to us. Put Joseph Willet down, sir. Destroy him. Crush him. And be happy.'

With these words, Mr Tappertit, who seemed to expect no reply, and to hold it as a necessary consequence of his eloquence that his hearer should be utterly stunned, dumb-foundered, and over-whelmed, folded his arms so that the palm of each hand rested on the opposite shoulder, and disappeared after the manner of those mysterious warners of whom he had read in cheap story-books.

'That fellow,' said Mr Chester, relaxing his face when he was fairly gone, 'is good practice. I *have* some command of my features, beyond all doubt. He fully confirms what I suspected, though; and blunt tools are sometimes found of use, where sharper instruments would fail. I fear I may be obliged to make great havoc among these worthy people. A troublesome necessity! I quite feel for them.'

With that he fell into a quiet slumber: – subsided into such a gentle, pleasant sleep, that it was quite infantine.

*

CHAPTER THE TWENTY-FIFTH

Leaving the favoured, and well-received, and flattered of the world; him of the world most worldly, who never compromised himself by an ungentlemanly action and was never guilty of a manly one; to lie smilingly asleep – for even sleep, working but little change in his dissembling face, became with him a piece of cold, conventional hypocrisy – we follow in the steps of two slow travellers on foot, making towards Chigwell.

Barnaby and his mother. Grip in their company, of course.

The widow, to whom each painful mile seemed longer than the last, toiled wearily along; while Barnaby, yielding to every inconstant impulse, fluttered here and there, now leaving her far behind, now lingering far behind himself, now darting into some by-lane or path and leaving her to pursue her way alone, until he stealthily emerged again and came upon her with a wild shout of merriment, as his wayward and capricious nature prompted. Now he would call to her from the topmost branch of some high tree by the roadside; now, using his tall staff as a leaping-pole, come flying over ditch or hedge or five-barred gate; now run with surprising swiftness for a mile or more on the straight road, and halting, sport upon a patch of grass with Grip till she came up. These were his delights; and when his patient mother heard his merry voice, or looked into his flushed and healthy face, she would not have abated them by one sad word or murmur, though each had been to her a source of suffering in the same degree as it was to him of pleasure.

It is something to look upon enjoyment, so that it be free and wild and in the face of nature, though it is but the enjoyment of an idiot. It is something to know that Heaven has left the capacity of gladness in such a creature's breast; it is something to be assured that, however lightly men may crush that faculty in their fellows, the Great Creator of mankind imparts it even to his despised and slighted work. Who would not rather see a poor idiot happy in the sunlight, than a wise man pining in a darkened jail!

Ye men of gloom and austerity, who paint the face of Infinite Benevolence with an eternal frown; read in the Everlasting Book, wide open to your view, the lesson it would teach. Its pictures are not in black and sombre hues, but bright and glowing tints; its music – save when ye drown it – is not in sighs and groans, but songs and cheerful sounds. Listen to the million voices in the summer air, and find one dismal as your own. Remember, if ye can, the sense of hope and pleasure which every glad return of day awakens in the breast of all your kind who have not changed their nature; and learn some wisdom even from the witless, when their hearts are lifted up they know not why, by all the mirth and happiness it brings.

The widow's breast was full of care, was laden heavily with secret dread and sorrow; but her boy's gaiety of heart gladdened her, and beguiled the long journey. Sometimes he would bid her lean upon his arm, and would keep beside her steadily for a short distance; but it was more his nature to be rambling to and fro, and she better liked to see him free and happy, even than to have him near her, because she loved him better than herself.

She had quitted the place to which they were travelling, directly after the event which had changed her whole existence; and for two-and-twenty years had never had courage to revisit it. It was her native village. How many recollections crowded on her mind when it appeared in sight!

Two-and-twenty years. Her boy's whole life and history. The last time she looked back upon those roofs among the trees, she carried him in her arms, an infant. How often since that time had she sat beside him night and day, watching for the dawn of mind that never came; how had she feared, and doubted, and yet hoped, long after conviction forced itself upon her! The little stratagems she had devised to try him, the little tokens he had given in his childish way – not of dullness but of something infinitely worse, so ghastly and unchild-like in its cunning – came back as vividly as if but yesterday had intervened. The room in which they used to be; the spot in which his cradle stood; he, old and elfin-like in face, but ever dear to her, gazing at her with a wild and vacant eye, and crooning some uncouth song as she sat by and rocked him; every circumstance of his infancy came thronging back, and the most trivial, perhaps, the most distinctly.

His older childhood, too; the strange imaginings he had; his terror of certain senseless things – familiar objects he endowed with life; the slow and gradual breaking out of that one horror, in which, before his birth, his darkened intellect began; how, in the midst of all, she had found some hope and comfort in his being unlike another child, and had gone on almost believing in the slow development of his mind until he grew a man, and then his childhood was complete and lasting; one after another, all these old thoughts sprung up within her, strong after their long slumber and bitterer than ever.

She took his arm and they hurried through the village street. It was the same as it was wont to be in old times, yet different too, and wore another air. The change was in herself, not it; but she never thought of that, and wondered at its alteration, and where it lay, and what it was.

The people all knew Barnaby, and the children of the place came flocking round him – as she remembered to have done with their fathers and mothers round some silly beggarman, when a child herself. None of them knew her; they passed each well-remembered house, and yard, and homestead; and striking into the fields, were soon alone again.

The Warren was the end of their journey. Mr Haredale was

walking in the garden, and seeing them as they passed the iron-gate, unlocked it, and bade them enter that way.

'At length you have mustered heart to visit the old place,' he said to the widow. 'I am glad you have.'

'For the first time, and the last, sir,' she replied.

'The first for many years, but not the last?'

'The very last.'

'You mean,' said Mr Haredale, regarding her with some surprise, 'that having made this effort, you are resolved not to persevere and are determined to relapse? This is unworthy of you. I have often told you, you should return here. You would be happier here than elsewhere, I know. As to Barnaby, it's quite his home.'

'And Grip's,' said Barnaby, holding the basket open. The raven hopped gravely out, and perching on his shoulder and addressing himself to Mr Haredale, cried – as a hint, perhaps, that some temperate refreshment would be acceptable – 'Polly put the ket-tle on, we'll all have tea!'

'Hear me, Mary,' said Mr Haredale kindly, as he motioned her to walk with him towards the house. 'Your life has been an example of patience and fortitude, except in this one particular which has often given me great pain. It is enough to know that you were cruelly involved in the calamity which deprived me of an only brother, and Emma of her father, without being obliged to suppose (as I sometimes am) that you associate us with the author of our joint misfortunes.'

'Associate *you* with him, sir!' she cried.

'Indeed,' said Mr Haredale, 'I think you do. I almost believe that because your husband was bound by so many ties to our relation, and died in his service and defence, you have come in some sort to connect us with his murder.'

'Alas!' she answered. 'You little know my heart, sir. You little know the truth!'

'It is natural you should do so; it is very probable you may, without being conscious of it,' said Mr Haredale, speaking more to himself than her. 'We are a fallen house. Money, dispensed with the most lavish hand, would be a poor recompense for sufferings like yours; and thinly scattered by hands so pinched and tied as ours, it becomes a miserable mockery. I feel it so, God knows,' he added, hastily. 'Why should I wonder if she does!'

'You do me wrong, dear sir, indeed,' she rejoined with great earnestness; 'and yet when you come to hear what I desire your leave to say –'

'I shall find my doubts confirmed?' he said, observing that she faltered and became confused. 'Well!'

He quickened his pace for a few steps, but fell back again to her side, and said:

'And have you come all this way at last, solely to speak to me?'

She answered, 'Yes.'

'A curse,' he muttered, 'upon the wretched state of us proud beggars, from whom the poor and rich are equally at a distance; the one being forced to treat us with a show of cold respect; the other condescending to us in their every deed and word, and keeping more aloof, the nearer they approach us. – Why, if it were pain to you (as it must have been) to break for this slight purpose the chain of habit forged through two-and-twenty years, could you not let me know your wish, and beg me come to you?'

'There was not time, sir,' she rejoined. 'I took my resolution but last night, and taking it, felt that I must not lose a day – a day! an hour – in having speech with you.'

They had by this time reached the house. Mr Haredale paused for a moment, and looked at her as if surprised by the energy of her manner. Observing, however, that she took no heed of him, but glanced up, shuddering, at the old walls with which such horrors were connected in her mind, he led her by a private stair into his library, where Emma was seated in a window, reading.

The young lady, seeing who approached, hastily rose and laid aside her book, and with many kind words, and not without tears, gave her a warm and earnest welcome. But the widow shrunk from her embrace as though she feared her, and sunk down trembling on a chair.

'It is the return to this place after so long an absence,' said Emma, gently. 'Pray ring, dear uncle – or stay – Barnaby will run himself and ask for wine –'

'Not for the world,' she cried. 'It would have another taste – I could not touch it. I want but a minute's rest. Nothing but that.'

Miss Haredale stood beside her chair, regarding her with silent pity. She remained for a little time quite still; then rose and turned to Mr Haredale, who had sat down in his easy chair, and was contemplating her with fixed attention.

The tale connected with the mansion borne in mind, it seemed, as has been already said, the chosen theatre for such a deed as it had known. The room in which this group were now assembled – hard by the very chamber where the act was done – dull, dark, and sombre; heavy with worm-eaten books; deadened and shut in by faded hangings, muffling every sound; shadowed mournfully by trees whose rustling boughs gave ever and anon a spectral knocking at the glass; wore, beyond all others in the house, a ghostly, gloomy air. Nor were the group assembled there, unfitting tenants of the spot. The widow, with her marked and startling face and downcast eyes; Mr Haredale stern and despondent ever; his niece beside him, like, yet most unlike, the picture of her father, which gazed reproachfully down upon them from the blackened wall; Barnaby, with his vacant look and restless eye; were all in keeping with the place, and actors in the legend. Nay, the very raven, who had hopped upon the table and with the air of some old necromancer appeared to be profoundly studying a great folio volume that lay open on a desk, was strictly in unison with the rest, and looked like the embodied spirit of evil biding his time of mischief.

'I scarcely know,' said the widow, breaking silence, 'how to begin. You will think my mind disordered.'

'The whole tenor of your quiet and reproachless life since you were last here,' returned Mr Haredale, mildly, 'shall bear witness for you. Why do you fear to awaken such a suspicion? You do not speak to strangers. You have not to claim our interest or consideration for the first time. Be more yourself. Take heart. Any advice or assistance that I can give you, you know is yours of right, and freely yours.'

'What if I came, sir,' she rejoined, 'I, who have but one other friend on earth, to reject your aid from this moment, and to say that henceforth I launch myself upon the world, alone and unassisted, to sink or swim as Heaven may decree!'

'You would have, if you came to me for such a purpose,' said Mr Haredale calmly, 'some reason to assign for conduct so extraordinary, which – if one may entertain the possibility of anything so wild and strange – would have its weight, of course.'

'That, sir,' she answered, 'is the misery of my distress. I can give no reason whatever. My own bare word is all that I can offer. It is my duty, my imperative and bounden duty. If I did not discharge it, I should be a base and guilty wretch. Having said that, my lips are sealed, and I can say no more.'

As though she felt relieved at having said so much, and had nerved herself to the remainder of her task, she spoke from this time with a firmer voice and heightened courage.

'Heaven is my witness, as my own heart is – and yours, dear young lady, will speak for me, I know – that I have lived, since that time we all have bitter reason to remember, in unchanging devotion, and gratitude to this family. Heaven is my witness that go where I may, I shall preserve those feelings unimpaired. And it is my witness, too, that they alone impel me to the course I must take, and from which nothing now shall turn me, as I hope for mercy.'

'These are strange riddles,' said Mr Haredale.

'In this world, sir,' she replied, 'they may, perhaps, never be explained. In another, the Truth will be discovered in its own good time. And may that time,' she added in a low voice, 'be far distant!'

'Let me be sure,' said Mr Haredale, 'that I understand you, for I am doubtful of my own senses. Do you mean that you are resolved voluntarily to deprive yourself of those means of support you have received from us so long – that you are determined to resign the annuity we settled on you twenty years ago – to leave house, and home, and goods, and begin life anew – and this, for some secret reason or monstrous fancy which is incapable of explanation, which only now exists, and has been dormant all this time? In the name of God, under what delusion are you labouring?'

'As I am deeply thankful,' she made answer, 'for the kindness of those, alive and dead, who have owned this house; and as I would not have its roof fall down and crush me, or its very walls drip blood, my name being spoken in their hearing; I never will again subsist upon their bounty, or let it help me to subsistence. You do not know,' she added, suddenly, 'to what uses it may be applied; into what hands it may pass. I do, and I renounce it.'

'Surely,' said Mr Haredale, 'its uses rest with you.'

'They did. They rest with me no longer. It may be – it *is* – devoted to purposes that mock the dead in their graves. It never can prosper with me. It will bring some other heavy judgment on the head of my dear son, whose innocence will suffer for his mother's guilt.'

'What words are these!' cried Mr Haredale, regarding her with wonder. 'Among what associates have you fallen? Into what guilt have you ever been betrayed?'

'I am guilty, and yet innocent; wrong, yet right; good in intention, though constrained to shield and aid the bad. Ask me no more

questions, sir; but believe that I am rather to be pitied than condemned. I must leave my house to-morrow, for while I stay there,
it is haunted. My future dwelling, if I am to live in peace, must be
a secret. If my poor boy should ever stray this way, do not tempt
him to disclose it or have him watched when he returns; for if we
are hunted, we must fly again. And now this load is off my mind, I
beseech you – and you, dear Miss Haredale, too – to trust me if
you can, and think of me kindly as you have been used to do. If I
die and cannot tell my secret even then (for that may come to pass),
it will sit the lighter on my breast in that hour for this day's work;
and on that day, and every day until it comes, I will pray for and
thank you both, and trouble you no more.'

With that, she would have left them, but they detained her, and
with many soothing words and kind entreaties besought her to
consider what she did, and above all to repose more freely upon
them, and say what weighed so sorely on her mind. Finding her
deaf to their persuasions, Mr Haredale suggested, as a last resource,
that she should confide in Emma, of whom, as a young person and
one of her own sex, she might stand in less dread than of himself.
From this proposal, however, she recoiled with the same indescribable repugnance she had manifested when they met. The utmost
that could be wrung from her was, a promise that she would receive
Mr Haredale at her own house next evening, and in the mean time
re-consider her determination and their dissuasions – though any
change on her part, as she told them, was quite hopeless. This
condition made at last, they reluctantly suffered her to depart, since
she would neither eat nor drink within the house; and she, and
Barnaby, and Grip, accordingly went out as they had come, by the
private stair and garden gate; seeing and being seen of no one by
the way.

It was remarkable in the raven that during the whole interview
he had kept his eye on his book with exactly the air of a very sly
human rascal, who, under the mask of pretending to read hard,
was listening to everything. He still appeared to have the conversation very strongly in his mind, for although, when they were
alone again, he issued orders for the instant preparation of inumer-
able kettles for purposes of tea, he was thoughtful, and rather
seemed to do so from an abstract sense of duty, than with any
regard to making himself agreeable, or being what is commonly
called good company.

They were to return by the coach. As there was an interval of full two hours before it started, and they needed rest and some refreshment, Barnaby begged hard for a visit to the Maypole. But his mother, who had no wish to be recognized by any of those who had known her long ago, and who feared besides that Mr Haredale might, on second thoughts, despatch some messenger to that place of entertainment in quest of her, proposed to wait in the church-yard instead. As it was easy for Barnaby to buy and carry thither such humble viands as they required, he cheerfully assented, and in the churchyard they sat down to take their frugal dinner.

Here again, the raven was in a highly reflective state; walking up and down when he had dined, with an air of elderly complacency which was strongly suggestive of his having his hands under his coat-tails; and appearing to read the tombstones with a very critical taste. Sometimes, after a long inspection of an epitaph, he would strop his beak upon the grave to which it referred, and cry in his hoarse tones, 'I'm a devil, I'm a devil, I'm a devil!' but whether he addressed his observations to any supposed person below, or merely threw them off as a general remark, is matter of uncertainty.

It was a quiet pretty spot, but a sad one for Barnaby's mother; for Mr Reuben Haredale lay there, and near the vault in which his ashes rested, was a stone to the memory of her own husband, with a brief inscription recording how and when he had lost his life. She sat here, thoughtful and apart, until their time was out, and the distant horn told that the coach was coming.

Barnaby, who had been sleeping on the grass, sprung up quickly at the sound; and Grip, who appeared to understand it equally well, walked into his basket straightway, entreating society in general (as though he intended a kind of satire upon them in connexion with churchyards) never to say die on any terms. They were soon on the coach-top and rolling along the road.

It went round by the Maypole, and stopped at the door. Joe was from home, and Hugh came sluggishly out to hand up the parcel that it called for. There was no fear of old John coming out. They could see him from the coach-roof fast asleep in his cosey bar. It was a part of John's character. He made a point of going to sleep at the coach's time. He despised gadding about; he looked upon coaches as things that ought to be indicted; as disturbers of the peace of mankind; as restless, bustling, busy, horn-blowing contrivances,

quite beneath the dignity of men, and only suited to giddy girls that did nothing but chatter and go a-shopping. 'We know nothing about coaches here, sir,' John would say, if any unlucky stranger made inquiry touching the offensive vehicles; 'we don't book for 'em; we'd rather not; they're more trouble than they're worth, with their noise and rattle. If you like to wait for 'em you can; but we don't know anything about 'em; they may call and they may not – there's a carrier – he was looked upon as quite good enough for us, when *I* was a boy.'

She dropped her veil as Hugh climbed up, and while he hung behind, and talked to Barnaby in whispers. But neither he nor any other person spoke to her, or noticed her, or had any curiosity about her; and so, an alien, she visited and left the village where she had been born, and had lived a merry child, a comely girl, a happy wife – where she had known all her enjoyment of life, and had entered on its hardest sorrows.

CHAPTER THE TWENTY-SIXTH

'And you're not surprised to hear this, Varden?' said Mr Haredale. 'Well! You and she have always been the best friends, and you should understand her if anybody does.'

'I ask your pardon, sir,' rejoined the locksmith. 'I didn't say I understood her. I wouldn't have the presumption to say that of any woman. It's not so easily done. But I am not so much surprised, sir, as you expected me to be, certainly.'

'May I ask why not, my good friend?'

'I have seen, sir,' returned the locksmith with evident reluctance, 'I have seen in connexion with her, something that has filled me with distrust and uneasiness. She has made bad friends; how, or when, I don't know; but that her house is a refuge for one robber and cut-throat at least, I am certain. There, sir! Now it's out.'

'Varden!'

'My own eyes, sir, are my witnesses, and for her sake I would be willingly half-blind, if I could but have the pleasure of mistrusting 'em. I have kept the secret till now, and it will go no further than yourself, I know; but I tell you that with my own eyes – broad awake – I saw, in the passage of her house one evening after dark, the highwayman who robbed and wounded Mr Edward Chester, and on the same night threatened me.'

'And you made no effort to detain him?' said Mr Haredale quickly.

'Sir,' returned the locksmith, 'she herself prevented me – held me, with all her strength, and hung about me until he had got clear off.' And having gone so far, he related circumstantially all that had passed upon the night in question.

This dialogue was held in a low tone in the locksmith's little parlour, into which honest Gabriel had shown his visitor on his arrival. Mr Haredale had called upon him to entreat his company to the widow's, that he might have the assistance of his persuasion and influence; and out of this circumstance the conversation had arisen.

'I forbore,' said Gabriel, 'from repeating one word of this to anybody, as it could do her no good and might do her great harm. I thought and hoped, to say the truth, that she would come to me, and talk to me about it, and tell me how it was; but though I have purposely put myself in her way more than once or twice, she has never touched upon the subject – except by a look. And indeed,' said the good-natured locksmith, 'there was a good deal in the look, more than could have been put into a great many words. It said among other matters "Don't ask me anything" so imploringly, that I didn't ask her anything. You'll think me an old fool I know, sir. If it's any relief to call me one, pray do.'

'I am greatly disturbed by what you tell me,' said Mr Haredale, after a silence. 'What meaning do you attach to it?'

The locksmith shook his head, and looked doubtfully out of window at the failing light.

'She cannot have married again,' said Mr Haredale.

'Not without our knowledge surely, sir.'

'She may have done so, in the fear that it would lead, if known, to some objection or estrangement. Suppose she married incautiously – it is not improbable, for her existence has been a lonely and monotonous one for many years – and the man turned out a ruffian, she would be anxious to screen him, and yet would revolt from his crimes. This might be. It bears strongly on the whole drift of her discourse yesterday, and would quite explain her conduct. Do you suppose Barnaby is privy to these circumstances?'

'Quite impossible to say, sir,' returned the locksmith, shaking his head again: 'and next to impossible to find out from him. If what you suppose is really the case, I tremble for the lad – a notable person, sir, to put to bad uses –'

'It is not possible, Varden,' said Mr Haredale, in a still lower tone of voice than he had spoken yet, 'that we have been blinded and deceived by this woman from the beginning? It is not possible that this connexion was formed in her husband's lifetime, and led to his and my brother's—'

'Good God, sir,' cried Gabriel, interrupting him, 'don't entertain such dark thoughts for a moment. Five-and-twenty years ago, where was there a girl like her? A gay, handsome, laughing, bright-eyed damsel! Think what she was, sir. It makes my heart ache now, even now, though I'm an old man with a woman for a daughter, to think what she was, and what she is. We all change, but that's with Time; Time does his work honestly, and I don't mind him. A fig for Time, sir. Use him well, and he's a hearty fellow, and scorns to have you at a disadvantage. But care and suffering (and those have changed her) are devils, sir – secret, stealthy, undermining devils – who tread down the brightest flowers in Eden, and do more havoc in a month than Time does in a year. Picture to yourself for one minute what Mary was before they went to work with her fresh heart and face – do her that justice – and say whether such a thing is possible.'

'You're a good fellow, Varden,' said Mr Haredale, 'and are quite right. I have brooded on that subject so long, that every breath of suspicion carries me back to it. You are quite right.'

'It isn't, sir,' cried the locksmith with brightened eyes, and sturdy, honest voice; 'it isn't because I courted her before Rudge, and failed, that I say she was too good for him. She would have been as much too good for me. But she *was* too good for him; he wasn't free and frank enough for her. I don't reproach his memory with it, poor fellow; I only want to put her before you as she really was. For myself, I'll keep her old picture in my mind; and thinking of that, and what has altered her, I'll stand her friend, and try to win her back to peace. And damme, sir,' cried Gabriel, 'with your pardon for the word, I'd do the same if she had married fifty highwaymen in a twelvemonth; and think it in the Protestant Manual too, though Martha said it wasn't, tooth and nail, till doomsday!'

If the dark little parlour had been filled with a dense fog, which, clearing away in an instant, left it all radiance and brightness, it could not have been more suddenly cheered than by this outbreak on the part of the hearty locksmith. In a voice nearly as full and round as his own, Mr Haredale cried 'Well said!' and bade him come away without more parley. The locksmith complied right willingly; and both getting into a hackney-coach which was waiting at the door, drove off straightway.

They alighted at the street corner, and dismissing their conveyance, walked to the house. To their first knock at the door there was no response. A second met with the like result. But in answer to the third, which was of a more vigorous kind, the parlour window-sash was gently raised, and a musical voice cried:

'Haredale, my dear fellow, I am extremely glad to see you. How very much you have improved in your appearance since our last meeting! I never saw you looking better. *How* do you do?'

Mr Haredale turned his eyes towards the casement whence the voice proceeded, though there was no need to do so, to recognize the speaker, and Mr Chester waved his hand, and smiled a courteous welcome.

'The door will be opened immediately,' he said. 'There is nobody but a very dilapidated female to perform such offices. You will excuse her infirmities? If she were in a more elevated station of society, she would be gouty. Being but a hewer of wood and drawer of water,[1] she is rheumatic. My dear Haredale, these are natural class distinctions, depend upon it.'

Mr Haredale, whose face resumed its lowering and distrustful look the moment he heard the voice, inclined his head stiffly, and turned his back upon the speaker.

'Not opened yet!' said Mr Chester. 'Dear me! I hope the aged soul has not caught her foot in some unlucky cobweb by the way. She is there at last! Come in, I beg!'

Mr Haredale entered, followed by the locksmith. Turning with a look of great astonishment to the old woman who had opened the door, he inquired for Mrs Rudge – for Barnaby. They were both gone, she replied, wagging her ancient head, for good. There was a gentleman in the parlour, who perhaps could tell them more. That was all *she* knew.

'Pray, sir,' said Mr Haredale, presenting himself before this new tenant, 'where is the person whom I came here to see?'

'My dear friend,' he returned, 'I have not the least idea.'

'Your trifling is ill-timed,' retorted the other in a suppressed tone and voice, 'and its subject ill-chosen. Reserve it for those who are your friends, and do not expend it on me. I lay no claim to the distinction, and have the self-denial to reject it.'

'My dear, good sir,' said Mr Chester, 'you are heated with walking. Sit down, I beg. Our friend is –'

'Is but a plain honest man,' returned Mr Haredale, 'and quite unworthy of your notice.'

'Gabriel Varden by name, sir,' said the locksmith bluntly.

'A worthy English yeoman!' said Mr Chester. 'A most worthy yeoman, of whom I have frequently heard my son Ned – darling fellow – speak, and have often wished to see. Varden, my good friend, I am glad to know you. You wonder now,' he said, turning languidly to Mr Haredale, 'to see me here. Now, I am sure you do.'

Mr Haredale glanced at him – not fondly or admiringly – smiled, and held his peace.

'The mystery is solved in a moment,' said Mr Chester; 'in a moment. Will you step aside with me one instant. You remember our little compact in reference to Ned, and your dear niece, Haredale? You remember the list of assistants in their innocent intrigue? You remember these two people being among them? My dear fellow, congratulate yourself, and me. I have bought them off.'

'You have done what?' said Mr Haredale.

'Bought them off,' returned his smiling friend. 'I have found it necessary to take some active steps towards setting this boy and girl attachment quite at rest, and have begun by removing these two agents. You are surprised? Who *can* withstand the influence of a little money! They wanted it, and have been bought off. We have nothing more to fear from them. They are gone.'

'Gone!' echoed Mr Haredale. 'Where?'

'My dear fellow – and you must permit me to say again, that you never looked so young; so positively boyish as you do to-night – the Lord knows where; I believe Columbus himself wouldn't find them. Between you and me they have their hidden reasons, but upon that point I have pledged myself to secrecy. She appointed to see you here to-night I know, but found it inconvenient, and couldn't wait. Here is the key of the door. I am afraid you'll find it inconveniently large; but as the tenement is yours, your good-nature will excuse that, Haredale, I am certain!'

*

CHAPTER THE TWENTY-SEVENTH

Mr Haredale stood in the widow's parlour with the door-key in his hand, gazing by turns at Mr Chester and at Gabriel Varden, and occasionally glancing downward at the key as in the hope that of its own accord it would unlock the mystery; until Mr Chester, putting on his hat and gloves, and sweetly inquiring whether they were walking in the same direction, recalled him to himself.

'No,' he said. 'Our roads diverge – widely, as you know. For the present, I shall remain here.'

'You will be hipped, Haredale; you will be miserable, melancholy, utterly wretched,' returned the other. 'It is a place of the very last description for a man of your temper. I know it will make you very miserable.'

'Let it,' said Mr Haredale, sitting down; 'and thrive upon the thought. Good night!'

Feigning to be wholly unconscious of the abrupt wave of the hand which rendered this farewell tantamount to a dismissal, Mr Chester retorted with a bland and heartfelt benediction, and inquired of Gabriel in what direction *he* was going.

'Yours, sir, would be too much honour for the like of me,' replied the locksmith, hesitating.

'I wish you to remain here a little while, Varden,' said Mr Haredale without looking towards them. 'I have a word or two to say to you.'

'I will not intrude upon your conference another moment,' said Mr Chester with inconceivable politeness. 'May it be satisfactory to you both! God bless you!' So saying, and bestowing upon the locksmith a most refulgent smile, he left them.

'A deplorably constituted creature, that rugged person,' he said, as he walked along the street; 'he is an atrocity that carries its own punishment along with it – a bear that gnaws himself. And here is one of the inestimable advantages of having a perfect command over one's inclinations. I have been tempted in these two short interviews, to draw upon that fellow, fifty times. Five men in six would have yielded to the impulse. By suppressing mine, I wound him deeper and more keenly than if I were the best swordsman in all Europe, and he the worst. You are the wise man's very last resource,' he said, tapping the hilt of his weapon; 'we can but appeal to you when all else is said and done. To come to you before, and thereby spare our adversaries so much, is a barbarian mode of warfare, quite unworthy any man with the remotest pretensions to delicacy of feeling, or refinement.'

He smiled so very pleasantly as he communed with himself after this manner, that a beggar was emboldened to follow him for alms, and to dog his footsteps for some distance. He was gratified by the circumstance, feeling it complimentary to his power of feature, and as a reward suffered the man to follow him until he called a chair, when he graciously dismissed him with a fervent blessing.

'Which is as easy as cursing,' he wisely added, as he took his seat, 'and more becoming to the face. – To Clerkenwell, my good creatures, if you please!' The chairmen were rendered quite vivacious by having such a courteous burden, and to Clerkenwell they went at a fair round trot.

Alighting at a certain point he had indicated to them upon the road, and paying them something less than they had expected from a fare of such gentle speech, he turned into the street in which the locksmith dwelt, and presently stood beneath the shadow of the Golden Key. Mr Tappertit, who was hard at work by lamp-light, in a corner of the workshop, remained unconscious of his presence until a hand upon his shoulder made him start and turn his head.

'Industry,' said Mr Chester, 'is the soul of business, and the key-stone of prosperity. Mr Tappertit, I shall expect you to invite me to dinner when you are Lord Mayor of London.'

'Sir,' returned the 'prentice, laying down his hammer, and rubbing his nose on the back of a very sooty hand, 'I scorn the Lord Mayor and everything that belongs to him. We must have another state of society, sir, before you catch me being Lord Mayor. How de do sir?'

'The better, Mr Tappertit, for looking into your ingenuous face once more. I hope you are well.'

'I am as well, sir,' said Sim, standing up to get nearer to his ear, and whispering hoarsely, 'as any man can be under the aggrawations to which I am exposed. My life's a burden to me. If it wasn't for wengeance, I'd play at pitch and toss with it on the losing hazard.'

'Is Mrs Varden at home?' said Mr Chester.

'Sir,' returned Sim, eyeing him over with a look of concentrated expression, – 'she is. Did you wish to see her?'

Mr Chester nodded.

'Then come this way, sir,' said Sim, wiping his face upon his apron. 'Follow me, sir. – Would you permit me to whisper in your ear, one half a second?'

'By all means.'

Mr Tappertit raised himself on tiptoe, applied his lips to Mr Chester's ear, drew back his head without saying anything, looked hard at him, applied them to his ear again, again drew back, and finally whispered – 'The name is Joseph Willet. Hush! I say no more.'

Having said that much, he beckoned the visitor with a mysterious aspect to follow him to the parlour door, where he announced him in the voice of a gentleman-usher. 'Mr Chester.'

'And not Mr Edd'ard, mind,' said Sim, looking into the door again and adding this by way of postscript in his own person; 'it's his father.'

'But do not let his father,' said Mr Chester, advancing hat in hand, as he observed the effect of this last explanatory announcement, 'do not let his father be any check or restraint on your domestic occupations, Miss Varden.'

'Oh! Now! There! An't I always a saying it!' exclaimed Miggs, clapping her hands. 'If he an't been and took Missis for her own daughter. Well, she *do* look like it, that she do. Only think of that, mim!'

'Is it possible,' said Mr Chester in his softest tones, 'that this is Mrs Varden! I am amazed. That is not your daughter, Mrs Varden? No, no. Your sister.'

'My daughter, indeed sir,' returned Mrs V., blushing with great juvenility.

'Ah, Mrs Varden!' cried the visitor. 'Ah, ma'am – humanity is indeed a happy lot, when we can repeat ourselves in others, and still be young as they. You must allow me to salute you – the custom of the country, my dear madam – your daughter too.'

Dolly showed some reluctance to perform this ceremony, but was sharply reproved by Mrs Varden, who insisted on her undergoing it that minute. For pride, she said with great severity, was one of the seven deadly sins,[1] and humility and lowliness of heart were virtues. Wherefore she desired that Dolly would be kissed immediately, on pain of her just displeasure; at the same time giving her to understand that whatever she saw her mother do, she might safely do herself, without being at the trouble of any reasoning or reflection on the subject – which, indeed, was offensive and undutiful, and in direct contravention of the church catechism.[2]

Thus admonished, Dolly complied, though by no means willingly; for there was a broad, bold look of admiration in Mr Chester's face, refined and polished though it sought to be, which distressed her very much. As she stood with downcast eyes, not liking to look up and meet his, he gazed upon her with an approving air, and then turned to her mother.

'My friend Gabriel (whose acquaintance I only made this very evening) should be a happy man, Mrs Varden.'

'Ah!' sighed Mrs V., shaking her head.

'Ah!' echoed Miggs.

'Is that the case?' said Mr Chester, compassionately. 'Dear me!'

'Master has no intentions sir,' murmured Miggs as she sidled up to him, 'but to be as grateful as his natur will let him, for everythink he owns which it is in his powers to appreciate. But we never sir' – said Miggs, looking sideways at Mrs Varden, and interlarding her discourse with a sigh – 'we never know the full value of *some* wines and fig-trees[3] till we lose 'em. So much the worse sir, for them as has the slighting of 'em on their consciences when they're gone to be in full blow elsewhere.' And Miss Miggs cast up her eyes to signify where that might be.

As Mrs Varden distinctly heard, and was intended to hear, all that Miggs said, and as these words appeared to convey in metaphorical terms a presage or foreboding that she would at some early period droop beneath her trials and take an easy flight towards the stars, she immediately began to languish, and taking a volume of the Manual from a neighbouring table, leant her arm upon it as though she were Hope and that her Anchor.[4] Mr Chester perceiving this, and seeing how the volume was lettered on the back, took it gently from her hand, and turned the fluttering leaves.

'My favourite book, dear madam. How often, how very often in his early life – before he can remember' – (this clause was strictly true) 'have I deduced little easy moral lessons from its pages, for my dear son Ned! You know Ned?'

Mrs Varden had that honour, and a fine affable young gentleman he was.

'You're a mother, Mrs Varden,' said Mr Chester, taking a pinch of snuff, 'and you know what I, as a father, feel, when he is praised.

He gives me some uneasiness – much uneasiness – he's of a roving nature, ma'am – from flower to flower – from sweet to sweet – but his is the butterfly time of life, and we must not be hard upon such trifling.'

He glanced at Dolly. She was attending evidently to what he said. Just what he desired!

'The only thing I object to in this little trait of Ned's, is,' said Mr Chester, ' – and the mention of his name reminds me, by the way, that I am about to beg the favour of a minute's talk with you alone – the only thing I object to in it, is, that it *does* partake of insincerity. Now, however I may attempt to disguise the fact from myself in my affection for Ned, still I always revert to this – that if we are not sincere, we are nothing. Nothing upon earth. Let us be sincere, my dear madam – '

' – and Protestant,' murmured Mrs Varden.

' – and Protestant above all things. Let us be sincere and Protestant, strictly moral, strictly just (though always with a leaning towards mercy), strictly honest, and strictly true, and we gain – it is a slight point, certainly, but still it is something tangible; we throw up a groundwork and foundation, so to speak, of goodness, on which we may afterwards erect some worthy superstructure.'

Now, to be sure, Mrs Varden thought, here is a perfect character. Here is a meek, righteous, thorough-going Christian, who, having mastered all these qualities, so difficult of attainment; who, having dropped a pinch of salt on the tails of all the cardinal virtues,[5] and caught them every one; makes light of their possession, and pants for more morality. For the good woman never doubted (as many good men and women never do), that this slighting kind of profession, this setting so little store by great matters, this seeming to say 'I am not proud, I am what you hear, but I consider myself no better than other people; let us change the subject, pray' – was perfectly genuine and true. He so contrived it, and said it in that way that it appeared to have been forced from him, and its effect was marvellous.

Aware of the impression he had made – few men were quicker than he at such discoveries – Mr Chester followed up the blow by propounding certain virtuous maxims, somewhat vague and general in their nature, doubtless, and occasionally partaking of the character of truisms, worn a little out at elbow, but delivered in so charming a voice and with such uncommon serenity and peace of mind, that they answered as well as the best. Nor is this to be wondered at; for as hollow vessels produce a far more musical sound in falling than those which are substantial, so it will oftentimes be found that sentiments which have nothing in them make the loudest ringing in the world, and are the most relished.

Mr Chester, with the volume gently extended in one hand, and with the other planted lightly on his breast, talked to them in the most delicious manner possible; and quite enchanted all his hearers, notwithstanding their conflicting interests and thoughts. Even Dolly, who, between his keen regards and her eyeing over by Mr Tappertit, was put quite out of countenance, could not help owning within herself that he was the sweetest-spoken gentleman she had ever seen. Even Miss Miggs, who was divided between admiration of Mr Chester and a mortal jealousy of her young mistress, had sufficient leisure to be propitiated. Even Mr Tappertit, though occupied as we have seen in gazing at his heart's delight, could not wholly divert his thoughts from the voice of the other charmer. Mrs Varden, to her own private thinking, had never been so improved in all her life; and when Mr Chester, rising and craving permission to speak with her apart, took her by the hand and led her at arm's length up stairs to the best sitting-room, she almost deemed him something more than human.

'Dear madam,' he said, pressing her hand delicately to his lips; 'be seated.'

Mrs Varden called up quite a courtly air, and became seated.

'You guess my object?' said Mr Chester, drawing a chair towards her. 'You divine my purpose? I am an affectionate parent, my dear Mrs Varden.'

'That I am sure you are sir,' said Mrs V.

'Thank you,' returned Mr Chester, tapping his snuff-box lid. 'Heavy moral responsibilities rest with parents, Mrs Varden.'

Mrs Varden slightly raised her hands, shook her head, and looked at the ground as though she saw straight through the globe, out at the other end, and into the immensity of space beyond.

'I may confide in you,' said Mr Chester, 'without reserve. I love my son, ma'am, dearly; and loving him as I do, I would save him from working certain misery. You know of his attachment to Miss Haredale. You have abetted him in it, and very kind of you it was to do so. I am deeply obliged to you – most deeply obliged to you

– for your interest in his behalf; but my dear ma'am, it is a mistaken one, I do assure you.'

Mrs Varden stammered that she was sorry –

'Sorry, my dear ma'am,' he interposed. 'Never be sorry for what is so very amiable, so very good in intention, so perfectly like yourself. But there are grave and weighty reasons, pressing family considerations, and apart even from these, points of religious difference, which interpose themselves, and render their union impossible; utterly im-possible. I should have mentioned these circumstances to your husband; but he has – you will excuse my saying this so freely – he has *not* your quickness of apprehension or depth of moral sense. What an extremely airy house this is, and how beautifully kept! For one like myself – a widower so long – these tokens of female care and superintendence have inexpressible charms.'

Mrs Varden began to think (she scarcely knew why) that the young Mr Chester must be in the wrong, and the old Mr Chester must be in the right.

'My son Ned,' resumed her tempter with his most winning air, 'has had, I am told, your lovely daughter's aid, and your open-hearted husband's.'

'– Much more than mine sir,' said Mrs Varden; 'a great deal more. I have often had my doubts. It's a –'

'A bad example,' suggested Mr Chester. 'It is. No doubt it is. Your daughter is at that age when to set before her an encouragement for young persons to rebel against their parents on this most important point, is particularly injudicious. You are quite right. I ought to have thought of that myself, but it escaped me, I confess – so far superior are your sex to ours, dear madam, in point of penetration and sagacity.'

Mrs Varden looked as wise as if she had really said something to deserve this compliment – firmly believed she had, in short – and her faith in her own shrewdness increased considerably.

'My dear ma'am,' said Mr Chester, 'you embolden me to be plain with you. My son and I are at variance on this point. The young lady and her natural guardian differ upon it, also. And the closing point is, that my son is bound by his duty to me, by his honour, by every solemn tie and obligation, to marry some one else.'

'Engaged to marry another lady!' quoth Mrs Varden, holding up her hands.

'My dear madam, brought up, educated, and trained, expressly for that purpose. Expressly for that purpose. – Miss Haredale, I am told, is a very charming creature.'

'I am her foster-mother, and should know – the best young lady in the world,' said Mrs Varden.

'I have not the smallest doubt of it. I am sure she is. And you, who have stood in that tender relation towards her, are bound to consult her happiness. Now, can I – as I have said to Haredale, who quite agrees – can I possibly stand by, and suffer her to throw herself away (although she *is* of a catholic family), upon a young fellow who, as yet, has no heart at all? It is no imputation upon him to say he has not, because young men who have plunged deeply into the frivolities and conventionalities of society, very seldom have. Their hearts never grow, my dear ma'am, till after thirty. I don't believe, no, I do *not* believe, that I had any heart myself when I was Ned's age.'

'Oh sir,' said Mrs Varden, 'I think you must have had. It's impossible that you, who have so much now, can ever have been without any.'

'I hope,' he answered, shrugging his shoulders meekly, 'I have a little; I hope, a very little – Heaven knows! But to return to Ned; I have no doubt you thought, and therefore interfered benevolently in his behalf, that I objected to Miss Haredale. How very natural! My dear madam, I object to him – to him – emphatically to Ned himself.'

Mrs Varden was perfectly aghast at the disclosure.

'He has, if he honourably fulfils this solemn obligation of which I have told you – and he must be honourable, dear Mrs Varden, or he is no son of mine – a fortune within his reach. He is of most expensive, ruinously expensive habits; and if, in a moment of caprice and wilfulness, he were to marry this young lady, and so deprive himself of the means of gratifying the tastes to which he has been so long accustomed, he would – my dear madam, he would break the gentle creature's heart. Mrs Varden, my good lady, my dear soul, I put it to you – is such a sacrifice to be endured? Is the female heart a thing to be trifled with in this way? Ask your own, my dear madam. Ask your own, I beseech you.'

'Truly,' thought Mrs Varden, 'this gentleman is a saint. But,' she added aloud, and not unnaturally, 'if you take Miss Emma's lover away, sir, what becomes of the poor thing's heart, then?'

'The very point,' said Mr Chester, not at all abashed, 'to which I wished to lead you. A marriage with my son, whom I should be compelled to disown, would be followed by years of misery; they would be separated, my dear madam, in a twelvemonth. To break off this attachment, which is more fancied than real, as you and I know very well, will cost the dear girl but a few tears, and she is happy again. Take the case of your own daughter, the young lady down stairs, who is your breathing image' – Mrs Varden coughed and simpered – 'there is a young man, (I am sorry to say, a dissolute fellow, of very indifferent character,) of whom I have heard Ned speak – Bullet was it – Pullet – Mullet –'

'There is a young man of the name of Joseph Willet, sir,' said Mrs Varden, folding her hands loftily.

'That's he,' cried Mr Chester. 'Suppose this Joseph Willet now, were to aspire to the affections of your charming daughter, and were to engage them.'

'It would be like his impudence,' interposed Mrs Varden, bridling, 'to dare to think of such a thing!'

'My dear madam, that's the whole case. I know it would be like his impudence. It is like Ned's impudence to do as he has done; but you would not on that account, or because of a few tears from your beautiful daughter, refrain from checking their inclinations in their birth. I meant to have reasoned thus with your husband when I saw him at Mrs Rudge's this evening –'

'My husband,' said Mrs Varden, interposing with emotion, 'would be a great deal better at home than going to Mrs Rudge's so often. I don't know what he does there. I don't see what occasion he has to busy himself in her affairs at all, sir.'

'If I don't appear to express my concurrence in those last sentiments of yours,' returned Mr Chester, 'quite so strongly as you might desire, it is because his being there, my dear madam, and not proving conversational, led me hither, and procured me the happiness of this interview with one, in whom the whole management, conduct, and prosperity of her family are centred, I perceive.'

With that he took Mrs Varden's hand again, and having pressed it to his lips with the high-flown gallantry of the day – a little burlesqued to render it the more striking in the good lady's unaccustomed eyes – proceeded in the same strain of mingled sophistry, cajolery, and flattery, to entreat that her utmost influence might be exerted to restrain her husband and daughter from any further promotion of Edward's suit to Miss Haredale, and from aiding or abetting either party in any way. Mrs Varden was but a woman, and had her share of vanity, obstinacy, and love of power. She entered into a secret treaty of alliance, offensive and defensive, with her insinuating visitor; and really did believe, as many others would have done who saw and heard him, that in so doing she furthered the ends of truth, justice, and morality, in a very uncommon degree.

Overjoyed by the success of his negotiation, and mightily amused within himself, Mr Chester conducted her down stairs in the same state as before; and having repeated the previous ceremony of salutation, which also as before comprehended Dolly, took his leave; first completing the conquest of Miss Miggs's heart, by inquiring if 'this young lady' would light him to the door.

'Oh, mim,' said Miggs, returning with the candle. 'Oh gracious me, mim, there's a gentleman! Was there ever such an angel to talk as he is – and such a sweet-looking man! So upright and noble, that he seems to despise the very ground he walks on; and yet so mild and condescending, that he seems to say "but I will take notice on it too." And to think of his taking you for Miss Dolly, and Miss Dolly for your sister – Oh, my goodness me, if I was master wouldn't I be jealous of him!'

Mrs Varden reproved her handmaid for this vain-speaking; but very gently and mildly – quite smilingly indeed – remarking that she was a foolish, giddy, light-headed girl, whose spirits carried her beyond all bounds, and who didn't mean half she said, or she would be quite angry with her.

'For my part,' said Dolly, in a thoughtful manner, 'I half believe Mr Chester is something like Miggs in that respect. For all his politeness and pleasant speaking, I am pretty sure he was making game of us, more than once.'

'If you venture to say such a thing again, and to speak ill of people behind their backs in my presence, Miss,' said Mrs Varden, 'I shall insist upon your taking a candle and going to bed directly. How dare you, Dolly? I'm astonished at you. The rudeness of your whole behaviour this evening has been disgraceful. Did anybody ever hear,' cried the enraged matron, bursting into tears, 'of a daughter telling her own mother she has been made game of!'

What a very uncertain temper Mrs Varden's was!

CHAPTER THE TWENTY-EIGHTH

Repairing to a noted coffee-house in Convent Garden[1] when he left the locksmith's, Mr Chester sat long over a late dinner, entertaining himself exceedingly with the whimsical recollection of his recent proceedings, and congratulating himself very much on his great cleverness. Influenced by these thoughts, his face wore an expression so benign and tranquil, that the waiter in immediate attendance upon him felt he could almost have died in his defence, and settled in his own mind (until the receipt of the bill, and a very small fee for very great trouble disabused it of the idea) that such an apostolic customer was worth half-a-dozen of the ordinary run of visitors, at least.

A visit to the gaming-table – not as a heated, anxious venturer, but one whom it was quite a treat to see staking his two or three pieces in deference to the follies of society, and smiling with equal benevolence on winners and losers – made it late before he reached home. It was his custom to bid his servant go to bed at his own time unless he had orders to the contrary, and to leave a candle on the common stair. There was a lamp on the landing by which he could always light it when he came home late, and having a key of the door about him he could enter and go to bed at his pleasure.

He opened the glass of the dull lamp, whose wick, burnt up and swollen like a drunkard's nose, came flying off in little carbuncles at the candle's touch, and scattering hot sparks about rendered it matter of some difficulty to kindle the lazy taper; when a noise, as of a man snoring deeply some steps higher up, caused him to pause and listen. It was the heavy breathing of a sleeper, close at hand. Some fellow had lain down on the open staircase, and was slumbering soundly. Having lighted the candle at length and opened his own door, he softly ascended, holding the taper high above his head, and peering cautiously about; curious to see what kind of man had chosen so comfortless a shelter for his lodging.

With his head upon the landing and his great limbs flung over half a dozen stairs, as carelessly as though he were a dead man whom drunken bearers had thrown down by chance, there lay Hugh, face uppermost, his long hair drooping like some wild weed upon his wooden pillow, and his huge chest heaving with the sounds which so unwontedly disturbed the place and hour.

He who came upon him so unexpectedly was about to break his rest by thrusting him with his foot, when, glancing at his upturned face, he arrested himself in the very action, and stooping down and shading the candle with his hand, examined his features closely. Close as his first inspection was, it did not suffice, for he passed the light, still carefully shaded as before, across and across his face, and yet observed him with a searching eye.

While he was thus engaged, the sleeper, without any starting or turning round, awoke. There was a kind of fascination in meeting his steady gaze so suddenly, which took from the other the presence of mind to withdraw his eyes, and forced him, as it were, to meet his look. So they remained staring at each other, until Mr Chester at last broke silence, and asked him in a low voice, why he lay sleeping there.

'I thought,' said Hugh, struggling into a sitting posture and gazing at him intently, still, 'that you were a part of my dream. It was a curious one. I hope it may never come true, master.'

'What makes you shiver?'

'The – the cold, I suppose,' he growled, as he shook himself, and rose. 'I hardly know where I am yet.'

'Do you know me?' said Mr Chester.

'Ay. I know you,' he answered. 'I was dreaming of you – we're not where I thought we were. That's a comfort.'

He looked round him as he spoke, and in particular looked above his head, as though he half expected to be standing under some object which had had existence in his dream. Then he rubbed his eyes and shook himself again, and followed his conductor into his own rooms.

Mr Chester lighted the candles which stood upon his dressing-table, and wheeling an easy chair towards the fire, which was yet burning, stirred up a cheerful blaze, sat down before it, and bade his uncouth visitor 'Come here,' and draw his boots off.

'You have been drinking again, my fine fellow,' he said, as Hugh went down on one knee, and did as he was told.

'As I'm alive, master, I've walked the twelve long miles, and waited here I don't know how long, and had no drink between my lips since dinner-time at noon.'

'And can you do nothing better, my pleasant friend, than fall asleep, and shake the very building with your snores?' said Mr Chester. 'Can't you dream in your straw at home, dull dog as you are, that you need come here to do it? – Reach me those slippers, and tread softly.'

Hugh obeyed in silence.

'And harkee, my dear young gentleman,' said Mr Chester, as he put them on, 'the next time you dream, don't let it be of me, but of some dog or horse with whom you are better acquainted. Fill the glass once – you'll find it and the bottle in the same place – and empty it to keep yourself awake.'

Hugh obeyed again – even more zealously – and having done so, presented himself before his patron.

'Now,' said Mr Chester, 'what do you want with me?'

'There was news to-day,' returned Hugh. 'Your son was at our house – came down on horseback. He tried to see the young woman, but couldn't get sight of her. He left some letter or some message which our Joe had charge of, but he and the old one quarrelled about it when your son had gone, and the old one wouldn't let it be delivered. He says (that's the old one does) that none of his people shall interfere and get him into trouble. He's a landlord he says, and lives on everybody's custom.'

'He is a jewel,' smiled Mr Chester, 'and the better for being a dull one. – Well?'

'Varden's daughter – that's the girl I kissed –'

'– and stole the bracelet from upon the king's highway,' said Mr Chester, composedly. 'Yes; what of her?'

'She wrote a note at our house to the young woman, saying she lost the letter I brought to you, and you burnt. Our Joe was to carry it, but the old one kept him at home all next day, on purpose that he shouldn't. Next morning he gave it to me to take; and here it is.'

'You didn't deliver it then, my good friend?' said Mr Chester, twirling Dolly's note between his finger and thumb, and feigning to be surprised.

'I supposed you'd want to have it,' retorted Hugh. 'Burn one, burn all, I thought.'

'My devil-may-care acquaintance,' said Mr Chester – 'really if you do not draw some nicer distinctions, your career will be cut short with most surprising suddenness. Don't you know that the letter you brought to me, was directed to my son who resides in this very place? And can you descry no difference between his letters and those addressed to other people?'

'If you don't want it,' said Hugh, disconcerted by this reproof, for he had expected high praise, 'give it me back, and I'll deliver it. I don't know how to please you, master.'

'I shall deliver it,' returned his patron, putting it away after a moment's consideration, 'myself. Does the young lady walk out, on fine mornings?'

'Mostly – about noon is her usual time.'

'Alone?'

'Yes, alone.'

'Where?'

'In the grounds before the house. – Them that the footpath crosses.'

'If the weather should be fine, I may throw myself in her way to-morrow, perhaps,' said Mr Chester, as coolly as if she were one of his ordinary acquaintance. 'Mr Hugh, if I should ride up to the Maypole door, you will do me the favour only to have seen me once. You must suppress your gratitude, and endeavour to forget my forbearance in the matter of the bracelet. It is natural it should break out, and it does you honour; but when other folks are by, you must, for your own sake and safety, be as like your usual self as though you owed me no obligation whatever, and had never stood within these walls. You comprehend me?'

Hugh understood him perfectly. After a pause he muttered that he hoped his patron would involve him in no trouble about this last letter; for he had kept it back solely with the view of pleasing him. He was continuing in this strain, when Mr Chester with a most beneficent and patronising air cut him short by saying:

'My good fellow, you have my promise, my word, my sealed bond (for a verbal pledge with me is quite as good), that I will always protect you so long as you deserve it. Now, do set your mind at rest. Keep it at ease, I beg of you. When a man puts himself in my power so thoroughly as you have done, I really feel as though he had a kind of claim upon me. I am more disposed to mercy and forbearance under such circumstances than I can tell you, Hugh. Do look upon me as your protector, and rest assured, I entreat you, that on the subject of that indiscretion, you may preserve, as long as you and I are friends, the lightest heart that ever beat within a human breast. Fill that glass once more to cheer you on your road homewards – I am really quite ashamed to think how far you have to go – and then God bless you for the night.'

'They think,' said Hugh, when he had tossed the liquor down, 'that I am sleeping soundly in the stable. Ha ha ha! The stable door is shut, but the steed's gone, master.'

'You are a most convivial fellow,' returned his friend, 'and I love your humour of all things. Good night! Take the greatest possible care of yourself, for my sake!'

It was remarkable that during the whole interview, each had endeavoured to catch stolen glances of the other's face, and had never looked full at it. They interchanged one brief and hasty glance as Hugh went out, averted their eyes directly, and so separated. Hugh closed the double doors behind him, carefully and without noise; and Mr Chester remained in his easy chair, with his gaze intently fixed upon the fire.

'Well!' he said, after meditating for a long time – and said with a deep sigh and an uneasy shifting of his attitude, as though he dismissed some other subject from his thoughts, and returned to that which had held possession of them all the day – 'the plot thickens; I have thrown the shell; it will explode, I think, in eight-and-forty hours, and should scatter these good folks amazingly. We shall see!'

He went to bed and fell asleep, but had not slept long when he started up and thought that Hugh was at the outer door, calling in a strange voice, very different from his own, to be admitted. The delusion was so strong upon him, and was so full of that vague terror of the night in which such visions have their being, that he rose, and taking his sheathed sword in his hand, opened the door, and looked out upon the staircase, and towards the spot where Hugh had lain asleep; and even spoke to him by name. But all was dark and quiet, and creeping back to bed again, he fell, after an hour's uneasy watching, into a second sleep, and woke no more till morning.

*

CHAPTER THE TWENTY-NINTH

The thoughts of worldly men are for ever regulated by a moral law of gravitation, which, like the physical one, holds them down to earth. The bright glory of day, and the silent wonders of a starlit night, appeal to their minds in vain. There are no signs in the sun, or in the moon, or in the stars, for their reading. They are like some wise men, who, learning to know each planet by its Latin name, have quite forgotten such small heavenly constellations as Charity, Forbearance, Universal Love, and Mercy, although they shine by night and day so brightly that the blind may see them; and who, looking upward at the spangled sky, see nothing there but the reflection of their own great wisdom and book-learning.

It is curious to imagine these people of the world, busy in thought, turning their eyes toward the countless spheres that shine above us, and making them reflect the only images their minds contain. The man who lives but in the breath of princes, has nothing in his sight but stars for courtiers' breasts. The envious man beholds his neighbours' honours even in the sky; to the money-hoarder, and the mass of worldly folk, the whole great universe above glitters with sterling coin – fresh from the mint – stamped with the sovereign's head – coming always between them and heaven, turn where they may. So do the shadows of our own desires stand between us and our better angels, and thus their brightness is eclipsed.

Everything was fresh and gay, as though the world were but that morning made, when Mr Chester rode at a tranquil pace along the Forest road. Though early in the season, it was warm and genial weather; the trees were budding into leaf, the hedges and the grass were green, the air was musical with songs of birds, and high above them all the lark poured out her richest melody. In shady spots, the morning dew sparkled on each young leaf and blade of grass; and where the sun was shining, some diamond drops yet glistened brightly, as in unwillingness to leave so fair a world, and have such brief existence. Even the light wind, whose rustling was as gentle to the ear as softly-falling water, had its hope and promise; and, leaving a pleasant fragrance in its track as it went fluttering by, whispered of its intercourse with Summer, and of his happy coming.

The solitary rider went glancing on among the trees, from sunlight into shade and back again, at the same even pace – looking about him, certainly, from time to time, but with no greater thought of the day or the scene through which he moved, than that he was fortunate (being choicely dressed) to have such favourable weather. He smiled very complacently at such times, but rather as if he were satisfied with himself than with anything else; and so went riding on, upon his chesnut cob, as pleasant to look upon as his own horse, and probably far less sensitive to the many cheerful influences by which he was surrounded.

In course of time, the Maypole's massive chimneys rose upon his view: but he quickened not his pace one jot, and with the same cool gravity rode up to the tavern porch. John Willet, who was toasting his red face before a great fire in the bar, and who, with surpassing foresight and quickness of apprehension, had been thinking, as he looked at the blue sky, that if that state of things lasted much longer, it might ultimately become necessary to leave off fires and throw the windows open, issued forth to hold his stirrup; calling lustily for Hugh.

'Oh, you're here, are you, sir?' said John, rather surprised by the quickness with which he appeared. 'Take this here valuable animal into the stable, and have more than particular care of him if you want to keep your place. A mortal lazy fellow, sir; he needs a deal of looking after.'

'But you have a son,' returned Mr Chester, giving his bridle to Hugh as he dismounted, and acknowledging his salute by a careless motion of his hand towards his hat. 'Why don't you make *him* useful?'

'Why, the truth is, sir,' replied John with great importance, 'that my son – what, you're a listening are you, villain?'

'Who's listening?' returned Hugh angrily. 'A treat, indeed, to hear *you* speak! Would you have me take him in till he's cool?'

'Walk him up and down further off then, sir,' cried old John, 'and when you see me and a noble gentleman entertaining ourselves with talk, keep your distance. If you don't know your distance, sir,' added Mr Willet, after an enormously long pause, during which he fixed his great dull eyes on Hugh, and waited with exemplary patience for any little property in the way of ideas that might be coming to him, 'we'll find a way to teach you, pretty soon.'

Hugh shrugged his shoulders scornfully, and in his reckless swaggering way, crossed to the other side of the little green, and there, with the bridle slung loosely over his shoulder, led the horse to and fro, glancing at his master every now and then from under his bushy eyebrows, with as sinister an aspect as one would desire to see.

Mr Chester, who, without appearing to do so, had eyed him attentively during this brief dispute, stepped into the porch, and turning abruptly to Mr Willet, said,

'You keep strange servants, John.'

'Strange enough to look at sir, certainly,' answered the host; 'but out of doors; for horses, dogs, and the like of that; there an't a better man in England than is that Maypole Hugh yonder. He an't fit for indoors,' added Mr Willet, with the confidential air of a man who felt his own superior nature, '*I* do that; but if that chap had only a little imagination, sir – '

'He's an active fellow now, I dare swear,' said Mr Chester, in a musing tone, which seemed to suggest that he would have said the same had there been nobody to hear him.

'Active, sir!' retorted John, with quite an expression in his face; 'that chap! Hallo, there! You, sir! Bring that horse here, and go and hang my wig on the weathercock, to show this gentleman whether you're one of the lively sort or not.'

Hugh made no answer, but throwing the bridle to his master, and snatching his wig from his head, in a manner so unceremonious and hasty that the action discomposed Mr Willet not a little, though performed at his own special desire, climbed nimbly to the very summit of the maypole before the house, and hanging the wig upon the weathercock, sent it twirling round like a roasting jack. Having achieved this performance, he cast it on the ground, and sliding down the pole with inconceivable rapidity, alighted on his feet almost as soon as it had touched the earth.

'There, sir,' said John, relapsing into his usual stolid state, 'you won't see that at many houses, besides the Maypole, where there's good accommodation for man and beast – nor that neither, though that with him is nothing.'

This last remark bore reference to his vaulting on horseback, as upon Mr Chester's first visit, and quickly disappearing by the stable gate.

'That with him is nothing,' repeated Mr Willet, brushing his wig with his wrist, and inwardly resolving to distribute a small charge for dust and damage to that article of dress, through the various items of his guest's bill; 'he'll get out of a'most any winder in the house. There never was such a chap for flinging himself about and never hurting his bones. It's my opinion, sir, that it's pretty nearly all owing to his not having any imagination; and that if imagination could be (which it can't) knocked into him, he'd never be able to do it any more. But we was a talking, sir, about my son.'

'True, Willet, true,' said his visitor, turning again towards the landlord with his accustomed serenity of face. 'My good friend, what about him?'

It has been reported that Mr Willet, previously to making answer, winked. But as he never was known to be guilty of such lightness of conduct either before or afterwards, this may be looked upon as a malicious invention of his enemies – founded, perhaps, upon the undisputed circumstance of his taking his guest by the third breast button of his coat, counting downwards from the chin, and pouring his reply into his ear:

'Sir,' whispered John, with dignity, 'I know my duty. We want no love-making here, sir, unbeknown to parents. I respect a certain young gentleman, taking him in the light of a young gentleman; I respect a certain young lady, taking her in the light of a young lady; but of the two as a couple, I have no knowledge, sir, none whatever. My son, sir, is upon his patrole.'

'I thought I saw him looking through the corner window but this moment,' said Mr Chester, who naturally thought that being on patrole implied walking about somewhere.

'No doubt you did, sir,' returned John. 'He is upon his patrole of honour, sir, not to leave the premises. Me and some friends of mine that use the Maypole of an evening, sir, considered what was best to be done with him, to prevent his doing anything unpleasant in opposing your desires; and we've put him on his patrole. And what's more, sir, he won't be off his patrole for a pretty long time to come, I can tell you that.'

When he had communicated this bright idea, which had had its origin in the perusal by the village cronies of a newspaper, containing, among other matters, an account of how some officer pending the sentence of some court-martial had been enlarged on parole, Mr Willet drew back from his guest's ear, and without any visible alteration of feature, chuckled thrice audibly. This nearest approach to a laugh in which he ever indulged (and that but seldom and only on extreme occasions), never even curled his lip or effected the smallest change in – no, not so much as a slight wagging of – his great, fat, double chin, which at these times, as at all others, remained a perfect desert in the broad map of his face; one changeless, dull, tremendous blank.

Lest it should be matter of surprise to any, that Mr Willet adopted this bold course in opposition to one whom he had often entertained, and who had always paid his way at the Maypole gallantly, it may be remarked that it was his very penetration and sagacity in this respect, which occasioned him to indulge in those unusual demonstrations of jocularity, just now recorded. For Mr Willet, after carefully balancing father and son in his mental scales, had arrived at the distinct conclusion that the old gentleman was a better sort of customer than the young one. Throwing his landlord into the same scale, which was already turned by this consideration, and heaping upon him, again, his strong desires to run counter to the unfortunate Joe, and his opposition as a general principle to all matters of love and matrimony, it went down to the very ground straightway, and sent the light cause of the younger gentleman flying upwards to the ceiling. Mr Chester was not the kind of man to be by any means dim-sighted to Mr Willet's motives, but he thanked him as graciously as if he had been one of the most disinterested martyrs that ever shone on earth; and leaving him, with many complimentary reliances on his great taste and judgment, to prepare whatever dinner he might deem most fitting the occasion, bent his steps towards the Warren.

Dressed with more than his usual elegance; assuming a gracefulness of manner, which, though it was the result of long study, sat easily upon him and became him well; composing his features into their most serene and prepossessing expression; and setting in short that guard upon himself, at every point, which denoted that he attached no slight importance to the impression he was about to make; he entered the bounds of Miss Haredale's usual walk. He had not gone far, or looked about him long, when he descried coming towards him, a female figure. A glimpse of the form and dress as she crossed a little wooden bridge which lay between them, satisfied him that he had found her whom he desired to see. He threw himself in her way, and a very few paces brought them close together.

He raised his hat from his head, and yielding the path, suffered her to pass him. Then, as if the idea had but that moment occurred to him, he turned hastily back and said in an agitated voice:

'I beg pardon – do I address Miss Haredale?'

She stopped in some confusion at being so unexpectedly accosted by a stranger; and answered 'Yes.'

'Something told me,' he said, *looking* a compliment to her beauty, 'that it could be no other. Miss Haredale, I bear a name which is not unknown to you – which it is a pride, and yet a pain to me to know, sounds pleasantly in your ears. I am a man advanced in life, as you see. I am the father of him whom you honour and distinguish above all other men. May I for weighty reasons which fill me with distress, beg but a minute's conversation with you here?'

Who that was inexperienced in deceit, and had a frank and youthful heart, could doubt the speaker's truth – could doubt it too, when the voice that spoke, was like the faint echo of one she knew so well, and so much loved to hear? She inclined her head, and stopping, cast her eyes upon the ground.

'A little more apart – among these trees. It is an old man's hand, Miss Haredale; an honest one, believe me.'

She put hers in it as he said these words, and suffered him to lead her to a neighbouring seat.

'You alarm me, sir,' she said in a low voice. 'You are not the bearer of any ill news, I hope?'

'Of none that you anticipate,' he answered, sitting down beside her. 'Edward is well – quite well. It is of him I wish to speak, certainly; but I have no misfortune to communicate.'

She bowed her head again, and made as though she would have begged him to proceed; but said nothing.

'I am sensible that I speak to you at a disadvantage, dear Miss Haredale. Believe me that I am not so forgetful of the feelings of my younger days as not to know that you are little disposed to view me with favour. You have heard me described as cold-hearted, calculating, selfish –'

'I have never, sir' – she interposed with an altered manner and a firmer voice; 'I have never heard you spoken of in harsh or disrespectful terms. You do a great wrong to Edward's nature if you believe him capable of any mean or base proceeding.'

'Pardon me, my sweet young lady, but your uncle –'

'Nor is it my uncle's nature either,' she replied, with a heightened colour in her cheek. 'It is not his nature to stab in the dark, nor is it mine to love such deeds.'

She rose as she spoke, and would have left him; but he detained her with a gentle hand, and besought her in such persuasive accents to hear him but another minute, that she was easily prevailed upon to comply, and so sat down again.

'And it is,' said Mr Chester, looking upward, and apostrophising the air; 'it is this frank, ingenuous, noble nature, Ned, that you can wound so lightly. Shame – shame upon you, boy!'

She turned towards him quickly, and with a scornful look and flashing eyes. There were tears in Mr Chester's, but he dashed them hurriedly away, as though unwilling that his weakness should be known, and regarded her with mingled admiration and compassion.

'I never until now,' he said, 'believed, that the frivolous actions of a young man could move me like these of my own son. I never knew till now, the worth of a woman's heart, which boys so lightly win, and lightly fling away. Trust me, dear young lady, that I never until now did know your worth; and though an abhorrence of deceit and falsehood has impelled me to seek you out, and would have done so had you been the poorest and least gifted of your sex, I should have lacked the fortitude to sustain this interview could I have pictured you to my imagination as you really are.'

Oh! If Mrs Varden could have seen the virtuous gentleman as he said these words, with indignation sparkling from his eyes – if she could have heard his broken, quavering voice – if she could have beheld him as he stood bareheaded in the sunlight, and with unwonted energy poured forth his eloquence!

With a haughty face, but pale and trembling too, Emma regarded him in silence. She neither spoke nor moved, but gazed upon him as though she would look into his heart.

'I throw off,' said Mr Chester, 'the restraint which natural affection would impose on some men, and reject all bonds but those of truth and duty. Miss Haredale, you are deceived; you are deceived by your unworthy lover, and my unworthy son.'

Still she looked at him steadily, and still said not one word.

'I have ever opposed his professions of love for you; you will do me the justice, dear Miss Haredale, to remember that. Your uncle and myself were enemies in early life, and if I had sought retaliation, I might have found it here. But as we grow older, we grow wiser – better, I would fain hope – and from the first, I have opposed him in this attempt. I foresaw the end, and would have spared you, if I could.'

'Speak plainly, sir,' she faultered. 'You deceive me, or are deceived yourself. I do not believe you – I cannot – I should not.'

'First,' said Mr Chester, soothingly, 'for there may be in your mind some latent angry feeling to which I would not appeal, pray take this letter. It reached my hands by chance, and by mistake, and should have accounted to you (as I am told) for my son's not answering some other note of yours. God forbid, Miss Haredale,' said the good gentleman, with great emotion, 'that there should be in your gentle breast one causeless ground of quarrel with him. You should know, and you will see, that he was in no fault here.'

There appeared something so very candid, so scrupulously honourable, so very truthful and just in this course – something which rendered the upright person who resorted to it, so worthy of belief – that Emma's heart, for the first time, sunk within her. She turned away, and burst into tears.

'I would,' said Mr Chester, leaning over her, and speaking in mild and quite venerable accents; 'I would, dear girl, it were my task to banish, not increase, those tokens of your grief. My son, my erring son, – I will not call him deliberately criminal in this, for men so young, who have been inconstant twice or thrice before, act without reflection, almost without a knowledge of the wrong they do, – will break his plighted faith to you; has broken it even now. Shall I stop here, and having given you this warning, leave it to be fulfilled; or shall I go on?'

'You will go on, sir,' she answered, 'and speak more plainly yet, in justice both to him and me.'

'My dear girl,' said Mr Chester, bending over her more affectionately still; 'whom I would call my daughter, but the fates forbid, Edward seeks to break with you upon a false and most unwarrantable pretence. I have it on his own showing; in his own hand. Forgive me, if I have had a watch upon his conduct; I am his father; I had a regard for your peace and his honour, and no better resource was left me. There lies on his desk at this moment, ready for transmission to you, a letter, in which he tells you that our poverty – our poverty; his and mine, Miss Haredale – forbids him to pursue his claim upon your hand; in which he offers, voluntarily proposes, to free you from your pledge; and talks magnanimously (men do so, very commonly, in such cases) of being in time more worthy your regard – and so forth. A letter, to be plain, in which he not only jilts you – pardon the word; I would summon to your aid your pride and dignity – not only jilts you, I fear, in favour of the object whose slighting treatment first inspired his brief passion for yourself and gave it birth in wounded vanity, but affects to make a merit and a virtue of the act.'

She glanced proudly at him once more, as by an involuntary impulse, and with a swelling breast rejoined, 'If what you say be true, he takes much needless trouble, sir, to compass his design. He is very tender of my peace of mind. I quite thank him.'

'The truth of what I tell you, dear young lady,' he replied, 'you will test by the receipt or non-receipt of the letter of which I speak. – Haredale, my dear fellow, I am delighted to see you, although we meet under singular circumstances, and upon a melancholy occasion. I hope you are very well.'

At these words the young lady raised her eyes, which were filled with tears; and seeing that her uncle indeed stood before them, and being quite unequal to the trial of hearing or of speaking one word more, hurriedly withdrew, and left them. They stood looking at each other, and at her retreating figure, and for a long time neither of them spoke.

'What does this mean? Explain it,' said Mr Haredale at length. 'Why are you here, and why with her?'

'My dear friend,' rejoined the other, resuming his accustomed manner with infinite readiness, and throwing himself upon the bench with a weary air, 'you told me not very long ago, at that delightful old tavern of which you are the esteemed proprietor (and a most charming establishment it is for persons of rural pursuits and in robust health, who are not liable to take cold), that I had the head and heart of an evil spirit in all matters of deception. I thought at the time; I really did think; you flattered me. But now I begin to wonder at your discernment, and vanity apart, do honestly believe you spoke the truth. Did you ever counterfeit extreme ingenuousness and honest indignation? My dear fellow, you have no conception if you never did, how faint the effort makes one.'

Mr Haredale surveyed him with a look of cold contempt. 'You may evade an explanation, I know,' he said, folding his arms. 'But I must have it. I can wait.'

'Not at all. Not at all, my good fellow. You shall not wait a moment,' returned his friend, as he lazily crossed his legs. 'The simplest thing in the world. It lies in a nutshell. Ned has written her a letter – a boyish, honest, sentimental composition, which remains as yet in his desk, because he hasn't had the heart to send it. I have taken a liberty, for which my parental affection and anxiety are a sufficient excuse, and possessed myself of the contents. I have described them to your niece (a most enchanting person, Haredale; quite an angelic creature), with a little colouring and description adapted to our purpose. It's done. You may be quite easy. It's all over. Deprived of their adherents and mediators; her pride and jealousy roused to the utmost; with nobody to undeceive her, and you to confirm me; you will find that their intercourse will close with her answer. If she receives Ned's letter by to-morrow noon, you may date their parting from to-morrow night. No thanks I beg; you owe me none. I have acted for myself; and if I have forwarded our compact with all the ardour even you could have desired, I have done so selfishly, indeed.'

'I curse the compact, as you call it, with my whole heart and soul,' returned the other. 'It was made in an evil hour. I have bound myself to a lie; I have leagued myself with you; and though I did so with a righteous motive, and though it cost me such an effort as haply few men know, I hate and despise myself for the deed.'

'You are very warm,' said Mr Chester with a languid smile.

'I *am* warm. I am maddened by your coldness. 'Death, Chester, if your blood ran warmer in your veins, and there were no restraints upon me, such as those that hold and drag me back – well; it is done; you tell me so, and on such a point I may believe you. When I am most remorseful for this treachery, I will think of you and your marriage, and try to justify myself in such remembrances, for having torn asunder Emma and your son, at any cost. Our bond is cancelled now, and we may part.'

Mr Chester kissed his hand gracefully; and with the same tranquil face he had preserved throughout – even when he had seen his companion so tortured and transported by his passion that his whole frame was shaken – lay in his lounging posture on the seat and watched him as he walked away.

'My scape-goat and my drudge at school,' he said, raising his head to look after him; 'my friend of later days, who could not keep his mistress when he had won her, and threw me in her way to carry off the prize; I triumph in the present and the past. Bark on, ill-favoured ill-conditioned cur; fortune has ever been with me – I like to hear you.'

The spot where they had met, was in an avenue of trees. Mr Haredale not passing out on either hand, had walked straight on. He chanced to turn his head when at some considerable distance, and seeing that his late companion had by that time risen and was looking after him, stood still as though he half expected him to follow, and waited for his coming up.

'It *may* come to that one day, but not yet,' said Mr Chester, waving his hand, as though they were the best of friends, and turning away. 'Not yet, Haredale. Life is pleasant enough to me; dull and full of heaviness to you. No. To cross swords with such a man – to indulge his humour unless upon extremity – would be weak indeed.'

For all that, he drew his sword as he walked along, and in an absent humour ran his eye from hilt to point full twenty times. But thoughtfulness begets wrinkles; remembering this, he soon put it up, smoothed his contracted brow, hummed a gay tune with greater gaiety of manner, and was his unruffled self again.

CHAPTER THE THIRTIETH

A homely proverb recognises the existence of a troublesome class of persons who, having an inch conceded them, will take an ell. Not to quote the illustrious examples of those heroic scourges of mankind, whose amiable path in life has been from birth to death through blood, and fire, and ruin, and who would seem to have existed for no better purpose than to teach mankind that as the absence of pain is pleasure, so the earth, purged of their presence, may be deemed a blessed place – not to quote such mighty instances, it will be sufficient to refer to old John Willet.

Old John having long encroached a good standard inch, full measure, on the liberty of Joe, and having snipped off a Flemish ell in the matter of the parole, grew so despotic and so great, that his thirst for conquest knew no bounds. The more young Joe submitted, the more absolute old John became. The ell soon faded into nothing. Yards, furlongs, miles, arose; and on went old John in the pleasant-est manner possible, trimming off an exuberance in this place, shearing away some liberty of speech or action in that, and con-ducting himself in his small way with as much high mightiness and majesty, as the most glorious tyrant that ever had his statue reared in the public ways, of ancient or of modern times.

As great men are urged on to the abuse of power (when they need urging, which is not often), by their flatterers and dependents, so old John was impelled to these exercises of authority by the applause and admiration of his Maypole cronies, who, in the intervals of their nightly pipes and pots, would shake their heads and say that Mr Willet was a father of the good old English sort; that there were no new-fangled notions or modern ways in him; that he put them in mind of what their fathers were when they were boys; that there was no mistake about him; that it would be well for the country if there were more like him, and more was the pity that there were not; with many other original remarks of that nature. Then they would condescendingly give Joe to understand that it was all for his good, and he would be thankful for it one day; and in particular, Mr Cobb would acquaint him, that when he was his age, his father thought no more of giving him a parental kick, or a box on the ears, or a cuff on the head, or some little admonition of that sort, than he did of any other ordinary duty of life; and he would further remark, with looks of great significance, that but for this judicious bringing up, he might have never been the man he was at that present speaking: which was probable enough, as he was, beyond all question, the dullest dog of the party. In short, between old John and old John's friends, there never was an unfortunate young fellow so bullied, badgered, worried, fretted, and brow-beaten; so constantly beset, or made so tired of his life, as poor Joe Willet.

This had come to be the recognised and established state of things; but as John was very anxious to flourish his supremacy before the eyes of Mr Chester, he did that day exceed himself, and did so goad and chafe his son and heir, that but for Joe's having made a solemn vow to keep his hands in his pockets when they were not otherwise engaged, it is impossible to say what he might have done with them. But the longest day has an end, and at length Mr Chester came down stairs to mount his horse, which was ready at the door.

As old John was not in the way at the moment, Joe, who was sitting in the bar ruminating on his dismal fate and the manifold perfections of Dolly Varden, ran out to hold the guest's stirrup and assist him to mount. Mr Chester was scarcely in the saddle, and Joe was in the very act of making him a graceful bow, when old John came diving out of the porch, and collared him.

'None of that, sir,' said John, 'none of that, sir. No breaking of patroles. How dare you come out of the door, sir, without leave? You're trying to get away, sir, are you, and to make a traitor of yourself again? What do you mean, sir?'

'Let me go, father,' said Joe, imploringly, as he marked the smile upon their visitor's face, and observed the pleasure his disgrace afforded him. 'This is too bad. Who wants to get away?'

'Who wants to get away!' cried John, shaking him. 'Why you do, sir, you do. You're the boy, sir,' added John, collaring with one hand, and aiding the effect of a farewell bow to the visitor with the other, 'that wants to sneak into houses, and stir up differences between noble gentlemen and their sons, are you, eh? Hold your tongue, sir.'

Joe made no effort to reply. It was the crowning circumstance of his degradation. He extricated himself from his father's grasp, darted an angry look at the departing guest, and returned into the house.

'But for her,' thought Joe, as he threw his arms upon a table in the common room, and laid his head upon them, 'but for Dolly, who I couldn't bear should think me the rascal they would make me out to be if I ran away, this house and I should part to-night.'

It being evening by this time, Solomon Daisy, Tom Cobb, and Long Parkes, were all in the common room too, and had from the window been witnesses of what had just occurred. Mr Willet joining them soon afterwards, received the compliments of the company with great composure, and lighting his pipe, sat down among them.

'We'll see, gentlemen,' said John, after a long pause, 'who's the master of this house, and who isn't. We'll see whether boys are to govern men, or men are to govern boys.'

'And quite right too,' assented Solomon Daisy with some approving nods; 'quite right, Johnny. Very good, Johnny. Well said, Mr Willet. Brayvo, sir.'

John slowly brought his eyes to bear upon him, looked at him for a long time, and finally made answer, to the unspeakable consternation of his hearers, 'When I want encouragement from you, sir, I'll ask you for it. You let me alone, sir. I can get on without you, I hope. Don't you tackle me, sir, if you please.'

'Don't take it ill, Johnny; I didn't mean any harm,' pleaded the little man.

'Very good, sir,' said John, more than usually obstinate after his late success. 'Never mind, sir. I can stand pretty firm of myself, sir, I believe, without being shored up by you.' And having given utterance to this retort, Mr Willet fixed his eyes upon the boiler, and fell into a kind of tobacco-trance.

The spirits of the company being somewhat damped by this embarrassing line of conduct on the part of their host, nothing more was said for a long time; but at length Mr Cobb took upon himself to remark, as he rose to knock the ashes out of his pipe, that he hoped Joe would thenceforth learn to obey his father in all things; that he had found, that day, he was not one of the sort of men who were to be trifled with; and that he would recommend him, poetically speaking, to mind his eye for the future.

'I'd recommend you, in return,' said Joe, looking up with a flushed face, 'not to talk to me.'

'Hold your tongue, sir,' cried Mr Willet, suddenly rousing himself, and turning round.

'I won't, father,' cried Joe, smiting the table with his fist, so that the jugs and glasses rung again; 'these things are hard enough to bear from you; from anybody else I never will endure them any more. Therefore I say, Mr Cobb, don't talk to me.'

'Why, who are you,' said Mr Cobb, sneeringly, 'that you're not to be talked to, eh, Joe?'

To which Joe returned no answer, but with a very ominous shake of the head, resumed his old position, which he would have peacefully preserved until the house shut up at night, but that Mr Cobb, stimulated by the wonder of the company at the young man's presumption, retorted with sundry taunts, which proved too much for flesh and blood to bear. Crowding into one moment the vexation and the wrath of years, Joe started up, overturned the table, fell upon his long enemy, pummelled him with all his might and main, and finished by driving him with surprising swiftness against a heap of spittoons in one corner; plunging into which, head foremost, with a tremendous crash, he lay at full length among the ruins, stunned and motionless. Then, without waiting to receive the compliments of the bystanders on the victory he had won, he retreated to his own bedchamber, and considering himself in a state of siege, piled all the portable furniture against the door by way of barricade.

'I have done it now,' said Joe, as he sat down upon his bedstead and wiped his heated face. 'I knew it would come at last. The Maypole and I must part company. I'm a roving vagabond – she hates me for evermore – it's all over!'

——— ✳ ———

CHAPTER THE THIRTY-FIRST

Pondering on his unhappy lot, Joe sat and listened for a long time, expecting every moment to hear their creaking footsteps on the stairs, or to be greeted by his worthy father with a summons to capitulate unconditionally, and deliver himself up straightway. But neither voice nor footstep came; and though some distant echoes, as of closing doors and people hurrying in and out of rooms, resounding from time to time through the great passages, and penetrating to his remote seclusion, gave note of unusual commotion down stairs, no nearer sound disturbed his place of retreat, which seemed the quieter for these far-off noises, and was as dull and full of gloom as any hermit's cell.

It came on darker and darker. The old-fashioned furniture of the chamber, which was a kind of hospital for all the invalided moveables in the house, grew indistinct and shadowy in its many shapes; chairs and tables, which by day were as honest cripples as need be, assumed a doubtful and mysterious character; and one old leprous screen of faded India leather and gold binding, which had kept out many a cold breath of air in days of yore and shut in many a jolly face, frowned on him with a spectral aspect, and stood at full height in its allotted corner, like some gaunt ghost who waited to be questioned. A portrait opposite the window – a queer, old grey-eyed general, in an oval frame – seemed to wink and dose as the light decayed, and at length, when the last faint glimmering speck of day went out, to shut its eyes in good earnest, and fall sound asleep. There was such a hush and mystery about everything, that Joe could not help following its example; and so went off into a slumber likewise, and dreamed of Dolly, till the clock of Chigwell church struck two.

Still nobody came. The distant noises in the house had ceased, and out of doors all was quiet too; save for the occasional barking of some deep-mouthed dog, and the shaking of the branches by the night wind. He gazed mournfully out of window at each well-known object as it lay sleeping in the dim light of the moon; and creeping back to his former seat, thought about the late uproar, until, with long thinking of, it seemed to have occurred a month ago. Thus, between dozing, and thinking, and walking to the window and looking out, the night wore away; the grim old screen, and the kindred chairs and tables, began slowly to reveal themselves in their accustomed forms; the grey-eyed general seemed to wink and yawn and rouse himself; and at last he was broad awake again, and very uncomfortable and cold and haggard he looked, in the dull grey light of morning.

The sun had begun to peep above the forest trees, and already flung across the curling mist bright bars of gold, when Joe dropped from his window on the ground below, a little bundle and his trusty stick, and prepared to descend himself.

It was not a very difficult task; for there were so many projections and gable ends in the way, that they formed a series of clumsy steps, with no greater obstacle than a jump of some few feet at last. Joe, with his stick and bundle on his shoulder, quickly stood on the firm earth, and looked up at the old Maypole, it might be for the last time.

He didn't apostrophise it, for he was no great scholar. He didn't curse it, for he had little ill-will to give to anything on earth. He felt more affectionate and kind to it than ever he had done in all his life before, so said with all his heart, 'God bless you!' as a parting wish, and turned away.

He walked along at a brisk pace, big with great thoughts of going for a soldier and dying in some foreign country where it was very hot and sandy, and leaving God knows what unheard-of wealth in prize-money to Dolly, who would be very much affected when she came to know of it; and full of such youthful visions, which were sometimes sanguine and sometimes melancholy, but always had her for their main point and centre, pushed on vigorously until the noise of London sounded in his ears, and the Black Lion hove in sight.

It was only eight o'clock then, and very much astonished the Black Lion was, to see him come walking in with dust upon his feet at that early hour, with no grey mare to bear him company. But as he ordered breakfast to be got ready with all speed, and on its being

set before him gave indisputable tokens of a hearty appetite, the
Lion received him, as usual, with a hospitable welcome; and treated
him with those marks of distinction, which, as a regular customer,
and one within the freemasonry of the trade, he had a right to
claim.

This Lion or landlord, – for he was called both man and beast,
by reason of his having instructed the artist who painted his sign,
to convey into the features of the lordly brute whose effigy it bore,
as near a counterpart of his own face as his skill could compass
and devise, – was a gentleman almost as quick of apprehension,
and of almost as subtle a wit, as the mighty John himself. But
the difference between them lay in this; that whereas Mr Willet's
extreme sagacity and acuteness were the efforts of unassisted
nature, the Lion stood indebted, in no small amount, to beer; of
which he swigged such copious draughts, that most of his faculties
were utterly drowned and washed away, except the one great
faculty of sleep, which he retained in surprising perfection. The
creaking Lion over the house-door was, therefore, to say the truth,
rather a drowsy, tame, and feeble lion; and as these social represen-
tatives of a savage class are usually of a conventional character
(being depicted, for the most part, in impossible attitudes and of
unearthly colours), he was frequently supposed by the more ignorant and uninformed among the neighbours, to be the veritable
portrait of the host as he appeared on the occasion of some great
funeral ceremony or public mourning.

'What noisy fellow is that in the next room?' said Joe, when
he had disposed of his breakfast, and had washed and brushed
himself.

'A recruiting serjeant,' replied the Lion.

Joe started involuntarily. Here was the very thing he had been
dreaming of, all the way along.

'And I wish,' said the Lion, 'he was anywhere else but here. The
party make noise enough, but they don't call for much. There's great
cry there, Mr Willet, but very little wool.[1] Your father wouldn't like
'em, I know.'

Perhaps not much under any circumstances. Perhaps if he could
have known what was passing at that moment in Joe's mind, he
would have liked them still less.

'Is he recruiting for a – for a fine regiment?' said Joe, glancing at
a little round mirror that hung in the bar.

'I believe he is,' replied the host. 'It's much the same thing, whatever regiment he's recruiting for. I'm told there an't a deal of difference between a fine man and another one, when they're shot through and through.'

'They're not all shot,' said Joe.

'No,' the Lion answered, 'not all. Those that are – supposing it's done easy – are the best off in my opinion.'

'Ah!' retorted Joe, 'but you don't care for glory.'

'For what?' said the Lion.

'Glory.'

'No,' returned the Lion, with supreme indifference. 'I don't. You're right in that, Mr Willet. When Glory comes here, and calls for anything to drink and changes a guinea to pay for it, I'll give it him for nothing. It's my belief, sir, that the Glory's arms wouldn't do a very strong business.'

These remarks were not at all comforting. Joe walked out, stopped at the door of the next room, and listened. The serjeant was describing a military life. It was all drinking, he said, except that there were frequent intervals of eating and love-making. A battle was the finest thing in the world – when your side won it – and Englishmen always did that. 'Supposing you should be killed, sir?' said a timid voice in one corner. 'Well, sir, supposing you should be,' said the serjeant, 'what then? Your country loves you, sir; his Majesty King George the Third loves you; your memory is honoured, revered, respected; everybody's fond of you, and grateful to you; your name's wrote down at full length in a book in the War-office.[2] Damme, gentlemen, we must all die some time, or another, eh?'

The voice coughed, and said no more.

Joe walked into the room. A group of half-a-dozen fellows had gathered together in the tap-room, and were listening with greedy ears. One of them, a carter in a smockfrock, seemed wavering and disposed to enlist. The rest, who were by no means disposed, strongly urged him to do so (according to the custom of mankind), backed the serjeant's arguments, and grinned among themselves. 'I say nothing, boys,' said the serjeant, who sat a little apart, drinking his liquor. 'For lads of spirit' – here he cast an eye on Joe – 'this is the time. I don't want to inveigle you. The king's not come to that, I hope. Brisk young blood is what we want; not milk and water. We won't take five men out of six. We want top-sawyers, we do.

I'm not a-going to tell tales out of school, but, damme, if every
gentleman's son that carries arms in our corps, through being under
a cloud and having little differences with his relations, was counted
up' – here his eye fell on Joe again, and so good-naturedly, that Joe
beckoned him out. He came directly.

'You're a gentleman, by G – !' was his first remark, as he slapped
him on the back. 'You're a gentleman in disguise. So am I. Let's
swear a friendship.'

Joe didn't exactly do that, but he shook hands with him, and
thanked him for his good opinion.

'You want to serve,' said his new friend. 'You shall. You were
made for it. You're one of us by nature. What'll you take to drink?'

'Nothing just now,' replied Joe, smiling faintly. 'I haven't quite
made up my mind.'

'A mettlesome fellow like you, and not made up his mind!' cried
the serjeant. 'Here – let me give the bell a pull, and you'll make up
your mind in half a minute, I know.'

'You're right so far' – answered Joe, 'for if you pull the bell here,
where I'm known, there'll be an end of my soldiering inclinations
in no time. Look in my face. You see me, do you?'

'I do,' replied the serjeant with an oath, 'and a finer young fellow
or one better qualified to serve his king and country, I never set
my –' he used an adjective in this place – 'eyes on.'

'Thank you,' said Joe, 'I didn't ask you for want of a compliment,
but thank you all the same. Do I look like a sneaking fellow or a
liar?'

The serjeant rejoined with many choice asseverations that he
didn't; and that if his (the serjeant's) own father were to say he did,
he would run the old gentleman through the body cheerfully, and
consider it a meritorious action.

Joe expressed his obligations, and continued, 'You can trust me
then, and credit what I say. I believe I shall enlist into your regiment
to-night. The reason I don't do so now is, because I don't want
until to-night, to do what I can't recal. Where shall I find you, this
evening?'

His friend replied with some unwillingness, and after much
ineffectual entreaty having for its object the immediate settlement
of the business, that his quarters would be at the Crooked Billet in
Tower-street;[3] where he would be found waking until midnight,
and sleeping until breakfast-time to-morrow.

'And if I do come – which it's a million to one, I shall – when will you take me out of London?' demanded Joe.

'To-morrow morning, at half after eight o' clock,' replied the serjeant. 'You'll go abroad – a country where it's all sunshine and plunder – the finest climate in the world.'

'To go abroad,' said Joe, shaking hands with him, 'is the very thing I want. You may expect me.'

'You're the kind of lad for us,' cried the serjeant, holding Joe's hand in his, in the excess of his admiration. 'You're the boy to push your fortune. I don't say it because I bear you any envy, or would take away from the credit of the rise you'll make, but if I had been bred and taught like you, I'd have been a colonel by this time.'

'Tush man!' said Joe, 'I'm not so young as that. Needs must when the devil drives;[4] and the devil that drives me is an empty pocket and an unhappy home. For the present, good-bye.'

'For king and country!' cried the serjeant, flourishing his cap.

'For bread and meat!' cried Joe, snapping his fingers. And so they parted.

He had very little money in his pocket; so little indeed, that after paying for his breakfast (which he was too honest and perhaps too proud to score up to his father's charge) he had but a penny left. He had courage, notwithstanding, to resist all the affectionate importunities of the serjeant, who waylaid him at the door with many protestations of eternal friendship, and did in particular request that he would do him the favour to accept of only one shilling as a temporary accommodation.[5] Rejecting his offers both of cash and credit, Joe walked away with stick and bundle as before, bent upon getting through the day as he best could, and going down to the locksmith's in the dusk of the evening; for it should go hard, he had resolved, but he would have a parting word with charming Dolly Varden.

He went out by Islington and so on to Highgate, and sat on many stones and gates, but there were no voices in the bells to bid him turn. Since the time of noble Whittington,[6] fair flower of merchants, bells have come to have less sympathy with humankind. They only ring for money and on state occasions. Wanderers have increased in number; ships leave the Thames for distant regions, carrying from stem to stern no other cargo; the bells are silent; they ring out no entreaties or regrets; they are used to it and have grown worldly.

Joe bought a roll, and reduced his purse to the condition (with a difference) of that celebrated purse of Fortunatus,[7] which, whatever were its favoured owner's necessities, had one unvarying amount in it. In these real times, when all the Fairies are dead and buried, there are still a great many purses which possess that quality. The sum total they contain is expressed in arithmetic by a circle, and whether it be added to or multiplied by its own amount, the result of the problem is more easily stated than any known in figures.

Evening drew on at last. With the desolate and solitary feeling of one who had no home or shelter, and was alone utterly in the world for the first time, he bent his steps towards the locksmith's house. He had delayed till now, knowing that Mrs Varden sometimes went out alone, or with Miggs for her sole attendant, to lectures in the evening; and devoutly hoping that this might be one of her nights of moral culture.

He had walked up and down before the house, on the opposite side of the way, two or three times, when as he returned to it again, he caught a glimpse of a fluttering skirt at the door. It was Dolly's – to whom else could it belong? no dress but hers had such a flow as that. He plucked up his spirits, and followed it into the workshop of the Golden Key.

His darkening the door caused her to look round. Oh that face! 'If it hadn't been for that,' thought Joe, 'I should never have walked into poor Tom Cobb. She's twenty times handsomer than ever. She might marry a Lord!'

He didn't say this. He only thought it – perhaps looked it also. Dolly was glad to see him, and was *so* sorry her father and mother were away from home. Joe begged she wouldn't mention it on any account.

Dolly hesitated to lead the way into the parlour, for there it was nearly dark; at the same time she hesitated to stand talking in the workshop, which was yet light and open to the street. They had got by some means, too, before the little forge; and Joe having her hand in his (which he had no right to have, for Dolly only gave it him to shake), it was so like standing before some homely altar being married, that it was the most embarrassing state of things in the world.

'I have come,' said Joe, 'to say good-bye – to say good-bye for I don't know how many years; perhaps for ever. I am going abroad.'

Now this was exactly what he should not have said. Here he was, talking like a gentleman at large who was free to come and go and roam about the world at his pleasure, when that gallant coachmaker had vowed but the night before that Miss Varden held him bound in adamantine chains;[8] and had positively stated in so many words that she was killing him by inches, and that in a fortnight more or thereabouts he expected to make a decent end and leave the business to his mother.

Dolly released her hand and said 'Indeed!' She remarked in the same breath that it was a fine night, and in short, betrayed no more emotion than the forge itself.

'I couldn't go,' said Joe, 'without coming to see you. I hadn't the heart to.'

Dolly was more sorry than she could tell, that he should have taken so much trouble. It was such a long way, and he must have such a deal to do. And how *was* Mr Willet – that dear old gentleman –

'Is this all you say!' cried Joe.

All! Good gracious, what did the man expect! She was obliged to take her apron in her hand and run her eyes along the hem from corner to corner, to keep herself from laughing in his face; – not because his gaze confused her – not at all.

Joe had small experience in love affairs, and had no notion how different young ladies are at different times; he had expected to take Dolly up again at the very point where he had left her after that delicious evening ride, and was no more prepared for such an alteration than to see the sun and moon change places. He had buoyed himself up all day with an indistinct idea that she would certainly say 'Don't go,' or 'Don't leave us,' or 'Why do you go?' or 'Why do you leave us?' or would give him some little encouragement of that sort; he had even entertained the possibility of her bursting into tears, of her throwing herself into his arms, of her falling down in a fainting fit without previous word or sign; but any approach to such a line of conduct as this, had been so far from his thoughts that he could only look at her in silent wonder.

Dolly in the mean while, turned to the corners of her apron, and measured the sides, and smoothed out the wrinkles, and was as silent as he. At last after a long pause, Joe said good-bye. 'Good-bye' – said Dolly – with as pleasant a smile as if he were going into the next street, and were coming back to supper; 'good-bye.'

'Come,' said Joe, putting out both his hands, 'Dolly, dear Dolly, don't let us part like this. I love you dearly, with all my heart and soul; with as much truth and earnestness as ever man loved woman in this world, I do believe. I am a poor fellow, as you know – poorer now than ever, for I have fled from home, not being able to bear it any longer, and must fight my own way without help. You are beautiful, admired, are loved by everybody, are well off and happy; and may you ever be so! Heaven forbid I should ever make you otherwise; but give me a word of comfort. Say something kind to me. I have no right to expect it of you, I know, but I ask it because I love you, and shall treasure the slightest word from you all through my life. Dolly, dearest, have you nothing to say to me?'

No. Nothing. Dolly was a coquette by nature, and a spoilt child. She had no notion of being carried by storm in this way. The coachmaker would have been dissolved in tears, and would have knelt down, and called himself names, and clasped his hands, and beat his breast, and tugged wildly at his cravat, and done all kinds of poetry. Joe had no business to be going abroad. He had no right to be able to do it. If he was in adamantine chains, he couldn't.

'I have said good-bye,' said Dolly, 'twice. Take your arm away directly, Mr Joseph, or I'll call Miggs.'

'I'll not reproach you,' answered Joe, 'it's my fault, no doubt. I have thought sometimes that you didn't quite despise me, but I was a fool to think so. Every one must, who has seen the life I have led – you most of all. God bless you!'

He was gone, actually gone. Dolly waited a little while, thinking he would return, peeped out at the door, looked up the street and down as well as the increasing darkness would allow, came in again, waited a little longer, went up stairs humming a tune, bolted herself in, laid her head down on her bed, and cried as if her heart would break. And yet such natures are made up of so many contradictions, that if Joe Willet had come back that night, next day, next week, next month, the odds are a hundred to one she would have treated him in the very same manner, and have wept for it afterwards with the very same distress.

She had no sooner left the workshop than there cautiously peered out from behind the chimney of the forge, a face which had already emerged from the same concealment twice or thrice, unseen, and which, after satisfying itself that it was now alone, was followed by a leg, a shoulder, and so on by degrees, until the form of Mr

Tappertit stood confessed, with a brown-paper cap struck negligently on one side of its head, and its arms very much a-kimbo.

'Have my ears deceived me,' said the 'Prentice, 'or do I dream! am I to thank thee, Fortun', or to cus thee – which?'

He gravely descended from his elevation, took down his piece of looking-glass, planted it against the wall upon the usual bench, twisted his head round, and looked closely at his legs.

'If they're a dream,' said Sim, 'let sculptures have such wisions, and chisel 'em out when they wake. This is reality. Sleep has no such limbs as them. Tremble, Willet, and despair. She's mine! She's mine!'

With these triumphant expressions, he seized a hammer and dealt a heavy blow at a vice, which in his mind's eye represented the sconce[9] or head of Joseph Willet. That done, he burst into a peal of laughter which startled Miss Miggs even in her distant kitchen, and dipping his head into a bowl of water, had recourse to a jack-towel inside the closet door, which served the double purpose of smothering his feelings and drying his face.

Joe, disconsolate and down-hearted, but full of courage too, on leaving the locksmith's house made the best of his way to the Crooked Billet, and there inquired for his friend the serjeant, who, expecting no man less, received him with open arms. In the course of five minutes after his arrival at that house of entertainment, he was enrolled among the gallant defenders of his native land; and within half an hour, was regaled with a steaming supper of boiled tripe and onions, prepared, as his friend assured him more than once, at the express command of his most Sacred Majesty the King. To this meal, which tasted very savoury after his long fasting, he did ample justice; and when he had followed it up, or down, with a variety of loyal and patriotic toasts, he was conducted to a straw mattress in a loft over the stable, and locked in there for the night.

The next morning, he found that the obliging care of his martial friend had decorated his hat with sundry parti-coloured streamers, which made a very lively appearance; and in company with that officer, and three other military gentlemen newly enrolled, who were under a cloud so dense that it only left three shoes, a boot, and a coat and a half visible among them, repaired to the river-side. Here they were joined by a corporal and four more heroes, of whom two were drunk and daring, and two sober and penitent, but each of whom, like Joe, had his dusty stick and bundle. The party embarked in a passage-boat bound for Gravesend, whence they were to proceed on foot to Chatham;[10] the wind was in their favour, and they soon left London behind them, a mere dark mist – a giant phantom in the air.

CHAPTER THE THIRTY-SECOND

Misfortunes, saith the adage, never come singly. There is little doubt that troubles are exceedingly gregarious in their nature, and flying in flocks, are apt to perch capriciously; crowding on the heads of some poor wights until there is not an inch of room left on their unlucky crowns, and taking no more notice of others who offer as good resting-places for the soles of their feet,[1] than if they had no existence. It may have happened that a flight of troubles brooding over London, and looking out for Joseph Willet, whom they couldn't find, darted down hap-hazard on the first young man that caught their fancy, and settled on him instead. However this may be, certain it is that on the very day of Joe's departure they swarmed about the ears of Edward Chester, and did so buzz and flap their wings, and persecute him, that he was most profoundly wretched.

It was evening, and just eight o'clock, when he and his father, having wine and dessert set before them, were left to themselves for the first time that day. They had dined together, but a third person had been present during the meal, and until they met at table they had not seen each other since the previous night.

Edward was reserved, and silent. Mr Chester was more than usually gay; but not caring, as it seemed, to open a conversation with one whose humour was so different, he vented the lightness of his spirit in smiles and sparkling looks, and made no effort to awaken his attention. So they remained for some time: the father lying on a sofa with his accustomed air of graceful negligence; the son seated opposite to him with downcast eyes, busied, it was plain, with painful and uneasy thoughts.

'My dear Edward,' said Mr Chester at length, with a most engaging laugh, 'do not extend your drowsy influence to the decanter. Suffer *that* to circulate, let your spirits be never so stagnant.'

Edward begged his pardon, passed it, and relapsed into his former state.

'You do wrong not to fill your glass,' said Mr Chester, holding up his own before the light. 'Wine in moderation – not in excess, for that makes men ugly – has a thousand pleasant influences. It brightens the eyes, improves the voice, imparts a new vivacity to one's thoughts and conversation: you should try it, Ned.'

'Ah father!' cried his son, 'if—'

'My good fellow,' interposed the parent hastily, as he set down his glass, and raised his eyebrows with a startled and horrified expression, 'for heaven's sake don't call me by that obsolete and ancient name. Have some regard for delicacy. Am I grey, or wrinkled, do I go on crutches, have I lost my teeth, that you adopt such a mode of address? Good God, how very coarse!'

'I was about to speak to you from my heart, sir,' returned Edward, 'in the confidence which should subsist between us; and you check me in the outset.'

'Now *do*, Ned, *do* not,' said Mr Chester, raising his delicate hand imploringly, 'talk in that monstrous manner. About to speak from your heart! Don't you know that the heart is an ingenious part of our formation – the centre of the blood-vessels and all that sort of thing – which has no more to do with what you say or think, than your knees have? How can you be so very vulgar and absurd? These anatomical allusions should be left to gentlemen of the medical profession. They are really not agreeable in society. You quite surprise me, Ned.'

'Well! there are no such things to wound, or heal, or have regard for. I know your creed, sir, and will say no more,' returned his son.

'There again,' said Mr Chester, sipping his wine, 'you are wrong. I distinctly say there are such things. We know there are. The hearts of animals – of bullocks, sheep, and so forth – are cooked and devoured, as I am told, by the lower classes, with a vast deal of relish. Men are sometimes stabbed to the heart, shot to the heart; but as to speaking from the heart, or to the heart, or being warm-hearted, or cold-hearted, or broken-hearted, or being all heart, or having no heart – pah! these things are nonsense, Ned.'

'No doubt, sir,' returned his son, seeing that he paused for him to speak. 'No doubt.'

'There's Haredale's niece, your late flame,' said Mr Chester, as a careless illustration of his meaning. 'No doubt in your mind she was all heart once. Now she has none at all. Yet she is the same person, Ned, exactly.'

'She is a changed person, sir,' cried Edward, reddening; 'and changed by vile means, I believe.'

'You have had a cool dismissal, have you?' said his father. 'Poor Ned! I told you last night what would happen. – May I ask you for the nut-crackers?'

'She has been tampered with, and most treacherously deceived,' cried Edward, rising from his seat. 'I never will believe that the knowledge of my real position, given her by myself, has worked this change. I know she is beset and tortured. But though our contract is at an end, and broken past all redemption; though I charge upon her want of firmness and want of truth, both to herself and me; I do not now, and never will believe, that any sordid motive, or her own unbiassed will, has led her to this course – never!'

'You make me blush,' returned his father gaily, 'for the folly of your nature, in which – but we never know ourselves – I devoutly hope there is no reflection of my own. With regard to the young lady herself, she has done what is very natural and proper, my dear fellow; what you yourself proposed, as I learn from Haredale; and what I predicted – with no great exercise of sagacity – she would do. She supposed you to be rich, or at least quite rich enough; and found you poor. Marriage is a civil contract; people marry to better their worldly condition and improve appearances; it is an affair of house and furniture, of liveries, servants, equipage, and so forth. The lady being poor and you poor also, there is an end of the matter. You cannot enter upon these considerations, and have no manner of business with the ceremony. I drink her health in this glass, and respect and honour her for her extreme good sense. It is a lesson to you. Fill yours, Ned.'

'It is a lesson,' returned his son, 'by which I hope I may never profit, and if years and their experience impress it on –'

'Don't say on the heart,' interposed his father.

'On men whom the world and its hypocrisy have spoiled,' said Edward warmly, 'Heaven keep me from its knowledge.'

'Come, sir,' returned his father, raising himself a little on the sofa, and looking straight towards him; 'we have had enough of this. Remember, if you please, your interest, your duty, your moral obligations, your filial affections, and all that sort of thing, which

it is so very delightful and charming to reflect upon; or you will repent it.'

'I shall never repent the preservation of my self-respect, sir,' said Edward. 'Forgive me if I say that I will not sacrifice it at your bidding, and that I will not pursue the track which you would have me take, and to which the secret share you have had in this late separation, tends.'

His father rose a little higher still, and looking at him as though curious to know if he were quite resolved and earnest, dropped gently down again, and said in the calmest voice – eating his nuts meanwhile,

'Edward, my father had a son, who being a fool like you, and, like you, entertaining low and disobedient sentiments, he disinherited and cursed one morning after breakfast. The circumstance occurs to me with a singular clearness of recollection this evening. I remember eating muffins at the time, with marmalade. He led a miserable life (the son, I mean) and died early; it was a happy release on all accounts; he degraded the family very much. It is a sad circumstance, Edward, when a father finds it necessary to resort to such strong measures.'

'It is,' replied Edward, 'and it is sad when a son, proffering him his love and duty in their best and truest sense, finds himself repelled at every turn, and forced to disobey. Dear father,' he added, more earnestly though in a gentler tone, 'I have reflected many times on what occurred between us when we first discussed this subject. Let there be a confidence between us; not in terms, but truth. Hear what I have to say.'

'As I anticipate what it is, and cannot fail to do so, Edward,' returned his father coldly, 'I decline. I couldn't possibly. I am sure it would put me out of temper, which is a state of mind I can't endure. If you intend to mar my plans for your establishment in life, and the preservation of that gentility and becoming pride, which our family have so long sustained – if, in short, you are resolved to take your own course, you must take it, and my curse with it. I am very sorry, but there's really no alternative.'

'The curse may pass your lips,' said Edward, 'but it will be but empty breath. I do not believe that any man on earth has greater power to call one down upon his fellow – least of all, upon his own child – than he has to make one drop of rain or flake of snow fall from the clouds above us at his impious bidding. Beware, sir, what you do.'

'You are so very irreligious, so exceedingly undutiful, so horribly profane,' rejoined his father, turning his face lazily towards him, and cracking another nut, 'that I positively must interrupt you here. It is quite impossible we can continue to go on, upon such terms as these. If you will do me the favour to ring the bell, the servant will show you to the door. Return to this roof no more, I beg you. Go, sir, since you have no moral sense remaining; and go to the Devil, at my express desire. Good day.'

Edward left the room without another word or look, and turned his back upon the house for ever.

The father's face was slightly flushed and heated, but his manner was quite unchanged, as he rang the bell again, and addressed his servant on his entrance.

'Peak – if that gentleman who has just gone out –'

'I beg your pardon, sir, Mr Edward?'

'Were there more than one, dolt, that you ask the question? – If that gentleman should send here for his wardrobe, let him have it, do you hear? If he should call himself at any time, I'm not at home. You'll tell him so, and shut the door.'

So, it soon got whispered about, that Mr Chester was very unfortunate in his son, who had occasioned him great grief and sorrow. And the good people who heard this and told it again, marvelled the more at his equanimity and even temper, and said what an amiable nature that man must have, who, having undergone so much, could be so placid and so calm. And when Edward's name was spoken, Society shook its head and laid its finger on its lip, and sighed, and looked very grave; and those who had sons about his age, waxed wrathful and indignant, and hoped, for Virtue's sake, that he was dead. And the world went on turning round, as usual, for five years, concerning which this Narrative is silent.

*

CHAPTER THE THIRTY-THIRD

One wintry evening, early in the year of our Lord one thousand
seven hundred and eighty, a keen north wind arose as it grew dark,
and night came on with black and dismal looks. A bitter storm of
sleet, sharp, dense, and icy-cold, swept the wet streets, and rattled
on the trembling windows. Signboards, shaken past endurance in
their creaking frames, fell crashing on the pavement; old tottering
chimneys reeled and staggered in the blast; and many a steeple
rocked again that night, as though the earth were troubled.

It was not a time for those who could by any means get light and
warmth, to brave the fury of the weather. In coffee-houses of the
better sort, guests crowded round the fire, forgot to be political,
and told each other with a secret gladness that the blast grew fiercer
every minute. Each humble tavern by the water-side, had its group
of uncouth figures round the hearth; who talked of vessels foun-
dering at sea, and all hands lost, related many a dismal tale of
shipwreck and drowned men, and hoped that some they knew were
safe, and shook their heads in doubt. In private dwellings, children
clustered near the blaze; listening with timid pleasure to tales of
ghosts and goblins, and tall figures clad in white standing by
bedsides, and people who had gone to sleep in old churches and
being overlooked had found themselves alone there at the dead
hour of the night: until they shuddered at the thought of the dark
rooms up-stairs, yet loved to hear the wind moan too, and hoped
it would continue bravely. From time to time these happy in-door
people stopped to listen, or one held up his finger and cried 'Hark!'
and then, above the rumbling in the chimney, and the fast pattering
on the glass, was heard a wailing, rushing sound, which shook the
walls as though a giant's hand were on them; then a hoarse roar as
if the sea had risen; then such a whirl and tumult that the air seemed
mad; and then, with a lengthened howl, the waves of wind swept
on, and left a moment's interval of rest.

Cheerily, though there were none abroad to see it, shone the
Maypole light that evening. Blessings on the red – deep, ruby,
glowing red – old curtain of the window; blending into one rich
stream of brightness, fire and candle, meat, drink, and company,
and gleaming like a jovial eye upon the bleak waste out of doors!
Within, what carpet like its crunching sand, what music merry as

its crackling logs, what perfume like its kitchen's dainty breath, what weather genial as its hearty warmth! Blessings on the old house, how sturdily it stood! How did the vexed wind chafe and roar about its stalwart roof; how did it pant and strive with its wide chimneys, which still poured forth from their hospitable throats, great clouds of smoke, and puffed defiance in its face; how above all, did it drive and rattle at the casement, emulous to extinguish that cheerful glow, which would not be put down and seemed the brighter for the conflict.

The profusion too, the rich and lavish bounty, of that goodly tavern! It was not enough that one fire roared and sparkled on its spacious hearth; in the tiles which paved and compassed it, five hundred flickering fires burnt brightly also. It was not enough that one red curtain shut the wild night out, and shed its cheerful influence on the room. In every saucepan lid, and candlestick, and vessel of copper, brass, or tin that hung upon the walls, were countless ruddy hangings, flashing and gleaming with every motion of the blaze, and offering, let the eye wander where it might, interminable vistas of the same rich colour. The old oak wainscoting, the beams, the chairs, the seats, reflected it in a deep, dull glimmer. There were fires and red curtains in the very eyes of the drinkers, in their buttons, in their liquor, in the pipes they smoked.

Mr Willet sat in what had been his accustomed place five years before, with his eyes on the eternal boiler; and had sat there since the clock struck eight, giving no other signs of life than breathing with a loud and constant snore (though he was wide awake), and from time to time putting his glass to his lips, or knocking the ashes out of his pipe, and filling it anew. It was now half-past ten. Mr Cobb and long Phil Parkes were his companions, as of old, and for two mortal hours and a half, none of the company had pronounced one word.

Whether people, by dint of sitting together in the same place and the same relative positions, and doing exactly the same things for a great many years, acquire a sixth sense, or some unknown power of influencing each other which serves them in its stead, is a question for philosophy to settle. But certain it is that old John Willet, Mr Parkes, and Mr Cobb, were one and all firmly of opinion that they were very jolly companions – rather choice spirits than otherwise; that they looked at each other every now and then as if there were a perpetual interchange of ideas going on among them;

that no man considered himself or his neighbour by any means silent; and that each of them nodded occasionally when he caught the eye of another, as if he would say 'You have expressed yourself extremely well, sir, in relation to that sentiment, and I quite agree with you.'

The room was so very warm, the tobacco so very good, and the fire so very soothing, that Mr Willet by degrees began to doze; but as he had perfectly acquired, by dint of long habit, the art of smoking in his sleep, and as his breathing was pretty much the same, awake or asleep, saving that in the latter case he sometimes experienced a slight difficulty in respiration (such as a carpenter meets with when he is planing and comes to a knot), neither of his companions was aware of the circumstance, until he met with one of these impediments and was obliged to try again.

'Johnny's dropped off,' said Mr Parkes in a whisper.

'Fast as a top,' said Mr Cobb.

Neither of them said any more until Mr Willet came to another knot – one of surpassing obduracy – which bade fair to throw him into convulsions, but which he got over at last without waking, by an effort quite superhuman.

'He sleeps uncommon hard,' said Mr Cobb.

Mr Parkes, who was possibly a hard-sleeper himself, replied with some disdain 'Not a bit on it;' and directed his eyes towards a handbill pasted over the chimney-piece, which was decorated at the top with a woodcut representing a youth of tender years running away very fast, with a bundle over his shoulder at the end of a stick, and – to carry out the idea – a finger-post and a mile-stone beside him. Mr Cobb likewise turned his eyes in the same direction, and surveyed the placard as if that were the first time he had ever beheld it. Now, this was a document which Mr Willet had himself indited on the disappearance of his son Joseph, acquainting the nobility and gentry and the public in general with the circumstances of his having left his home; describing his dress and appearance; and offering a reward of five pounds to any person or persons who would pack him up and return him safely to the Maypole at Chigwell, or lodge him in any of his Majesty's jails until such time as his father should come and claim him. In this advertisement Mr Willet had obstinately persisted, despite the advice and entreaties of his friends, in describing his son as a 'young boy;' and further-more as being from eighteen inches to a couple of feet shorter than he really was: two circumstances which perhaps accounted in some degree, for its never having been productive of any other effect than the transmission to Chigwell at various times and at a vast expense, of some five-and-forty runaways varying from six years old to twelve.

Mr Cobb and Mr Parkes looked mysteriously at this composition, at each other, and at old John. From the time he had pasted it up with his own hands, Mr Willet had never by word or sign alluded to the subject, or encouraged any one else to do so. Nobody had the least notion what his thoughts or opinions were, connected with it; whether he remembered it or forgot it; whether he had any idea that such an event had ever taken place. Therefore, even while he slept, no one ventured to refer to it in his presence; and for such sufficient reasons, these his chosen friends were silent now.

Mr Willet had got by this time into such a complication of knots, that it was perfectly clear he must wake or die. He chose the former alternative, and opened his eyes.

'If he don't come in five minutes,' said John, 'I shall have supper without him.'

The antecedent of this pronoun had been mentioned for the last time at eight o'clock. Messrs Parkes and Cobb being used to this style of conversation, replied without difficulty that to be sure Solomon was very late, and they wondered what had happened to detain him.

'He an't blown away, I suppose,' said Parkes. 'It's enough to carry a man of his figure off his legs, and easy too. Do you hear it? It blows great guns, indeed. There'll be many a crash in the Forest to-night, I reckon, and many a broken branch upon the ground to-morrow.'

'It won't break anything in the Maypole, I take it, sir,' returned old John. 'Let it try. I give it leave – what's that?'

'The wind,' cried Parkes. 'It's howling like a Christian, and has been all night long.'

'Did you ever, sir,' asked John, after a minute's contemplation, 'hear the wind say "Maypole?"'

'Why, what man ever did?' said Parkes.

'Nor "ahoy" perhaps?' added John.

'No. Nor that neither.'

'Very good, sir,' said Mr Willet, perfectly unmoved; 'then if that was the wind just now, and you'll wait a little time without speaking, you'll hear it say both words very plain.'

Mr Willet was right. After listening for a few moments, they could clearly hear, above the roar and tumult out of doors, this shout repeated; and that with a shrillness and energy, which denoted that it came from some person in great distress or terror. They looked at each other, turned pale, and held their breath. No man stirred.

It was in this emergency, that Mr Willet displayed something of that strength of mind and plenitude of mental resource, which rendered him the admiration of all his friends and neighbours. After looking at Messrs Parkes and Cobb for some time in silence, he clapped his two hands to his cheeks, and sent forth a roar which made the glasses dance and rafters ring – a long-sustained, discordant bellow, that rolled onward with the wind, and startling every echo, made the night a hundred times more boisterous – a deep, loud, dismal bray, that sounded like a human gong. Then, with every vein in his head and face swoln with the great exertion, and his countenance suffused with a lively purple, he drew a little nearer to the fire, and turning his back upon it, said with dignity:

'If that's any comfort to anybody, they're welcome to it. If it an't, I'm sorry for 'em. If either of you two gentlemen likes to go out and see what's the matter, you can. I'm not curious, myself.'

While he spoke the cry drew nearer and nearer, footsteps passed the window, the latch of the door was raised, it opened, was violently shut again, and Solomon Daisy, with a lighted lantern in his hand, and the rain streaming from his disordered dress, dashed into the room.

A more complete picture of terror than the little man presented, it would be difficult to imagine. The perspiration stood in beads upon his face, his knees knocked together, his every limb trembled, the power of articulation was quite gone; and there he stood, panting for breath, gazing on them with such livid ashy looks, that they were infected with his fear, though ignorant of its occasion, and, reflecting his dismayed and horror-stricken visage, stared back again without venturing to question him; until old John Willet, in a fit of temporary insanity, made a dive at his cravat, and, seizing him by that portion of his dress, shook him to and fro until his very teeth appeared to rattle in his head.

'Tell us what's the matter, sir,' said John, 'or I'll kill you. Tell us

GRAY. SC.

what's the matter, sir, or in another second, I'll have your head under the biler. How dare you look like that? Is anybody a following of you? What do you mean? Say something, or I'll be the death of you, I will.'

Mr Willet, in his frenzy, was so near keeping his word to the very letter (Solomon Daisy's eyes already beginning to roll in an alarming manner, and certain guttural sounds, as of a choking man, to issue from his throat), that the two bystanders, recovering in some degree, plucked him off his victim by main force, and placed the little clerk of Chigwell in a chair. Directing a fearful gaze all round the room, he implored them in a faint voice to give him some drink; and above all to lock the house-door and close and bar the shutters of the room, without a moment's loss of time. The latter request did not tend to re-assure his hearers, or to fill them with the most comfortable sensations; they complied with it, however, with the greatest expedition; and having handed him a bumper of brandy-and-water, nearly boiling hot, waited to hear what he might have to tell them.

'Oh, Johnny,' said Solomon, shaking him by the hand. 'Oh, Parkes. Oh, Tommy Cobb. Why did I leave this house to-night! On the nineteenth of March – of all nights in the year, on the nineteenth of March!'

They all drew closer to the fire. Parkes, who was nearest to the door, started and looked over his shoulder. Mr Willet, with great indignation, inquired what the devil he meant by that – and then said, 'God forgive me,' and glanced over his own shoulder, and came a little nearer.

'When I left here to-night,' said Solomon Daisy, 'I little thought what day of the month it was. I have never gone alone into the church after dark on this day, for seven-and-twenty years. I have heard it said that as we keep our birthdays when we are alive, so the ghosts of dead people, who are not easy in their graves, keep the day they died upon. – How the wind roars!'

Nobody spoke. All eyes were fastened on Solomon.

'I might have known,' he said, 'what night it was, by the foul weather. There's no such night in the whole year round as this is, always. I never sleep quietly in my bed on the nineteenth of March.'

'Go on,' said Tom Cobb, in a low voice. 'Nor I neither.'

Solomon Daisy raised his glass to his lips; put it down upon the floor with such a trembling hand that the spoon tinkled in it like a little bell; and continued thus.

'Have I ever said that we are always brought back to this subject in some strange way, when the nineteenth of this month comes round? Do you suppose it was by accident, I forgot to wind up the church-clock? I never forget it at any other time, though it's such a clumsy thing that it has to be wound up every day. Why should it escape my memory on this day of all others?

'I made as much haste down there as I could when I went from here, but I had to go home first for the keys; and the wind and rain being dead against me all the way, it was pretty well as much as I could do at times to keep my legs. I got there at last, opened the church-door, and went in. I had not met a soul all the way, and you may judge whether it was dull or not. Neither of you would bear me company. If you could have known what was to come, you'd have been in the right.

'The wind was so strong, that it was as much as I could do to shut the church-door by putting my whole weight against it; and even as it was, it burst wide open twice, with such strength that any of you would have sworn, if you had been leaning against it, as I was, that somebody was pushing on the other side. However, I got the key turned, went into the belfry, and wound up the clock – which was very near run down, and would have stood stock-still in half an hour.

'As I took up my lantern again to leave the church, it came upon me all at once that this was the nineteenth of March. It came upon me with a kind of shock, as if a hand had struck the thought upon my forehead; at the very same moment, I heard a voice outside the tower – rising from among the graves.'

Here old John precipitately interrupted the speaker, and begged that if Mr Parkes (who was seated opposite to him and was staring directly over his head) saw anything, he would have the goodness to mention it. Mr Parkes apologised, and remarked that he was only listening; to which Mr Willet angrily retorted, that his listening with that kind of expression in his face was not agreeable, and that if he couldn't look like other people, he had better put his pocket-handkerchief over his head. Mr Parkes with great submission pledged himself to do so, if again required, and John Willet turning to Solomon desired him to proceed. After waiting until a violent gust of wind and rain, which seemed to shake even that sturdy house to its foundation, had passed away, the little man complied:

'Never tell me that it was my fancy, or that it was any other sound which I mistook for that I tell you of. I heard the wind whistle through the arches of the church. I heard the steeple strain and creak. I heard the rain as it came driving against the walls. I felt the bells shake. I saw the ropes sway to and fro. And I heard that voice.'

'What did it say?' asked Tom Cobb.

'I don't know what; I don't know that it spoke. It gave a kind of cry, as any one of us might do, if something dreadful followed us in a dream, and came upon us unawares; and then it died off: seeming to pass quite round the church.'

'I don't see much in that,' said John, drawing a long breath, and looking round him like a man who felt relieved.

'Perhaps not,' returned his friend, 'but that's not all.'

'What more do you mean to say, sir, is to come?' asked John, pausing in the act of wiping his face upon his apron. 'What are you a going to tell us of next?'

'What I saw.'

'Saw!' echoed all three, bending forward.

'When I opened the church-door to come out,' said the little man, with an expression of face which bore ample testimony to the sincerity of his conviction, 'when I opened the church-door to come out, which I did suddenly, for I wanted to get it shut again before another gust of wind came up, there crossed me – so close, that by stretching out my finger I could have touched it – something in the likeness of a man. It was bare-headed to the storm. It turned its face without stopping, and fixed its eyes on mine. It was a ghost – a spirit.'

'Whose?' they all three cried together.

In the excess of his emotion (for he fell back trembling in his chair, and waved his hand as if entreating them to question him no further,) his answer was lost on all but old John Willet, who happened to be seated close beside him.

'Who!' cried Parkes and Tom Cobb, looking eagerly by turns at Solomon Daisy and at Mr Willet. 'Who was it?'

'Gentlemen,' said Mr Willet after a long pause, 'you needn't ask. The likeness of a murdered man. This is the nineteenth of March.'

A profound silence ensued.

'If you'll take my advice,' said John, 'we had better, one and all, keep this a secret. Such tales would not be liked at the Warren. Let us keep it to ourselves for the present time at all events, or we may get into trouble, and Solomon may lose his place. Whether it was really as he says, or whether it wasn't, is no matter. Right or wrong, nobody would believe him. As to the probabilities, I don't myself think,' said Mr Willet, eyeing the corners of the room in a manner which showed that, like some other philosophers, he was not quite easy in his theory, 'that a ghost as had been a man of sense in his lifetime, would be out a-walking in such weather – I only know that *I* wouldn't, if I was one.'

But this heretical doctrine was strongly opposed by the other three, who quoted a great many precedents to show that bad weather was the very time for such appearances; and Mr Parkes (who had had a ghost in his family, by the mother's side) argued the matter with so much ingenuity and force of illustration, that John was only saved from having to retract his opinion by the opportune appearance of supper, to which they applied themselves with a dreadful relish. Even Solomon Daisy himself, by dint of the elevating influences of fire, lights, brandy, and good company, so far recovered as to handle his knife and fork in a highly creditable manner, and to display a capacity both of eating and drinking, such as banished all fear of his having sustained any lasting injury from his fright.

Supper done, they crowded round the fire again, and, as is common on such occasions, propounded all manner of leading questions calculated to surround the story with new horrors and surprises. But Solomon Daisy, notwithstanding these temptations, adhered so steadily to his original account, and repeated it so often, with such slight variations, and with such solemn asseverations of its truth and reality, that his hearers were (with good reason) more astonished than at first. As he took John Willet's view of the matter in regard to the propriety of not bruiting the tale abroad, unless the spirit should appear to him again, in which case it would be necessary to take immediate counsel with the clergyman, it was solemnly resolved that it should be hushed up and kept quiet. And as most men like to have a secret to tell which may exalt their own importance, they arrived at this conclusion with perfect unanimity.

As it was by this time growing late, and was long past their usual hour of separating, the cronies parted for the night. Solomon Daisy, with a fresh candle in his lantern, repaired homewards under the escort of long Phil Parkes and Mr Cobb, who were rather more nervous than himself. Mr Willet, after seeing them to the door, returned to collect his thoughts with the assistance of the boiler, and to listen to the storm of wind and rain, which had not yet abated one jot of its fury.

CHAPTER THE THIRTY-FOURTH

Before old John had looked at the boiler quite twenty minutes, he got his ideas into a focus, and brought them to bear upon Solomon Daisy's story. The more he thought of it, the more impressed he became with a sense of his own wisdom, and a desire that Mr Haredale should be impressed with it likewise. At length, to the end that he might sustain a principal and important character in the affair; and might have the start of Solomon and his two friends, through whose means he knew the adventure, with a variety of exaggerations, would be known to at least a score of people, and most likely to Mr Haredale himself, by breakfast-time to-morrow; he determined to repair to the Warren before going to bed.

'He's my landlord,' thought John, as he took a candle in his hand, and setting it down in a corner out of the wind's way, opened a casement in the rear of the house, looking towards the stables. 'We haven't met of late years so often as we used to do – changes are taking place in the family – it's desirable that I should stand as well with them, in point of dignity, as possible – the whispering about of this here tale will anger him – it's good to have confidences with a gentleman of his natur', and set one's-self right besides. Halloa there! Hugh – Hugh. Hal-loa!'

When he had repeated this shout a dozen times, and startled every pigeon from its slumbers, a door in one of the ruinous old buildings opened, and a rough voice demanded what was amiss now, that a man couldn't even have his sleep in quiet.

'What! Haven't you sleep enough, growler, that you're not to be knocked up for once?' said John.

'No,' replied the voice, as the speaker yawned and shook himself. 'Not half enough.'

'I don't know how you *can* sleep, with the wind a bellowsing and roaring about you, making the tiles fly like a pack of cards,' said John; 'but no matter for that. Wrap yourself up in something or another, and come here, for you must go as far as the Warren with me. And look sharp about it.'

Hugh, with much low growling and muttering, went back into his lair; and presently re-appeared, carrying a lantern and a cudgel, and enveloped from head to foot in an old, frowsy, slouching horse-cloth. Mr Willet received this figure at the back door, and ushered him into the bar, while he wrapped himself in sundry greatcoats and capes, and so tied and knotted his face in shawls and handkerchiefs, that how he breathed was a mystery.

'You don't take a man out of doors at near midnight in such weather, without putting some heart into him, do you, master?' said Hugh.

'Yes I do, sir,' returned Mr Willet. 'I put the heart (as you call it) into him when he has brought me safe home again, and his standing steady on his legs an't of so much consequence. So hold that light up, if you please, and go on a step or two before, to show the way.'

Hugh obeyed with a very indifferent grace, and a longing glance at the bottles. Old John, laying strict injunctions on his cook to keep the doors locked in his absence, and to open to nobody but himself on pain of dismissal, followed him into the blustering darkness out of doors.

The way was wet and dismal, and the night so black, that if Mr Willet had been his own pilot, he would have walked into a deep horsepond within a few hundred yards of his own house, and would certainly have terminated his career in that ignoble sphere of action. But Hugh, who had a sight as keen as any hawk's, and, apart from that endowment, could have found his way blindfold to any place within a dozen miles, dragged old John along, quite deaf to his remonstrances, and took his own course without the slightest reference to, or notice of, his master. So they made head against the wind as they best could; Hugh crushing the wet grass beneath his heavy tread, and stalking on after his ordinary savage fashion; John Willet following at arm's length, picking his steps, and looking about him, now for bogs and ditches, and now for such stray ghosts as might be wandering abroad, with looks of as much dismay and uneasiness as his immoveable face was capable of expressing.

At length they stood upon the broad gravel-walk before the
Warren-house. The building was profoundly dark, and none were
moving near it save themselves. From one solitary turret-chamber,
however, there shone a ray of light; and towards this speck of
comfort in the cold, cheerless, silent scene, Mr Willet bade his pilot
lead him.

'The old room,' said John, looking timidly upward; 'Mr Reuben's
own apartment, God be with us! I wonder his brother likes to sit
there, so late at night – on this night too.'

'Why, where else should he sit?' asked Hugh, holding the lantern
to his breast, to keep the candle from the wind, while he trimmed
it with his fingers. 'It's snug enough, an't it?'

'Snug!' said John indignantly. 'You have a comfortable idea of
snugness, you have, sir. Do you know what was done in that room,
you ruffian?'

'Why, what is it the worse for that!' cried Hugh, looking into
John's fat face. 'Does it keep out the rain, and snow, and wind, the
less for that? Is it less warm or dry, because a man was killed there?
Ha, ha, ha! Never believe it, master. One man's no such matter as
that comes to.'

Mr Willet fixed his dull eyes on his follower, and began – by a
species of inspiration – to think it just barely possible that he was
something of a dangerous character, and that it might be advisable
to get rid of him one of these days. He was too prudent to say
anything, with the journey home before him; and therefore turned
to the iron gate before which this brief dialogue had passed, and
pulled the handle of the bell that hung beside it. The turret in which
the light appeared being at one corner of the building, and only
divided from the path by one of the garden-walks, upon which this
gate opened, Mr Haredale threw up the window directly, and
demanded who was there.

'Begging pardon, sir,' said John, 'I knew you sat up late, and
made bold to come round, having a word to say to you.'

'Willet – is it not?'

'Of the Maypole – at your service, sir.'

Mr Haredale closed the window, and withdrew. He presently
appeared at a door in the bottom of the turret, and coming across
the garden-walk, unlocked the gate and let them in.

'You are a late visitor, Willet. What is the matter?'

'Nothing to speak of, sir,' said John; 'an idle tale, I thought you ought to know of; nothing more.'

'Let your man go forward with the lantern, and give me your hand. The stairs are crooked and narrow. – Gently with your light, friend. You swing it like a censer.'

Hugh, who had already reached the turret, held it more steadily, and ascended first, turning round from time to time to shed his light downward on the steps. Mr Haredale following next, eyed his lowering face with no great favour; and Hugh, looking down on him, returned his glances with interest, as they climbed the winding stair.

It terminated in a little anti-room adjoining that from which they had seen the light. Mr Haredale entered first, and led the way through it into the latter chamber, where he seated himself at a writing-table from which he had risen when they rang the bell.

'Come in,' he said, beckoning to old John, who remained bowing at the door. 'Not you, friend,' he added hastily to Hugh, who entered also. 'Willet, why do you bring that fellow here?'

'Why, sir,' returned John, elevating his eyebrows, and lowering his voice to the tone in which the question had been asked him, 'he's a good guard, you see.'

'Don't be too sure of that,' said Mr Haredale, looking towards him as he spoke. 'I doubt it. He has an evil eye.'

'There's no imagination in his eye,' returned Mr Willet, glancing over his shoulder at the organ in question, 'certainly.'

'There is no good there, be assured,' said Mr Haredale. 'Wait in that little room, friend, and close the door between us.'

Hugh shrugged his shoulders, and with a disdainful look, which showed, either that he had overheard, or that he guessed the purport of their whispering, did as he was told. When he was shut out, Mr Haredale turned to John, and bade him go on with what he had to say, but not to speak too loud, for there were quick ears yonder.

Thus cautioned, Mr Willet, in an oily whisper, recited all that he had heard and said that night; laying particular stress upon his own sagacity, upon his great regard for the family, and upon his solicitude for their peace of mind and happiness. The story moved his auditor much more than he had expected. Mr Haredale often changed his attitude, rose and paced the room, returned again, desired him to repeat, as nearly as he could, the very words that

Solomon had used, and gave so many other signs of being disturbed and ill at ease, that even Mr Willet was surprised.

'You did quite right,' he said, at the end of a long conversation, 'to bid them keep this story secret. It is a foolish fancy on the part of this weak-brained man, bred in his fears and superstition. But Miss Haredale, though she would know it to be so, would be disturbed by it if it reached her ears; it is too nearly connected with a subject very painful to us all, to be heard with indifference. You were most prudent, and have laid me under a great obligation. I thank you very much.'

This was equal to John's most sanguine expectations; but he would have preferred Mr Haredale's looking at him when he spoke, as if he really did thank him, to his walking up and down, speaking by fits and starts, often stopping with his eyes fixed on the ground, moving hurriedly on again, like one distracted, and seeming almost unconscious of what he said or did.

This, however, was his manner; and it was so embarrassing to John that he sat quite passive for a long time, not knowing what to do. At length he rose. Mr Haredale stared at him for a moment as though he had quite forgotten his being present, then shook hands with him, and opened the door. Hugh, who was, or feigned to be, fast asleep on the anti-chamber floor, sprang up on their entrance, and throwing his cloak about him, grasped his stick and lantern, and prepared to descend the stairs.

'Stay,' said Mr Haredale. 'Will this man drink?'

'Drink! He'd drink the Thames up, if it was strong enough, sir,' replied John Willet. 'He'll have something when he gets home. He's better without it, now, sir.'

'Nay. Half the distance is done,' said Hugh. 'What a hard master you are! I shall go home the better for one glassful, half-way. Come!'

As John made no reply, Mr Haredale brought out a glass of liquor, and gave it to Hugh, who, as he took it in his hand, threw part of it upon the floor.

'What do you mean by splashing your drink about a gentleman's house, sir?' said John.

'I'm drinking a toast,' Hugh rejoined, holding the glass above his head, and fixing his eyes on Mr Haredale's face; 'a toast to this house and its master.' With that he muttered something to himself, and drank the rest, and setting down the glass, preceded them without another word.

John was a good deal scandalised by this observance, but seeing that Mr Haredale took little heed of what Hugh said or did, and that his thoughts were otherwise employed, he offered no apology, and went in silence down the stairs, across the walk, and through the garden-gate. They stopped upon the outer side for Hugh to hold the light while Mr Haredale locked it on the inner; and then John saw with wonder (as he often afterwards related), that he was very pale, and that his face had changed so much and grown so haggard since their entrance, that he almost seemed another man.

They were in the open road again, and John Willet was walking on behind his escort, as he had come, thinking very steadily of what he had just now seen, when Hugh drew him suddenly aside, and almost at the same instant three horsemen swept past – the nearest brushed his shoulder even then – who, checking their steeds as suddenly as they could, stood still, and waited for their coming up.

*

CHAPTER THE THIRTY-FIFTH

When John Willet saw that the horsemen wheeled smartly round, and drew up three abreast in the narrow road, waiting for him and his man to join them, it occurred to him with unusual precipitation that they must be highwaymen; and had Hugh been armed with a blunderbuss, in place of his stout cudgel, he would certainly have ordered him to fire it off at a venture, and would, while the word of command was obeyed, have consulted his own personal safety in immediate flight. Under the circumstances of disadvantage, however, in which he and his guard were placed, he deemed it prudent to adopt a different style of generalship, and therefore whispered his attendant to address them in the most peaceable and courteous terms. By way of acting up to the spirit and letter of this instruction, Hugh stepped forward, and flourishing his staff before the very eyes of the rider nearest to him, demanded roughly what he and his fellows meant by so nearly galloping over them, and why they scoured the king's highway at that late hour of night.

The man whom he addressed was beginning an angry reply in

the same strain, when he was checked by the horseman in the centre, who, interposing with an air of authority, inquired in a somewhat loud but not harsh or unpleasant voice:

'Pray, is this the London road?'

'If you follow it right, it is,' replied Hugh roughly.

'Nay, brother,' said the same person, 'you're but a churlish Englishman, if Englishman you be – which I should much doubt but for your tongue. Your companion, I am sure, will answer me more civilly. How say you, friend?'

'I say it *is* the London road, sir,' answered John. 'And I wish,' he added in a subdued voice, as he turned to Hugh, 'that you was in any other road, you vagabond. Are you tired of your life, sir, that you go a-trying to provoke three great neck-or-nothing chaps, that could keep on running over us, back'ards and for'ards, till we was dead, and then take our bodies up behind 'em, and drown us ten miles off?'

'How far is it to London?' inquired the same speaker.

'Why, from here sir,' answered John, persuasively, 'it's thirteen very easy mile.'

The adjective was thrown in, as an inducement to the travellers to ride away with all speed; but instead of having the desired effect, it elicited from the same person, the remark, 'Thirteen miles! That's a long distance!' which was followed by a short pause of indecision.

'Pray,' said the gentleman, 'are there any inns hereabouts?'

At the word 'inns,' John plucked up his spirit in a surprising manner; his fears rolled off like smoke; all the landlord stirred within him.

'There are no inns,' rejoined Mr Willet, with a strong emphasis on the plural number; 'but there's a Inn – one Inn – the Maypole Inn. That's a Inn indeed. You won't see the like of that Inn often.'

'You keep it perhaps?' said the horseman, smiling.

'I do, sir,' replied John, greatly wondering how he had found this out.

'And how far is the Maypole from here?'

'About a mile' – John was going to add that it was the easiest mile in all the world, when the third rider, who had hitherto kept a little in the rear, suddenly interposed:

'And have you one excellent bed, landlord? Hem! A bed that you can recommend – a bed that you are sure is well aired – a bed that has been slept in by some perfectly respectable and unexceptionable person?'

'We don't take in no tagrag and bobtail at our house, sir,' answered John. 'And as to the bed itself –'

'Say, as to three beds,' interposed the gentleman who had spoken before; 'for we shall want three if we stay, though my friend only speaks of one.'

'No, no, my lord; you are too good, you are too kind; but your life is of far too much importance to the nation in these portentous times, to be placed upon a level with one so useless and so poor as mine. A great cause, my lord, a mighty cause, depends on you. You are its leader and its champion, its advanced guard and its van. It is the cause of our altars and our homes, our country and our faith. Let *me* sleep on a chair – the carpet – anywhere. No one will repine if *I* take cold or fever. Let John Grueby pass the night beneath the open sky – no one will repine for *him*. But forty thousand men of this our island in the wave (exclusive of women and children) rivet their eyes and thoughts on Lord George Gordon;[1] and every day, from the rising up of the sun to the going down of the same,[2] pray for his health and vigour. My lord,' said the speaker, rising in his stirrups, 'it is a glorious cause, and must not be forgotten. My lord, it is a mighty cause, and must not be endangered. My lord, it is a holy cause, and must not be deserted.'

'It *is* a holy cause,' exclaimed his lordship, lifting up his hat with great solemnity. 'Amen!'

'John Grueby,' said the long-winded gentleman, in a tone of mild reproof, 'his lordship said Amen.'

'I heard my lord, sir,' said the man, sitting like a statue on his horse.

'And do not *you* say Amen, likewise?'

To which John Grueby made no reply at all, but sat looking straight before him.

'You surprise me, Grueby,' said the gentleman. 'At a crisis like the present, when Queen Elizabeth, that maiden monarch, weeps within her tomb, and Bloody Mary,[3] with a brow of gloom and shadow, stalks triumphant –'

'Oh, sir,' cried the man, gruffly, 'where's the use of talking of Bloody Mary, under such circumstances as the present, when my lord's wet through and tired with hard riding? Let's either go on to London, sir, or put up at once; or that unfort'nate Bloody Mary will have more to answer for – and she's done a deal more harm in her grave than she ever did in her lifetime, I believe.'

By this time Mr Willet, who had never heard so many words spoken together at one time, or delivered with such volubility and emphasis as by the long-winded gentleman; and whose brain, being wholly unable to sustain or compass them, had quite given itself up for lost; recovered so far as to observe that there was ample accommodation at the Maypole for all the party: good beds; neat wines; excellent entertainment for man and beast; private rooms for large or small parties; dinners dressed upon the shortest notice; choice stabling, and a lock-up coach-house: and, in short, to run over such recommendatory scraps of language as were painted up on various portions of the building, and which, in the course of some forty years, he had learnt to repeat with tolerable correctness. He was considering whether it was at all possible to insert any novel sentences to the same purpose, when the gentleman who had spoken first, turning to him of the long wind, exclaimed, 'What say you, Gashford? Shall we tarry at this house he speaks of, or press forward? You shall decide.'

'I would submit, my lord, then,' returned the person he appealed to, in a silky tone, 'that your health and spirits – so important, under Providence, to our great cause, our pure and truthful cause' – here his lordship pulled off his hat again, though it was raining hard – 'require refreshment and repose.'

'Go on before, landlord, and show the way,' said Lord George Gordon; 'we will follow at a footpace.'

'If you'll give me leave, my lord,' said John Grueby, in a low voice, 'I'll change my proper place, and ride before you. The looks of the landlord's friend are not over honest, and it may be as well to be cautious with him.'

'John Grueby is quite right,' interposed Mr Gashford, falling back hastily. 'My lord, a life so precious as yours must not be put in peril. Go forward, John, by all means. If you have any reason to suspect the fellow, blow his brains out.'

John made no answer, but looking straight before him, as his custom seemed to be when the secretary spoke, bade Hugh push on, and followed close behind him. Then came his lordship, with Mr Willet at his bridle rein; and, last of all, his lordship's secretary – for that, it seemed, was Gashford's office.

Hugh strode briskly on, often looking back at the servant, whose horse was close upon his heels, and glancing with a leer at his holster case of pistols, by which he seemed to set great store. He was a square-built, strong-made, bull-necked fellow, of the true English breed; and as Hugh measured him with his eye, he measured Hugh, regarding him meanwhile with a look of bluff disdain. He was much older than the Maypole man, being to all appearance five-and-forty; but was one of those self-possessed, hard-headed, imperturbable fellows, who, if they ever are beat at fisty-cuffs, or other kind of warfare, never know it, and go on coolly till they win.

'If I led you wrong now,' said Hugh, tauntingly, 'you'd – ha ha ha! – you'd shoot me through the head, I suppose.'

John Grueby took no more notice of this remark than if he had been deaf and Hugh dumb; but kept riding on, quite comfortably, with his eyes fixed on the horizon.

'Did you ever try a fall with a man when you were young, master?' said Hugh. 'Can you make any play at single-stick?'

John Grueby looked at him sideways with the same contented air, but deigned not a word in answer.

'– Like this?' said Hugh, giving his cudgel one of those skilful flourishes, in which the rustic of that time delighted. 'Whoop!'

'– Or that,' returned John Grueby, beating down his guard with his whip, and striking him on the head with its butt end. 'Yes, I played a little once. You wear your hair too long; I should have cracked your crown if it had been a little shorter.'

It was a pretty smart, loud-sounding rap, as it was, and evidently astonished Hugh; who, for the moment, seemed disposed to drag his new acquaintance from his saddle. But his face betokening neither malice, triumph, rage, nor any lingering idea that he had given him offence; his eyes gazing steadily in the old direction, and his manner being as careless and composed as if he had merely brushed away a fly; Hugh was so puzzled, and so disposed to look upon him as a customer of almost supernatural toughness, that he merely laughed, and cried 'Well done!' then, sheering off a little, led the way in silence.

Before the lapse of many minutes the party halted at the Maypole door. Lord George and his secretary quickly dismounting, gave their horses to their servant, who, under the guidance of Hugh, repaired to the stables. Right glad to escape from the inclemency of the night, they followed Mr Willet into the common room, and stood warming themselves and drying their clothes before the cheerful fire, while he busied himself with such orders and preparations as his guest's high quality required.

As he bustled in and out of the room, intent on these arrangements, he had an opportunity of observing the two travellers, of whom, as yet, he knew nothing but the voice. The Lord, the great personage, who did the Maypole so much honour, was about the middle height, of a slender make, and sallow complexion, with an aquiline nose, and long hair of a reddish brown, combed perfectly straight and smooth about his ears, and slightly powdered, but without the faintest vestige of a curl. He was attired, under his greatcoat, in a full suit of black, quite free from any ornament, and of the most precise and sober cut. The gravity of his dress, together with a certain lankness of cheek and stiffness of deportment, added nearly ten years to his age, but his figure was that of one not yet past thirty. As he stood musing in the red glow of the fire, it was striking to observe his very bright large eye, which betrayed a restlessness of thought and purpose, singularly at variance with the studied composure and sobriety of his mien, and with his quaint and sad apparel. It had nothing harsh or cruel in its expression; neither had his face, which was thin and mild, and wore an air of melancholy; but it was suggestive of an indefinable uneasiness, which infected those who looked upon him, and filled them with a kind of pity for the man: though why it did so, they would have had some trouble to explain.

Gashford, the secretary, was taller, angularly made, high-shouldered, bony, and ungraceful. His dress, in imitation of his superior, was demure and staid in the extreme; his manner, formal and constrained. This gentleman had an overhanging brow, great hands and feet and ears, and a pair of eyes that seemed to have made an unnatural retreat into his head, and to have dug themselves a cave to hide in. His manner was smooth and humble, but very sly and slinking. He wore the aspect of a man who was always lying in wait for something that *wouldn't* come to pass; but he looked patient – very patient – and fawned like a spaniel dog. Even now, while he warmed and rubbed his hands before the blaze, he had the air of one who only presumed to enjoy it in his degree as a commoner; and though he knew his lord was not regarding him, he looked into his face from time to time, and, with a meek and deferential manner, smiled as if for practice.

Such were the guests whom old John Willet, with a fixed and

leaden eye, surveyed a hundred times, and to whom he now advanced with a state candlestick in each hand, beseeching them to follow him into a worthier chamber. 'For my lord,' said John – it is odd enough, but certain people seem to have as great a pleasure in pronouncing titles as their owners have in wearing them – 'this room, my lord, isn't at all the sort of place for your lordship, and I have to beg your lordship's pardon for keeping you here, my lord, one minute.'

With this address, John ushered them up stairs into the state apartment, which, like many other things of state, was cold and comfortless. Their own footsteps, reverberating through the spacious room, struck upon their hearing with a hollow sound; and its damp and chilly atmosphere was rendered doubly cheerless by contrast with the homely warmth they had deserted.

It was of no use, however, to propose a return to the place they had quitted, for the preparations went on so briskly that there was no time to stop them. John, with the tall candlesticks in his hands, bowed them up to the fire-place; Hugh, striding in with a lighted brand and pile of fire-wood, cast it down upon the hearth, and set it in a blaze; John Grueby (who had a great blue cockade in his hat, which he appeared to despise mightily) brought in the portmanteau he had carried on his horse, and placed it on the floor; and presently all three were busily engaged in drawing out the screen, laying the cloth, inspecting the beds, lighting fires in the bedrooms, expediting the supper, and making everything as cosy and as snug as might be, on so short a notice. In less than an hour's time, supper had been served, and ate, and cleared away; and Lord George and his secretary, with slippered feet, and legs stretched out before the fire, sat over some hot mulled wine together.

'So ends, my lord,' said Gashford, filling his glass with great complacency, 'the blessed work of a most blessed day.'

'And of a blessed yesterday,' said his lordship, raising his head.

'Ah!' – and here the secretary clasped his hands – 'a blessed yesterday indeed! The Protestants of Suffolk are godly men and true. Though others of our countrymen have lost their way in darkness, even as we, my lord, did lose our road to-night, theirs is the light and glory.'

'Did I move them, Gashford?' said Lord George.

'Move them, my lord! Move them! They cried to be led on against

the Papists, they vowed a dreadful vengeance on their heads, they roared like men possessed – '

'But not by devils,' said his lord.

'By devils! my lord! By angels.'

'Yes – oh surely – by angels, no doubt,' said Lord George, thrusting his hands into his pockets, taking them out again to bite his nails, and looking uncomfortably at the fire. 'Of course by angels – eh Gashford?'

'You do not doubt it, my lord?' said the secretary.

'No – No,' returned his lord. 'No. Why should I? I suppose it would be decidedly irreligious to doubt it – wouldn't it Gashford? Though there certainly were,' he added, without waiting for an answer, 'some plaguy ill-looking characters among them.'

'When you warmed,' said the secretary, looking sharply at the other's downcast eyes, which brightened slowly as he spoke; 'when you warmed into that noble outbreak: when you told them that you were never of the lukewarm or the timid tribe, and bade them take heed that they were prepared to follow one who would lead them on, though to the very death; when you spoke of a hundred and twenty thousand men across the Scottish border[4] who would take their own redress at any time, if it were not conceded; when you cried "Perish the Pope and all his base adherents; the penal laws against them shall never be repealed while Englishmen have hearts and hands" – and waved your own and touched your sword; and when they cried "No Popery!" and you cried "No; not even if we wade in blood," and they threw up their hats and cried "Hurrah! not even if we wade in blood; No Popery! Lord George! Down with the Papists – Vengeance on their heads:" when this was said and done, and a word from you, my lord, could raise or still the tumult – ah! then I felt what greatness was indeed, and thought, When was there ever power like this of Lord George Gordon's!'

'It's a great power. You're right. It is a great power!' he cried with sparkling eyes. 'But – dear Gashford – did I really say all that?'

'And how much more!' cried the secretary, looking upwards. 'Ah! how much more!'

'And I told them what you say, about the one hundred and forty thousand men in Scotland, did I!' he asked with evident delight. 'That was bold.'

'Our cause is boldness. Truth is always bold.'

'Certainly. So is religion. She's bold, Gashford?'

'The true religion is, my lord.'

'And that's ours,' he rejoined, moving uneasily in his seat, and biting his nails as though he would pare them to the quick. 'There can be no doubt of ours being the true one. You feel as certain of that as I do, Gashford, don't you?'

'Does my lord ask *me*,' whined Gashford, drawing his chair nearer with an injured air, and laying his broad flat hand upon the table; '*me*,' he repeated, bending the dark hollows of his eyes upon him with an unwholesome smile, 'who, stricken by the magic of his eloquence in Scotland but a year ago, abjured the errors of the Romish church, and clung to him as one whose timely hand had plucked me from a pit?'

'True. No – No. I – I didn't mean it,' replied the other, shaking him by the hand, rising from his seat, and pacing restlessly about the room. 'It's a proud thing to lead the people, Gashford,' he added as he made a sudden halt.

'By force of reason too,' returned the pliant secretary.

'Ay, to be sure. They may cough, and jeer, and groan in Parliament, and call me fool and madman, but which of them can raise this human sea and make it swell and roar at pleasure? Not one.'

'Not one,' repeated Gashford.

'Which of them can say for his honesty, what I can say for mine; which of them has refused a minister's bribe of one thousand pounds a year, to resign his seat in favour of another? Not one.'

'Not one,' repeated Gashford again – taking the lion's share of the mulled wine between whiles.

'And as we are honest, true, and in a sacred cause, Gashford,' said Lord George with a heightened colour and in a louder voice, as he laid his fevered hand upon his shoulder, 'and are the only men who regard the mass of people out of doors, or are regarded by them, we will uphold them to the last; and will raise a cry against these un-English Papists which shall re-echo through the country, and roll with a noise like thunder. I will be worthy of the motto on my coat of arms, "Called and chosen and faithful." '[5]

'Called,' said the secretary, 'by Heaven.'

'I am.'

'Chosen by the people.'

'Yes.'

'Faithful to both.'

'To the block!'

It would be difficult to convey an adequate idea of the excited manner in which he gave these answers to the secretary's promptings; of the rapidity of his utterance, or the violence of his tone and gesture; in which, struggling through his Puritan's demeanour, was something wild and ungovernable which broke through all restraint. For some minutes he walked rapidly up and down the room, then stopping suddenly, exclaimed,

'Gashford – *You* moved them yesterday too. Oh yes! You did.'

'I shone with a reflected light my lord,' replied the humble secretary, laying his hand upon his heart. 'I did my best.'

'You did well,' said his master, 'and are a great and worthy instrument. If you will ring for John Grueby to carry the portmanteau into my room, and will wait here while I undress, we will dispose of business as usual, if you're not too tired.'

'Too tired my lord! – But this is his consideration! Christian from head to foot.' With which soliloquy, the secretary tilted the jug, and looked very hard into the mulled wine, to see how much remained.

John Willet and John Grueby appeared together. The one bearing the great candlesticks, and the other the portmanteau, showed the deluded lord into his chamber; and left the secretary alone, to yawn and shake himself, and finally to fall asleep before the fire.

'Now Mr Gashford sir,' said John Grueby in his ear, after what appeared to him a moment of unconsciousness; 'my lord's abed.'

'Oh. Very good John,' was his mild reply. 'Thank you John. Nobody need sit up. I know my room.'

'I hope you're not a going to trouble your head to-night, or my lord's head neither, with anything more about Bloody Mary,' said John. 'I wish the blessed old creetur had never been born.'

'I said you might go to bed, John,' returned the secretary. 'You didn't hear me, I think.'

'Between Bloody Marys, and blue cockades, and glorious Queen Besses, and no Poperys, and Protestant associations,[6] and making of speeches,' pursued John Grueby, looking, as usual, a long way off, and taking no notice of this hint, 'my lord's half off his head. When we go out o' doors, such a set of ragamuffins comes a shouting after us "Gordon for ever!" that I'm ashamed of myself and don't know where to look. When we're in-doors, they come a roaring and screaming about the house like so many devils; and my lord instead of ordering them to be drove away, goes out into the balcony and demeans himself by making speeches to 'em, and calls 'em "Men of England," and "Fellow-countrymen," as if he was fond of 'em and thanked 'em for coming. I can't make it out, but they're all mixed up somehow or another with that unfort'nate Bloody Mary, and call her name out till they're hoarse. They're all Protestants too – every man and boy among 'em: and Protestants is very fond of spoons I find, and silver plate in general, whenever area-gates is left open accidentally. I wish that was the worst of it, and that no more harm might be to come; but if you don't stop these ugly customers in time, Mr Gashford, (and I know you; you're the man that blows the fire) you'll find 'em grow a little bit too strong for you. One of these evenings, when the weather gets warmer and Protestants are thirsty, they'll be pulling London down, – and I never heerd that Bloody Mary went as far as *that*.'

Gashford had vanished long ago, and these remarks had been bestowed on empty air. Not at all discomposed by the discovery, John Grueby fixed his hat on, wrong side foremost that he might be unconscious of the shadow of the obnoxious cockade, and withdrew to bed; shaking his head in a very gloomy and prophetic manner until he reached his chamber.

CHAPTER THE THIRTY-SIXTH

Gashford, with a smiling face, but still with looks of profound deference and humility, betook himself towards his master's room, smoothing his hair down as he went, and humming a psalm tune. As he approached Lord George's door, he cleared his throat and hummed more vigorously.

There was a remarkable contrast between this man's occupation at the moment, and the expression of his countenance, which was singularly repulsive and malicious. His beetling brow almost obscured his eyes; his lip was curled contemptuously; his very shoulders seemed to sneer in stealthy whisperings with his great flapped ears.

'Hush!' he muttered softly, as he peeped in at the chamber-door.

'He seems to be asleep. Pray Heaven he is! Too much watching, too much care, too much thought – ah! Lord preserve him for a martyr! He is a saint, if ever saint drew breath on this bad earth.'

Placing his light upon a table, he walked on tiptoe to the fire, and sitting in a chair before it with his back towards the bed, went on communing with himself like one who thought aloud:

'The saviour of his country and his country's religion, the friend of his poor countrymen, the enemy of the proud and harsh; beloved of the rejected and oppressed, adored by forty thousand bold and loyal English hearts – what happy slumbers his should be!' And here he sighed, and warmed his hands, and shook his head as men do when their hearts are full, and heaved another sigh, and warmed his hands again.

'Why, Gashford?' said Lord George, who was lying broad awake, upon his side, and had been staring at him from his entrance.

'My – my lord,' said Gashford, starting and looking round as though in great surprise. 'I have disturbed you!'

'I have not been sleeping.'

'Not sleeping!' he repeated, with assumed confusion. 'What can I say for having in your presence given utterance to thoughts – but they were sincere – they were sincere!' exclaimed the secretary, drawing his sleeve in a hasty way across his eyes; 'and why should I regret your having heard them?'

'Gashford,' said the poor lord, stretching out his hand with manifest emotion. 'Do not regret it. You love me well, I know – too well. I don't deserve such homage.'

Gashford made no reply, but grasped the hand and pressed it to his lips. Then rising, and taking from the trunk a little desk, he placed it on a table near the fire, unlocked it with a key he carried in his pocket, sat down before it, took out a pen, and, before dipping it in the inkstand, sucked it – to compose the fashion of his mouth perhaps, on which a smile was hovering yet.

'How do our numbers stand since last enrolling-night?' inquired Lord George. 'Are we really forty thousand strong, or do we still speak in round numbers when we take the Association at that amount?'

'Our total now exceeds that number by a score and three,' Gashford replied, casting his eyes upon his papers.

'The funds?'

'Not *very* improving; but there is some manna in the wilderness, my lord. Hem! On Friday night the widows' mites[1] dropped in. "Forty scavengers, three and fourpence. An aged pew-opener of St Martin's parish, sixpence. A bell-ringer of the established church, sixpence. A Protestant infant, newly born, one halfpenny. The United Link Boys, three shillings – one bad. The anti-popish prisoners in Newgate,[2] five and fourpence. A friend in Bedlam,[3] half-a-crown. Dennis the hangman,[4] one shilling."'

'That Dennis,' said his lordship, 'is an earnest man. I marked him in the crowd in Welbeck Street,[5] last Friday.'

'A good man,' rejoined the secretary; 'a staunch, sincere, and truly zealous man.'

'He should be encouraged,' said Lord George. 'Make a note of Dennis. I'll talk with him.'

Gashford obeyed, and went on reading from his list:

' "The Friends of Reason, half-a-guinea. The Friends of Liberty, half-a-guinea. The Friends of Peace, half-a-guinea. The Friends of Charity, half-a-guinea. The Friends of Mercy, half-a-guinea. The Associated Rememberers of Bloody Mary, half-a-guinea. The United Bull-Dogs, half-a-guinea." '

'The United Bull-Dogs,' said Lord George, biting his nails most horribly, 'are a new society, are they not?'

'Formerly the 'Prentice Knights, my lord. The indentures of the old members expiring by degrees, they changed their name, it seems, though they still have 'prentices among them, as well as workmen.'

'What is their president's name?' inquired Lord George.

'President,' said Gashford, reading, 'Mr Simon Tappertit.'

'I remember him. The little man, who sometimes brings an elderly sister to our meetings, and sometimes another female too, who is conscientious, I have no doubt, but not well-favoured?'

'The very same, my lord.'

'Tappertit is an earnest man,' said Lord George thoughtfully. 'Eh, Gashford?'

'One of the foremost among them all, my lord. He snuffs the battle from afar, like the war-horse.[6] He throws his hat up in the street as if he were inspired, and makes most stirring speeches from the shoulders of his friends.'

'Make a note of Tappertit,' said Lord George Gordon. 'We may advance him to a place of trust.'

'That,' rejoined the secretary, doing as he was told, 'is all – except Mrs Varden's box (fourteenth time of opening), seven shillings and sixpence in silver and copper, and half-a-guinea in gold; and Miggs (being the saving of a quarter's wages), one-and-threepence.'

'Miggs,' said Lord George. 'Is that a man?'

'The name is entered on the list as a woman,' replied the secretary. 'I think she is the tall spare female of whom you spoke just now, my lord, as not being well-favoured, who sometimes comes to hear the speeches – along with Tappertit and Mrs Varden.'

'Mrs Varden is the elderly lady then, is she!'

The secretary nodded, and rubbed the bridge of his nose with the feather of his pen.

'She is a zealous sister,' said Lord George. 'Her collection goes on prosperously, and is pursued with fervour. Has her husband joined?'

'A malignant,'[7] returned the secretary, folding up his papers. 'Unworthy such a wife. He remains in outer darkness,[8] and steadily refuses.'

'The consequences be upon his own head! – Gashford!'

'My lord!'

'You don't think,' he turned restlessly in his bed as he spoke, 'these people will desert me, when the hour arrives? I have spoken boldly for them, ventured much, suppressed nothing. They'll not fall off, will they?'

'No fear of that, my lord,' said Gashford, with a meaning look, which was rather the involuntary expression of his own thoughts than intended as any confirmation of his words, for the other's face was turned away. 'Be sure there is no fear of that.'

'Nor,' he said with a more restless motion than before, 'of their – but they *can* sustain no harm from leaguing for this purpose. Right is on our side, though Might may be against us. You feel as sure of that as I – honestly, you do?'

The secretary was beginning with 'You do not doubt,' when the other interrupted him, and impatiently rejoined:

'Doubt. No. Who says I doubt? If I doubted, should I cast away relatives, friends, everything, for this unhappy country's sake; this unhappy country,' he cried, springing up in bed, after repeating the phrase 'unhappy country's sake' to himself, at least a dozen times, 'forsaken of God and man, delivered over to a dangerous confederacy of Popish powers; the prey of corruption, idolatry, and despotism! Who says I doubt? Am I called, and chosen, and faithful? Tell me. Am I, or am I not?'

'To God, the country, and yourself,' cried Gashford.

'I am. I will be. I say again, I will be: to the block. Who says as much! Do you? Does any man alive?'

The secretary drooped his head with an expression of perfect acquiescence in anything that had been said or might be; and Lord George gradually sinking down upon his pillow, fell asleep.

Although there was something very ludicrous in his vehement manner, taken in conjunction with his meagre aspect and ungraceful presence, it would scarcely have provoked a smile in any man of kindly feeling; or even if it had, he would have felt sorry and almost angry with himself next moment, for yielding to the impulse. This lord was sincere in his violence and in his wavering. A nature prone to false enthusiasm, and the vanity of being a leader, were the worst qualities apparent in his composition. All the rest was weakness – sheer weakness; and it is the unhappy lot of thoroughly weak men, that their very sympathies, affections, confidences – all the qualities which in better constituted minds are virtues – dwindle into foibles, or turn into downright vices.

Gashford, with many a sly look towards the bed, sat chuckling at his master's folly, until his deep and heavy breathing warned him that he might retire. Locking his desk, and replacing it within the trunk (but not before he had taken from a secret lining two printed handbills) he cautiously withdrew; looking back, as he went, at the pale face of the slumbering man, above whose head the dusty plumes that crowned the Maypole couch, waved drearily and sadly as though it were a bier.

Stopping on the staircase to listen that all was quiet, and to take off his shoes lest his footsteps should alarm any light sleeper who might be near at hand, he descended to the ground floor, and thrust one of his bills beneath the great door of the house. That done, he crept softly back to his own chamber, and from the window let another fall – carefully wrapped round a stone to save it from the wind – into the yard below.

They were addressed on the back 'To every Protestant into whose hands this shall come,' and bore within, what follows:

'Men and Brethren. Whoever shall find this letter, will take it as a warning to join, without delay, the friends of Lord George Gordon. There are great events at hand; and the times are dangerous and troubled. Read this carefully, keep it clean, and drop it somewhere else. For King and Country. Union.'

'More seed, more seed,' said Gashford as he closed the window. 'When will the harvest come!'

*

CHAPTER THE THIRTY-SEVENTH

To surround anything, however monstrous or ridiculous, with an air of mystery, is to invest it with a secret charm, and power of attraction which to the crowd is irresistible. False priests, false prophets,[1] false doctors, false patriots, false prodigies of every kind, veiling their proceedings in mystery, have always addressed themselves at an immense advantage to the popular credulity, and have been, perhaps, more indebted to that resource in gaining and keeping for a time the upper hand of Truth and Common Sense, than to any half-dozen items in the whole catalogue of imposture. Curiosity is, and has been from the creation of the world, a master-passion. To awaken it, to gratify it by slight degrees, and yet leave something always in suspense, is to establish the surest hold that can be had, in wrong, on the unthinking portion of mankind.

If a man had stood on London Bridge, calling till he was hoarse, upon the passers-by, to join with Lord George Gordon, although for an object which no man understood, and which in that very incident had a charm of its own, – the probability is, that he might have influenced a score of people in a month. If all zealous Protestants had been publicly urged to join an association for the avowed purpose of singing a hymn or two occasionally, and hearing some indifferent speeches made, and ultimately of petitioning Parliament[2] not to pass an act for abolishing the penal laws against Roman Catholic priests, the penalty of perpetual imprisonment denounced against those who educated children in that persuasion, and the disqualification of all members of the Romish church to inherit real property in the United Kingdom by right of purchase or descent, – matters so far removed from the business and bosoms of the mass, might perhaps have called together a hundred people. But when vague rumours got abroad, that in this Protestant association a secret power was mustering against the government for undefined and mighty purposes; when the air was filled with whispers of a confederacy among the Popish powers to degrade and enslave England, establish an inquisition in London, and turn the pens of Smithfield market[3] into stakes and cauldrons; when terrors and alarms which no man understood were perpetually broached, both in and out of Parliament, by one enthusiast who did not understand himself, and by-gone bugbears which had lain quietly in their graves for centuries, were raised again to haunt the ignorant and credulous; when all this was done, as it were, in the dark, and secret invitations to join the Great Protestant Association in defence of religion, life, and liberty, were dropped in the public ways, thrust under the house-doors, tossed in at windows, and pressed into the hands of those who trod the streets by night; when they glared from every wall, and shone on every post and pillar, so that stocks and stones[4] appeared infected with the common fear, urging all men to join together blindfold in resistance of they knew not what, they knew not why; – then the mania spread indeed, and the body, still increasing every day, grew forty thousand strong.

So said, at least, in this month of March 1780, Lord George Gordon, the association's president. Whether it was the fact or otherwise, few men knew, or cared to ascertain. It had never made any public demonstration; had scarcely ever been heard of, save through him; had never been seen; and was supposed by many to be the mere creature of his disordered brain. He was accustomed to talk largely about numbers of men – stimulated, as it was inferred, by certain successful disturbances, arising out of the same subject, which had occurred in Scotland in the previous year; was looked upon as a cracked-brained member of the lower house, who attacked all parties and sided with none, and was very little regarded. It was known that there was discontent abroad – there always is; he had been accustomed to address the people by placard, speech, and pamphlet, upon other questions; nothing had come, in England, of his past exertions, and nothing was apprehended from his present. Just as he has come upon the reader, he had come, from time to time, upon the public, and been forgotten in a day; as suddenly as he appears in these pages, after a blank of five long years, did he and his proceedings begin to force themselves, about this period, upon the notice of thousands of people, who had mingled in active life during the whole interval, and who, without being deaf or blind to passing events, had scarcely ever thought of him before.

'My lord,' said Gashford in his ear, as he drew the curtains of his bed betimes; 'my lord!'

'Yes – who's that? What is it?'

'The clock has struck nine,' returned the secretary, with meekly-folded hands. 'You have slept well? I hope you have slept well? If my prayers are heard, you are refreshed indeed.'

'To say the truth, I have slept so soundly,' said Lord George, rubbing his eyes and looking round the room, 'that I don't remember quite – what place is this?'

'My lord!' cried Gashford, with a smile.

'Oh!' returned his superior. 'Yes. You're not a Jew then?'

'A Jew!' exclaimed the pious secretary, recoiling.

'I dreamed that we were Jews, Gashford. You and I – both of us – Jews with long beards.'

'Heaven forbid, my lord! We might as well be Papists.'

'I suppose we might,' returned the other, very quickly. 'Eh? You really think so, Gashford?'

'Surely I do,' the secretary cried, with looks of great surprise.

'Humph!' he muttered. 'Yes, that seems reasonable.'

'I hope, my lord –' the secretary began.

'Hope!' he echoed, interrupting him. 'Why do you say, you hope? There's no harm in thinking of such things.'

'Not in dreams,' returned the secretary.

'In dreams! No, nor waking either.'

– ' "Called, and chosen, and faithful," ' said Gashford, taking up Lord George's watch which lay upon a chair, and seeming to read the inscription on the seal, abstractedly.

It was the slightest action possible, not obtruded on his notice, and apparently the result of a moment's absence of mind, not worth remark. But as the words were uttered, Lord George, who had been going on impetuously, stopped short, reddened, and was silent. Apparently quite unconscious of this change in his demeanour, the wily secretary stepped a little apart, under pretence of pulling up the window-blind, and returning, when the other had had time to recover, said:

'The holy cause goes bravely on, my lord. I was not idle, even last night. I dropped two of the hand-bills before I went to bed, and both are gone this morning. Nobody in the house has mentioned the circumstance of finding them, though I have been down stairs full half-an-hour. One or two recruits will be their first fruit, I predict; and who shall say how many more, with Heaven's blessing on your inspired exertions!'

'It was a famous device in the beginning,' replied Lord George; 'an excellent device, and did good service in Scotland. It was quite worthy of you. You remind me not to be a sluggard, Gashford, when the vineyard is menaced with destruction, and may be trodden down by papist feet. Let the horses be saddled in half-an-hour. We must be up and doing!'

He said this with a heightened colour, and in a tone of such enthusiasm, that the secretary deemed all further prompting needless, and withdrew.

– 'Dreamed he was a Jew,' he said thoughtfully, as he closed the bedroom door. 'He may come to that before he dies. It's like enough. Well! After a time, and provided I lost nothing by it, I don't see why that religion shouldn't suit me as well as any other. There are rich men among the Jews; shaving is very troublesome; – yes, it would suit me well enough. For the present, though, we must be Christian to the core. Our prophetic motto will suit all creeds in their turn, that's a comfort.' Reflecting on this source of consolation, he reached the sitting-room, and rang the bell for breakfast.

Lord George was quickly dressed (for his plain toilet was easily made), and as he was no less frugal in his repasts than in his Puritan attire, his share of the meal was soon despatched. The secretary, however, more devoted to the good things of this world, or more intent on sustaining his strength and spirits for the sake of the Protestant cause, ate and drank to the last minute, and required indeed some three or four reminders from John Grueby, before he could resolve to tear himself away from Mr Willet's plentiful providing.

At length he came down stairs, wiping his greasy mouth, and having paid John Willet's bill, climbed into his saddle. Lord George, who had been walking up and down before the house talking to himself with earnest gestures, mounted his horse; and returning old John Willet's stately bow, as well as the parting salutation of a dozen idlers whom the rumour of a live lord being about to leave the Maypole had gathered round the porch, they rode away, with stout John Grueby in the rear.

If Lord George Gordon had appeared in the eyes of Mr Willet

over-night, a nobleman of somewhat quaint and odd exterior, the impression was confirmed this morning, and increased a hundred fold. Sitting bolt upright upon his bony steed, with his long, straight hair, dangling about his face and fluttering in the wind; his limbs all angular and rigid, his elbows stuck out on either side ungracefully, and his whole frame jogged and shaken at every motion of his horse's feet; a more grotesque or more ungainly figure can hardly be conceived. In lieu of whip, he carried in his hand a great gold-headed cane, as large as any footman carries in these days; and his various modes of holding this unwieldy weapon – now upright before his face like the sabre of a horse-soldier, now over his shoulder like a musket, now between his finger and thumb, but always in some uncouth and awkward fashion – contributed in no small degree to the absurdity of his appearance. Stiff, lank, and solemn, dressed in an unusual manner, and ostentatiously exhibiting – whether by design or accident – all his peculiarities of carriage, gesture, and conduct; all the qualities, natural and artificial, in which he differed from other men; he might have moved the sternest looker-on to laughter, and fully provoked the smiles and whispered jests which greeted his departure from the Maypole inn.

Quite unconscious, however, of the effect he produced, he trotted on beside his secretary, talking to himself nearly all the way, until they came within a mile or two of London, when now and then some passenger went by who knew him by sight, and pointed him out to some one else, and perhaps stood looking after him, or cried in jest or earnest as it might be, 'Hurrah Geordie! No Popery!' At which he would gravely pull off his hat, and bow. When they reached the town and rode along the streets, these notices became more frequent; some laughed, some hissed, some turned their heads and smiled, some wondered who he was, some ran along the pavement by his side and cheered. When this happened in a crush of carts and chairs and coaches, he would make a dead stop, and pulling off his hat cry 'Gentlemen, No Popery!' to which the gentlemen would respond with lusty voices, and with three times three;[5] and then, on he would go again with a score or so of the raggedest, following at his horse's heels, and shouting till their throats were parched.

The old ladies too – there were a great many old ladies in the streets, and these all knew him. Some of them – not those of the highest rank, but such as sold fruit from baskets and carried burdens – clapped their shrivelled hands, and raised a weazen, piping, shrill 'Hurrah my Lord.' Others waved their hands, or handkerchiefs, or shook their fans or parasols, or threw up windows and called in haste to those within, to come and see. All these marks of popular esteem, he received with profound gravity and respect; bowing very low, and so frequently that his hat was more off his head than on; and looking up at the houses as he passed along, with the air of one who was making a public entry, and yet was not puffed-up or proud.

So they rode (to the deep and unspeakable disgust of John Grueby) the whole length of Whitechapel, Leadenhall-street, and Cheapside, and into Saint Paul's Churchyard. Arriving close to the cathedral, he halted; spoke to Gashford; and looking upward at its lofty dome, shook his head, as though he said 'The Church in Danger!' Then to be sure, the bystanders stretched their throats indeed; and he went on again with mighty acclamations from the mob, and lower bows than ever.

So along the Strand, up Swallow-street, into the Oxford-road, and thence to his house in Welbeck-street, near Cavendish-square, whither he was attended by a few dozen idlers; of whom he took leave on the steps with this brief parting 'Gentlemen, No Popery. Good day. God bless you.' This being rather a shorter address than they expected, was received with some displeasure, and cries of 'A speech! a speech!' which might have been complied with, but that John Grueby, making a mad charge upon them with all three horses, on his way to the stables, caused them to disperse into the adjoining fields, where they presently fell to pitch and toss, chuck-farthing, odd or even, dog-fighting, and other Protestant recreations.

In the afternoon Lord George came forth again, dressed in a black velvet coat, and trousers and waistcoat of the Gordon plaid, all of the same Quaker cut;[6] and in this costume, which made him look a dozen times more strange and singular than before, went down on foot to Westminster. Gashford, meanwhile, bestirred himself in business matters; with which he was still engaged when, shortly after dusk, John Grueby entered and announced a visitor.

'Let him come in,' said Gashford.

'Here! come in!' growled John to somebody without; 'You're a Protestant, an't you?'

'*I* should think so,' replied a deep, gruff voice.

'You've the looks of it,' said John Grueby. 'I'd have known you for one, anywhere.' With which remark he gave the visitor admission, retired, and shut the door.

The man who now confronted Gashford, was a squat, thickset personage, with a low retreating forehead, a coarse shock head of hair, and eyes so small and near together, that his broken nose alone seemed to prevent their meeting and fusing into one of the usual size. A dingy handkerchief twisted like a cord about his neck, left its great veins exposed to view, and they were swoln and starting, as though with gulping down strong passions, malice, and ill-will. His dress was of threadbare velveteen – a faded, rusty, whitened black, like the ashes of a pipe or a coal fire after a day's extinction; discoloured with the soils of many a stale debauch, and reeking yet with pot-house odours. In lieu of buckles at his knees, he wore unequal loops of packthread; and in his grimy hands he held a knotted stick, the knob of which was carved into a rough likeness of his own vile face. Such was the visitor who doffed his three-cornered hat in Gashford's presence, and waited, leering, for his notice.

'Ah! Dennis!' cried the secretary. 'Sit down.'

'I see my lord down yonder – ' cried the man, with a jerk of his thumb towards the quarter that he spoke of, 'and he says to me, says my lord, "If you've nothing to do, Dennis, go up to my house and talk with Muster Gashford." Of course I'd nothing to do, you know. These an't my working hours. Ha ha! I was a taking the air when I see my lord, that's what I was doing. I takes the air by night, as the howls does, Muster Gashford.'

'And sometimes in the day-time, eh?' said the secretary – 'when you go out in state,[7] you know.'

'Ha ha!' roared the fellow, smiting his leg; 'for a gentleman as 'ull say a pleasant thing in a pleasant way, give me Muster Gashford agin' all London and Westminster! My lord an't a bad 'un at that, but he's a fool to you. Ah to be sure, – when I go out in state.'

'And have your carriage,' said the secretary; 'and your chaplain, eh? and all the rest of it?'

'You'll be the death of me,' cried Dennis with another roar, 'you will. But what's in the wind now, Muster Gashford,' he asked hoarsely, 'Eh? Are we to be under orders to pull down one of them Popish chapels – or what?'

'Hush!' said the secretary, suffering the faintest smile to play upon his face. 'Hush! God bless me, Dennis! We associate, you know, for strictly peaceable and lawful purposes.'

'*I* know, bless you,' returned the man, thrusting his tongue into his cheek; 'I entered a' purpose, didn't I!'

'No doubt,' said Gashford, smiling as before. And when he said so, Dennis roared again, and smote his leg still harder, and falling into fits of laughter, wiped his eyes with the corner of his neckerchief, and cried 'Muster Gashford again all England – hollow!'

'Lord George and I were talking of you last night,' said Gashford, after a pause. 'He says you are a very earnest fellow.'

'So I am,' returned the hangman.

'And that you truly hate the Papists.'

'So I do,' and he confirmed it with a good round oath. 'Lookye here, Muster Gashford,' said the fellow, laying his hat and stick upon the floor, and slowly beating the palm of one hand with the fingers of the other; 'Ob-serve. I'm a constitutional officer that works for my living, and does my work creditable. Do I, or do I not?'

'Unquestionably.'

'Very good. Stop a minute. My work, is sound, Protestant, constitutional, English work. Is it, or is it not?'

'No man alive can doubt it.'

'Nor dead neither. Parliament says this here – says Parliament "If any man, woman, or child, does anything which goes again a certain number of our acts" – how many hanging laws may there be at this present time, Muster Gashford? Fifty?'[8]

'I don't exactly know how many,' replied Gashford, leaning back in his chair and yawning; 'a great number though.'

'Well; say fifty. Parliament says "If any man, woman, or child, does anything again any one of them fifty acts, that man, woman, or child, shall be worked off by Dennis." George the Third steps in when they number very strong at the end of a sessions, and says "These are too many for Dennis. I'll have half for *my*self and Dennis shall have half for *him*self;"[9] and sometimes he throws me in one over that I don't expect, as he did three year ago, when I got Mary Jones, a young woman of nineteen who come up to Tyburn with a infant at her breast, and was worked off for taking a piece of cloth off the counter of a shop in Ludgate-hill, and putting it down again when the shopman see her; and who had never done any harm before, and only tried to do that, in consequence of her husband having been pressed three weeks previous, and she being left to beg, with two young children – as was proved upon the trial. Ha ha! – Well! That being the law and the practice of England, is the glory of England, an't it Muster Gashford?'

'Certainly,' said the secretary.

'And in times to come,' pursued the hangman, 'if our grandsons should think of their grandfathers' times, and find these things altered, they'll say "Those were days indeed, and we've been going down hill ever since." – Won't they Muster Gashford?'

'I have no doubt they will,' said the secretary.

'Well then, look here,' said the hangman. 'If these papists gets into power, and begins to boil and roast instead of hang, what becomes of my work! If they touch my work that's a part of so many laws, what becomes of the laws in general, what becomes of the religion, what becomes of the country! – Did you ever go to church, Muster Gashford?'

'Ever!' repeated the secretary with some indignation; 'of course.'

'Well,' said the ruffian, 'I've been once – twice, counting the time I was christened – and when I heard the Parliament prayed for, and thought how many new hanging laws they made every sessions, I considered that *I* was prayed for. Now mind, Muster Gashford,' said the fellow, taking up his stick and shaking it with a ferocious air, 'I mustn't have my Protestant work touched, nor this here Protestant state of things altered in no degree, if I can help it; I mustn't have no Papists interfering with me, unless they come to me to be worked off in course of law; I mustn't have no biling, no roasting, no frying – nothing but hanging. My lord may well call me an earnest fellow. In support of the great Protestant principle of having plenty of that, I'll,' and here he beat his club upon the ground, 'burn, fight, kill – do anything you bid me, so that it's bold and devilish – though the end of it was, that I got hung myself. – There, Muster Gashford!'

He appropriately followed up this frequent prostitution of a noble word to the vilest purposes, by pouring out in a kind of ecstacy, at least a score of most tremendous oaths; then wiped his heated face upon his neckerchief, and cried, 'No Popery! I'm a religious man, by G – !'

Gashford had leant back in his chair, regarding him with eyes so sunken, and so shadowed by his heavy brows, that for aught the hangman saw of them, he might have been stone blind. He remained smiling in silence for a short time longer, and then said, slowly and distinctly:

'You are indeed an earnest fellow, Dennis – a most valuable fellow – the staunchest man I know of in our ranks. But you must calm yourself; you must be peaceful, lawful, mild as any lamb. I am sure you will be though.'

'Ay, ay, we shall see, Muster Gashford, we shall see. You won't have to complain of me,' returned the other, shaking his head.

'I am sure I shall not,' said the secretary in the same mild tone, and with the same emphasis. 'We shall have, we think, about next month, or May, when this Papist relief bill comes before the house, to convene our whole body for the first time. My lord has thoughts of our walking in procession through the streets – just as an innocent display of strength – and accompanying our petition down to the door of the House of Commons.'

'The sooner, the better,' said Dennis, with another oath.

'We shall have to draw up in divisions, our numbers being so large; and, I believe I may venture to say,' resumed Gashford, affecting not to hear the interruption, 'though I have no direct instructions to that effect – that Lord George has thought of you as an excellent leader for one of these parties. I have no doubt you would be an admirable one.'

'Try me,' said the fellow, with an ugly wink.

'You would be cool, I know,' pursued the secretary, still smiling, and still managing his eyes so that he could watch him closely, and really not be seen in turn, 'obedient to orders, and perfectly temperate. You would lead your party into no danger, I am certain.'

'I'd lead them, Muster Gashford' – the hangman was beginning in a reckless way, when Gashford started forward, laid his finger on his lips, and feigned to write, just as the door was opened by John Grueby.

'Oh!' said John, looking in; 'here's another Protestant.'

'Some other room, John,' cried Gashford in his blandest voice. 'I am engaged just now.'

But John had brought this new visitor to the door, and he walked in unbidden, as the words were uttered; giving to view the form and features, rough attire, and reckless air, of Hugh.

CHAPTER THE THIRTY-EIGHTH

The secretary put his hand before his eyes to shade them from the glare of the lamp, and for some moments looked at Hugh with a frowning brow, as if he remembered to have seen him lately, but could not call to mind where, or on what occasion. His uncertainty was very brief, for before Hugh had spoken a word, he said, as his countenance cleared up:

'Ay, ay, I recollect. It's quite right, John, you needn't wait. Don't go, Dennis.'

'Your servant, master,' said Hugh, as Grueby disappeared.

'Yours friend,' returned the secretary in his smoothest manner. 'What brings *you* here? We left nothing behind us, I hope?'

Hugh gave a short laugh, and thrusting his hand into his breast, produced one of the handbills, soiled and dirty from lying out of doors all night, which he laid upon the secretary's desk after flattening it upon his knee, and smoothing out the wrinkles with his heavy palm.

'Nothing but that, master. It fell into good hands, you see.'

'What is this!' said Gashford, turning it over with an air of perfectly natural surprise. 'Where did you get it from, my good fellow; what does it mean? I don't understand this at all.'

A little disconcerted by this reception, Hugh looked from the secretary to Dennis, who had risen and was standing at the table too, observing the stranger by stealth, and seeming to derive the utmost satisfaction from his manners and appearance. Considering himself silently appealed to by this action, Mr Dennis shook his head thrice, as if to say of Gashford, 'No. He don't know anything at all about it. I know he don't. I'll take my oath he don't;' and hiding his profile from Hugh with one long end of his frowzy neckerchief, nodded and chuckled behind this screen in extreme approval of the secretary's proceedings.

'It tells the man that finds it, to come here, don't it?' asked Hugh. 'I'm no scholar, myself, but I showed it to a friend, and he said it did.'

'It certainly does,' said Gashford, opening his eyes to their utmost width; 'really this is the most remarkable circumstance I have ever known. How did you come by this piece of paper, my good friend?'

'Muster Gashford,' wheezed the hangman under his breath, 'agin all Newgate!'

Whether Hugh heard him, or saw by his manner that he was being played upon, or perceived the secretary's drift of himself, he came in his blunt way to the point at once.

'Here!' he said, stretching out his hand and taking it back; 'never mind the bill, or what it says, or what it don't say. You don't know anything about it, master, – no more do I, – no more does he,' glancing at Dennis. 'None of us know what it means, or where it comes from; there's an end of that. Now, I want to make one against the Catholics, I'm a No-Popery man, and ready to be sworn in. That's what I've come here for.'

'Put him down on the roll, Muster Gashford,' said Dennis approvingly. 'That's the way to go to work – right to the end at once, and no palaver.'

'What's the use of shooting wide of the mark, eh, old boy!' cried Hugh.

'My sentiments all over!' rejoined the hangman. 'This is the sort of chap for my division, Muster Gashford. Down with him, sir. Put him on the roll. I'd stand godfather to him, if he was to be christened in a bonfire, made of the ruins of the Bank of England.'

With these and other expressions of confidence of the like flattering kind Mr Dennis gave him a hearty slap on the back, which Hugh was not slow to return.

'No Popery, brother!' cried the hangman.

'No Property, brother!' responded Hugh.

'Popery, Popery,' said the secretary with his usual mildness.

'It's all the same!' cried Dennis. 'It's all right. Down with him, Muster Gashford. Down with everybody, down with everything! Hurrah for the Protestant religion! That's the time of day, Muster Gashford!'

The secretary regarded them both with a very favourable expression of countenance, while they gave loose to these and other demonstrations of their patriotic purpose; and was about to make some remark aloud, when Dennis, stepping up to him, and shading his mouth with his hand, said, in a hoarse whisper, as he nudged him with his elbow:

'Don't split upon a constitutional officer's profession, Muster Gashford. There are popular prejudices, you know, and he mightn't like it. Wait till he comes to be more intimate with me. He's a fine-built chap, an't he?'

'A powerful fellow indeed!'

'Did you ever, Muster Gashford,' whispered Dennis, with a horrible kind of admiration, such as that with which a cannibal might regard his intimate friend, when hungry, – 'did you ever' – and here he drew still closer to his ear, and fenced his mouth with both his open hands – 'see such a throat as his? Do but cast your eye upon it. There's a neck for stretching, Muster Gashford!'

The secretary assented to this proposition with the best grace he could assume – it is difficult to feign a true professional relish: which is eccentric sometimes – and after asking the candidate a few unimportant questions, proceeded to enrol him a member of the Great Protestant Association of England. If anything could have exceeded Mr Dennis's joy on the happy conclusion of this ceremony, it would have been the rapture with which he received the announcement that the new member could neither read nor write: those two arts being (as Mr Dennis swore) the greatest possible curse a civilised community could know, and militating more against the professional emoluments and usefulness of the great constitutional office he had the honour to hold, than any adverse circumstances that could present themselves to his imagination.

The enrolment being completed, and Hugh having been informed by Gashford, in his peculiar manner, of the peaceful and strictly lawful objects contemplated by the body to which he now belonged – during which recital Mr Dennis nudged him very much with his elbow, and made divers remarkable faces – the secretary gave them both to understand that he desired to be alone. Therefore they took their leaves without delay, and came out of the house together.

'Are you walking, brother?' said Dennis.

'Ay!' returned Hugh. 'Where you will.'

'That's social,' said his new friend. 'Which way shall we take? Shall we go and have a look at doors that we shall make a pretty good clattering at, before long – eh, brother?'

Hugh answering in the affirmative, they went slowly down to Westminster, where both houses of Parliament[1] were then sitting. Mingling in the crowd of carriages, horses, servants, chairmen, link-boys, porters, and idlers of all kinds, they lounged about; while

Hugh's new friend pointed out to him significantly the weak parts of the building, how easy it was to get into the lobby, and so to the very door of the House of Commons; and how plainly, when they marched down there in grand array, their roars and shouts would be heard by the members inside; with a great deal more to the same purpose, all of which Hugh received with manifest delight.

He told him, too, who some of the Lords and Commons were, by name, as they came in and out; whether they were friendly to the Papists or otherwise; and bade him take notice of their liveries and equipages, that he might be sure of them, in case of need. Sometimes he drew him close to the windows of a passing carriage, that he might see its master's face by the light of the lamps; and, both in respect of people and localities, he showed so much acquaintance with everything around, that it was plain he had often studied there before; as indeed, when they grew a little more confidential, he confessed he had.

Perhaps the most striking part of all this was, the number of people – never in groups of more than two or three together – who seemed to be skulking about the crowd for the same purpose. To the greater part of these, a slight nod or a look from Hugh's companion was sufficient greeting; but, now and then, some man would come and stand beside him in the throng, and, without turning his head or appearing to communicate with him, would say a word or two in a low voice, which he would answer in the same cautious manner. Then they would part, like strangers. Some of these men often reappeared again unexpectedly in the crowd close to Hugh, and, as they passed by, pressed his hand, or looked him sternly in the face; but they never spoke to him, nor he to them; no, not a word.

It was remarkable, too, that whenever they happened to stand where there was any press of people, and Hugh chanced to be looking downward, he was sure to see an arm stretched out – under his own perhaps, or perhaps across him – which thrust some paper into the hand or pocket of a bystander, and was so suddenly withdrawn that it was impossible to tell from whom it came; nor could he see in any face, on glancing quickly round, the least confusion or surprise. They often trod upon a paper like the one he carried in his breast, but his companion whispered him not to touch it or to take it up, – not even to look towards it, – so there they let them lie, and passed on.

When they had paraded the street and all the avenues of the building in this manner for near two hours, they turned away, and his friend asked him what he thought of what he had seen, and whether he was prepared for a good hot piece of work if it should come to that. 'The hotter the better,' said Hugh, 'I'm prepared for anything.' – 'So am I,' said his friend, 'and so are many of us;' and they shook hands upon it with a great oath; and with many terrible imprecations on the Papists.

As they were thirsty by this time, Dennis proposed that they should repair together to the Boot,[2] where there was good company and strong liquor. Hugh yielding a ready assent, they bent their steps that way with no loss of time.

This Boot was a lone house of public entertainment, situated in the fields at the back of the Foundling Hospital;[3] a very solitary spot at that period, and quite deserted after dark. The tavern stood at some distance from any high road, and was approachable only by a dark and narrow lane; so that Hugh was much surprised to find several people drinking there, and great merriment going on. He was still more surprised to find among them almost every face that had caught his attention in the crowd; but his companion having whispered him outside the door, that it was not considered good manners at the Boot to appear at all curious about the company, he kept his own counsel, and made no show of recognition.

Before putting his lips to the liquor which was brought for them, Dennis drank in a loud voice the health of Lord George Gordon, President of the Great Protestant Association; which toast Hugh pledged likewise, with corresponding enthusiasm. A fiddler who was present, and who appeared to act as the appointed minstrel of the company, forthwith struck up a Scotch reel; and that in tones so invigorating, that Hugh and his friend (who had both been drinking before) rose from their seats as by previous concert, and, to the great admiration of the assembled guests, performed an extemporaneous No-Popery Dance.

— * —

CHAPTER THE THIRTY-NINTH

The applause which the performance of Hugh and his new friend elicited from the company at The Boot, had not yet subsided, and the two dancers were still panting from their exertions, which had been of a rather extreme and violent character, when the party was reinforced by the arrival of some more guests, who, being a detachment of United Bulldogs, were received with very flattering marks of distinction and respect.

The leader of this small party – for, including himself, they were but three in number – was our old acquaintance, Mr Tappertit, who seemed, physically speaking, to have grown smaller with years (particularly as to his legs, which were stupendously little), but who, in a moral point of view, in personal dignity and self-esteem, had swelled into a giant. Nor was it by any means difficult for the most unobservant person to detect this state of feeling in the quondam 'Prentice, for it not only proclaimed itself impressively and beyond mistake in his majestic walk and kindling eye, but found a striking means of revelation in his turned-up nose, which scouted all things of earth with deep disdain, and sought communion with its kindred skies.

Mr Tappertit, as chief or captain of the Bulldogs, was attended by his two lieutenants; one, the tall comrade of his younger life; the other, a 'Prentice Knight in days of yore – Mark Gilbert, bound in the olden time to Thomas Curzon of the Golden Fleece. These gentlemen, like himself, were now emancipated from their 'Prentice thraldom, and served as journeymen; but they were, in humble emulation of his great example, bold and daring spirits, and aspired to a distinguished state in great political events. Hence their connexion with the Protestant Association of England, sanctioned by the name of Lord George Gordon; and hence their present visit to The Boot.

'Gentlemen!' said Mr Tappertit, taking off his hat as a great General might in addressing his troops. 'Well met. My Lord does me and you the honour to send his compliments per self.'

'You've seen my Lord too, have you?' said Dennis. '*I* see him this afternoon.'

'My duty called me to the Lobby when our shop shut up; and I

saw him there, sir,' Mr Tappertit replied, as he and his Lieutenants took their seats. 'How do *you* do?'

'Lively, master, lively,' said the fellow. 'Here's a new brother, regularly put down in black and white by Muster Gashford; a credit to the cause; one of the stick-at-nothing sort; one arter my own heart. D'ye see him? Has he got the looks of a man that'll do, do you think?' he cried, as he slapped Hugh on the back.

'Looks or no looks,' said Hugh, with a drunken flourish of his arm, 'I'm the man you want. I hate the Papists, every one of 'em. They hate me and I hate them. They do me all the harm they can, and I'll do them all the harm *I* can. Hurrah!'

'Was there ever,' said Dennis, looking round the room, when the echo of his boisterous voice had died away; 'was there ever such a game boy! Why, I mean to say, brothers, that if Muster Gashford had gone a hundred mile and got together fifty men of the common run, they wouldn't have been worth this one.'

The greater part of the company implicitly subscribed to this opinion, and testified their faith in Hugh, by nods and looks of great significance. Mr Tappertit sat and contemplated him for a long time in silence, as if he suspended his judgment; then drew a little nearer to him, and eyed him over more carefully; then went close up to him, and took him apart into a dark corner.

'I say,' he began, with a thoughtful brow, 'haven't I seen you before?'

'It's like you may,' said Hugh, in his careless way. 'I don't know; shouldn't wonder.'

'No, but it's very easily settled,' returned Sim. 'Look at me. Did you ever see *me* before? You wouldn't be likely to forget it, you know, if you ever did. Look at me. Don't be afraid; I won't do you any harm. Take a good look – steady now.'

The encouraging way in which Mr Tappertit made this request, and coupled it with an assurance that he needn't be frightened, amused Hugh mightily – so much indeed, that he saw nothing at all of the small man before him, through closing his eyes in a fit of hearty laughter, which shook his great broad sides until they ached again.

'Come!' said Mr Tappertit, growing a little impatient under this disrespectful treatment. 'Do you know me, feller?'

'Not I,' cried Hugh. 'Ha ha ha! Not I! But I should like to.'

'And yet I'd have wagered a seven-shilling piece,'[1] said Mr Tappertit, folding his arms, and confronting him with his legs wide apart and firmly planted on the ground, 'that you once were hostler at the Maypole.'

Hugh opened his eyes on hearing this, and looked at him in great surprise.

'– And so you were, too,' said Mr Tappertit, pushing him away, with a condescending playfulness. 'When did *my* eyes ever deceive – unless it was a young woman! Don't you know me now?'

'Why it an't –' Hugh faltered.

'An't it,' said Mr Tappertit. 'Are you sure of that? You remember G. Varden, don't you?'

Certainly Hugh did, and he remembered D. Varden too; but that he didn't tell him.

'You remember coming down there, before I was out of my time, to ask after a vagabond that had bolted off, and left his disconsolate father a prey to the bitterest emotions, and all the rest of it – don't you?' said Mr Tappertit.

'Of course I do!' cried Hugh. 'And I saw you there.'

'Saw me there!' said Mr Tappertit. 'Yes, I should think you did see me there. The place would be troubled to go on without me. Don't you remember my thinking you liked the vagabond, and on that account going to quarrel with you; and then finding you detested him worse than poison, going to drink with you? Don't you remember that?'

'To be sure!' cried Hugh.

'Well! and are you in the same mind now?' said Mr Tappertit.

'Yes!' roared Hugh.

'You speak like a man,' said Mr Tappertit, 'and I'll shake hands with you.' With these conciliatory expressions he suited the action to the word; and Hugh meeting his advances readily, they performed the ceremony with a show of great heartiness.

'I find,' said Mr Tappertit, looking round on the assembled guests, 'that brother What's-his-name and I are old acquaintance. – You never heard anything more of that rascal, I suppose, eh?'

'Not a syllable,' replied Hugh. 'I never want to. I don't believe I ever shall. He's dead long ago, I hope.'

'It's to be hoped, for the sake of mankind in general and the happiness of society, that he is,' said Mr Tappertit, rubbing his palm upon his legs, and looking at it between whiles. 'Is your other hand at all cleaner? Much the same. Well, I'll owe you another shake. We'll suppose it done, if you've no objection.'

Hugh laughed again, and with such thorough abandonment to his mad humour, that his limbs seemed dislocated, and his whole frame in danger of tumbling to pieces; but Mr Tappertit, so far from receiving this extreme merriment with any irritation, was pleased to regard it with the utmost favour, and even to join in it, so far as one of his gravity and station could, with any regard to that decency and decorum which men in high places are expected to maintain.

Mr Tappertit did not stop here, as many public characters might have done, but calling up his brace of lieutenants, introduced Hugh to them with high commendation; declaring him to be a man who, at such times as those in which they lived, could not be too much cherished. Further, he did him the honour to remark, that he would be an acquisition of which even the United Bulldogs might be proud; and finding, upon sounding him, that he was quite ready and willing to enter the society (for he was not at all particular, and would have leagued himself that night with anything, or anybody, for any purpose whatsoever), caused the necessary preliminaries to be gone into upon the spot. This tribute to his great merit delighted no man more than Mr Dennis, as he himself proclaimed with several rare and surprising oaths; and indeed it gave unmingled satisfaction to the whole assembly.

'Make anything you like of me!' cried Hugh, flourishing the can he had emptied more than once. 'Put me on any duty you please. I'm your man. I'll do it. Here's my captain – here's my leader. Ha ha ha! Let him give me the word of command, and I'll fight the whole Parliament House single-handed, or set a lighted torch to the King's Throne itself!' With that, he smote Mr Tappertit on the back, with such violence that his little body seemed to shrink into a mere nothing; and roared again until the very foundlings near at hand were startled in their beds.

In fact, a sense of something whimsical in their companionship seemed to have taken entire possession of his rude brain. The bare fact of being patronised by a great man whom he could have crushed with one hand, appeared in his eyes so eccentric and humorous, that a kind of ferocious merriment gained the mastery over him, and quite subdued his brutal nature. He roared and roared again; toasted Mr Tappertit a hundred times; declared himself a Bulldog to the core; and vowed to be faithful to him to the last drop of blood in his veins.

All these compliments Mr Tappertit received as matters of course – flattering enough in their way, but entirely attributable to his vast superiority. His dignified self-possession only delighted Hugh the more; and in a word, this giant and dwarf struck up a friendship which bade fair to be of long continuance, as the one held it to be his right to command, and the other considered it an exquisite pleasantry to obey. Nor was Hugh by any means a passive follower, who scrupled to act without precise and definite orders; for when Mr Tappertit mounted on an empty cask which stood by way of rostrum in the room, and volunteered a speech upon the alarming crisis then at hand, he placed himself beside the orator, and though he grinned from ear to ear at every word he said, threw out such expressive hints to scoffers in the management of his cudgel, that those who were at first the most disposed to interrupt, became remarkably attentive, and were the loudest in their approbation.

It was not all noise and jest, however, at The Boot, nor were the whole party listeners to the speech. There were some men at the other end of the room (which was a long, low-roofed chamber) in earnest conversation all the time; and when any of this group went out, fresh people were sure to come in soon afterwards and sit down in their places, as though the others had relieved them on some watch or duty; which it was pretty clear they did, for these changes took place by the clock, at intervals of half an hour. These persons whispered very much among themselves, and kept aloof, and often looked round, as jealous of their speech being overheard; some two or three among them entered in books what seemed to be reports from the others; when they were not thus employed, one of them would turn to the newspapers which were strewn upon the table, and from the Saint James's Chronicle, the Herald, Chronicle, or Public Advertiser,[2] would read to the rest in a low voice some passage having reference to the topic in which they were all so deeply interested. But the great attraction was a pamphlet called The Thunderer,[3] which espoused their own opinions, and was supposed at that time to emanate directly from the Association. This was always in request; and whether read aloud, to an eager knot of listeners, or by some solitary man, was certain to be followed by stormy talking and excited looks.

In the midst of all his merriment, and admiration of his captain, Hugh was made sensible by these and other tokens, of the presence of an air of mystery, akin to that which had so much impressed

him out of doors. It was impossible to discard a sense that something serious was going on, and that under the noisy revel of the public-house, there lurked unseen and dangerous matter. Little affected by this, however, he was perfectly satisfied with his quarters and would have remained there till morning, but that his conductor rose soon after midnight, to go home; Mr Tappertit following his example, left him no excuse to stay. So they all three left the house together: roaring a No-Popery song until the fields resounded with the dismal noise.

'Cheer up, captain!' cried Hugh, when they had roared themselves out of breath. 'Another stave!'

Mr Tappertit, nothing loath, began again; and so the three went staggering on, arm-in-arm, shouting like madmen, and defying the watch with great valour. Indeed this did not require any unusual bravery or boldness, as the watchmen of that time, being selected for the office on account of excessive age and extraordinary infirm-ity, had a custom of shutting themselves up tight in their boxes on the first symptoms of disturbance, and remaining there until they disappeared. In these proceedings, Mr Dennis, who had a gruff voice and lungs of considerable power, distinguished himself very much, and acquired great credit with his two companions.

'What a queer fellow you are!' said Mr Tappertit. 'You're so precious sly and close. Why don't you ever tell what trade you're of?'

'Answer the captain instantly,' cried Hugh, beating his hat down on his head; 'why don't you ever tell what trade you're of?'

'I'm of as gen-teel a calling, brother, as any man in England – as light a business as any gentleman could desire.'

'Was you 'prenticed to it?' asked Mr Tappertit.

'No. Natural genius,' said Mr Dennis. 'No 'prenticing. It come by natur'. Muster Gashford knows my calling. Look at that hand of mine – many and many a job that hand has done, with a neatness and dex-terity, never known afore. When I look at that hand,' said Mr Dennis, shaking it in the air, 'and remember the helegant bits of work it has turned off, I feel quite molloncholy to think it should ever grow old and feeble. But sich is life!'

He heaved a deep sigh as he indulged in these reflections, and putting his fingers with an absent air on Hugh's throat, and particu-larly under his left ear, as if he were studying the anatomical development of that part of his frame, shook his head in a despondent manner and actually shed tears.

'You're a kind of artist, I suppose – eh!' said Mr Tappertit.

'Yes,' rejoined Dennis; 'yes – I may call myself a artist – a fancy workman – art improves natur' – that's my motto.'

'And what do you call this?' said Mr Tappertit taking his stick out of his hand.

'That's my portrait atop,' Dennis replied; 'd'ye think it's like?'

'Why – it's a little too handsome,' said Mr Tappertit. 'Who did it? You?'

'I!' repeated Dennis, gazing fondly on his image. 'I wish I had the talent. That was carved by a friend of mine, as is now no more. The very day afore he died, he cut that with his pocket-knife from memory! I'll die game, says my friend, and my last moments shall be dewoted to making Dennis's picter. That's it.'

'That was a queer fancy, wasn't it?' said Mr Tappertit.

'It *was* a queer fancy,' rejoined the other, breathing on his fictitious nose, and polishing it with the cuff of his coat, 'but he was a queer subject altogether – a kind of gipsy – one of the finest, stand-up men, you ever see. Ah! He told me some things that would startle you a bit, did that friend of mine, on the morning when he died.'

'You were with him at the time, were you?' said Mr Tappertit.

'Yes,' he answered with a curious look, 'I was there. Oh! yes certainly, I was there. He wouldn't have gone off half as comfortable without me. I had been with three or four of his family under the same circumstances. They were all fine fellows.'

'They must have been fond of you,' remarked Mr Tappertit, looking at him sideways.

'I don't know that they was exactly fond of me,' said Dennis, with a little hesitation, 'but they all had me near 'em when they departed. I come in for their wardrobes too. This very hankecher that you see round my neck, belonged to him that I've been speaking of – him as did that likeness.'

Mr Tappertit glanced at the article referred to, and appeared to think that the deceased's ideas of dress were of a peculiar and by no means an expensive kind. He made no remark upon the point, however, and suffered his mysterious companion to proceed without interruption.

'These smalls,' said Dennis, rubbing his legs; 'these very smalls –
they belonged to a friend of mine that's left off sich incumbrances
for ever: this coat too – I've often walked behind this coat, in the
streets, and wondered whether it would ever come to me: this pair
of shoes have danced a hornpipe for another man, afore my eyes,
full half-a-dozen times at least: and as to my hat,' he said, taking
it off, and twirling it round upon his fist – 'Lord! I've seen this hat
go up Holborn on the box of a hackney-coach – ah, many and many
a day!'

'You don't mean to say their old wearers are *all* dead, I
hope?' said Mr Tappertit, falling a little distance from him, as he
spoke.

'Every one of 'em,' replied Dennis. 'Every man Jack!'

There was something so very ghastly in this circumstance, and
it appeared to account, in such a very strange and dismal manner,
for his faded dress – which, in this new aspect, seemed discoloured
by the earth from graves – that Mr Tappertit abruptly found he
was going another way, and, stopping short, bade him good night
with the utmost heartiness. As they happened to be near the Old
Bailey,[4] and Mr Dennis knew there were turnkeys in the lodge with
whom he could pass the night, and discuss professional subjects of
common interest among them before a rousing fire, and over a
social glass, he separated from his companions without any great
regret, and warmly shaking hands with Hugh, and making an early
appointment for their meeting at The Boot, left them to pursue
their road.

'That's a strange sort of man,' said Mr Tappertit, watching the
hackney-coachman's hat as it went bobbing down the street. 'I
don't know what to make of him. Why can't he have his smalls
made to order, or wear live clothes at any rate?'

'He's a lucky man, captain,' cried Hugh. 'I should like to have
such friends as his.'

'I hope he don't get 'em to make their wills, and then knock 'em
on the head,' said Mr Tappertit, musing. 'But come. The United
B.'s expect me. On! – What's the matter?'

'I quite forgot,' said Hugh, who had started at the striking of a
neighbouring clock. 'I have somebody to see to-night – I must turn
back directly. The drinking and singing put it out of my head. It's
well I remembered it!'

Mr Tappertit looked at him as though he were about to give

utterance to some very majestic sentiments in reference to this act of desertion, but as it was clear, from Hugh's hasty manner, that the engagement was one of a pressing nature, he graciously forbore, and gave him his permission to depart immediately, which Hugh acknowledged with a roar of laughter.

'Good night, captain!' he cried. 'I am yours to the death, remember!'

'Farewell!' said Mr Tappertit, waving his hand. 'Be bold and vigilant!'

'No Popery, captain!' roared Hugh.

'England in blood first!' cried his desperate leader. Whereat Hugh cheered and laughed, and ran off like a greyhound.

'That man will prove a credit to my corps,' said Simon, turning thoughtfully upon his heel. 'And let me see. In an altered state of society – which must ensue if we break out and are victorious – when the locksmith's child is mine, Miggs must be got rid of somehow, or she'll poison the tea-kettle one evening when I'm out. He might marry Miggs, if he was drunk enough. It shall be done. I'll make a note of it.'

CHAPTER THE FORTIETH

Little thinking of the plan for his happy settlement in life which had suggested itself to the teeming brain of his provident commander, Hugh made no pause until Saint Dunstan's giants[1] struck the hour above him, when he worked the handle of a pump which stood hard by, with great vigour, and thrusting his head under the spout, let the water gush upon him until a little stream ran down from every uncombed hair, and he was wet to the waist. Considerably refreshed by this ablution, both in mind and body, and almost sobered for the time, he dried himself as he best could; then crossed the road, and plied the knocker of the Middle Temple gate.

The night-porter looked through a small grating in the portal with a surly eye, and cried 'Halloa!' which greeting Hugh returned in kind, and bade him open quickly.

'We don't sell beer here,' cried the man; 'what else do you want?'

'To come in,' Hugh replied, with a kick at the door.

'Where to go to?'

'Paper-Buildings.'

'Whose chambers?'

'Sir John Chester's.' Each of which answers, he emphasised with another kick.

After a little growling on the other side, the gate was opened, and he passed in: undergoing a close inspection from the porter as he did so.

'*You* wanting Sir John, at this time of night!' said the man.

'Ay!' said Hugh. 'I! What of that?'

'Why, I must go with you and see that you do, for I don't believe it.'

'Come along then.'

Eyeing him with suspicious looks, the man, with key and lantern, walked on at his side, and attended him to Sir John Chester's door, at which Hugh gave one knock, that echoed through the dark staircase like a ghostly summons, and made the dull light tremble in the drowsy lamp.

'Do you think he wants me now?' said Hugh.

Before the man had time to answer, a footstep was heard within, a light appeared, and Sir John, in his dressing-gown and slippers, opened the door.

'I ask you pardon, Sir John,' said the porter, pulling off his hat. 'Here's a young man says he wants to speak to you. It's late for strangers. I thought it best to see that all was right.'

'Aha!' cried Sir John, raising his eyebrows. 'It's you, messenger, is it? Go in. Quite right, friend. I commend your prudence highly. Thank you. God bless you. Good night.'

To be commended, thanked, God-blessed, and bade good night by one who carried 'Sir' before his name, and wrote himself M. P. to boot, was something for a porter. He withdrew with much humility and reverence. Sir John followed his late visitor into the dressing-room, and sitting in his easy chair before the fire, and moving it so that he could see him as he stood, hat in hand, beside the door, looked at him from head to foot.

The old face, calm and pleasant as ever; the complexion, quite juvenile in its bloom and clearness; the same smile; the wonted precision and elegance of dress; the white, well-ordered teeth; the delicate hands; the composed and quiet manner; everything as it used to be: no marks of age or passion, envy, hate, or discontent: all unruffled and serene, and quite delightful to behold.

He wrote himself M. P. – but how? Why, thus. It was a proud family – more proud, indeed, than wealthy. He had stood in danger of arrest; of bailiffs, and a jail – a vulgar jail, to which the common people with small incomes went. Gentlemen of ancient houses have no privilege of exemption from such cruel laws – unless they are of one great house, and then they have. A proud man of his stock and kindred had the means of sending him there. He offered – not indeed to pay his debts, but to let him sit for a close borough until his own son came of age, which, if he lived, would come to pass in twenty years. It was quite as good as an Insolvent Act,[2] and infinitely more genteel. So Sir John Chester was a member of Parliament.

But how Sir John? Nothing so simple, or so easy. One touch with a sword of state, and the transformation is effected. John Chester Esquire, M. P. attended court – went up with an address – headed a deputation. Such elegance of manner, so many graces of deportment, such powers of conversation, could never pass unnoticed. Mr was too common for such merit. A man so gentlemanly should have been – but Fortune is capricious – born a Duke: just as some dukes should have been born labourers. He caught the fancy of the king, knelt down a grub, and rose a butterfly. John Chester Esquire was knighted and became Sir John.

'I thought when you left me this evening, my esteemed acquaintance,' said Sir John after a pretty long silence, 'that you intended to return with all despatch?'

'So I did, Master.'

'And so you have?' he retorted, glancing at his watch. 'Is that what you would say?'

Instead of replying, Hugh changed the leg on which he leant, shuffled his cap from one hand to the other, looked at the ground, the wall, the ceiling, and finally at Sir John himself; before whose pleasant face he lowered his eyes again, and fixed them on the floor.

'And how have you been employing yourself in the mean while?' quoth Sir John, lazily crossing his legs. 'Where have you been? what harm have you been doing?'

'No harm at all, Master,' growled Hugh, with humility. 'I have only done as you ordered.'

'As I *what?*' returned Sir John.

'Well then,' said Hugh uneasily, 'as you advised, or said I ought, or said I might, or said that you would do, if you was me. Don't be so hard upon me, master.'

Something like an expression of triumph in the perfect control he had established over this rough instrument, appeared in the knight's face for an instant; but it vanished directly, as he said – paring his nails while speaking:

'When you say I ordered you, my good fellow, you imply that I directed you to do something for me – something I wanted done – something for my own ends and purposes – you see? Now I am sure I needn't enlarge upon the extreme absurdity of such an idea, however unintentional; so, please –' and here he turned his eyes upon him – 'to be more guarded. Will you?'

'I meant to give you no offence,' said Hugh. 'I don't know what to say. You catch me up so very short.'

'You will be caught up much shorter, my good friend – infinitely shorter – one of these days, depend upon it,' replied his patron, calmly. 'By-the-bye, instead of wondering why you have been so long, my wonder should be why you came at all. Why did you?'

'You know, master,' said Hugh, 'that I couldn't read the bill I found, and that supposing it to be something particular from the way it was wrapped up, I brought it here.'

'And could you ask no one else to read it, Bruin?'³ said Sir John.

'No one that I could trust with secrets, master. Since Barnaby Rudge was lost sight of for good and all – and that's five year ago – I haven't talked with any one but you.'

'You have done me honour, I am sure.'

'I have come to and fro, master, all through that time, when there was anything to tell, because I knew that you'd be angry with me if I stayed away,' said Hugh, blurting the words out, after an embarrassed silence; 'and because I wished to please you, if I could, and not to have you go against me. There. That's the true reason why I came to-night. You know that, master, I am sure.'

'You are a specious fellow,' returned Sir John, fixing his eyes upon him, 'and carry two faces under your hood, as well as the best. Didn't you give me in this room, this evening, any other reason; no dislike of anybody who has slighted you, lately, on all occasions, abused you, treated you with rudeness; acted towards you, more as if you were a mongrel dog than a man like himself?'

'To be sure I did!' cried Hugh, his passion rising, as the other meant it should; 'and I say it all over now, again. I'd do anything to have some revenge on him – anything. And when you told me that he and all the Catholics would suffer from those who joined together under that handbill, I said I'd make one of 'em, if their master was the devil himself. I *am* one of 'em. See whether I am as good as my word and turn out to be among the foremost, or no. I mayn't have much head, master, but I've head enough to remember those that use me ill. You shall see, and so shall he, and so shall hundreds more, how my spirit backs me when the time comes. My bark is nothing to my bite. Some that I know, had better have a wild lion among 'em than me, when I am fairly loose – they had!'

The knight looked at him with a smile of far deeper meaning than ordinary; and pointing to the old cupboard, followed him with his eyes while he filled and drank a glass of liquor; and smiled when his back was turned, with deeper meaning yet.

'You are in a blustering mood, my friend,' he said, when Hugh confronted him again.

'Not I, master!' cried Hugh. 'I don't say half I mean. I can't. I haven't got the gift. There are talkers enough among us; I'll be one of the doers.'

'Oh! you have joined those fellows then?' said Sir John, with an air of most profound indifference.

'Yes. I went up to the house you told me of, and got put down upon the muster. There was another man there, named Dennis – '

'Dennis, eh!' cried Sir John, laughing. 'Ay, ay! a pleasant fellow, I believe?'

'A roaring dog, master – one after my own heart – hot upon the matter too – red hot.'

'So I have heard,' replied Sir John carelessly. 'You don't happen to know his trade, do you?'

'He wouldn't say,' cried Hugh. 'He keeps it secret.'

'Ha ha!' laughed Sir John. 'A strange fancy – a weakness with some persons – you'll know it one day, I dare swear.'

'We're intimate already,' said Hugh.

'Quite natural! And have been drinking together, eh?' pursued Sir John. 'Did you say what place you went to in company, when you left Lord George's?'

Hugh had not said or thought of saying, but he told him; and this inquiry being followed by a long train of questions, he related all that had passed both in and out of doors, the kind of people he had seen, their numbers, state of feeling, mode of conversation, apparent expectations and intentions. His questioning was so artfully contrived, that he seemed even in his own eyes to volunteer all this information rather than to have it wrested from him; and he was brought to this state of feeling so naturally, that when Mr Chester[4] yawned at length and declared himself quite wearied out, he made a rough kind of excuse for having talked so much.

'There – get you gone,' said Sir John, holding the door open in his hand. 'You have made a pretty evening's work. I told you not to do this. You may get into trouble. You'll have an opportunity of revenging yourself on your proud friend Haredale, though, and for that, you'd hazard anything I suppose?'

'I would,' retorted Hugh, stopping in his passage out, and looking back; 'but what do *I* risk! What do I stand a chance of losing, master? Friends, home? A fig for 'em all; I have none; they are nothing to me. Give me a good scuffle; let me pay off old scores in a bold riot where there are men to stand by me; and then use me as you like – it don't matter much to me what the end is!'

'What have you done with that paper?' said Sir John.

'I have it here, master.'

'Drop it again as you go along; it's as well not to keep such things about you.'

Hugh nodded, and touching his cap with an air of as much respect as he could summon up, departed.

Sir John, fastening the doors behind him, went back to his dressing-room, and sat down once again before the fire, at which he gazed for a long time, in earnest meditation.

'This happens fortunately,' he said, breaking into a smile, 'and promises well. Let me see. My relative and I, who are the most Protestant fellows in the world, give our worst wishes to the Roman Catholic cause; and to Saville,[5] who introduces their bill, I have a personal objection besides; but as each of us has himself for the first article in his creed, we cannot commit ourselves by joining with a very extravagant madman, such as this Gordon most undoubtedly is. Now really, to foment his disturbances in secret, through the medium of such a very apt instrument as my savage friend here, may further our real ends; and to express at all becoming seasons, in moderate and polite terms, a disapprobation of his proceedings, though we agree with him in principle, will certainly be to gain a character for honesty and uprightness of purpose, which cannot fail to do us infinite service, and to raise us into some importance. Good! So much for public grounds. As to private considerations, I confess that if these vagabonds *would* make some riotous demonstration (which does not appear impossible), and *would* inflict some little chastisement on Haredale as a not inactive man among his sect, it would be extremely agreeable to my feelings, and would amuse me beyond measure. Good again! Perhaps better!'

When he came to this point, he took a pinch of snuff; then beginning slowly to undress, he resumed his meditations, by saying with a smile:

'I fear, I *do* fear exceedingly, that my friend is following fast in the footsteps of his mother. His intimacy with Mr Dennis is very ominous. But I have no doubt he must have come to that end any way. If I lend him a helping hand, the only difference is, that he may, upon the whole, possibly drink a few gallons, or puncheons, or hogsheads, less in this life than he otherwise would. It's no business of mine. It's a matter of very small importance!'

So he took another pinch of snuff, and went to bed.

*

CHAPTER THE FORTY-FIRST

From the workshop of the Golden Key, there issued forth a tinkling sound, so merry and good-humoured, that it suggested the idea of some one working blithely, and made quite pleasant music. No man who hammered on at a dull monotonous duty, could have brought such cheerful notes from steel and iron; none but a chirping, healthy, honest-hearted fellow, who made the best of everything, and felt kindly towards everybody, could have done it for an instant. He might have been a coppersmith, and still been musical. If he had sat in a jolting waggon, full of rods of iron, it seemed as if he would have brought some harmony out of it.

Tink, tink, tink – clear as a silver bell, and audible at every pause of the streets' harsher noises, as though it said, 'I don't care; nothing puts me out; I am resolved to be happy.' Women scolded, children squalled, heavy carts went rumbling by, horrible cries proceeded from the lungs of hawkers; still it struck in again, no higher, no lower, no louder, no softer; not thrusting itself on people's notice a bit the more for having been outdone by louder sounds – tink, tink, tink, tink, tink.

It was a perfect embodiment of the still small voice,[1] free from all cold, hoarseness, huskiness, or unhealthiness of any kind; foot-passengers slackened their pace, and were disposed to linger near it; neighbours who had got up splenetic that morning, felt good-humour stealing on them as they heard it, and by degrees became quite sprightly; mothers danced their babies to its ringing; still the same magical tink, tink, tink, came gaily from the workshop of the Golden Key.

Who but the locksmith could have made such music! A gleam of sun shining through the unsashed window, and chequering the dark workshop with a broad patch of light, fell full upon him, as though attracted by his sunny heart. There he stood working at his anvil, his face all radiant with exercise and gladness, his sleeves turned up, his wig pushed off his shining forehead – the easiest, freest, happiest man in all the world. Beside him sat a sleek cat, purring and winking in the light, and falling every now and then into an idle doze, as from excess of comfort. Toby looked on from a tall bench hard by; one beaming smile, from his broad nut-brown face down to the slack-baked buckles in his shoes. The very locks that hung around had something jovial in their rust, and seemed like gouty gentlemen of hearty natures, disposed to joke on their infirmities. There was nothing surly or severe in the whole scene. It seemed impossible that any one of the innumerable keys could fit a churlish strong-box or a prison-door. Cellars of beer and wine, rooms where there were fires, books, gossip, and cheering laughter – these were their proper sphere of action. Places of distrust, and cruelty, and restraint, they would have left quadruple-locked for ever.

Tink, tink, tink. The locksmith paused at last, and wiped his brow. The silence roused the cat, who, jumping softly down, crept to the door, and watched with tiger eyes a bird-cage in an opposite window. Gabriel lifted Toby to his mouth, and took a hearty draught.

Then, as he stood upright, with his head flung back, and his portly chest thrown out, you would have seen that Gabriel's lower man was clothed in military gear. Glancing at the wall beyond, there might have been espied, hanging on their several pegs, a cap and feather, broad-sword, sash, and coat of scarlet; which any man learned in such matters would have known from their make and pattern to be the uniform of a serjeant in the Royal East-London Volunteers.[2]

As the locksmith put his mug down, empty, on the bench whence it had smiled on him before, he glanced at these articles with a laughing eye, and looking at them with his head a little on one side, as though he would get them all into a focus, said, leaning on his hammer:

'Time was, now, I remember, when I was like to run mad with the desire to wear a coat of that colour. If any one (except my father) had called me a fool for my pains, how I should have fired and fumed! But what a fool I must have been, sure-ly!'

'Ah!' sighed Mrs Varden, who had entered unobserved. 'A fool indeed. A man at your time of life, Varden, should know better now.'

'Why, what a ridiculous woman you are, Martha,' said the locksmith, turning round with a smile.

'Certainly,' replied Mrs V. with great demureness. 'Of course I am. I know that, Varden. Thank you.'

'I mean –' began the locksmith.

'Yes,' said his wife, 'I know what you mean. You speak quite plain enough to be understood, Varden. It's very kind of you to adapt yourself to my capacity, I am sure.'

'Tut, tut, Martha,' rejoined the locksmith; 'don't take offence at nothing. I mean, how strange it is of you to run down volunteering, when it's done to defend you and all the other women, and our own fireside and everybody else's, in case of need.'

'It's unchristian,' cried Mrs Varden, shaking her head.

'Unchristian!' said the locksmith. 'Why, what the devil –'

Mrs Varden looked at the ceiling, as in expectation that the consequence of this profanity would be the immediate descent of the four-post bedstead on the second floor, together with the best sitting-room on the first; but no visible judgment occurring, she heaved a deep sigh, and begged her husband, in a tone of resignation, to go on, and by all means to blaspheme as much as possible, because he knew she liked it.

The locksmith did for a moment seem disposed to gratify her, but he gave a great gulp, and mildly rejoined:

'I was going to say, what on earth do you call it unchristian for? Which would be most unchristian, Martha – to sit quietly down and let our houses be sacked by a foreign army, or to turn out like men and drive 'em off? Shouldn't I be a nice sort of a Christian, if I crept into a corner of my own chimney and looked on while a parcel of whiskered savages bore off Dolly – or you – ?'

When he said 'or you,' Mrs Varden, despite herself, relaxed into
a smile. There was something complimentary in the idea. 'In such
a state of things as that, indeed –' she simpered.

'As that!' repeated the locksmith. 'Well, that would be the state
of things directly. Even Miggs would go. Some black tambourine-
player, with a great turban on, would be bearing *her* off, and,
unless the tambourine-player was proof against kicking and
scratching, it's my belief he'd have the worst of it. Ha ha ha! I'd
forgive the tambourine-player. I wouldn't have him interfered with
on any account, poor fellow.' And here the locksmith laughed again
so heartily, that tears came into his eyes – much to Mrs Varden's
indignation, who thought the capture of so sound a Protestant
and estimable a private character as Miggs by a pagan negro, a
circumstance too shocking and awful for contemplation.

The picture Gabriel had drawn, indeed, threatened serious consequences, and would indubitably have led to them, but luckily at
that moment a light footstep crossed the threshold, and Dolly,
running in, threw her arms round her old father's neck and hugged
him tight.

'Here she is at last!' cried Gabriel. 'And how well you look, Doll,
and how late you are, my darling!'

How well she looked? Well? Why, if he had exhausted every
laudatory adjective in the dictionary, it wouldn't have been praise
enough. When and where was there ever, such a plump, roguish,
comely, bright-eyed, enticing, bewitching, captivating, maddening
little puss in all this world, as Dolly! What was the Dolly of five
years ago, to the Dolly of that day! How many coachmakers,
saddlers, cabinet-makers, and professors of other useful arts, had
deserted their fathers, mothers, sisters, brothers, and, most of all,
their cousins, for the love of her! How many unknown gentlemen
– supposed to be of mighty fortunes, if not titles – had waited round
the corner after dark, and tempted Miggs the incorruptible, with
golden guineas, to deliver offers of marriage folded up in love-
letters! How many disconsolate fathers and substantial tradesmen
had waited on the locksmith for the same purpose, with dismal
tales of how their sons had lost their appetites, and taken to shut
themselves up in dark bedrooms, and wandering in desolate suburbs
with pale faces, and all because of Dolly Varden's loveliness and
cruelty! How many young men, in all previous times of unprecedented steadiness, had turned suddenly wild and wicked for the

same reason, and, in an ecstasy of unrequited love, taken to wrench off door-knockers, and invert the boxes of rheumatic watchmen! How had she recruited the king's service, both by sea and land, through rendering desperate his loving subjects between the ages of eighteen and twenty-five! How many young ladies had publicly professed, with tears in their eyes, that for their tastes she was much too short, too tall, too bold, too cold, too stout, too thin, too fair, too dark – too everything but handsome! How many old ladies, taking counsel together, had thanked Heaven their daughters were not like her, and had hoped she might come to no harm, and had thought she would come to no good, and had wondered what people saw in her, and had arrived at the conclusion that she was 'going off' in her looks, or had never come on in them, and that she was a thorough imposition and a popular mistake!

And yet here was this same Dolly Varden, so whimsical and hard to please that she was Dolly Varden still, all smiles and dimples and pleasant looks, and caring no more for the fifty or sixty young fellows who at that very moment were breaking their hearts to marry her, than if so many oysters had been crossed in love and opened afterwards.

Dolly hugged her father as has been already stated, and having hugged her mother also, accompanied both into the little parlour where the cloth was already laid for dinner, and where Miss Miggs – a trifle more rigid and bony than of yore – received her with a sort of hysterical gasp, intended for a smile. Into the hands of that young virgin, she delivered her bonnet and walking dress (all of a dreadful, artful, and designing kind), and then said with a laugh, which rivalled the locksmith's music, 'How glad I always am to be at home again!'

'And how glad we always are, Doll,' said her father, putting back the dark hair from her sparkling eyes, 'to have you at home. Give me a kiss.'

If there had been anybody of the male kind there to see her do it – but there was not – it was a mercy.

'I don't like your being at the Warren,' said the locksmith, 'I can't bear to have you out of my sight. And what is the news over yonder, Doll?'

'What news there is, I think you know already,' replied his daughter. 'I am sure you do though.'

'Ay?' cried the locksmith. 'What's that?'

'Come, come,' said Dolly, 'you know very well. I want you to tell me why Mr Haredale – oh, how gruff he is again, to be sure! – has been away from home for some days past, and why he is travelling about (we know he *is* travelling, because of his letters) without telling his own niece why or wherefore.'

'Miss Emma doesn't want to know, I'll swear,' returned the locksmith.

'I don't know that,' said Dolly; 'but *I* do, at any rate. Do tell me. Why is he so secret, and what is this ghost story, which nobody is to tell Miss Emma, and which seems to be mixed up with his going away? Now I see you know, by your colouring so.'

'What the story means, or is, or has to do with it, I know no more than you, my dear,' returned the locksmith, 'except that it's some foolish fear of little Solomon's – which has, indeed, no meaning in it, I suppose. As to Mr Haredale's journey, he goes, as I believe –'

'Yes,' said Dolly.

'As I believe,' resumed the locksmith, pinching her cheek, 'on business, Doll. What it may be, is quite another matter. Read Blue Beard,[3] and don't be too curious, pet; it's no business of yours or mine, depend upon that; and here's dinner, which is much more to the purpose.'

Dolly might have remonstrated against this summary dismissal of the subject, notwithstanding the appearance of dinner, but at the mention of Blue Beard Mrs Varden interposed, protesting she could not find it in her conscience to sit tamely by, and hear her child recommended to peruse the adventures of a Turk and Mussulman – far less of a fabulous Turk, which she considered that Potentate to be. She held that, in such stirring and tremendous times as those in which they lived, it would be much more to the purpose if Dolly became a regular subscriber to the Thunderer, where she would have an opportunity of reading Lord George Gordon's speeches word for word, which would be a greater comfort and solace to her, than a hundred and fifty Blue Beards ever could impart. She appealed in support of this proposition to Miss Miggs, then in waiting, who said that indeed the peace of mind she had derived from the perusal of that paper generally, but especially of one article of the very last week as ever was, entitled 'Great Britain drenched in gore,' exceeded all belief; the same composition, she added, had also wrought such a comforting effect on the mind of a married sister of hers, then resident at Golden Lion Court, number twenty-sivin, second bell-handle on the right-hand door-post, that, being in a delicate state of health, and in fact expecting an addition to her family, she had been seized with fits directly after its perusal, and had raved of the Inquisition[4] ever since; to the great improvement of her husband and friends. Miss Miggs went on to say that she would recommend all those whose hearts were hardened to hear Lord George themselves, whom she commended first, in respect of his steady Protestantism, then of his oratory, then of his eyes, then of his nose, then of his legs, and lastly of his figure generally, which she looked upon as fit for any statue, prince, or angel, to which sentiment Mrs Varden fully subscribed.

Mrs Varden having cut in, looked at a box upon the mantle-shelf, painted in imitation of a very red-brick dwelling-house, with a yellow roof; having at top a real chimney, down which voluntary subscribers dropped their silver, gold, or pence, into the parlour; and on the door the counterfeit presentment[5] of a brass plate, whereon was legibly inscribed 'Protestant Association:' – and looking at it, said, that it was to her a source of poignant misery to think that Varden never had, of all his substance, dropped anything into that temple, save once in secret – as she afterwards discovered – two fragments of tobacco-pipe, which she hoped would not be put down to his last account. That Dolly, she was grieved to say, was no less backward in her contributions, better loving, as it seemed, to purchase ribbons and such gauds, than to encourage the great cause, then in such heavy tribulation; and that she did entreat her (her father she much feared could not be moved) not to despise, but imitate, the bright example of Miss Miggs, who flung her wages, as it were, into the very countenance of the Pope, and bruised his features with her quarter's money.

'Oh, mim,' said Miggs, 'don't relude to that. I had no intentions, mim, that nobody should know. Such sacrifices as I can make, are quite a widder's mite. It's all I have,' cried Miggs with a great burst of tears – for with her they never came on by degrees – 'but it's made up to me in other ways; it's well made up.'

This was quite true, though not perhaps in the sense that Miggs intended. As she never failed to keep her self-denial full in Mrs Varden's view, it drew forth so many gifts of caps and gowns and other articles of dress, that upon the whole the red-brick house was perhaps the best investment for her small capital she could

possibly have hit upon; returning her interest, at the rate of seven
or eight per cent. in money, and fifty at least in personal repute and
credit.

'You needn't cry, Miggs,' said Mrs Varden, herself in tears;
'you needn't be ashamed of it, though your poor mistress *is* on the
same side.'

Miggs howled at this remark, in a peculiarly dismal way, and
said she knowed that master hated her. That it was a dreadful thing
to live in families and have dislikes, and not give satisfactions. That
to make divisions was a thing she could not abear to think of,
neither could her feelings let her do it. That if it was master's wishes
as she and him should part, it was best they should part, and she
hoped he might be the happier for it, and always wishes him well,
and that he might find somebody as would meet his dispositions.
It would be a hard trial, she said, to part from such a missis, but
she could meet any suffering when her conscience told her she was
in the rights, and therefore she was willing even to go that lengths.
She did not think, she added, that she could long survive the
separations, but, as she was hated and looked upon unpleasant,
perhaps her dying as soon as possible would be the best endings
for all parties. With this affecting conclusion, Miss Miggs shed
more tears, and sobbed abundantly.

'Can you bear this, Varden?' said his wife in a solemn voice,
laying down her knife and fork.

'Why, not very well, my dear,' rejoined the locksmith, 'but I try
to keep my temper.'

'Don't let there be words on my account, mim,' sobbed Miggs.
'It's much the best that we should part. I wouldn't stay – oh,
gracious me! – and make dissensions, not for a annual gold mine,
and found in tea and sugar.'[6]

Lest the reader should be at any loss to discover the cause
of Miss Miggs's deep emotion, it may be whispered apart that,
happening to be listening, as her custom sometimes was, when
Gabriel and his wife conversed together, she had heard the locksmith's joke relative to the foreign black who played the tambour-
ine, and bursting with the spiteful feelings which the taunt awoke
in her fair breast, exploded in the manner we have witnessed.
Matters having now arrived at a crisis, the locksmith as usual, and
for the sake of peace and quietness, gave in.

'What are you crying for, girl?' he said. 'What's the matter with you? What are you talking about hatred for? *I* don't hate you; I don't hate anybody. Dry your eyes and make yourself agreeable, in Heaven's name, and let us all be happy while we can.'

The allied powers deeming it good generalship to consider this a sufficient apology on the part of the enemy, and confession of having been in the wrong, did dry their eyes and take it in good part. Miss Miggs observed that she bore no malice, no not to her greatest foe, whom she rather loved the more indeed, the greater persecution she sustained. Mrs Varden approved of this meek and forgiving spirit in high terms, and incidentally declared as a closing article of agreement, that Dolly should accompany her to the Clerkenwell branch of the association, that very night. This was an extraordinary instance of her great prudence and policy; having had this end in view from the first, and entertaining a secret misgiving that the locksmith (who was bold when Dolly was in question) would object, she had backed Miss Miggs up to this point, in order that she might have him at a disadvantage. The manoeuvre succeeded so well that Gabriel only made a wry face, and with the warning he had just had, fresh in his mind, did not dare to say one word.

The difference ended, therefore, in Miggs being presented with a gown by Mrs Varden and half-a-crown by Dolly, as if she had eminently distinguished herself in the paths of morality and goodness. Mrs V., according to custom, expressed her hope that Varden would take a lesson from what had passed and learn more generous conduct for the time to come; and the dinner being now cold and nobody's appetite very much improved by what had passed, they went on with it, as Mrs Varden said, 'like Christians.'

As there was to be a grand parade of the Royal East London Volunteers that afternoon, the locksmith did no more work; but sat down comfortably with his pipe in his mouth, and his arm round his pretty daughter's waist, looking lovingly on Mrs V. from time to time, and exhibiting from the crown of his head to the sole of his foot, one smiling surface of good humour. And to be sure, when it was time to dress him in his regimentals, and Dolly, hanging about him in all kinds of graceful winning ways, helped to button and buckle and brush him up and get him into one of the tightest coats that ever was made by mortal tailor, he was the proudest father in all England.

'What a handy jade it is!' said the locksmith to Mrs Varden, who

stood by with folded hands – rather proud of her husband too –
while Miggs held his cap and sword at arm's length, as if mistrusting
that the latter might run some one through the body of its own
accord; 'but never marry a soldier Doll, my dear.'

Dolly didn't ask why not, or say a word indeed, but stooped her
head down very low to tie his sash.

'I never wear this dress,' said honest Gabriel, 'but I think of poor
Joe Willet. I loved Joe; he was always a favourite of mine. Poor Joe!
– Dear heart, my girl, don't tie me in so tight.'

Dolly laughed – not like herself at all – the strangest little laugh
that could be – and held her head down lower still.

'Poor Joe!' resumed the locksmith, muttering to himself; 'I always
wish he had come to me. I might have made it up between them, if
he had. Ah! old John made a great mistake in his way of acting by
that lad – a great mistake. – Have you nearly tied that sash, my
dear?'

What an ill-made sash it was! There it was, loose again and
trailing on the ground. Dolly was obliged to kneel down, and
recommence at the beginning.

'Never mind young Willet, Varden,' said his wife frowning; 'you
might find some one more deserving to talk about, I think.'

Miss Miggs gave a great sniff to the same effect.

'Nay, Martha,' cried the locksmith, 'don't let us bear too hard
upon him. If the lad is dead indeed, we'll deal kindly by his memory.'

'A runaway and a vagabond!' said Mrs Varden.

Miss Miggs expressed her concurrence as before.

'A runaway, my dear, but not a vagabond,' returned the locksmith in a gentle tone. 'He behaved himself well, did Joe – always
– and was a handsome manly fellow. Don't call him a vagabond,
Martha.'

Mrs Varden coughed – and so did Miggs.

'He tried hard to gain your good opinion, Martha, I can tell you,'
said the locksmith smiling, and stroking his chin. 'Ah! that he did.
It seems but yesterday that he followed me out to the Maypole door
one night, and begged me not to say how like a boy they used him
– say here, at home, he meant, though at the time, I recollect, I
didn't understand. "And how's Miss Dolly, sir?" says Joe,' pursued
the locksmith, musing sorrowfully, 'Ah! Poor Joe!'

'Well, I declare,' cried Miggs. 'Oh! Goodness gracious me!'

'What's the matter now?' said Gabriel, turning sharply to her.

'Why, if here an't Miss Dolly,' said the handmaid, stooping down to look into her face, 'a giving way to floods of tears. Oh mim! oh sir. Raly it's give me such a turn,' cried the susceptible damsel, pressing her hand upon her side to quell the palpitation of her heart, 'that you might knock me down with a feather.'

The locksmith, after glancing at Miss Miggs as if he could have wished to have a feather brought straightway, looked on with a broad stare while Dolly hurried away, followed by that sympathising young woman: then turning to his wife, stammered out, 'Is Dolly ill? Have *I* done anything? Is it my fault?'

'Your fault!' cried Mrs V. reproachfully. 'There – You had better make haste out.'

'What have I done?' said poor Gabriel. 'It was agreed that Mr Edward's name was never to be mentioned, and I have not spoken of him, have I!'

Mrs Varden merely replied that she had no patience with him, and bounced off after the other two. The unfortunate locksmith wound his sash about him, girded on his sword, put on his cap, and walked out.

'I am not much of a dab at my exercise,' he said under his breath, 'but I shall get into fewer scrapes at that work than at this. Every man came into the world for something; my department seems to be to make every woman cry without meaning it. It's rather hard!'

But he forgot it before he reached the end of the street, and went on with a shining face, nodding to the neighbours, and showering about his friendly greetings like mild spring rain.

CHAPTER THE FORTY-SECOND

The Royal East London Volunteers made a brilliant sight that day: formed into lines, squares, circles, triangles, and what not, to the beating of drums and the streaming of flags; and performed a vast number of complex evolutions, in all of which Serjeant Varden bore a conspicuous share. Having displayed their military prowess to the utmost in these warlike shows, they marched in glittering order to the Chelsea Bun-house,[1] and regaled in the adjacent taverns until dark. Then at sound of drum they fell in again, and returned amidst the shouting of His Majesty's lieges to the place from whence they came.

The homeward march being somewhat tardy, – owing to the un-soldierlike behaviour of certain corporals, who, being gentleman of sedentary pursuits in private life and excitable out of doors, broke several windows with their bayonets, and rendered it imperative on the commanding officer to deliver them over to a strong guard, with whom they fought at intervals as they came along, – it was nine o'clock when the locksmith reached home. A hackney-coach was waiting near his door; and as he passed it, Mr Haredale looked from the window and called him by his name.

'The sight of you is good for sore eyes, sir,' said the locksmith, stepping up to him. 'I wish you had walked in though, rather than waited here.'

'There is nobody at home, I find,' Mr Haredale answered; 'besides, I desired to be as private as I could.'

'Humph!' muttered the locksmith, looking round at his house. 'Gone with Simon Tappertit to that precious Branch, no doubt.'

Mr Haredale invited him to come into the coach, and, if he were not tired or anxious to go home, to ride with him a little way that they might have some talk together. Gabriel cheerfully complied, and the coachman mounting his box drove off.

'Varden,' said Mr Haredale after a minute's pause, 'you will be amazed to hear what errand I am on; it will seem a very strange one.'

'I have no doubt it's a reasonable one, sir, and has a meaning in it,' replied the locksmith; 'or it would not be yours at all. Have you just come back to town, sir?'

'But half an hour ago.'

'Bringing no news of Barnaby, or his mother?' said the locksmith dubiously. 'Ah! you needn't shake your head, sir. It was a wild-goose chase. I feared that, from the first. You exhausted all reasonable means of discovery when they went away. To begin again after so long a time has passed is hopeless, sir – quite hopeless.'

'Why, where are they?' he returned impatiently. 'Where can they be? Above ground?'

'God knows,' rejoined the locksmith, 'many that I knew above it five years ago, have their beds under the grass now. And the world is a wide place. It's a hopeless attempt, sir, believe me. We must leave the discovery of this mystery, like all others, to time, and accident, and Heaven's pleasure.'

'Varden, my good fellow,' said Mr Haredale, 'I have a deeper meaning in my present anxiety to find them out, than you can fathom. It is not a mere whim; it is not the casual revival of my old wishes and desires; but an earnest, solemn purpose. My thoughts and dreams all tend to it, and fix it in my mind. I have no rest by day or night; I have no peace or quiet; I am haunted.'

His voice was so altered from its usual tones, and his manner bespoke so much emotion, that Gabriel, in his wonder, could only sit and look towards him in the darkness, and fancy the expression of his face.

'Do not ask me,' continued Mr Haredale, 'to explain myself. If I were to do so, you would think me the victim of some hideous fancy. It is enough that this is so, and that I cannot – no, I can not – lie quietly in my bed, without doing what will seem to you incomprehensible.'

'Since when, sir,' said the locksmith after a pause, 'has this uneasy feeling been upon you?'

Mr Haredale hesitated for some moments, and then replied: 'Since the night of the storm. In short, since the last nineteenth of March.'

As though he feared that Varden might express surprise, or reason with him, he hastily went on:

'You will think, I know, I labour under some delusion. Perhaps I do. But it is not a morbid one; it is a wholesome action of the mind, reasoning on actual occurrences. You know the furniture remains in Mrs Rudge's house, and that it has been shut up, by my orders, since she went away, save once a-week or so, when an old neighbour visits it to scare away the rats. I am on my way there now.'

'For what purpose?' asked the locksmith.

'To pass the night there,' he replied; 'and not to-night alone, but many nights. This is a secret which I trust to you in case of any unexpected emergency. You will not come, unless in case of strong necessity, to me; from dusk to broad day, I shall be there. Emma, your daughter, and the rest, suppose me out of London, as I have been until within this hour. Do not undeceive them. This is the errand I am bound upon. I know I may confide it to you, and I rely upon your questioning me no further at this time.'

With that, as if to change the theme, he led the astounded locksmith back to the night of the Maypole highwayman, to the robbery of Edward Chester, to the reappearance of the man at Mrs Rudge's house, and to all the strange circumstances which afterwards occurred. He even asked him carelessly about the man's height, his face, his figure, whether he was like any one he had ever seen – like Hugh, for instance, or any man he had known at any time – and put many questions of that sort, which the locksmith, considering them as mere devices to engage his attention and prevent his expressing the astonishment he felt, answered pretty much at random.

At length they arrived at the corner of the street in which the house stood, where Mr Haredale, alighting, dismissed the coach. 'If you desire to see me safely lodged,' he said, turning to the locksmith with a gloomy smile, 'you can.'

Gabriel, to whom all former marvels had been nothing in comparison with this, followed him along the narrow pavement in silence. When they reached the door, Mr Haredale softly opened it with a key he had about him, and closing it when Varden entered, they were left in thorough darkness.

They groped their way into the ground-floor room. Here Mr Haredale struck a light, and kindled a pocket taper he had brought with him for the purpose. It was then, when the flame was full upon him, that the locksmith saw for the first time how haggard, pale, and changed he looked; how worn and thin he was; how perfectly his whole appearance coincided with all that he had said so strangely as they rode along. It was not an unnatural impulse in Gabriel, after what he had heard, to note curiously the expression of his eyes. It was perfectly collected and rational; – so much so, indeed, that he felt ashamed of his momentary suspicion, and drooped his own when Mr Haredale looked towards him, as if he feared they would betray his thoughts.

'Will you walk through the house?' said Mr Haredale, with a glance towards the window, the crazy shutters of which were closed and fastened. 'Speak low.'

There was a kind of awe about the place, which would have rendered it difficult to speak in any other manner. Gabriel whispered 'Yes,' and followed him up stairs.

Everything was just as they had seen it last. There was a sense of closeness from the exclusion of fresh air, and a gloom and heaviness around, as though long imprisonment had made the very silence sad. The homely hangings of the beds and windows had begun to droop; the dust lay thick upon their dwindling folds; and damps had made their way through ceiling, wall, and floor. The boards creaked beneath their tread as if resenting the unaccustomed intrusion; nimble spiders, paralysed by the taper's glare, checked the motion of their hundred legs upon the wall, or dropped like lifeless things upon the ground; the death-watch ticked aloud; and the scampering feet of rats and mice rattled behind the wainscot.

As they looked about them on the decaying furniture, it was strange to find how vividly it presented those to whom it had belonged, and with whom it was once familiar. Grip seemed to perch again upon his high-backed chair; Barnaby to crouch in his old favourite corner by the fire; the mother to resume her usual seat, and watch him as of old. Even when they could separate these objects from the phantoms of the mind which they invoked, the latter only glided out of sight, but lingered near them still; for then they seemed to lurk in closets and behind the doors, ready to start out and suddenly accost them in their well-remembered tones.

They went down stairs, and again into the room they had just now left. Mr Haredale unbuckled his sword and laid it on the table, with a pair of pocket pistols; then told the locksmith he would light him to the door.

'But this is a dull place, sir,' said Gabriel, lingering; 'may no one share your watch?'

He shook his head, and so plainly evinced his wish to be alone, that Gabriel could say no more. In another moment the locksmith was standing in the street, whence he could see that the light once more travelled up-stairs, and soon returning to the room below, shone brightly through the chinks in the shutters.

If ever man were sorely puzzled and perplexed, the locksmith was, that night. Even when snugly seated by his own fireside, with Mrs Varden opposite in a night-cap and night-jacket, and Dolly beside him (in a most distracting dishabille) curling her hair, and smiling as if she had never cried in all her life and never could – even then, with Toby at his elbow and his pipe in his mouth, and Miggs (but that perhaps was not much) falling asleep in the back-ground, he could not quite discard his wonder and uneasiness. So, in his dreams – still there was Mr Haredale, haggard and

careworn, listening in the solitary house to every sound that stirred, with the taper shining through the chinks until the day should turn it pale and end his lonely watching.

*

CHAPTER THE FORTY-THIRD

Next morning brought no satisfaction to the locksmith's thoughts, nor next day, nor the next, nor many others. Often after nightfall he entered the street, and turned his eyes towards the well-known house; and as surely as he did so, there was the solitary light, still gleaming through the crevices of the window-shutter, while all within was motionless, noiseless, cheerless, as a grave. Unwilling to hazard Mr Haredale's favour by disobeying his strict injunction, he never ventured to knock at the door or to make his presence known in any way. But whenever strong interest and curiosity attracted him to the spot – which was not seldom – the light was always there.

If he could have known what passed within, the knowledge would have yielded him no clue to this mysterious vigil. At twilight, Mr Haredale shut himself up, and at daybreak he came forth. He never missed a night, always came and went alone, and never varied his proceedings in the least degree.

The manner of his watch was this. At dusk, he entered the house in the same way as when the locksmith bore him company, kindled a light, went through the rooms, and narrowly examined them. That done, he returned to the chamber on the ground-floor, and laying his sword and pistols on the table, sat by it until morning.

He usually had a book with him, and often tried to read, but never fixed his eyes or thoughts upon it for five minutes together. The slightest noise without doors, caught his ear; a step upon the pavement seemed to make his heart leap.

He was not without some refreshment during the long lonely hours; generally carrying in his pocket a sandwich of bread and meat, and a small flask of wine. The latter, diluted with large quantities of water, he drank in a heated, feverish way, as though his throat were dried up; but he scarcely ever broke his fast, by so much as a crumb of bread.

If this voluntary sacrifice of sleep and comfort had its origin, as the locksmith on consideration was disposed to think, in any superstitious expectation of the fulfilment of a dream or vision connected with the event on which he had brooded for so many years, and if he waited for some ghostly visitor who walked abroad when men lay sleeping in their beds, he showed no trace of fear or wavering. His stern features expressed the most inflexible resolution; his brows were puckered, and his lips compressed, with deep and settled purpose; and when he started at a noise and listened, it was not with the start of fear but hope, and catching up his sword as though the hour had come at last, he would clutch it in his tight-clenched hand, and listen, with sparkling eyes and eager looks, until it died away.

These disappointments were numerous, for they ensued on almost every sound, but his constancy was not shaken. Still, every night he was at his post, the same stern, sleepless, sentinel; and still night passed and morning dawned, and he must watch again.

This went on for weeks; he had taken a lodging at Vauxhall in which to pass the day and rest himself; and from this place, when the tide served, he usually came to London Bridge from Westminster by water, in order that he might avoid the busy streets.

One evening, shortly before twilight, he came his accustomed road upon the river's bank, intending to pass through Westminster Hall[1] into Palace Yard, and there take boat to London Bridge as usual. There was a pretty large concourse of people assembled round the Houses of Parliament, looking at the members as they entered and departed, and giving vent to rather noisy demonstrations of approval or dislike, according to their known opinions. As he made his way among the throng, he heard once or twice the No-Popery cry, which was then becoming pretty familiar to the ears of most men; but holding it in very slight regard, and observing that the idlers were of the lowest grade, he neither thought nor cared about it, but made his way along, with perfect indifference.

There were many little knots and groups of persons in Westminster Hall: some few looking upward at its noble ceiling, and at the rays of evening light, tinted by the setting sun, which streamed in aslant through its small windows, and growing dimmer by degrees, were quenched in the gathering gloom below; some, noisy passengers, mechanics going home from work, and otherwise, who hurried quickly through, waking the echoes with their voices, and soon darkening the small door in the distance, as they passed into the street beyond; some, in busy conference together on political or private matters, pacing slowly up and down with eyes that sought the ground, and seeming, by their attitudes, to listen earnestly from head to foot. Here, a dozen squabbling urchins made a very Babel in the air; there, a solitary man, half clerk, half mendicant, paced up and down with hungry dejection in his look and gait; at his elbow passed an errand-lad, swinging his basket round and round, and with his shrill whistle riving the very timbers of the roof; while a more observant schoolboy, half-way through, pocketed his ball, and eyed the distant beadle as he came looming on. It was that time of evening when, if you shut your eyes and open them again, the darkness of an hour appears to have gathered in a second. The smooth-worn pavement, dusty with footsteps, still called upon the lofty walls to reiterate the shuffle and the tread of feet unceasingly, save when the closing of some heavy door resounded through the building like a clap of thunder, and drowned all other noises in its rolling sound.

Mr Haredale, glancing only at such of these groups as he passed nearest to, and then in a manner betokening that his thoughts were elsewhere, had nearly traversed the Hall, when two persons before him caught his attention. One of these, a gentleman in elegant attire, carried in his hand a cane, which he twirled in a jaunty manner as he loitered on; the other, an obsequious, crouching, fawning figure, listened to what he said – at times throwing in an humble word himself – and, with his shoulders shrugged up to his ears, rubbed his hands submissively, or answered at intervals by an inclination of the head, half-way between a nod of acquiescence, and a bow of most profound respect.

In the abstract there was nothing very remarkable in this pair, for servility waiting on a handsome suit of clothes and a cane – not to speak of gold and silver sticks, or wands of office – is common enough. But there was that about the well-dressed man, yes, and about the other likewise, which struck Mr Haredale with no pleasant feeling. He hesitated, stopped, and would have stepped aside and turned out of his path, but at the moment, the other two faced about quickly, and stumbled upon him before he could avoid them.

The gentleman with the cane lifted his hat and had begun to tender an apology, which Mr Haredale had begun as hastily to acknowledge and walk away, when he stopped short and cried, 'Haredale! Gad bless me, this is strange indeed!'

'It is,' he returned impatiently; 'yes – a – '

'My dear friend,' cried the other, detaining him, 'why such great speed? One minute, Haredale, for the sake of old acquaintance.'

'I am in haste,' he said. 'Neither of us has sought this meeting. Let it be a brief one. Good night!'

'Fie, fie!' replied Sir John (for it was he), 'how very churlish! We were speaking of you. Your name was on my lips – perhaps you heard me mention it? No? I am sorry for that. I am really sorry. – You know our friend here, Haredale? This is really a most remarkable meeting!'

The friend, plainly very ill at ease, had made bold to press Sir John's arm, and to give him other significant hints that he was desirous of avoiding this introduction. As it did not suit Sir John's purpose, however, that it should be evaded, he appeared quite unconscious of these silent remonstrances, and inclined his hand towards him as he spoke, to call attention to him more particularly.

The friend, therefore, had nothing for it, but to muster up the pleasantest smile he could, and to make a conciliatory bow, as Mr Haredale turned his eyes upon him. Seeing that he was recognised, he put out his hand in an awkward and embarrassed manner, which was not mended by its contemptuous rejection.

'Mr Gashford!' said Haredale, coldly. 'It is as I have heard then. You have left the darkness for the light, sir, and hate those whose opinions you formerly held, with all the bitterness of a renegade. You are an honour, sir, to any cause. I wish the one you espouse at present, much joy of the acquisition it has made.'

The secretary rubbed his hands and bowed, as though he would disarm his adversary by humbling himself before him. Sir John Chester again exclaimed, with an air of great gaiety, 'Now, really, this is a most remarkable meeting!' and took a pinch of snuff with his usual self-possession.

'Mr Haredale,' said Gashford, stealthily raising his eyes, and letting them drop again when they met the other's steady gaze, 'is too conscientious, too honourable, too manly, I am sure, to attach unworthy motives to an honest change of opinions, even though it implies a doubt of those he holds himself. Mr Haredale is too just, too generous, too clear-sighted in his moral vision, to – '

'Yes, sir?' he rejoined with a sarcastic smile, finding that the secretary stopped. 'You were saying' –

Gashford meekly shrugged his shoulders, and looking on the ground again, was silent.

'No, but let us really,' interposed Sir John at this juncture, 'let us really, for a moment, contemplate the very remarkable character of this meeting. Haredale, my dear friend, pardon me if I think you are not sufficiently impressed with its singularity. Here we stand, by no previous appointment or arrangement, three old school-fellows, in Westminster Hall: three old boarders in a remarkably dull and shady seminary at Saint Omer's,[2] where you, being Catholics and of necessity educated out of England, were brought up; and where I, being a promising young Protestant at that time, was sent to learn the French Tongue from a native of Paris!'

'Add to the singularity, Sir John,' said Mr Haredale, 'that some of you Protestants of promise are at this moment leagued in yonder building, to prevent our having the surpassing and unheard-of privilege of teaching our children to read and write – here – in this land, where thousands of us enter your service every year, and to preserve the freedom of which, we die in bloody battles abroad, in heaps: and that others of you, to the number of some thousands as I learn, are led on to look on all men of my creed as wolves and beasts of prey, by this man Gashford. Add to it, besides, the bare fact that this man lives in society, walks the streets in broad day – I was about to say, holds up his head, but that he does not – and it will be strange, and very strange, I grant you.'

'Oh! you are hard upon our friend,' replied Sir John, with an engaging smile. 'You are really very hard upon our friend!'

'Let him go on, Sir John,' said Gashford, fumbling with his gloves. 'Let him go on. I can make allowances, Sir John. I am honoured with your good opinion, and I can dispense with Mr Haredale's. Mr Haredale is a sufferer from the penal laws, and I can't expect his favour.'

'You have so much of my favour, sir,' retorted Mr Haredale, with a bitter glance at the third party in their conversation, 'that I am glad to see you in such good company. You are the essence of your great Association, in yourselves.'

'Now, there you mistake,' said Sir John, in his most benignant way. 'There – which is a most remarkable circumstance for a man of your punctuality and exactness, my dear Haredale – you fall into an error. I don't belong to the body; I have an immense respect for its members, but I don't belong to it; although I am, it is certainly true, the conscientious opponent of your being relieved. I feel it my duty to be so; it is a most unfortunate necessity; and cost me a bitter struggle. – Will you try this box? If you don't object to a trifling infusion of a very chaste scent, you'll find its flavour exquisite.'

'I ask your pardon, Sir John,' said Mr Haredale, declining the proffer with a motion of his hand, 'for having ranked you among the humble instruments who are obvious and in all men's sight. I should have done more justice to your genius. Men of your capacity plot in secrecy and safety, and leave exposed posts to the duller wits.'

'Don't apologise, for the world,' replied Sir John sweetly; 'old friends like you and I may be allowed some freedoms, or the deuce is in it.'

Gashford, who had been very restless all this time, but had not once looked up, now turned to Sir John, and ventured to mutter something to the effect that he must go, or my Lord would perhaps be waiting. 'Don't distress yourself, good sir,' said Mr Haredale, 'I'll take my leave, and put you at your ease –' which he was about to do without further ceremony, when he was stayed by a buzz and murmur at the upper end of the hall, and, looking in that direction, saw Lord George Gordon coming on, with a crowd of people round him.

There was a lurking look of triumph, though very differently expressed, in the faces of his two companions, which made it a natural impulse on Mr Haredale's part not to give way before this leader, but to stand there while he passed. He drew himself up to his full height, and, clasping his hands behind him, looked on with a proud and scornful aspect, while Lord George slowly advanced (for the press was great about him) towards the spot where they were standing.

He had left the House of Commons but that moment, and had come straight down into the Hall, bringing with him, as his custom was, intelligence of what had been said that night in reference to the Papists, and what petitions had been presented in their favour, and who had supported them, and when the bill was to be brought in, and when it would be advisable to present their own Great Protestant petition.[3] All this he told the persons about him in a loud voice, and with great abundance of ungainly gesture. Those who were nearest him made comments to each other, and vented threats and murmurings; those who were outside the crowd cried 'Silence,' and 'Stand back,' or closed in upon the rest, endeavouring to make a forcible exchange of places: and so they came driving on in a very disorderly and irregular way, as it is the manner of a crowd to do.

When they were very near to where the Secretary, Sir John, and Mr Haredale stood, Lord George turned round and, making a few remarks of a sufficiently violent and incoherent kind, concluded with the usual sentiment, and called for three cheers to back it. While these were in the act of being given with great energy, he extricated himself from the press, and stepped up to Gashford's side. Both he and Sir John being well known to the populace, they fell back a little, and left the four standing together.

'Mr Haredale, Lord George,' said Sir John Chester, seeing that the nobleman regarded him with an inquisitive look. 'A Catholic gentleman unfortunately – most unhappily a Catholic – but an esteemed acquaintance of mine, and once of Mr Gashford's. My dear Haredale, this is Lord George Gordon.'

'I should have known that, had I been ignorant of his lordship's person,' said Mr Haredale. 'I hope there is but one gentleman in England who, addressing an ignorant and excited throng, would speak of a large body of his fellow-subjects in such injurious language as I heard this moment. For shame, my lord, for shame!'

'I cannot talk to you, sir,' replied Lord George in a loud voice, and waving his hand in a disturbed and agitated manner; 'we have nothing in common.'

'We have much in common – many things – all that the Almighty gave us,' said Mr Haredale; 'and common charity, my lord, not to say common sense and common decency, should teach you to refrain from these proceedings. If every one of those men had arms in their hands at this moment, as they have them in their heads, I would not leave this place without telling you that you disgrace your station.'

'I don't hear you, sir,' he replied in the same manner as before; 'I can't hear you. It is indifferent to me what you say. Don't retort, Gashford,' for the secretary had made a show of wishing to do so; 'I can hold no communion with the worshippers of idols.'

As he said this, he glanced at Sir John, who lifted his hands and eyebrows, as if deploring the intemperate conduct of Mr Haredale, and smiled in admiration of the crowd, and of their leader.

'*He* retort!' cried Haredale. 'Look you here, my Lord. Do you know this man?'

Lord George replied by laying his hand upon the shoulder of his cringing secretary, and viewing him with a smile of confidence.

'This man,' said Mr Haredale, eyeing him from top to toe, 'who in his boyhood was a thief, and has been from that time to this, a servile, false, and truckling knave: this man, who has crawled and crept through life, wounding the hands he licked, and biting those he fawned upon: this sycophant, who never knew what honour, truth, or courage meant; who robbed his benefactor's daughter of her virtue, and married her to break her heart, and did it, with stripes and cruelty: this creature, who has whined at kitchen windows for the broken food, and begged for halfpence at our chapel doors: this apostle of the faith, whose tender conscience cannot bear the altars where his vicious life was publicly denounced – Do you know this man, my Lord?'

'Oh, really – you are very, very hard upon our friend!' exclaimed Sir John.

'Let Mr Haredale go on,' said Gashford, upon whose unwholesome face the perspiration had broken out during this speech, in blotches of wet; 'I don't mind him, Sir John; it's quite as indifferent to me what he says, as it is to my Lord; if he reviles my Lord, as you have heard, Sir John, how can *I* hope to escape?'

'Is it not enough, my Lord,' Mr Haredale continued, 'that I, as good a gentleman as you, must hold my property, such as it is, by a trick at which the state connives because of these hard laws;[4] and that we may not teach our youth in schools the common principles of right and wrong; but must we be denounced and ridden by such men as this! Here is a man to head your No-Popery cry, my Lord. For shame. For shame!'

The infatuated nobleman had glanced more than once at Sir John Chester, as if to inquire whether there was any truth in these statements concerning Gashford, and Sir John had as often plainly answered by a shrug or look, 'Oh dear me! no.' He now said, in the same loud key, and in the same strange manner as before:

'I have nothing to say, sir, in reply, and no desire to hear anything more. I beg you won't obtrude your conversation, or these personal attacks, upon me any further. I shall not be deterred from doing my duty to my country and my countrymen, by any such attempts, whether they proceed from emissaries of the Pope or not, I assure you. Come, Gashford!'

They had walked on a few paces while speaking, and were now at the Hall-door, through which they passed together. Mr Haredale, without any leave-taking, turned away to the river-stairs, which were close at hand, and hailed the only boatman who remained there.

But the throng of people – the foremost of whom had heard every word that Lord George Gordon said, and among all of whom the rumour had been rapidly dispersed that the stranger was a Papist who was bearding him for his advocacy of the popular cause – came pouring out pell-mell, and, forcing the nobleman, his secretary, and Sir John Chester on before them, so that they appeared to be at their head, crowded to the top of the stairs where Mr Haredale waited until the boat was ready, and there stood still, leaving him on a little clear space by himself.

They were not silent, however, though inactive. At first some indistinct mutterings arose among them, which were followed by a hiss or two, and these swelled by degrees into a perfect storm. Then one voice said, 'Down with the Papists!' and there was a pretty general cheer, but nothing more. After a lull of a few moments, one man cried out, 'Stone him;' another, 'Duck him;' another, in a stentorian voice, 'No Popery!' This favourite cry the rest re-echoed, and the mob, which might have been two hundred strong, joined in a general shout.

Mr Haredale had stood calmly on the brink of the steps, until they made this demonstration, when he looked round contemptuously, and walked at a slow pace down the stairs. He was pretty near the boat, when Gashford, as if without intention, turned about, and directly afterwards a great stone was thrown by some hand in the crowd, which struck him on the head, and made him stagger like a drunken man.

The blood sprung freely from the wound, and trickled down his coat. He turned directly, and rushing up the steps with a boldness and passion which made them all fall back, demanded:

'Who did that? Show me the man who hit me.'

Not a soul moved; except some in the rear who slunk off, and, escaping to the other side of the way, looked on like indifferent spectators.

'Who did that?' he repeated. 'Show me the man who did it. Dog, was it you? It was your deed, if not your hand – I know you.'

He threw himself on Gashford as he said the words, and hurled him to the ground. There was a sudden motion in the crowd, and some laid hands upon him, but his sword was out, and they fell off again.

'My Lord – Sir John' – he cried, 'draw, one of you – you are responsible for this outrage, and I look to you. Draw, if you are gentlemen.' With that he struck Sir John upon the breast with the flat of his weapon, and with a burning face and flashing eyes stood upon his guard; alone, before them all.

For an instant, for the briefest space of time the mind can readily conceive, there was a change in Sir John's smooth face, such as no man ever saw there. The next moment, he stepped forward, and laid one hand on Mr Haredale's arm, while with the other he endeavoured to appease the crowd.

'My dear friend, my good Haredale, you are blinded with passion – it's very natural, extremely natural – but you don't know friends from foes.'

'I know them all, sir, I can distinguish well –' he retorted, almost mad with rage. 'Sir John, my Lord – do you hear me? Are you cowards?'

'Never mind, sir,' said a man, forcing his way between and pushing him towards the stairs with friendly violence, 'never mind asking that. For God's sake, get away. What *can* you do against this number? And there are as many more in the next street, who'll be round directly' – indeed they began to pour in as he said the words – 'you'd be giddy from that cut, in the first heat of a scuffle. Now do retire, sir, or take my word for it you'll be worse used than you would be if every man in the crowd was a woman, and that woman Bloody Mary. Come, sir, make haste – as quick as you can.'

Mr Haredale, who began to turn faint and sick, felt how sensible this advice was, and descended the steps with his unknown friend's assistance. John Grueby (for John it was) helped him into the boat, and giving her a shove off which sent her thirty feet into the tide, bade the waterman pull away like a Briton; and walked up again as composedly as if he had just landed.

There was at first a slight disposition on the part of the mob to resent this interference; but John looking particularly strong and

cool, and wearing besides Lord George's livery, they thought better of it, and contented themselves with sending a shower of small missiles after the boat, which plashed harmlessly in the water, for she had by this time cleared the bridge, and was darting swiftly down the centre of the stream.

From this amusement, they proceeded to giving Protestant knocks at the doors of private houses, breaking a few lamps, and assaulting some stray constables. But it being whispered that a detachment of Life Guards had been sent for, they took to their heels with great expedition, and left the street quite clear.

CHAPTER THE FORTY-FOURTH

When the concourse separated, and, dividing into chance clusters, drew off in various directions, there still remained upon the scene of the late disturbance, one man. This man was Gashford, who, bruised by his late fall, and hurt in a much greater degree by the indignity he had undergone, and the exposure of which he had been the victim, limped up and down, breathing curses and threats of vengeance.

It was not the secretary's nature to waste his wrath in words. While he vented the froth of his malevolence in these effusions, he kept a steady eye on two men, who, having disappeared with the rest when the alarm was spread, had since returned, and were now visible in the moonlight, at no great distance, as they walked to and fro, and talked together.

He made no move towards them, but waited patiently on the dark side of the street, until they were tired of strolling backwards and forwards and walked away in company. Then he followed, but at some distance: keeping them in view, without appearing to have that object, or being seen by them.

They went up Parliament Street, past Saint Martin's church, and away by Saint Giles's to Tottenham Court Road, at the back of which, upon the western side, was then a place called the Green Lanes. This was a retired spot, not of the choicest kind, leading into the fields. Great heaps of ashes; stagnant pools, overgrown with rank grass and duckweed; broken turnstiles; and the upright posts of palings long since carried off for firewood, which menaced all heedless walkers with their jagged and rusty nails; were the leading features of the landscape: while here and there a donkey, or a ragged horse, tethered to a stake, and cropping off a wretched meal from the coarse stunted turf, were quite in keeping with the scene, and would have suggested (if the houses had not done so sufficiently, of themselves) how very poor the people were who lived in the crazy huts adjacent, and how fool-hardy it might prove for one who carried money, or wore decent clothes, to walk that way alone, unless by daylight.

Poverty has its whims and shows of taste, as wealth has. Some of these cabins were turreted, some had false windows painted on their rotten walls; one had a mimic clock, upon a crazy tower of four feet high, which screened the chimney; each in its little patch of ground had a rude seat or arbour. The population dealt in bones, in rags, in broken glass, in old wheels, in birds, and dogs. These, in their several ways of stowage, filled the gardens; and shedding a perfume, not of the most delicious nature, in the air, filled it besides with yelps, and screams, and howling.

Into this retreat, the secretary followed the two men whom he had held in sight; and here he saw them safely lodged, in one of the meanest houses, which was but a room, and that of small dimensions. He waited without, until the sound of their voices, joined in a discordant song, assured him they were making merry; and then approaching the door, by means of a tottering plank which crossed the ditch in front, knocked at it with his hand.

'Muster Gashford!' said the man who opened it, taking his pipe from his mouth, in evident surprise. 'Why, who'd have thought of this here honor! Walk in, Muster Gashford – walk in, sir.'

Gashford required no second invitation, and entered with a gracious air. There was a fire in the rusty grate (for though the spring was pretty far advanced, the nights were cold), and on a stool beside it Hugh sat smoking. Dennis placed a chair, his only one, for the secretary, in front of the hearth; and took his seat again upon the stool he had left, when he rose to give the visitor admission.

'What's in the wind now, Muster Gashford?' he said, as he resumed his pipe, and looked at him askew. 'Any orders from head-quarters? Are we going to begin? What is it, Muster Gashford?'

'Oh, nothing, nothing,' rejoined the secretary, with a friendly nod to Hugh. 'We have broken the ice, though. We had a little spurt to-day – eh, Dennis?'

'A very little one,' growled the hangman. 'Not half enough for me.'

'Nor me either!' cried Hugh. 'Give us something to do with life in it – with life in it, Master. Ha, ha!'

'Why, you wouldn't,' said the secretary, with his worst expression of face, and in his mildest tones, 'have anything to do, with – with death in it?'

'I don't know that,' replied Hugh. 'I'm open to orders. I don't care; not I.'

'Nor I!' vociferated Dennis.

'Brave fellows!' said the secretary, in as pastor-like a voice as if he were commending them for some uncommon act of valour and generosity. 'By the bye' – and here he stopped and warmed his hands: then suddenly looked up – 'who threw that stone to-day?'

Mr Dennis coughed and shook his head, as who should say, 'A mystery indeed!' Hugh sat and smoked in silence.

'It was well done!' said the secretary, warming his hands again. 'I should like to know that man.'

'Would you?' said Dennis, after looking at his face to assure himself that he was serious. 'Would you like to know that man, Muster Gashford?'

'I should indeed,' replied the secretary.

'Why then, Lord love you,' said the hangman, in his hoarsest chuckle, as he pointed with his pipe to Hugh, 'there he sets. That's the man. My stars and halters,[1] Muster Gashford,' he added in a whisper, as he drew his stool close to him and jogged him with his elbow, 'what a interesting blade he is! He wants as much holding in as a thorough-bred bulldog. If it hadn't been for me to-day, he'd have had that 'ere Roman down, and made a riot of it, in another minute.'

'And why not?' cried Hugh in a surly voice, as he overheard this last remark. 'Where's the good of putting things off? Strike while the iron's hot; that's what I say.'

'Ah!' retorted Dennis, shaking his head, with a kind of pity for his friend's ingenuous youth: 'but suppose the iron an't hot, brother? You must get people's blood up afore you strike, and have 'em in the humour. There wasn't quite enough to provoke 'em to-day, I tell you. If you'd had your way, you'd have spoilt the fun to come, and ruined us.'

'Dennis is quite right,' said Gashford, smoothly. 'He is perfectly correct. Dennis has great knowledge of the world.'

'I ought to have, Muster Gashford, seeing what a many people I've helped out of it, eh?' grinned the hangman, whispering the words behind his hand.

The secretary laughed at this jest as much as Dennis could desire, and when he had done, said, turning to Hugh:

'Dennis's policy was mine, as you may have observed. You saw, for instance, how I fell when I was set upon. I made no resistance. I did nothing to provoke an outbreak. Oh dear no!'

'No, by the Lord Harry!' cried Dennis with a noisy laugh, 'you went down very quiet, Muster Gashford – and very flat besides. I thinks to myself at the time "it's all up with Muster Gashford!" I never see a man lay flatter nor more still – with the life in him – than you did to-day. He's a rough 'un to play with, is that 'ere Papist, and that's the fact.'

The secretary's face, as Dennis roared with laughter, and turned his wrinkled eyes on Hugh who did the like, might have furnished a study for the devil's picture. He sat quite silent until they were serious again, and then said, looking round:

'We are very pleasant here; so very pleasant, Dennis, that but for my Lord's particular desire that I should sup with him, and the time being very near at hand, I should be inclined to stop, until it would be hardly safe to go homeward. I come upon a little business – yes, I do – as you supposed. It's very flattering to you; being this. If we ever should be obliged – and we can't tell, you know – this is a very uncertain world' –

'I believe you, Muster Gashford,' interposed the hangman with a grave nod. 'The uncertainties as I've seen in reference to this here state of existence, the unexpected contingencies as have come about! – Oh my eye!' And feeling the subject much too vast for expression, he puffed at his pipe again, and looked the rest.

'I say,' resumed the secretary, in a slow, impressive way; 'we can't tell what may come to pass; and if we should be obliged, against our wills, to have recourse to violence, my Lord (who has suffered terribly to-day, as far as words can go) consigns to you two – bearing in mind my recommendation of you both, as good staunch men, beyond all doubt and suspicion – the pleasant task of punishing this Haredale. You may do as you please with him, or his; provided that you show no mercy, and no quarter, and leave no two beams of his house standing where the builder placed them. You may sack it, burn it, do with it as you like, but it must come down; it must be razed to the ground; and he, and all belonging to him, left as shelterless as new-born infants whom their mothers have exposed. Do you understand me?' said Gashford, pausing, and pressing his hands together gently.

'Understand you, master!' cried Hugh. 'You speak plain now. Why, this *is* hearty!'

'I knew you would like it,' said Gashford, shaking him by the hand; 'I thought you would. Good night! Don't rise, Dennis: I would rather find my way alone. I may have to make other visits here, and it's pleasant to come and go without disturbing you. I can find my way perfectly well. Good night!'

He was gone, and had shut the door behind him. They looked at each other, and nodded approvingly: Dennis stirred up the fire.

'This looks a little more like business!' he said.

'Ay, indeed!' cried Hugh; 'this suits me!'

'I've heerd it said of Muster Gashford,' said the hangman, thoughtfully, 'that he'd a surprising memory and wonderful firmness – that he never forgot, and never forgave. – Let's drink his health!'

Hugh readily complied; pouring no liquor on the floor when he drank this toast; and they pledged the secretary as a man after their own hearts, in a bumper.

*

CHAPTER THE FORTY-FIFTH

While the worst passions of the worst men were thus working in the dark, and the mantle of religion, assumed to cover the ugliest deformities, threatened to become the shroud of all that was good and peaceful in society, a circumstance occurred which once more altered the position of two persons from whom this history has long been separated, and to whom it must now return.

In a small English country town, the inhabitants of which supported themselves by the labour of their hands in plaiting and preparing straw for those who made bonnets and other articles of dress and ornament from that material, – concealed under an assumed name, and living in a quiet poverty which knew no change, no pleasures, and few cares but that of struggling on from day to day in the one great toil for bread, – dwelt Barnaby and his mother. Their poor cottage had known no stranger's foot since they sought the shelter of its roof five years before; nor had they in all that time held any commerce or communication with the old world from which they had fled. To labour in peace, and devote her labour and her life to her poor son, was all the widow sought. If happiness can be said at any time to be the lot of one on whom a secret sorrow preys, she was happy now. Tranquillity, resignation, and her strong love of him who needed it so much, formed the small circle of her quiet joys; and while that remained unbroken, she was contented.

For Barnaby himself, the time which had flown by, had passed him like the wind. The daily suns of years had shed no brighter gleam of reason on his mind; no dawn had broken on his long, dark night. He would sit sometimes – often for days together – on a low seat by the fire or by the cottage door, busy at work (for he had learnt the art his mother plied), and listening, God help him, to the tales she would repeat, as a lure to keep him in her sight. He had no recollection of these little narratives; the tale of yesterday was new upon the morrow; but he liked them at the moment; and when the humour held him, would remain patiently within doors, hearing her stories like a little child, and working cheerfully from sunrise until it was too dark to see.

At other times, – and then their scanty earnings were barely sufficient to furnish them with food, though of the coarsest sort, – he would wander abroad from dawn of day until the twilight deepened into night. Few in that place, even of the children, could be idle, and he had no companions of his own kind. Indeed there were not many who could have kept up with him in his rambles, had there been a legion. But there were a score of vagabond dogs belonging to the neighbours, who served his purpose quite as well. With two or three of these, or sometimes with a full half-dozen barking at his heels, he would sally forth on some long expedition that consumed the day; and though, on their return at nightfall, the dogs would come home limping and sore-footed, and almost spent with their fatigue, Barnaby was up and off again at sunrise with some new attendants of the same class, with whom he would return in like manner. On all these travels, Grip, in his little basket at his master's back, was a constant member of the party, and when they set off in fine weather and in high spirits, no dog barked louder than the raven.

Their pleasures on these excursions were simple enough. A crust of bread and scrap of meat, with water from the brook or spring, sufficed for their repast. Barnaby's enjoyments were, to walk, and run, and leap, till he was tired; then to lie down in the long grass, or by the growing corn, or in the shade of some tall tree, looking upward at the light clouds as they floated over the blue surface of the sky, and listening to the lark as she poured out her brilliant song. There were wild-flowers to pluck – the bright red poppy, the gentle harebell, the cowslip, and the rose. There were birds to watch; fish; ants; worms; hares or rabbits, as they darted across the distant pathway in the wood and so were gone: millions of living things to have an interest in, and lie in wait for, and clap hands and shout in memory of, when they had disappeared. In default of these, or when they wearied, there was the merry sunlight to hunt out, as it crept in aslant through leaves and boughs of trees, and hid far down – deep, deep, in hollow places – like a silver pool, where nodding branches seemed to bathe and sport; sweet scents of summer air breathing over fields of beans or clover; the perfume of wet leaves or moss; the life of waving trees, and shadows always changing. When these or any of them tired, or in excess of pleasing tempted him to shut his eyes, there was slumber in the midst of all these soft delights, with the gentle wind murmuring like music in his ears, and everything around melting into one delicious dream.

Their hut – for it was little more – stood on the outskirts of the town, at a short distance from the high road, but in a secluded place, where few chance passengers strayed at any season of the year. It had a plot of garden-ground attached, which Barnaby, in fits and starts of working, trimmed, and kept in order. Within doors and without, his mother laboured for their common good; and hail, rain, snow, or sunshine, found no difference in her.

Though so far removed from the scenes of her past life, and with so little thought or hope of ever visiting them again, she seemed to have a strange desire to know what happened in the busy world. Any old newspaper, or scrap of intelligence from London, she caught at with avidity. The excitement it produced was not of a pleasurable kind, for her manner at such times expressed the keenest anxiety and dread; but it never faded in the least degree. Then, and in stormy winter nights, when the wind blew loud and strong, the old expression came into her face, and she would be seized with a fit of trembling, like one who had an ague. But Barnaby noted little of this; and putting a great constraint upon herself, she usually recovered her accustomed manner before the change had caught his observation.

Grip was by no means an idle or unprofitable member of the humble household. Partly by dint of Barnaby's tuition, and partly by pursuing a species of self-instruction common to his tribe, and exerting his powers of observation to the utmost, he had acquired a degree of sagacity which rendered him famous for miles round. His conversational powers and surprising performances were the universal theme: and as many persons came to see the wonderful raven, and none left his exertions unrewarded – when he condescended to exhibit, which was not always, for genius is capricious – his earnings formed an important item in the common stock. Indeed, the bird himself appeared to know his value well; for though he was perfectly free and unrestrained in the presence of Barnaby and his mother, he maintained in public an amazing gravity, and never stooped to any other gratuitous performances than biting the ankles of vagabond boys (an exercise in which he much delighted), killing a fowl or two occasionally, and swallowing the dinners of various neighbouring dogs, of whom the boldest held him in great awe and dread.

Time had glided on in this way, and nothing had happened to disturb or change their mode of life, when, one summer's night in June, they were in their little garden, resting from the labours of the day. The widow's work was yet upon her knee, and strewn upon the ground about her; and Barnaby stood leaning on his spade, gazing at the brightness in the west, and singing softly to himself.

'A brave evening, mother! If we had, chinking in our pockets, but a few specks of that gold which is piled up yonder in the sky, we should be rich for life.'

'We are better as we are,' returned the widow with a quiet smile. 'Let us be contented, and we do not want and need not care to have it, though it lay shining at our feet.'

'Ay!' said Barnaby, resting with crossed arms on his spade, and looking wistfully at the sunset, 'that's well enough, mother; but

gold's a good thing to have. I wish that I knew where to find it. Grip and I could do much with gold, be sure of that.'

'What would you do?' she asked.

'What! A world of things. We'd dress finely – you and I, I mean; not Grip – keep horses, dogs, wear bright colours and feathers, do no more work, live delicately and at our ease. Oh, we'd find uses for it, mother, and uses that would do us good. I would I knew where gold was buried. How hard I'd work to dig it up!'

'You do not know,' said his mother, rising from her seat and laying her hand upon his shoulder, 'what men have done to win it, and how they have found, too late, that it glitters brightest at a distance, and turns quite dim and dull when handled.'

'Ay, ay; so you say; so you think,' he answered, still looking eagerly in the same direction. 'For all that, mother, I should like to try.'

'Do you not see,' she said, 'how red it is? Nothing bears so many stains of blood, as gold. Avoid it. None have such cause to hate its name as we have. Do not so much as think of it, dear love. It has brought such misery and suffering on your head and mine as few have known, and God grant few may have to undergo. I would rather we were dead and laid down in our graves, than you should ever come to love it.'

For a moment Barnaby withdrew his eyes and looked at her with wonder. Then, glancing from the redness in the sky to the mark upon his wrist as if he would compare the two, he seemed about to question her with earnestness, when a new object caught his wandering attention, and made him quite forgetful of his purpose.

This was a man with dusty feet and garments, who stood, bareheaded, behind the hedge that divided their patch of garden from the pathway, and leant meekly forward as if he sought to mingle with their conversation, and waited for his time to speak. His face was turned towards the brightness, too, but the light that fell upon it showed that he was blind, and saw it not.

'A blessing on those voices!' said the wayfarer. 'I feel the beauty of the night more keenly, when I hear them. They are like eyes to me. Will they speak again, and cheer the heart of a poor traveller?'

'Have you no guide?' asked the widow, after a moment's pause.

'None but that,' he answered, pointing with his staff towards the sun. 'and sometimes a milder one at night, but she is idle now.'

'Have you travelled far?'

'A weary way and long,' rejoined the traveller as he shook his
head. 'A weary, weary, way. I struck my stick just now upon the
bucket of your well – be pleased to let me have a draught of water,
lady.'

'Why do you call me lady?' she returned. 'I am as poor as you.'

'Your speech is soft and gentle, and I judge by that,' replied the
man. 'The coarsest stuffs and finest silks, are – apart from the sense
of touch – alike to me. I cannot judge you by your dress.'

'Come round this way,' said Barnaby, who had passed out at the
garden gate and now stood close beside him. 'Put your hand in
mine. You're blind and always in the dark, eh? Are you frightened
in the dark? Do you see great crowds of faces, now? Do they grin
and chatter?'

'Alas!' returned the other, 'I see nothing. Waking or sleeping,
nothing.'

Barnaby looked curiously at his eyes, and touching them with
his fingers, as an inquisitive child might do, led him towards the
house.

'You have come a long distance,' said the widow, meeting him
at the door. 'How have you found your way so far?'

'Use and necessity are good teachers, as I have heard – the best
of any,' said the blind man, sitting down upon the chair to which
Barnaby had led him, and putting his hat and stick upon the
red-tiled floor. 'May neither you nor your son ever learn under
them. They are rough masters.'

'You have wandered from the road, too,' said the widow, in a
tone of pity.

'Maybe, maybe,' returned the blind man with a sigh, and yet
with something of a smile upon his face, 'that's likely. Handposts
and milestones are dumb, indeed, to me. Thank you the more for
this rest, and this refreshing drink!'

As he spoke, he raised the mug of water to his mouth. It was
clear, and cold, and sparkling, but not to his taste nevertheless, or
his thirst was not very great, for he only wetted his lips and put it
down again.

He wore, hanging with a long strap round his neck, a kind of
scrip or wallet, in which to carry food. The widow set some bread
and cheese before him, but he thanked her, and said that through
the kindness of the charitable he had broken his fast once since

morning, and was not hungry. When he had made her this reply, he opened his wallet, and took out a few pence, which was all it appeared to contain.

'Might I make bold to ask,' he said, turning towards where Barnaby stood looking on, 'that one who has the gift of sight, would lay this out for me in bread to keep me on my way? Heaven's blessing on the young feet that will bestir themselves in aid of one so helpless as a sightless man!'

Barnaby looked at his mother, who nodded assent; in another moment he was gone upon his charitable errand. The blind man sat listening with an attentive face, until long after the sound of his retreating footsteps was inaudible to the widow, and then said, suddenly, and in a very altered tone:

'There are various degrees and kinds of blindness, widow. There is the connubial blindness, ma'am, which perhaps you may have observed in the course of your own experience, and which is a kind of wilful and self-bandaging blindness. There is the blindness of party, ma'am, and public men, which is the blindness of a mad bull in the midst of a regiment of soldiers clothed in red. There is the blind confidence of youth, which is the blindness of young kittens, whose eyes have not yet opened on the world; and there is that physical blindness, ma'am, of which I am, contrairy to my own desire, a most illustrious example. Added to these, ma'am, is that blindness of the intellect, of which we have a specimen in your interesting son, and which, having sometimes glimmerings and dawnings of the light, is scarcely to be trusted as a total darkness. Therefore, ma'am, I have taken the liberty to get him out of the way for a short time, while you and I confer together, and this precaution arising out of the delicacy of my sentiments towards yourself, you will excuse me, ma'am, I know.'

Having delivered himself of this speech with many flourishes of manner, he drew from beneath his coat a flat stone bottle, and holding the cork between his teeth, qualified his mug of water with a plentiful infusion of the liquor it contained. He politely drained the bumper to her health, and the ladies, and setting it down empty, smacked his lips with infinite relish.

'I am a citizen of the world,[1] ma'am,' said the blind man, corking his bottle, 'and if I seem to conduct myself with freedom, it is the way of the world. You wonder who I am, ma'am, and what has brought me here. Such experience of human nature as I have, leads me to that conclusion, without the aid of eyes by which to read the movements of your soul as depicted in your feminine features. I will satisfy your curiosity immediately, ma'am; im-mediately.' With that he slapped his bottle on its broad back, and having put it under his garment as before, crossed his legs and folded his hands, and settled himself in his chair, previous to proceeding any further.

The change in his manner was so unexpected, the craft and nakedness of his deportment were so much aggravated by his condition – for we are accustomed to see in those who have lost a human sense, something in its place almost divine[2] – and this alteration bred so many fears in her whom he addressed, that she could not pronounce one word. After waiting, as it seemed, for some remark or answer, and waiting in vain, the visitor resumed:

'Madam, my name is Stagg. A friend of mine who has desired the honour of meeting with you any time these five years past, has commissioned me to call upon you. I should be glad to whisper that gentleman's name in your ear. – Zounds, ma'am, are you deaf? Do you hear me say that I should be glad to whisper my friend's name in your ear?'

'You need not repeat it,' said the widow, with a stifled groan; 'I see too well from whom you come.'

'But as a man of honour, ma'am,' said the blind man, striking himself on the breast, 'whose credentials must not be disputed, I take leave to say that I *will* mention that gentleman's name. Ay, ay,' he added, seeming to catch with his quick ear the very motion of her hand, 'but not aloud. With your leave ma'am, I desire the favour of a whisper.'

She moved towards him, and stooped down. He muttered a word in her ear; and, wringing her hands, she paced up and down the room like one distracted. The blind man, with perfect composure, produced his bottle again, mixed another glass-full; put it up as before; and, drinking from time to time, followed her with his face in silence.

'You are slow in conversation, widow,' he said after a time, pausing in his draught. 'We shall have to talk before your son.'

'What would you have me do?' she answered. 'What do you want?'

'We are poor, widow, we are poor,' he retorted, stretching out his right hand, and rubbing his thumb upon its palm.

'Poor!' she cried. 'And what am I?'

'Comparisons are odious,' said the blind man. 'I don't know, I don't care. I say that we are poor. My friend's circumstances are indifferent, and so are mine. We must have our rights, widow, or we must be bought off. But you know that, as well as I, so where's the use of talking?'

She still walked wildly to and fro. At length, stopping abruptly before him, she said:

'Is he near here?'

'He is. Close at hand.'

'Then I am lost!'

'Not lost, widow,' said the blind man, calmly; 'only found. Shall I call him?'

'Not for the world,' she answered, with a shudder.

'Very good,' he replied, crossing his legs again, for he had made as though he would rise and walk to the door. 'As you please, widow. His presence is not necessary that I know of. But both he and I must live; to live, we must eat and drink; to eat and drink, we must have money: – I say no more.'

'Do you know how pinched and destitute I am?' she retorted. 'I do not think you do, or can. If you had eyes, and could look around you on this poor cabin, you would have pity on me. Oh! let your heart be softened by your own affliction, friend, and have some sympathy with mine.'

The blind man snapped his fingers as he answered:

'– Beside the question, ma'am, beside the question. I have the softest heart in the world, but I can't live upon it. Many a gentleman lives well upon a soft head, who would find a heart of the same quality a very great drawback. Listen to me. This is a matter of business, with which sympathies and sentiments have nothing to do. As a mutual friend, I wish to arrange it in a satisfactory manner, if possible; and thus the case stands. – If you are very poor now, it's your own choice. You have friends who, in case of need, are always ready to help you. My friend is in a more destitute and desolate situation than most men, and, you and he being linked together in a common cause, he naturally looks to you to assist him. He has boarded and lodged with me a long time (for as I said just now, I am very soft-hearted), and I quite approve of his entertaining this opinion. You have always had a roof over your head; he has always been an outcast. You have your son to comfort and assist you; he has nobody at all. The advantages must not be

all one side. You are in the same boat, and we must divide the ballast a little more equally.'

She was about to speak, but he checked her, and went on.

'The only way of doing this, is by making up a little purse now and then for my friend; and that's what I advise. He bears you no malice that I know of, ma'am: so little, that although you have treated him harshly more than once, and driven him, I may say, out of doors, he has that regard for you that I believe, even if you disappointed him now, he would consent to take charge of your son, and to make a man of him.'

He laid a great stress on these latter words, and paused as if to find out what effect they had produced. She only answered by her tears.

'He is a likely lad,' said the blind man, thoughtfully, 'for many purposes, and not ill-disposed to try his fortune in a little change and bustle, if I may judge from what I heard of his talk with you to-night. – Come. In a word, my friend has pressing necessity for twenty pounds. You, who can give up an annuity, can get that sum for him. It's a pity you should be troubled. You seem very comfortable here, and it's worth that much to remain so. Twenty pounds, widow, is a moderate demand. You know where to apply for it; a post will bring it you. – Twenty pounds!'

She was about to answer him again, but again he stopped her.

'Don't say anything hastily; you might be sorry for it. Think of it a little while. Twenty pounds – of other people's money – how easy! Turn it over in your mind, I'm in no hurry. Night's coming on, and if I don't sleep here, I shall not go far. Twenty pounds! Consider of it, ma'am, for twenty minutes; give each pound a minute; that's a fair allowance. I'll enjoy the air the while, which is very mild and pleasant in these parts.'

With these words, he groped his way to the door, carrying his chair with him. Then seating himself, under a spreading honeysuckle, and stretching his legs across the threshold so that no person could pass in or out without his knowledge, he took from his pocket a pipe, flint, steel and tinder-box, and began to smoke. It was a lovely evening, of that gentle kind, and at that time of year, when the twilight is most beautiful. Pausing now and then to let his smoke curl slowly off, and to sniff the grateful fragrance of the flowers, he sat there at his ease – as though the cottage were his proper dwelling, and he had held undisputed possession of it all his life – waiting for the widow's answer and for Barnaby's return.

CHAPTER THE FORTY-SIXTH

When Barnaby returned with the bread, the sight of the pious old pilgrim smoking his pipe and making himself so thoroughly at home, appeared to surprise even him; the more so as that worthy person, instead of putting up the loaf in his wallet as a scarce and precious article, tossed it carelessly on the table, and producing his bottle, bade him sit down and drink.

'For I carry some comfort you see,' he said. 'Taste that. Is it good?'

The water stood in Barnaby's eyes as he coughed from the strength of the draught, and answered in the affirmative.

'Drink some more,' said the blind man; 'don't be afraid of it. You don't taste anything like that, often, eh?'

'Often!' cried Barnaby. 'Never!'

'Too poor?' returned the blind man with a sigh. 'Ay. That's bad. Your mother, poor soul, would be happier if she was richer, Barnaby.'

'Why, so I tell her – the very thing I told her just before you came to-night, when all that gold was in the sky,' said Barnaby, drawing his chair nearer to him, and looking eagerly in his face. 'Tell me. Is there any way of being rich, that I could find out?'

'Any way! A hundred ways.'

'Ay, ay?' he returned. 'Do you say so? What are they? – Nay, mother, it's for your sake I ask; not mine; – for yours, indeed. What are they?'

The blind man turned his face, on which there was a smile of triumph, to where the widow stood in great distress; and answered.

'Why, they are not to be found out by stay-at-homes, my good friend.'

'By stay-at-homes!' cried Barnaby, plucking at his sleeve. 'But I am not one. Now, there you mistake. I am often out before the sun, and travel home when he has gone to rest. I am away in the woods before the day has reached the shady places, and am often there when the bright moon is peeping through the boughs, and looking down upon the other moon that lives in water. As I walk along, I try to find, among the grass and moss, some of that small money for which she works so hard and used to shed so many tears. As I lie asleep in the shade, I dream of it – dream of digging it up in heaps; and spying it out, hidden under bushes; and seeing it sparkle, as the dew-drops do, among the leaves. But I never find it. Tell me where it is. I'd go there, if the journey were a whole year long, because I know she would be happier when I came home and brought some with me. Speak again. I'll listen to you if you talk all night.'

The blind man passed his hand lightly over the poor fellow's face, and finding that his elbows were planted on the table, that his chin rested on his two hands, that he leaned eagerly forward, and that his whole manner expressed the utmost interest and anxiety, paused for a minute as though he desired the widow to observe this fully, and then made answer:

'It's in the world, bold Barnaby, the merry world; not in solitary places like those you pass your time in, but in crowds, and where there's noise and rattle.'

'Good! good!' cried Barnaby, rubbing his hands. 'Yes! I love that. Grip loves it too. It suits us both. That's brave!'

' – The kind of places,' said the blind man, 'that a young fellow likes, and in which a good son may do more for his mother, and himself to boot, in a month, than he could here in all his life – that is, if he had a friend, you know, and some one to advise with.'

'You hear this, mother?' cried Barnaby, turning to her with delight. 'Never tell me we shouldn't heed it, if it lay shining at our feet. Why do we heed it so much now? Why do you toil from morning until night?'

'Surely,' said the blind man, 'surely. Have you no answer, widow? Is your mind,' he slowly added, 'not made up yet?'

'Let me speak with you,' she answered, 'apart.'

'Lay your hand upon my sleeve,' said Stagg, rising from the table; 'and lead me where you will. Courage, bold Barnaby. We'll talk more of this: I've a fancy for you. Wait there till I come back. Now, widow.'

She led him out at the door, and into the little garden, where they stopped.

'You are a fit agent,' she said, in a half breathless manner, 'and well represent the man who sent you here.'

'I'll tell him that you said so,' Stagg retorted. 'He has a regard for you, and will respect me the more (if possible) for your praise. We must have our rights, widow.'

'Rights! Do you know,' she said, 'that a word from me –'

'Why do you stop?' returned the blind man calmly, after a long pause. 'Do I know that a word from you would place my friend in the last position of the dance of life? Yes, I do. What of that? It will never be spoken, widow.'

'You are sure of that?'

'Quite – so sure, that I don't come here to discuss the question. I say we must have our rights, or we must be bought off. Keep to that point, or let me return to my young friend, for I have an interest in the lad, and desire to put him in the way of making his fortune. Bah! you needn't speak,' he added hastily; 'I know what you would say: you have hinted at it once already. Have I no feeling for you, because I am blind? No, I have not. Why do you expect me, being in darkness, to be better than men who have their sight – why should you? Is the hand of God more manifest in my having no eyes, than in your having two? It's the cant of you folks to be horrified if a blind man robs, or lies, or steals; oh yes, it's far worse in him, who can barely live on the few halfpence that are thrown to him in your crowded streets, than in you, who can see, and work, and are not dependent on the mercies of the world. A curse on you! You who have seven senses[1] may be wicked at your pleasure; we who have six, and want the most important, are to live and be moral on our affliction. The true charity and justice of rich to poor, all the world over!'

He paused a moment when he had said these words, and caught the sound of money, jingling in her hand.

'Well?' he cried, quickly resuming his former manner. 'That should lead to something. The point, widow?'

'First answer me one question,' she replied. 'You say he is close at hand. Has he left London?'

'Being close at hand, widow, it would seem he has,' returned the blind man.

'I mean, for good? You know that.'

'Yes, for good. The truth is, widow, that his making a longer stay there might have had disagreeable consequences. He has come away for that reason.'

'Listen,' said the widow, telling some money out, upon a bench beside them. 'Count.'

'Six,' said the blind man, listening attentively. 'Any more?'

'They are the savings,' she answered, 'of five years. Six guineas.'[2]

'He put out his hand for one of the coins; felt it carefully, put it between his teeth, rung it on the bench; and nodded to her to proceed.

'These have been scraped together and laid by, lest sickness or death should separate my son and me. They have been purchased at the price of much hunger, hard labour, and want of rest. If you *can* take them – do – on condition that you leave this place upon the instant, and enter no more into that room, where he sits now, expecting your return.'

'Six guineas,' said the blind man, shaking his head, 'though of the fullest weight that were ever coined, fall very far short of twenty pounds, widow.'

'For such a sum, as you know, I must write to a distant part of the country. To do that, and receive an answer, I must have time.'

'Two days?' said Stagg.

'More.'

'Four days?'

'A week. Return on this day week, at the same hour, but not to the house. Wait at the corner of the lane.'

'Of course,' said the blind man, with a crafty look, 'I shall find you there?'

'Where else can I take refuge? Is it not enough that you have made a beggar of me, and that I have sacrificed my whole store, so hardly earned, to preserve this home?'

'Humph!' said the blind man, after some consideration. 'Set me with my face towards the point you speak of, and in the middle of the road. Is this the spot?'

'It is.'

'On this day week at sunset. And think of him within doors. – For the present, good night.'

She made him no answer, nor did he stop for any. He went slowly away, turning his head from time to time, and stopping to listen, as if he were curious to know whether he was watched by any one. The shadows of night were closing fast around, and he was soon lost in the gloom. It was not, however, until she had traversed the lane from end to end, and made sure that he was gone, that she re-entered the cottage, and hurriedly barred the door and window.

'Mother!' said Barnaby. 'What is the matter? Where is the blind man?'

'He is gone.'

'Gone!' he cried, starting up. 'I must have more talk with him. Which way did he take?'

'I don't know,' she answered, folding her arms about him. 'You must not go out to-night. There are ghosts and dreams abroad.'

'Ay?' said Barnaby, in a frightened whisper.

'It is not safe to stir. We must leave this place to-morrow.'

'This place! This cottage – and the little garden mother!'

'Yes! To-morrow morning at sunrise. We must travel to London; lose ourselves in that wide place – there would be some trace of us in any other town – then travel on again, and find some new abode.'

Little persuasion was required to reconcile Barnaby to anything that promised change. In another minute, he was wild with delight; in another, full of grief at the prospect of parting with his friends the dogs; in another, wild again; then he was fearful of what she had said to prevent his wandering abroad that night, and full of terrors and strange questions. His light-heartedness in the end surmounted all his other feelings, and lying down in his clothes to the end that he might be ready on the morrow, he soon fell fast asleep before the poor turf fire.

His mother did not close her eyes, but sat beside him, watching. Every breath of wind sounded in her ears like that dreaded footstep at the door, or like that hand upon the latch, and made the calm summer night, a night of horror. At length the welcome day appeared. When she had made the little preparations which were needful for their journey, and had prayed upon her knees with many tears, she roused Barnaby, who jumped up gaily at her summons.

His clothes were few enough, and to carry Grip was a labour of love. As the sun shed his earliest beams upon the earth, they closed the door of their deserted home, and turned away. The sky was blue and bright. The air was fresh and filled with a thousand perfumes. Barnaby looked upward, and laughed with all his heart.

But it was a day he usually devoted to a long ramble, and one of the dogs – the ugliest of them all – came bounding up, and jumping round him in the fulness of his joy. He had to bid him go back in a surly tone, and his heart smote him while he did so. The dog retreated; turned with a half-incredulous, half-imploring look; came a little back; and stopped.

It was the last appeal of an old companion and a faithful friend – cast off. Barnaby could bear no more, and as he shook his head and waved his playmate home, he burst into tears.

'Oh mother, mother, how mournful he will be when he scratches at the door, and finds it always shut!'

There was such a sense of home in the thought, that though her own eyes overflowed she would not have obliterated the recollection of it, either from her own mind or from his, for the wealth of the whole wide world.

*

CHAPTER THE FORTY-SEVENTH

In the exhaustless catalogue of Heaven's mercies to mankind, the power we have of finding some germs of comfort in the hardest trials must ever occupy the foremost place; not only because it supports and upholds us when we most require to be sustained, but because in this source of consolation there is something, we have reason to believe, of the divine spirit; something of that goodness which detects amidst our own evil doings, a redeeming quality; something which, even in our fallen nature, we possess in common with the angels; which had its being in the old time when they trod the earth, and lingers on it yet, in pity.

How often, on their journey, did the widow remember with a grateful heart, that out of his deprivation Barnaby's cheerfulness and affection sprung! How often did she call to mind that but for that, he might have been sullen, morose, unkind, far removed from her – vicious, perhaps, and cruel! How often had she cause for comfort, in his strength, and hope, and in his simple nature! Those feeble powers of mind which rendered him so soon forgetful of the past, save in brief gleams and flashes, – even they were a comfort now. The world to him was full of happiness; in every tree, and plant, and flower, in every bird, and beast, and tiny insect whom a breath of summer wind laid low upon the ground, he had delight. His delight was hers; and where many a wise son would have made her sorrowful, this poor light-hearted idiot filled her breast with thankfulness and love.

Their stock of money was low, but from the hoard she had told into the blind man's hand, the widow had withheld one guinea. This, with the few pence she possessed besides, was to two persons of their frugal habits, a goodly sum in bank. Moreover they had Grip in company; and when they must otherwise have changed the guinea, it was but to make him exhibit outside an alehouse door, or in a village street, or in the grounds or gardens of a mansion of the better sort, and scores, who would have given nothing in charity, were ready to bargain for more amusement from the talking bird.

One day – for they moved slowly, and although they had many rides in carts and waggons, were on the road a week – Barnaby, with Grip upon his shoulder and his mother following, begged permission at a trim lodge to go up to the great house, at the other end of the avenue, and show his raven. The man within was inclined to give them admittance, and was indeed about to do so, when a stout gentleman with a long whip in his hand, and a flushed face which seemed to indicate that he had had his morning's draught, rode up to the gate, and called in a loud voice and with more oaths than the occasion seemed to warrant to have it opened directly.

'Who hast thou got here?' said the gentleman angrily, as the man threw the gate wide open, and pulled off his hat, 'who are these? Eh? ar't a beggar, woman?'

The widow answered with a curtsey, that they were poor travellers.

'Vagrants,' said the gentleman, 'vagrants and vagabonds. Thee wish to be made acquainted with the cage, dost thee – the cage, the stocks, and the whipping-post?[1] Where dost come from?'

She told him in a timid manner, – for he was very loud, hoarse, and red-faced, – and besought him not to be angry, for they meant no harm and would go upon their way that moment.

'Don't be too sure of that,' replied the gentleman, 'we don't allow vagrants to roam about this place. I know what thou want'st – stray linen drying on hedges, and stray poultry, eh? What hast got in that basket, lazy hound?'

'Grip, Grip, Grip – Grip the clever, Grip the wicked, Grip the knowing – Grip, Grip, Grip,' cried the raven, whom Barnaby had shut up on the approach of this stern personage. 'I'm a devil I'm a devil I'm a devil, Never say die Hurrah Bow wow wow, Polly put the kettle on we'll all have tea.'

'Take the virmin out, scoundrel,' said the gentleman, 'and let me see him.'

Barnaby, thus condescendingly addressed, produced his bird, but not without much fear and trembling,[2] and set him down upon the ground; which he had no sooner done than Grip drew fifty corks at least, and then began to dance; at the same time eyeing the gentleman with surprising insolence of manner, and screwing his head so much on one side that he appeared desirous of screwing it off upon the spot.

The cork-drawing seemed to make a greater impression on the gentleman's mind, than the raven's power of speech, and was indeed particularly adapted to his habits and capacity. He desired to have that done again, but despite his being very peremptory, and notwithstanding that Barnaby coaxed to the utmost, Grip turned a deaf ear to the request, and preserved a dead silence.

'Bring him along,' said the gentleman, pointing to the house. But Grip, who had watched the action, anticipated his master, by hopping on before them; – constantly flapping his wings, and screaming 'cook!' meanwhile, as a hint perhaps that there was company coming, and a small collation would be acceptable.

Barnaby and his mother walked on, on either side of the gentleman on horseback, who surveyed each of them from time to time in a proud and coarse manner, and occasionally thundered out some question, the tone of which alarmed Barnaby so much that he could find no answer, and, as a matter of course, could make him no reply. On one of these occasions, when the gentleman appeared disposed to exercise his horsewhip, the widow ventured to inform him in a low voice and with tears in her eyes, that her son was of weak mind.

'An idiot, eh?' said the gentleman looking at Barnaby as he spoke. 'And how long hast been an idiot?'

'She knows,' was Barnaby's timid answer, pointing to his mother – 'I – always, I believe.'

'From his birth,' said the widow.

'I don't believe it,' cried the gentleman, 'not a bit of it. It's an excuse not to work. There's nothing like flogging to cure that disorder. I'd make a difference in him in ten minutes, I'll be bound.'

'Heaven has made none in more than twice ten years, sir,' said the widow mildly.

'Then why don't you shut him up? we pay enough for county institutions, damn 'em. But thou'd rather drag him about to excite charity – of course. Ay, I know thee.'

Now, this gentleman had various endearing appellations among his intimate friends. By some he was called 'a country gentleman of the true school,' by some 'a fine old country gentleman,' by some 'a sporting gentleman,' by some 'a thorough-bred Englishman,' by some 'a genuine John Bull;'[3] but they all agreed in one respect, and that was, that it was a pity there were not more like him, and that because there were not, the country was going to rack and ruin every day. He was in the commission of the peace, and could write his name almost legibly; but his greatest qualifications were, that he was more severe with poachers, was a better shot, a harder rider, had better horses, kept better dogs, could eat more solid food, drink more strong wine, go to bed every night more drunk and get up every morning more sober, than any man in the county. In know-ledge of horseflesh he was almost equal to a farrier, in stable learning he surpassed his own head groom, and in gluttony not a pig on his estate was a match for him. He had no seat in Parliament himself, but he was extremely patriotic, and usually drove his voters up to the poll with his own hands. He was warmly attached to the church, and never appointed to the living in his gift any but a three-bottle man and a first-rate fox-hunter. He mistrusted the honesty of all poor people who could read and write, and had a secret jealousy of his own wife (a young lady whom he had married for what his friends called 'the good old English reason,' that her father's property adjoined his own) for possessing those accom-plishments in a greater degree than himself. In short, Barnaby being an idiot, and Grip a creature of mere brute instinct, it would be very hard to say what this gentleman was.

He rode up to the door of a handsome house approached by a great flight of steps, where a man was waiting to take his horse, and led the way into a large hall, which, spacious as it was, was tainted with the fumes of last night's stale debauch. Great-coats, riding-whips, bridles, topboots, spurs, and such gear, were strewn about on all sides, and formed, with some huge stags' antlers, and a few portraits of dogs and horses, its principal embellishments.

Throwing himself into a great chair (in which, by the bye, he often snored away the night, when he had been, according to his admirers, a finer country gentleman than usual) he bade the man tell his mistress to come down: and presently there appeared, a little flurried, as it seemed, by the unwonted summons, a lady much younger than himself, who had the appearance of being in delicate health, and not too happy.

'Here! Thou'st no delight in following the hounds as an English-woman should have,' said the gentleman. 'See to this here. That'll please thee perhaps.'

The lady smiled, sat down at a little distance from him, and glanced at Barnaby with a look of pity.

'He's an idiot, the woman says,' observed the gentleman, shaking his head; 'I don't believe it.'

'Are you his mother?' asked the lady.

She answered yes.

'What's the use of asking *her?*' said the gentleman, thrusting his hands into his breeches pockets. 'She'll tell thee so, of course. Most likely he's hired, at so much a day. There. Get on. Make him do something.'

Grip having by this time recovered his urbanity, condescended, at Barnaby's solicitation, to repeat his various phrases of speech, and to go through the whole of his performances with the utmost success. The corks, and the never say die, afforded the gentleman so much delight that he demanded the repetition of this part of the entertainment, until Grip got into his basket, and positively refused to say another word, good or bad. The lady too, was much amused with him; and the closing point of his obstinacy so delighted her husband that he burst into a roar of laughter, and demanded his price.

Barnaby looked as though he didn't understand his meaning. Probably he did not.

'His price,' said the gentleman, rattling the money in his pockets, 'what dost want for him? How much?'

'He's not to be sold,' replied Barnaby, shutting up the basket in a great hurry, and throwing the strap over his shoulder. 'Mother, come away.'

'Thou seest how much of an idiot he is, book-learner,' said the gentleman, looking scornfully at his wife. 'He can make a bargain. What dost want for him, old woman?'

'He is my son's constant companion,' said the widow. 'He is not to be sold, sir, indeed.'

'Not to be sold!' cried the gentleman, growing ten times redder, hoarser, and louder than before. 'Not to be sold!'

'Indeed no,' she answered. 'We have never thought of parting with him, sir, I do assure you.'

He was evidently about to make a very passionate retort, when a few murmured words from his wife happening to catch his ear, he turned sharply round, and said, 'Eh? What?'

'We can hardly expect them to sell the bird, against their own desire,' she faltered. 'If they prefer to keep him—'

'Prefer to keep him!' he echoed. 'These people, who go tramping about the country, a pilfering and vagabondizing on all hands, prefer to keep a bird, when a landed proprietor and a justice asks his price! That old woman's been to school. I know she has. Don't tell me no,' he roared to the widow, 'I say, yes.'

Barnaby's mother pleaded guilty to the accusation, and hoped there was no harm in it.

'No harm!' said the gentleman. 'No. No harm. No harm, ye old rebel, not a bit of harm. If my clerk was here, I'd set ye in the stocks, I would, or lay ye in jail for prowling up and down, on the look-out for petty larcenies, ye limb of a gipsy. Here, Simon, put these pilferers out, shove 'em into the road, out with 'em! Ye don't want to sell the bird, ye that come here to beg, don't ye? If they an't out in double-quick, set the dogs upon 'em!'

They waited for no further dismissal, but fled precipitately, leaving the gentleman to storm away by himself (for the poor lady had already retreated), and making a great many vain attempts to silence Grip, who, excited by the noise, drew corks enough for a city feast as they hurried down the avenue, and appeared to congratulate himself beyond measure on having been the cause of the disturbance. When they had nearly reached the lodge, another servant, emerging from the shrubbery, feigned to be very active in ordering them off, but this man put a crown into the widow's hand, and whispering that his lady sent it, thrust them gently from the gate.

This incident only suggested to the widow's mind, when they halted at an alehouse some miles further on, and heard the justice's character as given by his friends, that perhaps something more than capacity of stomach and tastes for the kennel and the stable, were required to form either a perfect country gentleman, a thorough-bred Englishman, or a genuine John Bull; and that possibly the terms were sometimes misappropriated, not to say disgraced. She little thought then, that a circumstance so slight would ever influence their future fortunes; but time and experience enlightened her in this respect.

'Mother,' said Barnáby, as they were sitting next day in a wagon which was to take them to within ten miles of the capital, 'we're going to London first, you said. Shall we see that blind man there?'

She was about to answer 'Heaven forbid!' but checked herself, and told him No, she thought not; why did he ask?

'He's a wise man,' said Barnaby, with a thoughtful countenance. 'I wish that we may meet with him again. What was it that he said of crowds? That gold was to be found where people crowded, and not among the trees and in such quiet places? He spoke as if he loved it; London is a crowded place; I think we shall meet him there.'

'But why do you desire to see him, love?' she asked.

'Because,' said Barnaby, looking wistfully at her, 'he talked to me about gold, which is a rare thing, and say what you will, a thing you would like to have, I know. And because he came and went away so strangely – just as white-headed old men come sometimes to my bed's foot in the night, and say what I can't remember when the bright day returns. He told me he'd come back. I wonder why he broke his word!'

'But you never thought of being rich or gay, before, dear Barnaby. You have always been contented.'

He laughed and bade her say that again, then cried, 'Ay ay – oh yes,' and laughed once more. Then something passed that caught his fancy, and the topic wandered from his mind, and was succeeded by another just as fleeting.

But it was plain from what he had said, and from his returning to the point more than once that day, and on the next, that the blind man's visit, and indeed his words, had taken strong possession of his mind. Whether the idea of wealth had occurred to him for the first time on looking at the golden clouds that evening – and images were often presented to his thoughts by outward objects quite as remote and distant; or whether their poor and humble way of life had suggested it, by contrast, long ago; or whether the accident (as he would deem it) of the blind man's pursuing the

current of his own remarks, had done so at the moment; or he had
been impressed by the mere circumstance of the man being blind,
and, therefore, unlike any one with whom he had talked before; it
was impossible to tell. She tried every means to discover, but in
vain; and the probability is that Barnaby himself was equally in
the dark.

It filled her with uneasiness to find him harping on this string,
but all that she could do, was to lead him quickly to some other
subject, and to dismiss it from his brain. To caution him against
their visitor, to show any fear or suspicion in reference to him,
would only be, she feared, to increase that interest with which
Barnaby regarded him, and to strengthen his desire to meet him
once again. She hoped, by plunging into the crowd, to rid herself
of her terrible pursuer, and then, by journeying to a distance and
observing increased caution, if that were possible, to live again
unknown, in secrecy and peace.

They reached, in course of time, their halting-place within ten
miles of London, and lay there for the night, after bargaining to
be carried on for a trifle next day, in a light van which was returning empty, and was to start at five o'clock in the morning. The
driver was punctual, the road good – save for the dust, the weather
being very hot and dry – and at seven in the forenoon of Friday the
second of June,[4] one thousand seven hundred and eighty, they
alighted at the foot of Westminster Bridge,[5] bade their conductor
farewell, and stood alone, together, on the scorching pavement.
For the freshness which night sheds upon such busy thoroughfares
had already departed, and the sun was shining with uncommon
lustre.

CHAPTER THE FORTY-EIGHTH

Uncertain where to go next, and bewildered by the crowd of people
who were already astir, they sat down in one of the recesses on the
bridge, to rest. They soon became aware that the stream of life was
all pouring one way, and that a vast throng of persons were crossing
the river from the Middlesex to the Surrey shore,[1] in unusual haste
and evident excitement. They were, for the most part, in knots of
two or three, or sometimes half-a-dozen; they spoke little together

— many of them were quite silent; and hurried on as if they had one
absorbing object in view, which was common to them all.

They were surprised to see that nearly every man in this great
concourse, which still came pouring past, without slackening in the
least, wore in his hat a blue cockade; and that the chance passengers
who were not so decorated, appeared timidly anxious to escape
observation or attack, and gave them the wall as if they would
conciliate them. This, however, was natural enough, considering
their inferiority in point of numbers; for the proportion of those
who wore blue cockades, to those who were dressed as usual, was
at least forty or fifty to one. There was no quarrelling, however:
the blue cockades went swarming on, passing each other when
they could, and making all the speed that was possible in such a
multitude; and exchanged nothing more than looks, and very often
not even those, with such of the passers-by as were not of their
number.

At first, the current of people had been confined to the two
pathways, and but a few more eager stragglers kept the road. But
after half an hour or so, the passage was completely blocked up by
the great press, which, being now closely wedged together, and
impeded by the carts and coaches it encountered, moved but slowly,
and was sometimes at a stand for five or ten minutes together.

After the lapse of nearly two hours, the numbers began to dimin-
ish visibly, and gradually dwindling away, by little and little, left
the bridge quite clear, save that, now and then, some hot and dusty
man with the cockade in his hat, and his coat thrown over his
shoulder, went panting by, fearful of being too late, or stopped to
ask which way his friends had taken, and being directed, hastened
on again like one refreshed. In this comparative solitude, which
seemed quite strange and novel after the late crowd, the widow had
for the first time an opportunity of inquiring of an old man who
came and sat beside them, what was the meaning of that great
assemblage.

'Why, where have you come from,' he returned, 'that you haven't
heard of Lord George Gordon's great association? This is the day
that he presents the petition against the Catholics, God bless him!'

'What have all these men to do with that?' she asked.

'What have they to do with it!' the old man replied. 'Why, how
you talk! Don't you know his Lordship has declared he won't
present it to the house at all, unless it is attended to the door

by forty thousand good and true men at least? There's a crowd
for you!'

'A crowd indeed!' said Barnaby. 'Do you hear that, mother!'

'And they're mustering yonder, as I am told,' resumed the old
man, 'nigh upon a hundred thousand strong. Ah! Let Lord George
alone. He knows his power. There'll be a good many faces inside
them three windows over there,' and he pointed to where the House
of Commons overlooked the river, 'that'll turn pale when good
Lord George gets up this afternoon, and with reason too. Ay, ay.
Let his Lordship alone. Let him alone. *He* knows!' And so, with
much mumbling and chuckling and shaking of his forefinger, he
rose, with the assistance of his stick, and tottered off.

'Mother!' said Barnaby, 'that's a brave crowd he talks of. Come!'

'Not to join it!' cried his mother.

'Yes, yes,' he answered, plucking at her sleeve. 'Why not? Come!'

'You don't know,' she urged, 'what mischief they may do, where
they may lead you, what their meaning is. Dear Barnaby, for my
sake –'

'For your sake!' he cried, patting her hand. 'Well! It *is* for your
sake, mother. You remember what the blind man said, about the
gold. Here's a brave crowd! Come! Or wait till I come back – yes,
yes, wait here.'

She tried with all the earnestness her fears engendered, to turn
him from his purpose, but in vain. He was stooping down to buckle
on his shoe, when a hackney-coach passed them rather quickly,
and a voice inside called to the driver to stop.

'Young man,' said a voice within.

'Who's that?' cried Barnaby, looking up.

'Do you wear this ornament?' returned the stranger, holding out
a blue cockade.

'In Heaven's name, no. Pray do not give it him!' exclaimed the
widow.

'Speak for yourself, woman,' said the man within the coach,
coldly. 'Leave the young man to his choice; he's old enough to
make it, and to snap your apron-strings. He knows, without your
telling, whether he wears the sign of a loyal Englishman or not.'

Barnaby, trembling with impatience, cried 'Yes! yes, yes, I do,'
as he had cried a dozen times already. The man threw him a
cockade, and crying 'Make haste to Saint George's Fields,'[2] ordered
the coachman to drive on fast; and left them.

With hands that trembled with his eagerness to fix the bauble in his hat, Barnaby was adjusting it as he best could, and hurriedly replying to the tears and entreaties of his mother, when two gentlemen passed on the opposite side of the way. Observing them, and seeing how Barnaby was occupied, they stopped, whispered together for an instant, turned back, and came over to them.

'Why are you sitting here?' said one of them, who was dressed in a plain suit of black, wore long lank hair, and carried a great cane. 'Why have you not gone with the rest?'

'I am going, sir,' replied Barnaby, finishing his task, and putting his hat on with an air of pride. 'I shall be there directly.'

'Say my Lord, young man, when his Lordship does you the honour of speaking to you,' said the second gentleman mildly. 'If you don't know Lord George Gordon when you see him, it's high time you should.'

'Nay, Gashford,' said Lord George, as Barnaby pulled off his hat again and made him a low bow, 'it's no great matter on a day like this which every Englishman will remember with delight and pride. Put on your hat, friend, and follow us, for you lag behind and are late. It's past ten now. Didn't you know that the hour of assembling was ten o'clock?'

Barnaby shook his head and looked vacantly from one to the other.

'You might have known it, friend,' said Gashford, 'it was perfectly understood. How came you to be so ill informed?'

'He cannot tell you, sir,' the widow interposed. 'It's of no use to ask him. We are but this morning come from a long distance in the country, and know nothing of these matters.'

'The cause has taken a deep root, and has spread its branches far and wide,' said Lord George to his secretary. 'This is a pleasant hearing. I thank Heaven for it!'

'Amen!' cried Gashford with a solemn face.

'You do not understand me, my Lord,' said the widow. 'Pardon me, but you cruelly mistake my meaning. We know nothing of these matters. We have no desire or right to join in what you are about to do. This is my son, my poor afflicted son, dearer to me than my own life. In mercy's name, my Lord, go your way alone, and do not tempt him into danger!'

'My good woman,' said Gashford, 'how can you! – Dear me! – What do you mean by tempting, and by danger? Do you think his

Lordship is a roaring lion, going about and seeking whom he may devour?[3] God bless me!'

'No, no, my Lord, forgive me,' implored the widow, laying both her hands upon his breast, and scarcely knowing what she did, or said, in the earnestness of her supplication, 'but there are reasons why you should hear my earnest, mother's prayer, and leave my son with me. Oh do! He is not in his right senses, he is not, indeed!'

'It is a bad sign of the wickedness of these times,' said Lord George, evading her touch, and colouring deeply, 'that those who cling to the truth and support the right cause, are set down as mad. Have you the heart to say this of your own son, unnatural mother!'

'I am astonished at you!' said Gashford, with a kind of meek severity. 'This is a very sad picture of female depravity.'

'He has surely no appearance,' said Lord George, glancing at Barnaby, and whispering in his secretary's ear, 'of being deranged? And even if he had, we must not construe any trifling peculiarity into madness. Which of us' – and here he turned red again – 'would be safe, if that were made the law!'

'Not one,' replied the secretary; 'in that case, the greater the zeal, the truth, and talent; the more direct the call from above; the clearer would be the madness. With regard to this young man, my Lord,' he added, with a lip that slightly curled as he looked at Barnaby, who stood twirling his hat, and stealthily beckoning them to come away, 'he is as sensible and self-possessed as any one I ever saw.'

'And you desire to make one of this great body?' said Lord George, addressing him; 'and intended to make one, did you?'

'Yes – yes,' said Barnaby, with sparkling eyes. 'To be sure I did! I told her so myself.'

'I see,' replied Lord George, with a reproachful glance at the unhappy mother. 'I thought so. Follow me and this gentleman, and you shall have your wish.'

Barnaby kissed his mother tenderly on the cheek, and bidding her be of good cheer, for their fortunes were both made now, did as he was desired. She, poor woman, followed too – with how much fear and grief it would be hard to tell.

They passed quickly through the Bridge-road, where the shops were all shut up (for the passage of the great crowd and the expectation of their return had alarmed the tradesmen for their goods and windows), and where, in the upper stories, all the inhabitants were congregated, looking down into the street below, with faces variously expressive of alarm, of interest, expectancy, and indignation. Some of these applauded, and some hissed; but regardless of these interruptions – for the noise of a vast congregation of people at a little distance, sounded in his ears like the roaring of a sea – Lord George Gordon quickened his pace, and presently arrived before St George's Fields.

They were really fields at that time, and of considerable extent. Here an immense multitude was collected, bearing flags of various kinds and sizes, but all of the same colour – blue, like the cockades – some sections marching to and fro in military array, and others drawn up in circles, squares, and lines. A large portion, both of the bodies which paraded the ground, and of those which remained stationary, were occupied in singing hymns or psalms. With whomsoever this originated, it was well done; for the sound of so many thousand voices in the air must have stirred the heart of any man within him, and could not fail to have a wonderful effect upon enthusiasts, however mistaken.

Scouts had been posted in advance of the great body, to give notice of their leader's coming. These falling back, the word was quickly passed through the whole host, and for a short interval there ensued a profound and death-like silence, during which the mass was so still and quiet, that the fluttering of a banner caught the eye, and became a circumstance of note. Then they burst into a tremendous shout, into another, and another; and the air seemed rent and shaken, as if by the discharge of cannon.

'Gashford!' cried Lord George, pressing his secretary's arm tight within his own, and speaking with as much emotion in his voice, as in his altered face, 'I am called indeed, now. I feel and know it. I am the leader of a host. If they summoned me at this moment with one voice to lead them on to death, I'd do it – Yes, and fall first myself!'

'It is a proud sight,' said the secretary. 'It is a noble day for England, and for the great cause throughout the world. Such homage, my Lord, as I, an humble but devoted man, can render –'

'What are you doing!' cried his master, catching him by both hands; for he had made a show of kneeling at his feet; 'Do not unfit me, dear Gashford, for the solemn duty of this glorious day –' the tears stood in the eyes of the poor gentleman as he said the words.

– 'Let us go among them; we have to find a place in some division for this new recruit – give me your hand.'

Gashford slid his cold insidious palm into his master's grasp, and so, hand in hand, and followed still by Barnaby and by his mother too, they mingled with the concourse.

They had by this time taken to their singing again, and as their leader passed between their ranks, they raised their voices to their utmost. Many of those who were banded together to support the religion of their country, even unto death, had never heard a hymn or psalm in all their lives. But these fellows having for the most part strong lungs, and being naturally fond of singing, chanted any ribaldry or nonsense that occurred to them, feeling pretty certain that it would not be detected in the general chorus, and not caring very much if it were. Many of these voluntaries were sung under the very nose of Lord George Gordon, who, quite unconscious of their burden, passed on with his usual stiff and solemn deportment, very much edified and delighted by the pious conduct of his followers.

So they went on and on, up this line, down that, round the exterior of this circle, and on every side of that hollow square; and still there were lines, and squares, and circles out of number to review. The day being now intensely hot, and the sun striking down his fiercest rays upon the field, those who carried heavy banners began to grow faint and weary; most of the number assembled were fain to pull off their neckcloths, and throw their coats and waistcoats open; and some, towards the centre, quite overpowered by the excessive heat, which was of course rendered more unendurable by the multitude around them, lay down upon the grass, and offered all they had about them for a drink of water. Still, no man left the ground, not even of these who were so distressed; still Lord George, streaming from every pore, went on with Gashford; and still Barnaby and his mother followed close behind them.

They had arrived at the top of a long line of some eight hundred men in single file, and Lord George had turned his head to look back, when a loud cry of recognition – in that peculiar and half-stifled tone which a voice has, when it is raised in the open air and in the midst of a great concourse of persons – was heard, and a man stepped with a shout of laughter from the rank, and smote Barnaby on the shoulders with his heavy hand.

'How now!' he cried. 'Barnaby Rudge! Why, where have you been hiding for these hundred years!'

Barnaby had been thinking within himself that the smell of the trodden grass brought back his old days at cricket, when he was a young boy and played on Chigwell Green. Confused by this sudden and boisterous address, he stared in a bewildered manner at the man, and could scarcely say 'What! Hugh!'

'Hugh!' echoed the other; 'ay, Hugh – Maypole Hugh! You remember my dog? He's alive now, and will know you, I warrant. What, you wear the colour, do you? Well done! Ha ha ha!'

'You know this young man, I see,' said Lord George.

'Know him, my Lord! as well as I know my own right hand. My captain knows him. We all know him.'

'Will you take him into your division?'

'It hasn't in it a better, nor a nimbler, nor a more active man, than Barnaby Rudge,' said Hugh. 'Show me the man who says it has. Fall in, Barnaby. He shall march, my Lord, between me and Dennis; and he shall carry,' he added, taking a flag from the hand of a tired man who tendered it, 'the gayest silken streamer in this valiant army.'

'In the name of God, no!' shrieked the widow, darting forward. 'Barnaby – my Lord – see – he'll come back – Barnaby – Barnaby!'

'Women in the field!' cried Hugh, stepping between them, and holding her off. 'Holloa! My captain there!'

'What's the matter here?' cried Simon Tappertit, bustling up in a great heat. 'Do you call this order?'

'Nothing like it, captain,' answered Hugh, still holding her back with his outstretched hand. 'It's against all orders. Ladies are carrying off our gallant soldiers from their duty. The word of command, captain! They're filing off the ground. Quick!'

'Close!' cried Simon, with the whole power of his lungs. 'Form! March!'

She was thrown to the ground; the whole field was in motion; Barnaby was whirled away into the heart of a dense mass of men, and she saw him no more.

—— * ——

CHAPTER THE FORTY-NINTH

The mob had been divided from its first assemblage into four divisions; the London, the Westminster, the Southwark, and the Scotch. Each of these divisions being subdivided into various bodies, and these bodies being drawn up in various forms and figures, the general arrangement was, except to the few chiefs and leaders, as unintelligible as the plan of a great battle to the meanest soldier in the field. It was not without its method, however; for, in a very short space of time after being put in motion, the crowd had resolved itself into three great parties, and were prepared, as had been arranged, to cross the river by different bridges, and make for the House of Commons in separate detachments.

At the head of that division which had Westminster Bridge for its approach to the scene of action, Lord George Gordon took his post; with Gashford at his right hand, and sundry ruffians, of most unpromising appearance, forming a kind of staff about him. The conduct of a second party, whose route lay by Blackfriars, was entrusted to a committee of management, including perhaps a dozen men: while the third, which was to go by London Bridge, and through the main streets, in order that their numbers, and their serious intentions might be the better known and appreciated by the citizens, were led by Simon Tappertit (assisted by a few subalterns, selected from the Brotherhood of United Bull-dogs), Dennis the hangman, Hugh, and some others.

The word of command being given, each of these great bodies took the road assigned to it, and departed on its way, in perfect order and profound silence. That which went through the City greatly exceeded the others in number, and was of such prodigious extent that when the rear began to move, the front was nearly four miles in advance, notwithstanding that the men marched three abreast and followed very close upon each other.

At the head of this party, in the place where Hugh, in the madness of his humour, had stationed him, and walking between that dangerous companion and the hangman, went Barnaby; as many a man among the thousands who looked on that day afterwards remembered well. Forgetful of all other things in the ecstacy of the moment, his face flushed and his eyes sparkling with delight, heedless of the weight of the great banner he carried, and mindful only of its flashing in the sun and rustling in the summer breeze, on he went, proud, happy, elated past all telling: – the only light-hearted, undesigning creature, in the whole assembly.

'What do you think of this?' asked Hugh, as they passed through the crowded streets, and looked up at the windows which were thronged with spectators. 'They have all turned out to see our flags and streamers? Eh, Barnaby? Why, Barnaby's the greatest man of all the pack! His flag's the largest of the lot, the brightest too. There's nothing in the show, like Barnaby. All eyes are turned on him. Ha ha ha!'

'Don't make that din, brother,' growled the hangman, glancing with no very approving eyes at Barnaby as he spoke: 'I hope he don't think there's nothing to be done, but carrying that there piece of blue rag, like a boy at a breaking-up.[1] You're ready for action I hope, eh? You, I mean,' he added, nudging Barnaby roughly with his elbow. 'What are you staring at? Why don't you speak?'

Barnaby had been gazing at his flag, and looked vacantly from his questioner to Hugh.

'He don't understand your way,' said the latter. 'Here, I'll explain it to him. Barnaby old boy, attend to me.'

'I'll attend,' said Barnaby, looking anxiously round; 'but I wish I could see her somewhere.'

'See who?' demanded Dennis in a gruff tone. 'You an't in love I hope, brother? That an't the sort of thing for us, you know. We mustn't have no love here.'

'She would be proud indeed to see me now, eh Hugh?' said Barnaby. 'Wouldn't it make her glad to see me at the head of this large show? She'd cry with joy, I know she would. Where *can* she be? She never sees me at my best, and what do I care to be gay and fine if *she's* not by?'

'Why, what palaver's this?' asked Mr Dennis with supreme disdain. 'We an't got no sentimental members among us, I hope.'

'Don't be uneasy, brother,' cried Hugh, 'he's only talking of his mother.'

'Of his what?' said Mr Dennis with a strong oath.

'His mother.'

'And have I combined myself with this here section, and turned out on this here memorable day, to hear men talk about their mothers!' growled Mr Dennis with extreme disgust. 'The notion of a man's sweetheart's bad enough, but a man's mother! –' and here his disgust was so extreme that he spat upon the ground, and could say no more.

'Barnaby's right,' cried Hugh with a grin, 'and I say it. Lookee, bold lad. If she's not here to see, it's because I've provided for her, and sent half a dozen gentlemen, every one of 'em with a blue flag (but not half as fine as yours), to take her, in state, to a grand house all hung round with gold and silver banners, and everything else you please, where she'll wait till you come, and want for nothing.'

'Ay!' said Barnaby, his face beaming with delight: 'have you indeed? That's a good hearing. That's fine! Kind Hugh!'

'But nothing to what will come, bless you,' retorted Hugh, with a wink at Dennis, who regarded his new companion in arms with great astonishment.

'No, indeed?' cried Barnaby.

'Nothing at all,' said Hugh. 'Money, cocked hats and feathers, red coats and gold lace; all the fine things there are, ever were, or will be; will belong to us if we are true to that noble gentleman – the best man in the world – carry our flags for a few days, and keep 'em safe. That's all we've got to do.'

'Is that all?' cried Barnaby with glistening eyes, as he clutched his pole the tighter; 'I warrant you I keep this one safe, then. You have put it in good hands. You know me, Hugh. Nobody shall wrest this flag away.'

'Well said!' cried Hugh. 'Ha ha! Nobly said! That's the old stout Barnaby, that I have climbed and leaped with many and many a day – I knew I was not mistaken in Barnaby. – Don't you see man,' he added in a whisper, as he slipped to the other side of Dennis, 'that the lad's a natural, and can be got to do anything, if you take him the right way. Letting alone the fun he is, he's worth a dozen men, in earnest, as you'd find if you tried a fall with him. Leave him to me. You shall soon see whether he's of use or not.'

Mr Dennis received these explanatory remarks with many nods and winks, and softened his behaviour towards Barnaby from that moment. Hugh, laying his finger on his nose, stepped back into his former place, and they proceeded in silence.

It was between two and three o'clock in the afternoon when the three great parties met at Westminster, and, uniting into one huge mass, raised a tremendous shout. This was not only done in token of their presence, but as a signal to those on whom the task devolved, that it was time to take possession of the lobbies of both

Houses, and of the various avenues of approach, and of the gallery stairs. To the last-named place, Hugh and Dennis, still with their pupil between them, rushed straightway; Barnaby having given his flag into the hands of one of their own party, who kept them at the outer door. Their followers pressing on behind, they were borne as on a great wave to the very doors of the gallery, whence it was impossible to retreat, even if they had been so inclined, by reason of the throng which choked up the passages. It is a familiar expression in describing a great crowd, that a person might have walked upon the people's heads. In this case it was actually done; for a boy who had by some means got among the concourse, and was in imminent danger of suffocation, climbed to the shoulders of a man beside him and walked upon the people's hats and heads into the open street; traversing in his passage the whole length of two staircases and a long gallery. Nor was the swarm without less dense; for a basket which had been tossed into the crowd, was jerked from head to head, and shoulder to shoulder, and went spinning and whirling on above them, until it was lost to view, without ever once falling in among them or coming near the ground.

Through this vast throng, sprinkled doubtless here and there with honest zealots, but composed for the most part of the very scum and refuse of London, whose growth was fostered by bad criminal laws, bad prison regulations, and the worst conceivable police, – such of the members of both Houses of Parliament as had not taken the precaution to be already at their posts, were compelled to fight and force their way. Their carriages were stopped and broken; the wheels wrenched off; the glasses shivered to atoms; the panels beaten in; drivers, footmen, and masters, pulled from their seats and rolled in the mud. Lords, commoners, and reverend Bishops, with little distinction of person or party, were kicked and pinched and hustled; passed from hand to hand through various stages of ill-usage; and sent to their fellow senators at last with their clothes hanging in ribands about them, their bagwigs torn off, themselves speechless and breathless, and their persons covered with the powder which had been cuffed and beaten out of their hair. One Lord was so long in the hands of the populace, that the Peers as a body resolved to sally forth and rescue him, and were in the act of doing so, when he happily appeared among them covered with dirt and bruises, and hardly to be recognized by those who knew him best. The noise and uproar were on the increase every moment. The air was filled with execrations, hoots, and howlings. The mob raged and roared, like a mad monster as it was, unceasingly, and each new outrage served to swell its fury.

Within doors, matters were even yet more threatening. Lord George – preceded by a man who carried the immense petition on a porter's knot through the lobby to the door of the House of Commons, where it was received by two officers of the house who rolled it up to the table ready for presentation – had taken his seat at an early hour, before the Speaker went to prayers. His followers pouring in at the same time, the lobby and all the avenues were immediately filled, as we have seen: thus the members were not only attacked in their passage through the streets, but were set upon within the very walls of Parliament; while the tumult, both within and without, was so great, that those who attempted to speak could scarcely hear their own voices; far less consult upon the course it would be wise to take in such extremity, or animate each other to dignified and firm resistance. So sure as any member, just arrived, with dress disordered and dishevelled hair, came struggling through the crowd in the lobby, it yelled and screamed in triumph; and when the door of the house, partially and cautiously opened by those within for his admission, gave them a momentary glimpse of the interior, they grew more wild and savage, like beasts at the sight of prey, and made a rush against the portal which strained its locks and bolts in their staples, and shook the very beams.

The strangers' gallery,[2] which was immediately above the door of the house, had been ordered to be closed on the first rumour of disturbance, and was empty; save that now and then Lord George took his seat there, for the convenience of coming to the head of the stairs which led to it, and repeating to the people what had passed within. It was on these stairs that Barnaby, Hugh, and Dennis were posted. There were two flights, short, steep, and narrow, running parallel to each other, and leading to two little doors communicating with a low passage which opened on the gallery. Between them was a kind of well, or unglazed skylight, for the admission of light and air into the lobby, which might be some eighteen or twenty feet below.

Upon one of these little staircases – not that at the head of which Lord George appeared from time to time, but the other – Gashford stood with his elbow on the bannister, and his cheek resting on his hand, with his usual crafty aspect. Whenever he varied this attitude in the slightest degree – so much as by the gentlest motion of his arm – the uproar was certain to increase, not merely there, but in the lobby below; from which place no doubt, some man who acted as fugleman to the rest, was constantly looking up and watching him.

'Order!' cried Hugh, in a voice which made itself heard even above the roar and tumult, as Lord George appeared at the top of the staircase. 'News! News from my Lord!'

The noise continued, notwithstanding his appearance, until Gashford looked round. There was silence immediately – even among the people in the passages without, and on the other staircases, who could neither see nor hear, but to whom, notwithstanding, the signal was conveyed with marvellous rapidity.

'Gentlemen,' said Lord George, who was very pale and agitated, 'We must be firm. They talk of delays, but we must have no delays. They talk of taking your petition into consideration next Tuesday, but we must have it considered now. Present appearances look bad for our success, but we must succeed and will!'

'We must succeed and will!' echoed the crowd. And so among their shouts and cheers and other cries, he bowed to them and retired, and presently came back again. There was another gesture from Gashford, and a dead silence directly.

'I am afraid,' he said, this time, 'that we have little reason, gentlemen, to hope for any redress from the proceedings of Parliament. But we must redress our own grievances, we must meet again, we must put our trust in Providence, and it will bless our endeavours.'

This speech being a little more temperate than the last, was not so favourably received. When the noise and exasperation were at their height, he came back once more, and told them that the alarm had gone forth for many miles round; that when the King heard of their assembling together in that great body, he had no doubt His Majesty would send down private orders to have their wishes complied with; and – with the manner of his speech as childish, irresolute, and uncertain as his matter – was proceeding further, when two gentlemen suddenly appeared at the door where he stood, and pressing past him and coming a step or two lower down upon the stairs, confronted the people.

The boldness of this action quite took them by surprise. They

were not the less disconcerted, when one of the gentlemen, turning
to Lord George, spoke thus – in a loud voice that they might hear
him well, but quite coolly and collectedly.

'You may tell these people, if you please, my Lord, that I am
General Conway[3] of whom they have heard; and that I oppose this
petition, and all their proceedings, and yours. I am a soldier, you
may tell them; and I will protect the freedom of this place with my
sword. You see, my Lord, that the members of this house are all
in arms to-day; you know that the entrance to it is a narrow one;
you cannot be ignorant that there are men within these walls who
are determined to defend that pass to the last, and before whom
many lives must fall if your adherents persevere. Have a care what
you do.'

'And my Lord George,' said the other gentleman, addressing him
in like manner, 'I desire them to hear this, from me – Colonel
Gordon[4] – your near relation. If a man among this crowd, whose
uproar strikes us deaf, crosses the threshold of the House of
Commons, I swear to run my sword that moment – not into his,
but into your body!'

With that, they stepped back again, keeping their faces towards
the crowd; took each an arm of the misguided nobleman; drew him
into the passage, and shut the door; which they directly locked and
fastened on the inside.

This was so quickly done, and the demeanour of both gentlemen
– who were not young men either – was so gallant and resolute,
that the crowd faltered and stared at each other with irresolute and
timid looks. Many tried to turn towards the door; some of the
faintest-hearted cried that they had best go back, and called to those
behind to give way; and the panic and confusion were increasing
rapidly, when Gashford whispered Hugh.

'What now!' Hugh roared aloud, turning towards them. 'Why
go back? Where can you do better than here, boys! One good rush
against these doors and one below at the same time, will do the
business. Rush on, then! As to the door below, let those stand back
who are afraid. Let those who are not afraid, try who shall be the
first to pass it. Here goes! Look out down there!'

Without the delay of an instant, he threw himself headlong over
the bannisters into the lobby below. He had hardly touched the
ground when Barnaby was at his side. The chaplain's assistant,
and some members who were imploring the people to retire,

immediately withdrew; and then, with a great shout, both crowds threw themselves against the doors pell-mell, and besieged the House in earnest.

At that moment, when a second onset must have brought them into collision with those who stood on the defensive within, in which case great loss of life and bloodshed would inevitably have ensued, – the hindmost portion of the crowd gave way, and the rumour spread from mouth to mouth that a messenger had been despatched by water for the military, who were forming in the street. Fearful of sustaining a charge in the narrow passages in which they were so closely wedged together, the throng poured out as impetuously as they had flocked in. As the whole stream turned at once, Barnaby and Hugh went with it: and so, fighting and struggling and trampling on fallen men and being trampled on in turn themselves, they and the whole mass floated by degrees into the open street, where a large detachment of the Guards, both horse and foot, came hurrying up; clearing the ground before them so rapidly that the people seemed to melt away as they advanced.

The word of command to halt being given, the soldiers formed across the street; the rioters, breathless and exhausted with their late exertions, formed likewise, though in a very irregular and disorderly manner. The commanding officer rode hastily into the open space between the two bodies, accompanied by a magistrate and an officer of the House of Commons, for whose accommodation a couple of troopers had hastily dismounted. The Riot Act[5] was read, but not a man stirred.

In the first rank of the insurgents, Barnaby and Hugh stood side by side. Somebody had thrust into Barnaby's hands when he came out into the street, his precious flag; which, being now rolled up and tied round the pole, looked like a giant quarter-staff as he grasped it firmly and stood upon his guard. If ever man believed with his whole heart and soul that he was engaged in a just cause, and that he was bound to stand by his leader to the last, poor Barnaby believed it of himself and Lord George Gordon.

After an ineffectual attempt to make himself heard, the magistrate gave the word and the Horse Guards came riding in among the crowd. But even then he galloped here and there, exhorting the people to disperse; and, although heavy stones were thrown at the men, and some were desperately cut and bruised, they had no orders but to make prisoners of such of the rioters as were the most active, and to drive the people back with the flat of their sabres. As the horses came in among them, the throng gave way at many points, and the Guards, following up their advantage, were rapidly clearing the ground, when two or three of the foremost, who were in a manner cut off from the rest by the people closing round them, made straight towards Barnaby and Hugh, who had no doubt been pointed out as the two men who dropped into the lobby; laying about them now with some effect, and inflicting on the more turbulent of their opponents, a few slight flesh wounds, under the influence of which a man dropped, here and there, into the arms of his fellows, amid much groaning and confusion.

At the sight of gashed and bloody faces, seen for a moment in the crowd, then hidden by the press around them, Barnaby turned pale and sick. But he stood his ground, and grasping his pole more firmly yet, kept his eye fixed upon the nearest soldier – nodding his head meanwhile, as Hugh, with a scowling visage, whispered in his ear.

The soldier came spurring on, making his horse rear as the people pressed about him, cutting at the hands of those who would have grasped his rein and forced his charger back, and waving to his comrades to follow – and still Barnaby, without retreating an inch, waited for his coming. Some called to him to fly, and some were in the very act of closing round him, to prevent his being taken, when the pole swept the air above the people's heads, and the man's saddle was empty in an instant.

Then he and Hugh turned and fled; the crowd opening to let them pass, and closing up again so quickly that there was no clue to the course they had taken. Panting for breath, hot, dusty, and exhausted with fatigue, they reached the river-side in safety, and getting into a boat with all despatch were soon out of any immediate danger.

As they glided down the river, they plainly heard the people cheering; and supposing they might have forced the soldiers to retreat, lay upon their oars for a few minutes, uncertain whether to return or not. But the crowd passing along Westminster Bridge, soon assured them that the populace were dispersing; and Hugh rightly guessed from this, that they had cheered the magistrate for offering to dismiss the military on condition of their immediate departure to their several homes; and that he and Barnaby were better where they were. He advised, therefore, that they should proceed to Blackfriars, and, going ashore at the bridge, make the best of their way to the Boot; where there was not only good entertainment and safe lodging, but where they would certainly be joined by many of their late companions. Barnaby assenting, they decided on this course of action, and pulled for Blackfriars accordingly.

They landed at a critical time, and fortunately for themselves at the right moment. For, coming into Fleet Street, they found it in an unusual stir; and inquiring the cause, were told that a body of Horse Guards had just galloped past, and that they were escorting some rioters whom they had made prisoners, to Newgate for safety. Not at all ill-pleased to have so narrowly escaped the cavalcade, they lost no more time in asking questions, but hurried to the Boot with as much speed as Hugh considered it prudent to make, without appearing singular or attracting an inconvenient share of public notice.

CHAPTER THE FIFTIETH

They were among the first to reach the tavern, but they had not been there many minutes, when several groups of men who had formed part of the crowd, came straggling in. Among them were Simon Tappertit and Mr Dennis; both of whom, but especially the latter, greeted Barnaby with the utmost warmth, and paid him many compliments on the prowess he had shown.

'Which,' said Dennis, with an oath, as he rested his bludgeon in a corner with his hat upon it, and took his seat at the same table with them, 'it does me good to think of. There was a opportunity! But it led to nothing. For my part, I don't know what would. There's no spirit among the people in these here times. Bring something to eat and drink here. I'm disgusted with humanity.'

'On what account?' asked Mr Tappertit, who had been quenching his fiery face in a half-gallon can. 'Don't you consider this a good beginning, mister?'

'Give me security that it an't an ending,' rejoined the hangman. 'When that soldier went down, we might have made London ours; but no; – we stand, and gape, and look on – the justice (I wish he had had a bullet in each eye, as he would have had, if we'd gone to work my way) says "My lads, if you'll give me your word to disperse, I'll order off the military," – our people set up a hurrah, throw up the game with the winning cards in their hands, and skulk away like a pack of tame curs as they are. Ah!' said the hangman, in a tone of deep disgust, 'it makes me blush for my feller creeturs. I wish I had been born a ox, I do!'

'You'd have been quite as agreeable a character if you had been, I think,' returned Simon Tappertit, going out in a lofty manner.

'Don't be too sure of that,' rejoined the hangman, calling after him; 'if I was a horned animal at the present moment, with the smallest grain of sense, I'd toss every man in this company, except-ing them two,' meaning Hugh and Barnaby, 'for his manner of conducting himself this day.'

With which mournful review of their proceedings, Mr Dennis sought consolation in cold boiled beef and beer; but without at all relaxing the grim and dissatisfied expression of his face, the gloom of which was rather deepened than dissipated by their grateful influence.

The company who were thus libelled might have retaliated by strong words, if not by blows, but they were dispirited and worn out. The greater part of them had fasted since morning; all had suffered extremely from the excessive heat; and, between the day's shouting, exertion, and excitement, many had quite lost their voices, and so much of their strength that they could hardly stand. Then they were uncertain what to do next, fearful of the conse-quences of what they had done already, and sensible that after all they had carried no point, but had indeed left matters worse than they had found them. Of those who had come to the Boot, many dropped off within an hour; such of them as were really honest and sincere, never, after the morning's experience, to return, or to hold any communication with their late companions. Others remained but to refresh themselves, and then went home desponding; others who had theretofore been regular in their attendance, avoided the place altogether. The half-dozen prisoners whom the Guards had taken, were magnified by report into half a hundred at least; and their friends, being faint and sober, so slackened in their energy, and so drooped beneath these dispiriting influences, that by eight o'clock in the evening, Dennis, Hugh, and Barnaby, were left alone.

Even they were fast asleep upon the benches, when Gashford's entrance roused them.

'Oh! You *are* here then?' said the secretary. 'Dear me!'

'Why, where should we be, Muster Gashford!' Dennis rejoined as he rose into a sitting posture.

'Oh nowhere, nowhere,' he returned with excessive mildness. 'The streets are filled with blue cockades. I rather thought you might have been among them. I am glad you are not.'

'You have orders for us, master, then?' said Hugh.

'Oh dear, no. Not I. No orders, my good fellow. What orders should I have? You are not in my service.'

'Muster Gashford,' remonstrated Dennis, 'we belong to the cause, don't we?'

'The cause!' repeated the secretary, looking at him in a sort of abstraction. 'There is no cause. The cause is lost.'

'Lost!'

'Oh yes. You have heard, I suppose? The petition is rejected by a hundred and ninety-two, to six. It's quite final. We might have spared ourselves some trouble: that, and my Lord's vexation, are the only circumstances I regret. I am quite satisfied in all other respects.'

As he said this, he took a penknife from his pocket, and putting his hat upon his knee, began to busy himself in ripping off the blue cockade which he had worn all day; at the same time humming a psalm tune which had been very popular in the morning, and dwelling on it with a gentle regret.

His two adherents looked at each other, and at him, as if they were at a loss how to pursue the subject. At length Hugh, after some elbowing and winking between himself and Mr Dennis, ventured to stay his hand, and to ask him why he meddled with that riband in his hat.

'Because,' said the secretary, looking up with something between a snarl and a smile, 'because to sit still and wear it, or fall asleep and wear it, or run away and wear it, is a mockery. That's all, friend.'

'What would you have us do, master!' cried Hugh.

'Nothing,' returned Gashford, shrugging his shoulders; 'nothing. When my Lord was reproached and threatened for standing by you, I, as a prudent man, would have had you do nothing. When the soldiers were trampling you under their horses' feet, I would have had you do nothing. When one of them was struck down by a daring hand, and I saw confusion and dismay in all their faces, I would have had you do nothing – just what you did, in short. This is the young man who had so little prudence and so much boldness. Ah! I am sorry for him.'

'Sorry, master!' cried Hugh.

'Sorry, Muster Gashford!' echoed Dennis.

'In case there should be a proclamation out to-morrow, offering five hundred pounds, or some such trifle, for his apprehension; and in case it should include another man who dropped into the lobby from the stairs above,' said Gashford, coldly; 'still, do nothing.'

'Fire and fury, master!' cried Hugh, starting up. 'What have we done, that you should talk to us like this!'

'Nothing,' returned Gashford with a sneer. 'If you are cast into prison; if the young man –' here he looked hard at Barnaby's attentive face – 'is dragged from us and from his friends; perhaps from people whom he loves, and whom his death would kill; is thrown into jail, brought out and hanged before their eyes; still, do nothing. You'll find it your best policy, I have no doubt.'

'Come on!' cried Hugh, striding towards the door. 'Dennis – Barnaby – come on!'

'Where? To do what?' said Gashford, slipping past him, and standing with his back against it.

'Anywhere! Anything!' cried Hugh. 'Stand aside, master, or the window will serve our turn as well. Let us out!'

'Ha ha ha! You are of such – of such an impetuous nature,' said Gashford, changing his manner for one of the utmost good fellowship and the pleasantest raillery; 'you are such an excitable creature – but you'll drink with me before you go?'

'Oh, yes – certainly,' growled Dennis, drawing his sleeve across his thirsty lips. 'No malice, brother. Drink with Muster Gashford!'

Hugh wiped his heated brow, and relaxed into a smile. The artful secretary laughed outright.

'Some liquor here! Be quick, or he'll not stop, even for that. He is a man of such desperate ardour!' said the smooth secretary, whom Mr Dennis corroborated with sundry nods and muttered oaths – 'Once roused, he is a fellow of such fierce determination!'

Hugh poised his sturdy arm aloft, and clapping Barnaby on the back, bade him fear nothing. They shook hands together – poor Barnaby evidently possessed with the idea that he was among the most virtuous and disinterested heroes in the world – and Gashford laughed again.

'I hear,' he said smoothly, as he stood among them with a great measure of liquor in his hand, and filled their glasses as quickly and as often as they chose, 'I hear – but I cannot say whether it be true or false – that the men who are loitering in the streets to-night, are half disposed to pull down a Romish chapel or two, and that they only want leaders. I even heard mention of those in Duke Street Lincoln's-Inn Fields, and in Warwick Street Golden Square;[1] but common report, you know – You are not going?'

– 'To do nothing, master, eh?' cried Hugh. 'No jails and halter for Barnaby and me. They must be frightened out of that. Leaders are wanted, are they? Now boys!'

'A most impetuous fellow!' cried the secretary. 'Ha ha! A courageous, boisterous, most vehement fellow! A man who –'

There was no need to finish the sentence, for they had rushed out of the house, and were far beyond hearing. He stopped in the middle of a laugh, listened, drew on his gloves, and, clasping his hands behind him, paced the deserted room for a long time, then bent his steps towards the busy town, and walked into the streets.

They were filled with people, for the rumour of that day's proceedings had made a great noise. Those persons who did not care to leave home, were at their doors or windows, and one topic of discourse prevailed on every side. Some reported that the riots were effectually put down; others that they had broken out again: some said that Lord George Gordon had been sent under a strong guard to the Tower; others that an attempt had been made upon the King's life, that the soldiers had been again called out, and that the noise of musketry in a distant part of the town had been plainly heard within an hour. As it grew darker, these stories became more direful and mysterious; and often, when some frightened passenger ran past with tidings that the rioters were not far off, and were coming up, the doors were shut and barred, lower windows made secure, and as much consternation engendered, as if the city were invaded by a foreign army.

Gashford walked stealthily about, listening to all he heard, and diffusing or confirming, whenever he had an opportunity, such false intelligence as suited his own purpose; and, busily occupied in this way, turned into Holborn for the twentieth time, when a great many women and children came flying along the street – often panting and looking back – and the confused murmur of numerous voices struck upon his ear. Assured by these tokens, and by the red light which began to flash upon the houses on either side, that some of his friends were indeed approaching, he begged a moment's shelter at a door which opened as he passed, and running with some other persons to an upper window, looked out upon the crowd.

They had torches among them, and the chief faces were distinctly visible. That they had been engaged in the destruction of some building was sufficiently apparent, and that it was a Catholic place of worship was evident from the spoils they bore as trophies, which were easily recognisable for the vestments of priests, and rich fragments of altar furniture. Covered with soot, and dirt, and dust, and lime; their garments torn to rags; their hair hanging wildly about them; their hands and faces jagged and bleeding with the wounds of rusty nails; Barnaby, Hugh, and Dennis hurried on before them all, like hideous madmen. After them, the dense throng came fighting on: some singing; some shouting in triumph; some quarreling among themselves; some menacing the spectators as they passed; some with great wooden fragments, on which they spent their rage as if they had been alive, rending them limb from limb, and hurling the scattered morsels high into the air; some in a drunken state, unconscious of the hurts they had received from falling bricks, and stones, and beams; one borne upon a shutter, in the very midst, covered with a dingy cloth, a senseless, ghastly heap. Thus – a vision of coarse faces, with here and there a blot of flaring, smoky light; a dream of demon heads and savage eyes, and sticks and iron bars uplifted in the air, and whirled about; a bewildering horror, in which so much was seen, and yet so little, which seemed so long and yet so short, in which there were so many phantoms, not to be forgotten all through life, and yet so many things that could not be observed in that distracting glimpse – it flitted onward, and was gone.

As it passed away upon its work of wrath and ruin, a piercing scream was heard. A knot of persons ran towards the spot; Gashford, who just then emerged into the street, among them. He was on the outskirts of the little concourse, and could not see or hear what passed within; but one who had a better place, informed him that a widow woman had descried her son among the rioters.

'Is that all?' said the secretary, turning his face homewards. 'Well! I think this looks a little more like business!'

*

CHAPTER THE FIFTY-FIRST

Promising as these outrages were to Gashford's view, and much like business as they looked, they extended that night no farther. The soldiers were again called out, again they took half-a-dozen prisoners, and again the crowd dispersed after a short and bloodless scuffle. Hot and drunken though they were, they had not yet broken all bounds and set all law and government at defiance. Something of their habitual deference to the authority erected by society for its own preservation yet remained among them, and had its majesty been vindicated in time, the secretary would have had to digest a bitter disappointment.

By midnight, the streets were clear and quiet, and, save that there stood in two parts of the town, a heap of nodding walls and pile of rubbish, where there had been at sunset a rich and handsome building, everything wore its usual aspect. Even the Catholic gentry and tradesmen, of whom there were many, resident in different parts of the City and its suburbs, had no fear for their lives or property, and but little indignation for the wrong they had already sustained in the plunder and destruction of their temples of worship. An honest confidence in the government under whose protection they had lived for many years, and a well-founded reliance on the good feeling and right thinking of the great mass of the community, with whom, notwithstanding their religious differences, they were every day in habits of confidential, affectionate, and friendly inter-course, re-assured them, even under the excesses that had been committed; and convinced them that they who were Protestants in anything but the name, were no more to be considered as abettors of these disgraceful occurrences, than they themselves were chargeable with the uses of the block, the rack, the gibbet, and the stake, in cruel Mary's reign.

The clock was on the stroke of one, when Gabriel Varden, with his lady and Miss Miggs, sat waiting in the little parlour. This fact; the toppling wicks of the dull, wasted candles; the silence that prevailed; and above all the nightcaps of both maid and matron, were sufficient evidence that they had been prepared for bed some time ago, and had some strong reason for sitting up so far beyond their usual hour.

If any other corroborative testimony had been required, it would have been abundantly furnished in the actions of Miss Miggs, who, having arrived at that restless state and sensitive condition of the nervous system which are the result of long watching, did, by a constant rubbing and tweaking of her nose, a perpetual change of position (arising from the sudden growth of imaginary knots and knobs in her chair), a frequent friction of her eyebrows, the incessant recurrence of a small cough, a small groan, a gasp, a sigh, a sniff, a spasmodic start, and by other demonstrations of that nature, so file down and rasp, as it were, the patience of the locksmith, that after looking at her in silence for some time, he at last broke out into this apostrophe:

'Miggs my good girl, go to bed – do go to bed. You're really worse than the dripping of a hundred water-butts outside the window, or the scratching of as many mice behind the wainscot. I can't bear it. Do go to bed, Miggs. To oblige me – do.'

'You haven't got nothing to untie sir,' returned Miss Miggs, 'and therefore your requests does not surprise me. But Missis has – and while you set up, mim' – she added, turning to the locksmith's wife, 'I couldn't, no not if twenty times the quantity of cold water was aperiently running down my back at this moment, go to bed with a quiet spirit.'

Having spoken these words, Miss Miggs made divers efforts to rub her shoulders in an impossible place, and shivered from head to foot; thereby giving the beholders to understand that the imaginary cascade was still in full flow, but that a sense of duty upheld her under that, and all other sufferings, and nerved her to endurance.

Mrs Varden being too sleepy to speak, and Miss Miggs having, as the phrase is, said her say, the locksmith had nothing for it but to sigh and be as quiet as he could.

But to be quiet with such a basilisk before him, was impossible. If he looked another way, it was worse to feel that she was rubbing her cheek, or twitching her ear, or winking her eye, or making all kinds of extraordinary shapes with her nose, than to see her do it. If she was for a moment free from any of these complaints, it was only because of her foot being asleep, or of her arm having got the fidgets, or of her leg being doubled up with the cramp, or of some other horrible disorder which racked her whole frame. If she did enjoy a moment's ease, then with her eyes shut and her mouth wide open she would be seen to sit very stiff and upright in her chair; then to nod a little way forward, and stop with a jerk; then to nod a little further forward, and stop with another jerk; then to recover herself; then to come forward again – lower – lower – lower – by very slow degrees, until, just as it seemed impossible that she could preserve her balance for another instant, and the locksmith was about to call out in an agony, to save her from dashing down upon her forehead and fracturing her skull, then, all of a sudden and without the smallest notice, she would come upright and rigid again with her eyes open, and in her countenance an expression of defiance, sleepy but yet most obstinate, which plainly said 'I've never once closed 'em since I looked at you last, and I'll take my oath of it!'

At length, after the clock had struck two, there was a sound at the street door as if somebody had fallen against the knocker by accident. Miss Miggs immediately jumping up and clapping her hands, cried with a drowsy mingling of the sacred and profane, 'Ally Looyer Mim! there's Simmuns's knock!'

'Who's there?' said Gabriel.

'Me!' cried the well-known voice of Mr Tappertit. Gabriel opened the door, and gave him admission.

He did not cut a very insinuating figure; for a man of his stature suffers in a crowd; and having been active in yesterday morning's work, his dress was literally crushed from head to foot: his hat being beaten out of all shape, and his shoes trodden down at heel like slippers. His coat fluttered in strips about him, the buckles were torn away both from his knees and feet, half his neckerchief was gone, and the bosom of his shirt was rent to tatters. Yet notwithstanding all these personal disadvantages; despite his being very weak from heat and fatigue; and so begrimed with mud and dust that he might have been in a case, for anything of the real texture (either of his skin or apparel) that the eye could discern; he stalked haughtily into the parlour, and throwing himself into a chair, and endeavouring to thrust his hands into the pockets of his small-clothes, which were turned inside out and displayed upon his legs, like tassels, surveyed the household with a gloomy dignity.

'Simon,' said the locksmith gravely, 'How comes it that you

return home at this time of night, and in this condition? Give me an assurance that you have not been among the rioters, and I am satisfied.'

'Sir,' replied Mr Tappertit, with a contemptuous look, 'I wonder at *your* assurance in making such demands.'

'You have been drinking,' said the locksmith.

'As a general principle, and in the most offensive sense of the words, sir,' returned his journeyman with great self-possession, 'I consider you a liar. In that last observation you have unintentionally – unintentionally, sir – struck upon the truth.'

'Martha,' said the locksmith, turning to his wife, and shaking his head sorrowfully, while a smile at the absurd figure before him still played upon his open face, 'I trust it may turn out that this poor lad is not the victim of the knaves and fools we have so often had words about, and who have done so much harm this day. If he has been at Warwick Street or Duke Street to-night – '

'He has been at neither, sir,' cried Mr Tappertit in a loud voice, which he suddenly dropped into a whisper as he repeated, with eyes fixed upon the locksmith, 'he has been at neither.'

'I am glad of it, with all my heart,' said the locksmith in a serious tone; 'for if he had been, and it could be proved against him, Martha, your great association would have been to him the cart that draws men to the gallows and leaves them hanging in the air. It would, as sure as we're alive!'

Mrs Varden was too much scared by Simon's altered manner and appearance, and by the accounts of the rioters which had reached her ears that night, to offer any retort, or to have recourse to her usual matrimonial policy. Miss Miggs wrung her hands, and wept.

'He was not at Duke Street or at Warwick Street, G. Varden,' said Simon, sternly; 'but he *was* at Westminster. Perhaps, sir, he kicked a county member, perhaps sir he tapped a lord – you may stare, sir, I repeat it – blood flowed from noses, and perhaps he tapped a lord. Who knows? This,' he added, putting his hand into his waistcoat-pocket, and taking out a large tooth, at sight of which both Miggs and Mrs Varden screamed, 'this was a bishop's. Beware, G. Varden!'

'Now, I would rather,' said the locksmith hastily, 'have paid five hundred pounds, than had this come to pass. You idiot, do you know what peril you stand in?'

'I know it, sir,' replied his journeyman, 'and it is my glory. I was there, everybody saw me there. I was conspicuous, and prominent. I will abide the consequences.'

The locksmith, really disturbed and agitated, paced to and fro in silence – glancing at his former 'prentice every now and then – and at length stopping before him, said:

'Get to bed, and sleep for a couple of hours that you may wake penitent, and with some of your senses about you. Be sorry for what you have done, and we will try to save you. If I call him by five o'clock,' said Varden, turning hurriedly to his wife, 'and he washes himself clean and changes his dress, he may get to the Tower Stairs,[1] and away by the Gravesend tide-boat, before any search is made for him. From there he can easily get on to Canterbury, where your cousin will give him work till this storm has blown over. I am not sure that I do right in screening him from the punishment he deserves, but he has lived in this house, man and boy, for a dozen years, and I should be sorry if for this one day's work he made a miserable end. Lock the front door Miggs, and show no light towards the street when you go up stairs. Quick, Simon! Get to bed!'

'And do you suppose, sir,' retorted Mr Tappertit, with a thickness and slowness of speech which contrasted forcibly with the rapidity and earnestness of his kind-hearted master – 'and do you suppose, sir, that I am base and mean enough to accept your servile proposition? – Miscreant!'

'Whatever you please, Sim, but get to bed. Every minute is of consequence. The light here, Miggs!'

'Yes yes, oh do! Go to bed directly,' cried the two women together.

Mr Tappertit stood upon his feet, and pushing his chair away to show that he needed no assistance, answered, swaying himself to and fro, and managing his head as if it had no connexion whatever with his body:

'You spoke of Miggs, sir – Miggs may be smothered!'

'Oh Simmun!' ejaculated that young lady in a faint voice. 'Oh mim! Oh sir! Oh goodness gracious, what a turn he has give me!'

'This family may *all* be smothered, sir,' returned Mr Tappertit, after glancing at her with a smile of ineffable disdain, 'excepting Mrs V. I have come here, sir, for her sake this night. Mrs Varden, take this piece of paper. It's a protection, ma'am. You may need it.'

With these words he held out at arm's length, a dirty, crumpled scrap of writing. The locksmith took it from him, opened it, and read as follows:

'All good friends to our cause, I hope will be particular, and do no injury to the property of any true Protestant. I am well assured that the proprietor of this house is a staunch and worthy friend to the cause.

'GEORGE GORDON.'

'What's this!' said the locksmith, with an altered face.

'Something that'll do you good service, young feller,' replied his journeyman, 'as you'll find. Keep that safe, and where you can lay your hand upon it in an instant. And chalk "No Popery" on your door to-morrow night, and for a week to come – that's all.'

'This is a genuine document,' said the locksmith, 'I know, for I have seen the hand before. What threat does it imply? What devil is abroad?'

'A fiery devil,' retorted Sim; 'a flaming, furious devil. Don't you put yourself in its way, or you're done for, my buck. Be warned in time, G. Varden. Farewell!'

But here the two women threw themselves in his way – especially Miss Miggs, who fell upon him with such fervour that she pinned him against the wall – and conjured him in moving words not to go forth till he was sober; to listen to reason; to think of it; to take some rest, and then determine.

'I tell you,' said Mr Tappertit, 'that my mind is made up. My bleeding country calls me, and I go! Miggs, if you don't get out of the way, I'll pinch you.'

Miss Miggs, still clinging to the rebel, screamed once vociferously – but whether in the distraction of her mind, or because of his having executed his threat, is uncertain.

'Release me,' said Simon, struggling to free himself from her chaste, but spider-like embrace. 'Let me go! I have made arrangements for you in an altered state of society, and mean to provide for you comfortably in life – there! Will that satisfy you?'

'Oh Simmun!' cried Miss Miggs. 'Oh my blessed Simmun! Oh mim, what are my feelings at this conflicting moment!'

Of a rather turbulent description, it would seem; for her nightcap had been knocked off in the scuffle, and she was on her knees upon the floor, making a strange revelation of blue and yellow curl-papers, straggling locks of hair, tags of staylaces, and strings of it's impossible to say what; panting for breath, clasping her hands, turning her eyes upwards, shedding abundance of tears, and exhibiting various other symptoms of the acutest mental suffering.

'I leave,' said Simon, turning to his master, with an utter disregard of Miggs's maidenly affliction, 'a box of things up stairs. Do what you like with 'em. *I* don't want 'em. I'm never coming back here, any more. Provide yourself, sir, with a journeyman; I'm my country's journeyman; henceforward that's *my* line of business.'

'Be what you like in two hours' time, but now go up to bed,' returned the locksmith, planting himself in the doorway. 'Do you hear me? Go to bed!'

'I hear you, and defy you, Varden,' rejoined Simon Tappertit. 'This night, sir, I have been in the country, planning an expedition which shall fill your bell-hanging soul with wonder and dismay. The plot demands my utmost energy. Let me pass!'

'I'll knock you down if you come near the door,' replied the locksmith. 'You had better go to bed!'

Simon made no answer, but gathering himself up as straight as he could, plunged head foremost at his old master, and the two went driving out into the workshop together, plying their hands and feet so briskly that they looked like half-a-dozen, while Miggs and Mrs Varden screamed for twelve.

It would have been easy for Varden to knock his old 'prentice down, and bind him hand and foot; but as he was loath to hurt him in his then defenceless state, he contented himself with parrying his blows when he could, taking them in perfect good part when he could not, and keeping between him and the door, until a favourable opportunity should present itself for forcing him to retreat up stairs, and shutting him up in his own room. But in the goodness of his heart, he calculated too much upon his adversary's weakness, and forgot that drunken men who have lost the power of walking steadily, can often run. Watching his time, Simon Tappertit made a cunning show of falling back, staggered unexpectedly forward, brushed past him, opened the door (he knew the trick of that lock well), and darted down the street like a mad dog. The locksmith paused for a moment in the excess of his astonishment, and then gave chace.

It was an excellent season for a run, for at that silent hour the streets were deserted, the air was cool, and the flying figure before him distinctly visible at a great distance, as it sped away, with a long gaunt shadow following at its heels. But the short-winded locksmith had no chance against a man of Sim's youth and spare figure, though the day had been when he could have run him down in no time. The space between them rapidly increased, and as the rays of the rising sun streamed upon Simon in the act of turning a distant corner, Gabriel Varden was fain to give up, and sit down on a door-step to fetch his breath. Simon meanwhile, without once stopping, fled at the same degree of swiftness to the Boot, where, as he well knew, some of his company were lying, and at which respectable hostelry – for he had already acquired the distinction of being in great peril of the law – a friendly watch had been expecting him all night, and was even now on the look-out for his coming.

'Go thy ways, Sim, go thy ways,' said the locksmith, as soon as he could speak. 'I have done my best for thee, poor lad, and would have saved thee, but the rope is round thy neck, I fear.'

So saying, and shaking his head in a very sorrowful and disconsolate manner, he turned back, and soon re-entered his own house, where Mrs Varden and the faithful Miggs had been anxiously expecting his return.

Now Mrs Varden (and by consequence Miss Miggs likewise) was impressed with a secret misgiving that she had done wrong; that she had, to the utmost of her small means, aided and abetted the growth of disturbances, the end of which it was impossible to foresee; that she had led remotely to the scene which had just passed; and that the locksmith's time for triumph and reproach had now arrived indeed. And so strongly did Mrs Varden feel this, and so crest-fallen was she in consequence, that while her husband was pursuing their lost journeyman, she secreted under her chair the little red-brick dwelling-house with the yellow roof, lest it should furnish new occasion for reference to the painful theme; and now hid the same still farther, with the skirts of her dress.

But it happened that the locksmith had been thinking of this very article on his way home, and that, coming into the room and not seeing it, he at once demanded where it was.

Mrs Varden had no resource but to produce it, which she did with many tears, and broken protestations that if she could have known –

'Yes, yes,' said Varden, 'of course – I know that. I don't mean to reproach you, my dear. But recollect from this time that all good things perverted to evil purposes, are worse than those which are naturally bad. A thoroughly wicked woman, is wicked indeed. When religion goes wrong, she is very wrong, for the same reason. Let us say no more about it, my dear.'

So he dropped the red-brick dwelling-house on the floor, and setting his heel upon it, crushed it into pieces. The halfpence, and sixpences, and other voluntary contributions, rolled about in all directions, but nobody offered to touch them, or to take them up.

'That,' said the locksmith, 'is easily disposed of, and I would to Heaven that everything growing out of the same society could be settled as easily.'

'It happens very fortunately, Varden,' said his wife, with her handkerchief to her eyes, 'that in case any more disturbances should happen – which I hope not; I sincerely hope not –'

'I hope so too, my dear.'

'– That in case any should occur, we have the piece of paper which that poor misguided young man brought.'

'Ay, to be sure,' said the locksmith, turning quickly round. 'Where is that piece of paper?'

Mrs Varden stood aghast as he took it from her outstretched hand, tore it into fragments, and threw them under the grate.

'Not use it!' she said.

'Use it!' cried the locksmith. 'No! Let them come and pull the roof about our ears; let them burn us out of house and home; I'd neither have the protection of their leader, nor chalk their howl upon my door, though, for not doing it, they shot me on my own threshold. Use it! Let them come and do their worst. The first man who crosses my door-step on such an errand as theirs, had better be a hundred miles away. Let him look to it. The others may have their will. I wouldn't beg or buy them off, if, instead of every pound of iron in the place, there was a hundred weight of gold. Get you to bed, Martha. I shall take down the shutters and go to work.'

'So early!' said his wife.

'Ay,' replied the locksmith cheerily, 'so early. Come when they may, they shall not find us skulking and hiding, as if we feared to take our portion of the light of day, and left it all to them. So pleasant dreams to you, my dear, and cheerful sleep!'

With that he gave his wife a hearty kiss, and bade her delay no longer, or it would be time to rise before she lay down to rest. Mrs Varden quite amiably and meekly walked up stairs, followed by Miggs, who, although a good deal subdued, could not refrain from sundry stimulative coughs and sniffs by the way, or from holding up her hands in astonishment at the daring conduct of master.

CHAPTER THE FIFTY-SECOND

A mob is usually a creature of very mysterious existence, particularly in a large city. Where it comes from or whither it goes, few men can tell. Assembling and dispersing with equal suddenness, it is as difficult to follow to its various sources as the sea itself; nor does the parallel stop here, for the ocean is not more fickle and uncertain, more terrible when roused, more unreasonable, or more cruel.

The people who were boisterous at Westminster upon the Friday morning, and were eagerly bent upon the work of devastation in Duke Street and Warwick Street at night, were, in the mass, the same. Allowing for the chance accessions of which any crowd is morally sure in a town where there must always be a large number of idle and profligate persons, one and the same mob was at both places. Yet they spread themselves in various directions when they dispersed in the afternoon, made no appointment for re-assembling, had no definite purpose or design, and indeed, for anything they knew, were scattered beyond the hope of future union.

At the Boot, which, as has been shown, was in a manner the head quarters of the rioters, there were not, upon this Friday night, a dozen people. Some slept in the stable and outhouses, some in the common room, some two or three in beds. The rest were in their usual homes or haunts. Perhaps not a score in all lay in the adjacent fields and lanes, and under haystacks, or near the warmth of brick-kilns, who had not their accustomed place of rest beneath the open sky. As to the public ways within the town, they had their ordinary nightly occupants, and no others: the usual amount of vice and wretchedness, but no more.

The experience of one evening, however, had taught the reckless leaders of disturbance, that they had but to show themselves in the streets, to be immediately surrounded by materials which they could only have kept together when their aid was not required, at great risk, expense, and trouble. Once possessed of this secret, they were as confident as if twenty thousand men, devoted to their will, had been encamped about them, and assumed a confidence which could not have been surpassed, though that had really been the case. All day, Saturday, they remained quiet. On Sunday, they rather studied how to keep their men within call, and in full hope, than to follow out, by any very fierce measure, their first day's proceedings.

'I hope,' said Dennis, as, with a loud yawn, he raised his body from a heap of straw on which he had been sleeping, and supporting his head upon his hand, appealed to Hugh on Sunday morning, 'that Muster Gashford allows some rest? Perhaps he'd have us at work again already, eh?'

'It's not his way to let matters drop, you may be sure of that,' growled Hugh in answer. 'I'm in no humour to stir yet, though. I'm as stiff as a dead body, and as full of ugly scratches as if I had been fighting all day yesterday with wild cats.'

'You've so much enthusiasm, that's it,' said Dennis, looking with great admiration at the uncombed head, matted beard, and torn hands and face of the wild figure before him; 'you're such a devil of a fellow. You hurt yourself a hundred times more than you need, because you will be foremost in everything, and will do more than the rest.'

'For the matter of that,' returned Hugh, shaking back his ragged hair and glancing towards the door of the stable in which they lay; 'there's one yonder as good as me. What did I tell you about him? Did I say he was worth a dozen, when you doubted him?'

Mr Dennis rolled lazily over upon his breast, and resting his chin upon his hand in imitation of the attitude in which Hugh lay, said, as he too looked towards the door:

'Ay ay, you knew him brother, you knew him. But who'd suppose to look at that chap now, that he could be the man he is! Isn't it a thousand cruel pities, brother, that instead of taking his nat'ral rest and qualifying himself for further exertions in this here *h*onorable

cause, he should be playing at soldiers like a boy? And his cleanliness too!' said Mr Dennis, who certainly had no reason to entertain a fellow feeling with anybody who was particular on that score: 'what weaknesses he's guilty of, with respect to his cleanliness! At five o'clock this morning, there he was at the pump, though any one would think he had gone through enough the day before yesterday, to be pretty fast asleep at that time. But no – when I woke for a minute or two, there he was at the pump, and if you'd have seen him sticking them peacock's feathers into his hat when he'd done washing – ah! I'm sorry he's such a imperfect character, but the best on us is incomplete in some pint of view or another.'

The subject of this dialogue and of these concluding remarks which were uttered in a tone of philosophical meditation, was, as the reader will have divined, no other than Barnaby, who, with his flag in his hand, stood sentry in the little patch of sunlight at the distant door, or walked to and fro outside, singing softly to himself, and keeping time to the music of some clear church bells. Whether he stood still, leaning with both hands on the flag-staff, or, bearing it upon his shoulder, paced slowly up and down, the careful arrangement of his poor dress, and his erect and lofty bearing, showed how high a sense he had of the great importance of his trust, and how happy and how proud it made him. To Hugh and his companion, who lay in a dark corner of the gloomy shed, he, and the sunlight, and the peaceful Sabbath sound to which he made response, seemed like a bright picture framed by the door, and set off by the stable's blackness. The whole formed such a contrast to themselves, as they lay wallowing, like some obscene animals, in their squalor and wickedness on the two heaps of straw, that for a few moments they looked on without speaking, and felt almost ashamed.

'Ah!' said Hugh at length, carrying it off with a laugh: 'He's a rare fellow is Barnaby, and can do more, with less rest, or meat, or drink, than any of us. As to his soldiering, *I* put him on duty there.'

'Then there was a object in it, and a proper good one too, I'll be sworn,' retorted Dennis with a broad grin, and an oath of the same quality. 'What was it, brother?'

'Why, you see,' said Hugh, crawling a little nearer to him, 'that our noble captain yonder, came in yesterday morning rather the worse for liquor, and was – like you and me – ditto last night.'

Dennis looked to where Simon Tappertit lay coiled upon a truss of hay, snoring profoundly, and nodded.

'And our noble captain,' continued Hugh with another laugh, 'our noble captain and I, have planned for to-morrow a roaring expedition, with good profit in it.'

'Against the papists?' asked Dennis, rubbing his hands.

'Ay, against the papists – against one of 'em at least, that some of us, and I for one, owe a good heavy grudge to.'

'Not Muster Gashford's friend that he spoke to us about in my house, eh?' said Dennis, brimfull of pleasant expectation.

'The same man,' said Hugh.

'That's your sort,' cried Mr Dennis, gaily shaking hands with him, 'that's the kind of game. Let's have revenges and injuries, and all that, and we shall get on twice as fast. Now you talk, indeed!'

'Ha ha ha! The captain,' added Hugh, 'has thoughts of carrying off a woman in the bustle, and – ha ha ha! – and so have I!'

Mr Dennis received this part of the scheme with a wry face, observing that as a general principle he objected to women altogether, as being unsafe and slippery persons on whom there was no calculating with any certainty, and who were never in the same mind for four-and-twenty hours at a stretch. He might have expatiated on this suggestive theme at much greater length, but that it occurred to him to ask what connexion existed between the proposed expedition and Barnaby's being posted at the stable door as sentry; to which Hugh cautiously replied in these words:

'Why, the people we mean to visit, were friends of his once upon a time, and I know that much of him to feel pretty sure that if he thought we were going to do them any harm, he'd be no friend to our side, but would lend a ready hand to the other. So I've persuaded him (for I know him of old) that Lord George has picked him out to guard this place to-morrow while we're away, and that it's a great honour – and so he's on duty now, and as proud of it as if he was a general. Ha ha! What do you say to me for a careful man as well as a devil of a one?'

Mr Dennis exhausted himself in compliments, and then added, 'But about the expedition itself – '

'About that,' said Hugh, 'you shall hear all particulars from me and the great captain conjointly and both together – for see, he's waking up. Rouse yourself lion-heart. Ha ha! Put a good face upon it, and drink again. Another hair of the dog that bit you, captain! Call for drink! There's enough of gold and silver cups and candle-sticks buried underneath my bed,' he added, rolling back the straw, and pointing to where the ground was newly turned, 'to pay for it, if it was a score of casks full. Drink captain!'

Mr Tappertit received these jovial promptings with a very bad grace, being much the worse, both in mind and body, for his two nights of debauch, and but indifferently able to stand upon his legs. With Hugh's assistance, however, he contrived to stagger to the pump; and having refreshed himself with an abundant draught of cold water, and a copious shower of the same refreshing liquid on his head and face, he ordered some rum and milk to be served; and upon that innocent beverage and some biscuits and cheese made a pretty hearty meal. That done, he disposed himself in an easy attitude on the ground beside his two companions (who were carousing after their own tastes), and proceeded to enlighten Mr Dennis in reference to to-morrow's project.

That their conversation was an interesting one, was rendered manifest by its length, and by the close attention of all three. That it was not of an oppressively grave character, but was enlivened by various pleasantries arising out of the subject, was clear from their loud and frequent roars of laughter, which startled Barnaby on his post, and made him wonder at their levity. But he was not sum-moned to join them, until they had eaten, and drunk, and slept, and talked together for some hours; not, indeed, until the twilight; when they informed him that they were about to make a slight demonstration in the streets – just to keep the people's hands in, as it was Sunday night, and the public might otherwise be disappointed – and that he was free to accompany them, if he would.

Without the slightest preparation, saving that they carried clubs and wore the blue cockade, they sallied out into the streets; and, with no more settled design than that of doing as much mischief as they could, paraded them at random. Their numbers rapidly increasing, they soon divided into parties; and agreeing to meet by-and-by, in the fields near Welbeck Street, scoured the town in various directions. The largest body, and that which augmented with the greatest rapidity, was the one to which Hugh and Barnaby belonged. This took its way towards Moorfields, where there was a rich chapel,[1] and in which neighbourhood several Catholic families were known to reside.

Beginning with the private houses so occupied, they broke open the doors and windows; and while they destroyed the furniture and left but the bare walls, made a sharp search for tools and engines of destruction, such as hammers, pokers, axes, saws, and such like instruments. Many of the rioters made belts of cord, of handker-chiefs, or any material they found at hand, and wore these weapons as openly as pioneers upon a field-day.[2] There was not the least disguise or concealment – indeed, on this night, very little excite-ment or hurry. From the chapels, they tore down and took away the very altars, benches, pulpits, pews, and flooring; from the dwelling-houses, the very wainscoting and stairs. This Sunday evening's recreation they pursued like mere workmen who had a certain task to do, and did it. Fifty resolute men might have turned them at any moment; a single company of soldiers could have scattered them like dust; but no man interposed, no authority restrained them, and, except by the terrified persons who fled from their approach, they were as little heeded as if they were pur-suing their lawful occupations with the utmost sobriety and good conduct.

In the same manner, they marched to the place of rendezvous agreed upon, made great fires in the fields, and reserving the most valuable of their spoils, burnt the rest. Priestly garments, images of saints, rich stuffs and ornaments, altar-furniture and household goods, were cast into the flames, and shed a glare on the whole country round; but they danced, and howled, and roared about these fires till they were tired, and were never for an instant checked.

As the main body filed off from this scene of action, and passed down Welbeck Street, they came upon Gashford, who had been a witness of their proceedings, and was walking stealthily along the pavement. Keeping up with him, and yet not seeming to speak, Hugh muttered in his ear:

'Is this better, master?'

'No,' said Gashford. 'It is not.'

'What would you have?' said Hugh. 'Fevers are never at their height at once. They must get on by degrees.'

'I would have you,' said Gashford, pinching his arm with such malevolence that his nails seemed to meet in the skin; 'I would have you put some meaning into your work. Fools! Can you make no better bonfires than of rags and scraps? Can you burn nothing whole?'

'A little patience, master,' said Hugh. 'Wait but a few hours, and you shall see. Look for a redness in the sky, to-morrow night.'

With that, he fell back into his place beside Barnaby; and when the secretary looked after him, both were lost in the crowd.

*

CHAPTER THE FIFTY-THIRD

The next day was ushered in by merry peals of bells, and by the firing of the Tower guns; flags were hoisted on many of the church-steeples; the usual demonstrations were made, in honour of the anniversary of the King's birth-day;[1] and every man went about his pleasure or business, as if the city were in perfect order, and there were no half-smouldering embers in its secret places which on the approach of night would kindle up again, and scatter ruin and dismay abroad. The leaders of the riot, rendered still more daring by the success of last night and by the booty they had acquired, kept steadily together, and only thought of implicating the mass of their followers so deeply that no hope of pardon or reward might tempt them to betray their more notorious confederates into the hands of justice.

Indeed, the sense of having gone too far to be forgiven, held the timid together no less than the bold. Many, who would readily have pointed out the foremost rioters and given evidence against them, felt that escape by that means was hopeless, when their every act had been observed by scores of people who had taken no part in the disturbances; who had suffered in their persons, peace, or property, by the outrages of the mob; who would be most willing witnesses; and whom the government would, no doubt, prefer to any King's evidence that might be offered. Many of this class had deserted their usual occupations on the Saturday morning; some had been seen by their employers, active in the tumult; others knew they must be suspected, and that they would be discharged if they returned; others had been desperate from the beginning, and comforted themselves with the homely proverb, that, being hung at all, they might as well be hung for a sheep as a lamb. They all hoped and believed, in a greater or less degree, that the government they seemed to have paralyzed, would, in its terror, come to terms with them in the end, and suffer them to make their own conditions. The least sanguine among them reasoned with himself that, at the worst, they were too many to be all punished, and that he had as good a chance of escape as any other man. The great mass never reasoned or thought at all, but were stimulated by their own headlong passions, by poverty, by ignorance, by the love of mischief, and the hope of plunder.

One other circumstance is worthy of remark; and that is, that from the moment of their first outbreak at Westminster, every symptom of order or preconcerted arrangement among them, vanished. When they divided into parties and ran to different quarters of the town, it was on the spontaneous suggestion of the moment. Each party swelled as it went along, like rivers as they roll towards the sea; new leaders sprang up as they were wanted, disappeared when the necessity was over, and reappeared at the next crisis. Each tumult took shape and form, from the circumstances of the moment; sober workmen going home from their day's labour, were seen to cast down their baskets of tools and become rioters in an instant; mere boys on errands did the like. In a word, a moral plague ran through the city. The noise, and hurry, and excitement, had for hundreds and hundreds an attraction they had no firmness to resist. The contagion spread, like a dread fever: an infectious madness, as yet not near its height, seized on new victims every hour, and society began to tremble at their ravings.

It was between two and three o'clock in the afternoon when Gashford looked into the lair described in the last chapter, and seeing only Barnaby and Dennis there, inquired for Hugh.

He was out, Barnaby told him; had gone out more than an hour ago; and had not yet returned.

'Dennis!' said the smiling secretary, in his smoothest voice, as he sat down cross-legged on a barrel, 'Dennis!'

The hangman struggled into a sitting posture directly, and with his eyes wide open, looked towards him.

'How do you do, Dennis?' said Gashford, nodding. 'I hope you have suffered no inconvenience from your late exertions, Dennis?'

'I always will say of you, Muster Gashford,' returned the hangman, staring at him, 'that that 'ere quiet way of yours might almost wake a dead man. It is,' he added with a muttered oath – still staring at him in a thoughtful manner – 'so awful sly!'

'So distinct, eh Dennis?'

'Distinct!' he answered, scratching his head, and keeping his eyes upon the secretary's face; 'I seem to hear it, Muster Gashford, in my wery bones.'

'I am very glad your sense of hearing is so sharp, and that I succeed in making myself so intelligible,' said Gashford, in his unvarying, even tone. 'Where is your friend?'

Mr Dennis looked round as in expectation of beholding him asleep upon his bed of straw; then remembering that he had seen him go out, replied:

'I can't say where he is, Muster Gashford, I expected him back afore now. I hope it isn't time that we was busy, Muster Gashford?'

'Nay,' said the secretary, 'who should know that as well as you? How can *I* tell you, Dennis? You are perfect master of your own actions, you know, and accountable to nobody – except sometimes to the law, eh?'

Dennis, who was very much baffled by the cool matter-of-course manner of this reply, recovered his self-possession on his professional pursuits being referred to, and pointing towards Barnaby, shook his head and frowned.

'Hush!' cried Barnaby.

'Ah! Do hush about that, Muster Gashford,' said the hangman in a low voice, 'pop'lar prejudices – you always forget – well, Barnaby, my lad, what's the matter?'

'I hear him coming,' he answered: 'Hark! Do you mark that? That's his foot! Bless you, I know his step, and his dog's too. Tramp, tramp, pit-pat, on they come together, and, ha ha ha! – and here they are!' he cried joyfully, welcoming Hugh with both hands, and then patting him fondly on the back, as if instead of being the rough companion he was, he had been one of the most prepossessing of men. 'Here he is, and safe too! I am glad to see him back again, old Hugh!'

'I'm a Turk if he don't give me a warmer welcome always than any man of sense,' said Hugh, shaking hands with him with a kind of ferocious friendship, strange enough to see. 'How are you, boy?'

'Hearty!' cried Barnaby, waving his hat. 'Ha ha ha! And merry too, Hugh! And ready to do anything for the good cause, and the right, and to help the kind, mild, pale-faced gentleman – the Lord they use so ill – eh, Hugh?'

'Ay!' returned his friend, dropping his hand, and looking at

Gashford for an instant with a changed expression before he spoke to him. 'Good day, master!'

'And good day to you,' replied the secretary, nursing his leg. 'And many good days – whole years of them, I hope. You are heated.'

'So would you have been, master,' said Hugh, wiping his face, 'if you'd been running here as fast as I have.'

'You know the news then? Yes, I supposed you would have heard it.'

'News! what news!'

'You don't?' cried Gashford, raising his eyebrows with an exclamation of surprise. 'Dear me! Come; then I *am* the first to make you acquainted with your distinguished position, after all. Do you see the King's Arms a-top?' he smilingly asked, as he took a large paper from his pocket, unfolded it, and held it out for Hugh's inspection.

'Well!' said Hugh. 'What's that to me?'

'Much. A great deal,' replied the secretary. 'Read it.'

'I told you, the first time I saw you, that I couldn't read,' said Hugh, impatiently. 'What in the Devil's name's inside of it?'

'It is a proclamation from The King in Council,' said Gashford, 'dated to-day, and offering a reward of five hundred pounds – five hundred pounds is a great deal of money, and a large temptation to some people – to any one who will discover the person or persons most active in demolishing those chapels on Saturday night.'[2]

'Is that all?' cried Hugh, with an indifferent air. 'I knew of that.'

'Truly I might have known you did,' said Gashford, smiling, and folding up the document again. 'Your friend, I might have guessed – indeed I did guess – was sure to tell you.'

'My friend!' stammered Hugh, with an unsuccessful effort to appear surprised. 'What friend?'

'Tut tut – do you suppose I don't know where you have been?' retorted Gashford, rubbing his hands, and beating the back of one on the palm of the other, and looking at him with a cunning eye. 'How dull you think me! Shall I say his name?'

'No,' said Hugh, with a hasty glance towards Dennis.

'You have also heard from him, no doubt,' resumed the secretary, after a moment's pause, 'that the rioters who have been taken (poor fellows) are committed for trial, and that some very active witnesses have had the temerity to appear against them. Among others –'

and here he clenched his teeth, as if he would suppress, by force, some violent words that rose upon his tongue; and spoke very slowly. 'Among others, a gentleman who saw the work going on in Warwick Street; a Catholic gentleman; one Haredale.'

Hugh would have prevented his uttering the word, but it was out already. Hearing the name, Barnaby turned swiftly round.

'Duty, duty, bold Barnaby!' cried Hugh, assuming his wildest and most rapid manner, and thrusting into his hand his staff and flag which leant against the wall. 'Mount guard without loss of time, for we are off upon our expedition. Up, Dennis, and get ready. Take care that no one turns the straw upon my bed, brave Barnaby; we know what's underneath it – eh? Now, master, quick! What you have to say, say speedily, for the little captain and a cluster of 'em are in the fields, and only waiting for us. Sharp's the word, and strike's the action. Quick!'

Barnaby was not proof against this bustle and despatch. The look of mingled astonishment and anger which had appeared in his face when he turned towards them, faded from it, as the words passed from his memory, like breath from a polished mirror; and grasping the weapon which Hugh forced upon him, he proudly took his station at the door, beyond their hearing.

'You might have spoiled our plans, master,' said Hugh. '*You*, too, of all men!'

'Who would have supposed that *he* would be so quick?' urged Gashford.

'He's as quick sometimes – I don't mean with his hands, for that you know, but with his head – as you, or any man,' said Hugh. 'Dennis, it's time we were going; they're waiting for us; I came to tell you. Reach me my stick and belt. Here! Lend a hand, master. Fling this over my shoulder, and buckle it behind, will you?'

'Brisk as ever!' said the secretary, adjusting it for him as he desired.

'A man need be brisk to-day; there's brisk work a-foot.'

'There is, is there?' said Gashford. He said it with such a provoking assumption of ignorance, that Hugh, looking over his shoulder and angrily down upon him, replied:

'Is there! You know there is! Who knows better than you, master, that the first great step to be taken is to make examples of these witnesses, and frighten all men from appearing against us or any of our body, any more?'

'There's one we know of,' returned Gashford, with an expressive smile, 'who is at least as well informed upon that subject as you or I.'

'If we mean the same gentleman, as I suppose we do,' Hugh rejoined, softly, 'I tell you this – he's as good and quick information about everything as –' here he paused and looked round, as if to make quite sure that the person in question was not within hearing – 'as Old Nick himself. Have you done that, master? How slow you are!'

'It's quite fast now,' said Gashford, rising. 'I say – you didn't find that your friend disapproved of to-day's little expedition? Ha ha ha! It is fortunate it jumps so well with the witness policy; for, once planned, it must have been carried out. And now you are going, eh?'

'Now we are going, master!' Hugh replied. 'Any parting words?'

'Oh dear, no,' said Gashford sweetly. 'None!'

'You're sure?' cried Hugh, nudging the grinning Dennis.

'Quite sure, eh, Muster Gashford?' chuckled the hangman.

Gashford paused a moment, struggling with his caution and his malice; then putting himself between the two men, and laying a hand upon the arm of each, said, in a cramped whisper:

'Do not, my good friends – I am sure you will not – forget our talk one night – in your house, Dennis – about this person. No merey, no quarter, no two beams of his house to be left standing where the builder placed them! Fire, the saying goes, is a good servant, but a bad master. Make it *his* master; he deserves no better. But I am sure you will be firm, I am sure you will be very resolute, I am sure you will remember that he thirsts for your lives, and those of all your brave companions. If you ever acted like stanch fellows, you will do so to-day. Won't you, Dennis – won't you, Hugh?'

The two looked at him, and at each other; then bursting into a roar of laughter, brandished their staves above their heads, shook hands, and hurried out.

When they had been gone a little time, Gashford followed. They were yet in sight, and hastening to that part of the adjacent fields in which their fellows had already mustered; Hugh was looking back, and flourishing his hat to Barnaby, who, delighted with his trust, replied in the same manner, and then resumed his pacing up and down before the stable-door, where his feet had worn a path already. And when Gashford himself was far distant, and looked back for the last time, he was still walking to and fro, with the same measured tread; the most devoted and the blithest champion that ever maintained a post, and felt his heart lifted up with a brave sense of duty, and determination to defend it to the last.

Smiling at the simplicity of the poor idiot, Gashford betook himself to Welbeck Street by a different path from that which he knew the rioters would take, and sitting down behind a curtain in one of the upper windows of Lord George Gordon's house, waited impatiently for their coming. They were so long, that although he knew it had been settled they should come that way, he had a misgiving they must have changed their plans and taken some other route. But at length the roar of voices was heard in the neighbouring fields, and soon afterwards they came thronging past, in a great body.

However, they were not all, nor nearly all, in one body, but were, as he soon found, divided into four parties, each of which stopped before the house to give three cheers, and then went on; the leaders crying out in what direction they were going, and calling on the spectators to join them. The first detachment, carrying, by way of banners, some relics of the havoc they had made in Moorfields, proclaimed that they were on their way to Chelsea, whence they would return in the same order, to make of the spoil they bore, a great bonfire, near at hand. The second gave out that they were bound for Wapping, to destroy a chapel; the third, that their place of destination was East Smithfield,³ and their object the same. All this was done in broad, bright, summer day. Gay carriages and chairs stopped to let them pass, or turned back to avoid them; people on foot stood aside in doorways, or perhaps knocked and begged permission to stand at a window, or in the hall, until the rioters had passed: but nobody interfered with them; and directly they had gone by, everything went on as usual.

There still remained the fourth body, and for that the secretary looked with a most intense eagerness. At last it came up. It was numerous, and composed of picked men; for as he gazed down among them, he recognised many upturned faces which he knew well – those of Simon Tappertit, Hugh, and Dennis in the front, of course. They halted and cheered, as the others had done; but when they moved again, they did not, like them, proclaim what

design they had. Hugh merely raised his hat upon the bludgeon he
carried, and glancing at a spectator on the opposite side of the way,
was gone.

Gashford followed the direction of his glance instinctively, and
saw, standing on the pavement, and wearing the blue cockade, Sir
John Chester. He held his hat an inch or two above his head, to
propitiate the mob; and, resting gracefully on his cane, smiling
pleasantly, and displaying his dress and person to the very
best advantage, looked on in the most tranquil state imaginable.
For all that, and quick and dexterous as he was, Gashford had
seen him recognise Hugh with the air of a patron. He had no
longer any eyes for the crowd, but fixed his keen regards upon
Sir John.

He stood in the same place and posture, until the last man in the
concourse had turned the corner of the street; then very deliberately
took the blue cockade out of his hat; put it carefully in his pocket,
ready for the next emergency; refreshed himself with a pinch of
snuff; put up his box; and was walking slowly off, when a passing
carriage stopped, and a lady's hand let down the glass. Sir John's
hat was off again immediately. After a minute's conversation at the
carriage-window, in which it was apparent that he was vastly
entertaining on the subject of the mob, he stepped lightly in, and
was driven away.

The secretary smiled, but he had other thoughts to dwell upon,
and soon dismissed the topic. Dinner was brought him, but he sent
it down untasted; and, in restless pacings up and down the room,
and constant glances at the clock, and many futile efforts to sit
down and read, or go to sleep, or look out of the window, consumed
four weary hours. When the dial told him thus much time had crept
away, he stole up stairs to the top of the house, and coming out
upon the roof sat down, with his face towards the east.

Heedless of the fresh air that blew upon his heated brow, of
the pleasant meadows from which he turned, of the piles of roofs
and chimneys upon which he looked, of the smoke and rising mist
he vainly sought to pierce, of the shrill cries of children at their
evening sports, the distant hum and turmoil of the town, the
cheerful country breath that rustled past to meet it, and to droop,
and die; he watched, and watched, till it was dark – save for the
specks of light that twinkled in the streets below and far away –

and, as the darkness deepened, strained his gaze and grew more eager yet.

'Nothing but gloom in that direction, still!' he muttered restlessly. 'Dog! where is the redness in the sky, you promised me!'

CHAPTER THE FIFTY-FOURTH

Rumours of the prevailing disturbances had by this time begun to be pretty generally circulated through the towns and villages round London, and the tidings were everywhere received with that appetite for the marvellous and love of the terrible which have probably been among the natural characteristics of mankind since the creation of the world. These accounts, however, appeared, to many persons at that day, as they would to us at the present, but that we know them to be matter of history, so monstrous and improbable, that a great number of those who were resident at a distance, and who were credulous enough on other points, were really unable to bring their minds to believe that such things could be; and rejected the intelligence they received on all hands, as wholly fabulous and absurd.

Mr Willet – not so much, perhaps, on account of his having argued and settled the matter with himself, as by reason of his constitutional obstinacy – was one of those who positively refused to entertain the current topic for a moment. On this very evening, and perhaps at the very time when Gashford kept his solitary watch, old John was so red in the face with perpetually shaking his head in contradiction of his three ancient cronies and pot companions, that he was quite a phenomenon to behold; and lighted up the Maypole Porch wherein they sat together, like a monstrous carbuncle in a fairy tale.[1]

'Do you think, sir,' said Mr Willet, looking hard at Solomon Daisy, for it was his custom in cases of personal altercation to fasten upon the smallest man in the party – 'do you think sir, that I'm a born fool?'

'No, no, Johnny,' returned Solomon, looking round upon the little circle of which he formed a part: 'We all know better than that. You're no fool Johnny. No, no!'

Mr Cobb and Mr Parkes shook their heads in unison, muttering 'No, no, Johnny, not you!' But as such compliments had usually the effect of making Mr Willet rather more dogged than before, he surveyed them with a look of deep disdain, and returned for answer:

'Then what do you mean by coming here, and telling me that this evening you're a going to walk up to London together – you three – you – and have the evidence of your own senses? An't,' said Mr Willet, putting his pipe in his mouth with an air of solemn disgust, 'an't the evidence of *my* senses enough for you?'

'But we haven't got it Johnny,' pleaded Parkes, humbly.

'You haven't got it sir?' repeated Mr Willet, eyeing him from top to toe. 'You haven't got it, sir? You *have* got it, sir. Don't I tell you that His blessed Majesty King George the Third would no more stand a rioting and rollicking in his streets, than he'd stand being crowed over by his own Parliament?'

'Yes Johnny, but that's your sense – not your senses,' said the adventurous Mr Parkes.

'How do *you* know,' retorted John with great dignity. 'You're a contradicting pretty free, you are sir. How do *you* know which it is? I'm not aware I ever told you, sir.'

Mr Parkes, finding himself in the position of having got into metaphysics without exactly seeing his way out of them, stammered forth an apology and retreated from the argument. There then ensued a silence of some ten minutes or quarter of an hour, at the expiration of which period Mr Willet was observed to rumble and shake with laughter, and presently remarked, in reference to his late adversary, 'that he hoped he had tackled him enough.' Thereupon Messrs Cobb and Daisy laughed, and nodded, and Parkes was looked upon as thoroughly and effectually put down.

'Do you suppose if all this was true, that Mr Haredale would be constantly away from home, as he is?' said John, after another silence. 'Do you think he wouldn't be afraid to leave his house with them two young women in it, and only a couple of men, or so?'

'Ay, but then you know,' returned Solomon Daisy, 'his house is a goodish way out of London, and they do say that the rioters won't go more than two mile, or three at farthest, off the stones. Besides, you know, some of the Catholic gentlefolks have actually sent trinkets and such-like down here for safety – at least, so the story goes.'

'The story goes!' said Mr Willet testily. 'Yes, sir. The story goes that you saw a ghost last March. But nobody believes it.'

'Well!' said Solomon, rising, to divert the attention of his two friends, who tittered at this retort: 'believed or disbelieved, it's true; and true or not, if we mean to go to London, we must be going at once. So shake hands, Johnny, and good night.'

'I shall shake hands,' returned the landlord, putting his into his pockets, 'with no man as goes to London on such nonsensical errands.'

The three cronies were therefore reduced to the necessity of shaking his elbows; having performed that ceremony, and brought from the house their hats, and sticks, and great-coats, they bade him good night and departed; promising to bring him on the morrow full and true accounts of the real state of the city, and if it were quiet, to give him the full merit of his victory.

John Willet looked after them, as they plodded along the road in the rich glow of a summer evening; and knocking the ashes out of his pipe, laughed inwardly at their folly, until his sides were sore. When he had quite exhausted himself – which took some time, for he laughed as slowly as he thought and spoke – he sat himself comfortably with his back to the house, put his legs upon the bench, then his apron over his face, and fell sound asleep.

How long he slept, matters not; but it was for no brief space, for when he awoke, the rich light had faded, the sombre hues of night were falling fast upon the landscape, and a few bright stars were already twinkling over-head. The birds were all at roost, the daisies on the green had closed their fairy hoods, the honeysuckle twining round the porch exhaled its perfume in a twofold degree, as though it lost its coyness at that silent time and loved to shed its fragrance on the night; the ivy scarcely stirred its deep green leaves. How tranquil, and how beautiful it was!

Was there no sound in the air, besides the gentle rustling of the trees and the grasshopper's merry chirp? Hark! Something very faint and distant, not unlike the murmuring in a sea-shell. Now it grew louder, fainter now, and now it altogether died away. Presently – it came again, subsided, came once more; grew louder, fainter, swelled into a roar. It was on the road, and varied with its windings. All at once it burst with a distinct sound – the voices, and the tramping feet of many men.

It is questionable whether old John Willet, even then, would have thought of the rioters, but for the cries of his cook and house-maid, who ran screaming up stairs and locked themselves into one of the old garrets, – shrieking dismally when they had done so, by way of rendering their place of refuge perfectly secret and secure. These two females did afterwards depone that Mr Willet in his consternation uttered but one word, and called that up the stairs in a stentorian voice, six distinct times. But as this word was a monosyllable, which, however inoffensive when applied to the quadruped it denotes, is highly reprehensible when used in con-nexion with females of unimpeachable character, many persons were inclined to believe that the young women laboured under some hallucination caused by excessive fear; and that their ears deceived them.

Be this as it may, John Willet, in whom the very uttermost extent of dull-headed perplexity supplied the place of courage, stationed himself in the porch, and waited for their coming up. Once, it dimly occurred to him that there was a kind of door to the house, which had a lock and bolts; and at the same time some shadowy ideas of shutters to the lower windows, flitted through his brain. But he stood stock still, looking down the road in the direction in which the noise was rapidly advancing, and did not so much as take his hands out of his pockets.

He had not to wait long. A dark mass, looming through a cloud of dust, soon became visible; the mob quickened their pace; shouting and whooping like savages, they came rushing on pell-mell; and in a few seconds he was bandied from hand to hand, in the heart of a crowd of men.

'Halloa!' cried a voice he knew, as the man who spoke came cleaving through the throng. 'Where is he? Give him to me. Don't hurt him. How now, old Jack! Ha ha ha!'

Mr Willet looked at him, and saw it was Hugh; but he said nothing, and thought nothing.

'These lads are thirsty and must drink!' cried Hugh, thrusting him back towards the house. 'Bustle, Jack, bustle. Show us the best – the very best – the over-proof that you keep for your own drink-ing, Jack!'

John faintly articulated the words, 'Who's to pay?'

'He says "Who's to pay!"' cried Hugh, with a roar of laughter which was loudly echoed by the crowd. Then turning to John, he added, 'Pay! Why, nobody.'

John stared round at the mass of faces – some grinning, some fierce, some lighted up by torches, some indistinct, some dusky and shadowy: some looking at him, some at his house, some at each other – and while he was, as he thought, in the very act of doing so, found himself, without any consciousness of having moved, in the bar; sitting down in an arm-chair, and watching the destruction of his property, as if it were some queer play or entertainment, of an astonishing and stupefying nature, but having no reference to himself – that he could make out – at all.

Yes. Here was the bar – the bar that the boldest never entered without special invitation – the sanctuary, the mystery, the hallowed ground: here it was, crammed with men, clubs, sticks, torches, pistols; filled with a deafening noise, oaths, shouts, screams, hootings; changed all at once into a bear-garden, a madhouse, an infernal temple: men darting in and out, by door and window, smashing the glass, turning the taps, drinking liquor out of China punchbowls, sitting astride of casks smoking private and personal pipes, cutting down the sacred grove of lemons, hacking and hewing at the celebrated cheese, breaking open inviolable drawers, putting things in their pockets which didn't belong to them, dividing his own money before his own eyes, wantonly wasting, breaking, pulling down and tearing up: nothing quiet, nothing private: men everywhere – above, below, overhead, in the bedrooms, in the kitchen, in the yard, in the stables – clambering in at windows when there were doors wide open; dropping out of windows when the stairs were handy; leaping over the banisters into chasms of passages: new faces and figures presenting themselves every instant – some yelling, some singing, some fighting, some breaking glass and crockery, some laying the dust with the liquor they couldn't drink, some ringing the bells till they pulled them down, others beating them with pokers till they beat them into fragments: more men still – more, more, more – swarming on like insects: noise, smoke, light, darkness, frolic, anger, laughter, groans, plunder, fear, and ruin!

Nearly all the time while John looked on at this bewildering scene, Hugh kept near him; and though he was the loudest, wildest,

most destructive villain there, he saved his old master's bones a score of times. Nay, even when Mr Tappertit, excited by liquor, came up, and in assertion of his prerogative politely kicked John Willet on the shins, Hugh bade him return the compliment; and if old John had had sufficient presence of mind to understand this whispered direction, and to profit by it, he might no doubt, under Hugh's protection, have done so with impunity.

At length the band began to reassemble outside the house, and to call to those within, to join them, for they were losing time. These murmurs increasing, and attaining a very high pitch, Hugh, and some of those who yet lingered in the bar, and who plainly were the leaders of the troop, took counsel together apart as to what was to be done with John, to keep him quiet until their Chigwell work was over. Some proposed to set the house on fire and leave him in it; others that he should be reduced to a state of temporary insensibility, by knocking on the head; others that he should be sworn to sit where he was until to-morrow at the same hour; others again that he should be gagged and taken off with them, under a sufficient guard. All these propositions being over-ruled, it was concluded, at last, to bind him in his chair, and the word was passed for Dennis.

'Look'ee here, Jack!' said Hugh, striding up to him: 'We're going to tie you, hand and foot, but otherwise you won't be hurt. D'ye hear?'

John Willet looked at another man, as if he didn't know which was the speaker, and muttered something about an ordinary every Sunday at two o'clock.

'You won't be hurt I tell you, Jack – do you hear me?' roared Hugh, impressing the assurance upon him by means of a heavy blow on the back. 'He's so dead scared, he's wool-gathering, I think. Ha ha! Give him a drop of something to drink here. Hand over, one of you.'

A glass of liquor being passed forward, Hugh poured the contents down old John's throat. Mr Willet feebly smacked his lips, thrust his hand into his pocket, and inquired what was to pay; adding, as he looked vacantly round, that he believed there was a trifle of broken glass –

'He's out of his senses for the time, it's my belief,' said Hugh, after shaking him, without any visible effect upon his system, until his keys rattled in his pocket. 'Where's that Dennis?'

The word was again passed, and presently Mr Dennis, with a long cord bound about his middle, something after the manner of a friar, came hurrying in, attended by a body-guard of half-a-dozen of his men.

'Come! Be alive here!' cried Hugh, stamping his foot upon the ground. 'Make haste!'

Dennis, with a wink and a nod, unwound the cord from about his person, and raising his eyes to the ceiling, looked all over it, and round the walls and cornice, with a curious eye; then shook his head.

'Move man, can't you!' cried Hugh, with another impatient stamp of his foot. 'Are we to wait here till the cry has gone for ten miles round, and our work's interrupted?'

'It's all very fine talking, brother,' answered Dennis, stepping towards him; 'but unless – ' and here he whispered in his ear – 'unless we do it over the door, it can't be done at all in this here room.'

'What can't?' Hugh demanded.

'What can't!' retorted Dennis. 'Why, the old man can't.'

'Why, you weren't going to hang him?' cried Hugh.

'No, brother!' returned the hangman, with a stare. 'What else?'

Hugh made no answer, but snatching the rope from his companion's hand, proceeded to bind old John himself; but his very first move was so bungling and unskilful, that Mr Dennis entreated, almost with tears in his eyes, that he might be permitted to perform the duty. Hugh consenting, he achieved it in a twinkling.

'There!' he said, looking mournfully at John Willet, who displayed no more emotion in his bonds than he had shown out of them. 'That's what I call pretty, and workmanlike. He's quite a picter now. But, brother, just a word with you – now that he's ready trussed, as one may say, wouldn't it be better for all parties if we was to work him off? It would read uncommon well in the newspapers, it would indeed. The public would think a great deal more on us!'

Hugh, inferring what his companion meant, rather from his gestures than his technical mode of expressing himself (to which, as he was ignorant of his calling, he wanted the clue), rejected this proposition for the second time, and gave the word 'Forward!' which was echoed by a hundred voices from without.

'To the Warren!' shouted Dennis as he ran out, followed by the rest. 'A witness's house, my lads!'

A loud yell followed, and the whole throng hurried off, mad for pillage and destruction. Hugh lingered behind for a few moments to stimulate himself with more drink, and to set all the taps running, a few of which had accidentally been spared; then glancing round the despoiled and plundered room, through whose shattered window the rioters had thrust the Maypole itself, – for even that had been sawn down, – lighted a torch; clapped the mute and motionless John Willet on the back; and waving it above his head, and uttering a fierce shout, hastened after his companions.

*

CHAPTER THE FIFTY-FIFTH

John Willet, left alone in his dismantled bar, continued to sit staring about him; awake as to his eyes, certainly, but with all his powers of reason and reflection in a sound and dreamless sleep. He looked round upon the room which had been for years, and was within an hour ago, the pride of his heart; and not a muscle of his face was moved. The night, without, looked black and cold through the dreary gaps in the casement; the precious liquids, now nearly leaked away, dripped with a hollow sound upon the floor; the Maypole peered ruefully in through the broken window, like the bowsprit of a wrecked ship; the ground might have been the bottom of the sea, it was so strewn with precious fragments. Currents of air rushed in, as the old doors jarred and creaked upon their hinges; the candles flickered and guttered down, and made long winding-sheets;[1] the cheery deep-red curtains flapped and fluttered idly in the road; even the stout Dutch kegs, overthrown and lying empty in dark corners, seemed the mere husks of good fellows whose jollity had departed, and who could kindle with a friendly glow no more. John saw this desolation, and yet saw it not. He was perfectly contented to sit there staring at it, and felt no more indignation or discomfort in his bonds than if they had been robes of honour. So far as he was personally concerned, old Time lay snoring, and the world stood still.

Save for the dripping from the barrels, the rustling of such light fragments of destruction as the wind affected, and the dull creaking of the open doors, all was profoundly quiet: indeed these sounds, like the ticking of the death-watch in the night, only made the silence they invaded deeper and more apparent. But quiet or noisy, it was all one to John. If a train of heavy artillery could have come up and commenced ball practice outside the window, it would have been all the same to him. He was a long way beyond surprise. A ghost couldn't have overtaken him.

By and by he heard a footstep – a hurried, and yet cautious footstep – coming on towards the house. It stopped, advanced again, then seemed to go quite round it. Having done that, it came beneath the window, and a head looked in.

It was strongly relieved against the darkness outside by the glare of the guttering candles. A pale, worn, withered face; the eyes – but that was owing to its gaunt condition – unnaturally large and bright; the hair a grizzled black. It gave a searching glance all round the room, and a deep voice said:

'Are you alone in this house?'

John made no sign, though the question was repeated twice, and he heard it distinctly. After a moment's pause, the man got in at the window. John was not at all surprised at this, either. There had been so much getting in and out of window in the course of the last hour or so, that he had quite forgotten the door, and seemed to have lived among such exercises from infancy.

The man wore a large, dark, faded cloak, and a slouched hat; he walked up close to John, and looked at him. John returned the compliment with interest.

'How long have you been sitting thus?' said the man.

John considered, but nothing came of it.

'Which way have the party gone?'

Some wandering speculations relative to the fashion of the stranger's boots, got into Mr Willet's mind by some accident or other, but they got out again in a hurry, and left him in his former state.

'You would do well to speak,' said the man: 'you may keep a whole skin, though you have nothing else left that can be hurt. Which way have the party gone?'

'That!' said John, finding his voice all at once, and nodding with perfect good faith – he couldn't point; he was so tightly bound – in exactly the opposite direction to the right one.

'You lie!' said the man angrily, and with a threatening gesture. 'I came that way. You would betray me.'

It was so evident that John's imperturbability was not assumed, but was the result of the late proceedings under his roof, that the man stayed his hand in the very act of striking him, and turned away.

John looked after him without so much as a twitch in a single nerve of his face. He seized a glass, and holding it under one of the little casks until a few drops were collected, drank them greedily off; then dashing it down upon the floor impatiently, he took the vessel in his hands and drained it into his throat. Some scraps of bread and meat were scattered about, and on these he fell next; eating them with great voracity, and pausing every now and then to listen for some fancied noise outside. When he had refreshed himself in this manner with violent haste, and raised another barrel to his lips, he pulled his hat upon his brow as though he were about to leave the house, and turned to John.

'Where are your servants?'

Mr Willet indistinctly remembered to have heard the rioters calling to them to throw the key of the room in which they were, out of window, for their keeping. He therefore replied, 'Locked up.'

'Well for them if they remain quiet, and well for you if you do the like,' said the man. 'Now show me the way the party went.'

This time Mr Willet indicated it correctly. The man was hurrying to the door, when suddenly there came towards them on the wind, the loud and rapid tolling of an alarm bell, and then a bright and vivid glare streamed up, which illumined, not only the whole chamber, but all the country.

It was not the sudden change from darkness to this dreadful light, it was not the sound of distant shrieks and shouts of triumph, it was not this dread invasion of the serenity and peace of night, that drove the man back as though a thunderbolt had struck him. It was the Bell. If the ghastliest shape the human mind has ever pictured in its wildest dreams had risen up before him, he could not have staggered backward from its touch, as he did from the first sound of that loud iron voice. With eyes that started from his head, his limbs convulsed, his face most horrible to see, he raised one arm high up into the air, and holding something visionary, back and down, with his other hand, drove at it as though he held a knife and stabbed it to the heart. He clutched his hair, and stopped his ears, and travelled madly round and round; then gave a frightful cry, and with it rushed away: still, still, the Bell tolled on and seemed to follow him – louder and louder, hotter and hotter yet. The glare grew brighter, the roar of voices deeper; the crash of heavy bodies falling, shook the air; bright streams of sparks rose up into the sky; but louder than them all – rising faster far, to Heaven – a million times more fierce and furious – pouring forth dreadful secrets after its long silence – speaking the language of the dead – the Bell – the Bell!

What hunt of spectres could surpass that dread pursuit and flight! Had there been a legion of them on his track, he could have better borne it. They would have had a beginning and an end, but here all space was full. The one pursuing voice was everywhere: it sounded in the earth, the air; shook the long grass, and howled among the trembling trees. The echoes caught it up, the owls hooted as it flew upon the breeze, the nightingale was silent and hid herself among the thickest boughs: it seemed to goad and urge the angry fire, and lash it into madness; everything was steeped in one prevailing red; the glow was everywhere; nature was drenched in blood: still the remorseless crying of that awful voice – the Bell, the Bell!

It ceased; but not in his ears. The knell was at his heart. No work of man had ever voice like that which sounded there, and warned him that it cried unceasingly to Heaven. Who could hear that bell, and not know what it said! There was murder in its every note – cruel, relentless, savage murder – the murder of a confiding man, by one who held his every trust. Its ringing summoned phantoms from their graves. What face was that, in which a friendly smile changed to a look of half incredulous horror, which stiffened for a moment into one of pain, then changed again into an imploring glance at Heaven, and so fell idly down with upturned eyes, like the dead stags he had often peeped at when a little child: shrinking and shuddering – there was a dreadful thing to think of now! – and clinging to an apron as he looked! He sank upon the ground, and grovelling down as if he would dig himself a place to hide in, covered his face and ears: but no, no, no – a hundred walls and roofs of brass would not shut out that bell, for in it spoke the wrathful voice of God, and from that, the whole wide universe could not afford a refuge!

While he rushed up and down, not knowing where to turn, and

while he lay crouching there, the work went briskly on indeed. When they left the Maypole, the rioters formed into a solid body, and advanced at a quick pace to the Warren. Rumour of their approach having gone before, they found the garden doors fast closed, the windows made secure, and the house profoundly dark: not a light being visible in any portion of the building. After some fruitless ringing at the bells, and beating at the iron gates, they drew off a few paces to reconnoitre, and confer upon the course it would be best to take.

Very little conference was needed, when all were bent upon one desperate purpose, infuriated with liquor, and flushed with successful riot. The word being given to surround the house, some climbed the gates, or dropped into the shallow trench and scaled the garden wall, while others pulled down the solid iron fence, and while they made a breach to enter by, made deadly weapons of the bars. The house being completely encircled, a small number of men were despatched to break open a tool-shed in the garden; and during their absence on this errand, the remainder contented themselves with knocking violently at the doors, and calling to those within, to come down and open them on peril of their lives.

No answer being returned to this repeated summons, and the detachment who had been sent away, coming back with an accession of pickaxes, spades, and hoes, they, – together with those who had such arms already, or carried (as many did) axes, poles, and crow-bars, – struggled into the foremost rank, ready to beset the doors and windows. They had not at this time more than a dozen lighted torches among them; but when these preparations were completed, flaming links were distributed and passed from hand to hand with such rapidity, that, in a minute's time, at least two-thirds of the whole roaring mass, bore, each man in his hand, a blazing brand. Whirling these about their heads they raised a loud shout, and fell to work upon the doors and windows.

Amidst the clattering of heavy blows, the rattling of broken glass, the cries and execrations of the mob, and all the din and turmoil of the scene, Hugh and his friends kept together at the turret door where Mr Haredale had last admitted him and old John Willet; and spent their united force on that. It was a strong old oaken door, guarded by good bolts and a heavy bar, but it soon went crashing in upon the narrow stairs behind, and made, as it were, a platform to facilitate their tearing up into the rooms above. Almost at the same moment, a dozen other points were forced, and at every one the crowd poured in like water.

A few armed servant-men were posted in the hall, and when the rioters forced an entrance there, they fired some half-a-dozen shots. But these taking no effect, and the concourse coming on like an army of devils, they only thought of consulting their own safety, and retreated, echoing their assailants' cries, and hoping in the confusion to be taken for rioters themselves; in which stratagem they succeeded, with the exception of one old man who was never heard of again, and was said to have had his brains beaten out with an iron bar (one of his fellows reported that he had seen the old man fall), and to have been afterwards burnt in the flames.

The besiegers being now in complete possession of the house, spread themselves over it from garret to cellar, and plied their demon labours fiercely. While some small parties kindled bonfires underneath the windows, others broke up the furniture and cast the fragments down to feed the flames below; where the apertures in the wall (windows no longer) were large enough, they hurled out tables, chests of drawers, beds, mirrors, pictures, and flung them whole into the fire; while every fresh addition to the blazing masses was received with shouts, and howls, and yells, which added new and dismal terrors to the conflagration. Those who had axes and had spent their fury on the moveables, chopped and tore down the doors and window frames, broke up the flooring, hewed away the rafters, and buried men who lingered in the upper rooms, in heaps of ruins. Some searched the drawers, the chests, the boxes, writing-desks, and closets, for jewels, plate, and money; while others less mindful of gain and more mad for destruction, cast their whole contents into the court-yard without examination, and called to those below, to heap them on the blaze. Men who had been into the cellars, and had staved the casks, rushed to and fro stark mad, setting fire to all they saw – often to the dresses of their own friends – and kindling the building in so many parts that some had no time for escape, and were seen, with drooping hands and blackened faces, hanging senseless on the window-sills to which they had crawled, until they were sucked and drawn into the burning gulf. The more the fire crackled and raged, the wilder and more cruel the men grew; as though moving in that element they became fiends, and changed their earthly nature for the qualities that give delight in hell.

The burning pile, revealing rooms and passages red hot, through gaps made in the crumbling walls; the tributary fires that licked the outer bricks and stones, with their long forked tongues, and ran up to meet the glowing mass within; the shining of the flames upon the villains who looked on and fed them; the roaring of the angry blaze, so bright and high that it seemed in its rapacity to have swallowed up the very smoke; the living flakes the wind bore rapidly away and hurried on with, like a storm of fiery snow; the noiseless breaking of great beams of wood, which fell like feathers on the heap of ashes, and crumbled in the very act to sparks and powder; the lurid tinge that overspread the sky, and the darkness, very deep by contrast, which prevailed around; the exposure to the coarse, common gaze, of every little nook which usages of home had made a sacred place, and the destruction by rude hands of every little household favourite which old associations made a dear and precious thing: all this taking place – not among pitying looks and friendly murmurs of compassion, but brutal shouts and exultations, which seemed to make the very rats who stood by the old house too long, creatures with some claim upon the pity and regard of those its roof had sheltered: – combined to form a scene never to be forgotten by those who saw it and were not actors in the work, so long as life endured.

And who were they? The alarm-bell rang – and it was pulled by no faint or hesitating hands – for a long time; but not a soul was seen. Some of the insurgents said that when it ceased, they heard the shrieks of women, and saw some garments fluttering in the air, as a party of men bore away no unresisting burdens. No one could say that this was true or false, in such an uproar; but where was Hugh? Who among them had seen him, since the forcing of the doors? The cry spread through the body. Where was Hugh?

'Here!' he hoarsely cried, appearing from the darkness; out of breath, and blackened with the smoke. 'We have done all we can; the fire is burning itself out; and even the corners where it hasn't spread, are nothing but heaps of ruins. Disperse my lads, while the coast's clear; get back by different ways; and meet as usual!' With that he disappeared again, – contrary to his wont, for he was always first to advance, and last to go away, – leaving them to follow homewards as they would.

It was not an easy task to draw off such a throng. If Bedlam gates had been flung open wide, there would not have issued forth such maniacs as the frenzy of that night had made. There were men there, who danced and trampled on the beds of flowers as though they trod down human enemies; and wrenched them from the stalks, like savages who twisted human necks. There were men who cast their lighted torches in the air, and suffered them to fall upon their heads and faces, blistering the skin with deep unseemly burns. There were men who rushed up to the fire, and paddled in it with their hands as if in water; and others who were restrained by force from plunging in, to gratify their deadly longing. On the skull of one drunken lad – not twenty, by his looks – who lay upon the ground with a bottle to his mouth, the lead from the roof came streaming down in a shower of liquid fire, white hot; melting his head like wax. When the scattered parties were collected, men – living yet, but singed as with hot irons – were plucked out of the cellars, and carried off upon the shoulders of others, who strove to wake them as they went along, with ribald jokes, and left them, dead, in the passages of hospitals. But of all the howling throng not one learnt mercy from, or sickened at, these sights; nor was the fierce, besotted, senseless rage of one man glutted.

Slowly, and in small clusters, with hoarse hurrahs and repetitions of their usual cry, the assembly dropped away. The last few red-eyed stragglers reeled after those who had gone before; the distant noise of men calling to each other, and whistling for others whom they missed, grew fainter and fainter; at length even these sounds died away, and silence reigned alone.

Silence indeed! The glare of the flames had sunk into a fitful, flashing light; and the gentle stars, invisible till now, looked down upon the blackening heap. A dull smoke hung upon the ruin, as though to hide it from those eyes of Heaven; and the wind forbore to move it. Bare walls, roof open to the sky – chambers, where the beloved dead had many and many a fair day risen to new life and energy; where so many dear ones had been sad and merry; which were connected with so many thoughts and hopes, regrets and changes – all gone. Nothing left but a dull and dreary blank – a smouldering heap of dust and ashes – the silence and solitude of utter desolation.

CHAPTER THE FIFTY-SIXTH

The Maypole cronies, little dreaming of the change so soon to come upon their favourite haunt, struck through the Forest path upon their way to London; and avoiding the main road, which was hot and dusty, kept to the bye paths and the fields. As they drew nearer to their destination, they began to make inquiries of the people whom they passed, concerning the riots, and the truth or falsehood of the stories they had heard. The answers went far beyond any intelligence that had spread to quiet Chigwell. One man told them that that afternoon the Guards, conveying to Newgate some rioters who had been re-examined, had been set upon by the mob and compelled to retreat; another, that the houses of two witnesses near Clare Market were about to be pulled down when he came away; another, that Sir George Saville's house in Leicester Fields[1] was to be burned that night, and that it would go hard with Sir George if he fell into the people's hands, as it was he who had brought in the Catholic bill. All accounts agreed that the mob were out, in stronger numbers and more numerous parties than had yet appeared; that the streets were unsafe; that no man's house or life was worth an hour's purchase; that the public consternation was increasing every moment; and that many families had already fled the city. One fellow who wore the popular colour, damned them for not having cockades in their hats, and bade them set a good watch to-morrow-night upon the prison doors, for the locks would have a straining; another asked if they were fire-proof, that they walked abroad without the distinguishing mark of all good and true men; and a third who rode on horseback, and was quite alone, ordered them to throw, each man a shilling, in his hat, towards the support of the rioters. Although they were afraid to refuse compliance with this demand, and were much alarmed by these reports, they agreed, having come so far, to go forward, and see the real state of things with their own eyes. So they pushed on quicker, as men do who are excited by portentous news; and ruminating on what they had heard, spoke little to each other.

It was now night, and as they came nearer to the city they had dismal confirmation of this intelligence in three great fires, all close together, which burnt fiercely and were gloomily reflected in the sky. Arriving in the immediate suburbs, they found that almost

every house had chalked upon its door in large characters "No
Popery," that the shops were shut, and that alarm and anxiety were
depicted in every face they passed.

Noting these things with a degree of apprehension which neither
of the three cared to impart, in its full extent, to his companions,
they came to a turnpike gate, which was shut. They were passing
through the turnstile on the path, when a horseman rode up from
London at a hard gallop, and called to the toll-keeper in a voice of
great agitation, to open quickly in the name of God.

The abjuration was so earnest and vehement, that the man, with
a lantern in his hand, came running out – toll-keeper though he
was – and was about to throw the gate open, when happening to
look behind him, he exclaimed, 'Good Heaven, what's that!
Another Fire!'

At this, the three turned their heads, and saw in the distance –
straight in the direction whence they had come – a broad sheet of
flame, casting a threatening light upon the clouds, which glimmered
as though the conflagration were behind them, and showed like a
wrathful sunset.

'My mind misgives me,' said the horseman, 'or I know from what
far building those flames come. Don't stand aghast, my good fellow.
Open the gate!'

'Sir,' cried the man, laying his hand upon his horse's bridle as he
let him through: 'I know you now, sir; be advised by me; do not go
on. I saw them pass, and know what kind of men they are. You
will be murdered.'

'So be it!' said the horseman, looking intently towards the fire,
and not at him who spoke.

'But Sir – Sir,' cried the man, grasping at his rein more tightly
yet, 'if you do go on, wear the blue riband. Here, sir,' he added,
taking one from his own hat, and speaking so earnestly that the
tears stood in his eyes: 'it's necessity, not choice, that makes me
wear it: it's love of life and home, sir. Wear it for this one night, sir;
only for this one night.'

'Do!' cried the three friends, pressing round his horse. 'Mr Haredale – worthy sir – good gentleman – pray be persuaded.'

'Who's that?' cried Mr Haredale, stooping down to look. 'Did I
hear Daisy's voice?'

'You did, sir,' cried the little man. 'Do be persuaded, sir. This
gentleman says very true. Your life may hang upon it.'

'Are you,' said Mr Haredale abruptly, 'afraid to come with me?'
'I, sir? – N-n-no.'

'Put that riband in your hat. If we meet the rioters, swear that I took you prisoner for wearing it. I will tell them so with my own lips; for as I hope for mercy when I die, I will take no quarter from them, nor shall they have quarter from me, if we come hand to hand to-night. Up here – behind me – quick! Clasp me tight round the body, and fear nothing.'

In an instant they were riding away, at full gallop, in a dense cloud of dust, and speeding on like hunters in a dream.

It was well the good horse knew the road he traversed, for never once – no, never once in all the journey – did Mr Haredale cast his eyes upon the ground, or turn them, for an instant, from the light towards which they sped so madly. Once he said in a low voice 'It *is* my house,' but that was the only time he spoke. When they came to dark and doubtful places, he never forgot to put his hand upon the little man to hold him more securely on his seat, but he kept his head erect and his eyes fixed on the fire, then, and always.

The road was dangerous enough, for they went the nearest way – headlong – far from the highway – by lonely lanes and paths, where waggon-wheels had worn deep ruts; where hedge and ditch hemmed in the narrow strip of ground; and tall trees, arching overhead, made it profoundly dark. But on, on, on, with neither stop nor stumble, till they reached the Maypole door, and could plainly see that the fire began to fade, as if for want of fuel.

'Down – for one moment – for but one moment,' said Mr Haredale, helping Daisy to the ground, and following himself. 'Willet – Willet – where are my niece and servants – Willet!'

Crying out to him distractedly, he rushed into the bar. – The landlord bound and fastened to his chair; the place dismantled, stripped, and pulled about his ears; – nobody could have taken shelter here.

He was a strong man, accustomed to restrain himself, and sup-press his strong emotions; but this preparation for what was to follow – though he had seen that fire burning, and knew that his house must be razed to the ground – was more than he could bear. He covered his face with his hands for a moment, and turned away his head.

'Johnny, Johnny,' said Solomon – and the simple-hearted fellow cried outright, and wrung his hands – 'Oh dear old Johnny, here's a change. That the Maypole bar should come to this, and we should live to see it! The old Warren too, Johnny – Mr Haredale – oh, Johnny, what a piteous sight this is!'

Pointing to Mr Haredale as he said these words, little Solomon Daisy put his elbows on the back of Mr Willet's chair, and fairly blubbered on his shoulder.

While Solomon was speaking, old John sat, mute as a stock-fish, staring at him with an unearthly glare, and displaying, by every possible symptom, entire and most complete unconsciousness. But when Solomon was silent again, John followed, with his great round eyes, the direction of his looks, and did appear to have some dawning distant notion that somebody had come to see him.

'You know us, don't you, Johnny?' said the little clerk, rapping himself on the breast. 'Daisy, you know – Chigwell Church – bell-ringer – little desk on Sundays – eh, Johnny?'

Mr Willet reflected for a few moments, and then muttered, as it were mechanically: 'Let us sing to the praise and glory of –'

'Yes, to be sure,' cried the little man, hastily; 'that's it – that's me, Johnny. You're all right now, an't you? Say you're all right, Johnny.'

'All right?' pondered Mr Willet, as if that were a matter entirely between himself and his conscience. 'All right? Ah!'

'They haven't been misusing you with sticks, or pokers, or any other blunt instruments, – have they, Johnny?' asked Solomon, with a very anxious glance at Mr Willet's head. 'They didn't beat you, did they?'

John knitted his brow; looked downwards, as if he were mentally engaged in some arithmetical calculation; then upwards, as if the total would not come at his call; then at Solomon Daisy, from his eyebrow to his shoe-buckle; then very slowly round the bar. And then a great, round, leaden-looking, and not at all transparent tear, came rolling out of each eye, and he said, as he shook his head:

'If they'd only had the goodness to murder me, I'd have thanked 'em kindly.'

'No, no, no, don't say that, Johnny,' whimpered his little friend. 'It's very – very bad, but not quite so bad as that. No, no!'

'Look'ee here, sir!' cried John, turning his rueful eyes on Mr Haredale, who had dropped on one knee, and was hastily beginning to untie his bonds. 'Look'ee here, sir! The very Maypole – the old dumb Maypole – stares in at the winder, as if it said, "John Willet,

John Willet, let's go and pitch ourselves in the nighest pool of water as is deep enough to hold us; for our day is over!"'

'Don't, Johnny, don't,' cried his friend: no less affected by this mournful effort of Mr Willet's imagination, than by the sepulchral tone in which he had spoken for the Maypole. 'Please don't, Johnny!'

'Your loss is great, and your misfortune a heavy one,' said Mr Haredale, looking restlessly towards the door: 'and this is not a time to comfort you. If it were, I am in no condition to do so. Before I leave you, tell me one thing, and try to tell me truly and plainly, I implore you. Have you seen, or heard of Emma?'

'No!' said Mr Willet.

'Nor any one, but these blood-hounds?'

'No!'

'They rode away, I trust in Heaven, before these dreadful scenes began,' said Mr Haredale, who, between his agitation, his eagerness to mount his horse again, and the dexterity with which the cords were tied, had scarcely yet undone one knot. 'A knife, Daisy.'

'You didn't,' said John, looking about, as though he had lost his pocket-handkerchief or some such slight article – 'either of you gentlemen – see a – a coffin anywheres, did you?'

'Willet!' cried Mr Haredale. Solomon dropped the knife, and instantly becoming limp from head to foot, exclaimed 'Good gracious!'

' – Because,' said John, not at all regarding them, 'a dead man called a little time ago, on his way yonder. I could have told you what name was on the plate, if he had brought his coffin with him, and left it behind. If he didn't, it don't signify.'

His landlord, who had listened to these words with breathless attention, started that moment to his feet; and, without a word, drew Solomon Daisy to the door, mounted his horse, took him up behind again, and flew rather than galloped towards the pile of ruins, which that day's sun had shone upon, a stately house. Mr Willet stared after them, listened, looked down upon himself to make quite sure that he was still unbound, and, without any manifestation of impatience, disappointment, or surprise, gently relapsed into the condition from which he had so imperfectly recovered.

Mr Haredale tied his horse to the trunk of a tree, and grasping his companion's arm, stole softly along the footpath, and into what had been the garden of his house. He stopped for an instant to look upon its smoking walls, and at the stars that shone through roof and floor upon the heap of crumbling ashes. Solomon glanced timidly in his face, but his lips were tightly pressed together, a resolute and stern expression sat upon his brow, and not a tear, a look, or gesture indicating grief, escaped him.

He drew his sword; felt for a moment in his breast, as though he carried other arms about him; then grasping Solomon by the wrist again, went with a cautious step all round the house. He looked into every doorway and gap in the wall; retraced his steps at every rustling of the air among the leaves; and searched in every shadowed nook with outstretched hands. Thus they made the circuit of the building: but they returned to the spot from which they had set out, without encountering any human being, or finding the least trace of any concealed straggler.

After a short pause, Mr Haredale shouted twice or thrice. Then cried aloud, 'Is there any one in hiding here, who knows my voice! There is nothing to fear now. If any of my people are near, I entreat them to answer!' He called them all by name; his voice was echoed in many mournful tones; then all was silent as before.

They were standing near the foot of the turret, where the alarm-bell hung. The fire had raged there, and the floors had been sawn, and hewn, and beaten down, besides. It was open to the night; but a part of the staircase still remained, winding upwards from a great mound of dust and cinders. Fragments of the jagged and broken steps offered an insecure and giddy footing here and there, and then were lost again, behind protruding angles of the wall, or in the deep shadows cast upon it by other portions of the ruin; for by this time the moon had risen, and shone brightly.

As they stood here, listening to the echoes as they died away, and hoping in vain to hear a voice they knew, some of the ashes in this turret slipped and rolled down. Startled by the least noise in that melancholy place, Solomon looked up at his companion's face, and saw that he had turned towards the spot, and that he watched and listened keenly.

He covered the little man's mouth with his hand, and looked again. Instantly, with kindling eyes, he bade him on his life keep still, and neither speak nor move. Then holding his breath, and stooping down, he stole into the turret, with his drawn sword in his hand, and disappeared.

Terrified to be left there by himself, under such desolate circumstances, and after all he had seen and heard that night, Solomon would have followed, but there had been something in Mr Haredale's manner and his look, the recollection of which held him spell-bound. He stood rooted to the spot; and scarcely venturing to breathe, looked up with mingled fear and wonder.

Again the ashes slipped and rolled – very, very softly – again – and then again, as though they crumbled underneath the tread of a stealthy foot. And now a figure was dimly visible; climbing very softly; and often stopping to look down: now it pursued its difficult way; and now it was hidden from the view again.

It emerged once more, into the shadowy and uncertain light – higher now, but not much, for the way was steep and toilsome, and its progress very slow. What phantom of the brain did he pursue; and why did he look down so constantly? He knew he was alone. Surely his mind was not affected by that night's loss and agony. He was not about to throw himself headlong from the summit of the tottering wall. Solomon turned sick, and clasped his hands. His limbs trembled beneath him, and a cold sweat broke out upon his pallid face.

If he complied with Mr Haredale's last injunction now, it was because he had not the power to speak or move. He strained his gaze, and fixed it on a patch of moonlight, into which, if he continued to ascend, he must soon emerge. When he appeared there, he would try to call to him.

Again the ashes slipped and crumbled; some stones rolled down, and fell with a dull heavy sound upon the ground below. He kept his eyes upon the piece of moonlight. The figure was coming on, for its shadow was already thrown upon the wall. Now it appeared – and now looked round at him – and now –

The horror-stricken clerk uttered a scream that pierced the air, and cried, 'The ghost again! The ghost!'

Long before the echo of that cry had died away, another form rushed out into the light, flung itself upon the foremost one, knelt down upon its breast, and clutched its throat with both hands.

'Villain!' cried Mr Haredale, in a terrible voice – for it was he. 'Dead and buried, as all men supposed through your infernal arts, but reserved by Heaven for this – at last – at last – I have you. You, whose hands are red with my brother's blood, and that of his faithful servant, shed to conceal your own atrocious guilt – You,

Rudge, double murderer and monster, I arrest you in the name of God, who has delivered you into my hands. Nay. Though you had the strength of twenty men,' he added, as he writhed and struggled, 'you could not escape me, or loosen my grasp to-night!'

— ❋ —

CHAPTER THE FIFTY-SEVENTH

Barnaby, armed as we have seen, continued to pace up and down before the stable-door; glad to be alone again, and heartily rejoicing in the unaccustomed silence and tranquillity. After the whirl of noise and riot in which the last two days had been passed, the pleasures of solitude and peace were enhanced a thousandfold. He felt quite happy; and as he leaned upon his staff and mused, a bright smile overspread his face, and none but cheerful visions floated into his brain.

Had he no thoughts of her, whose sole delight he was, and whom he had unconsciously plunged in such bitter sorrow and such deep affliction? Oh, yes. She was at the heart of all his cheerful hopes and proud reflections. It was she whom all this honour and distinction were to gladden; the joy and profit were for her. What delight it gave her to hear of the bravery of her poor boy! Ah! He would have known that without Hugh's telling him. And what a precious thing it was to know she lived so happily, and heard with so much pride (he pictured to himself her look when they told her) that he was in such high esteem: bold among the boldest, and trusted before them all. And when these frays were over, and the good Lord had conquered his enemies, and they were all at peace again, and he and she were rich, what happiness they would have in talking of these troubled times when he was a great soldier: and when they sat alone together in the tranquil twilight, and she had no longer reason to be anxious for the morrow, what pleasure would he have in the reflection that this was his doing – his – poor foolish Barnaby's; and in patting her on the cheek, and saying with a merry laugh, 'Am I silly now, mother – am I silly now?'

With a lighter heart and step, and eyes the brighter for the happy tear that dimmed them for a moment, Barnaby resumed his walk; and singing gaily to himself, kept guard upon his quiet post.

His comrade Grip, the partner of his watch, though fond of basking in the sunshine, preferred to-day to walk about the stable; having a great deal to do in the way of scattering the straw, hiding under it such small articles as had been casually left about, and haunting Hugh's bed, to which he seemed to have taken a particular attachment. Sometimes Barnaby looked in and called him, and then he came hopping out; but he merely did this as a concession to his master's weakness, and soon returned again to his own grave pursuits: peering into the straw with his bill, and rapidly covering up the place, as if he were whispering secrets to the earth and burying them;[1] constantly busying himself upon the sly; and affecting, whenever Barnaby came past, to look up in the clouds and have nothing whatever on his mind: in short, conducting himself, in many respects, in a more than usually thoughtful, deep, and mysterious manner.

As the day crept on, Barnaby, who had no directions forbidding him to eat and drink upon his post, but had been, on the contrary, supplied with a bottle of beer and a basket of provisions, determined to break his fast, which he had not done since morning. To this end, he sat down on the ground before the door, and putting his staff across his knees in case of alarm or surprise, summoned Grip to dinner.

This call, the bird obeyed with great alacrity; crying, as he sidled up to his master, 'I'm a devil, I'm a devil, I'm a Polly, I'm a kettle, I'm a Protestant, No Popery!' Having learnt this latter sentiment from the gentry among whom he had lived of late, he delivered it with uncommon emphasis.

'Well said, Grip!' cried his master, as he fed him with the daintiest bits. 'Well said, old boy!'

'Never say die, bow wow wow, keep up your spirits, Grip Grip Grip. Holloa! We'll all have tea, I'm a Protestant kettle, No Popery!' cried the raven.

'Gordon for ever, Grip!' cried Barnaby.

The raven, placing his head upon the ground, looked at his master sideways, as though he would have said, 'Say that again!' Perfectly understanding his desire, Barnaby repeated the phrase a great many times. The bird listened with profound attention; sometimes repeating the popular cry in a low voice, as if to compare the two, and try if it would at all help him to this new accomplishment; sometimes flapping his wings, or barking; and sometimes in a kind of desperation drawing a multitude of corks, with extraordinary viciousness.

Barnaby was so intent upon his favourite, that he was not at first aware of the approach of two persons on horseback, who were riding at a foot-pace, and coming straight towards his post. When he perceived them, however, which he did when they were within some fifty yards of him, he jumped hastily up, and ordering Grip within doors, stood with both hands on his staff, waiting until he should know whether they were friends or foes.

He had hardly done so, when he observed that those who advanced were a gentleman and his servant; almost at the same moment, he recognised Lord George Gordon, before whom he stood uncovered, with his eyes turned towards the ground.

'Good day!' said Lord George, not reining in his horse until he was close beside him. 'Well!'

'All quiet, sir, all safe!' cried Barnaby. 'The rest are away – they went by that path – that one. A grand party!'

'Ay?' said Lord George, looking thoughtfully at him. 'And you?' –

'Oh! They left me here to watch – to mount guard – to keep everything secure till they come back. I'll do it, sir, for your sake. You're a good gentleman; a kind gentleman – ay, you are. There are many against you, but we'll be a match for them, never fear!'

'What's that?' said Lord George – pointing to the raven who was peeping out of the stable-door – but still looking thoughtfully, and in some perplexity, it seemed, at Barnaby.

'Why, don't you know!' retorted Barnaby, with a wondering laugh. 'Not know what *he* is! A bird, to be sure. My bird – my friend – Grip.'

'A devil, a kettle, a Grip, a Polly, a Protestant – no Popery!' cried the raven.

'Though, indeed,' added Barnaby, laying his hand upon the neck of Lord George's horse, and speaking softly: 'you had good reason to ask me what he is, for sometimes it puzzles me – and I am used to him – to think he's only a bird. He ha ha! He's my brother, Grip is – always with me – always talking – always merry – eh, Grip?'

The raven answered by an affectionate croak, and hopping on his master's arm, which he held downward for that purpose, submitted with an air of perfect indifference to be fondled, and turned his restless, curious eye, now upon Lord George, and now upon his man.

Lord George, biting his nails in a discomfited manner, regarded Barnaby for some time in silence; then beckoning to his servant, said:

'Come hither, John.'

John Grueby touched his hat, and came.

'Have you ever seen this young man before?' his master asked, in a low voice.

'Twice, my Lord,' said John. 'I saw him in the crowd last night and Saturday.'

'Did – did it seem to you that his manner was at all wild, or strange?' Lord George demanded, faltering.

'Mad,' said John, with emphatic brevity.

'And why do you think him mad, sir?' said his master, speaking in a peevish tone. 'Don't use that word too freely. Why do you think him mad?'

'My Lord,' John Grueby answered, 'look at his dress, look at his eyes, look at his restless way, hear him cry "No Popery!" Mad, my Lord.'

'So because one man dresses unlike another,' returned his angry master, glancing at himself, 'and happens to differ from other men in his carriage and manner, and to advocate a great cause which the corrupt and irreligious desert, he is to be accounted mad, is he?'

'Stark, staring, raving mad, my Lord,' returned the unmoved John.

'Do you say this to my face?' cried his master, turning sharply upon him.

'To any man, my Lord, who asks me,' answered John.

'Mr Gashford, I find, was right,' said Lord George; 'I thought him prejudiced, though I ought to have known a man like him better, than to have supposed it possible!'

'I shall never have Mr Gashford's good word, my Lord,' replied John, touching his hat respectfully, 'and I don't covet it.'

'You are an ill-conditioned, most ungrateful fellow,' said Lord George: 'a spy, for anything I know. Mr Gashford is perfectly correct, as I might have felt convinced he was. I have done wrong to retain you in my service. It is a tacit insult to him as my choice and confidential friend to do so, remembering the cause you sided with, on the day he was maligned at Westminster. You will leave me to-night – nay, as soon as we reach home. The sooner, the better.'

'If it comes to that, I say so too, my Lord. Let Mr Gashford have his will. As to my being a spy, my Lord, you know me better than to believe it, I am sure. I don't know much about causes. My cause is the cause of one man against two hundred; and I hope it always will be.'

'You have said quite enough,' returned Lord George, motioning him to go back. 'I desire to hear no more.'

'If you'll let me add another word, my Lord,' returned John Grueby, 'I'd give this silly fellow a caution not to stay here by himself. The proclamation is in a good many hands already, and it's well known that he was concerned in the business it relates to. He had better get to a place of safety if he can, poor creature.'

'You hear what this man says?' cried Lord George, addressing Barnaby, who had looked on and wondered while this dialogue passed. 'He thinks you may be afraid to remain upon your post, and are kept here perhaps against your will. What do you say?'

'I think, young man,' said John, in explanation, 'that the soldiers may turn out and take you; and that if they do, you will certainly be hung by the neck till you're dead – dead – dead. And I think you'd better go from here, as fast as you can. That's what *I* think.'

'He's a coward, Grip, a coward!' cried Barnaby, putting the raven on the ground, and shouldering his staff. 'Let them come! Gordon for ever! Let them come!'

'Ay!' said Lord George, 'let them! Let us see who will venture to attack a power like ours; the solemn league of a whole people. *This* a madman! You have said well, very well. I am proud to be the leader of such men as you.'

Barnaby's heart swelled within his bosom as he heard these words. He took Lord George's hand and carried it to his lips; patted his horse's crest, as if the affection and admiration he had conceived for the man extended to the animal he rode; then unfurled his flag, and proudly waving it, resumed his pacing up and down.

Lord George, with a kindling eye and glowing cheek, took off his hat, and flourishing it above his head, bade him exultingly Farewell! – then cantered off at a brisk pace; after glancing angrily round to see that his servant followed. Honest John set spurs to his horse and rode after his master, but not before he had again warned Barnaby to retreat, with many significant gestures, which indeed he continued to make, and Barnaby to resist, until the windings of the road concealed them from each other's view.

Left to himself again with a still higher sense of the importance of his post, and stimulated to enthusiasm by the special notice and encouragement of his leader, Barnaby walked to and fro in a delicious trance rather than as a waking man. The sunshine which prevailed around was in his mind. He had but one desire ungratified. If she could only see him now!

The day wore on; its heat was gently giving place to the cool of evening; a light wind sprung up, fanning his long hair, and making the banner rustle pleasantly above his head. There was a freedom and freshness in the sound and in the time, which chimed exactly with his mood. He was happier than ever.

He was leaning on his staff looking towards the declining sun, and reflecting with a smile that he stood sentinel at that moment over buried gold, when two or three figures appeared in the distance, making towards the house at a rapid pace, and motioning with their hands as though they urged its inmates to retreat from some approaching danger. As they drew nearer, they became more earnest in their gestures; and they were no sooner within hearing, than the foremost among them cried that the soldiers were coming up.

At these words, Barnaby furled his flag, and tied it round the pole. His heart beat high while he did so, but he had no more fear or thought of retreating than the pole itself. The friendly stragglers hurried past him, after giving him notice of his danger, and quickly passed into the house, where the utmost confusion immediately prevailed. As those within hastily closed the windows and the doors, they urged him by looks and signs to fly without loss of time, and called to him many times to do so; but he only shook his head indignantly in answer, and stood the firmer on his post. Finding that he was not to be persuaded, they took care of themselves; and leaving the place with only one old woman in it, speedily withdrew.

As yet there had been no symptom of the news having any better foundation than in the fears of those who brought it, but the Boot had not been deserted five minutes, when there appeared, coming across the fields, a body of men who, it was easy to see, by the glitter of their arms and ornaments in the sun, and by their orderly and regular mode of advancing – for they came on as one man – were soldiers. In a very little time, Barnaby knew that they were a strong detachment of the Foot Guards, having along with them two gentlemen in private clothes, and a small party of Horse; the latter brought up the rear, and were not in number more than six or eight.

They advanced steadily; neither quickening their pace as they came nearer, nor raising any cry, nor showing the least emotion or anxiety. Though this was a matter of course in the case of regular troops, even to Barnaby, there was something particularly impressive and disconcerting in it to one accustomed to the noise and tumult of an undisciplined mob. For all that, he stood his ground not a whit the less resolutely, and looked on undismayed.

Presently, they marched into the yard, and halted. The commanding officer despatched a messenger to the horsemen, one of whom came riding back. Some words passed between them, and they glanced at Barnaby; who well remembered the man he had unhorsed at Westminster, and saw him now before his eyes. The man being speedily dismissed, saluted, and rode back to his comrades, who were drawn up apart at a short distance.

The officer then gave the word to prime and load. The heavy ringing of the musket-stocks upon the ground, and the sharp and rapid rattling of the ramrods in their barrels, were a kind of relief to Barnaby, deadly though he knew the purport of such sounds to be. When this was done, other commands were given, and the soldiers instantaneously formed in single file all round the house and stables; completely encircling them in every part, at a distance, perhaps, of some half-dozen yards; at least that seemed in Barnaby's eyes to be about the space left between himself and those who confronted him. The horsemen remained drawn up by themselves as before.

The two gentlemen in private clothes who had kept aloof, now rode forward, one on either side the officer. The proclamation having been produced and read by one of them, the officer called on Barnaby to surrender.

He made no answer, but stepping within the door, before which he had kept guard, held his pole crosswise to protect it. In the midst of a profound silence, he was again called upon to yield.

Still he offered no reply. Indeed he had enough to do, to run his eye backward and forward along the half-dozen men who immediately fronted him, and settle hurriedly within himself at which of them he would strike first, when they pressed on him. He caught the eye of one in the centre, and resolved to hew that fellow down, though he died for it.

Again there was a dead silence, and again the same voice called upon him to deliver himself up.

Next moment he was back in the stable, dealing blows about him like a madman. Two of the men lay stretched at his feet: the one he had marked, dropped first – he had a thought for that, even in the hot blood and hurry of the struggle. Another blow – another! Down, mastered, wounded in the breast by a heavy blow from the butt-end of a gun (he saw the weapon in the act of falling) – breathless – and a prisoner.

An exclamation of surprise from the officer recalled him, in some degree, to himself. He looked round. Grip, after working in secret all the afternoon, and with redoubled vigour while everybody's attention was distracted, had plucked away the straw from Hugh's bed, and turned up the loose ground with his iron bill. The hole had been recklessly filled to the brim, and was merely sprinkled with earth. Golden cups, spoons, candlesticks, coined guineas – all the riches were revealed.

They brought spades and a sack; dug up everything that was hidden there; and carried away more than two men could lift. They handcuffed him and bound his arms, searched him, and took away all he had. Nobody questioned or reproached him, or seemed to have much curiosity about him. The two men he had stunned, were carried off by their companions in the same business-like way in which everything else was done. Finally, he was left under a guard of four soldiers with fixed bayonets, while the officer directed in person the search of the house and the other buildings connected with it.

This was soon completed. The soldiers formed again in the yard; he was marched out, with his guard about him; and ordered to fall in, where a space was left. The others closed up all round, and so they moved away, with the prisoner in the centre.

When they came into the streets, he felt he was a sight; and looking up as they passed quickly along, could see people running to the windows a little too late, and throwing up the sashes to look after him. Sometimes he met a staring face beyond the heads about him, or under the arms of his conductors, or peering down upon him from a waggon-top or coach-box; but this was all he saw, being surrounded by so many men. The very noises of the streets

seemed muffled and subdued; and the air came stale and hot upon
him, like the sickly breath of an oven.

Tramp, tramp. Tramp, tramp. Heads erect, shoulders square,
every man stepping in exact time – all so orderly and regular –
nobody looking at him – nobody seeming conscious of his presence, – he could hardly believe he was a Prisoner. But at the word,
though only thought, not spoken, he felt the handcuffs galling his
wrists, the cord pressing his arms to his sides: the loaded guns
levelled at his head; and those cold, bright, sharp, shining points
turned towards him, the mere looking down at which, now that
he was bound and helpless, made the warm current of his life
run cold.

CHAPTER THE FIFTY-EIGHTH

They were not long in reaching the barracks, for the officer who
commanded the party was desirous to avoid rousing the people by
the display of military force in the streets, and was humanely
anxious to give as little opportunity as possible for any attempt at
rescue; knowing that it must lead to bloodshed and loss of life,
and that if the civil authorities by whom he was accompanied,
empowered him to order his men to fire, many innocent persons
would probably fall, whom curiosity or idleness had attracted to
the spot. He therefore led the party briskly on, avoiding with a
merciful prudence the more public and crowded thoroughfares,
and pursuing those which he deemed least likely to be infested by
disorderly persons. This wise proceeding not only enabled them to
gain their quarters without any interruption, but completely baffled
a body of rioters who had assembled in one of the main streets,
through which it was considered certain they would pass, and who
remained gathered together for the purpose of releasing the prisoner
from their hands, long after they had deposited him in a place of
security, closed the barrack gates, and set a double guard at every
entrance for its better protection.

Arrived at this place, poor Barnaby was marched into a stone-
floored room, where there was a very powerful smell of tobacco, a
strong thorough draft of air, and a great wooden bedstead, large
enough for a score of men. Several soldiers in undress were lounging

about, or eating from tin-cans; military accoutrements dangled on rows of pegs along the whitewashed wall; and some half-dozen men lay fast asleep upon their backs, snoring in concert. After remaining here just long enough to note these things, he was marched out again, and conveyed across the parade-ground to another portion of the building.

Perhaps a man never sees so much at a glance as when he is in a situation of extremity. The chances are a hundred to one, that if Barnaby had lounged in at the gate to look about him, he would have lounged out again with a very imperfect idea of the place, and would have remembered very little about it. But as he was taken handcuffed across the gravelled area, nothing escaped his notice. The dry, arid look of the dusty square, and of the bare brick building; the clothes hanging at some of the windows; and the men in their shirt-sleeves and braces, lolling with half their bodies out of the others; the green sun-blinds at the officers' quarters, and the little scanty trees in front; the drummer-boys practising in a distant court-yard; the men on drill on the parade; the two soldiers carrying a basket between them, who winked to each other as he went by, and slily pointed to their throats; the spruce Sergeant who hurried past with a cane in his hand, and under his arm a clasped book with a vellum cover; the fellows in the ground-floor rooms, furbishing and brushing up their different articles of dress, who stopped to look at him, and whose voices as they spoke together echoed loudly through the empty galleries and passages; – everything, down to the stand of muskets before the guard-house, and the drum with a pipe-clayed belt attached, in one corner, impressed itself upon his observation, as though he had noticed them in the same place a hundred times, or had been a whole day among them, in place of one brief hurried minute.

He was taken into a small paved back yard, and there they opened a great door, plated with iron, and pierced some five feet above the ground with a few holes to let in air and light. Into this dungeon he was walked straightway; and having locked him up there, and placed a sentry over him, they left him to his meditations.

The cell, or black hole, for it had those words painted on the door, was very dark, and having recently accommodated a drunken deserter, by no means clean. Barnaby felt his way to some straw at the further end, and looking towards the door, tried to accustom himself to the gloom, which, coming from the bright sunshine out of doors, was not an easy task.

There was a kind of portico or colonnade outside, and this obstructed even the little light that at the best could have found its way through the small apertures in the door. The footsteps of the sentinel echoed monotonously as he paced its stone pavement to and fro (reminding Barnaby of the watch he had so lately kept himself); and as he passed and repassed the door, he made the cell for an instant so black by the interposition of his body, that his going away again seemed like the appearance of a new ray of light, and was quite a circumstance to look for.

When the prisoner had sat sometime upon the ground, gazing at the chinks, and listening to the advancing and receding footsteps of his guard, the man stood still upon his post. Barnaby, quite unable to think, or to speculate on what would be done with him, had been lulled into a kind of doze by his regular pace; but his stopping roused him; and then he became aware that two men were in conversation under the colonnade, and very near the door of his cell.

How long they had been talking there, he could not tell, for he had fallen into an unconsciousness of his real position, and when the footsteps ceased, was answering aloud some question which seemed to have been put to him by Hugh in the stable, though of the fancied purport, either of question or reply, notwithstanding that he awoke with the latter on his lips, he had no recollection whatever. The first words that reached his ears, were these:

'Why is he brought here then, if he has to be taken away again, so soon?'

'Why where would you have him go! Damme, he's not as safe anywhere as among the king's troops, is he? What *would* you do with him? Would you hand him over to a pack of cowardly civilians, that shake in their shoes till they wear the soles out, with trembling at the threats of the ragamuffins he belongs to?'

'That's true enough.'

'True enough! – I'll tell you what. I wish, Tom Green, that I was a commissioned instead of a non-commissioned officer, and that I had the command of two companies – only two companies – of my own regiment. Call me out to stop these riots – give me the needful authority, and half-a-dozen rounds of ball cartridge –'

'Ay!' said the other voice. 'That's all very well, but they won't give the needful authority. If the magistrate won't give the word, what's the officer to do?'

Not very well knowing, as it seemed, how to overcome this difficulty, the other man contented himself with damning the magistrates.

'With all my heart,' said his friend.

'Where's the use of a magistrate?' returned the other voice. 'What's a magistrate in this case, but an impertinent, unnecessary, unconstitutional sort of interference? Here's a proclamation. Here's a man referred to in that proclamation. Here's proof against him, and a witness on the spot. Damme! Take him out and shoot him, sir. Who wants a magistrate?'

'When does he go before Sir John Fielding?'[1] asked the man who had spoken first.

'To-night at eight o'clock,' returned the other. 'Mark what follows. The magistrate commits him to Newgate. Our people take him to Newgate. The rioters pelt our people. Our people retire before the rioters. Stones are thrown, insults are offered, not a shot's fired. Why? Because of the magistrates. Damn the magistrates!'

When he had in some degree relieved his mind by cursing the magistrates in various other forms of speech, the man was silent, save for a low growling, still having reference to those authorities, which from time to time escaped him.

Barnaby, who had wit enough to know that this conversation concerned, and very nearly concerned, himself, remained perfectly quiet until they ceased to speak, when he groped his way to the door, and peeping through the air-holes, tried to make out what kind of men they were, to whom he had been listening.

The one who condemned the civil power in such strong terms, was a serjeant – engaged just then, as the streaming ribands in his cap announced, on the recruiting service. He stood leaning sideways against a pillar nearly opposite the door, and as he growled to himself, drew figures on the pavement with his cane. The other man had his back towards the dungeon, and Barnaby could only see his form. To judge from that, he was a gallant, manly, handsome fellow, but he had lost his left arm. It had been taken off between the elbow and the shoulder, and his empty coat-sleeve hung across his breast.

It was probably this circumstance which gave him an interest beyond any that his companion could boast of, and attracted

Barnaby's attention. There was something soldierly in his bearing, and he wore a jaunty cap and jacket. Perhaps he had been in the service at one time or other. If he had, it could not have been very long ago, for he was but a young fellow now.

'Well, well,' he said thoughtfully; 'let the fault be where it may, it makes a man sorrowful to come back to old England, and see her in this condition.'

'I suppose the pigs will join 'em next,' said the serjeant, with an imprecation on the rioters, 'now that the birds have set 'em the example.'

'The birds!' repeated Tom Green.

'Ah – birds,' said the serjeant testily; 'that's English, an't it?'

'I don't know what you mean.'

'Go to the guard-house, and see. You'll find a bird there, that's got their cry as pat as any of 'em, and bawls "No Popery," like a man – or like a devil, as he says he is. I shouldn't wonder. The devil's loose in London somewhere. Damme if I wouldn't twist his neck round, on the chance, if I had *my* way.'

The young man had taken two or three hasty steps away, as if to go and see this creature, when he was arrested by the voice of Barnaby.

'It's mine,' he called out, half laughing and half weeping – 'my pet, my friend Grip. Ha ha ha! Don't hurt him, he has done no harm. I taught him; it's my fault. Let me have him, if you please. He's the only friend I have left now. He'll not dance, or talk, or whistle for you, I know; but he will for me, because he knows me, and loves me – though you wouldn't think it – very well. You wouldn't hurt a bird, I'm sure. You're a brave soldier, sir, and wouldn't harm a woman or a child – no, no, nor a poor bird, I am certain.'

This latter adjuration was addressed to the serjeant, whom Barnaby judged from his red coat to be high in office, and able to seal Grip's destiny by a word. But that gentleman, in reply, surlily damned him for a thief and rebel as he was, and with many disinterested imprecations on his own eyes, liver, blood, and body, assured him that if it rested with him to decide, he would put a final stopper on the bird, and his master too.

'You talk boldly to a caged man,' said Barnaby, in anger. 'If I was on the other side of the door and there were none to part us, you'd change your note – ay, you may toss your head – you would!

Kill the bird – do. Kill anything you can, and so revenge yourself on those who with their bare hands untied could do as much to you!'

Having vented this defiance, he flung himself into the furthest corner of his prison, and muttering, 'Good bye, Grip – good bye, dear old Grip!' shed tears for the first time since he had been taken captive; and hid his face in the straw.

He had had some fancy at first, that the one armed man would help him, or would give him a kind word in answer. He hardly knew why, but he hoped and thought so. The young fellow had stopped when he called out, and checking himself in the very act of turning round, stood listening to every word he said. Perhaps he built his feeble trust on this; perhaps on his being young, and having a frank and honest manner. However that might be, he built on sand.[2] The other went away directly he had finished speaking, and neither answered him, nor returned. No matter. They were all against him here; he might have known as much. Good bye, old Grip, good bye!

After some time, they came and unlocked the door, and called to him to come out. He rose directly, and complied, for he would not have *them* think he was subdued or frightened. He walked out like a man, and looked haughtily from face to face.

None of them returned his gaze or seemed to notice it. They marched him back to the parade by the way they had brought him, and there they halted, among a body of soldiers, at least twice as numerous as that which had taken him prisoner in the afternoon. The officer he had seen before, bade him in a few brief words take notice that if he attempted to escape, no matter how favourable a chance he might suppose he had, certain of the men had orders to fire upon him, that moment. They then closed round him as before, and marched him off again.

In the same unbroken order they arrived at Bow-street, followed and beset on all sides by a crowd which was continually increasing. Here he was placed before a blind gentleman, and asked if he wished to say anything. Not he. What had he got to tell them? After a very little talking, which he was careless of and quite indifferent to, they told him he was to go to Newgate, and took him away.

He went out into the street, so surrounded and hemmed in on every side by soldiers, that he could see nothing; but he knew there was a great crowd of people, by the murmur; and that they were

not friendly to the soldiers, was soon rendered evident by their yells
and hisses. How often and how eagerly he listened for the voice
of Hugh! No. There was not a voice he knew among them all.
Was Hugh a prisoner too? Was there no hope!

As they came nearer and nearer to the prison, the hootings of the
people grew more violent; stones were thrown; and every now and
then, a rush was made against the soldiers, which they staggered
under. One of them, close before him, smarting under a blow upon
the temple, levelled his musket, but the officer struck it upwards
with his sword, and ordered him on peril of his life to desist.
This was the last thing he saw with any distinctness, for directly
afterwards he was tossed about, and beaten to and fro, as though
in a tempestuous sea. But go where he would, there were the same
guards about him. Twice or thrice he was thrown down, and so
were they; but even then, he could not elude their vigilance for a
moment. They were up again, and had closed about him, before
he, with his wrists so tightly bound, could scramble to his feet.
Fenced in, thus, he felt himself hoisted to the top of a low flight of
steps, and then for a moment he caught a glimpse of the fighting in
the crowd, and of a few red coats sprinkled together, here and
there, struggling to rejoin their fellows. Next moment, everything
was dark and gloomy, and he was standing in the prison lobby; the
centre of a group of men.

A smith was speedily in attendance, who rivetted upon him a set
of heavy irons. Stumbling on as well as he could, beneath the
unusual burden of these fetters, he was conducted to a strong stone
cell, where, fastening the door with locks, and bolts, and chains,
they left him, well secured; having first, unseen by him, thrust in
Grip, who, with his head drooping and his deep black plumes rough
and rumpled, appeared to comprehend and to partake, his master's
fallen fortunes.

*

CHAPTER THE FIFTY-NINTH

It is necessary at this juncture to return to Hugh, who, having, as we have seen, called to the rioters to disperse from about the Warren, and meet again as usual, glided back into the darkness from which he had emerged, and reappeared no more that night.

He paused in the copse which sheltered him from the observation of his mad companions, and waited to ascertain whether they drew off at his bidding, or still lingered and called to him to join them. Some few, he saw, were indisposed to go away without him, and made towards the spot where he stood concealed as though they were about to follow in his footsteps, and urge him to come back; but these men, being in their turn called to by their friends, and in truth not greatly caring to venture into the dark parts of the grounds where they might be easily surprised and taken, if any of the neighbours or retainers of the family were watching them from among the trees, soon abandoned the idea, and hastily assembling such men as they found of their mind at the moment, straggled off.

When he was satisfied that the great mass of the insurgents were imitating this example, and that the ground was rapidly clearing, he plunged into the thickest portion of the little wood; and crashing the branches as he went, made straight towards a distant light: guided by that, and by the sullen glow of the fire behind him.

As he drew nearer and nearer to the twinkling beacon towards which he bent his course, the red glare of a few torches began to reveal itself, and the voices of men speaking together in a subdued tone, broke the silence, which, save for a distant shouting now and then, already prevailed. At length he cleared the wood and, springing across a ditch, stood in a dark lane, where a small body of ill-looking vagabonds, whom he had left there some twenty minutes before, waited his coming with impatience.

They were gathered round an old post-chaise or chariot, driven by one of themselves, who sat postilion-wise upon the near horse. The blinds were drawn up, and Mr Tappertit and Dennis kept guard at the two windows. The former assumed the command of the party, for he challenged Hugh as he advanced towards them; and when he did so, those who were resting on the ground about the carriage rose to their feet and clustered round him.

'Well!' said Simon, in a low voice; 'is all right?'

'Right enough,' replied Hugh, in the same tone. 'They're dispersing now – had begun before I came away.'

'And is the coast clear?'

'Clear enough before our men, I take it,' said Hugh. 'There are not many who, knowing of their work over yonder, will want to meddle with 'em to-night. – Who's got some drink here?'

Everybody had some plunder from the cellar; half-a-dozen flasks and bottles were offered directly. He selected the largest, and putting it to his mouth, sent the wine gurgling down his throat. Having emptied it, he threw it down, and stretched out his hand for another, which he emptied likewise, at a draught. Another was given him, and this he half emptied too. Reserving what remained, to finish with, he asked:

'Have you got anything to eat, any of you? I'm as ravenous as a hungry wolf. Which of you was in the larder – come!'

'I was, brother,' said Dennis, pulling off his hat, and fumbling in the crown. 'There's a matter of cold venison pasty somewhere or another here, if that'll do.'

'Do!' cried Hugh, seating himself on the pathway. 'Bring it out! Quick! Show a light here, and gather round! Let me sup in state, my lads. Ha ha ha!'

Entering into his boisterous humour, for they all had drunk deeply and were as wild as he, they crowded about him, while two of their number who had torches, held them up, one on either side of him, that his banquet might not be despatched in the dark. Mr Dennis, having by this time succeeded in extricating from his hat a great mass of pasty, which had been wedged in so tightly that it was not easily got out, put it before him; and Hugh, having borrowed a notched and jagged knife from one of the company, fell to work upon it vigorously.

'I should recommend you to swallow a little fire every day, about an hour afore dinner, brother,' said Dennis, after a pause. 'It seems to agree with you, and to stimulate your appetite.'

Hugh looked at him, and at the blackened faces by which he was surrounded, and, stopping for a moment to flourish his knife above his head, answered with a roar of laughter.

'Keep order there, will you?' said Simon Tappertit.

'Why, isn't a man allowed to regale himself, noble captain,' retorted his lieutenant, parting the men who stood between them, with his knife, that he might see him, 'to regale himself a little bit, after such work as mine? What a hard captain! What a strict captain! What a tyrannical captain! Ha ha ha!'

'I wish one of you fellers would hold a bottle to his mouth to keep him quiet,' said Simon, 'unless you want the military to be down upon us.'

'And what if they are down upon us!' retorted Hugh. 'Who cares? Who's afraid? Let 'em come, I say, let 'em come. The more, the merrier. Give me bold Barnaby at my side, and we two will settle the military, without troubling any of you. Barnaby's the man for the military. Barnaby's health!'

But as the majority of those present, were by no means anxious for a second engagement that night, being already weary and exhausted, they sided with Mr Tappertit, and pressed him to make haste with his supper, for they had already delayed too long. Knowing, even in the height of his frenzy, that they incurred great danger by lingering so near the scene of the late outrages, Hugh made an end of his meal without more remonstrance, and rising, stepped up to Mr Tappertit and smote him on the back.

'Now then,' he cried, 'I'm ready. There are brave birds inside this cage, eh? Delicate birds, – tender, loving, little doves. I caged 'em – I caged 'em – one more peep!'

He thrust the little man aside as he spoke, and mounting on the steps which were half let down, pulled down the blind by force, and stared into the chaise like an ogre into his larder.

'Ha ha ha! and did you scratch, and pinch, and struggle, pretty mistress?' he cried, as he grasped a little hand that sought in vain to free itself from his gripe: 'you, so bright-eyed, and cherry-lipped, and daintily made? But I love you better for it, mistress. Ay, I do. You should stab me and welcome, so that it pleased you, and you had to cure me afterwards. I love to see you proud and scornful. It makes you handsomer than ever; and who so handsome as you at any time, my pretty one!'

'Come!' said Mr Tappertit, who had waited during this speech with considerable impatience. 'There's enough of that. Come down.'

The little hand seconded this admonition by thrusting Hugh's great head away with all its force, and drawing up the blind, amidst his noisy laughter, and vows that he must have another look, for the last glimpse of that sweet face had provoked him past all bearing. However, as the suppressed impatience of the party now broke out into open murmurs, he abandoned this design, and taking his seat upon the bar, contented himself with tapping at the front windows of the carriage, and trying to steal a glance inside; Mr Tappertit, mounting the steps and hanging on by the door, issued his directions to the driver with a commanding voice and attitude; the rest got up behind, or ran by the side of the carriage, as they could; some, in imitation of Hugh, endeavoured to see the face he had praised so highly, and were reminded of their impertinence by hints from the cudgel of Mr Tappertit. Thus they pursued their journey by circuitous and winding roads; preserving, except when they halted to take breath, or to quarrel about the best way of reaching London, pretty good order and tolerable silence.

In the mean time, Dolly – beautiful, bewitching, captivating little Dolly – her hair dishevelled, her dress torn, her dark eyelashes wet with tears, her bosom heaving – her face, now pale with fear, now crimsoned with indignation – her whole self a hundred times more beautiful in this heightened aspect than ever she had been before – vainly strove to comfort Emma Haredale, and to impart to her the consolation of which she stood in so much need herself. The soldiers were sure to come; they must be rescued; it would be impossible to convey them through the streets of London, when they set the threats of their guards at defiance, and shrieked to the passengers for help. If they did this, when they came into the more frequented ways, she was certain – she was quite certain – they must be released. So poor Dolly said, and so poor Dolly tried to think; but the invariable conclusion of all such arguments was, that Dolly burst into tears; cried, as she wrung her hands, what would they do or think, or who would comfort them, at home, at the Golden Key; and sobbed most piteously.

Miss Haredale, whose feelings were usually of a quieter kind than Dolly's, and not so much upon the surface, was dreadfully alarmed, and indeed had only just recovered from a swoon. She was very pale, and the hand which Dolly held was quite cold; but she bade her, nevertheless, remember that, under Providence, much must depend upon their own discretion; that if they remained quiet and lulled the vigilance of the ruffians into whose hands they had fallen, the chances of their being able to procure assistance when they reached the town, were very much increased; that unless society were quite unhinged, a hot pursuit must be immediately commenced; and that her uncle, she might be sure, would never

rest until he had found them out and rescued them. But as she said these latter words, the idea that he had fallen in a general massacre of the Catholics that night – no very wild or improbable supposition, after what they had seen and undergone – struck her dumb; and, lost in the horrors they had witnessed, and those they might be yet reserved for, she sat incapable of thought, or speech, or outward show of grief: as rigid, and almost as white and cold, as marble.

Oh, how many, many times, in that long ride, did Dolly think of her old lover – poor, fond, slighted Joe! How many, many times, did she recall that night when she ran into his arms from the very man now projecting his hateful gaze into the darkness where she sat, and leering through the glass, in monstrous admiration! And when she thought of Joe, and what a brave fellow he was, and how he would have rode boldly up, and dashed in among these villains now, yes, though they were double the number – and here she clenched her little hand, and pressed her foot upon the ground – the pride she felt for a moment in having won his heart, faded in a burst of tears, and she sobbed more bitterly than ever.

As the night wore on, and they proceeded by ways which were quite unknown to them – for they could recognise none of the objects of which they sometimes caught a hurried glimpse – their fears increased; nor were they without good foundation; it was not difficult for two beautiful young women to find, in their being borne they knew not whither, by a band of daring villains who eyed them as some among these fellows did, reasons for the worst alarm. When they at last entered London by a suburb with which they were wholly unacquainted, it was past midnight, and the streets were dark and empty. Nor was this the worst, for the carriage stopping in a lonely spot, Hugh suddenly opened the door, jumped in, and took his seat between them.

It was in vain they cried for help. He put his arm about the neck of each, and swore to stifle them with kisses if they were not as silent as the grave.

'I come here to keep you quiet,' he said, 'and that's the means I shall take. So don't be quiet, pretty mistresses – make a noise – do – and I shall like it all the better.'

They were proceeding at a rapid pace, and apparently with fewer attendants than before, though it was so dark (the torches being extinguished) that this was mere conjecture. They shrunk from his touch, each into the farthest corner of the carriage; but shrink as Dolly would, his arm encircled her waist, and held her fast. She neither cried nor spoke, for terror and disgust deprived her of the power; but she plucked at his hand as though she would die in the effort to disengage herself; and crouching on the ground, with her head averted and held down, repelled him with a strength she wondered at as much as he. The carriage stopped again.

'Lift this one out,' said Hugh to the man who opened the door, as he took Miss Haredale's hand, and felt how heavily it fell. 'She's fainted.'

'So much the better,' growled Dennis – it was that amiable gentleman. 'She's quiet. I always like 'em to faint, unless they're very tender and composed.'

'Can you take her by yourself?' asked Hugh.

'I don't know till I try. I ought to be able to; I've lifted up a good many in my time,' said the hangman. 'Up then! She's no small weight, brother; none of these here fine gals are. Up again! Now we have it.'

Having by this time hoisted the young lady into his arms, he staggered off with his burden.

'Look ye, pretty bird,' said Hugh, drawing Dolly towards him. 'Remember what I told you – a kiss for every cry. Scream, if you love me, darling. Scream once, mistress. Pretty mistress, only once, if you love me.'

Thrusting his face away with all her force, and holding down her head, Dolly submitted to be carried out of the chaise, and borne after Miss Haredale into a miserable cottage, where Hugh, after hugging her to his breast, set her gently down upon the floor.

Poor Dolly! Do what she would, she only looked the better for it, and tempted them the more. When her eyes flashed angrily, and her ripe lips slightly parted, to give her rapid breathing vent, who could resist it? When she wept and sobbed as though her heart would break, and bemoaned her miseries in the sweetest voice that ever fell upon a listener's ear, who could be insensible to the little winning pettishness which now and then displayed itself even in the sincerity and earnestness of her grief? When, forgetful for a moment of herself, as she was now, she fell on her knees beside her friend, and bent over her, and laid her cheek to hers, and put her arms about her, what mortal eyes could have avoided wandering to the delicate boddice, the streaming hair, the neglected dress, the perfect abandonment and unconsciousness of the blooming little beauty? Who could look on and see her lavish caresses and endearments, and not desire to be in Emma Haredale's place; to be either her or Dolly; either the hugging or the hugged? Not Hugh. Not Dennis.

'I tell you what it is, young women,' said Mr Dennis, 'I an't much of a lady's man myself, nor am I a party in the present business further than lending a willing hand to my friends: but if I see much more of this here sort of thing, I shall become a principal instead of an accessory. I tell you candidly.'

'Why have you brought us here?' said Emma. 'Are we to be murdered?'

'Murdered!' cried Dennis, sitting down upon a stool, and regarding her with great favour. 'Why, my dear, who'd murder sich chickabiddies as you? If you was to ask me, now, whether you was brought here to be married, there might be something in it.'

And here he exchanged a grin with Hugh, who removed his eyes from Dolly for the purpose.

'No, no,' said Dennis, 'there'll be no murdering, my pets. Nothing of that sort. Quite the contrary.'

'You are an older man than your companion, sir,' said Emma, trembling. 'Have you no pity for us? Do you not consider that we are women?'

'I do indeed, my dear,' retorted Dennis. 'It would be very hard not to, with two such specimens afore my eyes. Ha ha! Oh yes, I consider that. We all consider that, Miss.'

He shook his head waggishly, leered at Hugh again, and laughed very much, as if he had said a noble thing, and rather thought he was coming out.

'There'll be no murdering, my dear. Not a bit on it. I tell you what though, brother,' said Dennis, cocking his hat for the convenience of scratching his head, and looking gravely at Hugh, 'it's worthy of notice, as a proof of the amazing equalness and dignity of our law, that it don't make no distinction between men and women. I've heerd the judge say, sometimes, to a highwayman or housebreaker as had tied the ladies neck and heels – you'll excuse me making mention of it, my darlings – and put 'em in a cellar, that he showed no consideration to women. Now, I say that there judge didn't know his business, brother; and that if I had been that there highwayman or housebreaker, I should have made answer: "What are you a talking of, my lord? I showed the women as much consideration as the law does, and what more would you have me do?" If you was to count up in the newspapers the number of females as have been worked off in this here city alone, in the last ten year,' said Mr Dennis thoughtfully, 'you'd be surprised at the total – quite amazed, you would. There's a dignified and equal thing; a beautiful thing! But we've no security for its lasting. Now that they've begun to favour these here Papists, I shouldn't wonder if they went and altered even *that*, one of these days. Upon my soul, I shouldn't.'

This subject, perhaps from being of too exclusive and professional a nature, failed to interest Hugh as much as his friend had anticipated. But he had no time to pursue it, for at this crisis Mr Tappertit entered precipitately; at sight of whom Dolly uttered a scream of joy, and fairly threw herself into his arms.

'I knew it, I was sure of it!' cried Dolly. 'My dear father's at the door. Thank God, thank God! Bless you, Sim. Heaven bless you for this!'

Simon Tappertit, who had at first implicitly believed that the locksmith's daughter, unable any longer to suppress her secret passion for himself, was about to give it full vent in its intensity, and to declare that she was his for ever, looked extremely foolish when she said these words; – the more so, as they were received by Hugh and Dennis with a loud laugh, which made her draw back, and regard him with a fixed and earnest look.

'Miss Haredale,' said Sim, after a very awkward silence, 'I hope you're as comfortable as circumstances will permit of. Dolly Varden, my darling – my own, my lovely one – I hope *you're* pretty comfortable likewise.'

Poor little Dolly! She saw how it was; hid her face in her hands; and sobbed more bitterly than ever.

'You meet in me, Miss V.,' said Simon, laying his hand upon his breast, 'not a 'prentice, not a workman, not a slave, not the victim of your father's tyrannical behaviour, but the leader of a great people, the captain of a noble band, in which these gentlemen are, as I may say, corporals and serjeants. You behold in me, not a private individual, but a public character; not a mender of locks, but a healer of the wounds of his unhappy country. Dolly V., sweet Dolly V., for how many years have I looked forward to this meeting! For how many years has it been my intention to exalt and ennoble

you! I redeem it. Behold in me, your husband. Yes, beautiful Dolly
– charmer – enslaver – S. Tappertit is all your own!'

As he said these words he advanced towards her. Dolly retreated
till she could go no farther, and then sank down upon the floor.
Thinking it very possible that this might be maiden modesty, Simon
essayed to raise her; on which Dolly, goaded to desperation, wound
her hands in his hair, and crying out amidst her tears that he was a
dreadful little wretch, and always had been, shook, and pulled, and
beat him, until he was fain to call for help, most lustily. Hugh had
never admired her half so much as at that moment.

'She's in an excited state to-night,' said Simon, as he smoothed
his rumpled feathers, 'and don't know when she's well off. Let her
be by herself till to-morrow, and that'll bring her down a little.
Carry her into the next house!'

Hugh had her in his arms directly. It might be that Mr Tappertit's
heart was really softened by her distress, or it might be that he felt
it in some degree indecorous that his intended bride should be
struggling in the grasp of another man. He commanded him, on
second thoughts, to put her down again; and looked moodily on
as she flew to Miss Haredale's side, and clinging to her dress, hid
her flushed face in its folds.

'They shall remain here together till to-morrow,' said Simon,
who had now quite recovered his dignity – 'till to-morrow. Come
away!'

'Ay!' cried Hugh. 'Come away, captain. Ha ha ha!'

'What are you laughing at?' demanded Simon sternly.

'Nothing, captain, nothing,' Hugh rejoined; and as he spoke, and
clapped his hand upon the shoulder of the little man, he laughed
again, for some unknown reason, with tenfold violence.

Mr Tappertit surveyed him from head to foot with lofty scorn
(this only made him laugh the more), and turning to the prisoners,
said:

'You'll take notice, ladies, that this place is well watched on
every side, and that the least noise is certain to be attended with
unpleasant consequences. You'll hear – both of you – more of our
intentions to-morrow. In the mean time, don't show yourselves at
the window, or appeal to any of the people you may see pass it; for
if you do, it'll be known directly that you come from a Catholic
house, and all the exertions our men can make, may not be able to
save your lives.'

With this last caution, which was true enough, he turned to the
door, followed by Hugh and Dennis. They paused for a moment,
going out, to look at them clasped in each other's arms, and then
left the cottage; fastening the door, and setting a good watch upon
it, and indeed all round the house.

'I say,' growled Dennis, as they walked away in company, 'that's
a dainty pair. Muster Gashford's one is as handsome as the other,
eh?'

'Hush!' said Hugh, hastily. 'Don't you mention names. It's a bad
habit.'

'I wouldn't like to be *him*, then (as you don't like names), when
he breaks it out to her; that's all,' said Dennis. 'She's one of them
fine, black-eyed, proud gals, as I wouldn't trust at such times with
a knife too near 'em. I've seen some of that sort, afore now. I
recollect one that was worked off, many year ago – and there was
a gentleman in that case too – that says to me, with her lip a
trembling, but her hand as steady as ever I see one; "Dennis, I'm
near my end, but if I had a dagger in these fingers, and he was
within my reach, I'd strike him dead afore me;" – ah, she did – and
she'd have done it too!'

'Strike who dead?' demanded Hugh.

'How should I know, brother?' answered Dennis. '*She* never
said; not she.'

Hugh looked for a moment, as though he would have made
some further inquiry into this incoherent recollection; but Simon
Tappertit, who had been meditating deeply, gave his thoughts a
new direction.

'Hugh!' said Sim. 'You have done well to-day. You shall be
rewarded. So have you, Dennis. – There's no young woman *you*
want to carry off, is there?'

'N – no,' returned that gentleman, stroking his grizzled beard,
which was some two inches long. 'None in partickler, I think.'

'Very good,' said Sim; 'then we'll find some other way of making
it up to you. As to you, old boy' – he turned to Hugh – 'you shall
have Miggs (her that I promised you, you know) within three days.
Mind. I pass my word for it.'

Hugh thanked him heartily; and as he did so, his laughing fit
returned with such violence that he was obliged to hold his side
with one hand, and to lean with the other on the shoulder of his

small captain, without whose support he would certainly have
rolled upon the ground.

CHAPTER THE SIXTIETH

The three worthies turned their faces towards the Boot, with the
intention of passing the night in that place of rendezvous, and of
seeking the repose they so much needed in the shelter of their old
den; for now that the mischief and destruction they had purposed
were achieved, and their prisoners were safely bestowed for the
night, they began to be conscious of exhaustion, and to feel the
wasting effects of the madness which had led to such deplorable
results.

Notwithstanding the lassitude and fatigue which oppressed him
now, in common with his two companions, and indeed with all who
had taken an active share in that night's work, Hugh's boisterous
merriment broke out afresh whenever he looked at Simon
Tappertit, and vented itself – much to that gentleman's indignation
– in such shouts of laughter as bade fair to bring the watch upon
them, and involve them in a skirmish, to which in their present
worn-out condition they might prove by no means equal. Even Mr
Dennis, who was not at all particular on the score of gravity or
dignity, and who had a great relish for his young friend's eccentric
humours, took occasion to remonstrate with him on this imprudent
behaviour, which he held to be a species of suicide, tantamount
to a man's working himself off without being overtaken by the
law, than which he could imagine nothing more ridiculous or
impertinent.

Not abating one jot of his noisy mirth for these remonstrances,
Hugh reeled along between them, having an arm of each, until they
hove in sight of the Boot, and were within a field or two of that
convenient tavern. He happened by great good luck to have roared
and shouted himself into silence by this time. They were proceeding
onward without noise, when a scout who had been creeping about
the ditches all night, to warn any stragglers from encroaching
further on what was now such dangerous ground, peeped cautiously
from his hiding-place, and called to them to stop.

'Stop! and why?' said Hugh.

Because (the scout replied) the house was filled with constables and soldiers; having been surprised, that afternoon. The inmates had fled or been taken into custody, he could not say which. He had prevented a great many people from approaching nearer, and he believed they had gone to the markets and such places to pass the night. He had seen the distant fires, but they were all out now. He had heard the people who passed and repassed, speaking of them too, and could report that the prevailing opinion was one of apprehension and dismay. He had not heard a word of Barnaby – didn't even know his name – but it had been said in his hearing that some man had been taken and carried off to Newgate. Whether this was true or false, he could not affirm.

The three took counsel together, on hearing this, and debated what it might be best to do. Hugh, deeming it possible that Barnaby was in the hands of the soldiers, and at that moment under detention at the Boot, was for advancing stealthily, and firing the house; but his companions, who objected to such rash measures unless they had a crowd at their backs, represented that if Barnaby were taken he had assuredly been removed to a stronger prison: they would never have dreamed of keeping him all night in a place so weak and open to attack. Yielding to this reasoning, and to their persuasions, Hugh consented to turn back, and to repair to Fleet Market; for which place, it seemed, a few of their boldest associates had shaped their course, on receiving the same intelligence.

Feeling their strength recruited and their spirits roused now that there was a new necessity for action, they hurried away, quite forgetful of the fatigue under which they had been sinking but a few minutes before; and soon arrived at their place of destination.

Fleet Market, at that time, was a long irregular row of wooden sheds and pent-houses, occupying the centre of what is now called Farringdon Street.[1] They were jumbled together in a most unsightly fashion, in the middle of the road; to the great obstruction of the thoroughfare and the annoyance of passengers, who were fain to make their way, as they best could, among carts, baskets, barrows, trucks, casks, bulks, and benches, and to jostle with porters, hucksters, waggoners, and a motley crowd of buyers, sellers, pickpockets, vagrants, and idlers. The air was perfumed with the stench of rotten leaves and faded fruit; the refuse of the butchers' stalls, and offal and garbage of a hundred kinds: it was indispensable to most public conveniences in those days, that they should be public nuisances likewise; and Fleet Market maintained the principle to admiration.

To this place, perhaps because its sheds and baskets were a tolerable substitute for beds, or perhaps because it afforded the means of a hasty barricade in case of need, many of the rioters had straggled, not only that night, but for two or three nights before. It was now broad day, but the morning being cold, a group of them were gathered round a fire in a public-house, drinking hot purl, and smoking pipes, and planning new schemes for to-morrow.

Hugh and his two friends being known to most of these men, were received with signal marks of approbation, and inducted into the most honourable seats. The room-door was closed and fastened to keep intruders at a distance, and then they proceeded to exchange news.

'The soldiers have taken possession of the Boot, I hear,' said Hugh. 'Who knows anything about it?'

Several cried that they did; but the majority of the company having been engaged in the assault upon the Warren, and all present having been concerned in one or other of the night's expeditions, it proved that they knew no more than Hugh himself; having been merely warned by each other, or by the scout, and knowing nothing of their own knowledge.

'We left a man on guard there to-day,' said Hugh, looking round him, 'who is not here. You know who it is – Barnaby, who brought the soldier down, at Westminster. Has any man seen or heard of him?'

They shook their heads, and murmured an answer in the negative, as each man looked round and appealed to his fellow; when a noise was heard without, and a man was heard to say that he wanted Hugh – that he must see Hugh.

'He is but one man,' cried Hugh to those who kept the door; 'let him come in.'

'Ay, ay!' muttered the others. 'Let him come in. Let him come in.'

The door was accordingly unlocked and opened. A one-armed man, with his head and face tied up with a bloody cloth as though he had been severely beaten, his clothes torn, and his remaining hand grasping a thick stick, rushed in among them, and panting for breath, demanded which was Hugh.

'Here he is,' replied the person he inquired for. 'I am Hugh. What do you want with me?'

'I have a message for you,' said the man. 'You know one Barnaby.'

'What of him? Did he send the message?'

'Yes. He's taken. He's in one of the strong cells in Newgate. He defended himself as well as he could, but was overpowered by numbers. That's his message.'

'When did you see him?' asked Hugh, hastily.

'On his way to prison, where he was taken by a party of soldiers. They took a by-road, and not the one we expected. I was one of the few who tried to rescue him, and he called to me, and told me to tell Hugh where he was. We made a good struggle, though it failed. Look here!'

He pointed to his dress, and to his bandaged head, and still panting for breath, glanced round the room; then faced towards Hugh again.

'I know you by sight,' he said, 'for I was in the crowd on Friday, and on Saturday, and yesterday, but I didn't know your name. You're a bold fellow, I know. So is he. He fought like a lion to-night, but it was of no use. I did my best, considering that I want this limb.'

Again he glanced inquisitively round the room – or seemed to do so, for his face was nearly hidden by the bandage – and again facing sharply towards Hugh, grasped his stick as if he half expected to be set upon, and stood on the defensive.

If he had any such apprehension, however, he was speedily re-assured by the demeanour of all present. None thought of the bearer of the tidings. He was lost in the news he brought. Oaths, threats, and execrations, were vented on all sides. Some cried that if they bore this tamely, another day would see them all in jail; some, that they should have rescued the other prisoners, and this would not have happened. One man cried in a loud voice, 'Who'll follow me to Newgate!' and there was a loud shout, and a general rush towards the door.

But Hugh and Dennis stood with their backs against it, and kept them back, until the clamour had so far subsided that their voices could be heard, when they called to them together that to go now, in broad day, would be madness; and that if they waited until night and arranged a plan of attack, they might release, not only their own companions, but all the prisoners, and burn down the jail.

'Not that jail alone,' cried Hugh, 'but every jail in London. They shall have no place to put their prisoners in. We'll burn them all down; make bonfires of them every one! Here!' he cried, catching at the hangman's hand. 'Let all who're men here, join with us. Shake hands upon it. Barnaby out of jail, and not a jail left standing! Who joins?'

Every man there. And they swore a great oath to release their friends from Newgate next night; to force the doors and burn the jail; or perish in the fire themselves.

*

CHAPTER THE SIXTY-FIRST

On that same night – events so crowd upon each other in convulsed and distracted times, that more than the stirring incidents of a whole life often become compressed into the compass of four-and-twenty hours – on that same night, Mr Haredale, having strongly bound his prisoner, with the assistance of the sexton, and forced him to mount his horse, conducted him to Chigwell; bent upon procuring a conveyance to London from that place, and carrying him at once before a Justice. The disturbed state of the town would be, he knew, a sufficient reason for demanding the murderer's committal to prison before daybreak, as no man could answer for the security of any of the watch-houses or ordinary places of detention; and to convey a prisoner through the streets when the mob were again abroad, would not only be a task of great danger and hazard, but would be to challenge an attempt at rescue. Directing the sexton to lead the horse, he walked close by the murderer's side, and in this order they reached the village about the middle of the night.

The people were all awake and up, for they were fearful of being burnt in their beds, and sought to comfort and assure each other by watching in company. A few of the stoutest-hearted were armed and gathered in a body on the green. To these, who knew him well, Mr Haredale addressed himself, briefly narrating what had happened, and beseeching them to aid in conveying the criminal to London before the dawn of day.

But not a man among them dared to help him by so much as the motion of a finger. The rioters, in their passage through the village, had menaced with their fiercest vengeance any person who should aid in extinguishing the fire, or render the least assistance to him, or any catholic whomsoever. Their threats extended to their lives and all that they possessed. They were assembled for their own protection, and could not endanger themselves by lending any aid to him. This they told him, not without hesitation and regret, as they kept aloof in the moonlight and glanced fearfully at the ghostly rider, who, with his head drooping on his breast and his hat slouched down upon his brow, neither moved nor spoke.

Finding it impossible to persuade them, and indeed hardly knowing how to do so after what they had seen of the fury of the crowd, Mr Haredale besought them that at least they would leave him free to act for himself, and would suffer him to take the only chaise and pair of horses that the place afforded. This was not acceded to without some difficulty, but in the end they told him to do what he would, and to go away from them in heaven's name.

Leaving the sexton at the horse's bridle, he drew out the chaise with his own hands, and would have harnessed the horses, but that the postboy of the village – a soft-hearted, good-for-nothing, vagabond kind of fellow – was moved by his earnestness and passion, and, throwing down a pitchfork with which he was armed, swore that the rioters might cut him into mince-meat if they liked, but he would not stand by and see an honest gentleman who had done no wrong, reduced to such extremity, without doing what he could to help him. Mr Haredale shook him warmly by the hand, and thanked him from his heart. In five minutes' time the chaise was ready, and this good scapegrace in his saddle. The murderer was put inside, the blinds were drawn up, the sexton took his seat upon the bar, Mr Haredale mounted his horse and rode close beside the door; and so they started in the dead of night, and in profound silence, for London.

The consternation was so extreme that even the horses which had escaped the flames at the Warren, could find no friends to shelter them. They passed them on the road, browzing on the stunted grass; and the driver told them, that the poor beasts had wandered to the village first, but had been driven away, lest they should bring the vengeance of the crowd on any of the inhabitants.

Nor was this feeling confined to such small places, where the people were timid, ignorant, and unprotected. When they came near London they met, in the grey light of morning, more than one poor catholic family who, terrified by the threats and warnings of their neighbours, were quitting the city on foot, and who told them they could hire no cart or horse for the removal of their goods, and had been compelled to leave them behind, at the mercy of the crowd. Near Mile-end[1] they passed a house, the master of which, a catholic gentleman of small means, having hired a waggon to remove his furniture by midnight, had had it all brought down into the street, to wait the vehicle's arrival, and save time in the packing. But the man with whom he made the bargain, alarmed by the fires that night, and by the sight of the rioters passing his door, had refused to keep it: and the poor gentleman, with his wife and servant and their little children, were sitting trembling among their goods in the open street, dreading the arrival of day and not knowing where to turn or what to do.

It was the same, they heard, with the public conveyances. The panic was so great that the mails and stage-coaches were afraid to carry passengers who professed the obnoxious religion. If the drivers knew them, or they admitted that they held that creed, they would not take them, no, though they offered large sums; and yesterday, people had been afraid to recognise catholic acquaintance in the streets, lest they should be marked by spies, and burnt out, as it was called, in consequence. One mild old man – a priest, whose chapel was destroyed; a very feeble, patient, inoffensive creature – who was trudging away, alone, designing to walk some distance from town, and then try his fortune with the coaches, told Mr Haredale that he feared he might not find a magistrate who would have the hardihood to commit a prisoner to jail, on his complaint. But notwithstanding these discouraging accounts they went on, and reached the Mansion House[2] soon after sunrise.

Mr Haredale threw himself from his horse, but he had no need to knock at the door, for it was already open, and there stood upon the step a portly old man, with a very red, or rather purple face, who, with an anxious expression of countenance, was remonstrating with some unseen person up-stairs, while the porter essayed to close the door by degrees and get rid of him. With the intense impatience and excitement natural to one in his condition, Mr Haredale thrust himself forward and was about to speak, when the fat old gentleman interposed:

'My good sir,' said he, 'pray let me get an answer. This is the sixth time I have been here. I was here five times yesterday. My house is threatened with destruction. It is to be burned down to-night, and was to have been last night, but they had other business on their hands. Pray let me get an answer.'

'My good sir,' returned Mr Haredale, shaking his head, 'my house is burned to the ground. But God forbid that yours should be. Get your answer. Be brief, in mercy to me.'

'Now, you hear this, my Lord?' – said the old gentleman, calling up the stairs, to where the skirt of a dressing-gown fluttered on the landing-place. 'Here is a gentleman here, whose house was actually burnt down last night.'

'Dear me, dear me,' replied a testy voice, 'I am very sorry for it, but what am I to do? I can't build it up again. The chief magistrate of the city can't go and be a rebuilding of people's houses, my good sir. Stuff and nonsense!'

'But the chief magistrate of the city can prevent people's houses from having any need to be rebuilt, if the chief magistrate's a man, and not a dummy – can't he, my Lord?' cried the old gentleman in a choleric manner.

'You are disrespectable, sir,' said the Lord Mayor[3] – 'leastways, disrespectful I mean.'

'Disrespectful, my Lord!' returned the old gentleman. 'I was respectful five times yesterday. I can't be respectful for ever. Men can't stand on being respectful when their houses are going to be burnt over their heads, with them in 'em. What am I to do, my Lord? *Am* I to have any protection!'

'I told you yesterday, sir,' said the Lord Mayor, 'that you might have an alderman in your house, if you could get one to come.'

'What the devil's the good of an alderman?' returned the choleric old gentleman.

'– To awe the crowd, sir,' said the Lord Mayor.

'Oh Lord ha' mercy!' whimpered the old gentleman, as he wiped his forehead in a state of ludicrous distress, 'to think of sending an alderman to awe a crowd! Why, my Lord, if they were even so many babies, fed on mother's milk, what do you think they'd care for an alderman! Will *you* come?'

'I!' said the Lord Mayor, most emphatically: 'Certainly not.'

'Then what,' returned the old gentleman, 'what am I to do? Am

I a citizen of England? Am I to have the benefit of the laws? Am I to have any return for the King's Taxes?'

'I don't know, I am sure,' said the Lord Mayor; 'what a pity it is you're a catholic! Why couldn't you be a protestant, and then you wouldn't have got yourself into such a mess? I'm sure I don't know what's to be done. – There are great people at the bottom of these riots. – Oh dear me, what a thing it is to be a public character! – You must look in again in the course of the day. – Would a javelin-man do? – Or there's Philips the constable, – *he's* disengaged, – he's not very old for a man at his time of life, except in his legs, and if you put him up at a window he'd look quite young by candle-light, and might frighten 'em very much. – Oh dear! – well, – we'll see about it.'

'Stop!' cried Mr Haredale, pressing the door open as the porter strove to shut it, and speaking rapidly, 'My Lord Mayor, I beg you not to go away. I have a man here, who committed a murder eight-and-twenty years ago. Half-a-dozen words from me, on oath, will justify you in committing him to prison for re-examination. I only seek, just now, to have him consigned to a place of safety. The least delay may involve his being rescued by the rioters.'

'Oh dear me!' cried the Lord Mayor. 'God bless my soul – and body – oh Lor! – well I! – there are great people at the bottom of these riots, you know. – You really mustn't.'

'My Lord,' said Mr Haredale, 'the murdered gentleman was my brother; I succeeded to his inheritance; there were not wanting slanderous tongues at that time, to whisper that the guilt of this most foul and cruel deed was mine – mine, who loved him, as he knows, in Heaven, dearly. The time has come, after all these years of gloom and misery, for avenging him, and bringing to light a crime so artful and so devilish that it has no parallel. Every second's delay on your part loosens this man's bloody hands again, and leads to his escape. My Lord, I charge you hear me, and despatch this matter on the instant.'

'Oh dear me!' cried the chief magistrate; 'these an't business hours, you know – I wonder at you – how ungentlemanly it is of you – you mustn't – you really mustn't. – And I suppose *you* are a catholic too?'

'I am,' said Mr Haredale.

'God bless my soul, I believe people turn catholics a' purpose to vex and worrit me,' cried the Lord Mayor. I wish you wouldn't come here; they'll be setting the Mansion House afire next, and we shall have you to thank for it. You must lock your prisoner up, sir – give him to a watchman – and – and call again at a proper time. Then we'll see about it!'

Before Mr Haredale could answer, the sharp closing of a door and drawing of its bolts, gave notice that the Lord Mayor had retreated to his bedroom, and that further remonstrance would be unavailing. The two clients retreated likewise, and the porter shut them out into the street.

'That's the way he puts me off,' said the old gentleman, 'I can get no redress and no help. What are you going to do, sir?'

'To try elsewhere,' answered Mr Haredale, who was by this time on horseback.

'I feel for you, I assure you – and well I may, for we are in a common cause,' said the old gentleman. 'I may not have a house to offer you to-night; let me tender it while I can. On second thoughts though,' he added, putting up a pocket-book he had produced while speaking, 'I'll not give you a card, for if it was found upon you, it might get you into trouble. Langdale[4] – that's my name – vintner and distiller – Holborn Hill – you're heartily welcome, if you'll come.'

Mr Haredale bowed his head, and rode off, close beside the chaise as before; determining to repair to the house of Sir John Fielding, who had the reputation of being a bold and active magistrate, and fully resolved, in case the rioters should come upon them, to do execution on the murderer with his own hands, rather than suffer him to be released.

They arrived at the magistrate's dwelling, however, without molestation (for the mob, as we have seen, were then intent on deeper schemes), and knocked at the door. As it had been pretty generally rumoured that Sir John was proscribed by the rioters, a body of thief-takers[5] had been keeping watch in the house all night. To one of them, Mr Haredale stated his business, which appearing to the man of sufficient moment to warrant his arousing the justice, procured him an immediate audience.

No time was lost in committing the murderer to Newgate; then a new building, recently completed at a vast expense, and considered to be of enormous strength. The warrant being made out, three of the thief-takers bound him afresh (he had been struggling, it seemed, in the chaise, and had loosened his manacles); gagged him, lest they should meet with any of the mob, and he should call to them for help; and seated themselves, along with him, in the carriage. These men being all well armed, made a formidable escort; but they drew up the blinds again, as though the carriage were empty, and directed Mr Haredale to ride forward, that he might not attract attention by seeming to belong to it.

The wisdom of this proceeding was sufficiently obvious, for as they hurried through the city they passed among several groups of men, who, if they had not supposed the chaise to be quite empty, would certainly have stopped it. But those within keeping quite close, and the driver tarrying to be asked no questions, they reached the prison without interruption, and, once there, had him out, and safe within its gloomy walls, in a twinkling.

With eager eyes and strained attention, Mr Haredale saw him chained, and locked and barred up in his cell. Nay, when he had left the jail, and stood in the free street, without, he felt the iron plates upon the doors, with his hands, and drew them over the stone wall, to assure himself that it was real; and to exult in its being so strong, and rough, and cold. It was not until he turned his back upon the jail, and glanced along the empty streets, so lifeless and quiet in the bright morning, that he felt the weight upon his heart; that he knew he was tortured by anxiety for those he had left at home; and that home itself was but another bead in the long rosary of his regrets.

CHAPTER THE SIXTY-SECOND

The prisoner, left to himself, sat down upon his bedstead: and resting his elbows on his knees, and his chin upon his hands, remained in that attitude for hours. It would be hard to say, of what nature his reflections were. They had no distinctness, and, saving for some flashes now and then, no reference to his condition or the train of circumstances by which it had been brought about. The cracks in the pavement of his cell, the chinks in the wall where stone was joined to stone, the bars in the window, the iron ring upon the floor, – such things as these, subsiding strangely into one another, and awakening an indescribable kind of interest and amusement, engrossed his whole mind; and although at the bottom

of his every thought there was an uneasy sense of guilt, and dread
of death, he felt no more than that vague consciousness of it, which
a sleeper has of pain. It pursues him through his dreams, gnaws at
the heart of all his fancied pleasures, robs the banquet of its taste,
music of its sweetness, makes happiness itself unhappy, and yet is
no bodily sensation, but a phantom without shape, or form, or
visible presence; pervading everything, but having no existence;
recognizable everywhere, but nowhere seen, or touched, or met
with face to face, until the sleep is past, and waking agony
returns.

After a long time, the door of his cell opened. He looked up; saw
the blind man enter; and relapsed into his former position.

Guided by his breathing, the visitor advanced to where he sat;
and stopping beside him, and stretching out his hand to assure
himself that he was right, remained, for a good space, silent.

'This is bad, Rudge. This is bad,' he said at length.

The prisoner shuffled with his feet upon the ground in turning
his body from him, but made no other answer.

'How were you taken?' he asked. 'And where? You never told
me more than half your secret. No matter; I know it now. How
was it, and where, eh?' he asked again, coming still nearer to
him.

'At Chigwell,' said the other.

'At Chigwell! How came you there?'

'Because I went there, to avoid the man I stumbled on,' he
answered. 'Because I was chased and driven there, by him and Fate.
Because I was urged to go there, by something stronger than my
own will. When I found him watching in the house she used to live
in, night after night, I knew I never could escape him – never! and
when I heard the Bell –'

He shivered; muttered that it was very cold; paced quickly up
and down the narrow cell; and sitting down again, fell into his old
posture.

'You were saying,' said the blind man, after another pause, 'that
when you heard the Bell –'

'Let it be, will you?' he retorted in a hurried voice. 'It hangs there
yet.'

The blind man turned a wistful and inquisitive face towards him,
but he continued to speak, without noticing him.

'I went to Chigwell, in search of the mob. I have been so hunted and beset by this man, that I knew my only hope of safety lay in joining them. They had gone on before; I followed them, when it left off.'

'When what left off?'

'The Bell. They had quitted the place. I hoped that some of them might be still lingering among the ruins, and was searching for them when I heard – ' he drew a long breath, and wiped his forehead with his sleeve – 'his voice.'

'Saying what?'

'No matter what. I don't know. I was then at the foot of the turret, where I did the – '

'Ay,' said the blind man, nodding his head with perfect composure, 'I understand.'

'I climbed the stair, or so much of it as was left; meaning to hide till he had gone. But he heard me; and followed almost as soon as I set foot upon the ashes.'

'You might have hidden in the wall, and thrown him down, or stabbed him,' said the blind man.

'Might I? Between that man and me, was one who led him on – I saw it, though he did not – and raised above his head a bloody hand. It was in the room above that *he* and I stood glaring at each other on the night of the murder, and before he fell he raised his hand like that, and fixed his eyes on me. I knew the chase would end there.'

'You have a strong fancy,' said the blind man, with a smile.

'Strengthen yours with blood, and see what it will come to.'

He groaned, and rocked himself, and looking up for the first time, said, in a low, hollow voice:

'Eight-and-twenty years! Eight-and-twenty years! He has never changed in all that time, never grown older, nor altered in the least degree. He has been before me in the dark night, and the broad sunny day; in the twilight, the moonlight, the sunlight, the light of fire, and lamp, and candle; and in the deepest gloom. Always the same! In company, in solitude, on land, on shipboard; sometimes leaving me alone for months, and sometimes always with me. I have seen him, at sea, come gliding in the dead of night along the bright reflection of the moon in the calm water; and I have seen him, on quays and market-places, with his hand uplifted, towering, the centre of a busy crowd, unconscious of the terrible form that had its silent stand among them. Fancy! Are you real? Am I? Are these iron fetters, rivetted on me by the smith's hammer, or are they fancies I can shatter at a blow?'

The blind man listened in silence.

'Fancy! Do I fancy that I killed him? Do I fancy that as I left the chamber where he lay, I saw the face of a man peeping from a dark door, who plainly showed me by his fearful looks that he suspected what I had done? Do I remember that I spoke fairly to him – that I drew nearer – nearer yet – with the hot knife in my sleeve? Do I fancy how *he* died? Did he stagger back into the angle of the wall into which I had hemmed him, and, bleeding inwardly, stand, not fall, a corpse before me? Did I see him, as I see you now, erect and on his feet – but dead!'

The blind man, who knew that he had risen, motioned him to sit down again upon his bedstead; but he took no notice of the gesture.

'It was then I thought, for the first time, of fastening the murder upon him. It was then I dressed him in my clothes, and dragged him down the back stairs to the piece of water. Do I remember listening to the bubbles that came rising up when I had rolled him in? Do I remember wiping the water from my face, and because the body splashed it there, in its descent, feeling as if it *must* be blood?

'Did I go home when I had done? And oh, my God! how long it took to do! Did I stand before my wife, and tell her? Did I see her fall upon the ground; and, when I stooped to raise her, did she thrust me back with a force that cast me off as if I had been a child, staining the hand with which she clasped my wrist? Is *that* fancy?

'Did she go down upon her knees, and call on Heaven to witness that she and her unborn child renounced me from that hour; and did she, in words so solemn that they turned me cold – me, fresh from the horrors my own hands had made – warn me to fly while there was time; for though she would be silent, being my wretched wife, she would not shelter me? Did I go forth that night, abjured of God and man, and anchored deep in hell; to wander at my cable's length about the earth, and surely be drawn down at last?'

'Why did you return?' said the blind man.

'Why is blood red? I could no more help it, than I could live without breath. I struggled against the impulse, but I was drawn back, through every difficult and adverse circumstance, as by a mighty engine. Nothing could stop me. The day and hour were none of my choice. Sleeping and waking, I had been among the old haunts for years – had visited my own grave. Why did I come back? Because this jail was gaping for me, and he stood beckoning at the door.'

'You were not known?' said the blind man.

'I was a man who had been twenty-two years dead. No. I was not known.'

'You should have kept your secret better.'

'*My* secret? *Mine?* It was a secret, any breath of air could whisper at its will. The stars had it in their twinkling, the water in its flowing, the leaves in their rustling, the seasons in their return. It lurked in strangers' faces, and their voices. Everything had lips on which it always trembled – *My* secret!'

'It was revealed by your own act at any rate,' said the blind man.

'The act was not mine. I did it, but it was not mine. I was obliged at times to wander round, and round, and round that spot. If you had chained me up when the fit was on me, I should have broken away, and gone there. As truly as the loadstone draws iron towards it, so he, lying at the bottom of his deep grave, could draw me near him when he would. Was that fancy? Did I like to go there, or did I strive and wrestle with the power that forced me?'

The blind man shrugged his shoulders, and smiled incredulously. The prisoner again resumed his old attitude, and for a long time both were mute.

'I suppose then,' said his visitor, at length breaking silence, 'that you are penitent and resigned; that you desire to make peace with everybody (in particular, with your wife who has brought you to this); and that you ask no greater favour than to be carried to Tyburn as soon as possible? That being the case, I had better take my leave. I am not good enough to be company for you.'

'Have I not told you,' said the other fiercely, 'that I have striven and wrestled with the power that brought me here? Has my whole life, for eight-and-twenty years, been one perpetual struggle and resistance, and do you think I want to lie down and die? Do all men shrink from death – I most of all!'

'That's better said. That's better spoken, Rudge – but I'll not call you that again – than anything you have said yet,' returned the blind man, speaking more familiarly, and laying his hand upon his arm. 'Lookye, – I never killed a man myself, for I have never been placed in a position that made it worth my while. Farther, I am not an advocate for killing men, and I don't think I should recommend it or like it – for it's very hazardous – under any circumstances. But as you had the misfortune to get into this trouble before I made your acquaintance, and as you have been my companion, and have been of use to me for a long time now, I overlook that part of the matter, and am only anxious that you shouldn't die unnecessarily. Now I do not consider that at present it is at all necessary.'

'What else is left me?' returned the prisoner. 'To eat my way through these walls with my teeth?'

'Something easier than that,' returned his friend. 'Promise me that you will talk no more of these fancies of yours – idle, foolish things, quite beneath a man – and I'll tell you what I mean.'

'Tell me,' said the other.

'Your worthy lady with the tender conscience; your scrupulous, virtuous, punctilious, but not blindly affectionate wife –'

'What of her?'

'Is now in London.'

'A curse upon her, be she where she may!'

'That's natural enough. If she had taken her annuity as usual, you would not have been here, and we should have been better off. But that's apart from the business. She's in London. Scared, as I suppose, and have no doubt, by my representation when I waited upon her, that you were close at hand (which I, of course, urged only as an inducement to compliance, knowing that she was not pining to see you), she left that place, and travelled up to London.'

'How do you know?'

'From my friend the noble captain – the illustrious general – the bladder, Mr Tappertit. I learnt from him the last time I saw him, which was yesterday, that your son who is called Barnaby – not after his father I suppose –'

'Death! does that matter now!'

'– You are impatient,' said the blind man calmly; 'it's a good sign, and looks like life – that your son Barnaby had been lured away from her by one of his companions who knew him of old, at Chigwell; and that he is now among the rioters.'

'And what is that to me? If father and son be hanged together, what comfort shall I find in that?'

'Stay – stay, my friend,' returned the blind man, with a cunning look, 'you travel fast to journeys' ends. Suppose I track my lady out, and say thus much: "You want your son, ma'am – good. I, knowing those who tempt him to remain among them, can restore him to you, ma'am – good. You must pay a price, ma'am, for his restoration – good again. The price is small, and easy to be paid – dear ma'am, that's best of all." '

'What mockery is this?'

'Very likely, she may reply in those words. "No mockery at all," I answer. "Madam, a person said to be your husband (identity is difficult of proof after the lapse of many years) is in prison, his life in peril – the charge against him, murder. Now, ma'am, your husband has been dead a long, long time. The gentleman never can be confounded with him, if you will have the goodness to say a few words, on oath, as to when he died, and how; and that this person (who I am told resembles him in some degree) is no more he than I am. Such testimony will set the question quite at rest. Pledge yourself to me to give it, ma'am, and I will undertake to keep your son (a fine lad) out of harm's way until you have done this trifling service, when he shall be delivered up to you, safe and sound. On the other hand, if you decline to do so, I fear he will be betrayed, and handed over to the law, which will assuredly sentence him to suffer death. It is, in fact, a choice between his life and death. If you refuse, he swings. If you comply, the timber is not grown, nor the hemp sown, that shall do him any harm." '

'There is a gleam of hope in this!' cried the prisoner, starting up.

'A gleam!' returned his friend, 'a noon-blaze; a full and glorious daylight. Hush! I hear the tread of distant feet. Rely on me.'

'When shall I hear more?'

'As soon as I do. I should hope, to-morrow. They are coming to say that our time for talk is over. I hear the jingling of the keys. Not another word of this just now, or they may overhear us.'

As he said these words, the lock was turned, and one of the prison turnkeys appearing at the door, announced that it was time for visitors to leave the jail.

'So soon!' said Stagg, meekly. 'But it can't be helped. Cheer up, friend. This mistake will soon be set at rest, and then you are a man again![1] If this charitable gentleman will lead a blind man (who has nothing in return but prayers) to the prison-porch, and set him with his face towards the west, he will do a worthy deed. Thank you, good sir. I thank you very kindly.'

So saying, and pausing for an instant at the door to turn his grinning face towards his friend, he departed.

When the officer had seen him to the porch, he returned, and again unlocking and unbarring the door of the cell, set it wide open, informing its inmate that he was at liberty to walk in the adjacent yard, if he thought proper, for an hour.

The prisoner answered with a sullen nod; and being left alone again, sat brooding over what he had heard, and pondering upon the hopes the recent conversation had awakened; gazing abstractedly, the while he did so, on the light without, and watching the shadows thrown by one wall on another, and on the stone-paved ground.

It was a dull, square yard, made cold and gloomy by high walls, and seeming to chill the very sunlight. The stone, so bare, and rough, and obdurate, filled even him with longing thoughts of meadow-land and trees; and with a burning wish to be at liberty. As he looked, he rose, and leaning against the door-post, gazed up at the bright blue sky, smiling even on that dreary home of crime. He seemed, for a moment, to remember lying on his back in some sweet-scented place, and gazing at it through moving branches, long ago.

His attention was suddenly attracted by a clanking sound – he knew what it was, for he had startled himself by making the same noise in walking to the door. Presently a voice began to sing, and he saw the shadow of a figure on the pavement. It stopped – was silent all at once, as though the person for a moment had forgotten where he was, but soon remembered – and so, with the same clanking noise, the shadow disappeared.

He walked out into the court and paced it to and fro; startling the echoes, as he went, with the harsh jangling of his fetters. There was a door near his, which, like his, stood ajar.

He had not taken half-a-dozen turns up and down the yard, when, standing still to observe this door, he heard the clanking sound again. A face looked out of the grated window – he saw it very dimly, for the cell was dark and the bars were heavy – and directly afterwards, a man appeared, and came towards him.

For the sense of loneliness he had, he might have been in the jail a year. Made eager by the hope of companionship, he quickened his pace, and hastened to meet the man half way –

What was this! His son!

They stood face to face, staring at each other. He shrinking and cowed, despite himself; Barnaby struggling with his imperfect memory, and wondering where he had seen that face, before. He

was not uncertain long, for suddenly he laid hands upon him, and striving to bear him to the ground, cried:

'Ah! I know! You are the robber!'

He said nothing in reply at first, but held down his head, and struggled with him silently. Finding the younger man too strong for him, he raised his face, looked close into his eyes, and said,

'I am your father.'

God knows what magic the name had for his ears; but Barnaby released his hold, fell back, and looked at him aghast. Suddenly he sprung towards him, put his arms about his neck, and pressed his head against his cheek.

Yes, yes, he was; he was sure he was. But where had he been so long, and why had he left his mother by herself, or worse than by herself, with her poor foolish boy? And had she really been as happy as they said? And where was she? Was she near there? She was not happy now, and he in jail? Ah, no.

Not a word was said in answer; but Grip croaked loudly, and hopped about them, round and round, as if enclosing them in a magic circle, and invoking all the powers of mischief.

*

CHAPTER THE SIXTY-THIRD

During the whole of this day, every regiment in or near the metropolis was on duty in one or other part of the town; and the regulars and militia, in obedience to the orders which were sent to every barrack and station within twenty-four hours' journey, began to pour in by all the roads. But the disturbances had attained to such a formidable height, and the rioters had grown, with impunity, to be so audacious and so daring, that the sight of this great force, continually augmented by new arrivals, instead of operating as a check, stimulated them to outrages of greater hardihood than any they had yet committed; and helped to kindle a flame in London, the like of which had never been beheld, even in its ancient and rebellious times.

All yesterday, and on this day likewise, the commander-in-chief[1] endeavoured to arouse the magistrates to a sense of their duty, and in particular the Lord Mayor, who was the faintest-hearted and most timid of them all. With this object, large bodies of the soldiery were several times despatched to the Mansion House to await his orders: but as he could, by no threats or persuasions, be induced to give any; and as the men remained in the open street, fruitlessly for any good purpose, and thrivingly for a very bad one; these laudable attempts did harm rather than good. For the crowd, becoming speedily acquainted with the Lord Mayor's temper, did not fail to take advantage of it, by boasting that even the civil authorities were opposed to the Papists, and could not find it in their hearts to molest those who were guilty of no other offence. These vaunts they took care to make within the hearing of the soldiers; and they, being naturally loath to quarrel with the people, received their advances kindly enough: answering, when they were asked if they desired to fire upon their countrymen, 'No, they would be damned if they did;' and showing much honest simplicity, and good-nature. The feeling that the military were No Popery men, and were ripe for disobeying orders and joining the mob, soon became very prevalent in consequence. Rumours of their disaffection, and of their leaning towards the popular cause, spread from mouth to mouth with astonishing rapidity; and whenever they were drawn up idly in the streets or squares, there was sure to be a crowd about them, cheering, and shaking hands, and treating them with a great show of confidence and affection.

By this time, the crowd was everywhere; all concealment and disguise were laid aside, and they pervaded the whole town. If any man among them wanted money, he had but to knock at the door of a dwelling-house, or walk into a shop, and demand it in the rioters' name; and his demand was instantly complied with. The peaceable citizens being afraid to lay hands upon them, singly and alone, it may be easily supposed that when gathered together in bodies, they were perfectly secure from interruption. They assembled in the streets, traversed them at their will and pleasure, and publicly concerted their plans. Business was quite suspended; the greater part of the shops were closed; most of the houses displayed a blue flag in token of their adherence to the popular side; and even the Jews in Houndsditch,[2] Whitechapel, and those quarters, wrote upon their doors or window-shutters 'This House is a True Protestant.' The crowd was the law, and never was the law held in greater dread, or more implicitly obeyed.

It was about six o'clock in the evening, when a vast mob poured

into Lincoln's Inn Fields by every avenue, and divided – evidently
in pursuance of a previous design – into several parties. It must not
be understood that this arrangement was known to the whole
crowd, but that it was the work of a few leaders; who, mingling
with the men as they came upon the ground, and calling to them to
fall into this or that party, effected it as rapidly as if it had been
determined on by a council of the whole number, and every man
had known his place.

It was perfectly notorious to the assemblage that the largest body,
which comprehended about two-thirds of the whole, was designed
for the attack on Newgate. It comprehended all the rioters who
had been conspicuous in any of their former proceedings; all those
whom they recommended as daring hands and fit for the work; all
those whose companions had been taken in the riots; and a great
number of people who were relatives or friends of felons in the jail.
This last class included, not only the most desperate and utterly
abandoned villains in London, but some who were comparatively
innocent. There was more than one woman there, disguised in
man's attire, and bent upon the rescue of a child or brother. There
were the two sons of a man who lay under sentence of death, and
who was to be executed along with three others, on the next day
but one. There was a great party of boys whose fellow pickpockets
were in the prison; and at the skirts of all, a score of miserable
women, outcasts from the world, seeking to release some other
fallen creature as miserable as themselves, or moved by a general
sympathy perhaps – God knows – with all who were without hope,
and wretched.

Old swords, and pistols without ball or powder; sledge-hammers,
knives, axes, saws, and weapons pillaged from the butchers' shops;
a forest of iron bars and wooden clubs; long ladders for scaling the
walls, each carried on the shoulders of a dozen men; lighted torches;
tow smeared with pitch, and tar, and brimstone; staves roughly
plucked from fence and paling; and even crutches torn from
crippled beggars in the streets; composed their arms. When all was
ready, Hugh and Dennis, with Simon Tappertit between them, led
the way. Roaring and chafing like an angry sea, the crowd pressed
after them.

Instead of going straight down Holborn to the jail, as all
expected, their leaders took the way to Clerkenwell, and rushing

down a quiet street, halted before a locksmith's house – the Golden Key.

'Beat at the door,' cried Hugh to the men about him. 'We want one of his craft to-night. Beat it in, if no one answers.'

The shop was shut. Both door and shutters were of a strong and sturdy kind, and they knocked without effect. But the impatient crowd raising a cry of 'Set fire to the house!' and torches being passed to the front, an upper window was thrown open, and the stout old locksmith stood before them.

'What now, ye villains!' he demanded. 'Where is my daughter?'

'Ask no questions of us, old man,' retorted Hugh, waving his comrades to be silent, 'but come down, and bring the tools of your trade. We want you.'

'Want me!' cried the locksmith, glancing at the regimental dress he wore: 'Ay, and if some that I could name possessed the hearts of mice, ye should have had me long ago. Mark me, my lad – and you about him do the same. There are a score among ye whom I see now and know, who are dead men from this hour. Begone! and rob an undertaker's while you can! You'll want some coffins before long.'

'Will you come down?' cried Hugh.

'Will you give me my daughter, ruffian?' cried the locksmith.

'I know nothing of her,' Hugh rejoined. 'Burn the door!'

'Stop!' cried the locksmith, in a voice that made them falter – presenting, as he spoke, a gun. 'Let an old man do that. You can spare him better.'

The young fellow who held the light, and who was stooping down before the door, rose hastily at these words, and fell back. The locksmith ran his eye along the upturned faces, and kept the weapon levelled at the threshold of his house. It had no other rest than his shoulder, but was as steady as the house itself.

'Let the man who does it, take heed to his prayers,' he said firmly; 'I warn him.'

Snatching a torch from one who stood near him, Hugh was stepping forward with an oath, when he was arrested by a shrill and piercing shriek, and, looking upward, saw a fluttering garment on the house-top.

There was another shriek, and another, and then a shrill voice cried, 'Is Simmun below!' At the same moment a lean neck was

stretched over the parapet, and Miss Miggs, indistinctly seen in the
gathering gloom of evening, screeched in a frenzied manner, 'Oh!
dear gentlemen, let me hear Simmuns's answer from his own lips.
Speak to me, Simmun. Speak to me!'

Mr Tappertit, who was not at all flattered by this compliment,
looked up, and bidding her hold her peace, ordered her to come
down and open the door, for they wanted her master, and would
take no denial.

'Oh good gentlemen!' cried Miss Miggs. 'Oh my own precious,
precious Simmun –'

'Hold your nonsense, will you!' retorted Mr Tappertit; 'and come
down and open the door. – G. Varden, drop that gun, or it will be
worse for you.'

'Don't mind his gun,' screamed Miggs. 'Simmun and gentlemen,
I poured a mug of table-beer right down the barrel.'

The crowd gave a loud shout, which was followed by a roar of
laughter.

'It wouldn't go off, not if you was to load it up to the muzzle,'
screamed Miggs. 'Simmun and gentlemen, I'm locked up in the
front attic, through the little door on the right hand when you think
you've got to the very top of the stairs – and up the flight of corner
steps, being careful not to knock your heads against the rafters,
and not to tread on one side in case you should fall into the two-pair
bed-room through the lath and plasture, which do not bear, but
the contrairy. Simmun and gentlemen, I've been locked up here for
safety, but my endeavours has always been, and always will be, to
be on the right side – the blessed side – and to prenounce the Pope
of Babylon,[3] and all her inward and her outward workings, which
is Pagin. My sentiments is of little consequences, I know,' cried
Miggs, with additional shrillness, 'for my positions is but a servant,
and as sich, of humilities; still I gives expressions to my feelings,
and places my reliances on them which entertains my own
opinions!'

Without taking much notice of these outpourings of Miss Miggs
after she had made her first announcement in relation to the gun,
the crowd raised a ladder against the window where the locksmith
stood, and notwithstanding that he closed, and fastened, and
defended it manfully, soon forced an entrance by shivering the glass
and breaking in the frames. After dealing a few stout blows about
him, he found himself defenceless, in the midst of a furious crowd,

which overflowed the room and softened off in a confused heap of faces at the door and window.

They were very wrathful with him (for he had wounded two men), and even called out to those in front, to bring him forth and hang him on a lamp-post. But Gabriel was quite undaunted, and looked from Hugh and Dennis, who held him by either arm, to Simon Tappertit, who confronted him.

'You have robbed me of my daughter,' said the locksmith, 'who is far, far dearer to me than my life; and you may take my life, if you will. I bless God that I have been enabled to keep my wife free of this scene; and that He has made me a man who will not ask mercy at such hands as yours.'

'And a wery game old gentleman you are,' said Mr Dennis, approvingly; 'and you express yourself like a man. What's the odds, brother, whether it's a lamp-post to-night, or a feather-bed ten year to come, eh?'

The locksmith glanced at him disdainfully, but returned no other answer.

'For my part,' said the hangman, who particularly favoured the lamp-post suggestion, 'I honour your principles. They're mine exactly. In such sentiments as them,' and here he emphasized his discourse with an oath, 'I'm ready to meet you or any man half-way. – Have you got a bit of cord anywheres handy? Don't put yourself out of the way, if you haven't. A handkecher will do.'

'Don't be a fool, master,' whispered Hugh, seizing Varden roughly by the shoulder; 'but do as you're bid. You'll soon hear what you're wanted for. Do it!'

'I'll do nothing at your request, or that of any scoundrel here,' returned the locksmith. 'If you want any service from me, you may spare yourselves the pains of telling me what it is. I tell you, beforehand, I'll do nothing for you.'

Mr Dennis was so affected by this constancy on the part of the staunch old man, that he protested – almost with tears in his eyes – that to balk his inclinations would be an act of cruelty and hard dealing to which he, for one, never could reconcile his conscience. The gentleman, he said, had avowed in so many words that he was ready for working off; such being the case, he considered it their duty, as a civilised and enlightened crowd, to work him off. It was not often, he observed, that they had it in their power to accommodate themselves to the wishes of those from whom they had the misfortune to differ. Having now found an individual who expressed a desire which they could reasonably indulge, (and for himself he was free to confess that in his opinion that desire did honour to his feelings), he hoped they would decide to accede to his proposition before going any further. It was an experiment which, skilfully and dexterously performed, would be over in five minutes, with great comfort and satisfaction to all parties; and though it did not become him (Mr Dennis) to speak well of himself, he trusted he might be allowed to say that he had practical knowledge of the subject, and, being naturally of an obliging and friendly disposition, would work the gentleman off with a deal of pleasure.

These remarks, which were addressed in the midst of a frightful din and turmoil to those immediately about him, were received with great favour; not so much, perhaps, because of the hangman's eloquence, as on account of the locksmith's obstinacy. Gabriel was in imminent peril, and he knew it; but he preserved a steady silence; and would have done so, if they had been debating whether they should roast him at a slow fire.

As the hangman spoke, there was some stir and confusion on the ladder; and directly he was silent – so immediately upon his holding his peace, that the crowd below had no time to learn what he had been saying, or to shout in response – some one at the window cried:

'He has a grey head. He is an old man: Don't hurt him!'

The locksmith turned, with a start, towards the place from which the words had come, and looked hurriedly at the people who were hanging on the ladder and clinging to each other.

'Pay no respect to my grey hair, young man,' he said, answering the voice and not any one he saw. 'I don't ask it. My heart is green enough to scorn and despise every man among you, – band of robbers that you are!'

This incautious speech by no means tended to appease the ferocity of the crowd. They cried again to have him brought out; and it would have gone hard with the honest locksmith, but that Hugh reminded them, in answer, that they wanted his services, and must have them.

'So, tell him what we want,' he said to Simon Tappertit, 'and quickly. And open your ears, master, if you would ever use them after to-night.'

Gabriel folded his arms, which were now at liberty, and eyed his old 'prentice in silence.

'Lookye, Varden,' said Sim, 'we're bound for Newgate.'

'I know you are,' returned the locksmith. 'You never said a truer word than that.'

'To burn it down, I mean,' said Simon, 'and force the gates, and set the prisoners at liberty. You helped to make the lock of the great door.'

'I did,' said the locksmith. 'You owe me no thanks for that – as you'll find before long.'

'Maybe,' returned his journeyman, 'but you must show us how to force it.'

'Must I!'

'Yes; for you know, and I don't. You must come along with us, and pick it with your own hands.'

'When I do,' said the locksmith quietly, 'my hands shall drop off at the wrists, and you shall wear them, Simon Tappertit, on your shoulders for epaulettes.'

'We'll see that,' cried Hugh, interposing, as the indignation of the crowd again burst forth. 'You fill a basket with the tools he'll want, while I bring him down stairs. Open the doors below, some of you. And light the great captain, others! Is there no business afoot, my lads, that you can do nothing but stand and grumble?'

They looked at one another, and quickly dispersing, swarmed over the house, plundering and breaking, according to their custom, and carrying off such articles of value as happened to please their fancy. They had no great length of time for these proceedings, for the basket of tools was soon prepared and slung over a man's shoulders. The preparations being now completed, and everything ready for the attack, those who were pillaging and destroying in the other rooms were called down to the workshop. They were about to issue forth, when the man who had been last up stairs, stepped forward, and asked if the young woman in the garret (who was making a terrible noise, he said, and kept on screaming without the least cessation) was to be released?

For his own part, Simon Tappertit would certainly have replied in the negative, but the mass of his companions, mindful of the good service she had done in the matter of the gun, being of a different opinion, he had nothing for it but to answer, Yes. The man, accordingly, went back again to the rescue, and presently returned with Miss Miggs, limp and doubled up, and very damp from much weeping.

As the young lady had given no tokens of consciousness on their way down stairs, the bearer reported her either dead or dying; and being at some loss what to do with her, was looking round for a convenient bench or heap of ashes on which to place her senseless form, when she suddenly came upon her feet by some mysterious means, thrust back her hair, stared wildly at Mr Tappertit, cried 'My Simmuns's life is not a wictim!' and dropped into his arms with such promptitude that he staggered and reeled some paces back, beneath his lovely burden.

'Oh bother!' said Mr Tappertit. 'Here. Catch hold of her, somebody. Lock her up again; she never ought to have been let out.'

'My Simmun!' cried Miss Miggs, in tears, and faintly. 'My for ever, ever blessed Simmun!'

'Hold up, will you,' said Mr Tappertit, in a very unresponsive tone, 'I'll let you fall if you don't. What are you sliding your feet off the ground for?'

'My angel Simmuns!' murmured Miggs – 'he promised –'

'Promised! Well, and I'll keep my promise,' answered Simon, testily. 'I mean to provide for you, don't I? Stand up!'

'Where am I to go? What is to become of me after my actions of this night!' cried Miggs. 'What resting-places now remains but in the silent tombs!'

'I wish you was in the silent tombs, I do,' cried Mr Tappertit, 'and boxed up tight, in a good strong one. Here,' he cried to one of the by-standers, in whose ear he whispered for a moment: 'Take her off, will you. You understand where?'

The fellow nodded; and taking her in his arms, notwithstanding her broken protestations, and her struggles (which latter species of opposition, involving scratches, was much more difficult of resistance), carried her away. They who were in the house poured out into the street; the locksmith was taken to the head of the crowd, and required to walk between his two conductors; the whole body was put in rapid motion; and without any shouting or noise they bore down straight on Newgate, and halted in a dense mass before the prison gate.

CHAPTER THE SIXTY-FOURTH

Breaking the silence they had hitherto preserved, they raised a great cry as soon as they were ranged before the jail, and demanded to speak with the governor. Their visit was not wholly unexpected, for his house, which fronted the street, was strongly barricaded, the wicket-gate of the prison was closed up, and at no loophole or grating was any person to be seen. Before they had repeated their summons many times, a man appeared upon the roof of the governor's house, and asked what it was they wanted.

Some said one thing, some another, and some only groaned and hissed. It being now nearly dark, and the house high, many persons in the throng were not aware that any one had come to answer them, and continued their clamour until the intelligence was gradually diffused through the whole concourse. Ten minutes or more elapsed before any one voice could be heard with tolerable distinctness; during which interval the figure remained perched alone, against the summer-evening sky, looking down into the troubled street.

'Are you,' said Hugh at length, 'Mr Akerman,[1] the head jailer here?'

'Of course he is, brother,' whispered Dennis. But Hugh, without minding him, took his answer from the man himself.

'Yes,' he said. 'I am.'

'You have got some friends of ours in your custody, master.'

'I have a good many people in my custody.' He glanced downward, as he spoke, into the jail: and the feeling that he could see into the different yards, and that he overlooked everything which was hidden from their view by the rugged walls, so lashed and goaded the mob, that they howled like wolves.

'Deliver up our friends,' said Hugh, 'and you may keep the rest.'

'It's my duty to keep them all. I shall do my duty.'

'If you don't throw the doors open, we shall break 'em down,' said Hugh; 'for we will have the rioters out.'

'All I can do, good people,' Akerman replied, 'is to exhort you to disperse; and to remind you that the consequences of any disturbance in this place, will be very severe, and bitterly repented by most of you, when it is too late.'

He made as though he would retire when he had said these words, but he was checked by the voice of the locksmith.

'Mr Akerman,' cried Gabriel, 'Mr Akerman.'

'I will hear no more from any of you,' replied the governor, turning towards the speaker, and waving his hand.

'But I am not one of them,' said Gabriel. 'I am an honest man, Mr Akerman; a respectable tradesman – Gabriel Varden, the locksmith. You know me?'

'You among the crowd!' cried the governor in an altered voice.

'Brought here by force – brought here to pick the lock of the great door for them,' rejoined the locksmith. 'Bear witness for me, Mr Akerman, that I refuse to do it; and that I will not do it, come what may of my refusal. If any violence is done to me, please to remember this.'

'Is there no way of helping you?' said the governor.

'None, Mr Akerman. You'll do your duty, and I'll do mine. Once again, you robbers and cut-throats,' said the locksmith, turning round upon them, 'I refuse. Howl till you're hoarse. I refuse.'

'Stay – stay!' said the jailer, hastily. 'Mr Varden, I know you for a worthy man, and one who would do no unlawful act except upon compulsion –'

'Upon compulsion, sir,' interposed the locksmith, who felt that the tone in which this was said, conveyed the speaker's impression that he had ample excuse for yielding to the furious multitude who beset and hemmed him in, on every side, and among whom he stood, an old man, quite alone; 'upon compulsion, sir, I'll do nothing.'

'Where is that man,' said the keeper, anxiously, 'who spoke to me just now?'

'Here!' Hugh replied.

'Do you know what the guilt of murder is, and that by keeping that honest tradesman at your side you endanger his life!'

'We know it very well,' he answered, 'for what else did we bring him here? Let's have our friends, master, and you shall have your friend. Is that fair, lads?'

The mob replied to him with a loud Hurrah!

'You see how it is, sir?' cried Varden. 'Keep 'em out, in King George's name. Remember what I have said. Good night!'

There was no more parley. A shower of stones and other missiles compelled the keeper of the jail to retire; and the mob, pressing on, and swarming round the walls, forced Gabriel Varden close up to the door.

In vain the basket of tools was laid upon the ground before him, and he was urged in turn by promises, by blows, by offers of reward, and threats of instant death, to do the office for which they had brought him there. 'No,' cried the sturdy locksmith, 'I will not!'

He had never loved his life so well as then, but nothing could move him. The savage faces that glared upon him, look where he would; the cries of those who thirsted, like wild animals, for his blood; the sight of men pressing forward, and trampling down their fellows, as they strove to reach him, and struck at him above the heads of other men, with axes and with iron bars; all failed to daunt him. He looked from man to man, and face to face, and still, with quickened breath and lessening colour, cried firmly, 'I will not!'

Dennis dealt him a blow upon the face which felled him to the ground. He sprung up again like a man in the prime of life, and with the crimson pouring from his forehead, caught him by the throat.

'You cowardly dog!' he said: 'Give me my daughter. Give me my daughter.'

They struggled together. Some cried 'Kill him,' and some (but they were not near enough) strove to trample him to death. Tug as he would at the old man's wrists, the hangman could not force him to unclench his hands.

'Is this all the return you make me, you ungrateful monster?' he articulated with great difficulty, and with many oaths.

'Give me my daughter!' cried the locksmith, who was now as fierce as those who gathered round him: 'Give me my daughter!'

He was down again, and up, and down once more, and buffeting with a score of them, who bandied him from hand to hand, when one tall fellow, fresh from a slaughter-house, whose dress and great thigh-boots smoked hot with grease and blood, raised a pole-axe, and swearing a horrible oath, aimed it at the old man's uncovered head. At that instant, and in the very act, he fell himself, as if struck by lightning, and over his body a one-armed man came darting to the locksmith's side. Another man was with him, and both caught the locksmith roughly in their grasp.

'Leave him to us!' they cried to Hugh – struggling, as they spoke, to force a passage backward through the crowd. 'Leave him to us. Why do you waste your whole strength on such as he, when a couple of men can finish him in as many minutes! You lose time. Remember the prisoners! remember Barnaby!'

The cry ran through the mob. Hammers began to rattle on the walls; and every man strove to reach the prison, and be among the foremost rank. Fighting their way through the press and struggle, as desperately as if they were in the midst of enemies rather than their own friends, the two men retreated with the locksmith between them, and dragged him through the very heart of the concourse.

And now the strokes began to fall like hail upon the gate, and on the strong building; for those who could not reach the door, spent their fierce rage on anything – even on the great blocks of stone, which shivered their weapons into fragments, and made their hands and arms to tingle as if the walls were active in their stout resistance, and dealt them back their blows. The clash of iron ringing upon iron, mingled with the deafening tumult and sounded high above it, as the great sledge-hammers rattled on the nailed and plated door: the sparks flew off in showers; men worked in gangs, and at short intervals relieved each other, that all their strength might be devoted to the work; but there stood the portal still, as grim and dark and strong as ever, and, saving for the dints upon its battered surface, quite unchanged.

While some brought all their energies to bear upon this toilsome task; and some, rearing ladders against the prison, tried to clamber to the summit of the walls they were too short to scale; and some again engaged a body of police a hundred strong, and beat them back and trod them under foot by force of numbers; others besieged the house on which the jailer had appeared, and, driving in the door, brought out his furniture, and piled it up against the prison gate, to make a bonfire which should burn it down. As soon as this device was understood, all those who had laboured hitherto, cast down their tools and helped to swell the heap; which reached half-way across the street, and was so high, that those who threw more fuel on the top, got up by ladders. When all the keeper's goods were flung upon this costly pile, to the last fragment, they smeared it with the pitch, and tar, and rosin they had brought, and sprinkled it with turpentine. To all the woodwork round the prison doors they did the like, leaving not a joist or beam un- touched. This infernal christening performed, they fired the pile with lighted matches and with blazing tow, and then stood by, awaiting the result.

The furniture being very dry, and rendered more combustible by wax and oil, besides the arts they had used, took fire at once. The flames roared high and fiercely, blackening the prison wall, and twining up its lofty front like burning serpents. At first, they crowded round the blaze, and vented their exultation only in their looks: but when it grew hotter and fiercer – when it crackled, leaped, and roared, like a great furnace – when it shone upon the opposite houses, and lighted up not only the pale and wondering faces at the windows, but the inmost corners of each habitation – when, through the deep red heat and glow, the fire was seen sporting and toying with the door, now clinging to its obdurate surface, now gliding off with fierce inconstancy and soaring high into the sky, anon returning to fold it in its burning grasp and lure it to its ruin – when it shone and gleamed so brightly that the church clock of St Sepulchre's,[2] so often pointing to the hour of death, was legible as in broad day, and the vane upon its steeple-top glittered in the unwonted light like something richly jewelled – when blackened stone and sombre brick grew ruddy in the deep reflection, and windows shone like burnished gold, dotting the longest distance in the fiery vista with their specks of brightness – when wall and tower, and roof and chimney-stack, seemed drunk, and in the flickering glare appeared to reel and stagger – when scores of objects, never seen before, burst out upon the view, and things the most familiar put on some new aspect – then the mob began to join the whirl, and with loud yells, and shouts, and clamour, such as happily is seldom heard, bestirred themselves to feed the fire, and keep it at its height.

Although the heat was so intense that the paint on the houses over against the prison, parched and crackled up, and swelling into boils, as it were from excess of torture, broke and crumbled away; although the glass fell from the window-sashes, and the lead and iron on the roofs blistered the incautious hand that touched them, and the sparrows in the eaves took wing, and, rendered giddy by the smoke, fell fluttering down upon the blazing pile; still the fire was tended unceasingly by busy hands, and round it, men were going always. They never slackened in their zeal, or kept aloof, but pressed upon the flames so hard, that those in front had much ado to save themselves from being thrust in; if one man swooned or dropped, a dozen struggled for his place, and that, although they knew the pain, and thirst, and pressure, to be unendurable. Those who fell down in fainting-fits, and were not crushed or burnt, were carried to an inn-yard close at hand, and dashed with water from a pump; of which buckets full were passed from man to man among the crowd; but such was the strong desire of all to drink, and such the fighting to be first, that, for the most part, the whole contents were spilled upon the ground, without the lips of one man being moistened.

Meanwhile, and in the midst of all the roar and outcry, those who were nearest to the pile, heaped up again the burning fragments that came toppling down, and raked the fire about the door, which, although a sheet of flame, was still a door fast locked and barred, and kept them out. Great pieces of blazing wood were passed, besides, above the people's heads to such as stood about the ladders, and some of these, climbing up to the topmost stave, and holding on with one hand by the prison wall, exerted all their skill and force to cast these firebrands on the roof, or down into the yards within. In many instances their efforts were successful; which occasioned a new and appalling addition to the horrors of the scene: for the prisoners within, seeing from between their bars that the fire caught in many places and thrived fiercely, and being all locked up in strong cells for the night, began to know that they were in danger of being burnt alive. This terrible fear, spreading from cell to cell and from yard to yard, vented itself in such dismal cries and wailings, and in such dreadful shrieks for help, that the whole jail resounded with the noise; which was loudly heard even above the shouting of the mob and roaring of the flames, and was so full of agony and despair, that it made the boldest tremble.

It was remarkable that these cries began in that quarter of the jail which fronted Newgate Street, where, it was well known, the men who were to suffer death on Thursday were confined. And not only were these four who had so short a time to live, the first to whom the dread of being burnt occurred, but they were, throughout, the most importunate of all: for they could be plainly heard, notwithstanding the great thickness of the walls, crying that the wind set that way, and that the flames would shortly reach them; and calling to the officers of the jail to come and quench the fire from a cistern which was in their yard, and full of water. Judging from what the crowd without the walls could hear from time to time, these four doomed wretches never ceased to call for help; and that with as much distraction, and in as great a frenzy of attachment to existence, as though each had an honoured, happy life before him, instead of eight-and-forty hours of miserable imprisonment, and then a violent and shameful death.

But the anguish and suffering of the two sons of one of these men, when they heard, or fancied that they heard, their father's voice, is past description. After wringing their hands and rushing to and fro as if they were stark mad, one mounted on the shoulders of his brother and tried to clamber up the face of the high wall, guarded at the top with spikes and points of iron. And when he fell among the crowd, he was not deterred by his bruises, but mounted up again, and fell again, and, when he found the feat impossible, began to beat the stones and tear them with his hands, as if he could that way make a breach in the strong building, and force a passage in. At last, they clove their way among the mob about the door, though many men, a dozen times their match, had tried in vain to do so, and were seen, in – yes, in – the fire, striving to prize it down, with crowbars.

Nor were they alone affected by the outcry from within the prison. The women who were looking on, shrieked loudly, beat their hands together, stopped their ears; and many fainted: the men who were not near the walls and active in the siege, rather than do nothing, tore up the pavement of the street, and did so with a haste and fury they could not have surpassed if that had been the jail, and they were near their object. Not one living creature in the throng was for an instant still. The whole great mass were mad.

A shout! Another! Another yet, though few knew why, or what it meant. But those around the gate had seen it slowly yield, and drop from its topmost hinge. It hung on that side by but one, but it was upright still, because of the bar, and its having sunk, of its own weight, into the heap of ashes at its foot. There was now a gap at the top of the doorway, through which could be descried a gloomy passage, cavernous and dark. Pile up the fire!

It burnt fiercely. The door was red-hot, and the gap wider. They vainly tried to shield their faces with their hands, and standing as if in readiness for a spring, watched the place. Dark figures, some crawling on their hands and knees, some carried in the arms of others, were seen to pass along the roof. It was plain the jail could hold out no longer. The keeper, and his officers, and their wives and children, were escaping. Pile up the fire!

The door sank down again: it settled deeper in the cinders – tottered – yielded – was down!

As they shouted again, they fell back, for a moment, and left a clear space about the fire that lay between them and the jail entry. Hugh leapt upon the blazing heap, and scattering a train of sparks into the air, and making the dark lobby glitter with those that hung upon his dress, dashed into the jail.

The hangman followed. And then so many rushed upon their track, that the fire got trodden down and thinly strewn about the street; but there was no need of it now, for, inside and out, the prison was in flames.

—— * ——

CHAPTER THE SIXTY-FIFTH

During the whole course of the terrible scene which was now at its height, one man in the jail suffered a degree of fear and mental torment which had no parallel in the endurance, even of those who lay under sentence of death.

When the rioters first assembled before the building, the murderer was roused from sleep – if such slumbers as his, may have that blessed name – by the roar of voices, and the struggling of a great crowd. He started up as these sounds met his ear, and, sitting on his bedstead, listened.

After a short interval of silence the noise burst out again. Still listening attentively, he made out, in course of time, that the jail was besieged by a furious multitude. His guilty conscience instantly arrayed these men against himself, and brought the fear upon him that he would be singled out, and torn to pieces.

Once impressed with the terror of this conceit, everything tended to confirm and strengthen it. His double crime, the circumstances under which it had been committed, the length of time that had elapsed, and its discovery in spite of all, made him as it were, the visible object of the Almighty's wrath. In all the crime and vice and moral gloom of the great pest-house of the capital, he stood alone, marked and singled out by his great guilt, a Lucifer among the devils.[1] The other prisoners were a host, hiding and sheltering each other – a crowd like that without the walls. He was one man against the whole united concourse; a single, solitary, lonely man, from whom the very captives in the jail fell off and shrunk appalled.

It might be that the intelligence of his capture having been bruited abroad, they had come there purposely to drag him out and kill him in the street; or it might be that they were the rioters, and, in pursuance of an old design, had come to sack the prison. But in either case he had no belief or hope that they would spare him. Every shout they raised, and every sound they made, was a blow upon his heart. As the attack went on, he grew more wild and frantic in his terror: tried to pull away the bars that guarded the chimney and prevented him from climbing up: called loudly on the turnkeys to cluster round the cell and save him from the fury of the rabble; or put him in some dungeon underground, no matter of what depth, how dark it was, or loathsome, or beset with rats and creeping things, so that it hid him and was hard to find.

But no one came, or answered him. Fearful, even while he cried to them, of attracting attention, he was silent. By and bye, he saw, as he looked from his grated window, a strange glimmering on the stone walls and pavement of the yard. It was feeble at first, and came and went, as though some officers with torches were passing to and fro upon the roof of the prison. Soon it reddened, and lighted brands came whirling down, spattering the ground with fire, and burning sullenly in corners. One rolled beneath a wooden bench, and set it in a blaze; another caught a water-spout, and so went climbing up the wall, leaving a long straight track of fire behind it. After a time, a slow thick shower of burning fragments, from some upper portion of the prison which was blazing nigh, began to fall before his door. Remembering that it opened outwards, he knew that every spark which fell upon the heap, and in the act lost its bright life, and died an ugly speck of dust and rubbish, helped to entomb him in a living grave. Still, though the jail resounded with shrieks and cries for help, – though the fire bounded up as if each separate flame had had a tiger's life, and roared as though, in every one, there were a hungry voice – though the heat began to grow intense, and the air suffocating, and the clamour without increased, and the danger of his situation even from one merciless element was every moment more extreme, – still he was afraid to raise his voice again, lest the crowd should break in, and should, of their own ears or from the information given them by the other prisoners, get the clue to his place of confinement. Thus fearful alike, of those within the prison and of those without; of noise and silence; light and darkness; of being released, and being left there to die; he was so tortured and tormented, that nothing man has ever done to man in the horrible caprice of power and cruelty, exceeds his self-inflicted punishment.

Now, now, the door was down. Now they came rushing through the jail, calling to each other in the vaulted passages; clashing the iron gates dividing yard from yard; beating at the doors of cells and wards; wrenching off bolts and locks and bars; tearing down the doorposts to get men out; endeavouring to drag them by main force through gaps and windows where a child could scarcely pass; whooping and yelling without a moment's rest; and running through the heat and flames as if they were cased in metal. By their legs, their arms, the hair upon their heads, they dragged the prisoners out. Some threw themselves upon the captives as they got towards the door, and tried to file away their irons; some danced about them with a frenzied joy, and rent their clothes, and were ready, as it seemed, to tear them limb from limb. Now a party of a dozen men came darting through the yard into which the murderer cast fearful glances from his darkened window; dragging a prisoner along the ground whose dress they had nearly torn from his body in their mad eagerness to set him free, and who was bleeding and senseless in their hands. Now a score of prisoners ran to and fro, who had lost themselves in the intricacies of the prison, and were so bewildered with the noise and glare that they knew not where to turn or what to do, and still cried out for help, as loudly as before. Anon some famished wretch whose theft had been a loaf of bread, or scrap of butcher's meat, came skulking past, barefooted, – going slowly away because that jail, his house, was burning; not because he had any other, or had friends to meet, or old haunts to revisit, or any liberty to gain, but liberty to starve and die. And then a knot of highwaymen went trooping by, conducted by the friends they had among the crowd, who muffled their fetters as they went along, with handkerchiefs and bands of hay, and wrapped them up in coats and cloaks, and gave them drink from bottles, and held it to their lips, because of their handcuffs which there was no time to remove. All this, and Heaven knows how much more, was done amidst a noise, a hurry, and distraction, like nothing that we know of, even in our dreams; which seemed for ever on the rise, and never to decrease for the space of a single instant.

He was still looking down from his window upon these things, when a band of men with torches, ladders, axes, and many kinds of weapons, poured into the yard, and hammering at his door, enquired if there were any prisoner within. He left the window when he saw them coming, and drew back into the remotest corner of the cell; but although he returned them no answer, they had a fancy that some one was within, for they presently set ladders against it, and began to tear away the bars at the casement; not only that, indeed, but with pickaxes to hew down the very stones in the wall.

As soon as they had made a breach at the window, large enough for the admission of a man's head, one of them thrust in a torch and looked all round the room. He followed this man's gaze until it rested on himself, and heard him demand why he had not answered, but made him no reply.

In the general surprise and wonder, they were used to this; for without saying anything more, they enlarged the breach until it was large enough to admit the body of a man, and then came dropping down upon the floor, one after another, until the cell was full. They caught him up among them, handed him to the window, and those who stood upon the ladders cast him down upon the pavement of the yard. Then the rest came out, one after another, and, bidding him fly, and lose no time, or the way would be choaked up, hurried away to rescue others.

It seemed not a minute's work from first to last. He staggered to his feet, incredulous of what had happened, when the yard was filled again, and a crowd rushed on, hurrying Barnaby among them. In another minute – not so much: another minute! the same instant, with no lapse or interval between! he and his son were being passed from hand to hand, through the dense crowd in the street, and were glancing backward at a burning pile which some one said was Newgate.

From the moment of their first entrance into the prison, the crowd dispersed themselves about it, and swarmed into every chink and crevice, as if they had a perfect acquaintance with its innermost parts, and bore in their minds an exact plan of the whole. For this immediate knowledge of the place, they were, no doubt, in a great degree indebted to the hangman, who stood in the lobby, directing some to go this way, some that, and some the other; and who materially assisted in bringing about the wonderful rapidity with which the release of the prisoners was effected.

But this functionary of the law reserved one important piece of intelligence, and kept it snugly to himself. When he had issued his instructions relative to every other part of the building, and the mob were dispersed from end to end, and busy at their work, he took a bundle of keys from a kind of cupboard in the wall, and going by a private passage near the chapel (it joined the governor's house, and was then on fire), betook himself to the condemned cells, which were a series of small, strong, dismal rooms, opening on a low gallery, guarded, at the end at which he entered, by a strong iron wicket, and at its opposite extremity by two doors and a thick grate. Having double locked the wicket, and assured himself that the other entrances were well secured, he sat down on a bench in the gallery, and sucked the head of his stick, with an air of the utmost complacency, tranquillity, and contentment.

It would have been strange enough, a man's enjoying himself in this quiet manner, while the prison was burning, and such a tumult was cleaving the air, though he had been outside the walls. But here, in the very heart of the building, and moreover with the prayers and cries of the four men under sentence sounding in his ears, and their hands, stretched out through the gratings in their cell doors, clasped in frantic entreaty before his very eyes, it was particularly remarkable. Indeed, Mr Dennis appeared to think it an uncommon circumstance, and to banter himself upon it; for he thrust his hat on one side as some men do when they are in a waggish humour, sucked the head of his stick with a higher relish, and smiled as though he would say, 'Dennis, you're a rum dog; you're a queer fellow; you're capital company, Dennis, and quite a character!'

He sat in this way for some minutes, while the four men in the cells, who were certain that somebody had entered the gallery, but could not see who, gave vent to such piteous entreaties as wretches in their miserable condition may be supposed to have been inspired with: urging, whoever it was, to set them at liberty, for the love of Heaven; and protesting, with great fervour, and truly enough, perhaps, for the time, that if they escaped, they would amend their ways, and would never, never, never again do wrong before God or man, but would lead penitent and sober lives, and sorrowfully repent the crimes they had committed. The terrible energy with which they spoke, would have moved any person, no matter how good or just (if any good or just person could have strayed into

that sad place that night), to have set them at liberty; and, while he would have left any other punishment to its free course, to have saved them from this last dreadful and repulsive penalty; which never turned a man inclined to evil, and has hardened thousands who were half inclined to good.

Mr Dennis, who had been bred and nurtured in the good old school, and had administered the good old laws on the good old plan,[2] always once and sometimes twice every six weeks, for a long time, bore these appeals with a deal of philosophy. Being at last, however, rather disturbed in his pleasant reflection by their repetition, he rapped at one of the doors with his stick, and cried:

'Hold your noise there, will you?'

At this they all cried together that they were to be hanged on the next day but one; and again implored his aid.

'Aid! For what!' said Mr Dennis, playfully rapping the knuckles of the hand nearest him.

'To save us!' they cried.

'Oh, certainly,' said Mr Dennis, winking at the wall in the absence of any friend with whom he could humour the joke. 'And so you're to be worked off, are you brothers?'

'Unless we are released to-night,' one of them cried, 'we are dead men!'

'I tell you what it is,' said the hangman, gravely; 'I'm afraid my friend that you're not in that 'ere state of mind that's suitable to your condition, then; you're not a going to be released: don't think it – Will you leave off that 'ere indecent row? I wonder you an't ashamed of yourselves, I do.'

He followed up this reproof by rapping every set of knuckles one after the other, and having done so, resumed his seat again with a cheerful countenance.

'You've had law,' he said, crossing his legs and elevating his eyebrows: 'laws have been made a' purpose for you; a wery handsome prison's been made a' purpose for you; a parson's kept a' purpose for you; a constitootional officer's appointed a' purpose for you; carts is maintained a' purpose for you – and yet you're not contented! – *Will* you hold that noise, you sir in the furthest?'

A groan was the only answer.

'So well as I can make out,' said Mr Dennis, in a tone of mingled badinage and remonstrance, 'there's not a man among you. I begin to think I'm on the opposite side, and among the ladies; though for the matter of that, I've seen a many ladies face it out, in a manner that did honour to the sex. – You in number two, don't grind them teeth of yours. Worse manners,' said the hangman, rapping at the door with his stick, 'I never see in this place afore. I'm ashamed on you. You're a disgrace to the Bailey!'

After pausing for a moment to hear if anything could be pleaded in justification, Mr Dennis resumed, in a sort of coaxing tone:

'Now look'ee here, you four. I'm come here to take care of you, and see that you an't burnt instead of the other thing. It's no use your making any noise, for you won't be found out by them as has broken in, and you'll only be hoarse when you come to the speeches, – which is a pity. What I say in respect to the speeches always is, "Give it mouth." That's my maxim. Give it mouth. I've heerd,' said the hangman, pulling off his hat to take his handkerchief from the crown and wipe his face, and then putting it on again a little more on one side than before, 'I've heerd a eloquence on them boards – you know what boards I mean – and have heerd a degree of mouth given to them speeches, that they was as clear as a bell, and as good as a play. There's a pattern! And always, when a thing of this nature's to come off, what I stand up for, is, a proper frame of mind. Let's have a proper frame of mind, and we can go through with it, creditable – pleasant – sociable. Whatever you do, and I address myself, in particular, to you in the furthest, never snivel. I'd sooner by half, though I lose by it, see a man tear his clothes a' purpose to spile 'em before they come to me, than find him snivelling. It's ten to one a better frame of mind, every way!'

While the hangman addressed them to this effect, in the tone and with the air of a pastor in familiar conversation with his flock, the noise had been in some degree subdued; for the rioters were busy in conveying the prisoners to the Sessions House,[3] which was beyond the main walls of the prison, though connected with it, and the crowd were busy, too, in passing them from thence along the street. But when he had got thus far in his discourse, the sound of voices in the yard showed plainly that the mob had returned and were coming that way; and directly afterwards a violent crashing at the grate below, gave note of their attack upon the cells (as they were called) at last.

It was in vain the hangman ran from door to door, and covered the grates, one after another, with his hat, in futile efforts to stifle the cries of the four men within; it was in vain he dogged their outstretched hands, and beat them with his stick, or menaced them with new and lingering pains in the execution of his office; the place resounded with their cries. These, together with the feeling that they were now the last men in the jail, so worked upon and stimulated the besiegers, that in an incredibly short space of time they forced the strong grate down below, which was formed of iron rods two inches square, drove in the two other doors, as if they had been but deal partitions, and stood at the end of the gallery with only a bar or two between them and the cells.

'Halloa!' cried Hugh, who was the first to look into the dusky passage: 'Dennis before us! Well done, old boy. Be quick, and open here, for we shall be suffocated in the smoke, going out.'

'Go out at once, then,' said Dennis. 'What do you want here?'

'Want!' echoed Hugh. 'The four men.'

'Four devils!' cried the hangman. 'Don't you know they're left for death on Thursday? Don't you respect the law – the constitootion – nothing? Let the four men be.'

'Is this a time for joking?' cried Hugh. 'Do you hear 'em? Pull away these bars that have got fixed between the door and the ground; and let us in.'

'Brother,' said the hangman in a low voice, as he stooped under pretence of doing what Hugh desired, but only looked up in his face, 'can't you leave these here four men to me, if I've the whim? You do what you like, and have what you like of everything for your share, give me my share. I want these four men left alone, I tell you!'

'Pull the bars down, or stand out of the way,' was Hugh's reply.

'You can turn the crowd if you like, you know that well enough, brother,' said the hangman, slowly. 'What! You *will* come in, will you?'

'Yes.'

'You won't let these men alone, and leave 'em to me? You've no respect for nothing – haven't you?' said the hangman, retreating to the door by which he had entered, and regarding his companion with an ugly scowl. 'You *will* come in, will you, brother?'

'I tell you, yes. What the devil ails you? Where are you going?'

'No matter where I'm going,' rejoined the hangman, looking in again at the iron wicket, which he had nearly shut upon himself, and held ajar. 'Remember where you're coming. That's all!'

With that, he shook his likeness at Hugh, and giving him a grin, compared with which his usual smile was amiable, disappeared, and shut the door.

Hugh paused no longer, but goaded alike by the cries of the convicts, and by the impatience of the crowd, warned the man immediately behind him – the way was only wide enough for one abreast – to stand back, and wielded a sledge hammer with such strength, that after a few blows the iron bent and broke, and gave them free admittance.

If the two sons of one of these men, of whom mention has been made, were furious in their zeal before, they had now the wrath and vigour of lions. Calling to the man within each cell, to keep as far back as he could, lest the axes crashing through the door should wound him, a party went to work upon each one, to beat it in by sheer strength, and force the bolts and staples from their hold. But although these two lads had the weakest party, and the worst armed, and did not begin until after the others, having stopped to whisper to him through the grate, that door was the first open, and that man the first out. As they dragged him into the gallery to knock off his irons, he fell down among them, a mere heap of chains, and was carried out in that state on men's shoulders with no sign of life.

The release of these four wretched creatures, and conveying them, astounded and bewildered, into the street so full of life – a spectacle they had never thought to see again, until they emerged from solitude and silence upon that last journey, when the air should be heavy with the pent-up breath of thousands, and the streets and houses should be built and roofed with human faces, not with bricks and tiles and stones – was the crowning horror of the scene. Their pale and haggard looks, and hollow eyes; their staggering feet, and hands stretched out as if to save themselves from falling; their wandering and uncertain air; the way they heaved and gasped for breath, as though in water, when they were first plunged into the crowd; all marked them for the men. No need to say 'this one was doomed to die;' there were the words broadly stamped and branded on his face. The crowd fell off, as if they had been laid out for burial, and had risen in their shrouds; and many were seen to shudder, as though they had been actually dead men, when they chanced to touch or brush against their garments.

At the bidding of the mob, the houses were all illuminated that night – lighted up from top to bottom as at a time of public gaiety and joy. Many years afterwards, old people who lived in their youth near this part of the city, remembered being in a great glare of light, within doors and without, and as they looked, timid and frightened children, from the windows, seeing *a face* go by.[4] Though the whole great crowd and all its other terrors had faded from their recollection, this one object remained; alone, distinct, and well-remembered. Even in the unpractised minds of infants, one of these doomed men darting by, and but an instant seen, was an image of force enough to dim the whole concourse; to find itself an all-absorbing place, and hold it ever after.

When this last task had been achieved, the shouts and cries grew fainter; the clank of fetters, which had resounded on all sides as the prisoners escaped, was heard no more; all the noises of the crowd subsided into a hoarse and sullen murmur as it passed into the distance; and when the human tide had rolled away, a melancholy heap of smoking ruins marked the spot where it had lately chafed and roared.

CHAPTER THE SIXTY-SIXTH

Although he had had no rest upon the previous night, and had watched with little intermission for some weeks past, sleeping only in the day by starts and snatches, Mr Haredale, from the dawn of morning until sunset, sought his niece in every place where he deemed it possible she could have taken refuge. All day long, nothing, save a draught of water, passed his lips; though he prosecuted his inquiries far and wide, and never so much as sat down, once.

In every quarter he could think of; at Chigwell and in London; at the houses of the trades-people with whom he dealt, and of the friends he knew; he pursued his search. A prey to the most harrowing anxieties and apprehensions, he went from magistrate to magistrate, and finally to the Secretary of State.[1] The only comfort he received was from this minister, who assured him that the Government, being now driven to the exercise of the extreme prerogatives of the Crown, were determined to exert them; that a proclamation would probably be out upon the morrow, giving to the military, discretionary and unlimited power in the suppression of the riots; that the sympathies of the King, the Administration, and both Houses of Parliament, and indeed of all good men of every religious persuasion, were strongly with the Catholics; and that justice should be done them at any cost or hazard. He told him, further, that other persons whose houses had been burnt, had for a time lost sight of their children or their relatives, but had in every case, within his knowledge, succeeded in discovering them; that his complaint should be remembered, and fully stated in the instructions given to the officers in command, and to all the inferior myrmidons of justice;[2] and that everything that could be done to help him, should be done, with a good-will and in good faith.

Grateful for this consolation, feeble as it was in its reference to the past, and little hope as it afforded him in connexion with the subject of distress which lay nearest to his heart; and really thankful for the interest the minister expressed, and seemed to feel, in his condition; Mr Haredale withdrew. He found himself, with the night coming on, alone in the streets; and destitute of any place in which to lay his head.

He entered an hotel near Charing Cross; and ordered some refreshment and a bed. He saw that his faint and worn appearance attracted the attention of the landlord and his waiters; and thinking that they might suppose him to be penniless, took out his purse, and laid it on the table. It was not that, the landlord said, in a faltering voice. If he were one of those who had suffered by the rioters, he durst not give him entertainment. He had a family of children, and had been twice warned to be careful in receiving guests. He heartily prayed his forgiveness, but what could he do?

Nothing. No man felt that, more sincerely than Mr Haredale. He told the man as much, and left the house.

Feeling that he might have anticipated this occurrence, after what he had seen at Chigwell in the morning, where no man dared to touch a spade, though he offered a large reward to all who would come and dig among the ruins of his house, he walked along the Strand; too proud to expose himself to another refusal, and of too generous a spirit to involve in distress or ruin any honest tradesman who might be weak enough to give him shelter. He wandered into one of the streets by the side of the river, and was pacing in a thoughtful manner up and down, thinking, strangely, of things that had happened long ago, when he heard a servant-man at an upper window call to another on the opposite side of the street, that the mob were setting fire to Newgate.

To Newgate! where that man was! His failing strength returned, his energies came back with tenfold vigour, on the instant. If it were possible – if they should set the murderer free – was he, after all he had undergone, to die with the suspicion of having slain his own brother, dimly gathering about him –

He had no consciousness of going to the jail; but there he stood, before it. There was the crowd, wedged and pressed together in a dense, dark, moving mass; and there were the flames soaring up into the air. His head turned round and round, lights flashed before his eyes, and he struggled hard with two men.

'Nay, nay,' said one. 'Be more yourself, my good sir. We attract attention here. Come away. What can you do among so many men?'

'The gentleman's always for doing something,' said the other, forcing him along as he spoke. 'I like him for that. I do like him for that.'

They had by this time got him into a court, hard by the prison. He looked from one to the other, and as he tried to release himself, felt that he tottered on his feet. He who had spoken first, was the old gentleman whom he had seen at the Lord Mayor's. The other was John Grueby, who had stood by him so manfully at Westminster.

'What does this mean?' he asked them, faintly. 'How came we together?'

'On the skirts of the crowd,' returned the distiller; 'but come with us. Pray come with us. You seem to know my friend here?'

'Surely,' said Mr Haredale, looking in a kind of stupor at John.

'He'll tell you then,' returned the old gentleman, 'that I am a man to be trusted. He's my servant. He was lately (as you know, I have no doubt) in Lord George Gordon's service; but he left it, and brought, in pure good-will to me and others, who are marked by the rioters, such intelligence as he had picked up, of their designs.'

– 'On one condition, please, sir,' said John, touching his hat. 'No evidence against my Lord – a misled man – a kind-hearted man, sir. My Lord never intended this.'

'The condition will be observed, of course,' rejoined the old distiller. 'It's a point of honour. But come with us, sir; pray come with us.'

John Grueby added no entreaties, but he adopted a different kind of persuasion, by putting his arm through one of Mr Haredale's, while his master took the other, and leading him away with all speed.

Sensible, from a strange lightness in his head, and a difficulty in fixing his thoughts on anything, even to the extent of bearing his companions in his mind for a minute together without looking at them, that his intellect was affected by the agitation and suffering through which he had passed, and to which he was still a prey, Mr Haredale let them lead him where they would. As they went along, he was conscious of having no command over what he said or thought, and that he had a fear of going mad.

The distiller lived, as he had told him when they first met, on Holborn Hill, where he had great storehouses and drove a large trade. They approached his house by a back entrance, lest they should attract the notice of the crowd, and went into an upper room which faced towards the street; the windows, however, in common with those of every other room in the house, were boarded up inside, that out of doors all might appear quite dark.

By the time they had laid him on a sofa in this chamber, Mr Haredale was perfectly insensible; but John immediately fetching a surgeon, who took from him a large quantity of blood,[3] he gradually came to himself. As he was for the time too weak to walk, they had no difficulty in persuading him to remain there all night, and got him to bed without loss of time. That done, they gave him a cordial and some toast, and presently a pretty strong composing-draught, under the influence of which he soon fell into a lethargy, and, for a time, forgot his troubles.

The vintner, who was a very hearty old fellow and a worthy man, had no thoughts of going to bed himself, for he had received several threatening warnings from the rioters, and had indeed gone out that evening to try and gather from the conversation of the mob whether his house was to be the next attacked. He sat all night in an easy-chair in the same room – dozing a little now and then – and received from time to time the reports of John Grueby and two or three other trust-worthy persons in his employ, who went out into the streets as scouts; and for whose entertainment an ample allowance of good cheer (which the old vintner, despite his anxiety, now and then attacked himself) was set forth in an adjoining chamber.

These accounts were of a sufficiently alarming nature from the first; but as the night wore on, they grew so much worse, and involved such a fearful amount of riot and destruction, that in comparison with these new tidings all the previous disturbances sunk to nothing.

The first intelligence that came, was of the taking of Newgate, and the escape of all the prisoners, whose track, as they made up Holborn and into the adjacent streets, was proclaimed to those citizens who were shut up in their houses, by the rattling of their chains, which formed a dismal concert, and was heard in every direction: as though so many forges were at work. The flames too shone so brightly through the vintner's skylights, that the rooms and staircases below were nearly as light as in broad day; while the distant shouting of the mob seemed to shake the very walls and ceilings.

At length they were heard approaching the house, and some minutes of terrible anxiety ensued. They came close up, and stopped before it; but after giving three loud yells, went on. And although they returned several times that night, creating new alarms each time, they did nothing there; having their hands full. Shortly after they had gone away for the first time, one of the scouts came running in with the news that they had stopped before Lord Mansfield's house in Bloomsbury square.[4]

Soon afterwards there came another, and another, and then the first returned again: and so, by little and little, their tale was this: – That the mob gathering round Lord Mansfield's house, had called on those within to open the door, and receiving no reply (for Lord and Lady Mansfield were at that moment escaping by the backway), forced an entrance according to their usual custom. That they then began to demolish it with great fury, and setting fire to it in several parts, involved in a common ruin the whole of the costly furniture, the plate and jewels, a beautiful gallery of pictures, the rarest collection of manuscripts ever possessed by any one private person in the world, and worse than all, because nothing could replace this loss, the great Law Library, on almost every page of which were notes in the Judge's own hand, of inestimable value, – being the results of the study and experience of his whole life. That while they were howling and exulting round the fire, a troop of soldiers, with a magistrate among them, came up, and being too late (for the mischief was by that time done), began to disperse the crowd.

That the riot act being read, and the crowd still resisting, the soldiers received orders to fire, and levelling their muskets shot dead at the first discharge six men and a woman, and wounded many persons; and loading again directly, fired another volley, but over the people's heads it was supposed, as none were seen to fall. That thereupon, and daunted by the shrieks and tumult, the crowd began to disperse, and the soldiers went away: leaving the killed and wounded on the ground: which they had no sooner done than the rioters came back again, and taking up the dead bodies, and the wounded people, formed into a rude procession, having the bodies in the front. That in this order, they paraded off with a horrible merriment; fixing weapons in the dead men's hands to make them look as if alive; and preceded by a fellow ringing Lord Mansfield's dinner-bell with all his might.

The scouts reported further, that this party meeting with some others who had been at similar work elsewhere, they all united into one, and drafting off a few men with the killed and wounded, marched away to Lord Mansfield's country seat at Caen Wood,[5] between Hampstead and Highgate; bent upon destroying that house likewise, and lighting up a great fire there, which from that height should be seen all over London. But in this, they were disappointed, for a party of horse having arrived before them, they retreated faster than they went, and came straight back to town.

There being now a great many parties in the streets, each went to work according to its humour, and a dozen houses were quickly blazing, including those of Sir John Fielding and two other justices, and four in Holborn – one of the greatest thoroughfares in London – which were all burning at the same time, and burned until they went out of themselves, for the people cut the engine hose, and would not suffer the firemen to play upon the flames. At one house near Moorfields, they found in one of the rooms some canary birds[6] in cages, and these they cast into the fire alive. The poor little creatures screamed, it was said, like infants, when they were flung upon the blaze; and one man was so touched that he tried in vain to save them, which roused the indignation of the crowd, and nearly cost him his life.

At this same house, one of the fellows who went through the rooms, breaking the furniture and helping to destroy the building, found a child's doll – a poor toy – which he exhibited at the window to the mob below, as the image of some unholy saint which the late

occupants had worshipped. While he was doing this, another man
with an equally tender conscience (they had both been foremost in
throwing down the canary birds for roasting alive), took his seat
on the parapet of the house, and harangued the crowd from a
pamphlet circulated by the association, relative to the true principles of Christianity. Meanwhile the Lord Mayor, with his hands
in his pockets, looked on as an idle man might look at any other
show, and seemed mightily satisfied to have got a good
place.

Such were the accounts brought to the old vintner by his servants
as he sat at the side of Mr Haredale's bed; having been unable even
to doze, after the first part of the night; being too much disturbed
by his own fears; by the cries of the mob, the light of the fires, and
the firing of the soldiers. Such, with the addition of the release of
all the prisoners in the New Jail at Clerkenwell,[7] and as many
robberies of passengers in the streets, as the crowd had leisure to
indulge in, were the scenes of which Mr Haredale was happily
unconscious, and which were all enacted before midnight.

*

CHAPTER THE SIXTY-SEVENTH

When darkness broke away and morning began to dawn, the town
wore a strange aspect indeed.

Sleep had scarcely been thought of all night. The general alarm
was so apparent in the faces of the inhabitants, and its expression
was so aggravated by want of rest (few persons, with any property
to lose, having dared to go to bed since Monday), that a stranger
coming into the streets would have supposed some mortal pest or
plague was raging. In place of the usual cheerfulness and animation
of morning, everything was dead and silent. The shops remained
closed, offices and warehouses were shut, the coach and chair
stands were deserted, no carts or waggons rumbled through the
slowly waking streets, the early cries were all hushed; a universal
gloom prevailed. Great numbers of people were out, even at daybreak, but they flitted to and fro as though they shrank from the
sound of their own footsteps; the public ways were haunted rather
than frequented; and round the smoking ruins people stood apart

from one another and in silence; not venturing to condemn the rioters, or to be supposed to do so, even in whispers.

At the Lord President's in Piccadilly, at Lambeth Palace, at the Lord Chancellor's in Great Ormond Street, in the Royal Exchange, the Bank,[1] the Guildhall, the Inns of Court, the Courts of Law, and every chamber fronting the streets near Westminster Hall and the Houses of Parliament, parties of soldiers were posted before daylight. A body of Horse-Guards paraded Palace-yard; an encampment was formed in the Park, where fifteen hundred men and five battalions of Militia were under arms; the Tower was fortified, the draw-bridges were raised, the cannon loaded and pointed, and two regiments of artillery busied in strengthening the fortress and preparing it for defence. A numerous detachment of soldiers were stationed to keep guard at the New-River Head, which the people had threatened to attack, and where, it was said, they meant to cut off the main-pipes, so that there might be no water for the extinction of the flames. In the Poultry, and on Cornhill, and at several other leading points, iron chains were drawn across the street; parties of soldiers were distributed in some of the old city churches while it was yet dark; and in several private houses (among them, Lord Rockingham's in Grosvenor Square);[2] which were blockaded as though to sustain a siege, and had guns pointed from the windows. When the sun rose, it shone into handsome apartments filled with armed men; the furniture hastily heaped away in corners, and made of little or no account, in the terror of the time – on arms glittering in city chambers, among desks and stools, and dusty books – into little smoky church-yards in odd lanes and byeways, with soldiers lying down among the tombs, or lounging under the shade of the one old tree, and their pile of muskets sparkling in the light – on solitary sentries pacing up and down in court-yards, silent now, but yesterday resounding with the din and hum of business – everywhere on guard-rooms, garrisons, and threatening preparations.

As the day crept on, still stranger things were witnessed in the streets. The gates of the King's Bench and Fleet Prisons[3] being opened at the usual hour, were found to have notices affixed to them, announcing that the rioters would come that night to burn them down. The Wardens, too well knowing the likelihood there was of this promise being fulfilled, were fain to set their prisoners at liberty, and give them leave to move their goods; so, all day, such

of them as had any furniture were occupied in conveying it, some
to this place, some to that, and not a few to the brokers' shops,
where they gladly sold it, for any wretched price those gentry chose
to give. There were some broken men among these debtors who
had been in jail so long, and were so miserable and destitute of
friends, so dead to the world, and utterly forgotten and uncared
for, that they implored their jailors not to set them free, and to send
them, if need were, to some other place of custody. But they,
refusing to comply, lest they should incur the anger of the mob,
turned them into the streets, where they wandered up and down
hardly remembering the ways untrodden by their feet so long, and
crying – such abject things those rotten-hearted jails had made
them – as they slunk off in their rags, and dragged their slip-shod
feet along the pavement.

Even of the three hundred prisoners who had escaped from
Newgate, there were some – a few, but there were some – who
sought their jailors out and delivered themselves up: preferring
imprisonment and punishment to the horrors of such another night
as the last. Many of the convicts, drawn back to their old place of
captivity by some indescribable attraction, or by a desire to exult
over it in its downfall and glut their revenge by seeing it in ashes,
actually went back in broad noon, and loitered about the cells.
Fifty were retaken at one time on this next day, within the prison
walls; but their fate did not deter others, for there they went in spite
of everything, and there they were taken in twos and threes, twice
or thrice a day, all through the week. Of the fifty just mentioned,
some were occupied in endeavouring to rekindle the fire; but in
general they seemed to have no object in view but to prowl and
lounge about the old place: being often found asleep in the ruins,
or sitting talking there, or even eating and drinking, as in a choice
retreat.

Besides the notices on the gates of the Fleet and the King's Bench,
many similar announcements were left, before one o'clock at noon,
at the houses of private individuals; and further, the mob proclaimed their intention of seizing on the Bank, the Mint, the Arsenal
at Woolwich, and the Royal Palaces.[4] The notices were seldom
delivered by more than one man, who, if it were at a shop, went in,
and laid it, with a bloody threat perhaps, upon the counter; or if it
were at a private house, knocked at the door, and thrust it in the
servant's hand. Notwithstanding the presence of the military in

every quarter of the town, and the great force in the Park, these messengers did their errands with impunity all through the day. So did two boys who went down Holborn alone, armed with bars taken from the railings of Lord Mansfield's house, and demanded money for the rioters. So did a tall man on horseback who made a collection for the same purpose in Fleet Street, and refused to take anything but gold.

A rumour had now got into circulation, too, which diffused a greater dread all through London, even than these publicly-announced intentions of the rioters, though all men knew that if they were successfully effected, there must ensue a national bankruptcy and general ruin. It was said that they meant to throw the gates of Bedlam open, and let all the madmen loose. This suggested such dreadful images to the people's minds, and was indeed an act so fraught with new and unimaginable horrors in the contemplation, that it beset them more than any loss or cruelty of which they could foresee the worst, and drove many sane men nearly mad themselves.

So the day passed on: the prisoners moving their goods; people running to and fro in the streets, carrying away their property; groups standing in silence round the ruins; all business suspended; and the soldiers disposed as has been already mentioned, remaining quite inactive. So the day passed on, and dreaded night drew near again.

At last, at seven o'clock in the evening, the privy council[5] issued a solemn proclamation that it was now necessary to employ the military, and that the officers had most direct and effectual orders, by an immediate exertion of their utmost force, to repress the disturbances; and warning all good subjects of the king to keep themselves, their servants, and apprentices, within doors that night. There was then delivered out to every soldier on duty, thirty-six rounds of powder and ball; the drums beat; and the whole force was under arms at sunset.

The city authorities, stimulated by these vigorous measures, held a common council; passed a vote thanking the military associations who had tendered their aid to the civil authorities; accepted it; and placed them under the direction of the two sheriffs. At the queen's palace,[6] a double guard, the yeomen on duty, the groom-porters, and all other attendants, were stationed in the passages and on the staircases at seven o'clock, with strict instructions to be watchful on

their posts all night; and all the doors were locked. The gentlemen of
the Temple, and the other Inns,[7] mounted guard within their gates,
and strengthened them with the great stones of the pavement, which
they took up for the purpose. In Lincoln's Inn, they gave up the
hall and commons to the Northumberland militia, under the command of Lord Algernon Percy;[8] in some few of the city wards, the
burgesses turned out, and without making a very fierce show,
looked brave enough. Some hundreds of stout gentlemen threw
themselves, armed to the teeth, into the halls of the different companies,[9] double-locked and bolted all the gates, and dared the
rioters (among themselves) to come on at their peril. These arrangements being all made simultaneously, or nearly so, were completed
by the time it got dark; and then the streets were comparatively
clear, and were guarded at all the great corners and chief avenues
by the troops: while parties of the officers rode up and down in all
directions, ordering chance stragglers home, and admonishing the
residents to keep within their houses, and, if any firing ensued, not
to approach the windows. More chains were drawn across such of
the thoroughfares as were of a nature to favour the approach of a
great crowd, and at each of these points a considerable force was
stationed. All these precautions having been taken and it being now
quite dark, those in command awaited the result in some anxiety:
and not without a hope that such vigilant demonstrations might
of themselves dishearten the populace, and prevent any further
outrages.

But in this reckoning they were cruelly mistaken, for in half an
hour, or less, as though the setting in of night had been their
preconcerted signal, the rioters having previously, in small parties,
prevented the lighting of the street lamps, rose like a great sea; and
that in so many places at once, and with such inconceivable fury,
that those who had the direction of the troops knew not, at first,
where to turn or what to do. One after another, new fires blazed
up in every quarter of the town, as though it were the intention of
the insurgents to wrap the city in a circle of flames, which, contracting by degrees, should burn the whole to ashes; the crowd
swarmed and roared in every street; and none but rioters and
soldiers being out of doors, it seemed to the latter as if all London
were arrayed against them, and they stood alone against the town.

In two hours, six-and-thirty fires were raging – six-and-thirty
great conflagrations: among them the Borough Clink in Tooley-

street,[10] the King's Bench, the Fleet, and the New Bridewell. In almost every street, there was a battle; and in every quarter the muskets of the troops were heard above the shouts and tumult of the mob. The firing began in the Poultry, where the chain was drawn across the road, where nearly a score of people were killed on the first discharge. Their bodies having been hastily carried into St Mildred's church[11] by the soldiers, they fired again, and following fast upon the crowd, who began to give way when they saw the execution that was done, formed across Cheapside, and charged them at the point of the bayonet.

The streets were now a dreadful spectacle indeed: while the shouts of the rabble, the shrieks of women, the cries of the wounded, and the constant firing, formed a deafening and an awful accompaniment to the sights which every corner presented. Wherever the road was obstructed by the chains, there the fighting and the loss of life were greatest; but there was hot work and bloodshed in almost every leading thoroughfare, and in every one the same appalling scenes occurred.

At Holborn Bridge,[12] and on Holborn Hill, the confusion was greater than in any other part; for the crowd that poured out of the city in two great streams, one by Ludgate Hill, and one by Newgate-street, united at that spot, and formed a mass so dense, that at every volley the people seemed to fall in heaps. At this place a large detachment of soldiery were posted, who fired, now up Fleet Market, now up Holborn, now up Snow Hill – constantly raking the streets in each direction. At this place too, several large fires were burning, so that all the terrors of that terrible night seemed to be concentrated in this one spot.

Full twenty times, the rioters, headed by one man who wielded an axe in his right hand, and bestrode a brewer's horse of great size and strength, caparisoned with fetters taken out of Newgate, which clanked and jingled as he went, made an attempt to force a passage at this point, and fire the vintner's house. Full twenty times they were repulsed with loss of life, and still came back again: and though the fellow at their head was marked and singled out by all, and was a conspicuous object as the only rioter on horseback, not a man could hit him. So surely as the smoke cleared away, so surely there was he; calling hoarsely to his companions, brandishing his axe above his head, and dashing on as though he bore a charmed life,[13] and was proof against ball and powder.

This man was Hugh; and in every part of the riot, he was seen. He headed two attacks upon the Bank, helped to break open the Toll-houses on Blackfriars Bridge, and cast the money into the street: fired two of the prisons with his own hand: was here, and there, and everywhere – always foremost – always active – striking at the soldiers, cheering on the crowd, making his horse's iron music heard through all the yell and uproar: but never hurt or stopped. Turn him at one place, and he made a new struggle in another; force him to retreat at this point, and he advanced on that, directly. Driven from Holborn for the twentieth time, he rode at the head of a great crowd straight upon Saint Paul's, attacked a guard of soldiers who kept watch over a body of prisoners within the iron railings, forced them to retreat, rescued the men they had in custody, and with this accession to his party, came back again, mad with liquor and excitement, and hallooing them on like a demon.

It would have been no easy task for the most careful rider to sit a horse in the midst of such a throng and tumult; but though this madman rolled upon his back (he had no saddle) like a boat upon the sea, he never for an instant lost his seat, or failed to guide him where he would. Through the very thickest of the press, over dead bodies and burning fragments, now on the pavement, now in the road, now riding up a flight of steps to make himself the more conspicuous to his party, and now forcing a passage through a mass of human beings, so closely wedged together that it seemed as if the edge of a knife would scarcely part them, – on he went, as though he could surmount all obstacles by the mere exercise of his will. And perhaps his not being shot was in some degree attributable to this very circumstance; for his extreme audacity, and the conviction that he must be one of those to whom the proclamation referred, inspired the soldiers with a desire to take him alive, and diverted many an aim which otherwise might have been more near the mark.

The vintner and Mr Haredale, unable to sit quietly listening to the terrible noise without seeing what went on, had climbed to the roof of the house; and hiding behind a stack of chimneys, were looking cautiously down into the street, almost hoping that after so many repulses the rioters would be foiled, when a great shout proclaimed that a party were coming round the other way; and the dismal jingling of those accursed fetters warned them next moment that they too were led by Hugh. The soldiers had advanced into Fleet Market and were dispersing the people there; so that they came on with hardly any check, and were soon before the house.

'All's over now,' said the vintner. 'Fifty thousand pounds will be scattered in a minute. We must save ourselves. We can do no more, and shall have reason to be thankful if we do as much.'

Their first impulse was, to clamber along the roofs of the houses, and, knocking at some garret window for admission, pass down that way into the street, and so escape. But another fierce cry from below, and a general upturning of the faces of the crowd, apprised them that they were discovered, and even that Mr Haredale was recognised; for Hugh, seeing him plainly in the bright glare of the flames, which in that part made it as light as day, called to him by his name, and swore to have his life.

'Leave me here,' said Mr Haredale, 'and in Heaven's name, my good friend, save yourself! Come on!' he muttered, as he turned towards Hugh and faced him without any further effort at conceal- ment: 'This roof is high, and if we grapple, we will die together!'

'Madness,' said the honest vintner, pulling him back, 'sheer madness. Hear reason sir. My good sir, hear reason. I could never make myself heard by knocking at a window now; and even if I could, no one would be bold enough to connive at my escape. Through the cellars, there's a kind of passage into the back street by which we roll casks in and out. We shall have time to get down there, before they can force an entry. Do not delay an instant, but come with me – for both our sakes – for mine – my dear good sir!'

As he spoke, and drew Mr Haredale back, they had both a glimpse of the street. It was but a glimpse, but it showed them the crowd, gathering and clustering round the house: some of the armed men pressing to the front to break down the doors and windows, some bringing brands from the nearest fire, some with lifted faces following their course upon the roof and pointing them out to their companions, all raging and roaring like the flames they lighted up. They saw some men howling and thirsting for the treasures of strong liquor which they knew were stored within; they saw others, who had been wounded, sinking down into the opposite doorways and dying, solitary wretches, in the midst of all the vast assemblage; here a frightened woman trying to escape; and there a lost child; and there a drunken ruffian, unconscious of the death-wound on his head, raving and fighting to the last. All these things, and even such trivial incidents as a man with his hat off, or turning round, or stooping down, or shaking hands with another, they marked distinctly; yet in a glance so brief, that, in the act of stepping back, they lost the whole, and saw but the pale faces of each other, and the red sky above them.

Mr Haredale yielded to the entreaties of his companion – more because he was resolved to defend him to the last, than for any thought he had of his own life, or any care he entertained for his own safety – and quickly re-entering the house, they descended the stairs together. Loud blows were thundering on the shutters, crowbars were already thrust beneath the door, the glass fell from the sashes, a deep light shone through every crevice, and they heard the voices of the foremost in the crowd so close to every chink and keyhole, that they seemed to be hoarsely whispering their threats into their very ears. They had but a moment reached the bottom of the cellar-steps and shut the door behind them, when the mob broke in.

The vaults were profoundly dark, and having no torch or candle – for they had been afraid to carry one, lest it should betray their place of refuge – they were obliged to grope with their hands. But they were not long without light, for they had not gone far when they heard the crowd forcing the door; and, looking back among the low-arched passages, could see them in the distance, hurrying to and fro with flashing links, broaching the casks, staving the great vats, turning off upon the right hand and the left, into the different cellars, and lying down to drink at the channels of strong spirits which were already flowing fast upon the ground.

They hurried on, not the less quickly for this; and had reached the only vault which lay between them and the passage out, when suddenly, from the direction in which they were going, a strong light gleamed upon their faces; and before they could slip aside, or turn back, or hide themselves, two men (one bearing a torch) came upon them, and cried in an astonished whisper, 'Here they are!'

At the same instant they pulled off what they wore upon their heads. Mr Haredale saw before him Edward Chester, and then saw, when the vintner gasped his name, Joe Willet.

Ay, the same Joe, though with an arm the less, who used to make the quarterly journey on the grey mare to pay the bill to the purple-faced vintner; and that very same purple-faced vintner,

formerly of Thames Street, now looked him in the face, and challenged him by name.

'Give me your hand,' said Joe softly, taking it whether the astonished vintner would or no. 'Don't fear to shake it, man; it's a friendly one and a hearty one, though it has no fellow. Why, how well you look and how bluff you are! And you – God bless you, sir. Take heart, take heart. We'll find them. Be of good cheer; we have not been idle.'

There was something so honest and frank in Joe's speech, that Mr Haredale put his hand in his involuntarily, though their meeting was suspicious enough. But his glance at Edward Chester, and that gentleman's keeping aloof, were not lost upon Joe, who said bluntly, glancing at Edward while he spoke:

'Times are changed, Mr Haredale, and times have come when we ought to know friends from enemies, and make no confusion of names. Let me tell you that but for this gentleman, you would most likely have been dead by this time, or badly wounded at the best.'

'What do you say?' asked Mr Haredale.

'I say,' said Joe, 'first, that it was a bold thing to be in the crowd at all disguised as one of them; though I won't say much about that, on second thoughts, for that's my case too. Secondly, that it was a brave and glorious action – that's what I call it – to strike that fellow off his horse before their eyes!'

'What fellow! Whose eyes!'

'What fellow, sir!' cried Joe: 'a fellow who has no good-will to you, and who has the daring and devilry in him of twenty fellows. I know him of old. Once in the house, *he* would have found you, here or anywhere. The rest owe you no particular grudge, and, unless they see you, will only think of drinking themselves dead. But we lose time. Are you ready?'

'Quite,' said Edward. 'Put out the torch, Joe, and go on. And be silent, there's a good fellow.'

'Silent or not silent,' murmured Joe, as he dropped the flaring link upon the ground, crushed it with his foot, and gave his hand to Mr Haredale, 'it was a brave and glorious action; – no man can alter that.'

Both Mr Haredale and the worthy vintner were too amazed and too much hurried to ask any further questions, so followed their conductors in silence. It seemed, from a short whispering which presently ensued between them and the vintner relative to the best way of escape, that they had entered by the back-door, with the connivance of John Grueby, who watched outside with the key in his pocket, and whom they had taken into their confidence. A part of the crowd coming up that way, just as they entered, John had double-locked the door again, and made off for the soldiers, so that means of retreat was cut from under them.

However, as the front door had been forced, and this minor crowd, being anxious to get at the liquor, had no fancy for losing time in breaking down another, but had gone round and got in from Holborn with the rest, the narrow lane in the rear was quite free of people. So when they had crawled through the passage indicated by the vintner (which was a mere shelving-trap for the admission of casks), and had managed with some difficulty to unchain and raise the door at the upper end, they emerged into the street without being observed or interrupted. Joe still holding Mr Haredale tight, and Edward taking the same care of the vintner, they hurried through the streets at a rapid pace; occasionally standing aside to let some fugitives go by, or to keep out of the way of the soldiers who followed them, and whose questions, when they halted to put any, were speedily stopped by one whispered word from Joe.

CHAPTER THE SIXTY-EIGHTH

While Newgate was burning on the previous night, Barnaby and his father, having been passed among the crowd from hand to hand, stood in Smithfield, on the outskirts of the mob, gazing at the flames like men who had been suddenly roused from sleep. Some moments elapsed before they could distinctly remember where they were, or how they got there; or recollected that while they were standing idle and listless spectators of the fire, they had tools in their hands which had been hurriedly given them that they might free themselves from their fetters.

Barnaby, heavily ironed as he was, if he had obeyed his first impulse, or if he had been alone, would have made his way back to the side of Hugh, who to his clouded intellect now shone forth with the new lustre of being his preserver and truest friend. But his father's terror of remaining in the streets, communicated itself to him when he comprehended the full extent of his fears, and impressed him with the same eagerness to fly to a place of safety.

In a corner of the market among the pens for cattle, Barnaby knelt down, and pausing every now and then to pass his hand over his father's face, or look up to him with a smile, knocked off his irons. When he had seen him spring, a free man, to his feet, and had given vent to the transport of delight which the sight awakened, he went to work upon his own, which soon fell rattling down upon the ground, and left his limbs unfettered.

Gliding away together when this task was accomplished, and passing several groups of men, each gathered round a stooping figure to hide him from those who passed, but unable to repress the clanking sound of hammers, which told that they too were busy at the same work, – the two fugitives made towards Clerkenwell, and passing thence to Islington, as the nearest point of egress, were quickly in the fields. After wandering about for a long time, they found in a pasture near Finchley[1] a poor shed, with walls of mud, and roof of grass and brambles, built for some cow-herd, but now deserted. Here they lay down for the rest of the night.

They wandered up and down when it was day, and once Barnaby went off alone to a cluster of little cottages two or three miles away, to purchase bread and milk. But finding no better shelter, they returned to the same place, and lay down again to wait for night.

Heaven alone can tell, with what vague thoughts of duty, and affection; with what strange promptings of nature, intelligible to him as to a man of radiant mind and most enlarged capacity; with what dim memories of children he had played with when a child himself, who had prattled of their fathers, and of loving them, and being loved; with how many half-remembered, dreamy associations of his mother's grief and tears and widowhood; he watched and tended this man. But that a vague and shadowy crowd of such ideas came slowly on him; that they taught him to be sorry when he looked upon his haggard face, that they overflowed his eyes when he stooped to kiss him on the cheek, that they kept him waking in a tearful gladness, shading him from the sun, fanning him with leaves, soothing him when he started in his sleep – ah! what a troubled sleep it was – and wondering when *she* would come to join them and be happy, is the Truth. He sat beside him all that day; listening for her footstep in every breath of air, looking for her shadow on the gently-waving grass, twining the hedge flowers for her pleasure when she came, and his when he awoke; and stooping down from time to time to listen to his mutterings, and wonder why he was so restless in that quiet place. The sun went down, and night came on, and he was still quite tranquil; busied with these thoughts, as if there were no other people in the world, and the dull cloud of smoke hanging on the immense city in the distance, hid no vices, no crimes, no life or death, or causes of disquiet – nothing but clear air.

But the hour had now come when he must go alone to find out the blind man, (a task that filled him with delight,) and bring him to that place; taking especial care that he was not watched or followed on his way back. He listened to the directions he must observe, repeated them again and again; and after twice or thrice returning to surprise his father with a light-hearted laugh, went forth, at last, upon his errand: leaving Grip, whom he had carried from the jail in his arms, to his care.

Fleet of foot, and anxious to return, he sped swiftly on towards the city, but could not reach it before the fires began and made the night angry with their dismal lustre. When he entered the town – it might be that he was changed by going there without his late companions, and on no violent errand; or by the beautiful solitude in which he had passed the day, or by the thoughts that had come upon him, – but it seemed peopled by a legion of devils. This flight and pursuit, this cruel burning and destroying, these dreadful cries and stunning noises, were they the good Lord's noble cause!

Though almost stupefied by the bewildering scene, still he found the blind man's house. It was shut up and tenantless. He waited for a long while, but no one came. At last he withdrew; and as he knew by this time that the soldiers were firing, and many people must have been killed, he went down into Holborn, where he heard the great crowd was, to try if he could find Hugh, and persuade him to avoid the danger, and return with him.

If he had been stunned and shocked before, his horror was increased a thousand-fold when he got into this vortex of the riot, and not being an actor in the terrible spectacle, had it all before his eyes. But there, in the midst, towering above them all, close before the house they were attacking now, was Hugh on horseback, calling to the rest!

Sickened by the sights surrounding him on every side, and by the heat and roar, and crash, he forced his way among the crowd (where many recognised him, and with shouts pressed back to let him pass), and in time was nearly up with Hugh, who was savagely threatening some one, but whom, or what he said he could not, in the great confusion, understand. At that moment the crowd forced their way into the house, and Hugh – it was impossible to see by what means, in such a concourse – fell headlong down.

Barnaby was beside him when he staggered to his feet. It was well he made him hear his voice, or Hugh, with his uplifted axe, would have cleft his skull in twain.

'Barnaby – you! Whose hand was that, that struck me down?'

'Not mine.'

'Whose! – I say, whose!' he cried, reeling back, and looking wildly round. 'What are we doing? Where is he? Show me!'

'You are hurt,' said Barnaby – as indeed he was, in the head, both by the blow he had received, and by his horse's hoof. 'Come away with me.'

As he spoke, he took the horse's bridle in his hand, turned him, and dragged Hugh several paces. This brought them out of the crowd, which was pouring from the street into the vintner's cellars.

'Where's – where's Dennis?' said Hugh, coming to a stop, and checking Barnaby with his strong arm. 'Where has he been all day? What did he mean by leaving me as he did, in the jail, last night? Tell me, you – d'ye hear!'

With a flourish of his dangerous weapon, he fell down upon the ground like a log. After a minute, though already frantic with drinking and with the wound in his head, he crawled to a stream of burning spirit which was pouring down the kennel, and began to drink at it as if it were a brook of water.

Barnaby drew him away, and forced him to rise. Though he could neither stand nor walk, he involuntarily staggered to his horse, climbed upon his back, and clung there. After vainly attempting to divest the animal of his clanking trappings, Barnaby sprang up behind him, snatched the bridle, turned into Leather Lane, which was close at hand, and urged the frightened horse into a heavy gallop.

He looked back once before he left the street; and looked upon a sight not easily to be erased, even from his remembrance, so long as he had life.

The vintner's house, with half a dozen others near at hand, was one great, glowing blaze. All night, no one had essayed to quench the flames or stop their progress; but now a body of soldiers were actively engaged in pulling down two old wooden houses, which were every moment in danger of taking fire, and which could scarcely fail, if they were left to burn, to extend the conflagration immensely. The tumbling down of nodding walls and heavy blocks of wood, the hooting and the execrations of the crowd, the distant firing of other military detachments, the distracted looks and cries of those whose habitations were in danger, the hurrying to and fro of frightened people with their goods; the reflections in every quarter of the sky, of deep, red, soaring flames, as though the last day had come and the whole universe were burning; the dust, and smoke, and drift of fiery particles, scorching and kindling all it fell upon; the hot unwholesome vapour, the blight on everything; the stars, and moon, and very sky, obliterated; – made up such a sum of dreariness and ruin, that it seemed as if the face of Heaven were blotted out, and night, in its rest and quiet, and softened light, never could look upon the earth again.

But there was a worse spectacle than this – worse by far than fire and smoke, or even the rabble's unappeasable and maniac rage. The gutters of the street and every crack and fissure in the stones, ran with scorching spirit; which, being dammed up by busy hands, overflowed the road and pavement, and formed a great pool, in which the people dropped down dead by dozens. They lay in heaps all round this fearful pond, husbands and wives, fathers and sons, mothers and daughters, women with children in their arms and babies at their breasts, and drank until they died.[2] While some stooped with their lips to the brink and never raised their heads again, others sprang up from their fiery draught, and danced, half in a mad triumph, and half in the agony of suffocation, until they fell, and steeped their corpses in the liquor that had killed them. Nor was even this the worst or most appalling kind of death that happened on this fatal night. From the burning cellars, where they drank out of hats, pails, buckets, tubs, and shoes, some men were drawn, alive, but all alight from head to foot; who, in their unendurable anguish and suffering, making for anything that had the look of water, rolled, hissing, in this hideous lake, and splashed up liquid fire which lapped in all it met with as it ran along the surface, and neither spared the living nor the dead. On this last night of the great

riots – for the last night it was – the wretched victims of a senseless outcry, became themselves the dust and ashes of the flames they had kindled, and strewed the public streets of London.

With all he saw in this last glance fixed indelibly upon his mind, Barnaby hurried from the city which inclosed such horrors; and, holding down his head that he might not even see the glare of the fires upon the quiet landscape, was soon in the still country roads.

He stopped at about half-a-mile from the shed where his father lay, and with some difficulty making Hugh sensible that he must dismount, sunk the horse's furniture in a pool of stagnant water, and turned the animal loose. That done, he supported his companion as well as he could, and led him slowly forward.

*

CHAPTER THE SIXTY-NINTH

It was the dead of night, and very dark, when Barnaby, with his stumbling companion, approached the place where he had left his father; but he could see him stealing away into the gloom, distrustful even of him, and rapidly retreating. After calling to him twice or thrice that there was nothing to fear, but without effect, he suffered Hugh to sink upon the ground, and followed, to bring him back.

He continued to creep away, until Barnaby was close upon him; then turned, and said in a terrible, though suppressed voice:

'Let me go. Do not lay hands upon me. Stand back. You have told her; and you and she together, have betrayed me!'

Barnaby looked at him, in silence.

'You have seen your mother!'

'No,' cried Barnaby, eagerly. 'Not for a long time – longer than I can tell. A whole year, I think. Is she here?'

His father looked upon him stedfastly for a few moments, then said – drawing nearer to him as he spoke, for, seeing his face, and hearing his words, it was impossible to doubt his truth:

'What man is that?'

'Hugh – Hugh. Only Hugh. You know him. *He* will not harm you. Why, you're afraid of Hugh! Ha ha ha! Afraid of gruff, old, noisy Hugh!'

'What man is he, I ask you,' he rejoined so fiercely, that Barnaby stopped in his laugh, and shrinking back, surveyed him with a look of terrified amazement.

'Why, how stern you are! You make me fear you, though you are my father – I never feared her. Why do you speak to me so?'

– 'I want,' he answered, putting away the hand which his son, with a timid desire to propitiate him, laid upon his sleeve, – 'I want an answer, and you give me only jeers and questions. Who have you brought with you to this hiding-place, poor fool; and where is the blind man?'

'I don't know where. His house was close shut. I waited, but no person came; that was no fault of mine. This is Hugh – brave Hugh, who broke into that ugly jail, and set us free. Aha! You like him now, do you? You like him now!'

'Why does he lie upon the ground?'

'He has had a fall, and has been drinking. The fields and trees go round, and round, and round, with him, and the ground heaves under his feet. You know him? You remember? See!'

They had by this time returned to where he lay, and both stooped over him to look into his face.

'I recollect the man,' his father murmured. 'Why did you bring him here?'

'Because he would have been killed if I had left him over yonder. They were firing guns, and shedding blood. Does the sight of blood turn you sick, father? I see it does, by your face. That's like me – What are you looking at?'

'At nothing!' said the murderer softly, as he started back a pace or two, and gazed with sunken jaw and staring eyes above his son's head. 'At nothing!'

He remained in the same attitude and with the same expression on his face for a minute or more; then glanced slowly round as if he had lost something; and went shivering back, towards the shed.

'Shall I bring him in, father?' asked Barnaby, who had looked on, wondering.

He only answered with a suppressed groan, and lying down upon the ground, wrapped his cloak about his head, and shrunk into the darkest corner.

Finding that nothing would rouse Hugh now, or make him sensible for a moment, Barnaby dragged him along the grass, and laid him on a little heap of refuse hay and straw which had been his own bed; first having brought some water from a running stream hard by, and washed his wound, and laved his hands and face. Then he lay down himself, between the two, to pass the night; and looking at the stars, fell fast asleep.

Awakened early in the morning, by the sunshine, and the songs of birds, and hum of insects, he left them sleeping in the hut, and walked into the sweet and pleasant air. But he felt that on his jaded senses, oppressed and burdened with the dreadful scenes of last night, and many nights before, all the beauties of opening day, which he had so often tasted, and in which he had had such deep delight, fell heavily. He thought of the blithe mornings when he and the dogs went bounding on together through the woods and fields; and the recollection filled his eyes with tears. He had no consciousness, God help him, of having done wrong, nor had he any new perception of the merits of the cause in which he had been engaged, or those of the men who advocated it; but he was full of cares now, and regrets, and dismal recollections, and wishes (quite unknown to him before) that this or that event had never happened, and that the sorrow and suffering of so many people had been spared. And now he began to think how happy they would be – his father, mother, he, and Hugh – if they rambled away together, and lived in some lonely place, where there were none of these troubles; and that perhaps the blind man, who had talked so wisely about gold, and told him of the great secrets he knew, could teach them how to live without being pinched and griped by want. As this occurred to him, he was the more sorry that he had not seen him last night; and he was still brooding over this regret, when his father came, and touched him on the shoulder.

'Ah!' cried Barnaby, starting from his fit of thoughtfulness. 'Is it only you?'

'Who should it be?'

'I almost thought,' he answered, 'it was the blind man. I must have some talk with him, father.'

'And so must I, for without seeing him, I don't know where to fly or what to do; and lingering here, is death. You must go to him again, and bring him here.'

'Must I!' cried Barnaby, delighted; 'that's brave, father. That's what I want to do.'

'But you must bring only him, and none other. And though you wait at his door a whole day and night, still you must wait, and not come back without him.'

'Don't you fear that,' he cried gaily. 'He shall come, he shall come.'

'Trim off these gewgaws,' said his father, plucking the scraps of ribbon and the feathers from his hat, 'and over your own dress, wear my cloak. Take heed how you go, and they will be too busy in the streets to notice you. Of your coming back you need take no account, for he'll manage that, safely.'

'To be sure!' said Barnaby. 'To be sure he will! A wise man, father, and one who can teach us to be rich! Oh! I know him, I know him.'

He was speedily dressed; and, as well disguised as he could be, with a lighter heart he then set off upon his second journey; leaving Hugh, who was still in a drunken stupor, stretched upon the ground within the shed, and his father walking to and fro before it.

The murderer, full of anxious thoughts, looked after him, and paced up and down, disquieted by every breath of air that whispered among the boughs, and by every light shadow thrown by the passing clouds upon the daisied ground. He was anxious for his safe return, and yet, though his own life and safety hung upon it, felt a relief while he was gone. In the intense selfishness which the constant presence before him of his great crimes, and their consequences here and hereafter, engendered, every thought of Barnaby, as his son, was swallowed up and lost. Still, his presence was a torture and reproach; in his wild eyes, there were terrible images of that guilty night; with his unearthly aspect, and his half-formed mind, he seemed to the murderer a creature who had sprung into existence from his victim's blood. He could not bear his look, his voice, his touch; and yet was forced, by his own desperate condition and his only hope of cheating the gibbet, to have him by his side, and to know that he was inseparable from his single chance of escape.

He walked to and fro, with little rest, all day, revolving these things in his mind; and still Hugh lay, unconscious, in the shed. At length, when the sun was setting, Barnaby returned, leading the blind man, and talking earnestly to him as they came along together.

The murderer advanced to meet them, and bidding his son go on and speak to Hugh, who had just then staggered to his feet, took his place at the blind man's elbow, and slowly followed, towards the shed.

'Why did you send *him?*' said Stagg. 'Don't you know it was the way to have him lost, as soon as found?'

'Would you have had me come myself?' returned the other.

'Humph! Perhaps not. I was before the jail on Tuesday night, but missed you in the crowd. I was out last night, too. There was good work last night – gay work – profitable work' – he added, rattling the money in his pockets.

'Have you –'

– 'Seen your good lady? Yes.'

'Do you mean to tell me more, or not?'

'I'll tell you all,' returned the blind man, with a laugh. 'Excuse me – but I love to see you so impatient. There's energy in it.'

'Does she consent to say the word that may save me?'

'No,' returned the blind man emphatically, as he turned his face towards him. 'No. Thus it is. She has been at death's door since she lost her darling – has been insensible, and I know not what. I tracked her to a hospital, and presented myself (with your leave) at her bed-side. Our talk was not a long one, for she was weak, and there being people near, I was not quite easy. But I told her all that you and I agreed upon; and pointed out the young gentleman's position, in strong terms. She tried to soften me, but that, of course (as I told her), was lost time. She cried and moaned, you may be sure; all women do. Then, of a sudden, she found her voice and strength, and said that Heaven would help her and her innocent son; and that to Heaven she appealed against us – which she did; in really very pretty language, I assure you. I advised her, as a friend, not to count too much upon assistance from any such distant quarter – recommended her to think of it – told her where I lived – said I knew she would send to me before noon, next day – and left her, either in a faint or shamming.'

When he had concluded this narration, during which he had made several pauses, for the convenience of cracking and eating nuts, of which he seemed to have a pocketful, the blind man pulled a flask from his pocket, took a draught himself, and offered it to his companion.

'You won't, won't you?' he said, feeling that he pushed it from him. 'Well! Then the gallant gentleman who's lodging with you, will. Hallo, bully!'

'Death!' said the other, holding him back. 'Will you tell me what I am to do!'

'Do! Nothing easier. Make a moonlight flitting in two hours' time with the young gentleman (he's quite ready to go; I have been giving him good advice as we came along), and get as far from London as you can. Let me know where you are, and leave the rest to me. She *must* come round; she can't hold out long; and as to the chances of your being retaken in the meanwhile, why it wasn't one man who got out of Newgate, but three hundred. Think of that, for your comfort.'

'We must support life. – How?'

'How!' repeated the blind man. 'By eating and drinking. And how get meat and drink, but by paying for it! Money!' he cried, slapping his pocket. 'Is money the word? Why, the streets have been running money. Devil send that the sport's not over yet, for these are jolly times; golden, rare, roaring, scrambling times. Hallo, bully! Hallo! Hallo! Drink, bully, drink. Where are ye there! Hallo!'

With such vociferations, and with a boisterous manner which bespoke his perfect abandonment to the general licence and disorder, he groped his way towards the shed, where Hugh and Barnaby were sitting on the ground, and entered.

'Put it about!' he cried, handing his flask to Hugh. 'The kennels run with wine and gold. Guineas and strong water flow from the very pumps. About with it, don't spare it!'

Exhausted, unwashed, unshorn; begrimed with smoke and dust; his hair clotted with blood; his voice quite gone, so that he spoke in whispers; his skin parched up by fever; his whole body bruised, and cut, and beaten about; Hugh still took the flask, and raised it to his lips. He was in the act of drinking, when the front of the shed was suddenly darkened, and Dennis stood before them.

'No offence, no offence,' said that personage in a conciliatory tone, as Hugh stopped in his draught, and eyed him, with no pleasant look, from head to foot. 'No offence, brother. Barnaby here too, eh? How are you, Barnaby? And two other gentlemen! Your humble servant, gentlemen. No offence to *you* either, I hope. Eh, brothers?'

Notwithstanding that he spoke in this very friendly and confident manner, he seemed to have considerable hesitation about entering, and remained outside the roof. He was rather better dressed than usual: wearing the same suit of thread-bare black, it is true, but having round his neck an unwholesome-looking cravat of a yellowish white; and on his hands great leather gloves, such as a gardener might wear in following his trade. His shoes were newly greased, and ornamented with a pair of rusty iron buckles; the packthread at his knees had been renewed; and where he wanted buttons, he wore pins. Altogether, he had something the look of a tipstaff, or a bailiff's follower, desperately faded, but who had a notion of keeping up the appearance of a professional character, and making the best of the worst means.

'You're very snug here,' said Mr Dennis, pulling out a mouldy pocket-handkerchief, which looked like a decomposed halter; and wiping his forehead in a nervous manner.

'Not snug enough to prevent your finding us, it seems,' Hugh answered, sulkily.

'Why, I'll tell you what, brother,' said Dennis, with a friendly smile, 'when you don't want me to know which way you're riding, you must wear another sort of bells on your horse. Ah! I know the sound o' them you wore last night, and have got quick ears for 'em, that's the truth. Well, but how are you, brother?'

He had by this time approached, and now ventured to sit down by him.

'How am I?' answered Hugh. 'Where were you yesterday? Where did you go when you left me in the jail? Why did you leave me? And what did you mean by rolling your eyes and shaking your fist at me, eh?'

'I shake my fist! – at you, brother!' said Dennis, gently checking Hugh's uplifted hand, which looked threatening.

'Your stick, then; it's all one.'

'Lord love you, brother, I meant nothing. You don't understand me by half. I shouldn't wonder now,' he added, in the tone of a desponding and an injured man, 'but you thought, because I wanted them chaps left in the prison, that I was a going to desert the banners?'

Hugh told him, with an oath, that he did.

'Well!' said Mr Dennis mournfully, 'if you an't enough to make a man mistrust his feller-creeturs, I don't know what is. Desert the banners, eh! Me! Ned Dennis, as was so christened by his own father! – Is this axe your'n, brother?'

'Yes, that's mine,' said Hugh, in the same sullen manner as before; 'it might have hurt you, if you had come in its way once or twice last night. Put it down.'

'Might have hurt me!' said Mr Dennis, still keeping it in his hand,

and feeling the edge with an air of abstraction. 'Might have hurt me! and me exerting myself all the time to the wery best advantage. Here's a world! And you're not a going to ask me to take a sup out of that 'ere bottle, eh?'

Hugh tossed it towards him. As he raised it to his lips, Barnaby jumped up, and motioning them to be silent, looked eagerly out.

'What's the matter, Barnaby?' said Dennis, glancing at Hugh and dropping the flask, but still holding the axe in his hand.

'Hush!' he answered softly. 'What do I see glittering behind the hedge?'

'What!' cried the hangman, raising his voice to its highest pitch, and laying hold of him and Hugh. 'Not – not SOLDIERS, surely!'

That moment, the shed was filled with armed men; and a body of horse, galloping into the field, drew up before it.

'There!' said Dennis, who remained untouched among them when they had seized their prisoners; 'it's them two young ones, gentlemen, that the proclamation puts a price on. This other's an escaped felon. – I'm sorry for it, brother,' he added, in a tone of resignation, addressing himself to Hugh; 'but you've brought it on yourself; you forced me to do it; you wouldn't respect the soundest constitootional principles, you know; you went and wiolated the wery frame-work of society. I had sooner have given away a trifle in charity than done this, I would upon my soul. – If you'll keep fast hold on 'em, gentlemen, I think I can make a shift to tie 'em better than you can.'

But this operation was postponed for a few moments by a new occurrence. The blind man, whose ears were quicker than most people's sight, had been alarmed, before Barnaby, by a rustling in the bushes, under cover of which the soldiers had advanced. He retreated instantly – had hidden somewhere for a minute – and probably in his confusion mistaking the point at which he had emerged, was now seen running across the open meadow.

An officer cried directly that he had helped to plunder a house last night. He was loudly called on, to surrender. He ran the harder, and in a few seconds would have been out of gun-shot. The word was given, and the men fired.

There was a breathless pause and a profound silence, during which all eyes were fixed upon him. He had been seen to start at the discharge, as if the report had frightened him. But he neither stopped nor slackened his pace in the least, and ran on full forty yards further. Then, without one reel or stagger, or sign of faintness, or quivering of any limb, he dropped.

Some of them hurried up to where he lay; – the hangman with them. Everything had passed so quickly, that the smoke was not yet scattered, but curled slowly off in a little cloud, which seemed like the dead man's spirit moving solemnly away. There were a few drops of blood upon the grass – more, when they turned him over – that was all.

'Look here! Look here!' said the hangman, stooping one knee beside the body, and gazing up with a disconsolate face at the officer and men. 'Here's a pretty sight!'

'Stand out of the way,' replied the officer. 'Serjeant! see what he had about him.'

The man turned his pockets out upon the grass, and counted, besides some foreign coins and two rings, five-and-forty guineas in gold. These were bundled up in a handkerchief and carried away; the body remained there for the present, but six men and the serjeant were left to take it to the nearest public-house.

'Now then, if you're going,' said the serjeant, clapping Dennis on the back, and pointing after the officer who was walking towards the shed.

To which Mr Dennis only replied, 'Don't talk to me!' and then repeated what he had said before, namely 'Here's a pretty sight!'

'It's not one that you care for much, I should think,' observed the serjeant coolly.

'Why, who,' said Mr Dennis, rising, 'should care for it, if I don't?'

'Oh! I didn't know you was so tender-hearted,' said the serjeant. 'That's all!'

'Tender-hearted!' echoed Dennis. 'Tender-hearted! Look at this man. Do you call *this* constitootional? Do you see him shot through and through instead of being worked off like a Briton? Damme, if I know which party to side with. You're as bad as the other. What's to become of the country if the military power's to go a superseding the ciwilians in this way? Where's this poor fellow-creetur's rights as a citizen, that he didn't have *me* in his last moments! I was here. I was willing. I was ready. These are nice times, brother, to have

the dead crying out against us in this way, and sleep comfortably in our beds arterwards; wery nice!'

Whether he derived any material consolation from binding the prisoners, is uncertain; most probably he did. At all events his being summoned to that work, diverted him, for the time, from these painful reflections, and gave his thoughts a more congenial occupation.

They were not all three carried off together, but in two parties; Barnaby and his father, going by one road in the centre of a body of foot; and Hugh, fast bound upon a horse, and strongly guarded by a troop of cavalry, being taken by another.

They had no opportunity for the least communication, in the short interval which preceded their departure; being kept strictly apart. Hugh only observed that Barnaby walked with a drooping head among his guard, and, without raising his eyes, that he tried to wave his fettered hand when he passed. For himself, he buoyed up his courage as he rode along, with the assurance that the mob would force his jail wherever it might be, and set him at liberty. But when they got into London, and more especially into Fleet Market, lately the stronghold of the rioters, where the military were rooting out the last remnant of the crowd, he saw that this hope was gone, and felt that he was riding to his death.

CHAPTER THE SEVENTIETH

Mr Dennis having despatched this piece of business without any personal hurt or inconvenience, and having now retired into the tranquil respectability of private life, resolved to solace himself with half an hour or so of female society. With this amiable purpose in his mind, he bent his steps towards the house where Dolly and Miss Haredale were still confined, and whither Miss Miggs had also been removed by order of Mr Simon Tappertit.

As he walked along the streets with his leather gloves clasped behind him, and his face indicative of cheerful thought and pleasant calculation, Mr Dennis might have been likened unto a farmer ruminating among his crops, and enjoying by anticipation the bountiful gifts of Providence. Look where he would, some heap of ruins afforded him rich promise of a working off; the whole town appeared to have been ploughed, and sown, and nurtured by most genial weather; and a goodly harvest was at hand.

Having taken up arms and resorted to deeds of violence, with the great main object of preserving the Old Bailey in all its purity, and the gallows in all its pristine usefulness and moral grandeur, it would perhaps be going too far to assert that Mr Dennis had ever distinctly contemplated and foreseen this happy state of things. He rather looked upon it as one of those beautiful dispensations which are inscrutably brought about for the behoof and advantage of good men. He felt, as it were, personally referred to, in this prosperous ripening for the gibbet; and had never considered himself so much the pet and favourite child of Destiny, or loved that lady so well or with such a calm and virtuous reliance, in all his life.

As to being taken up, himself, for a rioter, and punished with the rest, Mr Dennis dismissed that possibility from his thoughts as an idle chimera; arguing that the line of conduct he had adopted at Newgate, and the service he had rendered that day, would be more than a set-off against any evidence which might identify him as a member of the crowd: that any charge of companionship which might be made against him by those who were themselves in danger, would certainly go for nought: and that if any trivial indiscretion on his part should unluckily come out, the uncommon usefulness of his office, at present, and the great demand for the exercise of its functions, would certainly cause it to be winked at, and passed over. In a word, he had played his cards throughout, with great care; had changed sides at the very nick of time; had delivered up two of the most notorious rioters, and a distinguished felon to boot; and was quite at his ease.

Saving – for there is a reservation; and even Mr Dennis was not perfectly happy – saving for one circumstance; to wit, the forcible detention of Dolly and Miss Haredale, in a house almost adjoining his own. This was a stumbling-block, for if they were discovered and released, they could, by the testimony they had it in their power to give, place him in a situation of great jeopardy; and to set them at liberty, first extorting from them an oath of secrecy and silence, was a thing not to be thought of. It was more, perhaps, with an eye to the danger which lurked in this quarter, than from his abstract love of conversation with the sex, that the hangman, quickening his steps, now hastened into their society; cursing the amorous natures of Hugh and Mr Tappertit with great heartiness, at every step he took.

When he entered the miserable room in which they were confined, Dolly and Miss Haredale withdrew in silence to the furthest corner. But Miss Miggs, who was particularly tender of her reputation, immediately fell upon her knees and began to scream very loud, crying 'What will become of me!' – 'Where is my Simmuns!' 'Have mercy, good gentleman, on my sex's weakness!' – with other doleful lamentations of that nature, which she delivered with great propriety and decorum.

'Miss, Miss,' whispered Dennis, beckoning to her with his forefinger, 'come here – I won't hurt you. Come here, my lamb, will you?'

On hearing this tender epithet, Miss Miggs, who had left off screaming directly he opened his lips, and had listened to him attentively, began again: crying 'Oh I'm his lamb! He says I'm his lamb! Oh gracious, why wasn't I born old and ugly? Why was I ever made to be the youngest of six, and all of 'em dead and in their blessed graves, excepting one married sister, which is settled in Golden Lion Court, number twenty-sivin, second bell-handle on the –!'

'Don't I say I an't a going to hurt you?' said Dennis, pointing to a chair. 'Why Miss, what's the matter?'

'I don't know what mayn't be the matter!' cried Miggs, clasping her hands distractedly. 'Anything may be the matter!'

'But nothing is, I tell you,' said the hangman. 'First stop that noise and come and sit down here, will you, chuckey?'

The coaxing tone in which he said these latter words might have failed in its object, if he had not accompanied them with sundry sharp jerks of his thumb over one shoulder, and with divers winks and thrustings of his tongue into his cheek, from which signals the damsel gathered that he sought to speak to her apart, concerning Miss Haredale and Dolly. Her curiosity being very powerful, and her jealousy by no means inactive, she arose, and with a great deal of shivering and starting back, and much muscular action among all the small bones in her throat, gradually approached him.

'Sit down,' said the hangman.

Suiting the action to the word, he thrust her rather suddenly and prematurely into a chair; and designing to reassure her by a little harmless jocularity, such as is adapted to please and fascinate the sex, converted his right forefinger into an ideal bradawl or gimlet, and made as though he would screw the same into her side – whereat Miss Miggs shrieked again, and discovered symptoms of faintness.

'Lovey, my dear,' whispered Dennis, drawing his chair close to hers. 'When was your young man here last, eh?'

'My young man, good gentleman!' answered Miggs in a tone of exquisite distress.

'Ah! Simmuns, you know – him?' said Dennis.

'Mine indeed!' cried Miggs, with a burst of bitterness – and as she said it, she glanced towards Dolly. 'Mine, good gentleman!'

This was just what Mr Dennis wanted, and expected.

'Ah!' he said, looking so soothingly, not to say amorously on Miggs, that she sat, as she afterwards remarked, on pins and needles of the sharpest Whitechapel kind; not knowing what intentions might be suggesting that expression to his features: 'I was afraid of that. I saw as much, myself. It's her fault. She will entice 'em.'

'I wouldn't,' cried Miggs, folding her hands and looking upwards with a kind of devout blankness, 'I wouldn't lay myself out as she does; I wouldn't be as bold as her; I wouldn't seem to say to all male creeturs "come and kiss me"' – and here a shudder quite convulsed her frame – 'for any earthly crowns as might be offered. Worlds,' Miggs added solemnly, 'should not reduce me. No. Not if I was Wenis.'[1]

'Well but you are Wenus you know,' said Mr Dennis, confidentially.

'No, I am not, good gentleman,' answered Miggs, shaking her head with an air of self-denial which seemed to imply that she might be if she chose, but she hoped she knew better. 'No I am not, good gentleman. Don't charge me with it.'

Up to this time, she had turned round every now and then to where Dolly and Miss Haredale had retired, and uttered a scream, or groan, or laid her hand upon her heart and trembled excessively, with a view of keeping up appearances, and giving them to understand that she conversed with the visitor, under protest and on compulsion, and at a great personal sacrifice, for their common good. But at this point, Mr Dennis looked so very full of meaning, and gave such a singularly expressive twitch to his face as a request to her to come still nearer to him, that she abandoned these little arts and gave him her whole and undivided attention.

'When was Simmuns here, I say?' quoth Dennis, in her ear.

'Not since yesterday morning; and then only for a few minutes. Not all day, the day before.'

'You know he meant all along to carry off that one?' said Dennis, indicating Dolly by the slightest possible jerk of his head: – 'And to hand you over to somebody else.'

Miss Miggs, who had fallen into a terrible state of grief when the first part of this sentence was spoken, recovered a little at the second, and seemed by the sudden check she put upon her tears, to intimate that possibly this arrangement might meet her views; and that it might, perhaps, remain an open question.

' – But unfort'nately,' pursued Dennis, who observed this: 'somebody else was fond of her too, you see; and even if he wasn't, somebody else is took for a rioter, and it's all over with him.'

Miss Miggs relapsed.

'Now, I want,' said Dennis, 'to clear this house, and to see you righted. What if I was to get her off, out of the way, eh?'

Miss Miggs, brightening again, rejoined, with many breaks and pauses from excess of feeling, that temptations had been Simmuns's bane. That it was not his faults, but hers (meaning Dolly's). That men did not see through these dreadful arts as women did, and therefore was caged and trapped, as Simmun had been. That she had no personal motives to serve – far from it – on the contrary, her intentions was good towards all parties. But forasmuch as she knowed that Simmun, if united to any designing and artful minxes (she would name no names, for that was not her dispositions) – to *any* designing and artful minxes – must be made miserable and unhappy for life, she *did* incline towards prewentions. Such, she added, was her free confessions. But as this was private feelings, and might perhaps be looked upon as wengeance, she begged the gentleman would say no more. Whatever he said, wishing to do her duty by all mankind, even by them as had ever been her bitterest enemies, she would not listen to him. With that she stopped her ears, and shook her head from side to side, to intimate to Mr Dennis that though he talked until he had no breath left, she was as deaf as any adder.[2]

'Lookee here, my sugar-stick,' said Mr Dennis; 'if your view's the same as mine, and you'll only be quiet and slip away at the right time, I can have the house clear to-morrow, and be out of this trouble. – Stop though! there's the other.'

'Which other, sir?' asked Miggs – still with her fingers in her ears and her head shaking obstinately.

'Why, the tallest one, yonder,' said Dennis, as he stroked his chin, and added, in an under tone to himself, something about not crossing Muster Gashford.

Miss Miggs replied (still being profoundly deaf) that if Miss Haredale stood in the way at all, he might make himself quite easy on that score; as she had gathered, from what passed between Hugh and Mr Tappertit when they were last there, that she was to be removed alone (not by them, by somebody else), to-morrow night.

Mr Dennis opened his eyes very wide at this piece of information, whistled once, considered once, and finally slapped his head once and nodded once, as if he had got the clue to this mysterious removal, and so dismissed it. Then he imparted his design concerning Dolly to Miss Miggs, who was taken more deaf than before, when he began; and so remained, all through.

The notable scheme was this. Mr Dennis was immediately to seek out from among the rioters, some daring young fellow (and he had one in his eye, he said), who, terrified by the threats he could hold out to him, and alarmed by the capture of so many who were no better and no worse than he, would gladly avail himself of any help to get abroad, and out of harm's way, with his plunder, even though his journey were incumbered by an unwilling companion; indeed, the unwilling companion being a beautiful girl, would probably be an additional inducement and temptation. Such a person found, he proposed to bring him there on the ensuing night, when the tall one was taken off, and Miss Miggs had purposely retired; and then that Dolly should be gagged, muffled in a cloak, and carried in any handy conveyance down to the river's side; where there were abundant means of getting her smuggled snugly off in any small craft of doubtful character, and no questions asked. With regard to the expense of this removal, he would say, at a rough calculation, that two or three silver tea or coffee pots, with something additional for drink (such as a muffineer, or toast-rack), would more than cover it. Articles of plate of every kind having been buried by the rioters in several lonely parts of London, and particularly, as he knew, in St James's Square, which, though easy of access, was little frequented after dark, and had a convenient piece of water in the midst,[3] the needful funds were close at hand, and could be had upon the shortest notice. With regard to Dolly, the gentleman would exercise his own discretion. He would be bound to do nothing but take her away, and keep her away; all other arrangements and dispositions would rest entirely with himself.

If Miss Miggs had had her hearing, no doubt she would have been greatly shocked by the indelicacy of a young female's going away with a stranger, by night (for her moral feelings, as we have said, were of the tenderest kind); but directly Mr Dennis ceased to speak, she reminded him that he had only wasted breath. She then went on to say (still with her fingers in her ears) that nothing less than a severe practical lesson would save the locksmith's daughter from utter ruin; and that she felt it, as it were, a moral obligation and a sacred duty to the family, to wish that some one would devise one for her reformation. Miss Miggs remarked, and very justly, as an abstract sentiment which happened to occur to her at the moment, that she dared to say the locksmith and his wife would murmur, and repine, if they were ever, by forcible abduction, or otherwise, to lose their child: but that we seldom knew, in this world, what was best for us; such being our sinful and imperfect natures, that very few arrived at that clear understanding.

Having brought their conversation to this satisfactory end, they parted: Dennis, to further his design, and take another walk about his farm; Miss Miggs, to launch, when he left her, into such a burst of mental anguish (which she gave them to understand was occasioned by certain tender things he had had the presumption and audacity to say), that little Dolly's heart was quite melted. Indeed, she said and did so much to soothe the outraged feelings of Miss Miggs, and looked so beautiful while doing so, that if that young maid had not had ample vent for her surpassing spite, in a knowledge of the mischief that was brewing, she must have scratched her features, on the spot.

*

CHAPTER THE SEVENTY-FIRST

All next day, Emma Haredale, Dolly, and Miggs, remained cooped up together in what had now been their prison for so many days, without seeing any person, or hearing any sound but the murmured conversation, in an outer room, of the men who kept watch over them. There appeared to be more of these fellows than there had been hitherto; and they could no longer hear the voices of women, which they had before plainly distinguished. Some new excitement, too, seemed to prevail among them; for there was much stealthy going in and out, and a constant questioning of those who were newly arrived. They had previously been quite reckless in their behaviour; often making a great uproar; quarrelling among themselves, fighting, dancing, and singing. They were now very subdued and silent; conversing almost in whispers, and stealing in and out with a soft and stealthy tread, very different from the boisterous trampling in which their arrivals and departures had hitherto been announced to the trembling captives.

Whether this change was occasioned by the presence among them of some person of authority in their ranks, or by any other cause, they were unable to decide. Sometimes they thought it was in part attributable to there being a sick man in the chamber, for last night there had been a shuffling of feet, as though a burden were brought in, and afterwards a moaning noise. But they had no means of ascertaining the truth: for any question or entreaty on their parts only provoked a storm of brutal execrations, or something worse; and they were too happy to be left alone, unassailed by threats or admiration, to risk even that comfort, by any voluntary communication with those who held them in durance.

It was sufficiently evident, both to Emma and to the locksmith's poor little daughter herself, that she, Dolly, was the great object of attraction; and that so soon as they should have leisure to indulge in the softer passion, Hugh and Mr Tappertit would certainly fall to blows for her sake: in which latter case, it was not very difficult to foresee whose prize she would become. With all her old horror of that man revived, and deepened into a degree of aversion and abhorrence which no language can describe; with a thousand old recollections and regrets, and causes of distress, anxiety, and fear, besetting her on all sides; poor Dolly Varden – sweet, blooming, buxom Dolly – began to hang her head, and fade, and droop, like a beautiful flower. The colour fled from her cheeks, her courage forsook her, her gentle heart failed. Unmindful of all her provoking caprices, forgetful of all her conquests and inconstancy, with all her winning little vanities quite gone, she nestled all the livelong day in Emma Haredale's bosom; and, sometimes calling on her

dear old grey-haired father, sometimes on her mother, and sometimes even on her old home, pined slowly away, like a poor bird in
its cage.

Light hearts, light hearts, that float so gaily on a smooth stream,
that are so sparkling and buoyant in the sunshine – down upon
fruit, bloom upon flowers, blush in summer air, life of the winged
insect, whose whole existence is a day – how soon ye sink in
troubled water! Poor Dolly's heart – a little, gentle, idle, fickle
thing; giddy, restless, fluttering; constant to nothing but bright
looks, and smiles, and laughter – Dolly's heart was breaking.

Emma had known grief, and could bear it better. She had little
comfort to impart, but she could soothe and tend her, and she did
so; and Dolly clung to her like a child to its nurse. In endeavouring
to inspire her with some fortitude, she increased her own; and
though the nights were long, and the days dismal and she felt the
wasting influence of watching and fatigue, and had perhaps a more
defined and clear perception of their destitute condition and its
worst dangers, she uttered no complaint. Before the ruffians, in
whose power they were, she bore herself so calmly, and with such
an appearance, in the midst of all her terror, of a secret conviction
that they dared not harm her, that there was not a man among
them but held her in some degree of dread; and more than one
believed she had a weapon hidden in her dress, and was prepared
to use it.

Such was their condition when they were joined by Miss Miggs;
who gave them to understand that she too had been taken prisoner,
because of her charms; and detailed such feats of resistance she had
performed (her virtue having given her supernatural strength), that
they felt it quite a happiness to have her for a champion. Nor was
this the only comfort they derived at first from Miggs's presence
and society: for that young lady displayed such resignation and
long-suffering, and so much meek endurance, under her trials; and
breathed in all her chaste discourse a spirit of such holy confidence
and resignation, and devout belief that all would happen for the
best; that Emma felt her courage strengthened by the bright
example, never doubting but that everything she said was true, and
that she, like them, was torn from all she loved, and agonized by
doubt and apprehension. As to poor Dolly, she was roused, at first,
by seeing one who came from home; but when she heard under
what circumstances she had left it, and in whose hands her father

had fallen, she wept more bitterly than ever, and refused all comfort.

Miss Miggs was at some trouble to reprove her for this state of mind, and to entreat her to take example by herself, who, she said, was now receiving back, with interest, tenfold the amount of her subscriptions to the red-brick dwelling-house, in the articles of peace of mind and a quiet conscience. And, while on serious topics, Miss Miggs considered it her duty to try her hand at the conversion of Miss Haredale; for whose improvement she launched into a polemical address of some length, in the course whereof, she likened herself unto a chosen missionary, and that young lady to a cannibal in darkness. Indeed she returned so often to these subjects, and so frequently called upon them to take a lesson from her, – at the same time vaunting and, as it were, rioting in, her huge unworthiness, and abundant excess of sin, – that, in the course of a short time, she became, in that small chamber, rather a nuisance than a comfort, and rendered them, if possible, even more unhappy than they had been before.

The night had now come; and for the first time (for their jailers had been regular in bringing food and candles), they were left in darkness. Any change in their condition in such a place inspired new fears; and when some hours had passed, and the gloom was still unbroken, Emma could no longer repress her alarm.

They listened attentively. There was the same murmuring in the outer room, and now and then a moan which seemed to be wrung from a person in great pain, who made an effort to subdue it, but could not. Even these men seemed to be in darkness too; for no light shone through the chinks in the door, nor were they moving, as their custom was, but quite still: the silence being unbroken by so much as the creaking of a board.

At first, Miss Miggs wondered greatly in her own mind who this sick person might be; but arriving, on second thoughts, at the conclusion that he was a part of the schemes on foot, and an artful device soon to be employed with great success, she opined, for Miss Haredale's comfort, that it must be some misguided Papist who had been wounded: and this happy supposition encouraged her to say, under her breath, 'Ally Looyer!' several times.

'Is it possible,' said Emma, with some indignation, 'that you who have seen these men committing the outrages you have told us of, and who have fallen into their hands, like us, can exult in their cruelties!'

'Personal considerations, Miss,' rejoined Miggs, 'sinks into nothing, afore a noble cause. Ally Looyer! Ally Looyer! Ally Looyer, good gentlemen!'

It seemed, from the shrill pertinacity with which Miss Miggs repeated this form of acclamation, that she was calling the same through the keyhole of the door; but in the profound darkness she could not be seen.

'If the time has come – Heaven knows it may come at any moment – when they are bent on prosecuting the designs, whatever they may be, with which they have brought us here, can you still encourage, and side with them?' demanded Emma.

'I thank my goodness-gracious-blessed-stars I can, Miss,' returned Miggs, with increased energy. 'Ally Looyer, good gentlemen!'

Even Dolly, cast down and disappointed as she was, revived at this, and bade Miggs hold her tongue directly.

'*Which*, was you pleased to observe, Miss Varsen?' said Miggs, with a strong emphasis on the irrelative pronoun.

Dolly repeated her request.

'Ho, gracious me!' cried Miggs, with hysterical derision. 'Ho, gracious me! Yes, to be sure I will. Ho yes! I am a abject slave, and a toiling, moiling, constant-working, always-being-found-fault-with, never-giving-satisfactions,   nor-having-no-time-to-clean-oneself, potter's wessel[1] – an't I, Miss! Ho yes! My situations is lowly, and my capacities is limited, and my duties is to humble myself afore the base degenerating daughters of their blessed mothers as is fit to keep companies with holy saints but is born to persecutions from wicked relations – and to demean myself before them as is no better than Infidels – an't it, Miss! Ho yes! My only becoming occupations is to help young flaunting pagins to brush and comb and titivate themselves into whitening and suppulchres,[2] and leave the young men to think that there an't a bit of padding in it nor no pinching ins nor fillings out nor pomatums nor deceits nor earthly wanities – an't it, Miss! Yes, to be sure it is – ho yes!'

Having delivered these ironical passages with a most wonderful volubility, and with a shrillness perfectly deafening (especially when she jerked out the interjections), Miss Miggs, from mere habit, and not because weeping was at all appropriate to the occasion, which was one of triumph, concluded by bursting into a flood of tears, and calling in an impassioned manner on the name of Simmuns.

What Emma Haredale and Dolly would have done, or how long Miss Miggs, now that she had hoisted her true colours, would have gone on waving them before their astonished senses, it is impossible to tell. Nor is it necessary to speculate on these matters, for a startling interruption occurred at that moment, which took their whole attention by storm.

This was a violent knocking at the door of the house, and then its sudden bursting open; which was immediately succeeded by a scuffle in the room without, and the clash of weapons. Transported with the hope that rescue had at length arrived, Emma and Dolly shrieked aloud for help; nor were their shrieks unanswered; for after a hurried interval, a man, bearing in one hand a drawn sword, and in the other a taper, rushed into the chamber where they were confined.

It was some check upon their transport to find in this person an entire stranger, but they appealed to him, nevertheless, and besought him, in impassioned language, to restore them to their friends.

'For what other purpose am I here?' he answered, closing the door, and standing with his back against it. 'With what object have I made my way to this place, through difficulty and danger, but to preserve you?'

With a joy for which it was impossible to find adequate expression, they embraced each other, and thanked Heaven for this most timely aid. Their deliverer stepped forward for a moment to put the light upon the table, and immediately returning to his former position against the door, bared his head, and looked on smilingly.

'You have news of my uncle, Sir?' said Emma, turning hastily towards him.

'And of my father and mother?' added Dolly.

'Yes,' he said. 'Good news.'

'They are alive and unhurt?' they both cried at once.

'Yes, and unhurt,' he rejoined.

'And close at hand?'

'I did not say close at hand,' he answered smoothly; 'they are at no great distance. *Your* friends, sweet one,' he added, addressing Dolly, 'are within a few hours' journey. You will be restored to them, I hope, to-night.'

'My uncle, Sir –' faltered Emma.

'Your uncle, dear Miss Haredale, happily – I say happily, because he has succeeded where many of our creed have failed, and is safe – has crossed the sea, and is out of Britain.'

'I thank God for it,' said Emma, faintly.

'You say well. You have reason to be thankful: greater reason than it is possible for you, who have seen but one night of these cruel outrages, to imagine.'

'Does he desire,' said Emma, 'that I should follow him?'

'Do you ask if he desires it?' cried the stranger in surprise. 'If he desires it! But you do not know the danger of remaining in England, the difficulty of escape, or the price hundreds would pay to secure the means, when you make that inquiry. Pardon me. I had forgotten that you could not, being prisoner here.'

'I gather, Sir,' said Emma, after a moment's pause, 'from what you hint at, but fear to tell me, that I have witnessed but the beginning, and the least, of the violence to which we are exposed; and that it has not yet slackened in its fury?'

He shrugged his shoulders, shook his head, lifted up his hands; and with the same smooth smile, which was not a pleasant one to see, cast his eyes upon the ground, and remained silent.

'You may venture, Sir, to speak plain,' said Emma, 'and to tell me the worst. We have undergone some preparation for it already.'

But here Dolly interposed, and entreated her not to hear the worst, but the best; and besought the gentleman to tell them the best, and to keep the remainder of his news until they were safe among their friends again.

'It is told in three words,' he said, glancing at the locksmith's daughter with a look of some displeasure. 'The people have risen, to a man, against us; the streets are filled with soldiers, who support them and do their bidding. We have no protection but from above, and no safety but in flight; and that is a poor resource; for we are watched on every hand, and detained here, both by force and fraud. Miss Haredale, I cannot bear – believe me, that I cannot bear – by speaking of myself, or what I have done, or am prepared to do, to seem to vaunt my services before you. But, having powerful Protestant connexions, and having my whole wealth embarked with theirs in shipping and commerce, I happily possessed the means of saving your uncle. I have the means of saving you; and in redemption of my sacred promise, made to him, I am here; pledged not to leave you until I have placed you in his arms. The treachery or penitence of one of the men about you, led to the discovery of your place of confinement; and that I have forced my way here, sword in hand, you see.'

'You bring,' said Emma, faltering, 'some note or token from my uncle?'

'No, he doesn't,' cried Dolly, pointing at him earnestly: 'now I am sure he doesn't. Don't go with him for the world!'

'Hush, pretty fool – be silent,' he replied, frowning angrily upon her. 'No, Miss Haredale, I have no letter, nor any token of any kind; for while I sympathise with you, and such as you, on whom misfortune so heavy and so undeserved has fallen, I value my life. I carry, therefore, no writing which, found upon me, would lead to its certain loss. I never thought of bringing any other token, nor did Mr Haredale think of entrusting me with one: possibly because he had good experience of my faith and honesty, and owed his life to me.'

There was a reproof conveyed in these words, which, to a nature like Emma Haredale's, was well addressed. But Dolly, who was differently constituted, was by no means touched by it; and still conjured her, in all the terms of affection and attachment she could think of, not to be lured away.

'Time presses,' said their visitor, who, although he sought to express the deepest interest, had something cold and even in his speech, that grated on the ear; 'and danger surrounds us. If I have exposed myself to it, in vain, let it be so; but if you and he should ever meet again, do me justice. If you decide to remain (as I think you do), remember, Miss Haredale, that I left you, with a solemn caution, and acquitting myself of all the consequences to which you expose yourself.'

'Stay, sir!' cried Emma – 'one moment, I beg you. Cannot we' – and she drew Dolly closer to her – 'cannot we go together?'

'The task of conveying one female in safety through such scenes as we must encounter, to say nothing of attracting the attention of those who crowd the streets,' he answered, 'is enough. I have said that she will be restored to her friends to-night. If you accept the service I tender, Miss Haredale, she shall be instantly placed in safe conduct, and that promise redeemed. Do you decide to remain? People of all ranks and creeds are flying from the town, which is sacked from end to end. Let me be of use in some quarter. Do you stay, or go?'

'Dolly,' said Emma, in a hurried manner, 'my dear girl, this is our last hope. If we part now, it is only that we may meet again in happiness and honour. I will trust to this gentleman.'

'No – no – no!' cried Dolly, clinging to her. 'Pray, pray, do not!'

'You hear,' said Emma, 'that to-night – only to-night – within a few hours – oh, think of that! – you will be among those who would die of grief to lose you, and are now plunged in the deepest misery for your sake. Pray for me, dear girl, as I will for you; and never forget the many quiet hours we have passed together. Say one "God bless you!" Say that at parting, sister!'

But Dolly could say nothing; no, not when Emma kissed her cheek a hundred times, and covered it with tears, could she do more than hang upon her neck, and sob, and clasp, and hold her tight.

'We have time for no more of this,' cried the man, unclenching her hands and throwing her roughly off, as he drew Emma Haredale towards the door: 'Now! Quick, outside there! are you ready?'

'Ay!' cried a loud voice, which made him start. 'Quite ready! Stand back here, for your lives!'

And in an instant he was felled like an ox in the butcher's shambles – struck down as though a block of marble had fallen from the roof and crushed him – and cheerful light, and beaming faces came pouring in – and Emma was clasped in her uncle's embrace; and Dolly, with a shriek that pierced the air, fell into the arms of her father and mother.

What fainting there was, what laughing, what crying, what sobbing, what smiling; how much questioning, no answering, all talking together, all beside themselves with joy; what kissing, congratulating, embracing, shaking of hands; and falling into all these raptures, over and over and over again; no language can describe.

At length, and after a long time, the old locksmith went up and fairly hugged two strangers, who had stood apart and left them to themselves; and then they saw – whom? Yes, Edward Chester and Joseph Willet.

'See here!' cried the locksmith. 'See here! where would any of us have been without these two? Oh, Mr Edward, Mr Edward – oh, Joe, Joe, how light, and yet how full, you have made my old heart to-night!'

'It was Mr Edward that knocked him down, sir,' said Joe: 'I longed to do it, but I gave it up to him. Come, you brave and honest

gentleman! Get your senses together, for you haven't long to lie
here.'

He had his foot upon the breast of their sham deliverer, in the
absence of a spare arm; and gave him a gentle roll as he spoke.
Gashford, for it was no other, crouching yet malignant, raised his
scowling face, like sin subdued, and pleaded to be gently used.

'I have access to all my lord's papers, Mr Haredale,' he said, in
a submissive voice: Mr Haredale keeping his back towards him,
and not once looking round: 'there are very important documents
among them. There are a great many in secret drawers, and distributed in various places, known only to my lord and me. I can give
some very valuable information, and render important assistance
to any inquiry. You will have to answer it, if I receive ill usage.'

'Pah!' cried Joe, in deep disgust. 'Get up, man; you're waited for,
outside. Get up, do you hear?'

Gashford slowly rose; and picking up his hat, and looking with
a baffled malevolence, yet with an air of despicable humility, all
round the room, crawled out.

'And now, gentlemen,' said Joe, who seemed to be the spokesman
of the party, for all the rest were silent; 'the sooner we get back to
the Black Lion, the better, perhaps.'

Mr Haredale nodded assent; and drawing his niece's arm through
his, and taking one of her hands between his own, passed out
straightway; followed by the locksmith, Mrs Varden, and Dolly –
who would scarcely have presented a sufficient surface for all the
hugs and caresses they bestowed upon her though she had been a
dozen Dollys. Edward Chester and Joe followed.

And did Dolly never once look behind – not once? Was there not
one little fleeting glimpse of the dark eyelash, almost resting on her
flushed cheek, and of the downcast sparkling eye it shaded? Joe
thought there was – and he is not likely to have been mistaken; for
there were not many eyes like Dolly's, that's the truth.

The outer room, through which they had to pass, was full of
men; among them, Mr Dennis in safe keeping; and there, had been
since yesterday, lying in hiding behind a wooden screen which was
now thrown down, Simon Tappertit, the recreant 'Prentice; burnt
and bruised, and with a gun-shot wound in his body; and his legs
– his perfect legs, the pride and glory of his life, the comfort of his
whole existence – crushed into shapeless ugliness.[3] Wondering no
longer at the moans they had heard, Dolly crept closer to her father,

and shuddered at the sight: but neither bruises, burns, nor gun-shot wound, nor all the torture of his shattered limbs, sent half so keen a pang to Simon's breast, as Dolly passing out, with Joe for her preserver.

A coach was ready at the door, and Dolly found herself safe and whole inside, between her father and mother; with Emma Haredale and her uncle, quite real, sitting opposite. But there was no Joe, no Edward; and they had said nothing. They had only bowed once, and kept at a distance. Dear heart! what a long way it was, to the Black Lion.

CHAPTER THE SEVENTY-SECOND

The Black Lion was so far off, and occupied such a length of time in the getting at, that notwithstanding the strong presumptive evidence she had about her of the late events being real and of actual occurrence, Dolly could not divest herself of the belief that she must be in a dream which was lasting all night. Nor was she quite certain that she saw and heard with her own proper senses, even when the coach, in the fullness of time, stopped at the Black Lion, and the host of that tavern approached in a gush of cheerful light to help them to dismount, and give them hearty welcome.

There too, at the coach door, one on one side, one upon the other, were already Edward Chester and Joe Willet, who must have followed in another coach: and this was such a strange and unaccountable proceeding, that Dolly was the more inclined to favour the idea of her being fast asleep. But when Mr Willet appeared – old John himself – so heavy-headed and obstinate, and with such a double chin as the liveliest imagination could never in its boldest flights have conjured up in all its vast proportions – then she stood corrected, and unwillingly admitted to herself that she was broad awake.

And Joe had lost an arm – he – that well-made, handsome, gallant fellow! As Dolly glanced towards him, and thought of the pain he must have suffered, and the far-off places in which he had been wandering; and wondered who had been his nurse, and hoped that whoever it was, she had been as kind and gentle and considerate as she would have been; the tears came rising to her bright eyes, one by one, little by little, until she could keep them back no longer, and so, before them all, wept bitterly.

'We are all safe now, Dolly,' said her father, kindly. 'We shall not be separated any more. Cheer up, my love, cheer up!'

The locksmith's wife knew better perhaps, than he, what ailed her daughter. But Mrs Varden being quite an altered woman – for the riots had done that good – added her word to his, and comforted her with similar representations.

'Mayhap,' said Mr Willet senior, looking round upon the company, 'she's hungry. That's what it is, depend upon it – I am, myself.'

The Black Lion, who, like old John, had been waiting supper past all reasonable and conscionable hours, hailed this as a philosophical discovery of the profoundest and most penetrating kind; and the table being already spread, they sat down to supper straightway.

The conversation was not of the liveliest nature, nor were the appetites of some among them very keen. But in both these respects, old John more than atoned for any deficiency on the part of the rest, and very much distinguished himself.

It was not in point of actual talkativeness that Mr Willet shone so brilliantly, for he had none of his old cronies to 'tackle,' and was rather timorous of venturing on Joe; having certain vague misgivings within him, that he was ready on the shortest notice, and on receipt of the slightest offence, to fell the Black Lion to the floor of his own parlour, and immediately withdraw to China or some other remote and unknown region, there to dwell for evermore; or at least until he had got rid of his remaining arm and both legs, and perhaps an eye or so, into the bargain. It was with a peculiar kind of pantomime that Mr Willet filled up every pause; and in this he was considered by the Black Lion, who had been his familiar for some years, quite to surpass and go beyond himself, and outrun the expectations of his most admiring friends.

The subject that worked in Mr Willet's mind, and occasioned these demonstrations, was no other than his son's bodily disfigurement, which he had never yet got himself thoroughly to believe, or comprehend. Shortly after their first meeting, he had been observed to wander, in a state of great perplexity, to the kitchen, and to direct his gaze towards the fire, as if in search of his usual adviser in all matters of doubt and difficulty. But there being no boiler at the Black Lion, and the rioters having so beaten and battered his own that it was quite unfit for further service, he wandered out again, in a perfect bog of uncertainty and mental confusion; and in that state took the strangest means of resolving his doubts: such as feeling the sleeve of his son's great-coat as deeming it possible that his arm might be there; looking at his own arms and those of everybody else, as if to assure himself that two and not one was the usual allowance; sitting by the hour together in a brown study, as if he were endeavouring to recal Joe's image in his younger days, and to remember whether he really had in those times one arm or a pair; and employing himself in many other speculations of the same kind.

Finding himself, at this supper, surrounded by faces with which he had been so well acquainted in old times, Mr Willet recurred to the subject with uncommon vigour; apparently resolved to understand it now or never. Sometimes, after every two or three mouthfuls, he laid down his knife and fork, and stared at his son with all his might – particularly at his maimed side; then he looked slowly round the table until he caught some person's eye, when he shook his head with great solemnity, patted his shoulder, winked, or as one may say – for winking was a very slow process with him – went to sleep with one eye for a minute or two; and so, with another solemn shaking of his head, took up his knife and fork again, and went on eating. Sometimes he put his food into his mouth abstractedly, and, with all his faculties concentrated on Joe, gazed at him in a fit of stupefaction as he cut his meat with one hand, until he was recalled to himself by symptoms of choking on his own part, and was by that means restored to consciousness. At other times he resorted to such small devices as asking him for the salt, the pepper, the vinegar, the mustard – anything that was on his maimed side – and watching him as he handed it. By dint of these experiments, he did at last so satisfy and convince himself, that, after a longer silence than he had yet maintained, he laid down his knife and fork on either side his plate, drank a long draught from a tankard beside him, still keeping his eyes on Joe, and, leaning backward in his chair and fetching a long breath, said, as he looked all round the board:

'It's been took off!'

'By George!' said the Black Lion, striking the table with his hand, 'he's got it!'

'Yes sir,' said Mr Willet, with the look of a man who felt that he had earned a compliment, and deserved it. 'That's where it is. It's been took off.'

'Tell him where it was done,' said the Black Lion to Joe.

'At the defence of the Savannah,[1] father.'

'At the defence of the Salwanner,' repeated Mr Willet, softly; again looking round the table.

'In America, where the war is,' said Joe.

'In America where the war is,' repeated Mr Willet. 'It was took off in the defence of the Salwanners in America where the war is.' Continuing to repeat these words to himself in a low tone of voice (the same information had been conveyed to him in the same terms, at least fifty times before), Mr Willet arose from table; walked round to Joe; felt his empty sleeve all the way up, from the cuff, to where the stump of his arm remained; shook his hand; lighted his pipe at the fire, took a long whiff, walked to the door; turned round once when he had reached it, wiped his left eye with the back of his forefinger, and said, in a faltering voice; 'My son's arm – was took off – at the defence of the – Salwanners – in America – where the war is' – with which words he withdrew, and returned no more that night.

Indeed, on various pretences, they all withdrew one after another, save Dolly, who was left sitting there alone. It was a great relief to be alone, and she was crying to her heart's content, when she heard Joe's voice at the end of the passage, bidding somebody good night.

Good night! Then he was going elsewhere – to some distance, perhaps. To what kind of home *could* he be going, now that it was so late!

She heard him walk along the passage, and pass the door. But there was a hesitation in his footsteps. He turned back – Dolly's heart beat high – he looked in.

'Good night!' – he didn't say Dolly, but there was comfort in his not saying Miss Varden.

'Good night!' sobbed Dolly.

'I am sorry you take on so much, for what is past and gone,' said Joe kindly. 'Don't. I can't bear to see you do it. Think of it no longer. You are safe and happy now.'

Dolly cried the more.

'You must have suffered very much within these few days – and yet you're not changed, unless it's for the better. They said you were, but I don't see it. You were – you were always very beautiful,' said Joe, 'but you are more beautiful than ever, now. You are indeed. There can be no harm in my saying so, for you must know it. You are told so very often, I am sure.'

As a general principle, Dolly *did* know it, and *was* told so, very often. But the coach-maker had turned out, years ago, to be a special donkey; and whether she had been afraid of making similar discoveries in others, or had grown by dint of long custom to be careless of compliments generally, certain it is that although she cried so much, she was better pleased to be told so now, than ever she had been in all her life.

'I shall bless your name,' sobbed the locksmith's little daughter, 'as long as I live. I shall never hear it spoken without feeling as if my heart would burst. I shall remember it in my prayers every night and morning till I die!'

'Will you?' said Joe, eagerly. 'Will you indeed? It makes me – well, it makes me very glad and proud to hear you say so.'

Dolly still sobbed, and held her handkerchief to her eyes. Joe still stood, looking at her.

'Your voice,' said Joe, 'brings up old times so pleasantly, that for the moment, I feel as if that night – there can be no harm in talking of that night now – had come back, and nothing had happened in the mean time. I feel as if I hadn't suffered any hardships, but had knocked down poor Tom Cobb only yesterday, and had come to see you with my bundle on my shoulder before running away. – You remember?'

Remember! But she said nothing. She raised her eyes for an instant. It was but a glance; a little, tearful, timid glance. It kept Joe silent though, for a long time.

'Well!' he said stoutly, 'it was to be otherwise, and was. I have been abroad, fighting all the summer and frozen up all the winter, ever since. I have come back as poor in purse as I went, and crippled for life besides. But, Dolly, I would rather have lost this other arm – ay, I would rather have lost my head – than have come back to find you dead, or anything but what I always pictured you to myself, and what I always hoped and wished to find you. Thank God for all!'

Oh how much, and how keenly, the little coquette of five years ago, felt now! She had found her heart at last. Never having known its worth till now, she had never known the worth of his. How priceless it appeared!

'I did hope once,' said Joe, in his homely way, 'that I might come back a rich man, and marry you. But I was a boy then, and have long known better than that. I am a poor, maimed, discharged soldier, and must be content to rub through life as I can. I can't say, even now, that I shall be glad to see you married, Dolly; but I *am* glad – yes, I am, and glad to think I can say so – to know that you are admired and courted, and can pick and choose for a happy life. It's a comfort to me to know that you'll talk to your husband about me; and I hope the time will come when I may be able to like him, and to shake hands with him, and to come and see you as a poor friend who knew you when you were a girl. God bless you!'

His hand *did* tremble; but for all that, he took it away again, and left her.

*

CHAPTER THE SEVENTY-THIRD

By this Friday night – for it was on Friday in the riot week, that Emma and Dolly were rescued, by the timely aid of Joe and Edward Chester – the disturbances were entirely quelled, and peace and order were restored to the affrighted city. True, after what had happened, it was impossible for any man to say how long this better state of things might last, or how suddenly new outrages, exceeding even those so lately witnessed, might burst forth and fill its streets with ruin and bloodshed; for this reason, those who had fled from the recent tumults still kept at a distance, and many families, hitherto unable to procure the means of flight, now availed themselves of the calm, and withdrew into the country. The shops, too, from Tyburn to Whitechapel, were still shut; and very little business was transacted in any of the places of great commercial resort. But, notwithstanding, and in spite of the melancholy forebodings of that numerous class of society who see with the greatest clearness into the darkest perspectives; the town remained profoundly quiet. The strong military force disposed in every advantageous quarter, and stationed at every commanding point, held the scattered fragments of the mob in check; the search after rioters was prosecuted with unrelenting vigour; and if there were any among them so desperate and reckless as to be inclined, after the terrible scenes they had beheld, to venture forth again, they were so daunted by these resolute measures, that they quickly shrunk into their hiding-places, and had no thought but for their personal safety.

In a word, the crowd was utterly routed. Upwards of two hundred had been shot dead in the streets. Two hundred and fifty more were lying, badly wounded, in the hospitals; of whom seventy or eighty died within a short time afterwards. A hundred were already in custody, and more were taken every hour. How many perished in the conflagrations, or by their own excesses, is unknown; but that numbers found a terrible grave in the hot ashes of the flames they had kindled, or crept into vaults and cellars to drink in secret or to nurse their sores, and never saw the light again, is certain. When the embers of the fires had been black and cold for many weeks, the labourers' spades proved this beyond a doubt.

Seventy-two private houses and four strong jails were destroyed in the four great days of these riots. The total loss of property, as estimated by the sufferers, was one hundred and fifty-five thousand pounds; at the lowest and least partial estimate of disinterested persons, it exceeded one hundred and twenty-five thousand pounds.[1] For this immense loss, compensation was soon afterwards made out of the public purse, in pursuance of a vote of the House of Commons; the sum being levied on the various wards in the city, on the county, and the borough of Southwark. Both Lord Mansfield and Lord Saville, however, who had been great sufferers, refused to accept of any compensation whatever.

The House of Commons, sitting on Tuesday with locked and guarded doors, had passed a resolution to the effect that, as soon as the tumults subsided, it would immediately proceed to consider the petitions presented from many of his majesty's Protestant subjects, and would take the same into its serious consideration. While this question was under debate, Mr Herbert,[2] one of the members present, indignantly rose and called upon the House to observe that Lord George Gordon was then sitting under the gallery with the blue cockade, the signal of rebellion, in his hat. He was not only obliged, by those who sat near, to take it out; but, offering to go into the street to pacify the mob with the somewhat indefinite assurance that the House was prepared to give them 'the satisfaction they sought,' was actually held down in his seat by the combined force of several members. In short, the disorder and violence which reigned triumphant out of doors, penetrated into the senate, and there, as elsewhere, terror and alarm prevailed, and ordinary forms were for the time forgotten.

On the Thursday, both Houses had adjourned until the following Monday se'ennight,[3] declaring it impossible to pursue their deliberations with the necessary gravity and freedom, while they were surrounded by armed troops. And now that the rioters were dispersed, the citizens were beset with a new fear; for, finding the public thoroughfares and all their usual places of resort filled with soldiers entrusted with the free use of fire and sword, they began to lend a greedy ear to the rumours which were afloat of martial law being declared, and to dismal stories of prisoners having been seen hanging on lamp-posts in Cheapside and Fleet-street. These terrors being promptly dispelled by a Proclamation declaring that all the rioters in custody would be tried by a special commission in due course of law, a fresh alarm was engendered by its being whispered abroad that French money had been found on some of the rioters, and that the disturbances had been fomented by foreign powers who sought to compass the overthrow and ruin of England. This report, which was strengthened by the diffusion of anonymous hand-bills, but which, if it had any foundation at all, probably owed its origin to the circumstance of some few coins which were not English money having been swept into the pockets of the insurgents with other miscellaneous booty, and afterwards discovered on the prisoners or the dead bodies, – caused a great sensation; and men's minds being in that excited state when they are most apt to catch at any shadow of apprehension, was bruited about with much industry.

All remaining quiet, however, during the whole of this Friday, and on this Friday night, and no new discoveries being made, confidence began to be restored, and the most timid and desponding breathed again. In Southwark, no fewer than three thousand of the inhabitants formed themselves into a watch, and patrolled the streets every hour. Nor were the citizens slow to follow so good an example: and it being the manner of peaceful men to be very bold when the danger is over, they were abundantly fierce and daring; not scrupling to question the stoutest passenger with great severity, and carrying it with a very high hand over all errand-boys, servant-girls, and 'prentices.

As day deepened into evening, and darkness crept into the nooks and corners of the town as if it were mustering in secret and gathering strength to venture into the open ways, Barnaby sat in his dungeon, wondering at the silence, and listening in vain for the noise and outcry which had ushered in the night of late. Beside him, with his hand in hers, sat one in whose companionship he felt at peace and tranquil. She was worn, and altered; full of grief; and heavy-hearted; but the same to him.

'Mother,' he said, after a long silence: 'how long, – how many days and nights, – shall I be kept here?'

'Not many, dear. I hope not many.'

'You hope! Ay, but your hoping will not undo these chains. *I* hope, but they don't mind that. Grip hopes, but who cares for Grip?'

The raven gave a short, dull, melancholy croak. It said 'Nobody,' as plainly as a croak could speak.

'Who cares for Grip, excepting you and me?' said Barnaby, smoothing the bird's rumpled feathers with his hand. 'He never speaks in this place; he never says a word in jail; he sits and mopes all day in this dark corner, dozing sometimes, and sometimes looking at the light that creeps in through the bars, and shines in his bright eye as if a spark from those great fires had fallen into the room and was burning yet. But who cares for Grip?'

The raven croaked again – Nobody.

'And by the way,' said Barnaby, withdrawing his hand from the bird, and laying it upon his mother's arm, as he looked eagerly in her face; 'if they kill me – they may, I heard it said they would – what will become of Grip when I am dead?'

The sound of the word, or the current of his own thoughts, suggested to Grip his old phrase 'Never say die!' But he stopped short in the middle of it, drew a dismal cork, and subsided into a faint croak, as if he lacked the heart to get through the shortest sentence.

'Will they take *his* life as well as mine?' said Barnaby. 'I wish they would. If you and I and he could die together, there would be none to feel sorry, or to grieve for us. But do what they will, I don't fear them, mother.'

'They will not harm you,' she said, her tears choking her utterance. 'They never will harm you when they know all. I am sure they never will.'

'Oh! Don't you be too sure of that,' cried Barnaby, with a strange pleasure in the belief that she was self-deceived, and in his own sagacity. 'They have marked me, mother, from the first. I heard them say so to each other when they brought me to this place last night; and I believe them. Don't you cry for me. They said that I was bold, and so I am, and so I will be. You may think that I am silly, but I can die as well as another. – I have done no harm, have I?' he added quickly.

'None before Heaven,' she answered.

'Why then,' said Barnaby, 'let them do their worst. You told me once – you – when I asked you what death meant, that it was nothing to be feared, if we did no harm – Aha! mother, you thought I had forgotten that!'

His merry laugh and playful manner smote her to the heart. She drew him closer to her, and besought him to talk to her in whispers and to be very quiet, for it was getting dark, and their time was short, and she would soon have to leave him for the night.

'You will come to-morrow?' said Barnaby.

Yes. And every day. And they would never part again.

He joyfully replied that this was well, and what he wished, and what he had felt quite certain she would tell him: and then he asked her where she had been so long; and why she had not come to see him when he was a great soldier; and ran through the wild schemes he had had for their being rich and living prosperously; and, with some faint notion in his mind that she was sad and he had made her so, tried to console and comfort her, and talked of their former life and his old sports and freedom: little dreaming that every word he uttered only increased her sorrow, and that her tears fell faster at the freshened recollection of their lost tranquillity.

'Mother,' said Barnaby, as they heard the man approaching to close the cells for the night, 'when I spoke to you just now about my father you cried "Hush!" and turned away your head. Why did you do so? Tell me why, in a word. You thought *he* was dead. You are not sorry that he is alive and has come back – to us. Where is he? Here?'

'Do not ask any one where he is, or speak about him,' she made answer.

'Why not?' said Barnaby. 'Because he is a stern man and talks roughly? Well! I don't like him, or want to be with him by myself; but why not speak about him?'

'Because I am sorry that he is alive; sorry that he has come back; and sorry that he and you have ever met. Because, dear Barnaby, the endeavour of my life has been to keep you two asunder.'

'Father and son asunder! Why?'

'He has,' she whispered in his ear, 'he has shed blood. The time has come when you must know it. He has shed the blood of one who loved him well, and trusted him, and never did him wrong in word or deed.'

Barnaby recoiled in horror, and glancing at his stained wrist for an instant, wrapped it, shuddering, in his dress.

'But,' she added hastily as the key turned in the lock, 'and although we shun him, he is your father, dearest, and I am his wretched wife. They seek his life, and he will lose it. It must not be by our means; nay, if we could win him back to penitence, we should be bound to love him yet. Do not seem to know him, except as one who fled with you from the jail; and if they question you about him, do not answer them. God be with you through the night, dear boy! God be with you!'

She tore herself away, and in a few seconds Barnaby was alone. He stood for a long time rooted to the spot, with his face hidden in his hands; then flung himself, sobbing, upon his miserable bed.

But the moon came slowly up in all her gentle glory, and the stars looked out; and through the small compass of the grated window, as through the narrow crevice of one good deed in a murky life of guilt,[4] the face of Heaven shone bright and merciful. He raised his head; gazed upward at the quiet sky, which seemed to smile upon the earth in sadness, as if the night, more thoughtful than the day, looked down in sorrow on the sufferings and evil deeds of men; and felt its peace sink deep into his heart. He, a poor idiot, caged in his narrow cell, was as much lifted up to God, while gazing on that mild light, as the freest and most favoured man in all the spacious city; and in his ill-remembered prayer, and in the fragment of the childish hymn, with which he sung and crooned himself asleep, there breathed as true a spirit as ever studied homily expressed, or old cathedral arches echoed.

As his mother crossed a yard on her way out, she saw, through a grated door which separated it from another court, her husband, walking round and round, with his hands folded on his breast, and his head hung down. She asked the man who conducted her, if she might speak a word with this prisoner. Yes, but she must be quick, for he was locking up for the night, and there was but a minute or so to spare. Saying this, he unlocked the door, and bade her go in.

It grated harshly as it turned upon its hinges, but he was deaf to the noise, and still walked round and round the little court, without raising his head or changing his attitude in the least. She spoke to him, but her voice was weak, and failed her. At length she put herself in his track, and when he came near, stretched out her hand and touched him.

He started backward, trembling from head to foot; but seeing who it was, demanded why she came there. Before she could reply, he spoke again.

'Am I to live or die? Do you do murder too, or spare?'

'My son – our son,' she answered, 'is in this prison.'

'What is that to me?' he cried, stamping impatiently on the stone pavement. 'I know it. He can no more aid me than I can aid him. If you are come to talk of him, begone!'

As he spoke he resumed his walk, and hurried round the court as before. When he came again to where she stood, he stopped, and said,

'Am I to live or die? Do you repent?'

'Oh! – do *you*?' she answered. 'Will you, while time remains? Do not believe that I could save you, if I dared.'

'Say if you would,' he answered with an oath, as he tried to disengage himself and pass on. 'Say if you would.'

'Listen to me for one moment,' she returned; 'for but a moment. I am but newly risen from a sick-bed, from which I never hoped to rise again. The best among us think at such a time of good intentions half-performed and duties left undone. If I have ever, since that fatal night, omitted to pray for your repentance before death – if I omitted, even then, anything which might tend to urge it on you when the horror of your crime was fresh – if, in our later meeting, I yielded to the dread that was upon me, and forgot to fall upon my knees and solemnly adjure you, in the name of him you sent to his account with Heaven, to prepare for the retribution which must come, and which is stealing on you now – I humbly before you, and in the agony of supplication in which you see me, beseech that you will let me make atonement.'

'What is the meaning of your canting words?' he answered roughly. 'Speak so that I may understand you.'

'I will,' she answered, 'I desire to. Bear with me for a moment more. The hand of Him who set his curse on murder, is heavy on us now. You cannot doubt it. Our son, our innocent boy, on whom His anger fell before his birth, is in this place in peril of his life – brought here by your guilt; yes, by that alone, as Heaven sees and knows, for he has been led astray in the darkness of his intellect, and that the terrible consequence of your crime.'

'If you come, woman-like, to load me with reproaches –' he muttered, again endeavouring to break away.

'– I do not. I have a different purpose. You must hear it. If not to-night, to-morrow; if not to-morrow, at another time. You *must* hear it. Husband, escape is hopeless – impossible.'

'You tell me so, do you?' he said, raising his manacled hand, and shaking it. 'You!'

'Yes,' she said, with indescribable earnestness. 'But why?'

'To make me easy in this jail. To make the time 'twixt this and death, pass pleasantly. Ha ha! For my good – yes, for my good, of course,' he said, grinding his teeth, and smiling at her with a livid face.

'Not to load you with reproaches,' she replied; 'not to aggravate the tortures and miseries of your condition; not to give you one hard word; but to restore you to peace and hope. Husband, dear husband, if you will but confess this dreadful crime; if you will but implore forgiveness of Heaven and of those whom you have wronged on earth; if you will dismiss these vain uneasy thoughts, which never can be realised, and will rely on Penitence and on the Truth; I promise you, in the great name of the Creator, whose image you have defaced, that He will comfort and console you. And for myself,' she cried, clasping her hands, and looking upward, 'I swear before Him, as He knows my heart and reads it now, that from that hour I will love and cherish[5] you as I did of old, and watch you night and day in the short interval that will remain to us, and soothe you with my truest love and duty, and pray, with you, that one threatening judgment may be arrested, and that our boy may be spared to bless God, in his poor way, in the free air and sunlight!'

He fell back and gazed at her while she poured out these words, as though he were for a moment awed by her manner, and knew not what to do. But rage and fear soon got the mastery of him, and he spurned her from him.

'Begone!' he cried. 'Leave me! You plot, do you! You plot to get speech with me, and let them know I am the man they say I am. A curse on you and on your boy.'

'On him the curse has already fallen,' she replied, wringing her hands.

'Let it fall heavier. Let it fall on one and all. I hate ye both. The worst has come to me. The only comfort that I seek or I can have, will be the knowledge that it comes to you. Begone!'

She would have urged him gently, even then, but he menaced her with his chain.

'I say begone – I say it for the last time; and do not tempt me. The gallows has me in its grasp, and it is a black phantom that may urge me on to something more, before it coils its arm about my throat. Begone! I curse the hour that I was born, the man I slew, and all the living world!'

In a paroxysm of wrath, and terror, and the fear of death, he broke from her, and rushed into the darkness of his cell, where he cast himself jangling down upon the stone floor, and smote it with his ironed hands. The man returned to lock the dungeon door, and having done so, carried her away.

On that warm, balmy night in June, there were glad faces and light hearts in all quarters of the town; and sleep, banished by the late horrors, was doubly welcomed. On that night, families made merry in their houses, and greeted each other on the common danger they had escaped; and those who had been denounced, ventured into the streets; and they who had been plundered, got good shelter. Even the timorous Lord Mayor, who was summoned that night before the Privy Council to answer for his conduct, came back contented; observing to all his friends that he had got off very well with a reprimand, and repeating with huge satisfaction his memorable defence before the Council, 'that such was his temerity, he thought death would have been his portion.'[6]

On that night, too, more of the scattered remnants of the mob were traced to their lurking-places, and taken; and in the hospitals, and deep among the ruins they had made, and in the ditches, and the fields, many unshrouded wretches lay dead: envied by those who had been active in the disturbances, and pillowed their doomed heads in the temporary jails.

And in the Tower, in a dreary room, whose thick stone walls shut out the hum of life, and made a stillness which the records left by former prisoners with those silent witnesses seemed to deepen

and intensify; remorseful for every act that had been done by every man among the cruel crowd; feeling for the time their guilt his own, and their lives put in peril by himself; and finding, amidst such reflections, little comfort in fanaticism, or in his fancied call; sat the unhappy author of all – Lord George Gordon.

He had been made prisoner that evening. 'If you are sure it's me you want,' he said to the officer, who waited outside with the warrant for his arrest on a charge of High Treason, 'I am ready to accompany you –' which he did without resistance. He was conducted first before the Privy Council, and afterwards to the Horse Guards, and then was taken by way of Westminster Bridge, and back over London Bridge (for the purpose of avoiding the main streets), to the Tower, under the strongest guard ever known to enter its gates with a single prisoner.

Of all his forty thousand men, not one remained to bear him company. Friends, dependents, followers, – none were there. His fawning secretary had played the traitor; and he whose weakness had been goaded and urged on by so many for their own purposes, was desolate and alone.

CHAPTER THE SEVENTY-FOURTH

Mr Dennis, having been made prisoner late in the evening, was removed to a neighbouring round-house for that night, and carried before a justice for examination on the next day, Saturday. The charges against him being numerous and weighty, and it being in particular proved, by the testimony of Gabriel Varden, that he had shown a special desire to take his life, he was committed for trial. Moreover he was honoured with the distinction of being considered a chief among the insurgents, and received from the magistrate's lips the complimentary assurance that he was in a position of imminent danger, and would do well to prepare himself for the worst.

To say that Mr Dennis's modesty was not somewhat startled by these honours, or that he was altogether prepared for so flatter-ing a reception, would be to claim for him a greater amount of stoical philosophy than even he possessed. Indeed this gentleman's stoicism was of that not uncommon kind, which enables a man to bear with exemplary fortitude the afflictions of his friends, but renders him, by way of counterpoise, rather selfish and sensitive in respect of any that happen to befall himself. It is therefore no disparagement to the great officer in question to state, without disguise or concealment, that he was at first very much alarmed, and that he betrayed divers emotions of fear, until his reasoning powers came to his relief, and set before him a more hopeful prospect.

In proportion as Mr Dennis exercised these intellectual qualities with which he was gifted, reviewing his best chances of coming off handsomely and with small personal inconvenience, his spirits rose, and his confidence increased. When he remembered the great estimation in which his office was held, and the constant demand for his services; when he bethought himself, how the Statute Book regarded him as a kind of Universal Medicine applicable to men, women, and children, of every age and variety of criminal constitution; and how high he stood, in his official capacity, in the favour of the Crown, and both Houses of Parliament, the Mint, the Bank of England, and the Judges of the land; when he recollected that whatever ministry was in or out, he remained their peculiar pet and panacea, and that for his sake England stood single and conspicuous among the civilised nations of the earth: when he called these things to mind and dwelt upon them, he felt certain that the national gratitude *must* relieve him from the consequences of his late proceedings, and would certainly restore him to his old place in the happy social system.

With these crumbs, or as one may say, with these whole loaves of comfort to regale upon, Mr Dennis took his place among the escort that awaited him, and repaired to jail with a manly indifference. Arriving at Newgate, where some of the ruined cells had been hastily fitted up for the safe keeping of rioters, he was warmly received by the turnkeys, as an unusual and interesting case, which agreeably relieved their monotonous duties. In this spirit, he was fettered with great care, and conveyed into the interior of the prison.

'Brother,' cried the hangman, as, following an officer, he traversed under these novel circumstances the remains of passages with which he was well acquainted, 'am I going to be along with anybody?'

'If you'd have left more walls standing, you'd have been alone,' was the reply. 'As it is, we're cramped for room, and you'll have company.'

'Well,' returned Dennis, 'I don't object to company, brother. I rather like company. I was formed for society,[1] I was.'

'That's rather a pity, an't it?' said the man.

'No,' answered Dennis, 'I'm not aware that it is. Why should it be a pity, brother?'

'Oh! I don't know,' said the man carelessly. 'I thought that was what you meant. Being formed for society, and being cut off in your flower,[2] you know –'

'I say,' interposed the other quickly, 'what are you talking of? Don't! Who's a going to be cut off in their flowers?'

'Oh, nobody particular. I thought you was, perhaps,' said the man.

Mr Dennis wiped his face, which had suddenly grown very hot, and remarking in a tremulous voice to his conductor that he had always been fond of his joke, followed him in silence until he stopped at a door.

'This is my quarters, is it?' he asked, facetiously.

'This is the shop, sir,' replied his friend.

He was walking in, but not with the best possible grace, when he suddenly stopped, and started back.

'Halloa!' said the officer. 'You're nervous.'

'Nervous!' whispered Dennis in great alarm. 'Well I may be. Shut the door.'

'I will, when you're in,' returned the man.

'But I can't go in there,' whispered Dennis. 'I can't be shut up with that man. Do you want me to be throttled, brother?'

The officer seemed to entertain no particular desire on the subject one way or other, but briefly remarking that he had his orders, and intended to obey them, pushed him in, turned the key, and retired.

Dennis stood trembling with his back against the door, and involuntarily raising his arm to defend himself, stared at a man, the only other tenant of the cell, who lay, stretched at his full length, upon a stone bench, and who paused in his deep breathing as if he were about to wake. But he rolled over on one side, let his arm fall negligently down, drew a long sigh, and murmuring indistinctly, fell fast asleep again.

Relieved in some degree by this, the hangman took his eyes for an instant from the slumbering figure, and glanced round the cell in search of some 'vantage-ground or weapon of defence. There was nothing moveable within it, but a clumsy table which could not be displaced without noise, and a heavy chair. Stealing on tiptoe towards this latter piece of furniture, he retired with it into the remotest corner, and intrenching himself behind it, watched the enemy with the utmost vigilance and caution.

The sleeping man was Hugh; and perhaps it was not unnatural for Dennis to feel in a state of very uncomfortable suspense, and to wish with his whole soul that he might never wake again. Tired of standing, he crouched down in his corner after some time, and rested on the cold pavement; but although Hugh's breathing still proclaimed that he was sleeping soundly, he could not trust him out of his sight for an instant. He was so afraid of him, and of some sudden onslaught, that he was not content to see his closed eyes through the chair-back, but every now and then, rose stealthily to his feet, and peered at him with outstretched neck, to assure himself that he really was still asleep, and was not about to spring upon him when he was off his guard.

He slept so long and so soundly, that Mr Dennis began to think he might sleep on until the turnkey visited them. He was congratulating himself upon these promising appearances, and blessing his stars with much fervour, when one or two unpleasant symptoms manifested themselves: such as another motion of the arm, another sigh, a restless tossing of the head. Then, just as it seemed that he was about to fall heavily to the ground from his narrow bed, Hugh's eyes opened.

It happened that his face was turned directly towards his unexpected visitor. He looked lazily at him for some half-dozen seconds without any aspect of surprise or recognition; then suddenly jumped up, and with a great oath pronounced his name.

'Keep off, brother, keep off!' cried Dennis, dodging behind the chair. 'Don't do me a mischief. I'm a prisoner like you. I haven't the free use of my limbs. I'm quite an old man. Don't hurt me!'

He whined out the last three words in such piteous accents, that Hugh, who had dragged away the chair, and aimed a blow at him with it, checked himself, and bade him get up.

'I'll get up certainly, brother,' cried Dennis, anxious to propitiate him by any means in his power. 'I'll comply with any request of yours, I'm sure. There – I'm up now. What can I do for you? Only say the word, and I'll do it.'

'What can you do for me!' cried Hugh, clutching him by the collar with both hands, and shaking him as though he were bent on stopping his breath by that means. 'What have you done for me?'

'The best. The best that could be done,' returned the hangman.

Hugh made him no answer, but shaking him in his strong gripe until his teeth chattered in his head, cast him down upon the floor, and flung himself on the bench again.

'If it wasn't for the comfort it is to me, to see you here,' he muttered, 'I'd have crushed your head against it; I would.'

It was some time before Dennis had breath enough to speak, but as soon as he could resume his propitiatory strain, he did so.

'I did the best that could be done, brother,' he whined; 'I did indeed. I was forced with two bayonets and I don't know how many bullets on each side of me, to point you out. If you hadn't been taken, you'd have been shot; and what a sight that would have been – a fine young man like you!'

'Will it be a better sight now?' asked Hugh, raising his head, with such a fierce expression, that the other durst not answer him just then.

'A deal better,' said Dennis meekly, after a pause. 'First, there's all the chances of the law, and they're five hundred strong. We may get off scot-free. Unlikelier things than that, have come to pass. Even if we shouldn't, and the chances fail, we can but be worked off once: and when it's well done, it's so neat, so skilful, so captivating, if that don't seem too strong a word, that you'd hardly believe it could be brought to sich perfection. Kill one's fellow-creeturs off, with muskets! – Pah!' and his nature so revolted at the bare idea, that he spat upon the dungeon pavement.

His warming on this topic, which to one unacquainted with his pursuits and tastes appeared like courage; together with his artful suppression of his own secret hopes, and mention of himself as being in the same condition with Hugh; did more to soothe that ruffian than the most elaborate arguments could have done, or the most abject submission. He rested his arms upon his knees, and stooping forward, looked from beneath his shaggy hair at Dennis, with something of a smile upon his face.

'The fact is, brother,' said the hangman, in a tone of greater confidence, 'that you got into bad company. The man that was with you was looked after more than you, and it was him I wanted.

As to me, what have I got by it? Here we are, in one and the same plight.'

'Lookee, rascal,' said Hugh, contracting his brows, 'I'm not altogether such a shallow blade but I know you expected to get something by it, or you would not have done it. But it's done, and you're here, and it will soon be all over with you and me; and I'd as soon die as live, or live as die. Why should I trouble myself to have revenge on you? To eat, and drink, and go to sleep, as long as I stay here, is all I care for. If there was but a little more sun to bask in, than can find its way into this cursed place, I'd lie in it all day, and not trouble myself to sit or stand up once. That's all the care I have for myself. Why should I care for *you?*'

Finishing this speech with a growl like the yawn of a wild beast, he stretched himself upon the bench again, and closed his eyes once more.

After looking at him in silence for some moments, Dennis, who was greatly relieved to find him in this mood, drew the chair towards his rough couch and sat down near him – taking the precaution, however, to keep out of the range of his brawny arm.

'Well said, brother; nothing could be better said,' he ventured to observe. 'We'll eat and drink of the best, and sleep our best, and make the best of it every way. Anything can be got for money. Let's spend it merrily.'

'Ay,' said Hugh, coiling himself into a new position. – 'Where is it?'

'Why, they took mine from me at the lodge,' said Mr Dennis; 'but mine's a peculiar case.'

'Is it? They took mine too.'

'Why then, I tell you what, brother,' Dennis began. 'You must look up your friends –'

'My friends!' cried Hugh, starting up and resting on his hands. 'Where are my friends?'

'Your relations then,' said Dennis.

'Ha ha ha!' laughed Hugh, waving one arm above his head. 'He talks of friends to me – talks of relations to a man whose mother died the death in store for her son, and left him, a hungry brat, without a face he knew in all the world! He talks of this to me!'

'Brother,' cried the hangman, whose features underwent a sudden change, 'you don't mean to say –'

'I mean to say,' Hugh interposed, 'that they hung her up at

Tyburn. What was good enough for her, is good enough for me. Let them do the like by me as soon as they please – the sooner the better. Say no more to me. I'm going to sleep.'

'But I want to speak to you; I want to hear more about that,' said Dennis, changing colour.

'If you're a wise man,' growled Hugh, raising his head to look at him with a savage frown, 'you'll hold your tongue. I tell you I'm going to sleep.'

Dennis venturing to say something more in spite of this caution, the desperate fellow struck at him with all his force; and missing him, lay down again with many muttered oaths and imprecations, and turned his face towards the wall. After two or three ineffectual twitches at his dress, which he was hardy enough to venture upon, notwithstanding his dangerous humour, Mr Dennis, who burnt, for reasons of his own, to pursue the conversation, had no alternative but to sit as patiently as he could: waiting his further pleasure.

—— ✳ ——

CHAPTER THE SEVENTY-FIFTH

A month has elapsed, – and we stand in the bed-chamber of Sir John Chester. Through the half-opened window, the Temple Garden looks green and pleasant, the placid river, gay with boat and barge, and dimpled with the plash of many an oar, sparkles in the distance; the sky is blue and clear; and the summer air steals gently in, filling the room with perfume. The very town, the smoky town, is radiant. High roofs and steeple tops, wont to look black and sullen, smile a cheerful grey; every old gilded vane, and ball, and cross, glitters anew in the bright morning sun; and high among them all Saint Paul's towers up, showing its lofty crest in burnished gold.

Sir John was breakfasting in bed. His chocolate and toast stood upon a little table at his elbow; books and newspapers lay ready to his hand, upon the coverlet; and, sometimes pausing to glance with an air of tranquil satisfaction round the well-ordered room, and sometimes to gaze indolently at the summer sky, he ate, and drank, and read the news, luxuriously.

The cheerful influence of the morning seemed to have some effect, even upon his equable temper. His manner was unusually gay; his smile more placid and agreeable than usual; his voice more clear and pleasant. He laid down the newspaper he had been reading; leaned back upon his pillow with the air of one who resigned himself to a train of charming recollections; and after a pause, soliloquized as follows:

'And my friend the centaur, goes the way of his mama! I am not surprised. And his mysterious friend Mr Dennis, likewise! I am not surprised. And my old postman, the exceedingly free-and-easy young madman of Chigwell! I am quite rejoiced. It's the very best thing that could possibly happen to him.'

After delivering himself of these remarks, he fell again into his smiling train of reflection; from which he roused himself at length to finish his chocolate, which was getting cold, and ring the bell for more.

The new supply arriving, he took the cup from his servant's hand; and saying, with a charming affability, 'I am obliged to you, Peak,' dismissed him.

'It is a remarkable circumstance,' he said, dallying lazily with the teaspoon, 'that my friend the madman should have been within an ace of escaping, on his trial; and it was a good stroke of chance (or, as the world would say, a providential occurrence) that the brother of my Lord Mayor should have been in court, with other country justices, into whose very dense heads curiosity had penetrated. For though the brother of my Lord Mayor was decidedly wrong; and established his near relationship to that amusing person beyond all doubt, in stating that my friend was sane, and had, to his knowledge, wandered about the country with a vagabond parent, avowing revolutionary and rebellious sentiments; I am not the less obliged to him for volunteering that evidence. These insane creatures make such very odd and embarrassing remarks, that they really ought to be hanged, for the comfort of society.'

The country justice had indeed turned the wavering scale against poor Barnaby, and solved the doubt that trembled in his favour. Grip little thought how much he had to answer for.

'They will be a singular party,' said Sir John, leaning his head upon his hand, and sipping his chocolate; 'a very curious party. The hangman himself; the centaur; and the madman. The centaur would make a very handsome preparation in Surgeons' Hall,[1] and would benefit science extremely. I hope they have taken care to bespeak him. – Peak, I am not at home, of course, to anybody but the hair-dresser.'

This reminder to his servant was called forth by a knock at the door, which the man hastened to open. After a prolonged murmur of question and answer, he returned; and as he cautiously closed the room-door behind him, a man was heard to cough in the passage.

'Now, it is of no use, Peak,' said Sir John, raising his hand in deprecation of his delivering any message; 'I am not at home. I cannot possibly hear you. I told you I was not at home, and my word is sacred. Will you never do as you are desired?'

Having nothing to oppose to this reproof, the man was about to withdraw, when the visitor who had given occasion to it, probably rendered impatient by delay, knocked with his knuckles at the chamber-door, and called out that he had urgent business with Sir John Chester, which admitted of no delay.

'Let him in,' said Sir John. 'My good fellow,' he added, when the door was opened, 'how came you to intrude yourself in this extraordinary manner upon the privacy of a gentleman? How can you be so wholly destitute of self-respect as to be guilty of such remarkable ill-breeding?'

'My business, Sir John, is not of a common kind, I do assure you,' returned the person he addressed. 'If I have taken any uncommon course to get admission to you, I hope I shall be pardoned on that account.'

'Well! we shall see; we shall see;' returned Sir John, whose face cleared up when he saw who it was, and whose prepossessing smile was now restored. 'I am sure we have met before,' he added in his winning tone, 'but really I forget your name.'

'My name is Gabriel Varden, sir.'

'Varden, of course, Varden,' returned Sir John, tapping his forehead. 'Dear me, how very defective my memory becomes! Varden to be sure – Mr Varden the locksmith. You have a charming wife, Mr Varden, and a most beautiful daughter. They are well?'

Gabriel thanked him, and said they were.

'I rejoice to hear it,' said Sir John. 'Commend me to them when you return, and say that I wished I were fortunate enough to convey, myself, the salute which I entrust you to deliver. And what,' he asked very sweetly, after a moment's pause, 'can I do for you? You may command me, freely.'

'I thank you Sir John,' said Gabriel, with some pride in his manner, 'but I have come to ask no favour of you, though I come on business. – Private,' he added, with a glance at the man who stood looking on, 'and very pressing business.'

'I cannot say you are the more welcome for being independent, and having nothing to ask of me,' returned Sir John, graciously, 'for I should have been happy to render you a service; still, you are welcome on any terms. Oblige me with some more chocolate, Peak – and don't wait.'

The man retired, and left them alone.

'Sir John,' said Gabriel, 'I am a working-man, and have been, all my life. If I don't prepare you enough for what I have to tell; if I come to the point too abruptly; and give you a shock, which a gentleman could have spared you, or at all events lessened very much, I hope you will give me credit for meaning well. I wish to be careful and considerate, and I trust that in a straight-forward person like me, you'll take the will for the deed.'

'Mr Varden,' returned the other, perfectly composed under this exordium; 'I beg you'll take a chair. Chocolate, perhaps, you don't relish? Well! it *is* an acquired taste, no doubt.'

'Sir John,' said Gabriel, who had acknowledged with a bow the invitation to be seated, but had not availed himself of it; 'Sir John' – he dropped his voice and drew nearer to the bed – 'I am just now come from Newgate –'

'Good Gad!' cried Sir John, hastily sitting up in bed; 'from Newgate, Mr Varden! How could you be so very imprudent as to come from Newgate! Newgate, where there are jail-fevers, and ragged people, and bare-footed men and women, and a thousand horrors! Peak, bring the camphor, quick! Heaven and earth, Mr Varden, my dear, good soul, how *could* you come from Newgate?'

Gabriel returned no answer, but looked on in silence while Peak (who had entered opportunely with the hot chocolate) ran to a drawer, and returning with a bottle, sprinkled his master's dressing-gown and the bedding; and besides moistening the locksmith himself, plentifully, described a circle round about him on the carpet. When he had done this, he again retired; and Sir John, reclining in an easy attitude upon his pillow, once more turned a smiling face towards his visitor.

'You will forgive me, Mr Varden, I am sure, for being at first a

LANDELLS

little sensitive both on your account and my own. I confess I was startled, notwithstanding your delicate preparation. Might I ask you to do me the favour not to approach any nearer? – You have really come from Newgate!'

The locksmith inclined his head.

'In-deed! And now, Mr Varden, all exaggeration and embellishment apart,' said Sir John Chester, confidentially, as he sipped his chocolate, 'what kind of place *is* Newgate?'

'A strange place, Sir John,' returned the locksmith, 'of a sad and doleful kind. A strange place, where many strange things are heard and seen; but few more strange than that I come to tell you of. The case is urgent. I am sent here.'

'Not – no, no – not from the jail?'

'Yes, Sir John; from the jail.'

'And my good, credulous, open-hearted friend,' said Sir John, setting down his cup, and laughing, – 'by whom?'

'By a man called Dennis – for many years the hangman, and to-morrow morning the hanged,' returned the locksmith.

Sir John had expected – had been quite certain from the first – that he would say he had come from Hugh, and was prepared to meet him on that point. But this answer occasioned him a degree of astonishment, which for the moment he could not, with all his command of feature, prevent his face from expressing. He quickly subdued it, however, and said in the same light tone:

'And what does the gentleman require of me? My memory may be at fault again, but I don't recollect that I ever had the pleasure of an introduction to him, or that I ever numbered him among my personal friends, I do assure you, Mr Varden.'

'Sir John,' returned the locksmith, gravely, 'I will tell you, as nearly as I can, in the words he used to me, what he desires that you should know, and what you ought to know without a moment's loss of time.'

Sir John Chester settled himself in a position of greater repose, and looked at his visitor with an expression of face which seemed to say, 'This is an amusing fellow! I'll hear him out.'

'You may have seen in the newspapers, Sir,' said Gabriel, pointing to the one which lay by his side, 'that I was a witness against this man upon his trial some days since; and that it was not his fault I was alive, and able to speak to what I knew.'

'*May* have seen!' cried Sir John. 'My dear Mr Varden, you

are quite a public character, and live in all men's thoughts most deservedly. Nothing can exceed the interest with which I read your testimony, and remembered that I had the pleasure of a slight acquaintance with you. – I hope we shall have your portrait published?'

'This morning, Sir,' said the locksmith, taking no notice of these compliments, 'early this morning, a message was brought to me from Newgate, at this man's request, desiring that I would go and see him, for he had something particular to communicate. I needn't tell you that he is no friend of mine, and that I had never seen him, until the rioters beset my house.'

Sir John fanned himself gently with the newspaper, and nodded.

'I knew, however, from the general report,' resumed Gabriel, 'that the order for his execution to-morrow, went down to the prison last night; and looking upon him as a dying man, I complied with his request.'

'You are quite a Christian, Mr Varden,' said Sir John; 'and in that amiable capacity, you increase my desire that you should take a chair.'

'He said,' continued Gabriel, looking steadily at the knight, 'that he had sent to me, because he had no friend or companion in the whole world, (being the common hangman), and because he believed, from the way in which I had given my evidence, that I was an honest man, and would act truly by him. He said that, being shunned by every one who knew his calling, even by people of the lowest and most wretched grade; and finding, when he joined the rioters, that the men he acted with had no suspicion of it (which I believe is true enough, for a poor fool of an old 'prentice of mine was one of them); he had kept his own counsel, up to the time of his being taken and put in jail.'

'Very discreet of Mr Dennis,' observed Sir John with a slight yawn, though still with the utmost affability, 'but – except for your admirable and lucid manner of telling it, which is perfect – not very interesting to me.'

'When,' pursued the locksmith, quite unabashed and wholly regardless of these interruptions, 'when he was taken to the jail, he found that his fellow-prisoner, in the same room, was a young man, Hugh by name, a leader in the riots, who had been betrayed and given up by himself. From something which fell from this unhappy creature in the course of the angry words they had at meeting, he discovered that his mother had suffered the death to which they both are now condemned. – The time is very short, Sir John.'

The knight laid down his paper fan, replaced his cup upon the table at his side, and, saving for the smile that lurked about his mouth, looked at the locksmith with as much steadiness as the locksmith looked at him.

'They have been in prison now, a month. One conversation led to many more; and the hangman soon found, from a comparison of time, and place, and dates, that he had executed the sentence of the law upon this woman, himself. She had been tempted by want – as so many people are – into the easy crime of passing forged notes. She was young and handsome; and the traders who employ men, women, and children in this traffic, looked upon her as one who was well adapted for their business, and who would probably go on without suspicion for a long time. But they were mistaken; for she was stopped in the commission of her very first offence, and died for it. She was of gipsy blood, Sir John –'

It might have been the effect of a passing cloud which obscured the sun, and cast a shadow on his face; but the knight turned deadly pale. Still he met the locksmith's eye, as before.

'She was of gipsy blood, Sir John,' repeated Gabriel, 'and had a high, free spirit. This, and her good looks, and her lofty manner, interested some gentlemen who were easily moved by dark eyes; and efforts were made to save her. They might have been successful, if she would have given them any clue to her history. But she never would, or did. There was reason to suspect that she would make an attempt upon her life. A watch was set upon her night and day; and from that time she never spoke again –'

Sir John stretched out his hand towards his cup. The locksmith going on, arrested it half way.

– 'Until she had but a minute to live. Then she broke silence, and said, in a low firm voice which no one heard but this executioner, for all other living creatures had retired and left her to her fate, "If I had a dagger within these fingers and he was within my reach, I would strike him dead before me, even now!" The man asked "Who?" – she said, The father of her boy.'

Sir John drew back his outstretched hand, and seeing that the locksmith paused, signed to him with easy politeness and without any new appearance of emotion, to proceed.

'It was the first word she had ever spoken, from which it could be understood that she had any relative on earth. "Was the child alive?" he asked. "Yes." He asked her where it was, its name, and whether she had any wish respecting it. She had but one, she said. It was that the boy might live and grow, in utter ignorance of his father, so that no arts might teach him to be gentle and forgiving. When he became a man, she trusted to the God of their tribe to bring the father and the son together, and revenge her through her child. He asked her other questions, but she spoke no more. Indeed, he says she scarcely said this much to him, but stood with her face turned upwards to the sky, and never looked towards him once.'

Sir John took a pinch of snuff; glanced approvingly at an elegant little sketch, entitled 'Nature,' on the wall; and raising his eyes to the locksmith's face again, said, with an air of courtesy and patronage, 'You were observing, Mr Varden –'

'That she never,' returned the locksmith, who was not to be diverted by any artifice from his firm manner, and his steady gaze, 'that she never looked towards him once, Sir John; and so she died, and he forgot her. But, some years afterwards, a man was sentenced to die the same death, who was a gipsy too; a sunburnt, swarthy fellow, almost a wild man; and while he lay in prison, under sentence, he, who had seen the hangman more than once while he was free, cut an image of him on his stick, by way of braving death, and showing those who attended on him, how little he cared or thought about it. He gave this stick into his hands at Tyburn, and told him then, that the woman I have spoken of had left her own people to join a fine gentleman, and that, being deserted by him, and cast off by her old friends, she had sworn within her own proud breast, that whatever her misery might be, she would ask no help of any human being. He told him that she had kept her word to the last; and that, meeting even him in the streets – he had been fond of her once, it seems – she had slipped from him by a trick, and he never saw her again, until, being in one of the frequent crowds at Tyburn, with some of his rough companions, he had been driven almost mad by seeing, in the criminal under another name, whose death he had come to witness, herself. Standing in the same place in which she had stood, he told the hangman this, and told him, too, her real name, which only her own people and the gentleman for whose sake she had left them, knew. – That name he will tell again, Sir John, to none but you.'

'To none but me!' exclaimed the knight, pausing in the act of raising his cup to his lips with a perfectly steady hand, and curling up his little finger for the better display of a brilliant ring with which it was ornamented: 'but me! – My dear Mr Varden, how very preposterous, to select me for his confidence! With you at his elbow, too, who are so perfectly trustworthy.'

'Sir John, Sir John,' returned the locksmith, 'at twelve to-morrow, these men die. Hear the few words I have to add, and do not hope to deceive me; for though I am a plain man of humble station, and you are a gentleman of rank and learning, the truth raises me to your level, and by its power I KNOW that you anticipate the disclosure with which I am about to end, and that you believe this doomed man, Hugh, to be your son.'

'Nay,' said Sir John, bantering him with a gay air; 'the wild gentleman, who died so suddenly, scarcely went as far as that, I think?'

'He did not,' returned the locksmith, 'for she had bound him by some pledge, known only to these people, and which the worst among them respect, not to tell your name: but, in a fantastic pattern on the stick, he had carved some letters, and when the hangman asked it, he bade him, especially if he should ever meet with her son in after life, remember that place well.'

'What place?'

'Chester.'

The knight finished his cup of chocolate with an appearance of infinite relish, and carefully wiped his lips upon his handkerchief.

'Sir John,' said the locksmith, 'this is all that has been told to me; but since these two men have been left for death, they have conferred together, closely. See them, and hear what they can add. See this Dennis, and learn from him what he has not trusted to me. If you, who hold the clue to all, want corroboration (which you do not), the means are easy.'

'And to what,' said Sir John Chester, rising on his elbow, after smoothing the pillow for its reception; 'my dear, good-natured, estimable Mr Varden – with whom I cannot be angry if I would – to what does all this tend?'

'I take you for a man, Sir John, and I suppose to some pleading of natural affection in your breast,' returned the locksmith indignantly. 'I suppose to the straining of every nerve, and the exertion of all the influence you have, or can make, in behalf of your miserable son, and the man who has disclosed his existence to you.

At the worst, I suppose to your seeing your son, and awakening him to a sense of his crime and danger. He has no such sense now. Think what his life must have been, when he said in my hearing, that if I moved you to anything, it would be to hastening his death, and ensuring his silence, if you had it in your power!'

'And have you, my good Mr Varden,' said Sir John in a tone of mild reproof, 'have you really lived to your present age, and remained so very simple and credulous, as to approach a gentleman of established character with such credentials as these, from desperate men in their last extremity, catching at any straw? Oh dear! Oh fie, fie!'

The locksmith was going to interpose, but he stopped him:

'On any other subject, Mr Varden, I shall be delighted – I shall be charmed – to converse with you, but I owe it to my own character not to pursue this topic for another moment.'

'Think better of it, Sir, when I am gone,' returned the locksmith; 'think better of it, Sir. Although you have, thrice within as many weeks, turned your lawful son, Mr Edward, from your door; you may have time, you may have years, to make your peace with *him*, Sir John: but that twelve o'clock will soon be here, and soon be past for ever.'

'I thank you very much,' returned the knight, kissing his delicate hand to the locksmith, 'for your guileless advice; and I only wish, my good soul, although your simplicity is quite captivating, that you had a little more worldly wisdom.[2] I never so much regretted the arrival of my hair-dresser as I do at this moment. God bless you! Good morning! You'll not forget my message to the ladies, Mr Varden? Peak, show Mr Varden to the door.'

Gabriel said no more, but gave the knight a parting look, and left him. As he quitted the room, Sir John's face changed; and the smile gave place to a haggard and anxious expression, like that of a weary actor jaded by the performance of a difficult part. He rose from his bed with a heavy sigh, and wrapped himself in his morning-gown.

'So, she kept her word,' he said, 'and was constant to her threat! I would I had never seen that dark face of hers, – I might have read these consequences in it, from the first. This affair would make a noise abroad, if it rested on better evidence; but as it is, and by not joining the scattered links of the chain, I can afford to slight it. – Extremely distressing to be the parent of such an uncouth creature!

Still, I gave him very good advice: I told him he would certainly be
hanged: I could have done no more if I had known of our relationship; and there are a great many fathers who have never done as
much for *their* natural children. – The hair-dresser may come in,
Peak!'

The hair-dresser came in; and saw in Sir John Chester (whose
accommodating conscience was soon quieted by the numerous
precedents that occurred to him in support of his last observation),
the same imperturbable, fascinating, elegant gentleman he had seen
yesterday, and many yesterdays before.

CHAPTER THE SEVENTY-SIXTH

As the locksmith walked slowly away from Sir John Chester's
chambers, he lingered under the trees which shaded the path,
almost hoping that he might be summoned to return. He had turned
back thrice, and still loitered at the corner, when the clocks struck
twelve.

It was a solemn sound, and not merely for its reference to to-
morrow; for he knew that in that chime the murderer's knell was
rung. He had seen him pass along the crowded street, amidst
the execrations of the throng: had marked his quivering lip, and
trembling limbs; the ashy hue upon his face, his clammy brow, the
wild distraction of his eye – the fear of death that swallowed up all
other thoughts, and gnawed without cessation at his heart and
brain. He had marked the wandering look, seeking for hope, and
finding, turn where it would, despair. He had seen the remorseful,
pitiful, desolate creature, riding, with his coffin by his side, to the
gibbet. He knew that to the last he had been an unyielding, obdurate
man; that in the savage terror of his condition he had hardened,
rather than relented, to his wife and child; and that the last words
which had passed his white lips were curses on them as his foes.

Mr Haredale had determined to be there, and see it done. Nothing
but the evidence of his own senses could satisfy that gloomy thirst
for retribution which had been gathering upon him for so many
years. The locksmith knew this, and when the chimes had ceased
to vibrate, hurried away to meet him.

'For these two men,' he said, as he went, 'I can do no more.

Heaven have mercy on them! – Alas! I say I can do no more for them, but whom *can* I help? Mary Rudge will have a home, and a firm friend when she most wants one; but Barnaby – poor Barnaby – willing Barnaby – what aid can I render him? There are many, many men of sense, God forgive me,' cried the honest locksmith, stopping in a narrow court to pass his hand across his eyes, 'I could better afford to lose than Barnaby. We have always been good friends, but I never knew, till now, how much I loved the lad.'

There were not many in the great city who thought of Barnaby that day, otherwise than as an actor in a show which was to take place to-morrow. But if the whole population had had him in their minds, and had wished his life to be spared, not one among them could have done so with a purer zeal or greater singleness of heart than the good locksmith.

Barnaby was to die. There was no hope. It is not the least evil attendant upon the frequent exhibition of this last dread punishment, of Death, that it hardens the minds of those who deal it out, and makes them, though they be amiable men in other respects, indifferent to, or unconscious of, their great responsibility. The word had gone forth that Barnaby was to die. It went forth every month, for lighter crimes. It was a thing so common, that very few were startled by the awful sentence, or cared to question its propriety. Just then, too, when the law had been so flagrantly outraged, its dignity must be asserted. The symbol of its dignity, – stamped upon every page of the criminal statute-book, – was the gallows; and Barnaby was to die.

They had tried to save him. The locksmith had carried petitions and memorials to the fountain-head, with his own hands. But the well was not one of mercy, and Barnaby was to die.

From the first She had never left him, save at night, and with her beside him, he was as usual contented. On this last day, he was more elated and more proud than he had been yet; and when she dropped the book she had been reading to him aloud, and fell upon his neck, he stopped in his busy task of folding a piece of crape about his hat, and wondered at her anguish. Grip uttered a feeble croak, half in encouragement, it seemed, and half remonstrance, but he wanted heart to sustain it, and lapsed abruptly into silence.

With them, who stood upon the brink of the great gulf which none can see beyond, Time, so soon to lose itself in vast Eternity, rolled on like a mighty river, swoln and rapid as it nears the sea. It

was morning but now; they had sat and talked together in a dream; and here was evening. The dreadful hour of separation, which even yesterday had seemed so distant, was at hand.

They walked out into the court-yard, clinging to each other, but not speaking. Barnaby knew that the jail was a dull, sad, miserable place, and looked forward to to-morrow, as to a passage from it to something bright and beautiful. He had a vague impression too, that he was expected to be brave – that he was a man of great consequence, and that the prison people would be glad to make him weep: he trod the ground more firmly as he thought of this, and bade her take heart and cry no more, and feel how steady his hand was. 'They call me silly, mother. They shall see – to-morrow!'

Dennis and Hugh were in the court-yard. Hugh came forth from his cell as they did, stretching himself as though he had been sleeping. Dennis sat upon a bench in a corner, with his knees and chin huddled together, and rocked himself to and fro like a person in severe pain.

The mother and son remained on one side of the court, and these two men upon the other. Hugh strode up and down, glancing fiercely every now and then at the bright summer sky, and looking round, when he had done so, at the walls.

'No reprieve, no reprieve! Nobody comes near us. There's only the night left now!' moaned Dennis faintly, as he wrung his hands. 'Do you think they'll reprieve me in the night, brother? I've known reprieves come in the night, afore now. I've known 'em come as late as five, six, and seven o'clock in the morning. Don't you think there's a good chance yet, – don't you? Say you do. Say *you* do, young man,' whined the miserable creature, with an imploring gesture towards Barnaby, 'or I shall go mad!'

'Better be mad than sane, here,' said Hugh. '*Go* mad.'

'But tell me what you think. Somebody tell me what he thinks!' cried the wretched object, – so mean, and wretched, and despicable, that even Pity's self might have turned away at sight of such a being in the likeness of a man – 'isn't there a chance for me, – isn't there a good chance for me? Isn't it likely they may be doing this to frighten me? Don't you think it is? Oh!' he almost shrieked, as he wrung his hands, 'won't anybody give me comfort?'

'You ought to be the best, instead of the worst,' said Hugh, stopping before him. 'Ha, ha, ha! See the hangman, when it comes home to him!'

'You don't know what it is,' cried Dennis, actually writhing as he spoke: 'I do. That I should come to be worked off! I! I! That *I* should come!'

'And why not?' said Hugh, as he thrust back his matted hair to get a better view of his late associate. 'How often, before I knew your trade, did I hear you talking of this as if it was a treat?'

'I an't inconsistent,' screamed the miserable creature; 'I'd talk so again, if I was hangman. Some other man has got my old opinions at this minute. That makes it worse. Somebody's longing to work me off. I know by myself that somebody must be!'

'He'll soon have his longing,' said Hugh, resuming his walk. 'Think of that, and be quiet.'

Although one of these men displayed, in his speech and bearing, the most reckless hardihood; and the other, in his every word and action, testified such an extreme of abject cowardice that it was humiliating to see him; it would be difficult to say which of them would most have repelled and shocked an observer. Hugh's was the dogged desperation of a savage at the stake; the hangman was reduced to a condition little better, if any, than that of a hound with the halter round his neck. Yet, as Mr Dennis knew and could have told them, these were the two commonest states of mind in persons brought to their pass. Such was the wholesome growth of the seed sown by the law, that this kind of harvest was usually looked for, as a matter of course.

In one respect they all agreed. The wandering and uncontrollable train of thought, suggesting sudden recollections of things distant and long forgotten and remote from each other – the vague restless craving for something undefined, which nothing could satisfy – the swift flight of the minutes, fusing themselves into hours, as if by enchantment – the rapid coming of the solemn night – the shadow of death always upon them, and yet so dim and faint, that objects the meanest and most trivial started from the gloom beyond, and forced themselves upon the view – the impossibility of holding the mind, even if they had been so disposed, to penitence and preparation, or of keeping it to any point while that hideous fascination tempted it away – these things were common to them all, and varied only in their outward tokens.

'Fetch me the book I left within – upon your bed,' she said to Barnaby, as the clock struck. 'Kiss me first!'

He looked in her face, and saw there, that the time was come. After a long embrace, he tore himself away, and ran to bring it to her; bidding her not stir till he came back. He soon returned, for a shriek recalled him, – but she was gone.

He ran to the yard gate, and looked through. They were carrying her away. She had said her heart would break. It was better so.

'Don't you think,' whimpered Dennis, creeping up to him, as he stood with his feet rooted to the ground, gazing at the blank walls – 'don't you think there's still a chance? It's a dreadful end; it's a terrible end for a man like me. Don't you think there's a chance? I don't mean for you, I mean for me. Don't let *him* hear us' (meaning Hugh); 'he's so desperate.'

'Now then,' said the officer, who had been lounging in and out with his hands in his pockets, and yawning as if he were in the last extremity for some subject of interest: 'it's time to turn in, boys.'

'Not yet,' cried Dennis, 'not yet. Not for an hour yet.'

'I say, – your watch goes different from what it used to,' returned the man. 'Once upon a time it was always too fast. It's got the other fault now.'

'My friend,' cried the wretched creature, falling on his knees, 'my dear friend – you always were my dear friend – there's some mistake. Some letter has been mislaid, or some messenger has been stopped upon the way. He may have fallen dead. I saw a man once, fall down dead in the street, myself, and he had papers in his pocket. Send to enquire. Let somebody go to enquire. They never will hang me. They never can. – Yes, they will,' he cried, starting to his feet with a terrible scream. 'They'll hang me by a trick, and keep the pardon back. It's a plot against me. I shall lose my life!' And uttering another yell, he fell in a fit upon the ground.

'See the hangman when it comes home to him!' cried Hugh again, as they bore him away – 'Ha ha ha! Courage, bold Barnaby, what care we? Your hand! They do well to put us out of the world, for if we got loose a second time, we wouldn't let them off so easy, eh? Another shake! A man can die but once. If you wake in the night, sing that out lustily, and fall asleep again. Ha ha ha!'

Barnaby glanced once more through the grate into the empty

yard; and then watched Hugh as he strode to the steps leading to
his sleeping-cell. He heard him shout, and burst into a roar of
laughter, and saw him flourish his hat. Then he turned away himself,
like one who walked in his sleep; and, without any sense of fear or
sorrow, lay down on his pallet, listening for the clock to strike
again.

*

CHAPTER THE SEVENTY-SEVENTH

The time wore on: the noises in the streets became less frequent by
degrees, until silence was scarcely broken save by the bells in church
towers, marking the progress – softer and more stealthy while the
city slumbered – of that Great Watcher with the hoary head, who
never sleeps or rests. In the brief interval of darkness and repose
which feverish towns enjoy, all busy sounds were hushed; and those
who awoke from dreams lay listening in their beds, and longed for
dawn, and wished the dead of the night were past.

Into the street outside the jail's main wall, workmen came straggling at this solemn hour, in groups of two or three, and meeting
in the centre cast their tools upon the ground and spoke in whispers.
Others soon issued from the jail itself, bearing on their shoulders,
planks, and beams: these materials being all brought forth, the rest
bestirred themselves, and the dull sound of hammers began to echo
through the stillness.

Here and there among this knot of labourers, one, with a lantern
or a smoky link, stood by to light his fellows at their work, and by
its doubtful aid, some might be dimly seen taking up the pavement
of the road, while others held great upright posts, or fixed them in
the holes thus made for their reception. Some dragged slowly on
towards the rest, an empty cart, which they brought rumbling from
the prison yard; while others erected strong barriers across the
street. All were busily engaged. Their dusky figures moving to and
fro, at that unusual hour, so active and so silent, might have been
taken for those of shadowy creatures toiling at midnight on some
ghostly unsubstantial work, which, like themselves, would vanish
with the first gleam of day, and leave but morning mist and vapour.

While it was yet dark, a few lookers-on collected, who had plainly come there for the purpose and intended to remain: even those who had to pass the spot on their way to some other place, lingered, and lingered yet, as though the attraction of that were irresistible. Meanwhile the noise of saw and mallet went on briskly, mingled with the clattering of boards on the stone pavement of the road, and sometimes with the workmen's voices as they called to one another. Whenever the chimes of the neighbouring church were heard – and that was every quarter of an hour – a strange sensation, instantaneous and indescribable, but perfectly obvious, seemed to pervade them all.

Gradually, a faint brightness appeared in the east, and the air, which had been very warm all through the night, felt cool and chilly. Though there was no daylight yet, the darkness was diminished, and the stars looked pale. The prison, which had been a mere black mass with little shape or form, put on its usual aspect; and ever and anon a solitary watchman could be seen upon its roof, stopping to look down upon the preparations in the street. This man, from forming, as it were, a part of the jail, and knowing or being supposed to know all that was passing within, became an object of as much interest, and was as eagerly looked for, and as awfully pointed out, as if he had been a spirit.

By and bye, the feeble light grew stronger, and the houses with their sign-boards and inscriptions stood plainly out, in the dull grey morning. Heavy stage waggons crawled from the Inn-yard opposite; and travellers peeped out; and as they rolled sluggishly away, cast many a backward look towards the jail. And now the sun's first beams came glancing into the street; and the night's work, which, in its various stages and in the varied fancies of the lookers-on had taken a hundred shapes, wore its own proper form – a scaffold, and a gibbet.

As the warmth of cheerful day began to shed itself upon the scanty crowd, the murmur of tongues was heard, shutters were thrown open, and blinds drawn up, and those who had slept in rooms over against the prison, where places to see the execution were let at high prices, rose hastily from their beds. In some of the houses people were busy taking out the window sashes for the better accommodation of spectators; in others the spectators were already seated, and beguiling the time with cards, or drink, or jokes among themselves. Some had purchased seats upon the house-tops, and were already crawling to their stations from parapet and garret window. Some were yet bargaining for good places, and stood in them in a state of indecision: gazing at the slowly-swelling crowd, and at the workmen as they rested listlessly against the scaffold; and affecting to listen with indifference to the proprietor's eulogy of the commanding view his house afforded, and the surpassing cheapness of his terms.

A fairer morning never shone. From the roofs and upper stories of these buildings, the spires of city churches and the great cathedral dome were visible, rising up beyond the prison, into the blue sky: clad in the colour of light summer clouds, and showing in the clear atmosphere their every scrap of tracery and fretwork, and every niche and loophole. All was brightness and promise, excepting in the street below, into which (for it yet lay in shadow) the eye looked down as into a dark trench, where, in the midst of so much life, and hope, and renewal of existence, stood the terrible instrument of death. It seemed as if the very sun forbore to look upon it.

But it was better, grim and sombre in the shade, than when, the day being more advanced, it stood confessed in the full glare and glory of the sun, with its black paint blistering, and its nooses dangling in the light like loathsome garlands. It was better in the solitude and gloom of midnight with a few forms clustering about it, than in the freshness and the stir of morning: the centre of an eager crowd. It was better haunting the street like a spectre, when men were in their beds; and influencing perchance the city's dreams; than braving the broad day, and thrusting its obscene presence upon their waking senses.

Five o'clock had struck – six – seven – and eight. Along the two main streets at either end of the cross-way, a living stream had now set in: rolling towards the marts of gain and business. Carts, coaches, waggons, trucks, and barrows, forced a passage through the outskirts of the throng, and clattered onward in the same direction. Some of these which were public conveyances and had come from a short distance in the country, stopped; and the driver pointed to the gibbet with his whip, though he might have spared himself the pains, for the heads of all the passengers were turned that way without his help, and the coach windows were stuck full of staring eyes. In some of the carts and waggons, women might be seen glancing fearfully at the same unsightly thing; and even little children were held up above the people's heads to see what kind of toy a gallows was, and learn how men were hanged.

Two rioters were to die before the prison, who had been concerned in the attack upon it; and one directly afterwards in Bloomsbury Square. At nine o'clock, a strong body of military marched into the street, and formed and lined a narrow passage into Holborn, which had been indifferently kept all night by constables. Through this, another cart was brought (the one already mentioned had been employed in the construction of the scaffold), and wheeled up to the prison gate. These preparations made, the soldiers stood at ease; the officers lounged to and fro, in the alley they had made, or talked together at the scaffold's foot; and the concourse, which had been rapidly augmenting for some hours, and still received additions every minute, waited with an impatience which increased with every chime of St Sepulchre's clock, for twelve at noon.

Up to this time they had been very quiet, comparatively silent, save when the arrival of some new party at a window, hitherto unoccupied, gave them something new to look at or to talk of. But as the hour approached, a buzz and hum arose, which, deepening every moment, soon swelled into a roar, and seemed to fill the air. No words or even voices could be distinguished in this clamour, nor did they speak much to each other; though such as were better informed upon the topic than the rest, would tell their neighbours, perhaps, that they might know the hangman when he came out, by his being the shorter one: and that the man who was to suffer with him was named Hugh: and that it was Barnaby Rudge who would be hanged in Bloomsbury Square. As it is the nature of men in a great heat to perspire spontaneously, so this wild murmur, floating up and down, seemed born of their intense impatience, and quite beyond their restraint or control.

It grew, as the time drew near, so loud, that those who were at the windows could not hear the church-clock strike, though it was close at hand. Nor had they any need to hear it, either, for they could see it in the people's faces. So surely as another quarter chimed, there was a movement in the crowd – as if something had passed over it – as if the light upon them had been changed – in which the fact was readable as on a brazen dial, figured by a giant's hand.

Three quarters past eleven! The murmur now was deafening, yet every man seemed mute. Look where you would among the crowd, you saw strained eyes and lips compressed; it would have been difficult for the most vigilant observer to point this way or that, and say that yonder man had cried out: it were as easy to detect the motion of lips in a sea-shell.

Three quarters past eleven! Many spectators who had retired from the windows, came back refreshed, as though their watch had just begun. Those who had fallen asleep roused themselves; and every person in the crowd made one last effort to better his position – which caused a press against the sturdy barriers that made them bend and yield like twigs. The officers, who until now had kept together, fell into their several positions, and gave the words of command. Swords were drawn, muskets shouldered, and the bright steel winding its way among the crowd, gleamed and glittered in the sun like a river. Along this shining path two men came hurrying on, leading a horse, which was speedily harnessed to the cart at the prison door. Then a profound silence replaced the tumult that had so long been gathering, and a breathless pause ensued. Every window was now choked up with heads; the house-tops teemed with people – clinging to chimneys, peering over gable-ends, and holding on where the sudden loosening of any brick or stone would dash them down into the street. The church tower, the church roof, the church yard, the prison leads, the very water-spouts and lamp-posts – every inch of room – swarmed with human life.

At the first stroke of twelve the prison bell began to toll. Then the roar – mingled now with cries of 'Hats off!' and 'Poor fellows!' and, from some specks in the great concourse, with a shriek or groan – burst forth again. It was terrible to see – if any one in that distraction of excitement could have seen – the world of eager eyes, all strained upon the scaffold and the beam.

The hollow murmuring was heard within the jail as plainly as without. The three were brought forth into the yard, together, as it resounded through the air: and knew its import well.

'D'ye hear?' cried Hugh, undaunted by the sound. 'They expect us! I heard them gathering when I woke in the night, and turned over on t'other side and fell asleep again. We shall see how they welcome the hangman, now that it comes home to him. Ha, ha, ha!'

The ordinary coming up at this moment, reproved him for his indecent mirth, and advised him to alter his demeanour.

'And why, master?' said Hugh. 'Can I do better than bear it easily? *You* bear it easily enough. Oh! never tell me,' he cried, as the other would have spoken, 'for all your sad look and your

solemn air, you think little enough of it! They say you're the best
maker of lobster salads in London. Ha, ha, ha! I've heard that, you
see, before now. Is it a good one, this morning – is your hand in?
How does the breakfast look? I hope there's enough, and to spare,
for all this hungry company that'll sit down to it, when the sight's
over.'

'I fear,' observed the clergyman, shaking his head, 'that you are
incorrigible.'

'You're right. I am,' rejoined Hugh sternly. 'Be no hypocrite,
master. You make a merry-making of this, every month; let me be
merry, too. If you want a frightened fellow, there's one that'll suit
you. Try your hand upon him.'

He pointed, as he spoke, to Dennis, who, with his legs trailing
on the ground, was held between two men; and who trembled so,
that all his joints and limbs seemed racked by spasms. Turning
from this wretched spectacle, he called to Barnaby, who stood
apart.

'What cheer, Barnaby? Don't be downcast, lad. Leave that to
him.'

'Bless you,' cried Barnaby, stepping lightly towards him, 'I'm not
frightened, Hugh. I'm quite happy. I wouldn't desire to live now,
if they'd let me. Look at me! Am I afraid to die? Will they see *me*
tremble?'

Hugh gazed for a moment at his face, on which there was a
strange, unearthly smile; and at his eye, which sparkled brightly;
and interposing between him and the ordinary, gruffly whispered
to the latter:

'I wouldn't say much to him, master, if I was you. He may spoil
your appetite for breakfast, though you *are* used to it.'

He was the only one of the three, who had washed or trimmed
himself that morning. Neither of the others had done so, since their
doom was pronounced. He still wore the broken peacock's feathers
in his hat; and all his usual scraps of finery were carefully disposed
about his person. His kindling eye, his firm step, his proud and
resolute bearing, might have graced some lofty act of heroism; some
voluntary sacrifice, born of a noble cause and pure enthusiasm;
rather than that felon's death.

But all these things increased his guilt. They were mere assumptions. The law had declared it so, and so it must be. The good
minister had been greatly shocked, not a quarter of an hour before,

at his parting with Grip. For one in his condition, to fondle a bird! —

The yard was filled with people; bluff civic functionaries, officers of justice, soldiers, the curious in such matters, and guests who had been bidden as to a wedding. Hugh looked about him, nodded gloomily to some person in authority, who indicated with his hand in what direction he was to proceed; and clapping Barnaby on the shoulder, passed out with the gait of a lion.

They entered a large room, so near to the scaffold that the voices of those who stood about it, could be plainly heard: some beseeching the javelin-men to take them out of the crowd: others crying to those behind to stand back, for they were pressed to death, and suffocating for want of air.

In the middle of this chamber, two smiths, with hammers, stood beside an anvil. Hugh walked straight up to them, and set his foot upon it with a sound as though it had been struck by a heavy weapon. Then, with folded arms, he stood to have his irons knocked off: scowling haughtily round, as those who were present eyed him narrowly and whispered to each other.

It took so much time to drag Dennis in, that this ceremony was over with Hugh, and nearly over with Barnaby, before he appeared. He no sooner came into the place he knew so well, however, and among faces with which he was so familiar, than he recovered strength and sense enough to clasp his hands, and make a last appeal.

'Gentlemen, good gentlemen,' cried the abject creature, grovelling down upon his knees, and actually prostrating himself upon the stone floor: 'Governor, dear governor – honourable sheriffs – worthy gentlemen – have mercy upon a wretched man that has served His Majesty, and the Law, and Parliament, for so many years, and don't – don't let me die – because of a mistake.'

'Dennis,' said the governor of the jail, 'you know what the course is, and that the order came with the rest. You know that we could do nothing, even if we would.'

'All I ask, sir, – all I want and beg, is time, to make it sure,' cried the trembling wretch, looking wildly round for sympathy. 'The King and Government can't know it's me; I'm sure they can't know it's me; or they never would bring me to this dreadful slaughter-house. They know my name, but they don't know it's the same man. Stop my execution – for charity's sake stop my execution, gentlemen – till they can be told that I've been hangman here, nigh thirty year. Will no one go and tell them?' he implored, clenching his hands and glaring round, and round, and round again – 'will no charitable person go and tell them!'

'Mr Akerman,' said a gentleman who stood by, after a moment's pause; 'since it may possibly produce in this unhappy man a better frame of mind, even at this last minute, let me assure him that he was well known to have been the hangman, when his sentence was considered.'

' – But perhaps they think on that account that the punishment's not so great,' cried the criminal, shuffling towards this speaker on his knees, and holding up his folded hands; 'whereas it's worse, it's worse a hundred times, to me than any man. Let them know that, sir. Let them know that. They've made it worse to me by giving me so much to do. Stop my execution till they know that!'

The governor beckoned with his hand, and the two men, who had supported him before, approached. He uttered a piercing cry:

'Wait! Wait. Only a moment – only one moment more! Give me a last chance of reprieve. One of us three is to go to Bloomsbury Square. Let me be the one. It may come in that time; it's sure to come. In the Lord's name let me be sent to Bloomsbury Square. Don't hang me here. It's murder!'

They took him to the anvil: but even then he could be heard above the clinking of the smith's hammers, and the hoarse raging of the crowd, crying that he knew of Hugh's birth – that his father was living, and was a gentleman of influence and rank – that he had family secrets in his possession – that he could tell nothing unless they gave him time, but must die with them on his mind; and he continued to rave in this sort until his voice failed him, and he sank down a mere heap of clothes between the two attendants.

It was at this moment that the clock struck the first stroke of twelve, and the bell began to toll. The various officers, with the two sheriffs at their head, moved towards the door. All was ready when the last chime came upon the ear.

They told Hugh this, and asked if he had anything to say.

'To say!' he cried. 'Not I. I'm ready. – Yes,' he added, as his eye fell upon Barnaby, 'I have a word to say, too. Come hither, lad.'

There was, for the moment, something kind, and even tender, struggling in his fierce aspect, as he wrung his poor companion by the hand.

'I'll say this,' he cried, looking firmly round, 'that if I had ten lives to lose, and the loss of each would give me ten times the agony of the hardest death, I'd lay them all down – ay I would, though you gentlemen may not believe it – to save this one. This one,' he added, wringing his hand again, 'that will be lost through me.'

'Not through you,' said the idiot, mildly. 'Don't say that. You were not to blame. You have been always very good to me. – Hugh, we shall know what makes the stars shine, *now!*'

'I took him from her in a reckless mood, and didn't think what harm would come of it,' said Hugh, laying his hand upon his head, and speaking in a lower voice. 'I ask her pardon, and his. – Look here,' he added roughly, in his former tone. 'You see this lad?'

They murmured 'Yes,' and seemed to wonder why he asked.

'That gentleman yonder –' pointing to the clergyman – 'has often in the last few days spoken to me of faith, and strong belief. You see what I am – more brute than man, as I have been often told – but I had faith enough to believe, and did believe as strongly as any of you gentlemen can believe anything, that this one life would be spared. See what he is! – Look at him!'

Barnaby had moved towards the door, and stood beckoning him to follow.

'If this was not faith, and strong belief!' cried Hugh, raising his right arm aloft, and looking upward like a savage prophet whom the near approach of Death had filled with inspiration, 'where are they! What else should teach me – me, born as I was born, and reared as I have been – to hope for any mercy in this hardened, cruel, unrelenting place! Upon these human shambles, I, who never raised this hand in prayer till now, call down the wrath of God! On that black tree, of which I am the ripened fruit, I do invoke the curse of all its victims, past, and present, and to come. On the head of that man, who, in his conscience, owns me for his son, I leave the wish that he may never sicken in his bed of down, but die a violent death as I do now, and have the night-wind for his only mourner. To this I say, Amen, amen!'

His arm fell downward by his side; he turned; and moved towards them with a steady step: the man he had been before.

'There is nothing more?' said the Governor.

Hugh motioned Barnaby not to come near him (though without looking in the direction where he stood) and answered, 'There is nothing more.'

'Move forward!'

'– Unless,' said Hugh, glancing hurriedly back, – 'unless some person has a fancy for a dog; and not then, unless he means to use him well. There's one, belongs to me, at the house I came from; and it wouldn't be easy to find a better. He'll whine at first, but he'll soon get over that. – You wonder that I think about a dog just now,' he added, with a kind of laugh. 'If any man deserved it of me half as well, I'd think of him.'

He spoke no more, but moved onward in his place, with a careless air, though listening at the same time to the Service for the Dead,[1] with something between sullen attention, and quickened curiosity. As soon as he had passed the door, his miserable associate was carried out; and the crowd beheld the rest.

Barnaby would have mounted the steps at the same time – indeed he would have gone before them, but in both attempts he was restrained, as he was to undergo the sentence elsewhere. In a few minutes the sheriffs reappeared, the same procession was again formed, and they passed through various rooms and passages to another door – that at which the cart was waiting. He held down his head to avoid seeing what he knew his eyes must otherwise encounter, and took his seat sorrowfully, – and yet with something of a childish pride and pleasure, – in the vehicle. The officers fell into their places at the sides, in front, and in the rear; the sheriffs' carriages rolled on; a guard of soldiers surrounded the whole; and they moved slowly forward through the throng and pressure toward Lord Mansfield's ruined house.

It was a sad sight – all that show, and strength, and glitter, assembled round one helpless creature: and sadder yet to note, as he rode along, how his wandering thoughts found strange encouragement in the crowded windows and the concourse in the streets; and how, even then, he felt the influence of the bright sky, and looked up smiling into its deep unfathomable blue. But there had been many such sights since the riots were over – some so moving in their nature, and so repulsive too, that they were far more calculated to awaken pity for the sufferers, than respect for that law whose strong arm seemed in more than one case to be as wantonly stretched forth now that all was safe, as it had been basely paralysed in time of danger.

Two cripples – both mere boys – one with a leg of wood, one who dragged his twisted limbs along by the help of a crutch, were hanged in this same Bloomsbury Square. As the cart was about to glide from under them, it was observed that they stood with their faces from, not to, the house they had assisted to despoil; and their misery was protracted that this omission might be remedied. Another boy was hanged in Bow Street; other young lads in various quarters of the town. Four wretched women, too, were put to death. In a word, those who suffered as rioters were for the most part the weakest, meanest, and most miserable among them. It was an exquisite satire upon the false religious cry which led to so much misery, that some of these people owned themselves to be catholics, and begged to be attended by their own priests.

One young man was hanged in Bishopsgate Street, whose aged grey-headed father waited for him at the gallows, kissed him at its foot when he arrived, and sat there, on the ground, until they took him down. They would have given him the body of his child; but he had no hearse, no coffin, nothing to remove it in, being too poor; and walked meekly away beside the cart that took it back to prison, trying, as he went, to touch its lifeless hand.

But the crowd had forgotten these matters, or cared little about them if they lived in their memory: and while one great multitude fought and hustled to get near the gibbet before Newgate, for a parting look, another followed in the train of poor lost Barnaby, to swell the throng that waited for him on the spot.

CHAPTER THE SEVENTY-EIGHTH

On this same day, and about this very hour, Mr Willet, the elder, sat smoking his pipe in a chamber of the Black Lion. Although it was hot summer weather, Mr Willet sat close to the fire. He was in a state of profound cogitation, with his own thoughts, and it was his custom at such times to stew himself slowly, under the impression that that process of cookery was favourable to the melting out of his ideas, which, when he began to simmer, sometimes oozed forth so copiously as to astonish even himself.

Mr Willet had been several thousand times comforted by his friends and acquaintance, with the assurance that for the loss he had sustained in the damage done to the Maypole, he could 'come

upon the county.' But as this phrase happened to bear an unfortunate resemblance to the popular expression of 'coming on the
parish,' it suggested to Mr Willet's mind no more consolatory
visions than pauperism on an extensive scale, and ruin in its most
capacious aspect. Consequently, he had never failed to receive the
intelligence with a rueful shake of the head, or a dreary stare, and
had been always observed to appear much more melancholy after
a visit of condolence than at any other time in the whole four-and-
twenty hours.

It chanced, however, that sitting over the fire on this particular
occasion – perhaps because he was, as it were, done to a turn;
perhaps because he was in an unusually bright state of mind;
perhaps because he had considered the subject so long; or perhaps
because of all these favouring circumstances, taken together – it
chanced that, sitting over the fire on this particular occasion, Mr
Willet did, afar off and in the remotest depths of his intellect,
perceive a kind of lurking hint or faint suggestion, that out of the
public purse there might issue funds for the restoration of the
Maypole to its former high place among the taverns of the earth.
And this dim ray of light did so diffuse itself within him, and did
so kindle up and shine, that at last he had it as plainly and visibly
before him as the blaze by which he sat: and, fully persuaded that
he was the first to make the discovery, and that he had started,
hunted down, fallen upon, and knocked on the head, a perfectly
original idea which had never presented itself to any other man,
alive or dead, he laid down his pipe, rubbed his hands, and chuckled
audibly.

'Why, father!' cried Joe, entering at the moment, 'you're in spirits
to-day!'

'It's nothing partickler,' said Mr Willet, chuckling again. 'It's
nothing at all partickler, Joseph. Tell me something about the
Salwanners.' Having preferred this request, Mr Willet chuckled a
third time; and after these unusual demonstrations of levity, he put
his pipe in his mouth again.

'What shall I tell you, father?' asked Joe, laying his hand upon
his sire's shoulder, and looking down into his face. 'That I have
come back, poorer than a church mouse? You know that. That I
have come back, maimed and crippled? You know that.'

'It was took off,' muttered Mr Willet, with his eyes upon the fire, 'at the defence of the Salwanners, in America, where the war is.'

'Quite right,' returned Joe, smiling, and leaning with his remaining elbow on the back of his father's chair; 'the very subject I came to speak to you about. A man with one arm, father, is not of much use in the busy world.'

This was one of those vast propositions which Mr Willet had never considered for an instant, and required time to 'tackle.' Wherefore he made no answer.

'At all events,' said Joe, 'he can't pick and choose his means of earning a livelihood, as another man may. He can't say "I will turn my hand to this," or "I won't turn my hand to that," but must take what he can do, and be thankful it's no worse. – What did you say?'

Mr Willet had been softly repeating to himself, in a musing tone, the words 'defence of the Salwanners:' but he seemed embarrassed at having been overheard, and answered 'Nothing.'

'Now look here, father. – Mr Edward has come to England from the West Indies. When he was lost sight of (I ran away on the same day, father), he made a voyage to one of the islands, where a school-friend of his had settled; and finding him, wasn't too proud to be employed on his estate; and – and in short, got on well, and is prospering, and has come over here on business of his own, and is going back again speedily. Our returning nearly at the same time, and meeting in the course of the late troubles, has been a good thing every way; for it has not only enabled us to do old friends some service, but has opened a path in life for me which I may tread without being a burden upon you. To be plain, father, he can employ me; I have satisfied myself that I can be of real use to him; and I am going to carry my one arm away with him, and to make the most of it.'

In the mind's eye of Mr Willet, the West Indies, and indeed all foreign countries, were inhabited by savage nations, who were perpetually burying pipes of peace, flourishing tomahawks, and puncturing strange patterns in their bodies. He no sooner heard this announcement, therefore, than he leaned back in his chair, took his pipe from his lips, and stared at his son with as much dismay as if he already beheld him tied to a stake, and tortured for the entertainment of a lively population. In what form of expression

his feelings would have found a vent, it is impossible to say. Nor is
it necessary: for before a syllable occurred to him, Dolly Varden
came running into the room, in tears; threw herself on Joe's breast
without a word of explanation; and clasped her white arms round
his neck.

'Dolly!' cried Joe. 'Dolly!'

'Ay, call me that; call me that always,' exclaimed the locksmith's
little daughter; 'never speak coldly to me, never be distant, never
again reprove me for the follies I have long repented, or I shall die.'

'*I* reprove you!' said Joe.

'Yes – for every kind and honest word you uttered, went to my
heart. For you, who have borne so much from me – for you, who
owe your sufferings and pain to my caprice – for you to be so kind
– so noble to me, Joe –'

He could say nothing to her. Not a syllable. There was an odd
sort of eloquence in his one arm, which had crept round her waist:
but his lips were mute.

'If you had reminded me by a word – only by one short word,'
sobbed Dolly, clinging yet closer to him, 'how little I deserved that
you should treat me with so much forbearance; if you had exulted
only for one moment in your triumph, I could have borne it better.'

'Triumph!' repeated Joe, with a smile which seemed to say, 'I am
a pretty figure for that.'

'Yes, triumph,' she cried, with her whole heart and soul in her
earnest voice, and gushing tears; 'for it *is* one. I am glad to think
and know it is. I wouldn't be less humbled, dear; I wouldn't be
without the recollection of that last time we spoke together in this
place – no, not if I could recal the past, and make our parting,
yesterday.'

Did ever lover look as Joe looked now!

'Dear Joe,' said Dolly, 'I always loved you – in my own heart I
always did, although I was so vain and giddy. I hoped you would
come back that night. I made quite sure you would; I prayed for it
on my knees. Through all these long, long years, I have never once
forgotten you, or left off hoping that this happy time might come.'

The eloquence of Joe's arm surpassed the most impassioned
language; and so did that of his lips – yet he said nothing, either.

'And now, at last,' cried Dolly, trembling with the fervour of her
speech, 'if you were sick, and shattered in your every limb; if you
were ailing, weak, and sorrowful; if, instead of being what you are,

you were in everybody's eyes but mine, the wreck and ruin of a man; I would be your wife, dear love, with greater pride and joy, than if you were the stateliest lord in England!'

'What have I done,' cried Joe, 'what have I done, to meet with this reward?'

'You have taught me,' said Dolly, raising her pretty face to his, 'to know myself, and your worth; to be something better than I was; to be more deserving of your true and manly nature. In years to come, dear Joe, you shall find that you have done so; for I will be, not only now, when we are young and full of hope, but when we have grown old and weary, your patient, gentle, never-tiring wife. I will never know a wish or care beyond our home and you, and always study how to please you with my best affection and my most devoted love. I will: indeed I will.'

Joe could only repeat his former eloquence – but it was very much to the purpose.

'They know of this, at home,' said Dolly. 'For your sake, I would leave even them; but they know it, and are glad of it, and are proud of you, as I am, and full of gratitude. – You'll not come and see me as a poor friend who knew me when I was a girl, will you?'

Well, well! It don't matter what Joe said in answer, but he said a great deal; and Dolly said a great deal too: and he folded Dolly in his one arm pretty tight, considering that it was but one; and Dolly made no resistance: and if ever two people were happy in this world – which is not an utterly miserable one, with all its faults – we may, with some appearance of certainty, conclude that they were.

To say that during these proceedings Mr Willet the elder underwent the greatest emotions of astonishment of which our common nature is susceptible – to say that he was in a perfect paralysis of surprise, and that he wandered into the most stupendous and theretofore unattainable heights of complicated amazement – would be to shadow forth his state of mind in the feeblest and lamest terms. If a roc, an eagle, a griffin, a flying elephant, or winged sea-horse, had suddenly appeared, and, taking him on its back, carried him bodily into the very heart of the 'Salwanners,' it would have been to him as an every-day occurrence, in comparison with what he now beheld. To be sitting quietly by, seeing and hearing these things; to be completely overlooked, unnoticed, and disregarded, while his son and a young lady were talking to each other in the most impassioned manner, kissing each other, and making themselves in all respects perfectly at home; was a position so tremendous, so inexplicable, so utterly beyond the widest range of his capacity of comprehension, that he fell into a lethargy of wonder, and could no more rouse himself than an enchanted sleeper in the first year of his fairy lease, a century long.

'Father,' said Joe, presenting Dolly. 'You know who this is?'

Mr Willet looked first at her, then at his son, then back again at Dolly, and then made an ineffectual effort to extract a whiff from his pipe, which had gone out long ago.

'Say a word, father, if it's only "how d'ye do,"' urged Joe.

'Certainly, Joseph,' answered Mr Willet. 'Oh yes! Why not?'

'To be sure,' said Joe. 'Why not?'

'Ah!' replied his father. 'Why not?' and with this remark, which he uttered in a low voice as though he were discussing some grave question with himself, he used the little finger – if any of his fingers can be said to have come under that denomination – of his right hand, as a tobacco-stopper, and was silent again.

And so he sat for half an hour at least, although Dolly, in the most endearing of manners, hoped, a dozen times, that he was not angry with her. So he sat for half an hour, quite motionless, and looking all the while like nothing so much as a great Dutch Pin or Skittle. At the expiration of that period, he suddenly, and without the least notice, burst, to the great consternation of the young people, into a very loud and very short laugh; and repeating 'Certainly, Joseph. Oh yes! Why not?' went out for a walk.

*

CHAPTER THE SEVENTY-NINTH

Old John did not walk near the Golden Key, for between the Golden Key and the Black Lion there lay a wilderness of streets – as everybody knows who is acquainted with the relative bearings of Clerkenwell and Whitechapel – and he was by no means famous for pedestrian exercises. But the Golden Key lies in our way, though it was out of his; so to the Golden Key this chapter goes.

The Golden Key itself, fair emblem of the locksmith's trade, had been pulled down by the rioters, and roughly trampled under foot.

But now it was hoisted up again in all the glory of a new coat of paint, and showed more bravely even than in days of yore. Indeed the whole house-front was spruce and trim, and so freshened up throughout, that if there yet remained at large any of the rioters who had been concerned in the attack upon it, the sight of the old, goodly, prosperous dwelling, so revived, must have been to them as gall and wormwood.[1]

The shutters of the shop were closed, however, and the window-blinds above were all pulled down, and in place of its usual cheerful appearance, the house had a look of sadness and an air of mourning; which the neighbours who in old days had often seen poor Barnaby go in and out, were at no loss to understand. The door stood partly open; but the locksmith's hammer was unheard: the cat sat moping on the ashy forge; all was deserted, dark, and silent.

On the threshold of this door, Mr Haredale and Edward Chester met. The younger man gave place; and both passing in with a familiar air, which seemed to denote that they were tarrying there, or were well-accustomed to go to and fro unquestioned, shut it behind them.

Entering the old back parlour, and ascending the flight of stairs, abrupt and steep, and quaintly fashioned as of old, they turned into the best room; the pride of Mrs Varden's heart, and erst the scene of Miggs's household labours.

'Varden brought the mother here last evening, he told me?' said Mr Haredale.

'She is above stairs now – in the room over here,' Edward rejoined. 'Her grief, they say, is past all telling. I needn't add – for that you know beforehand – that the care, humanity, and sympathy of these good people have no bounds.'

'I am sure of that. Heaven repay them for it, and for much more! Varden is out?'

'He returned with your messenger, who arrived almost at the moment of his coming home himself. He was out the whole night – but that of course you knew. He was with you the greater part of it?'

'He was. Without him, I should have lacked my right hand. He is an older man than I; but nothing can conquer him.'

'The cheeriest, stoutest-hearted fellow in the world.'

'He has a right to be. He has a right to be. A better creature never lived. He reaps what he has sown – no more.'

'It is not all men,' said Edward, after a moment's hesitation, 'who have the happiness to do that.'

'More than you imagine,' returned Mr Haredale. 'We note the harvest more than the seed-time. You do so in me.'

In truth his pale and haggard face, and gloomy bearing, had so far influenced the remark, that Edward was, for the moment, at a loss to answer him.

'Tut, tut,' said Mr Haredale, ' 'twas not very difficult to read a thought so natural. But you are mistaken nevertheless. I have had my share of sorrows – more than the common lot, perhaps – but I have borne them ill. I have broken where I should have bent; and have mused and brooded, when my spirit should have mixed with all God's great creation. The men who learn endurance, are they who call the whole world, brother. I have turned *from* the world, and I pay the penalty.'

Edward would have interposed, but he went on without giving him time.

'It is too late to evade it now. I sometimes think, that if I had to live my life once more, I would amend this fault – not so much, I discover when I search my mind, for the love of what is right, as for my own sake. But even when I make these better resolutions, I instinctively recoil from the idea of suffering again what I have undergone; and in this circumstance I find the unwelcome assurance that I should still be the same man, though I could cancel the past, and begin anew, with its experience to guide me.'

'Nay, you make too sure of that,' said Edward.

'You think so,' Mr Haredale answered, 'and I am glad you do. I know myself better, and therefore distrust myself more. Let us leave this subject for another – not so far removed from it as it might, at first sight, seem to be. Sir, you still love my niece, and she is still attached to you.'

'I have that assurance from her own lips,' said Edward, 'and you know – I am sure you know – that I would not exchange it for any blessing life could yield me.'

'You are frank, honourable, and disinterested,' said Mr Haredale; 'you have forced the conviction that you are so, even on my once-jaundiced mind; and I believe you. Wait here till I come back.'

He left the room as he spoke; but soon returned, with his niece.

'On that first and only time,' he said, looking from the one to the other, 'when we three stood together under her father's roof, I bade you quit it, and charged you never to return.'

'It is the only circumstance arising out of our love,' observed Edward, 'that I have forgotten.'

'You own a name,' said Mr Haredale, 'I had deep reason to remember. I was moved and goaded by recollections of personal wrong and injury, I know: but even now I cannot charge myself with having then, or ever, lost sight of a heartfelt desire for her true happiness; or with having acted – however much I was mistaken – with any other impulse than the one pure, single, earnest wish to be to her, as far as in my inferior nature lay, the father she had lost.'

'Dear uncle,' cried Emma, 'I have known no parent but you. I have loved the memory of others, but I have loved you all my life. Never was father kinder to his child than you have been to me, without the interval of one harsh hour, since I can first remember.'

'You speak too fondly,' he answered, 'and yet I cannot wish you were less partial; for I have a pleasure in hearing those words, and shall have in calling them to mind when we are far asunder, which nothing else could give me. Bear with me for a moment longer, sir, for she and I have been together many years; and although I believe that in resigning her to you I put the seal upon her future happiness, I find it needs an effort.'

He pressed her tenderly to his bosom, and after a minute's pause, resumed:

'I have done you wrong, sir, and I ask your forgiveness – in no common phrase, or show of sorrow; but with earnestness and sincerity. In the same spirit, I acknowledge to you both that the time has been when I connived at treachery and falsehood – which if I did not perpetrate myself, I still permitted – to rend you two asunder.'

'You judge yourself too harshly,' said Edward. 'Let these things rest.'

'They rise up in judgment against me when I look back, and not now for the first time,' he answered. 'I cannot part from you without your full forgiveness; for busy life and I have little left in common now, and I have regrets enough to carry into solitude, without addition to the stock.'

'You bear a blessing from us both,' said Emma. 'Never mingle thoughts of me – of me who owe you so much love and duty – with anything but undying affection and gratitude for the past, and bright hopes for the future.'

'The future,' returned her uncle, with a melancholy smile, 'is a bright word for you, and its image should be wreathed with cheerful hopes. Mine is of another kind, but it will be one of peace; and free, I trust, from care or passion. When you quit England I shall leave it too. There are cloisters abroad; and now that the two great objects of my life are set at rest, I know no better home. You droop at that, forgetting I am growing old, and that my course is nearly run. Well, we will speak of it again – not once or twice, but many times; and you shall give me cheerful counsel, Emma.'

'And you will take it?' asked his niece.

'I'll listen to it,' he answered, kissing her fair brow, 'and it will have its weight, be certain. What have I left to say? You have of late been much together. It is better and more fitting that the circumstances attendant on the past, which wrought your separation, and sowed between you suspicion and distrust, should not be entered on by me.'

'Much, much better,' whispered Emma. 'Remember them no more!'

'I avow my share in them,' said Mr Haredale, 'though I held it at the time in detestation. Let no man turn aside, ever so slightly, from the broad path of honour, on the plausible pretence that he is justified by the goodness of his end. All good ends can be worked out by good means. Those that cannot, are bad; and may be counted so at once, and left alone.'

He looked from her to Edward, and said in a gentler tone:

'In goods and fortune you are now nearly equal; I have been her faithful steward, and to that remnant of a richer property which my brother left her, I desire to add, in token of my love, a poor pittance, scarcely worth the mention, for which I have no longer any need. I am glad you go abroad. Let our ill-fated house remain the ruin it is. When you return after a few thriving years, you will command a better, and more fortunate one. We are friends?'

Edward took his extended hand, and grasped it heartily.

'You are neither slow nor cold in your response,' said Mr Haredale, doing the like by him, 'and when I look upon you now, and know you, I feel that I would choose you for her husband. Her father had a generous nature, and you would have pleased him well. I give her to you in his name, and with his blessing. If the

world and I part in this act, we part on happier terms than we have
lived for many a day.'

He placed her in his arms, and would have left the room, but
that he was stopped in his passage to the door by a great noise at a
distance, which made them start and pause.

It was a loud shouting, mingled with boisterous acclamations,
that rent the very air. It drew nearer and nearer every moment, and
approached so rapidly, that even while they listened, it burst into
a deafening confusion of sounds at the street corner.

'This must be stopped – quieted,' said Mr Haredale, hastily. 'We
should have foreseen this, and provided against it. I will go out to
them at once.'

But before he could reach the door, and before Edward could
catch up his hat and follow him, they were again arrested by a loud
shriek from above stairs: and the locksmith's wife, bursting in, and
fairly running into Mr Haredale's arms, cried out:

'She knows it all, dear sir! – she knows it all! We broke it out
to her by degrees, and she is quite prepared.' Having made this
communication, and furthermore thanked Heaven with great
fervour and heartiness, the good lady, according to the custom of
matrons on all occasions of excitement, fainted away directly.

They ran to the window, threw up the sash, and looked into the
crowded street. Among a dense mob of persons, of whom not one
was for an instant still, the locksmith's ruddy face and burly form
could be descried, beating about as though he were struggling with
a rough sea. Now he was carried back a score of yards, now onward
nearly to the door, now back again, now forced against the opposite
houses, now against those adjoining his own: now carried up a
flight of steps, and greeted by the outstretched hands of half a
hundred men, while the whole tumultuous concourse stretched
their throats, and cheered with all their might. Though he was
really in a fair way to be torn to pieces in the general enthusiasm,
the locksmith, nothing discomposed, echoed their shouts till he was
hoarse as they, and in a glow of joy and right good-humour, waved
his hat until the daylight shone between its brim and crown.

But in all the bandyings from hand to hand, and strivings to and
fro, and sweepings here and there, which – saving that he looked
more jolly and more radiant after every struggle – troubled his
peace of mind no more than if he had been a straw upon the water's
surface, he never once released his firm grasp of an arm, drawn

tight through his. He sometimes turned to clap this friend upon the back, or whisper in his ear a word of staunch encouragement, or cheer him with a smile; but his great care was to shield him from the pressure, and force a passage for him to the Golden Key. Passive and timid, scared, pale, and wondering, and gazing at the throng as if he were newly risen from the dead, and felt himself a ghost among the living, Barnaby – not Barnaby in the spirit, but in flesh and blood, with pulses, sinews, nerves, and beating heart, and strong affections – clung to his stout old friend, and followed where he led.

And thus, in course of time, they reached the door, held ready for their entrance by no unwilling hands. Then slipping in, and shutting out the crowd by main force, Gabriel stood between Mr Haredale and Edward Chester, and Barnaby, rushing up the stairs, fell upon his knees beside his mother's bed.

'Such is the blessed end, sir,' cried the panting locksmith, to Mr Haredale, 'of the best day's work we ever did. The rogues! it's been hard fighting to get away from 'em. I almost thought, once or twice, they'd have been too much for us with their kindness!'

They had striven all the previous day to rescue Barnaby from his impending fate. Failing in their attempts, in the first quarter to which they addressed themselves, they renewed them in another. Failing there, likewise, they began afresh at midnight; and made their way, not only to the judge and jury who had tried him, but to men of influence at court, to the young Prince of Wales,[2] and even to the antechamber of the king himself. Successful, at last, in awakening an interest in his favour, and an inclination to inquire more dispassionately into his case, they had had an interview with the minister, in his bed, so late as eight o'clock that morning. The result of a searching inquiry (in which they, who had known the poor fellow from his childhood, did other good service, besides bringing it about) was, that between eleven and twelve o'clock, a free pardon to Barnaby Rudge was made out and signed, and entrusted to a horse-soldier for instant conveyance to the place of execution. This courier reached the spot just as the cart appeared in sight; and Barnaby being carried back to jail, Mr Haredale, assured that all was safe, had gone straight from Bloomsbury Square to the Golden Key, leaving to Gabriel the grateful task of bringing him home in triumph.

'I needn't say,' observed the locksmith, when he had shaken

hands with all the males in the house, and hugged all the females, five-and-forty times, at least, 'that, except among ourselves, *I* didn't want to make a triumph of it. But directly we got into the streets we were known, and this hubbub began. Of the two,' he added, as he wiped his crimson face, 'and after experience of both, I think I'd rather be taken out of my house by a crowd of enemies, than escorted home by a mob of friends!'

It was plain enough, however, that this was mere talk on Gabriel's part, and that the whole proceeding afforded him the keenest delight; for the people continuing to make a great noise without, and to cheer as if their voices were in the freshest order, and good for a fortnight, he sent up stairs for Grip (who had come home at his master's back, and had acknowledged the favours of the multitude by drawing blood from every finger that came within his reach), and with the bird upon his arm, presented himself at the first-floor window, and waved his hat again until it dangled by a shred, between his fingers and thumb. This demonstration having been received with appropriate shouts, and silence being in some degree restored, he thanked them for their sympathy; and taking the liberty to inform them that there was a sick person in the house, proposed that they should give three cheers for King George, three more for Old England, and three more for nothing particular, as a closing ceremony. The crowd assenting, substituted Gabriel Varden for the nothing particular; and giving him one over, for good measure, dispersed in high good-humour.

What congratulations they exchanged when they were left alone; what an overflowing of joy and happiness there was among them; how incapable it was of expression in Barnaby's own person; and how he went wildly from one to another, until he became so far tranquillized as to stretch himself on the ground beside his mother's couch, and fall into a deep sleep; are matters that need not be told. And it is well they happen to be of this class, for they would be very hard to tell, were their narration ever so indispensable.

Before leaving this bright picture, it may be well to glance at a dark and very different one which was presented to only a few eyes, that same night.

The scene was a churchyard; the time, midnight; the persons, Edward Chester, a clergyman, a grave-digger, and the four bearers of a homely coffin. They stood about a grave which had been newly dug, and one of the bearers held up a dim lantern, – the only light there – which shed its feeble ray upon the book of prayer. He placed it for a moment on the coffin, when he and his companions were about to lower it down. There was no inscription on the lid.

The mould fell solemnly upon the last house of this nameless man; and the rattling dust left a dismal echo even in the accustomed ears of those who had borne it to its resting-place. The grave was filled in to the top, and trodden down. They all left the spot together.

'You never saw him, living?' asked the priest, of Edward.

'Often, years ago; not knowing him for my brother.'

'Never since?'

'Never. Yesterday, he steadily refused to see me. It was urged upon him, many times, at my desire.'

'Still he refused? That was hardened and unnatural.'

'Do you think so?'

'I infer that you do not.'

'You are right. We hear the world wonder every day at monsters of ingratitude. Did it never occur to you that it often looks for monsters of affection, as though they were things of course?'

They had reached the gate by this time, and bidding each other good night, departed on their separate ways.

CHAPTER THE EIGHTIETH

That afternoon, when he had slept off his fatigue; had shaved, and washed, and dressed, and freshened himself from top to toe; when he had dined, comforted himself with a pipe, an extra Toby, a nap in the great arm-chair, and a quiet chat with Mrs Varden on everything that had happened, was happening, or about to happen, within the sphere of their domestic concern; the locksmith sat himself down at the tea-table in the little back parlour: the rosiest, cosiest, merriest, heartiest, best-contented old buck, in Great Britain or out of it.

There he sat, with his beaming eye on Mrs V., and his shining face suffused with gladness, and his capacious waistcoat smiling in every wrinkle, and his jovial humour peeping from under the table in the very plumpness of his legs: a sight to turn the vinegar of misanthropy into purest milk of human kindness.[1] There he sat, watching his wife as she decorated the room with flowers for the greater honour of Dolly and Joseph Willet, who had gone out walking, and for whom the tea-kettle had been singing gaily on the hob full twenty minutes, chirping as never kettle chirped before; for whom the best service of real undoubted china, patterned with divers round-faced mandarins holding up broad umbrellas, was now displayed in all its glory; to tempt whose appetites a clear, transparent, juicy ham, garnished with cool green lettuce leaves and fragrant cucumber, reposed upon a shady table, covered with a snow white cloth; for whose delight, preserves and jams, crisp cakes and other pastry, short to eat, with cunning twists and cottage loaves, and rolls of bread both white and brown, were all set forth in rich profusion; in whose youth Mrs V. herself had grown quite young, and stood there in a gown of red and white; symmetrical in figure, buxom in boddice, ruddy in cheek and lip, faultless in ankle, laughing in face and mood, in all respects delicious to behold – there sat the locksmith among all and every these delights, the sun that shone upon them all: the centre of the system: the source of light, heat, life, and frank enjoyment in the bright household world.

And when had Dolly ever been the Dolly of that afternoon? To see how she came in arm-in-arm with Joe; and how she made an effort not to blush or seem at all confused; and how she made believe she didn't care to sit on his side of the table; and how she coaxed the locksmith in a whisper not to joke; and how her colour came and went in a little restless flutter of happiness, which made her do everything wrong, and yet so charmingly wrong that it was much better than right! – why, the locksmith could have looked on at this (as he mentioned to Mrs Varden when they retired for the night) for four-and-twenty hours at a stretch, and never wished it done.

The recollections, too, with which they made merry over that long protracted tea! The glee with which the locksmith asked Joe if he remembered that stormy night at the Maypole when he first asked after Dolly – the laugh they all had about that night when she was going out to the party in the sedan-chair – the unmerciful manner in which they rallied Mrs Varden about putting those flowers outside that very window – the difficulty Mrs Varden found in joining the laugh against herself at first, and the extraordinary perception she had of the joke when she overcame it – the confidential statements of Joe concerning the precise day and hour when he was first conscious of being fond of Dolly, and Dolly's blushing admissions, half volunteered, and half extorted, as to the time from which she dated the discovery that she 'didn't mind' Joe – here was an exhaustless fund of mirth and conversation!

Then there was a great deal to be said regarding Mrs Varden's doubts, and motherly alarms, and shrewd suspicions; and it appeared that from Mrs Varden's penetration and extreme sagacity nothing had ever been hidden. She had known it all along. She had seen it from the first. She had always predicted it. She had been aware of it before the principals. She had said within herself (for she remembered the exact words) 'that young Willet is certainly looking after our Dolly, and I must look after *him*.' Accordingly she had looked after him, and had observed many little circumstances (all of which she named) so exceedingly minute that nobody else could make anything out of them even now; and had, it seemed from first to last, displayed the most unbounded tact and most consummate generalship.

Of course the night when Joe *would* ride homeward by the side of the chaise, and when Mrs Varden *would* insist upon his going back again, was not forgotten – nor the night when Dolly fainted on his name being mentioned – nor the times upon times when Mrs Varden, ever watchful and prudent, had found her pining in her own chamber. In short, nothing was forgotten; and everything by some means or other brought them back to the conclusion, that that was the happiest hour in all their lives; consequently, that everything must have occurred for the best, and nothing could be suggested which would have made it better.

While they were in the full glow of such discourse as this, there came a startling knock at the door, opening from the street into the workshop, which had been kept closed all day that the house might be more quiet. Joe, as in duty bound, would hear of nobody but himself going to open it; and accordingly left the room for that purpose.

It would have been odd enough, certainly, if Joe had forgotten the way to this door; and even if he had, as it was a pretty large one and stood straight before him, he could not easily have missed it. But Dolly, perhaps because she was in the flutter of spirits before mentioned, or perhaps because she thought he would not be able to open it with his one arm – she could have had no other reason – hurried out after him; and they stopped so long in the passage – no doubt owing to Joe's entreaties that she would not expose herself to the draught of July air which must infallibly come rushing in on this same door being opened – that the knock was repeated, in a yet more startling manner than before.

'Is anybody going to open that door?' cried the locksmith. 'Or shall I come?'

Upon that, Dolly went running back into the parlour, all dimples and blushes; and Joe opened it with a mighty noise, and other superfluous demonstrations of being in a violent hurry.

'Well,' said the locksmith, when he reappeared: 'what is it? eh Joe? what are you laughing at?'

'Nothing sir. It's coming in.'

'Who's coming in? what's coming in?' Mrs Varden, as much at a loss as her husband, could only shake her head in answer to his inquiring look: so the locksmith wheeled his chair round to command a better view of the room door, and stared at it with his eyes wide open, and a mingled expression of curiosity and wonder shining in his jolly face.

Instead of some person or persons straightway appearing, divers remarkable sounds were heard, first in the workshop and afterwards in the little dark passage between it and the parlour, as though some unwieldy chest or heavy piece of furniture were being brought in, by an amount of human strength inadequate to the task. At length after much struggling and bumping, and bruising of the wall on both sides, the door was forced open as by a battering-ram; and the locksmith, steadily regarding what appeared beyond, smote his thigh, elevated his eyebrows, opened his mouth, and cried in a loud voice expressive of the utmost consternation:

'Damme, if it an't Miggs come back!'

The young damsel whom he named no sooner heard these words, than deserting a very small boy and a very large box by whom she was accompanied, and advancing with such precipitation that her bonnet flew off her head, burst into the room, clasped her hands (in which she held a pair of pattens, one in each), raised her eyes devotedly to the ceiling, and shed a flood of tears.

'The old story!' cried the locksmith, looking at her in inexpressible desperation. 'She was born to be a damper, this young woman! nothing can prevent it!'

'Ho master, ho mim!' cried Miggs, 'can I constrain my feelings in these here once agin united moments! Ho Mr Warsen, here's blessedness among relations, Sir, here's forgivenesses of injuries, here's amicablenesses!'

The locksmith looked from his wife to Dolly, and from Dolly to Joe, and from Joe to Miggs, with his eyebrows still elevated and his mouth still open: when his eyes got back to Miggs, they rested on her; fascinated.

'To think,' cried Miggs with hysterical joy, 'that Mr Joe, and dear Miss Dolly, has raly come together after all as has been said and done contrairy! To see them two a settin' along with him and her, so pleasant and in all respects so affable and mild; and me not knowing of it, and not being in the ways to make no preparations for their teas. Ho what a cutting thing it is, and yet what sweet sensations is awoke within me!'

Either in clasping her hands again, or in an ecstacy of pious joy, Miss Miggs clinked her pattens after the manner of a pair of cymbals, at this juncture; and then resumed in the softest accents:

'And did my missis think – ho goodness, did she think – as her own Miggs, which supported her under so many trials, and understood her natur' when them as intended well but acted rough, went so deep into her feelings – did she think as her own Miggs would ever leave her? Did she think as Miggs, though she was but a servant, and knowed that servitudes was no inheritances, would forgit that she was the humble instruments as always made it comfortable between them two when they fell out, and always told master of the meekness and forgiveness of her blessed dispositions. Did she think as Miggs had no attachments? Did she think the wages was her only object?'

To none of these interrogatories, whereof every one was more pathetically delivered than the last, did Mrs Varden answer one word: but Miggs, not at all abashed by this circumstance, turned to the small boy in attendance – her eldest nephew; son of her own married sister; born in Golden Lion Court, number twenty-sivin; and bred in the very shadow of the second bell handle on the right hand door post – and with a plentiful use of her pocket handkerchief, addressed herself to him: requesting that on his return home he would console his parents for the loss of her, his aunt, by delivering to them a faithful statement of his having left her in the bosom of that family, with which, as his aforesaid parents well knew, her best affections were incorporated; that he would remind them that nothing less than her imperious sense of duty, and devoted

attachment to her old master and missis, likewise Miss Dolly and young Mr Joe, should ever have induced her to decline that pressing invitation which they, his parents, had, as he could testify, given her, to lodge and board with them, free of all cost and charge, for evermore; lastly, that he would help her with her box up stairs, and then repair straight home, bearing her blessing and her strong injunctions to mingle in his prayers a supplication that he might in course of time grow up a locksmith, or a Mr Joe, and have Mrs Vardens, and Miss Dollys for his relations and friends.

Having brought this admonition to an end, upon which, to say the truth, the young gentleman for whose benefit it was designed, bestowed little or no heed, having to all appearance his faculties absorbed in the contemplation of the sweetmeats, – Miss Miggs signified to the company in general that they were not to be uneasy, for she would soon return; and, with her nephew's aid, prepared to bear her wardrobe up the staircase.

'My dear,' said the locksmith to his wife. 'Do you desire this?'

'I desire it!' she answered. 'I am astonished – I am amazed – at her audacity. Let her leave the house this moment.'

Miggs, hearing this, let her end of the box fall heavily to the floor, gave a very loud sniff, crossed her arms, screwed down the corners of her mouth, and cried, in an ascending scale, 'Ho, good gracious!' three distinct times.

'You hear what your mistress says, my love,' remarked the locksmith. 'You had better go, I think. Stay; take this with you, for the sake of old service.'

Miss Miggs clutched the bank-note[2] he took from his pocketbook and held out to her; deposited it in a small, red leather purse; put the purse in her pocket (displaying, as she did so, a considerable portion of some undergarment, made of flannel, and more black cotton stocking than is commonly seen in public); and, tossing her head, as she looked at Mrs Varden, repeated –

'Ho good gracious!'

'I think you said that once before, my dear,' observed the locksmith.

'Times is changed, is they, mim!' cried Miggs, bridling; 'you can spare me now, can you? You can keep 'em down without me? You're not in wants of any one to scold, or throw the blame upon, no longer, an't you, mim? I'm glad to find you've grown so independent. I wish you joy, I'm sure!'

With that she dropped a curtsey, and keeping her head erect, her ear towards Mrs Varden, and her eye on the rest of the company, as she alluded to them in her remarks, proceeded:

'I'm quite delighted, I'm sure, to find sich independency, feeling sorry though, at the same time mim, that you should have been forced into submissions when you couldn't help yourself – he he he! It must be great vexations, 'specially considering how ill you always spoke of Mr Joe – to have him for a son-in-law at last; and I wonder Miss Dolly can put up with him, either, after being off and on for so many years with a coach-maker. But I *have* heerd say that the coachmaker thought twice about it – he he he! – and that he told a young man as was a frind of his, that he hoped he knowed better than to be drawed into that; though she and all the family *did* pull uncommon strong!'

Here she paused for a reply, and receiving none, went on as before.

'I *have* heerd say, mim, that the illnesses of some ladies was all pretensions, and that they could faint away stone dead whenever they had the inclinations so to do. Of course I never see sich cases with my own eyes – ho no! He he he! Nor master neither – ho no! He he he! I *have* heerd the neighbours make remark as some one as they was acquainted with, was a poor good-natur'd mean-spirited creetur, as went out fishing for a wife one day, and caught a Tartar. Of course I never to my knowledge see the poor person himself. Nor did you neither, mim – ho no. I wonder who it can be – don't you, mim? No doubt you do, mim. Ho yes. He he he!'

Again Miggs paused for a reply; and none being offered, was so oppressed with teeming spite and spleen, that she seemed like to burst.

'I'm glad Miss Dolly can laugh,' cried Miggs with a feeble titter. 'I like to see folks a laughing – so do you, mim, don't you? You was always glad to see people in spirits, wasn't you, mim? And you always did your best to keep 'em cheerful, didn't you, mim? Though there an't such a great deal to laugh at now either; is there, mim? It an't so much of a catch after looking out so sharp ever since she was a little chit, and costing such a deal in dress and show, to get a poor, common soldier, with one arm, is it, mim? He he! I wouldn't have a husband with one arm, anyways. I would have two arms. I would have two arms, if it was me, though instead of hands they'd only got hooks at the end, like our dustman.'

Miss Miggs was about to add, and had, indeed, begun to add, that, taking them in the abstract, dustmen were far more eligible matches than soldiers, though, to be sure, when people were past choosing they must take the best they could get, and think themselves well off too; but her vexation and chagrin being of that internally bitter sort which finds no relief in words, and is aggravated to madness by want of contradiction, she could hold out no longer, and burst into a storm of sobs and tears.

In this extremity she fell on the unlucky nephew, tooth and nail, and plucking a handful of hair from his head, demanded to know how long she was to stand there to be insulted, and whether or no he meant to help her to carry out the box again, and if he took a pleasure in hearing his family reviled, with other inquiries of that nature: at which disgrace and provocation, the small boy, who had been all this time gradually lashed into rebellion by the sight of unattainable pastry, walked off indignant, leaving his aunt and the box to follow at their leisure. Somehow or other, by dint of pushing and pulling, they did attain the street at last; where Miss Miggs, all blowzed with the exertion of getting there, and with her sobs and tears, sat down upon her property; to rest and grieve until she could ensnare some other youth to help her home.

'It's a thing to laugh at, Martha, not to care for,' whispered the locksmith, as he followed his wife to the window, and good-humouredly dried her eyes. 'What does it matter? You had seen your fault before. Come! Bring up Toby again, my dear; Dolly shall sing us a song; and we'll be all the merrier for this interruption.'

*

CHAPTER THE EIGHTY-FIRST

Another month had passed, and the end of August had nearly come, when Mr Haredale stood alone in the mail-coach office at Bristol. Although but a few weeks had intervened since his conversation with Edward Chester and his niece, in the locksmith's house, and he had made no change, in the mean time, in his accustomed style of dress, his appearance was greatly altered. He looked much older, and more care-worn. Violent agitation and anxiety of mind scatter wrinkles and grey hairs with no unsparing hand; but deeper traces follow on the silent uprooting of old habits, and severing of dear, familiar ties. The affections are not so easily wounded as the passions, but their hurts are deeper, and more lasting. He was now a solitary man, and the heart within him was dreary and lonesome.

He was not the less alone for having spent so many years in seclusion and retirement. This was no better preparation than a round of social cheerfulness: perhaps it even increased the keenness of his sensibility. He had been so dependent upon her for companionship and love; she had come to be so much a part and parcel of his existence; they had had so many cares and thoughts in common, which no one else had shared; that losing her was beginning life anew, and being required to summon up the hope and elasticity of youth, amid the doubts, distrusts, and weakened energies of age.

The effort he had made to part from her with seeming cheerfulness and hope – and they had parted only yesterday – left him the more depressed. With these feelings, he was about to revisit London for the last time, and look once more upon the walls of their old home, before turning his back upon it, for ever.

The journey was a very different one in those days from what the present generation find it; but it came to an end, as the longest journey will, and he stood again in the streets of the metropolis. He lay at the inn where the coach stopped, and resolved, before he went to bed, that he would make his arrival known to no one; would spend but another night in London; and would spare himself the pang of parting even with the honest locksmith.

Such conditions of the mind as that to which he was a prey when he lay down to rest, are favourable to the growth of disordered fancies, and uneasy visions. He knew this, even in the horror with which he started from his first sleep, and threw up the window to dispel it by the presence of some object, beyond the room, which had not been, as it were, the witness of his dream. But it was not a new terror of the night; it had been present to him before, in many shapes; it had haunted him in bygone times; and visited his pillow again and again. If it had been but an ugly object, a childish spectre, haunting his sleep, its return, in its old form, might have awakened a momentary sensation of fear, which, almost in the act of waking, would have passed away. This disquiet, however, lingered about him, and would yield to nothing. When he closed his eyes again, he felt it hovering near; as he slowly sunk into a slumber, he was conscious of its gathering strength and purpose, and gradually assuming its recent shape; when he sprang up from his bed, the same phantom vanished from his heated brain, and left him filled with a dread against which reason and waking thought were powerless.

The sun was up before he could shake it off. He rose late, but not refreshed, and remained within doors all that day. He had a fancy for paying his last visit to the old spot in the evening, for he had been accustomed to walk there at that season, and desired to see it under the aspect that was most familiar to him. At such an hour as would afford him time to reach it a little before sunset, he left the inn, and turned into the busy street.

He had not gone far, and was thoughtfully making his way among the noisy crowd, when he felt a hand upon his shoulder, and, turning, recognised one of the waiters from the inn, who begged his pardon, but he had left his sword behind him.

'Why have you brought it to me?' he asked, stretching out his hand, and yet not taking it from the man, but looking at him in a disturbed and agitated manner.

The man was sorry to have disobliged him, and would carry it back again. The gentleman had said that he was going a little way into the country, and that he might not return till late. The roads were not very safe for single travellers after dark; and since the riots, gentlemen had been more careful than ever not to trust themselves unarmed in lonely places. 'We thought you were a stranger, sir,' he added, 'and that you might believe our roads to be better than they are; but perhaps you know them well, and carry fire-arms –'

He took the sword, and putting it up at his side, thanked the man, and resumed his walk.

It was long remembered that he did this in a manner so strange, and with such a trembling hand, that the messenger stood looking after his retreating figure, doubtful whether he ought not to follow, and watch him. It was long remembered that he had been heard pacing his bed-room in the dead of the night; that the attendants had mentioned to each other in the morning, how fevered and how pale he looked; and that when this man went back to the inn, he told a fellow-servant that what he had observed in this short interview lay very heavy on his mind, and that he feared the gentleman intended to destroy himself, and would never come back alive.

With a half consciousness that his manner had attracted the man's attention (remembering the expression of his face when they parted), Mr Haredale quickened his steps; and arriving at a stand of coaches, bargained with the driver of the best to carry him so far on his road as the point where the foot-way struck across the fields, and to await his return at a house of entertainment which was within a stone's-throw of that place. Arriving there in due course, he alighted and pursued his way on foot.

He passed so near the Maypole, that he could see its smoke rising from among the trees, while a flock of pigeons – some of its old inhabitants, doubtless – sailed gaily home to roost, between him and the unclouded sky. 'The old house will brighten up now,' he said, as he looked towards it, 'and there will be a merry fireside beneath its ivied roof. It is some comfort to know that everything will not be blighted hereabouts. I shall be glad to have one picture of life and cheerfulness to turn to!'

He resumed his walk, and bent his steps towards the Warren. It was a clear, calm, silent evening, with hardly a breath of wind to stir the leaves, or any sound to break the stillness of the time, but drowsy sheep-bells tinkling in the distance, and at intervals the far-off lowing of cattle, or bark of village dogs. The sky was radiant with the softened glory of sunset; and on the earth, and in the air, a deep repose prevailed. At such an hour, he arrived at the deserted mansion which had been his home so long, and looked for the last time upon its blackened walls.

The ashes of the commonest fire are melancholy things, for in them there is an image of death and ruin, – of something that has been bright, and is but dull, cold, dreary dust, – with which our nature forces us to sympathise. How much more sad the crumbled embers of a home: the casting down of that great altar, where the worst among us sometimes perform the worship of the heart; and where the best have offered up such sacrifices, and done such deeds of heroism as, chronicled, would put the proudest temples of old Time, with all their vaunting annals, to the blush!

He roused himself from a long train of meditation, and walked slowly round the house. It was by this time almost dark.

He had nearly made the circuit of the building, when he uttered a half-suppressed exclamation, started, and stood still. Reclining, in an easy attitude, with his back against a tree, and contemplating the ruin with an expression of exquisite pleasure, – a pleasure so keen that it overcame his habitual indolence and command of feature, and displayed itself utterly free from all restraint or reserve, – before him, on his own ground, and triumphing over him then, as he had done in every misfortune and disappointment of his life, there stood the man whose presence, of all mankind, in any place, and least of all in that, he could the least endure.

Although his blood so rose against this man, and his wrath so stirred within him, that he could have struck him dead, he put such fierce constraint upon himself that he passed him without a word or look. Yes, and he would have gone on, and not turned, though to resist the Devil who poured such hot temptation in his brain, required an effort scarcely human, if this man had not himself summoned him to stop: and that, with an assumed compassion in his voice which drove him well-nigh mad, and in an instant routed all the self-command it had been anguish – acute, poignant anguish – to sustain.

All consideration, reflection, mercy, forbearance; everything by which a goaded man can curb his rage and passion; fled from him as he turned back. And yet he said, slowly and quite calmly – far more calmly than he had ever spoken to him before:

'Why have you called to me?'

'To remark,' said Sir John Chester with his wonted composure, 'what an odd chance it is, that we should meet here!'

'It *is* a strange chance.'

'Strange! The most remarkable and singular thing in the world. I never ride in the evening; I have not done so for years. The whim seized me, quite unaccountably, in the middle of last night. – How very picturesque this is!' – He pointed, as he spoke, to the dismantled house, and raised his glass to his eye.

'You praise your own work very freely.'

Sir John let fall his glass; inclined his face towards him with an air of the most courteous inquiry; and slightly shook his head as though he were remarking to himself, 'I fear this animal is going mad!'

'I say you praise your own work very freely,' repeated Mr Haredale.

'Work!' echoed Sir John, looking smilingly round. 'Mine! – I beg your pardon, I really beg your pardon –'

'Why you see,' said Mr Haredale, 'those walls. You see those tottering gables. You see on every side where fire and smoke have raged. You see the destruction that has been wanton here. Do you not?'

'My good fellow,' returned the knight, gently checking his impatience with his hand, 'of course I do. I see everything you speak of, when you stand aside, and do not interpose yourself between the view and me. I am very sorry for you. If I had not had the pleasure to meet you here, I think I should have written to tell you so. But you don't bear it as well as I had expected – excuse me – no, you don't indeed.'

He pulled out his snuff-box, and addressing him with the superior air of a man who by reason of his higher nature has a right to read a moral lesson to another, continued:

'For you are a philosopher, you know – one of that stern and rigid school who are far above the weaknesses of mankind in general. You are removed, a long way, from the frailties of the crowd. You contemplate them from a height, and rail at them with a most impressive bitterness. I have heard you.'

– 'And shall again,' said Mr Haredale.

'Thank you,' returned the other. 'Shall we walk as we talk? The damp falls rather heavily. Well, – as you please. But I grieve to say that I can spare you only a very few moments.'

'I would,' said Mr Haredale, 'you had spared me none. I would, with all my soul, you had been in Paradise (if such a monstrous lie could be enacted), rather than here to-night.'

'Nay,' returned the other – 'really – you do yourself injustice. You are a rough companion, but I would not go so far to avoid you.'

'Listen to me,' said Mr Haredale. 'Listen to me.'

'While you rail?' inquired Sir John.

'While I deliver your infamy. You urged and stimulated to do your work a fit agent, but one who in his nature – in the very essence of his being – is a traitor, and who has been false to you, despite the sympathy you two should have together, as he has been to all others. With hints, and looks, and crafty words, which told again are nothing, you set on Gashford to this work – this work before us now. With these same hints, and looks, and crafty words, which told again are nothing, you urged him on to gratify the deadly hate he owes me – I have earned it, I thank Heaven – by the abduction and dishonour of my niece. You did. I see denial in your looks' – he cried, abruptly pointing in his face, and stepping back. 'Denial is a lie!'

He had his hand upon his sword; but the knight, with a contemptuous smile, replied to him as coldly as before.

'You will take notice sir – if you can discriminate sufficiently – that I have taken the trouble to deny nothing. Your discernment is hardly fine enough for the perusal of faces, not of a kind as coarse as your speech; nor has it ever been, that I remember; or, in one face that I could name, you would have read indifference, not to say disgust, somewhat sooner than you did. I speak of a long time ago, – but you understand me.'

'Disguise it as you will, you mean denial. Denial explicit or reserved, expressed or left to be inferred, is still a lie. You say you don't deny. Do you admit?'

'You yourself,' returned Sir John, suffering the current of his speech to flow as smoothly as if it had been stemmed by no one word of interruption, 'publicly proclaimed the character of the gentleman in question (I think it was in Westminster Hall) in terms which relieve me from the necessity of making any further allusion to him. You may have been warranted; you may not have been; I can't say. Assuming the gentleman to be what you described, and to have made to you or any other person any statements that may have happened to suggest themselves to him, for the sake of his own security, or for the sake of money, or for his own amusement, or for any other consideration, – I have nothing to say of him, except that his extremely degrading situation appears to me to be shared with his employers. You are so very plain yourself, that you will excuse a little freedom in me, I am sure.'

'Attend to me again Sir John – but once,' cried Mr Haredale; 'in your every look, and word, and gesture, you tell me this was not your act. I tell you that it was, and that you tampered with the man I speak of, and with your wretched son (whom God forgive), to do this deed. You talk of degradation and character. You told me once that you had purchased the absence of the poor idiot and his mother, when (as I have discovered since, and then suspected) you had gone to tempt them, and had found them flown. To you I traced the insinuation that I alone reaped any harvest from my brother's death; and all the foul attacks and whispered calumnies that followed in its train. In every action of my life, from that first hope which you converted into grief and desolation, you have stood, like an adverse fate, between me and peace. In all, you have ever been the same cold-blooded, hollow, false, unworthy villain. For the second time, and for the last, I cast these charges in your teeth, and spurn you from me as I would a faithless dog!'

With that, he raised his arm, and struck him on the breast so that he staggered back. Sir John, the instant he recovered, drew his sword, threw away the scabbard and his hat, and rushing on his adversary made a desperate lunge at his heart, which, but that his guard was quick and true, would have stretched him dead upon the grass.

In the act of striking him, the torrent of his opponent's rage had reached a stop. He parried his rapid thrusts, without returning them, and called to him with a frantic kind of terror in his face to keep back.

'Not to-night! not to-night!' he cried. 'In God's name, not to-night!'

Seeing that he lowered his weapon, and that he would not thrust in turn, Sir John lowered his.

'I warn you, not to-night!' his adversary cried. 'Be warned in time!'

'You told me – it must have been in a sort of inspiration –' said Sir John, quite deliberately, though now he dropped his mask, and showed his bitter hatred in his face, 'that this was the last time. Be assured it is! Did you believe our last meeting was forgotten? Did you believe that your every word and look was not to be accounted for, and was not well remembered? Do you believe that I have waited your time, or you mine? What kind of man is he who entered, with all his sickening cant of honesty and truth, into a bond with me to prevent a marriage he affected to dislike, and when I had redeemed my part to the spirit and the letter, skulked from his, and brought the match about in his own time, to rid himself of a burden he had grown tired of, and cast a spurious lustre on his house?'

'I have acted,' cried Mr Haredale, 'with honour and in good faith. I do so now. Do not force me to renew this duel to-night!'

'You said my "wretched" son, I think?' said Sir John, with a smile. 'Poor fool! The dupe of such a shallow knave – trapped into marriage by such an uncle and by such a niece – he well deserves your pity. But he is no longer son of mine: you are welcome to the prize your craft has made, sir.'

'Once more,' cried his opponent, wildly stamping on the ground, 'although you tear me from my better angel, I implore you not to come within the reach of my sword to-night. Oh! why were you here at all! Why have we met! To-morrow would have cast us far apart for ever!'

'That being the case,' returned Sir John, without the least emotion, 'it is very fortunate we have met to-night. Haredale, I have always despised you, as you know, but I have given you credit for a species of brute courage. For the honour of my judgment, which I had thought a good one, I am sorry to find you a coward.'

Not another word was spoken on either side. They crossed swords, though it was now quite dusk, and attacked each other fiercely. They were well matched. Each was skilled in the management of his weapon. Mr Haredale had the advantage in strength and height; on the other hand his adversary could boast superior address, and certainly a greater share of coolness.

After a few seconds they grew hotter and more furious, and pressing on each other inflicted and received several slight wounds. It was directly after receiving one of these in his arm, that Mr Haredale, making a keener thrust as he felt the warm blood spirting out, plunged his sword through his opponent's body to the hilt.

Their eyes met, and were on each other as he drew it out. He put his arm about the dying man, who repulsed him, feebly, and dropped upon the turf. Raising himself upon his hands, he gazed at him for an instant, with scorn and hatred in his look: but seeming to remember, even then, that this expression would distort his features after death, he tried to smile; and, faintly moving his right hand, as if to hide his bloody linen in his vest, fell back dead – the phantom of last night.

CHAPTER THE LAST

A parting glance at such of the actors in this little history as it has not, in the course of its events, dismissed, will bring it to an end.

Mr Haredale fled that night. Before pursuit could be begun, indeed before Sir John was traced or missed, he had left the kingdom. Repairing straight to a religious establishment, known

throughout Europe for the rigour and severity of its discipline, and for the merciful penitence it exacted from those who sought its shelter as a refuge from the world, he took the vows which thenceforth shut him out from nature and his kind, and after a few remorseful years was buried in its gloomy cloisters.

Two days elapsed before the body of Sir John was found. As soon as it was recognised and carried home, the faithful valet, true to his master's creed, eloped with all the cash and moveables he could lay his hands on, and started as a finished gentleman upon his own account. In this career he met with great success, and would certainly have married an heiress in the end, but for an unlucky check which led to his premature decease. He sank under a contagious disorder, very prevalent at that time, and vulgarly termed the jail fever.

Lord George Gordon, remaining in his prison in the Tower until Monday the Fifth of February in the following year, was on that day solemnly tried at Westminster for High Treason. Of this crime he was, after a patient investigation, declared Not Guilty; upon the ground that there was no proof of his having called the multitude together with any traitorous or unlawful intentions. Yet so many people were there still, to whom those riots taught no lesson of reproof or moderation, that a public subscription was set on foot in Scotland to defray the cost of his defence.

For seven years afterwards he remained, at the strong intercession of his friends, comparatively quiet; saving that he every now and then took occasion to display his zeal for the Protestant faith in some extravagant proceeding which was the delight of its enemies; and saving, besides, that he was formally excommunicated by the Archbishop of Canterbury,[1] for refusing to appear as a witness in the Ecclesiastical Court when cited for that purpose. In the year 1788 he was stimulated by some new insanity to write and publish an injurious pamphlet, reflecting on the Queen of France, in very violent terms. Being indicted for the libel, and (after various strange demonstrations in court) found guilty, he fled into Holland in place of appearing to receive sentence: from whence, as the quiet burgomasters of Amsterdam had no relish for his company, he was sent home again with all speed. Arriving in the month of July at Harwich, and going thence to Birmingham, he made in the latter place, in August, a public profession of the Jewish religion; and figured there as a Jew until he was arrested, and brought back to

London to receive the sentence he had evaded. By virtue of this sentence he was, in the month of December, cast into Newgate for five years and ten months, and required besides to pay a large fine, and to furnish heavy securities for his future good behaviour.

After addressing, in the midsummer of the following year, an appeal to the commiseration of the National Assembly of France, which the English minister refused to sanction, he composed himself to undergo his full term of punishment; and suffering his beard to grow nearly to his waist, and conforming in all respects to the ceremonies of his new religion, he applied himself to the study of history, and occasionally to the art of painting, in which, in his younger days, he had shown some skill. Deserted by his former friends, and treated in all respects like the worst criminal in the jail, he lingered on, quite cheerful and resigned, until the 1st of November 1793, when he died in his cell, being then only three-and-forty years of age.

Many men with fewer sympathies for the distressed and needy, with less abilities and harder hearts, have made a shining figure and left a brilliant fame. He had his mourners. The prisoners bemoaned his loss, and missed him; for though his means were not large his charity was great, and in bestowing alms among them he considered the necessities of all alike, and knew no distinction of sect or creed. There are wise men in the highways of the world who may learn something, even from this poor crazy Lord who died in Newgate.

To the last, he was truly served by bluff John Grueby. He was at his side before he had been four-and-twenty hours in the Tower, and he never left him until he died. He had one other constant attendant, in the person of a beautiful Jewish girl; who attached herself to him from feelings half religious, half romantic, but whose virtuous and disinterested character appears to have been beyond the censure even of the most censorious.

Gashford deserted him, of course. He subsisted for a time upon his traffic in his master's secrets; and, this trade failing when the stock was quite exhausted, procured an appointment in the honourable corps of spies and eaves-droppers employed by the government. As one of these wretched underlings, he did his drudgery, sometimes abroad, sometimes at home; and long endured the various miseries of such a station. Ten or a dozen years ago[2] – not more – a meagre, wan old man, diseased and miserably poor, was found dead in his bed at an obscure inn in the Borough, where he was quite unknown. He had taken poison. There was no clue to his name; but it was discovered from certain entries in a pocket-book he carried, that he had been secretary to Lord George Gordon in the time of the famous riots.

Many months after the re-establishment of peace and order; and even when it had ceased to be the town talk, that every military officer, kept at free quarters by the city during the late alarms, had cost for his board and lodging four pounds four per day, and every private soldier two and twopence halfpenny; many months after even this engrossing topic was forgotten, and the United Bull-Dogs were to a man all killed, imprisoned or transported; Mr Simon Tappertit, being removed from a hospital to prison, and thence to his place of trial, was discharged by proclamation, on two wooden legs. Shorn of his graceful limbs, and brought down from his high estate to circumstances of utter destitution, and the deepest misery, he made shift to stump back to his old master, and beg for some relief. By the locksmith's advice and aid, he was established in business as a shoe-black, and opened shop under an archway near the Horse Guards. This being a central quarter, he quickly made a very large connection; and on levee days, was sometimes known to have as many as twenty half-pay officers waiting their turn for polishing. Indeed his trade increased to that extent, that in course of time he entertained no less than two apprentices, besides taking for his wife the widow of an eminent bone and rag collector, formerly of Millbank.[3] With this lady (who assisted in the business) he lived in great domestic happiness, only chequered by those little storms which serve to clear the atmosphere of wedlock, and brighten its horizon. In some of these gusts of bad weather, Mr Tappertit would, in the assertion of his prerogative, so far forget himself, as to correct his lady with a brush, or boot, or shoe; while she (but only in extreme cases) would retaliate by taking off his legs, and leaving him exposed to the derision of those urchins who delight in mischief.

Miss Miggs, baffled in all her schemes, matrimonial and otherwise, and cast upon a thankless, undeserving world, turned very sharp and sour; and did at length become so acid, and did so pinch and slap and tweak the hair and noses of the youth of Golden Lion Court, that she was by one consent expelled that sanctuary, and desired to bless some other spot of earth, in preference. It chanced at that moment, that the justices of the peace for Middlesex proclaimed by public placard that they stood in need of a female turnkey for the County Bridewell, and appointed a day and hour for the inspection of candidates. Miss Miggs, attending at the time appointed, was instantly chosen and selected from one hundred and twenty-four competitors, and at once promoted to the office; which she held until her decease, more than thirty years afterwards, remaining single all that time. It was observed of this lady that while she was inflexible and grim to all her female flock, she was particularly so to those who could establish any claim to beauty: and it was often remarked as a proof of her indomitable virtue and severe chastity, that to such as had been frail she showed no mercy; always falling upon them on the slightest occasion, or on no occasion at all, with the fullest measure of her wrath. Among other useful inventions which she practised upon this class of offenders and bequeathed to posterity, was the art of inflicting an exquisitely vicious poke or dig with the wards of a key in the small of the back, near the spine. She likewise originated a mode of treading by accident (in pattens) on such as had small feet; also very remarkable for its ingenuity, and previously quite unknown.

It was not very long, you may be sure, before Joe Willet and Dolly Varden were made husband and wife, and with a handsome sum in bank (for the locksmith could afford to give his daughter a good dowry), reopened the Maypole. It was not very long, you may be sure, before a red-faced little boy was seen staggering about the Maypole passage, and kicking up his heels on the green before the door. It was not very long, counting by years, before there was a red-faced little girl, another red-faced little boy, and a whole troop of girls and boys: so that, go to Chigwell when you would, there would surely be seen, either in the village street, or on the green, or frolicking in the farm-yard – for it was a farm now, as well as a tavern – more small Joes and small Dollys than could be easily counted. It was not a very long time before these appearances ensued; but it *was* a *very* long time before Joe looked five years older, or Dolly either, or the locksmith either, or his wife either: for cheerfulness and content are great beautifiers, and are famous preservers of youthful looks, depend upon it.

It was a long time, too, before there was such a country inn as the Maypole, in all England: indeed it is a great question whether there has ever been such another to this hour, or ever will be. It was a long time too – for Never, as the proverb says, is a long day –

before they forgot to have an interest in wounded soldiers at the
Maypole; or before Joe omitted to refresh them, for the sake of his
old campaign; or before the serjeant left off looking in there, now
and then; or before they fatigued themselves, or each other, by
talking on these occasions of battles and sieges, and hard weather
and hard service, and a thousand things belonging to a soldier's
life. As to the great silver snuff-box which the King sent Joe with
his own hand, because of his conduct in the Riots, what guest ever
went to the Maypole without putting finger and thumb into that
box, and taking a great pinch, though he had never taken a pinch
of snuff before, and almost sneezed himself into convulsions even
then? As to the purple-faced vintner, where is the man who lived
in those times and never saw *him* at the Maypole: to all appearance
as much at home in the best room, as if he lived there? And as to
the feastings and christenings, and revellings at Christmas, and
celebrations of birth-days, wedding-days, and all manner of days,
both at the Maypole and the Golden Key, – if they are not notorious,
what facts are?

Mr Willet the elder, having been by some extraordinary means
possessed with the idea that Joe wanted to be married, and that it
would be well for him, his father, to retire into private life, and
enable him to live in comfort, took up his abode in a small cottage
at Chigwell; where they widened and enlarged the fire-place for
him, hung up the boiler, and furthermore planted in the little garden
outside the front-door, a fictitious Maypole: so that he was quite
at home directly. To this, his new habitation, Tom Cobb, Phil
Parkes, and Solomon Daisy went regularly every night: and in the
chimney-corner, they all four quaffed, and smoked, and prosed,
and dozed, as they had done of old. It being accidentally discovered
after a short time that Mr Willet still appeared to consider himself
a landlord by profession, Joe provided him with a slate, upon which
the old man regularly scored up vast accounts for meat, drink, and
tobacco. As he grew older this passion increased upon him; and it
became his delight to chalk against the name of each of his cronies
a sum of enormous magnitude, and impossible to be paid: and such
was his secret joy in these entries, that he would be perpetually seen
going behind the door to look at them, and coming forth again,
suffused with the liveliest satisfaction.

He never recovered the surprise the Rioters had given him, and
remained in the same mental condition down to the last moment

of his life. It was like to have been brought to a speedy termination by the first sight of his first grandchild, which appeared to fill him with the belief that a miracle had happened to Joe, and that something alarming had occurred. Being promptly blooded, however, by a skilful surgeon, he rallied; and although the doctors all agreed, on his being attacked with symptoms of apoplexy six months afterwards, that he ought to die, and took it very ill that he did not, he remained alive – possibly on account of his constitutional slowness – for nearly seven years more, when he was one morning found speechless in his bed. He lay in this state, free from all tokens of uneasiness, for a whole week, when he was suddenly restored to consciousness by hearing the nurse whisper in his son's ear that he was going. 'I'm a-going, Joseph,' said Mr Willet, turning round upon the instant, 'to the Salwanners' – and immediately gave up the ghost.

He left a large sum of money behind him; even more than he was supposed to have been worth, although the neighbours, according to the custom of mankind in calculating the wealth that other people ought to have saved, had estimated his property in good round numbers. Joe inherited the whole; so that he became a man of great consequence in those parts, and was perfectly independent.

Some time elapsed before Barnaby got the better of the shock he had sustained, or regained his old health and gaiety. But he recovered by degrees: and although he could never separate his condemnation and escape from the idea of a terrific dream, he became, in other respects, more rational. Dating from the time of his recovery, he had a better memory and greater steadiness of purpose; but a dark cloud overhung his whole previous existence, and never cleared away.

He was not the less happy for this; for his love of freedom and interest in all that moved or grew, or had its being[4] in the elements, remained to him unimpaired. He lived with his mother on the Maypole farm, tending the poultry and the cattle, working in a garden of his own, and helping everywhere. He was known to every bird and beast about the place, and had a name for every one. Never was there a lighter-hearted husbandman, a creature more popular with young and old, a blither or more happy soul than Barnaby: and though he was free to ramble where he would, he never quitted Her, but was for evermore her stay and comfort.

It was remarkable that although he had that dim sense of the past, he sought out Hugh's dog, and took him under his care; and that he never could be tempted into London. When the Riots were many years old, and Edward and his wife came back to England with a family almost as numerous as Dolly's, and one day appeared at the Maypole porch, he knew them instantly, and wept and leaped for joy. But neither to visit them, nor on any other pretence, no matter how full of promise and enjoyment, could he be persuaded to set foot in the streets: nor did he ever conquer this repugnance or look upon the town again.

Grip soon recovered his looks, and became as glossy and sleek as ever. But he was profoundly silent. Whether he had forgotten the art of Polite Conversation in Newgate, or had made a vow in those troubled times to forego, for a period, the display of his accomplishments, is matter of uncertainty; but certain it is that for a whole year he never indulged in any other sound than a grave, decorous croak. At the expiration of that term, the morning being very bright and sunny, he was heard to address himself to the horses in the stable upon the subject of the Kettle, so often mentioned in these pages; and before the witness who overheard him could run into the house with the intelligence, and add to it upon his solemn affirmation the statement that he had heard him laugh, the bird himself advanced with fantastic steps to the very door of the bar, and there cried 'I'm a devil, I'm a devil, I'm a devil!' with extraordinary rapture.

From that period (although he was supposed to be much affected by the death of Mr Willet senior), he constantly practised and improved himself in the vulgar tongue;⁵ and as he was a mere infant for a raven, when Barnaby was grey, he has very probably gone on talking to the present time.

END OF 'BARNABY RUDGE.'

Appendix I: On the Illustrations

A. THE ILLUSTRATIONS AND THEIR ARTISTS

The illustrations to *Barnaby Rudge* were not given titles in *Master Humphrey's Clock* or the first volume publication. They were given titles in the Library edition of 1858, but not by Dickens, and various later editions have supplied their own. The nearest thing to a standard list of titles is in Thomas Hatton's 'A Bibliographical List of the Original Illustrations to the Works of Charles Dickens', in *The Nonesuch Dickens: Retrospectus and Prospectus* (London: Nonesuch, 1937, pp. 64–6), and I have used them below (see *The Letters of Charles Dickens, Volume 2, 1840–1*, ed. Madeline House and Graham Storey (Oxford: Clarendon Press, 1969), p. xiv). Hatton is not altogether reliable however: for example, he misascribes 'Widow Rudge's cottage' to Cattermole, although it is signed by Browne (see *Letters*, p. xiv).

Hablot K. Browne ('Phiz') created the majority of the illustrations (see A Note on the Text and Illustrations). The following were by George Cattermole: Chapter 1 'The Maypole Inn'; Chapter 4 'Sim in the Forge'; Chapters 10, 13, 16, 22; Chapter 25 'John Willet dozing'; Chapters 29, 42; Chapter 43 'In Westminster Hall'; Chapter 52 'The "Boot" Inn'; Chapters 54, 56; Chapter 59 'The Chariot'; Chapters 69, 73, 81.

B. ILLUSTRATED CAPITALS FROM THE FIRST EDITION

The ten monthly numbers had ornamental initial letters (Chapter 33 also has one), which sometimes comment on or illuminate the action of the novel. The initial 'I' of Chapter the First, for example, runs the length of the first paragraph of the novel and shows the maypole after which John Willet's inn is named. The most poignant is the initial 'T' at beginning of Chapter the Forty-ninth, in the shape of the gallows to which the rioters (who begin their work in earnest in that chapter) are heading.

CHAPTER THE
SIXTH

CHAPTER THE
THIRTEENTH

CHAPTER THE
FIRST

CHAPTER THE
TWENTY-THIRD

CHAPTER THE
THIRTY-FIRST

CHAPTER THE
THIRTY-THIRD

CHAPTER THE
THIRTY-NINTH

CHAPTER THE
FORTY-NINTH

CHAPTER THE
FIFTY-SEVENTH

CHAPTER THE
SIXTY-FIFTH

CHAPTER THE
SEVENTY-FIFTH

Appendix II: *Master Humphrey's Clock* Material

Barnaby Rudge was first published in Dickens's weekly journal *Master Humphrey's Clock*, which contained introductory and concluding material to the novel, as well as illustrations, that were not included when the novel was published as a separate volume.

A. BETWEEN *THE OLD CURIOSITY SHOP* AND *BARNABY RUDGE*, FROM *MASTER HUMPHREY'S CLOCK*, NO. 45, 6 FEBRUARY 1841

The original idea of *Master Humphrey's Clock* was that it would consist of stories told by Master Humphrey which he had found (see Introduction, section 4). By the conclusion of *The Old Curiosity Shop*, this framework had become vestigial, but the transition between the two novels has an interesting linking section (no. 45, 6 February 1841) in which Humphrey confesses that he personally had a role in the story of *The Old Curiosity Shop* and hints that one of the assembled company – we later learn that it is Jack Redburn – may have had a role in *Barnaby Rudge*.

MASTER HUMPHREY FROM HIS CLOCK SIDE IN THE CHIMNEY-CORNER

I was musing the other evening upon the characters and incidents with which I had been so long engaged; wondering how I could ever have looked forward with pleasure to the completion of my tale, and reproaching myself for having done so, as if it were a kind of cruelty to those companions of my solitude whom I had now dismissed, and could never again recall; when my clock struck ten. Punctual to the hour, my friends appeared.

On our last night of meeting, we had finished the story which the reader has just concluded. Our conversation took the same current as the meditations which the entrance of my friends had interrupted, and the Old Curiosity Shop was the staple of our discourse.

I may confide to the reader now, that in connexion with this little history I had something upon my mind – something to communicate which I had all along with difficulty repressed – something I had deemed it, during the progress of the story, necessary to its interest to disguise, and which, now that it was over, I wished, and was yet reluctant to disclose.

To conceal anything from those to whom I am attached, is not in my nature. I can never close my lips where I have opened my heart. This temper and the consciousness of having done some violence to it in my narrative, laid me under a restraint which I should have had great difficulty in overcoming, but for a timely remark from Mr Miles,[1] who, as I hinted in a former paper, is a gentleman of business habits, and of great exactness and propriety in all his transactions.

'I could have wished,' my friend objected; 'that we had been made acquainted with the single gentleman's name.[2] I don't like his withholding his name. It made me look upon him at first with suspicion, and caused me to doubt his moral character, I assure you. I am fully satisfied by this time of his being a worthy creature, but in this respect he certainly would not appear to have acted at all like a man of business.'

'My friends,' said I, drawing to the table at which they were by this time seated in their usual chairs, 'do you remember that this story bore another title besides that one we have so often heard of late?'

Mr Miles had his pocket-book out in an instant, and referring to an entry therein, rejoined 'Certainly. Personal adventures of Master Humphrey. Here it is. I made a note of it at the time.'

I was about to resume what I had to tell them, when the same Mr Miles again interrupted me, observing that the narrative originated in a personal adventure of my own, and that was no doubt the reason for its being thus designated.

This led me to the point at once.

'You will one and all forgive me,' I returned, 'if, for the greater convenience of the story, and for its better introduction, that adventure was fictitious. I had my share indeed – no light or trivial one – in the pages we have read, but it was not the share I feigned to have at first. The younger brother, the single gentleman, the nameless actor in this little drama, stands before you now.'

It was easy to see they had not expected this disclosure.

'Yes,' I pursued. 'I can look back upon my part in it with a calm, half-smiling pity for myself as for some other man. But I am he indeed; and now the chief sorrows of my life are yours.'

I need not say what true gratification I derived from the sympathy and kindness with which this acknowledgment was received; nor how often it had risen to my lips before; nor how difficult I had found it – how impossible, when I came to those passages which touched me most, and most nearly concerned me – to sustain the character I had assumed. It is enough to say that I replaced in the clock-case the record of so many trials – sorrowfully, it is true, but with a softened sorrow which was almost pleasure; and felt that in living through the past again, and communicating to others the lesson it had helped to teach me, I had been a happier man.

We lingered so long over the leaves from which I had read, that as I consigned them to their former resting-place, the hand of my trusty clock pointed to twelve, and there came towards us upon the wind the voice of the deep and distant bell of St Paul's[3] as it struck the hour of midnight.

'This,' said I, returning with a manuscript I had taken, at the moment, from the same repository, 'to be opened to such music, should be a tale where London's face by night is darkly seen, and where some deed of such a time as this is dimly shadowed out. Which of us here has seen the working of that great machine whose voice has just now ceased?'

Mr Pickwick had, of course, and so had Mr Miles. Jack and my deaf friend[4] were in the minority.

I had seen it but a few days before, and could not help telling them of the fancy I had had about it.

I paid my fee of twopence upon entering, to one of the money-changers who sit within the Temple;[5] and falling, after a few turns up and down, into the quiet train of thought which such a place awakens, paced the echoing stones like some old monk whose present world lay all within its walls. As I looked afar up into the lofty dome, I could not help wondering what were his reflections whose genius reared that mighty pile, when, the last small wedge of timber fixed, the last nail driven into its home for many centuries, the clang of hammers, and the hum of busy voices, gone, and the Great Silence whole years of noise had helped to make, reigning undisturbed around, he mused as I did now, upon his work, and lost himself amid its vast extent. I could not quite determine whether the contemplation of it would impress him with a sense of greatness or of insignificance; but when I remembered how long a time it had taken to erect, in how short a space it might be traversed even to its remotest parts, for how brief a term he, or any of those who cared to bear his name, would live to see it, or know of its existence, I imagined him far more melancholy than proud, and looking with regret upon his labour done. With these thoughts in my mind, I began to ascend, almost unconsciously, the flight of steps leading to the several wonders of the building, and found myself before a barrier where another money-taker sat, who demanded which among them I would choose to see. There were the stone-gallery, he said, and the whispering gallery, the geometrical staircase, the room of models, the clock – the clock being quite in my way, I stopped him there, and chose that sight from all the rest.

I groped my way into the Turret which it occupies, and saw before me, in a kind of loft, what seemed to be a great, old, oaken press with folding doors. These being thrown back by the attendant (who was sleeping when I came upon him, and looked a drowsy fellow, as though his close companionship with Time had made him quite indifferent to it) disclosed a complicated crowd of wheels and chains in iron and brass – great, sturdy, rattling engines – suggestive of breaking a finger put in here or there, and grinding the bone to powder – and these were the Clock! Its very pulse, if I may use the word, was like no other clock. It did not mark the flight of every moment with a gentle second stroke as though it would check old Time, and have him stay his pace in pity, but measured it with one sledge-hammer beat, as if its business were to crush the seconds as they came trooping on, and remorselessly to clear a path before the Day of Judgment.[6]

I sat down opposite to it, and hearing its regular and never-changing voice, that one deep constant note, uppermost amongst all the noise and clatter in the streets below – marking that, let that tumult rise or fall, go on or stop – let it be night or noon, to-morrow or to-day, this year or next – it still performed its functions with the same dull constancy, and regulated the progress of the life around, the fancy came upon me that this was London's Heart, and that when it should cease to beat, the City would be no more.

It is night. Calm and unmoved amidst the scenes that darkness favours, the great heart of London throbs in its Giant breast. Wealth and beggary, vice and virtue, guilt and innocence, repletion and the direst hunger, all treading on each other and crowding together, are gathered round it. Draw but a little circle above the clustering house-tops, and you shall have within its space, everything with its opposite extreme and contradiction, close beside. Where yonder feeble light is shining, a man is but this moment dead. The taper at a few yards' distance, is seen by eyes that have this instant opened on the world. There are two houses separated by but an inch or two of wall. In one, there are quiet minds at rest; in the other a waking conscience that one might think would trouble the very air. In that close corner where the roofs shrink down and cower together as if to hide their secrets from the handsome street hard by, there are such dark crimes, such miseries and horrors, as could be hardly told in whispers. In the handsome street, there are folks asleep who have dwelt there all their lives, and have no more knowledge of these things than if they had never been, or were transacted at the remotest limits of the world – who, if they were hinted at, would shake their heads, look wise, and frown, and say they were impossible, and out of Nature – as if all great towns were not. Does not this Heart of London, that nothing moves, nor stops, nor quickens – that goes on the same, let what will be done – does it not express the city's character well?

The day begins to break, and soon there is the hum and noise of life. Those who have spent the night on door-steps and cold stones, crawl off to beg; they who have slept in beds, come forth to their occupation too, and business is astir. The fog of sleep rolls slowly off, and London shines awake. The streets are filled with carriages, and people gaily clad. The jails are full, too, to the throat, nor have the workhouses or hospitals much room to spare. The courts of law are crowded. Taverns have their regular frequenters by this time, and every mart of traffic has its throng. Each of these places is a world, and has its own inhabitants; each is distinct from, and almost unconscious of the existence of any other. There are some few people well to do, who remember to have heard it said, that numbers of men and women – thousands they think it was – get up in London every day, unknowing where to lay their heads at night; and that there are quarters of the town where misery and famine always are. They don't believe it quite – there may be some truth in it, but it is exaggerated of course. So, each of these thousand worlds goes on, intent upon itself, until night comes again – first with its lights and pleasures, and its cheerful streets; then with its guilt and darkness.

Heart of London, there is a moral in thy every stroke! as I look on at thy indomitable working, which neither death, nor press of life, nor grief, nor gladness out of doors will influence one jot, I seem to hear a voice within thee which sinks into my heart, bidding me, as I elbow my way among the crowd, have some thought for the meanest wretch that passes, and, being a man, to turn away with scorn and pride from none that bear the human shape.

I am by no means sure that I might not have been tempted to enlarge upon this subject, had not the papers that lay before me on the table, been a silent reproach for even this digression. I took them up again when I had got thus far, and seriously prepared to read.

The hand-writing was strange to me, for the manuscript had been fairly copied. As it is against our rules in such a case to inquire into the authorship until the reading is concluded, I could only glance at the different faces round me, in search of some expression which should betray the writer. Whoever he might be, he was prepared for this, and gave no sign for my enlightenment.

I had the papers in my hand, when my deaf friend interposed with a suggestion.

'It has occurred to me,' he said, 'bearing in mind your sequel to the tale we have finished, that if such of us as have anything to relate of our own lives, could interweave it with our contribution to the Clock, it would be well to do so. This need be no restraint upon us, either as to time, or place, or incident, since any real passage of this kind may be surrounded by fictitious circumstances, and represented by fictitious characters. What if we made this, an article of agreement among ourselves?'

The proposition was cordially received, but the difficulty appeared to be that here was a long story written before we had thought of it.

'Unless,' said I, 'it should have happened that the writer of this tale – which is not impossible, for men are apt to do so when they write – has actually mingled with it something of his own endurance and experience.'

Nobody spoke, but I thought I detected in one quarter that this was really the case.

'If I have no assurance to the contrary,' I added therefore, 'I shall take it for granted that he has done so, and that even these papers come within our new agreement. Everybody being mute, we hold that understanding if you please.'

And here I was about to begin again, when Jack informed us softly, that during the progress of our last narrative, Mr Weller's Watch[7] had adjourned its sittings from the kitchen, and regularly met outside our door, where he had no doubt that august body would be found at the present moment. As this was for the convenience of listening to our stories, he submitted that they might be suffered to come in, and hear them more pleasantly.

To this we one and all yielded a ready assent, and the party being discovered as Jack had supposed, and invited to walk in, entered (though not without great confusion at having been detected) and were accommodated with chairs at a little distance.

Then, the lamp being trimmed, the fire well-stirred and burning brightly, the hearth clean swept, the curtains closely drawn, the clock wound up, we entered on our new story – BARNABY RUDGE.

B. DICKENS'S ANNOUNCEMENT TO HIS READERS OF THE CONCLUSION OF *MASTER HUMPHREY'S CLOCK*, OCTOBER 1841

In October 1841, Dickens announced to his readers that *Master Humphrey's Clock* would come to an end with the conclusion of *Barnaby Rudge* and in three revealing paragraphs showed how frustrating he found the rigours of weekly publication. The manuscript draft and corrected proof of the address can be found in the Forster Collection in the Victoria and Albert Museum. (This text is taken from John Butt and Kathleen Tillotson, *Dickens at Work* (London: Methuen, 1957), pp. 88–9.)

I should not regard the anxiety, the close confinement, or the constant attention, inseparable from the weekly form of publication (for to commune with you, in any form, is to me a labour of love), if I had found it advantageous to the conduct of my stories, the elucidation of my meaning, or the gradual development of my characters. But I have not done so. I have often felt cramped and confined in a very irksome and harassing degree, by the space in which I have been constrained to move. I have wanted you to know more at once than I could tell you; and it has frequently been of the greatest importance to my cherished intention, that you should do so. I have been sometimes strongly tempted (and have been at some pains to resist the temptation) to hurry incidents on, lest they should appear to you who waited from week to week, and had not, like me, the result and purpose in your minds, too long delayed. In a word, I have found this form of publication most anxious, perplexing, and difficult. I cannot bear these jerking confidences which are no sooner begun than ended, and no sooner ended than begun again.

Many passages in a tale of any length, depend materially for their interest on the intimate relation they bear to what has gone before, or to what is to follow. I sometimes found it difficult when I issued thirty-two closely-printed pages once a month, to sustain in your mind this needful connexion; in the present form of publication it is often, especially in the first half of a story, quite impossible to preserve it sufficiently through the current numbers. And although in my progress I am gradually able to set you right, and to show you what my meaning has been, and to work it out, I see no reason why you should ever be wrong when I have it in my power, by resorting to a better means of communication between us, to prevent it.

Considerations of immediate profit and advantage, ought, in such a case, to be of secondary importance. *They* would lead me, at all hazards, to hold my present course. But, for the reasons I have just now mentioned, I have, after long consideration, and with especial reference to the next new Tale I bear in my mind, arrived at the conclusion that it will be better to abandon this scheme of publication, in favour of our old and well-tried plan, which has only twelve gaps in a year, instead of fifty-two.

C. AT THE END OF *BARNABY RUDGE*, FROM *MASTER HUMPHREY'S CLOCK*, NO. 88, 27 NOVEMBER 1841

At the conclusion of *Barnaby Rudge*, which was also the final number of *Master Humphrey's Clock*, Dickens rapidly wrapped up the narrative framework that he had established so carefully in the journal's opening numbers. Humphrey reflects briefly on the power of time and memory, and we then learn that he has died, leaving his property, apart from some charitable legacies, to the Deaf Gentleman and Jack Redburn. Mr

Pickwick and the Wellers make their farewell, and the final words are those of the Deaf Gentleman who is 'From certain allusions which Jack has dropped, to his having been deserted and cast off in early life, ... inclined to believe that some passages of his youth may possibly be shadowed out in the history of Mr Chester and his son'. After this intriguing, if rather implausible, suggestion, we learn that: 'The chamber ... is deserted: our happy hour of meeting strikes no more: the chimney corner has grown cold: and MASTER HUMPHREY'S CLOCK has stopped for ever.'

NOTES

1. *Mr Miles*: Owen Miles, a former merchant and one of Humphrey's friends. See A Note on the Text and Illustrations for house styling applied here.

2. *the single gentleman's name*: The brother of Little Nell's grandfather in *The Old Curiosity Shop*, who arrives too late to save her, is known as the 'single gentleman'.

3. *St Paul's*: St Paul's Cathedral, designed by Sir Christopher Wren and completed in 1710.

4. *Mr Pickwick ... Jack and my deaf friend*: Members of Master Humphrey's circle: Mr Pickwick, whose adventures in *The Pickwick Papers* (1837) had made Dickens's reputation, was revived, not altogether successfully, in the early numbers of *Master Humphrey's Clock*; Jack Redburn is Humphrey's 'librarian, secretary, steward, and first minister: director of all my affairs and inspector-general of my household'.

5. *money-changers ... the Temple*: 'And Jesus went into the temple of God, and cast out all them that sold and bought in the temple, and overthrew the tables of the moneychangers, and the seats of them that sold doves' (Matthew 21:12).

6. *Day of Judgment*: See note 3 to ch. 23.

7. *Mr Weller's Watch*: Dickens also revived Mr Pickwick's celebrated servant, Sam Weller, and his father, Tony. While Humphrey, Pickwick and their friends meet upstairs, Tony Weller convenes a parallel group of storytellers, known as 'Mr Weller's Watch', in the servants' quarters.

Appendix III: Preface to the Cheap Edition (1849)

As it is Mr Waterton's opinion that ravens are gradually becoming extinct in England,[1] I offer a few words here about mine.

The raven in this story[2] is a compound of two great originals, of whom I have been, at different times, the proud possessor. The first was in the bloom of his youth, when he was discovered in a modest retirement in London, by a friend of mine, and given to me. He had from the first, as Sir Hugh Evans says of Anne Page,[3] 'good gifts,' which he improved by study and attention in a most exemplary manner. He slept in a stable – generally on horseback – and so terrified a Newfoundland dog by his preternatural sagacity, that he has been known, by the mere superiority of his genius, to walk off unmolested with the dog's dinner, from before his face. He was rapidly rising in acquirements and virtues, when, in an evil hour, his stable was newly painted. He observed the workmen closely, saw that they were careful of the paint, and immediately burned to possess it. On their going to dinner, he ate up all they had left behind, consisting of a pound or two of white lead; and this youthful indiscretion terminated in death.

While I was yet inconsolable for his loss, another friend of mine in Yorkshire discovered an older and more gifted raven at a village public-house, which he prevailed upon the landlord to part with for a consideration, and sent up to me. The first act of this Sage, was, to administer to the effects of his predecessor, by disinterring all the cheese and halfpence he had buried in the garden – a work of immense labour and research, to which he devoted all the energies of his mind. When he had achieved this task, he applied himself to the acquisition of stable language, in which he soon became such an adept, that he would perch outside my window and drive imaginary horses with great skill, all day. Perhaps even I never saw him at his best, for his former master sent his duty with him, 'and if I wished the bird to come out very strong, would I be so good as show him a drunken man' – which I never did, having (unfortunately) none but sober people at hand. But I could hardly have respected him more, whatever the stimulating influences of this sight might have been. He had not the least respect, I am sorry to say, for me in return, or for anybody but the cook; to whom he was attached – but only, I fear, as a Policeman might have been. Once, I met him unexpectedly, about half-a-mile off, walking down the middle of the public street, attended by a pretty large crowd, and spontaneously exhibiting the whole of his accomplishments. His gravity under those trying circumstances, I never can forget, nor the extraordinary gallantry with which, refusing to be brought home, he defended himself behind a pump, until overpowered by numbers. It may have been that he was too bright a genius to live long, or it may have been that he took some pernicious substance into his bill, and thence into his maw – which is not improbable, seeing that he new-pointed the greater part of the garden-wall by digging out the mortar, broke countless squares of glass by scraping away the putty all round the frames, and tore up and swallowed, in splinters, the greater part of a wooden staircase of six steps and a landing – but after some three years he too was taken ill, and died before the kitchen fire. He kept his eye to the last upon the meat as it roasted, and suddenly turned over on his back with a sepulchral cry of 'Cuckoo!' Since then I have been ravenless.[4]

Of the story of BARNABY RUDGE itself, I do not think I can say anything here, more to the purpose than the following passages from the original Preface.

'No account of the Gordon Riots having been to my knowledge introduced into any Work of Fiction, and the subject presenting very extraordinary and remarkable features, I was led to project this Tale.

'It is unnecessary to say, that those shameful tumults, while they reflect indelible disgrace upon the time in which they occurred, and all who had act or part in them, teach a good lesson. That what we falsely call a religious cry is easily raised by men who have no religion, and who in their daily practice set at nought the commonest principles of right and wrong; that it is begotten of intolerance and persecution; that it is senseless, besotted, inveterate, and unmerciful; all History teaches us. But perhaps we do not know it in our hearts too well, to profit by even so humble an example as the "No Popery" riots of Seventeen Hundred and Eighty.

'However imperfectly those disturbances are set forth in the following pages, they are impartially painted by one who has no sympathy with the Romish Church, although he acknowledges, as most men do, some esteemed friends among the followers of its creed.

'It may be observed that, in the description of the principal outrages, reference has been had to the best authorities of that time, such as they are; and that the account given in this Tale, of all the main features of the Riots, is substantially correct.

'It may be further remarked, that Mr Dennis's allusions to the flourishing condition of his trade in those days, have their foundation in Truth, and not in the Author's fancy. Any file of old Newspapers, or odd volume of the Annual Register, will prove this, with terrible ease.

'Even the case of Mary Jones, dwelt upon with so much pleasure by the same character, is no effort of invention. The facts were stated, exactly as they are stated here, in the House of Commons. Whether they afforded as much entertainment to the merry gentlemen assembled there, as some other most affecting circumstances of a similar nature mentioned by Sir Samuel Romilly,[5] is not recorded.'

That the case of Mary Jones may speak the more emphatically for itself, I now subjoin it, as related by SIR WILLIAM MEREDITH[6] in a speech in Parliament, 'on Frequent Executions,' made in 1777.

'Under this act,' the Shop-lifting Act, 'one Mary Jones was executed, whose case I shall just mention; it was at the time when press-warrants were issued, on the alarm about Falkland Islands.[7] The woman's husband was pressed, their goods seized for some debts of his, and she, with two small children, turned into the streets a-begging. It is a circumstance not to be forgotten, that she was very young (under nineteen), and most remarkably handsome. She went to a linen-draper's shop, took some coarse linen off the counter, and slipped it under her cloak; the shopman saw her, and she laid it down: for this she was hanged. Her defence was (I have the trial in my pocket), "that she had lived in credit, and wanted for nothing, till a press-gang came and stole her husband from her; but, since then, she had no bed to lie on; nothing to give her children to eat; and they were almost naked; and perhaps she might have done something wrong, for she hardly knew what she did." The parish officers testified the truth of this story; but it seems, there had been a good deal of shop-lifting about Ludgate; an example was thought necessary; and this woman was hanged for the comfort and satisfaction of shopkeepers in Ludgate Street. When brought to receive sentence, she behaved in such a frantic manner, as proved her mind to be in a distracted and desponding state; and the child was sucking at her breast when she set out for Tyburn.'

LONDON,
    March, 1849.

NOTES

1. *Mr Waterton's ... extinct in England*: Charles Waterton (1782–1865), naturalist and author of three sets of essays on natural history. Dickens owned a copy of his *Essays on Natural History, Chiefly Ornithology* (1838), with this argument that the raven was becoming extinct.

2. *The raven in this story*: Dickens owned three different ravens in the 1840s. The first, called Grip, died in March 1841 and was the subject of a number of letters by Dickens to his friends (see *The Letters of Charles Dickens, Volume 2, 1840–1*, ed. Madeline House and Graham Storey (Oxford: Clarendon Press, 1969), pp. 230–34, 266–7). He was then stuffed and, after Dickens's death, sold at auction for £126. He is now on display in the Rare Book Department of the Free Library of Philadelphia. His replacement was 'comparitively of weak intellects' (*Letters of Charles Dickens*, p. 304) but was replaced after his death by a third 'Yorkshire' raven 'before whom *the* raven (the dead one) sinks into insignificance' (*Letters of Charles Dickens*, p. 412).

3. *Sir Hugh Evans says of Anne Page*: Slender says: 'I know the young gentlewoman; she has good gifts'; and Evans responds: 'Seven hundred pounds, and possibilities, is goot gifts' *Merry Wives of Windsor*, I.i.54–5 (Alexander edition).

4. *ravenless*: The 1858 Library Edition replaces this sentence with Dicken's commemoration of a later bird: 'After this mournful deprivation, I was, for a long time, ravenless. The kindness of another friend at length provided me with another raven; but he is not a genius. He leads the life of a hermit, in my little orchard, on the summit of SHAKESPEARE'S Gad's Hill; he has no relish for society; he gives no evidence of ever cultivating his mind; and he has picked up nothing but meat since I have known him – except the faculty of barking like a dog.' Gad's Hill Place, near Rochester, was Dickens's home from 1857.

5. *Mary Jones . . . Sir Samuel Romilly*: See notes 3 and 4 to 1841 preface.

6. SIR WILLIAM MEREDITH: (d. 1790), third baronet, Whig politician and MP. Dickens quotes from Meredith's speech in the House of Commons, 13 May 1777, which argued against the death penalty on the grounds of its ineffectiveness and cruelty.

7. *Falkland Islands*: In the South Atlantic, about 300 miles from the coast of South America. The British garrison, established in 1765, was expelled by the Spanish in 1770 and restored in 1771.

Appendix IV: Running Titles from the Charles Dickens Edition (1867–8)

The Charles Dickens Edition of Dickens's works (1867–8) includes running heads on right-hand pages; a Prospectus, which remarks upon the author's 'present watchfulness over his own Edition', indicates that they were composed by Dickens himself (*Athenaeum*, 4 May 1867, p. 600; Robert L. Patten, *Charles Dickens and His Publishers* (Oxford: Clarendon Press, 1978, pp. 311–12)). Later editions sometimes draw upon the running heads, adapting them as convenient. They are given here in their original form.

CHAPTER 1 Maypole Company.
 Maypole Talk.
 On such a night as this.
CHAPTER 2 Rough Riding.
 Gabriel Varden.
CHAPTER 3 Joe Willet, the boy.
 A man lying on the road.
 Barnaby's foregone conclusion.
CHAPTER 4 The Locksmith's 'Prentice.
 About young Mr. Chester.
 The Green-eyed Monster.
CHAPTER 5 Who is it?
CHAPTER 6 The Widow's Secret.
 How it happened.
 The Locksmith lies.
CHAPTER 7 Domestic Bliss.
CHAPTER 8 Sim Tappertit.
 The 'Prentice's Glory.
 Solemnities of the 'Prentice Knights.
CHAPTER 9 Miss Miggs.
 Miss Miggs's watch.
CHAPTER 10 A Guest at the Maypole.
 The Maypole's Messenger.
 Barnaby's late.

CHAPTER 11 Hugh.
            Mr. Haredale arrives.
CHAPTER 12 Mr. Haredale and Mr. Chester.
            Quite a good understanding.
CHAPTER 13 The Boy again.
            The Warren.
            Diplomacy of Miss Miggs.
CHAPTER 14 Respecting Dolly.
            Comfortable in Bed.
CHAPTER 15 Father and Son.
            Family affairs.
            A Parent's blessing.
CHAPTER 16 A Spectral Man.
CHAPTER 17 Again, who is it?
            Barnaby and Grip.
            Barnaby thinks it must be his Birthday.
            Barnaby used as a lever.
CHAPTER 18 A late Lodger.
CHAPTER 19 Mrs. V.
            Never faint, my darling.
            The Maypole Bar.
CHAPTER 20 Dolly and Miss Haredale.
            The bracelet and the bushes.
CHAPTER 21 Dolly frightened and rescued.
            What was he like?
CHAPTER 22 Roads not safe.
            Duett for female voices.
CHAPTER 23 Mr. Chester on Lord Chesterfield.
            Valentine and Orson.
            Orson tamed.
CHAPTER 24 A Friend desires a conference.
            Mr. Tappertit comes to the point.
CHAPTER 25 The first time and the last.
            Strange riddles.
            A Sad spot.
CHAPTER 26 Quite at home.
CHAPTER 27 To Clerkenwell!
            A perfect character.
            A mere matter of heart.
CHAPTER 28 Hugh asleep on the stairs.
            Patron and Client.
CHAPTER 29 John Willet and his retainer.
            Mr. Chester and Miss Haredale.
            Lord Chesterfield's letters.

CHAPTER 30 The irrepressible boy.
The boy turns – like the worm.

CHAPTER 31 A recruiting Serjeant.
Good-Bye to the Golden Key.
Enlisted.

CHAPTER 32 Mr. Chester blushes.

CHAPTER 33 Glories of the Maypole Kitchen.
Maypole ahoy!
Solomon Daisy's fright.

CHAPTER 34 John Willet and Hugh.
Hugh drinks a toast.

CHAPTER 35 Lord George Gordon and Suite.
Lodged in state at the Maypole.
Called, chosen, and faithful.

CHAPTER 36 Make a note of Dennis.
More Seed for Sowing.

CHAPTER 37 The Holy Cause.
A representative man.
Mr. Dennis's vested interests.

CHAPTER 38 Mr. Dennis's sentiments, all over.

CHAPTER 39 Adhesion of the United Bull-dogs.
Hugh Joins the Brotherhood.
Mr. Dennis's Wardrobe.

CHAPTER 40 Sir John Chester, M.P.
Orson examined and dismissed.

CHAPTER 41 The Harmonious Locksmith.
Dolly Varden still!
Hysterical magnanimity of Miss Miggs.
The Locksmith's Mission.

CHAPTER 42 A grim Watchman.

CHAPTER 43 The No-Popery Cry arises.
Freedom among friends.
A stone from an unseen hand.

CHAPTER 44 The Green Lanes.
Muster Gashford's health!

CHAPTER 45 All is not gold that glitters.
There are several sorts of blindness.

CHAPTER 46 Blind, but open-eyed.
Au revoir!

CHAPTER 47 Two Poor Travellers.
The old school.

CHAPTER 48 Arrival among the Cockades.
Barnaby enrolled.
Barnaby made a Banner Bearer.

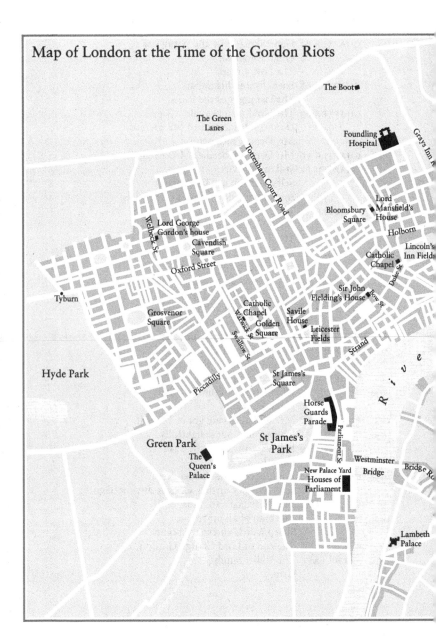

Map of London at the Time of the Gordon Riots

The Boot

The Green Lanes

Foundling Hospital

Grays Inn R

Tottenham Court Road

Lord Mansfield's House

Bloomsbury Square

Holborn

Lord George Gordon's house

Welbeck St

Cavendish Square

Lincoln's Inn Field

Oxford Street

Catholic Chapel

Duke St

Tyburn

Sir John Fielding's House

Bow St

Grosvenor Square

Catholic Chapel

Savile House

Warwick St

Golden Square

Leicester Fields

Swallow St

Strand

Hyde Park

St James's Square

River

Piccadilly

Horse Guards Parade

Parliament St

Green Park

St James's Park

The Queen's Palace

Westminster Bridge

Bridge R

New Palace Yard

Houses of Parliament

Lambeth Palace

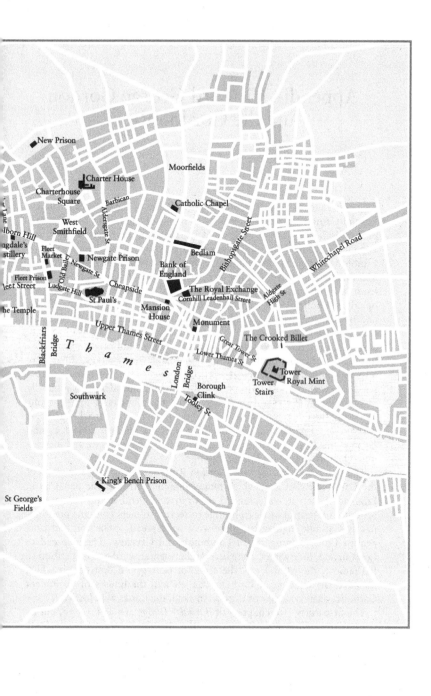

Appendix VI: Lord George Gordon and the Gordon Riots

As a consequence of the Protestant Reformation of the sixteenth century, Roman Catholics were often subject to forms of legal discrimination and persecution. The Corporation Act of 1661 and the Test Acts of 1673 and 1678 debarred Roman Catholics and others who were not members of the Established Church from public office, and prevented them from becoming Members of Parliament. Catholics were not allowed to vote, were excluded from the Universities, suffered punitive taxation and could not worship openly. Catholic priests were forbidden from performing religious offices, and no Roman Catholic could purchase land or inherit it if a Protestant relative made a claim. Although these penal laws were not always strictly enforced, they nevertheless imposed considerable handicaps on Catholics' lives and freedoms. In the course of the eighteenth century, there were attempts to lift some of the restrictions, but these moves often inspired resistance within a population whose 'British' national identity was heavily identified with Protestantism. There were many bursts of anti-Catholic agitation, the most important and dramatic of which occurred in 1780. It was led by Lord George Gordon (b. 1751), the younger son of Cosmo George, third Duke of Gordon, and forms the background to, and increasingly the foreground of, *Barnaby Rudge*.

The immediate cause of the Gordon Riots was the passage in 1778 of the Catholic Relief Act, which removed some anti-Catholic penalties in England. When it was planned in 1779 to extend its provisions into Scotland (in part in order to be able to recruit soldiers from the predominantly Catholic highlands), there were widespread opposition and riots against Catholic property in Edinburgh and Glasgow. These spread to London and, following the unsuccessful presentation of a mass petition to Parliament, the capital was the scene of rioting and destruction which included the burning of Catholic chapels and the houses of prominent Catholics as well as that of Lord Mansfield, the Lord Chief Justice.

The first thirty-two chapters of *Barnaby Rudge* are set in 1775, but its main action takes place in 1780 as the characters become increasingly caught up in the agitation against the Catholic Relief Act and the riots in London. Opposition to the Act was co-ordinated by the Protestant

Association, of which Gordon was President. He was educated at Eton and served as a junior officer in the Navy before his election as MP for the pocket borough of Ludgershall in 1774. His career in Parliament was notable for its independence, and, under his leadership, the Protestant Association demanded the repeal of the Act. The ministry under the Prime Minister, Lord North, made several attempts to bribe Gordon, either directly or through his family, to give up his seat in Parliament or desert the Association. Gordon rejected these offers (and revealed the first to the House of Commons). The figure of Gashford is Dickens's invention.

Matters reached a head when the Association called a mass meeting in St George's Fields, London, on Friday 2 June 1780 (ch. 48), and all marched in four divisions to the Houses of Parliament to present a monster petition, containing more than 100,000 signatures. There the crowd attacked a number of peers and bishops, some of whom were plastered with mud and excrement, but Gordon's motion within the House to consider the petition was rejected overwhelmingly (ch. 49). That evening, two Catholic chapels were attacked and looted (ch. 50), but the next day was relatively calm (ch. 52). On the Sunday, however, the violence broke out even more strongly and more chapels and houses were attacked with no intervention by the Lord Mayor or magistrates. Trouble then spread rapidly through the town and continued over the next few days. On the evening of Tuesday 6 June, Newgate prison was attacked and the prisoners released, as were Bridewell and New Jail in Clerkenwell (chs. 64–6). The following night the other London prisons were attacked and their prisoners released, although an assault on the Bank of England was unsuccessful. That evening also saw the burning of Langdale's distillery, one of the largest in London (chs. 67–8). By Thursday, following a declaration the previous day by the Privy Council, permitting soldiers to open fire on the rioters, the military had established some control, and violence was more sporadic. By 12 June normal life had been re-established and many of the released convicts had been re-arrested. Several hundred people were killed in the course of the riots, and twenty-five executed. (On the public hangman, see n. 4 to ch. 36.)

Gordon was arrested on Friday 9 June and imprisoned in the Tower of London, but at his trial for treason in February 1781, he was found not guilty. In 1786, however, he was arrested on charges of libelling the Queen of France, Marie Antoinette, and the 'Judges and Administration of the Laws of England' (Chapter the Last). He was found guilty, but fled to Amsterdam before sentence was passed. Gordon was discovered seven months later, hiding in a poor house in a Jewish area in Birmingham. He had converted to Judaism at some point (see the prophetic dream in ch. 37) and gave his name as Israel bar Abraham George Gordon. On his return to court, he was sentenced to five years' imprisonment in Newgate and ordered to pay substantial fines for the two libels. On 23 July 1789 he petitioned the National Assembly of France, asking its members to apply for his release from prison, and received a sympathetic reply from its secretary. At the end of the period of imprisonment Gordon was unable or unwilling to produce sureties for his good behaviour and so was returned to Newgate, where he died of jail fever, aged forty-one, in November 1793.

Glossary

SOED *The Shorter Oxford English Dictionary on Historical Principles*, ed. C. T. Onions (Oxford: Clarendon Press, 1973)
For other sources, see introductory note to Notes.

address: Skill, dexterity (ch. 81).

anchorite: Religious hermit or recluse.

area-head: An area is a court-yard enclosed by gates (ch. 35) at the front of a house which gives access to the basement. The area-head is the opening into this court-yard.

bag-wig: Peruke attached to an elaborate silk bag or purse, tied at the back with a silk bow.

basilisk: Fabulous serpent in Hellenistic and Roman legend, also known as the cockatrice, whose look and breath were thought to be fatal to all living creatures, except the weasel.

bearding: Defying or affronting.

blowzed: Slatternly, frowzy, ruddy in the face.

bob-wig: 'A wig having the bottom locks turned up into bobs or short curls' (*SOED*).

boot-jack: Device for pulling off boots.

bradawl or gimlet: Tools for boring small holes.

broadcloth: High quality, plainly woven, dressed, double-width black cloth, mainly used for men's clothes.

browzing: Feeding on leaves and shoots of trees and bushes; in ch. 61 used as a synonym of grazing.

bulk: 'A framework projecting from the front of a shop; a stall' (*SOED*).

bumper with a bead in the middle: Full glass with a foaming head.

burden: Refrain or chorus (chs. 22, 48).

chaf: Banter or ridicule.

chair: Sedan chair, carried on poles (ch. 13).

chuckey: Term of endearment.

chuck-farthing: Gambling game, in which the winner keeps all the coins s/he can successfully throw into a hole.

close borough: Or pocket borough, a parliamentary constituency under the control of a single person or family, usually with a small number of electors who could be readily controlled.

'come upon the county': To make a demand or claim, or become a burden, upon.

'coming over her': Deceiving her.

commission of the peace: Justice of the Peace or magistrate, responsible for the local administration of justice.

composing-draught: Dose of liquid medicine to make someone calm.

conformation: Structure or form.

corpse candles: Lambent flames seen in a churchyard and believed to portend a death or funeral.

crow to pluck: Grievance to sort out, dispute to settle.

crown: Silver coin, worth five shillings (25p).

depone: Declare upon oath.

dog sleep: Light or fitful sleep.

domino: Costume for masquerades, consisting of a loose cloak and a small mask over the top of the face.

drums: A drum was 'an evening assembly of fashionable people at a private house' (*SOED*).

dumb-foundered: Dumbfounded, struck dumb.

dun-haunted: Followed by creditors.

Dutch Pin: Ninepin or skittle.

ell: The universal measure for wool cloth in the medieval period, but varied in length in different places. An English ell was forty-five inches; a Flemish ell twenty-seven inches.

equipage: Furniture, retinue or carriage.

fire-dogs: Horizontal bars placed on either side of a hearth to support burning wood, also known as andirons.

flip: Mixture of small beer, brandy and sugar, heated with a hot iron.

footpads: Highway robbers who worked on foot.

foster-mother: Foster-nurse (ch. 27), rather than adoptive mother.

frail: Sexually unchaste.

frowzy: Unkempt, musty.

fugleman: Soldier, particularly skilled in drill, chosen as an example to his regiment or company; so an orchestrator or rabble-rouser.

full blow: In full blossom.

gave them the wall: Allowed them to pass on the side farthest from the road 'to acknowledge inferiority of station, or to shew courtesy, or to act from fear of reprisal' (Hill).

'Give it mouth': 'A rude request to an actor or orator [to] speak up' (J. C. Hotten, *A Dictionary of Modern Slang, Cant, and Vulgar Words* (London: J. C. Hotten, 1860)).

griffin: In Greek myth, fabulous creature with the body of a lion and the wings of an eagle.

hackney-chairs: Sedan chairs for hire.

half-pay officers: Retired military or naval officers, or those not on active service, who drew half their pay.

hartshorning: Applying hartshorn, a strong-smelling substance deriving from the horns of hart (i.e. deer) and a common source of ammonia.

henbane: The plant *Hyoscyamus niger*; in ch. 9 the drug extracted from it, with narcotic and poisonous properties.

hipped: Morbidly depressed or low-spirited.

hogshead: Large cask of liquor, holding sixty-three old wine gallons, the equivalent of fifty-two and a half imperial gallons.

hooped and furbelowed: Wearing a skirt held out with hoops and covered in trimmings and flounces.

hot purl: Warm beer infused with sugar, spices and gin.

in twig: In a good state, in good fettle: 'I have gone to work this morning in good twig, strong hope, and cheerful spirits' (Pilgrim, 2, p. 198).

indenters: Indentures, a written contract which bound the apprentice to his master for seven years, regulated by the Statute of Artificers of 1563.

jack-towel: Roller-towel.

jade: Originally a worthless horse, it came to be applied to women, sometimes with a playful sense as in ch. 41.

jail fever: Virulent form of typhoid which killed hundreds of Newgate prisoners each year.

javelin-man: Spear- or pike-bearer in the retinue of a sheriff or judge.

journeymen: Those who had successfully completed an apprenticeship to a particular trade, and were therefore superior to apprentices, but were not independent masters.

kennel: Street gutter.

King's evidence: A criminal would give evidence against his fellow-accused in order to gain immunity from prosecution or a more lenient treatment.

knocked up: Awakened (ch. 34).

leads: Sheets of lead forming a roof.

light guinea: A guinea was a gold coin, minted between 1663 and 1813, worth 21s (£1.05). A light guinea would be one short in weight, either through usage or deliberate reduction.

link-boy: Boy employed to carry a link or torch made of tow and pitch to light the street for pedestrians.

loadstone: Oxide of iron with magnetic properties.

mace: Strike with a mace or heavy club.

mere assumptions: Unwarrantable claims.

mooncalf: Foolish, or mooning and absent-minded person.

muffineer: 'A small castor with a perforated top for sprinkling sugar or salt on muffins; also a covered dish to keep muffins hot' (*SOED*).

mumchance: Silent or tongue-tied.

Mussulman: Muslim, follower of Islam.

natural: One naturally deficient in intellect, a fool or idiot.

natural children: Illegitimate children.

odd or even: Gambling game, in which one player holds in his or her hands a small number of hidden pieces, and the opponent tries to guess if there are an odd or even number of them.

off the stones: 'A colloquialism, popular in 1830–1880 for "outside London"' (Hawes).

ordinary: Chaplain of Newgate prison (chs. 16, 77); regular meal at a fixed price in an eating-house or inn (ch. 54).

over-proof: Drink above the standard strength.

packthread: Stout twine for tying up packs or bundles.

pattens: Wooden overshoes.

pent-houses: Sheds, or other structures, usually with a sloping roof, attached to a main building.

pitch and toss: Gambling game, in which pennies are pitched at a target. The winner is the player whose coin comes closest to the target.

pomatums: Pomades, or scented ointments for the skin or hair.

porter's knot: Knotted rope harness worn across the shoulders and back with a loop around the forehead, used by porters for carrying heavy loads.

post octavo: A size of paper smaller than octavo (sheets of paper folded to make 16 pages in books).

poussetting: To dance round and round with joined hands, as in a country dance.

pressed: Press-ganged, compulsorily enlisted in the armed forces.

Progress: A journey in state made by a royal or noble person (ch. 19).

providing yourself: Finding yourself a new job.

puncheons: Large casks for liquids, of varying capacity; used to age spirits, particularly rum.

quadrille: Both a card-game for four players and a square dance, of French origin, for four couples.

quarter-days: 'The four days fixed by custom as marking off the quarters of the year, on which the tenancy of houses usually begins and ends, and the payment of rents and other quarterly charges falls due' (*SOED*).

quartern loaf: Loaf of bread weighing four pounds.

ranger: Gamekeeper.

roasting-jack: Device for turning meat on a spit.

roc: Or rukh, a fabulous bird of stupendous size that appears several times in *The Arabian Nights*.

round-house: Lock-up or place of detention.

runts, fantails, tumblers, and pouters: Kinds of pigeon.

satyr: In Greek myth, a wood-spirit or demon, partly human and partly animal. Satyrs were associated with the god Bacchus, and with sexual license.

scavengers: Street-cleaners or dirt-collectors.

score up: Get drink on credit.

shay: Chaise.

single-stick: Fighting game with a stick held in one hand, like a fencing foil.

slack-baked: Only partly baked, so in ch. 41 of a lighter brown than the Toby's face.

small ale: Weak beer.

smalls: Small-clothes, close-fitting knee-breeches.

spatterdashes: 'A kind of long gaiter or legging made of leather, cloth etc. to keep the trousers or stockings from being spattered, especially in riding' (*SOED*).

standish: Stand containing ink, pens and other writing materials and accessories.

tagrag and bobtail: The rabble. 'Tagrag', from the sixteenth century, is now 'ragtag' (from about 1820).

tags of staylaces: The ends of cords used to tighten a woman's stays or bodice.

tap-room: The room in an inn or public house where drinks are kept on tap.

Tartar: Violent or intractable person; vixen or shrew.

Templars: Inhabitants of the Temple (see note 2 to ch. 15), including law students.

three-bottle man: Someone capable of drinking three bottles of wine at a sitting.

tie-wig: Wig tied with a ribbon at the back.

tipstaff: An Officer of the Court, who had powers of arrest, and so called from his rod tipped with a badge of office.

tiring equipage: Apparatus or case of articles for dressing.

toast in a tankard: Piece of bread, toasted and sometimes spiced, placed in a drink and thought to improve its flavour.

top-sawyers: Men who take the upper position in a saw pit and draw higher wages; hence, one who is superior or comes first.

tosspot: Heavy drinker, drunkard.

travelling post: With post-horses, so express, with speed or haste.

triple bob major: Peal rung on eight bells, repeated three times.

truckle-bed: 'A low bed running on truckles or castors, usually pushed beneath a high or "standing" bed when not in use' (*SOED*).

turnkey: Prison guard in charge of the keys.

two-pair: Second storey.

usquebaugh: Whisky (Irish and Scots Gaelic for Water of Life).

voluntaries: Extempore singing.

worked off: Hanged.

yeoman: Man of respectable standing, below the rank of a gentleman.

Yorkshire cake: 'A speciality of the county, this is a sweet teacake, often toasted and buttered', as in ch. 4 (Hawes).

Notes

I am greatly indebted to previous editions of the novel, in particular those of Gordon Spence for Penguin and Donald Hawes for Everyman, as well as to T. W. Hill for his 'Notes on *Barnaby Rudge*', in the *Dickensian*. I have also found *The Dickens Index*, ed. Nicolas Bentley, Michael Slater and Nina Burgis (Oxford: Oxford University Press, 1990); *The London Encyclopedia*, ed. Ben Weinreb and Christopher Hibbert (London: Macmillan, 1993); and the Pilgrim edition of Dickens's letters, ed. Madeline House, Graham Storey and Kathleen Tillotson, most helpful. The following editions and abbreviations have been used:

Hawes Charles Dickens, *Barnaby Rudge*, ed. Donald Hawes (London: Everyman, 1990)

Hill T. W. Hill, 'Notes on *Barnaby Rudge*', *Dickensian* 50–53 (1954–7)

Pilgrim *The Pilgrim Edition of the Letters of Charles Dickens*, vols. 1 and 2 ed. Madeline House and Graham Storey, (Oxford: Clarendon, 1965, 1969); vol. 4 ed. Kathleen Tillotson (Oxford: Clarendon, 1977)

Spence Charles Dickens, *Barnaby Rudge*, ed. Gordon Spence (London: Penguin, 1973)

(Biblical quotations are from the Authorized Version.)

PREFACE

1. *Work of Fiction*: Thomas Gaspey's novel *The Mystery or, Forty Years Ago* (3 vols, 1820) has three chapters concerned with the Gordon Riots, but it is not clear if Dickens knew of this work. See John Butt and Kathleen Tillotson, '*Barnaby Rudge*: the first projected novel', *Dickens at Work* (London: Methuen, 1957), pp. 77–8.

2. *old Newspapers ... Annual Register*: Dickens names several newspapers of the period in ch. 39 and is known to have consulted the newspapers of 1780 in the British Museum when writing this novel (see Butt and Tillotson, *Dickens at Work*, pp. 84–5). The *Annual Register; or A View of the History, Politics, and Literature For the Year* is a

record of all the notable events of a year, first published in 1759 and edited for many years by Edmund Burke. Dickens owned a set in eighty volumes, 1759–1827 (Pilgrim, 4, p. 717), and is known to have consulted the 1780 number in the writing of *Barnaby Rudge*.

3. *Mary Jones*: 'Was hanged by Edward Dennis, the public hangman, on 16 October 1771 for stealing four pieces of muslin worth £5. 10s.' (Hawes). See ch. 37 and Appendix III. For similar cases see Peter Linebaugh, *The London Hanged: Crime and Civil Society in the Eighteenth Century* (London: Allen Lane, 1991), pp. 338–9.

4. *Sir Samuel Romilly*: (1757–1818), criminal law reformer who made great efforts to lessen the severity of the English criminal law.

5. *Mr Rogers ... knew not what.'*: Samuel Rogers (1763–1855), poet and friend of Dickens. In ch. 72 of *The Old Curiosity Shop* (which was dedicated to Rogers), Dickens describes how, following Nell's death, her grandfather 'pined and moped away the time, and wandered here and there as seeking something, and had no comfort'. 'And long might'st ... knew not what' comes from Rogers's poem 'Ginevra' from *Italy* (1822–8), ll. 78–80. Appropriately, the poem describes the sudden death on her wedding-night of Ginevra, and the grief of her father at the loss. The italics are Dickens's.

CHAPTER THE FIRST

1. *Epping Forest ... the Maypole*: The forest is a remnant of ancient woodland, north-east of London; through enclosure, it had shrunk to 12,000 acres by 1777 and by the mid-nineteenth century to half of that. The Standard is 'A water-standard at the junction of Cornhill with Gracechurch street, Bishopsgate, and Leadenhall Street. Though the water had ceased to flow by 1603, the Standard remained for many years after, and was used as a point of measurement of distances from the City' (Spence); (see also note 1 to ch. 18). The Maypole is probably based on the old King's Head Inn, Chigwell. On 25 March 1841, Dickens wrote to John Forster: 'Chigwell, my dear fellow, is the greatest place in the world. Name your day for going. Such a delicious old inn opposite the churchyard – such a lovely ride – such beautiful forest scenery – such an out of the way, rural, place – such a sexton!' (Pilgrim, 2, p. 243).

2. *sixty-six years ago*: In 1775, sixty-six years before the publication of *Barnaby Rudge* in 1841. In later editions, Dickens amends the phrase to 'at that time' (but not in chapter 4).

3. *King Henry the Eighth ... Queen Elizabeth*: Henry VIII (1491–1547), second son of Henry VII, and King of England from 1509. Elizabeth I (1533–1603), Queen of England, daughter of Henry VIII and Anne Boleyn, proclaimed Queen in 1588 in succession to Mary I, and a heroine to Protestants (see note 3 to ch. 35).

4. *Chigwell*: Village in Essex, twelve miles north-east of London and a favourite resort for Londoners. Dickens describes an expedition to Chigwell in 'The Young Ladies' Young Gentleman', *Sketches of Young Gentlemen* (1838).

5. *Warren*: A significant name for Dickens, who as a boy had worked at Warren's Blacking Warehouse at Hungerford Stairs and later Covent Garden.

6. *King George*: King George III (1738–1820), grandson of George II and King of Great Britain and Ireland from 1760.

7. *swine ... scattering pearls before*: From the Sermon on the Mount: 'neither cast ye your pearls before swine' (Matthew 7:6).

8. *King George the Second*: (1683–1760), son of George I and King of Great Britain and Ireland from 1727.

9. *young princes*: King George III and Queen Charlotte had nine sons, seven of whom were born by 1775.

CHAPTER THE SECOND

1. *who ride the whirlwind and direct the storm*: From Joseph Addison's poem 'The Campaign' (1705), ll. 290–91: 'And, pleased th'Almighty's orders to perform, / Rides in the whirlwind, and directs the storm.'

CHAPTER THE THIRD

1. *Great Mogul*: The Great (or Grand) Mogul was the European name for the Emperor of Delhi, and was popularly used to mean any autocratic or despotic ruler. The mogul dynasty ruled large parts of India from the early sixteenth century, and the last Mogul Emperor was exiled by the British in 1857.

CHAPTER THE FOURTH

1. *Clerkenwell ... Charter House*: Clerkenwell is a suburb of London, north and slightly uphill from the City of London, rapidly urbanized in the eighteenth century and a centre for clock- and watch-makers, and other craftsmen. The Charter House is a historic school and hospital in Clerkenwell, founded in 1611, and originally a Carthusian monastery.

2. *Highgate ... Whitechapel*: Highgate is a village about five miles to the north of the City, Whitechapel an area just to the east of the boundary of the City.

3. *New River*: Channel more than thirty-eight miles long cut in the early

seventeenth century to bring spring water from Amwell and Chadwell in Hertfordshire to London. The New River Head was at Clerkenwell (ch. 67).

4. *'Prentice's Garland ... Guide to the Gallows*: 'A number of books with similar titles were published, e.g., *The Apprentice's Vade Mecum* (1734), *The Apprentices' Companion* (1795) and *The Warbler* (1772)' (Hawes).

5. *the liver of Prometheus*: In Greek mythology, Prometheus was imprisoned on a rock in the Caucasus by Zeus, for daring to bring fire to mankind. His liver was eaten every day by an eagle, and grew back each night.

6. *George Barnwell*: In the play *The History of George Barnwell, or The London Merchant* (1731) by George Lillo (1693–1739), George Barnwell is a London apprentice who is seduced by the prostitute Sarah Millwood and induced to rob his master and kill his uncle. The two villains then quarrel, inform on each other and are hanged. Dickens refers to the play several times in his work, most notably in ch. 15 of *Great Expectations*.

7. *Lion Heart*: King Richard the First (1157–99) was known as Coeur de Lion or Lion Heart.

8. *Carlisle House*: In Soho Square, occupied from 1760 by Theresa Cornelys, a Viennese opera singer and courtesan, it was a popular and fashionable location for dancing, cards, operatic concerts and masquerades.

9. *Protestant Manual*: *The Protestant Manual of Christian Devotions, composed of instructions, offices, and forms of prayer, in a plain, rational and scriptural method, etc.*, 2 pts (London, 1750).

CHAPTER THE FIFTH

1. *Southwark ... London Bridge*: Southwark is a London borough, south of the Thames, and the main entry to London from that direction. Old London Bridge, the first stone bridge across the Thames, was built in 1176 and remodelled several times, particularly in 1758–62, when the two central arches were replaced with a single navigation span. (It was finally replaced in 1831.)

2. *the patient composure of long effort and quiet resignation*: cf. 'he is one by whom / All effort seems forgotten, one to whom / Long patience has such mild composure given, / That patience now doth seem a thing, of which / He hath no need', William Wordsworth (1770–1850), 'Old Man Travelling: Animal Tranquility and Decay, A Sketch', ll. 8–12, in *Lyrical Ballads* (1798). The poem appears in the same volume as Wordsworth's 'The Idiot Boy', which has often been compared to Barnaby Rudge.

3. *smear of blood*: The doctrine of maternal impression, which was widely current in the nineteenth century, was that the mother's mental impressions could be transmitted to the child in the womb.

CHAPTER THE SIXTH

1. *accommodating his action to his speech*: cf. *Hamlet* III.ii.17. See also chs. 24, 39, 70.
2. *a large raven*: See Appendix III (and its note 2).

CHAPTER THE SEVENTH

1. *wise . . . neutral*: *Macbeth* II.iii.108–9.

CHAPTER THE EIGHTH

1. *Barbican*: Street leading off Aldersgate in the City of London, named after a fortification or watchtower that once stood there. In the eighteenth century, it was inhabited by tradesmen, especially new and second-hand clothes dealers.
2. *ready for his reception*: 'Dickens based his picture of trade union ritual on various reports of trials of striking union members charged with conspiracy or with administering illegal oaths. The Annual Register for 1838 summarizes what was discovered about union rituals from the union trials of the 1830s and the Select Committee on Combinations of 1837–8' (Patrick Brantlinger, *The Spirit of Reform: British Literature and Politics 1832–1867* (Cambridge: Harvard University Press, 1977), p. 92). E. P. Thompson, in *The Making of the English Working Class* (Harmondsworth: Penguin, 1968), p. 185, notes that a secret committee of the London Corresponding Society met in the cellars of Furnival's Inn in the 1790s, where Dickens was to live some forty years later. For a description of trade union initiation ceremonies, see Brantlinger, pp. 92–3 and Thompson p. 559.
3. *Atlas-wise*: In Greek mythology, Atlas was a Titan, the son of Iapetus and Clymene, who held up the sky on his shoulders.
4. *Dutch cheese . . . eating Cheshire sir, himself*: Dutch cheese was a small round cheese made on the Continent from skimmed milk; Cheshire a traditional English cheese, presumably considered to be of higher quality.
5. *marry her at the Fleet*: Irregular marriages took place without a licence within the Fleet prison and its environs from the late sixteenth

century until they were outlawed in 1753. This is therefore an anachronistic reference by Dickens or Mark Gilbert.

6. *the court of aldermen*: The Court of Aldermen of the City of London dates from 1200. Aldermen represented wards of the City, were justices of the peace responsible for the administration of justice and had a particular responsibility for the regulation of the City Livery Companies.

7. *Temple Bar*: At the junction of Fleet Street and the Strand, Temple Bar was rebuilt by Christopher Wren in the early 1670s and marked the western limits of the City of London. Until the mid eighteenth century, the heads of executed traitors were displayed there. In ch. 1 of *Bleak House*, it is described as 'That leaden-headed old obstruction, appropriate ornament for the threshold of a leaden-headed old corporation.' (It was removed to Theobalds Park in Hertfordshire in 1878 as it had become an obstruction to traffic.)

8. *Fleet Market*: Meat and vegetable market, designed by George Dance, between Fleet Street and Holborn. It was built in the 1730s on top of the Fleet Ditch and cleared in the 1820s.

CHAPTER THE NINTH

1. *undone*: Undressed, but Dickens is playing on its sense of 'ruined by seduction'.

2. *green as chemists' lamps*: 'Chemists displayed large illuminated green, yellow, red and sometimes blue glass bottles in their windows' (Hawes).

3. *mourning-coach and feathers*: I.e. a more elaborate funeral, with a carriage drawn by horses with ostrich plumes dyed black on their heads.

CHAPTER THE ELEVENTH

1. *passing bad Notes*: Circulating forged banknotes, a capital offence at this period.

CHAPTER THE THIRTEENTH

1. *Black Lion*: The Black Lion Inn was at 75, Whitechapel Road in the East End, now demolished.

2. *the Monument*: Tall Doric column erected 1671–6 to commemorate the Great Fire of London. A popular place for suicide, it features in *Nicholas Nickleby*, *Martin Chuzzlewit* and *Little Dorrit*.

3. *publicans coupled with sinners*: Publicans in the Bible are tax-gatherers

and much-hated figures, often coupled with sinners, as in Matthew 9:11, Mark 2:16, Luke 5:30. Mrs Varden here confuses them with inn-keepers.

CHAPTER THE FIFTEENTH

1. *'Who enters . . . noise behind'*: Possible echo of the inscription at the gate of Hell in *Inferno* by Dante (1265–1321), III, 1: 'Lasciate ogni speranza voi ch'entrata' ('Abandon all hope, ye who enter').

2. *the Temple . . . the Strand . . . Fountain Court*: *Temple*: The Inner and Middle Temples are two of the Inns of Court (see note 7 to ch. 67), and the residence of lawyers since the fourteenth century. The Temple, named after the Temple Church which was built by the Knights Templar in 1185, is located between Fleet Street and the Thames. It frequently appears in Dickens's work, most notably in *Martin Chuzzlewit*, *Our Mutual Friend* and *A Tale of Two Cities*. *The Strand*: Important street, originally a bridlepath running alongside the north bank of the River Thames, which links Westminster to the City of London. *Fountain Court*: Court in the Middle Temple, with a single-jet fountain, which also features in chapter 45 of *Martin Chuzzlewit*.

3. *Paper Buildings*: Part of the Inner Temple, erected in 1610 and rebuilt in 1838.

4. *Valentine and Orson*: An old French romance and a favourite children's story. Valentine and Orson are twin brothers, nephews of King Pepin. Orson is carried off by a bear and becomes a wild man, whereas Valentine is brought up at court and becomes an elegant gentleman.

5. *centaurs*: Wild and bestial creatures in Greek mythology, having the upper part of human beings and the lower part of horses. Centaurs often drink to excess and are representative of wildness and animal desire.

CHAPTER THE SIXTEENTH

1. *the watch*: Patrolled and guarded the streets of the town, and announced the hours. Although from 1705 the City had the first professional paid watch in the country, the members of it were old, otherwise unemployable and notoriously ineffectual. It was only with the establishment of the Metropolitan Police in 1829 that a more efficient force was established; the watch system was finally abandoned ten years later. See also ch. 49.

2. *Tyburn*: The main place of execution in London between 1388 and 1783; the location is marked by a stone at the junction of Edgware Road, Oxford Street and Bayswater Road.

3. *they who dealt in bodies with the surgeons*: It was illegal at this

period for surgeons to obtain bodies for dissection and so a lucrative but illegal trade arose in grave-robbing.

4. *turnpike*: From the mid seventeenth century onwards, turnpike trusts were permitted to erect gates and tollbars on roads and travellers were required to pay a toll to pass through. By the mid eighteenth century, there were turnpikes on all the main roads into and around London.

CHAPTER THE SEVENTEENTH

1. '*Polly put the ket* –': 'Polly put the kettle on', a well-known nursery rhyme.

CHAPTER THE EIGHTEENTH

1. *Cornhill ... Smithfield*: Cornhill is the highest hill in the City, and Smithfield was the City's largest meat market. It was not until 1855 that the sale of live cattle and horses was stopped.

2. *the city jail*: This is most likely to be the Bridewell prison on the banks of the Fleet River, which was under the control of the City rather than the Crown. Originally a palace, Bridewell became a prison in 1556, was rebuilt after the Great Fire and eventually closed in 1855. Alternatively, it could be one of the sheriff's prisons, the Poultry Compter or the Wood Street Compter.

CHAPTER THE NINETEENTH

1. *love among the roses*: Hill quotes a ballad by J. C. Doyle, 'Young love flew to the Paphian bower ... / The Graces there were cutting posies, / And found young Love among the roses' (Hill).

2. *her maiden meditation*: 'In maiden meditation, fancy-free', *A Midsummer Night's Dream* II.i.164.

3. *the plagues of Egypt*: As described in Exodus 7–11.

4. *Gretna Green*: Village in Dumfriesshire, which lies just north of the River Sark, the dividing line between England and Scotland. Following the Marriage Act of 1754, English couples wishing to marry quickly were obliged to go to Scotland, where the law only required them to declare their wish to marry before witnesses. The marriages were usually performed by the local blacksmith.

5. *hath been informed and verily believes*: Dickens is here parodying legal jargon.

CHAPTER THE TWENTIETH

1. *crossed afterwards*: Because of the cost of postage, it was common in the period to write both down the page and then across it, at a right angle.

CHAPTER THE TWENTY-FIRST

1. *the nothingness of good works*: 'Justification by faith and not by works was an essential component of Protestant doctrine' (Hawes).

CHAPTER THE TWENTY-SECOND

1. *Saint Paul's*: St Paul's Cathedral, designed by Sir Christopher Wren and completed in 1710.
2. *a shining light*: John 5:35.
3. *Jezebel*: The infamous wife of Ahab, King of Israel (1 Kings 16), and used for any wicked woman, or one who used cosmetics.

CHAPTER THE TWENTY-THIRD

1. *Lord Chesterfield*: Philip Dormer Stanhope (1694–1773), fourth Earl of Chesterfield. His *Letters to his son Philip Stanhope* gave instruction in manners and morals and were published after Chesterfield's death in two and then four volumes in 1774. Chester is therefore reading a recently published book, and a popular one. (Eleven editions were published in London and Dublin by the end of the century.) As David Roberts notes, the principles he taught

proved easy to caricature: self-interest above morality, adultery above marriage, cynicism above patriotism, breeding above all. Chesterfield badgers his son to find a mature society beauty to 'polish' him; tells him to seem trustworthy but never to trust; advises him that his dancing-master is more important than Aristotle. He favours smutty repartee with fifteen-year-old girls; prefers deceitful high-society liaisons, sometimes two or more at a time, to affairs of the heart; encourages the boy to enjoy his father's old flames.

(*Lord Chesterfield's Letters*, ed. David Roberts
(Oxford: Oxford University Press, 1992), pp. x–xi)

Samuel Johnson famously described the letters as teaching 'the morals of a whore, and the manners of a dancing-master' (James Boswell, *The Life of Samuel Johnson*, ed. R. W. Chapman (Oxford: Oxford University Press, 1970), p. 188).

2. *the Graces*: Goddesses of fertility in Greek mythology, usually said to be three in number: Aglaia (Brightness), Euphrosyne (Joyfulness) and Thalia (Bloom). Often associated with Aphrodite, the goddess of love.

3. *Day of Judgment*: The end of the world in Christian belief, when there will be a universal judgement of the living and the dead. See 2 Peter 2:9. Also 'the last day' (ch. 68).

4. *the cart and ladder*: Prisoners condemned to death would travel to the place of execution in a cart and ascend the scaffold by a ladder.

CHAPTER THE TWENTY-FOURTH

1. *the Gunpowder Plot*: Conspiracy of English Roman Catholics, led by Robert Catesby, to blow up the Houses of Parliament on 5 November 1605.

2. *E. C.*: Dickens or Sim is making a mistake here, as Chester's initials are 'J. C.', unless, as Spence suggests, 'he is wearing his son's nightcap'.

3. *playing upon him*: cf. *Hamlet* III.ii.352–4.

4. *Horse Guards*: The regiments of the Household Cavalry, which date back to the seventeenth century and are responsible for the protection of the sovereign.

CHAPTER THE TWENTY-SIXTH

1. *hewer of wood and drawer of water*: After Joshua conquered Canaan, the inhabitants of Gibeon attempted to deceive him, and were in consequence made menial bondsmen, 'hewers of wood and drawers of water' (Joshua 9:21–3).

CHAPTER THE TWENTY-SEVENTH

1. *pride . . . one of the seven deadly sins*: The others are avarice, lust, anger, gluttony, envy and sloth.

2. *the church catechism*: From the *Book of Common Prayer*.

3. *wines and fig-trees*: Miggs's pronunciation of the biblical phrase 'vines and fig-trees', found for example in Psalm 105:33, Jeremiah 5:17, Hosea 2:12. She means the wealth and pleasure Mrs Varden brings to the household.

4. *as though she were Hope and that her Anchor*: Hebrews 6:19 refers

to hope as 'an anchor of the soul'; this has given rise to a number of allegorical paintings, to which Dickens alludes here.

5. *the cardinal virtues*: The cardinal (from Latin *cardo*, 'hinge') or natural virtues: prudence, temperance, fortitude and justice.

CHAPTER THE TWENTY-EIGHTH

1. *Covent Garden*: Built in 1639 and at first was one of the most fashionable addresses in London. It soon started to decline with the growth of the fruit and vegetable market from the later seventeenth century. Coffee-houses began to spring up there from the middle of the eighteenth century, of which the best known was the Bedford, frequented by Pope, Fielding, Goldsmith and Boswell. The area was also a centre for gambling dens, Turkish baths and brothels.

CHAPTER THE THIRTY-FIRST

1. *great cry . . . but very little wool*: Adaptation of the proverbial 'Much cry, little wool'.

2. *War-office*: The government department responsible for the Army.

3. *the Crooked Billet in Tower-street*: Eighteenth-century inn near the Tower of London, in fact at No. 1, Little Tower Hill. (It was demolished in 1912.)

4. *Needs must when the devil drives*: *All's Well that Ends Well* I.iii.29.

5. *a temporary accommodation*: If Joe had taken the shilling, he would have enlisted himself.

6. *Since the time of noble Whittington*: Richard Whittington (1358–1423), popularly known as Dick, four times Lord Mayor of London. The popular story of Dick Whittington who turned at the sound of Bow Bells chiming 'turn again Whittington, thrice Lord Mayor of London' cannot be found earlier than 1605. Whittington is mentioned in several Dickens novels, including *Bleak House* and *David Copperfield*.

7. *purse of Fortunatus*: In the German folktale, Fortunatus, a beggar, is given a purse by Fortune which produces an inexhaustible supply of money. The story was made popular in English by Thomas Dekker in *The pleasant Comedie of Old Fortunatus* (1600), and is referred to in several Dickens novels and stories.

8. *adamantine chains*: 'In Adamantine chains and penal fire', Milton, *Paradise Lost* (1667) I, 48.

9. *in his mind's eye . . . sconce*: *Hamlet* I.ii.184. Valerie Gager notes in *Shakespeare and Dickens: The Dynamics of Influence* (Cambridge: Cambridge University Press, 1996), p. 278 that 'Dickens's unusual use of the word "sconce", used by Hamlet at V, i, 99 in a similarly violent

manner, as well as the ghostly beginning and ending of this chapter, strengthen the connection with the play.'

10. *Chatham*: Port and important naval base on the Kent coast, adjacent to the city of Rochester. Dickens spent several years of his childhood in Chatham.

CHAPTER THE THIRTY-SECOND

1. *the soles of their feet*: 'But the dove found no rest for the sole of her foot' (Genesis 8:9).

CHAPTER THE THIRTY-FIFTH

1. *Lord George Gordon*: For his background and life, see Appendix VI. Dickens wrote to John Forster during the composition of the novel:

Say what you please of Gordon, he must have been at heart a kind man, and a lover of the despised and rejected, after his own fashion. He lived upon a small income, and always within it; was known to relieve the necessities of many people; exposed in his place the corrupt attempt of a minister to buy him out of Parliament; and did great charities in Newgate. He always spoke on the people's side, and tried against his muddled brains to expose the profligacy of both parties. (Pilgrim, 2, pp. 294–5)

2. *rising up of the sun to the going down of the same*: 'from the rising of the sun unto the going down thereof' (Psalms 50:1).

3. *Bloody Mary*: Mary I (1516–58), Queen of England, 1553–8, only surviving child of Henry VIII and Catherine of Aragon and a Catholic. She gained the nickname because of her persecution of Protestants, some 300 of whom were executed during her reign. In *A Child's History of England* (1851–3), Dickens wrote: 'as Bloody Queen Mary, she will ever be justly remembered with horror and detestation in Great Britain'.

4. *across the Scottish border*: On the Gordon Riots, see Appendix VI.

5. *'Called and chosen and faithful'*: Taken from Revelation 17:14.

6. *blue cockades, and glorious Queen Besses … and Protestant associations*: Blue cockades were worn by supporters of the Protestant Association, founded in London in February 1779 to oppose Catholic emancipation. Gordon became its president on 12 November of the same year. Queen Bess was an affectionate nickname for Queen Elizabeth I.

CHAPTER THE THIRTY-SIXTH

1. *manna in the wilderness . . . widows' mites*: Manna was the food that miraculously sustained the Israelites between their Exodus from Egypt and their arrival in the Promised Land (Exodus 16:15). A 'mite' is a very small coin; on the widow's mite, see Mark 12:42.

2. *Newgate*: There had been a gaol at Newgate since the twelfth century, but it had been recently rebuilt (1770–78) at a cost of £45,000. It was described by George Crabbe as 'a very large, strong, and beautiful building' (George Crabbe, *The Poetical Works of the Rev. George Crabbe* (London: John Murray, 1851), 1, p. 82).

3. *Bedlam*: Bethlehem Royal Hospital in Moorfields, the most famous of all lunatic asylums. See also chs. 55 and 67.

4. *Dennis the hangman*: The public hangman at this period (1771–86) was Edward Dennis, who was tried on 3 July 1780 for his part in the attack on 7 June on the house of a certain Mr Boggis. His defence was that he was compelled to do so by the mob. He was convicted and condemned to death, but was reprieved and pardoned, to allow him to execute his fellow-rioters. Other than in his name and occupation, Dickens's character does not seem to resemble the historical Dennis.

5. *Welbeck Street*: Gordon lived at 64, Welbeck Street.

6. *He snuffs the battle from afar, like the war-horse*: Job 39:25.

7. *A malignant*: Rebellious, disaffected, a term particularly current during the Protectorate (1653–9) and used by supporters of Parliament and the Commonwealth to describe their political and religious enemies. It was also used as a term by early Protestants to describe the Roman Catholic Church.

8. *in outer darkness*: Matthew 8:12.

CHAPTER THE THIRTY-SEVENTH

1. *false prophets*: Matthew 7:15 and elsewhere.

2. *petitioning Parliament*: In fact the act had already been passed on 3 June 1778. Gordon's petition was to repeal it.

3. *Smithfield market into . . . cauldrons*: Between 1554 and 1558, over 200 Protestants were burned to death at Smithfield (see also note 1 to ch. 18.) in the reign of Mary I.

4. *stocks and stones*: 'When all our fathers worshiped stocks and stones': from Milton's sonnet 'On the Late Massacre in Piedmont' (1655).

5. *three times three*: Three cheers, three times.

6. *Quaker cut*: Simply and severely cut. Quakers, members of the Society of Friends, dress plainly. Gordon, known for the simplicity of his attire, was in mourning following the death of his mother in December 1779.

7. *out in state*: As the public hangman.

8. *Fifty*: A distinct underestimate, as there were more than two hundred capital offences at this period.

9. *I'll have half for myself and Dennis shall have half for himself*: Some criminals were pardoned at this period on condition that they joined the Army or Navy.

CHAPTER THE THIRTY-EIGHTH

1. *houses of Parliament*: In the old Palace of Westminster, destroyed by fire in 1834.

2. *the Boot*: On Cromer Street, rebuilt in 1801. The current inn would have been known to Dickens, whose home in Doughty Street from 1837 to 1839 is only a short distance away.

3. *the fields at the back of the Foundling Hospital*: The Foundling Hospital was established in 1741 by Captain Thomas Coram for illegitimate children. In 1745, it moved to a new site on land north of Lamb's Conduit Street, not far from Doughty Street, where Dickens lived. (It was demolished in 1926.)

CHAPTER THE THIRTY-NINTH

1. *seven-shilling piece*: In fact the seven-shilling piece only began to be issued in 1797.

2. *Saint James's Chronicle . . . Public Advertiser*: All of these were current newspapers at the time of the Riots, except the *Herald*, which first appeared in November 1780.

3. *The Thunderer*: Contemporary pamphlet by C. Thompson, which is reprinted in Thomas Vincent (William Holcroft), *A Plain and Succinct Narrative of the Late Riots and Disturbances* (Fielding and Walker, 1780), one of Dickens's major sources. There is a contemporary engraving of the riots reproduced in J. P. de Castro, *The Gordon Riots* (London: Oxford University Press, 1926), facing p. 92, with a bystander holding a copy of *The Thunderer*.

4. *Old Bailey*: The Central Criminal Court, first built beside Newgate prison in 1539 and replaced in 1774.

CHAPTER THE FORTIETH

1. *Saint Dunstan's giants*: The Fire of London had stopped just short of the Church of St Dunstan in the West, Fleet Street, and in gratitude the parishioners erected a clock with two giants that struck a bell every

fifteen minutes. It was a famous London landmark which also appears in Goldsmith's *The Vicar of Wakefield* (1766) and Scott's *The Fortunes of Nigel* (1822). (The church was demolished in 1830.)

2. *Insolvent Act*: The Insolvent Debtors Act allowed those imprisoned for debt to apply for release by stating all their debts and liabilities and surrendering their property. Dickens's father, John Dickens, applied for release from the Marshalsea Prison in 1824 under this act.

3. *Bruin*: The bear in the fable of Reynard the Fox, hence a boor.

4. *Mr Chester*: In fact, Sir John.

5. *Saville*: Sir George Savile (1726–84), eighth baronet, introduced the bill for Catholic relief to the House of Commons and was 'a likable and uncontroversial member, who had so far had nothing to do with Catholic relief' (Christopher Hibbert, *King Mob* (London: Longman, 1958), p. 18). Dickens misspells his name here and in chs. 56 and 73.

CHAPTER THE FORTY-FIRST

1. *still small voice*: The voice of God, as heard by Elijah in 1 Kings 19:12.

2. *Royal East-London Volunteers*: An imaginary company, although militia regiments played a important role in the suppression of the Riots. See Tony Hayter, *The Army and the Crowd in Mid-Georgian England* (London: Macmillan, 1978), pp. 151–3.

3. *Blue Beard*: In the fairy-story, first recorded by Charles Perrault in 1697, the wealthy Blue Beard gives his seventh bride the keys to all the rooms in the castle except one, which she is forbidden to enter. When she does so, she discovers the corpses of his previous wives. A favourite story of Dickens, it appears in many of his novels.

4. *Inquisition*: Founded by Pope Innocent III in the thirteenth century, the Inquisition was charged with investigating, suppressing and punishing heresy and heretics. For many Protestants, its name was synonymous with torture and cruelty.

5. *counterfeit presentment*: *Hamlet* III.iv.54.

6. *found in*: Provided with tea and sugar by her employer.

CHAPTER THE FORTY-SECOND

1. *Chelsea Bun-house*: Famous cake shop in Jew's Row (Pimlico Road), Chelsea, with many celebrated customers, including Jonathan Swift and several members of the royal family. (It was demolished in 1839.)

CHAPTER THE FORTY-THIRD

1. *Westminster Hall*: Built in 1097, it was the location of the chief courts of England from the thirteenth century until 1825. The late fourteenth-century oak hammer-beam roof has the widest unsupported span in the country. (It is now the vestibule of the House of Commons.)

2. *Saint Omer's*: Jesuit College, founded in 1592 in St Omer in north-eastern France.

3. *Great Protestant petition*: The petition begged Parliament to repeal the Catholic Relief Act of 1778, which had removed some forms of legal discrimination against Catholics. It was claimed to have more than 100,000 signatures.

4. *these hard laws*: See Appendix VI.

CHAPTER THE FORTY-FOURTH

1. *My stars and halters*: Dennis's variation on the mild oath or expletive 'My stars and garters'.

CHAPTER THE FORTY-FIFTH

1. *a citizen of the world*: 'If a man be gracious and courteous to strangers, it shows he is a citizen of the world', Francis Bacon, 'Of Goodness, and Goodness of Nature', *Essays* (1625). It is also the title of Oliver Goldsmith's *The Citizen of the World, or, Letters from a Chinese Philosopher* (1762).

2. *for we are . . . almost divine*: These lines are added to the manuscript in small letters above the line. The Pilgrim editors suggest that they were added in response to a letter protesting against his treatment of Stagg. Dickens wrote in reply:

My intention in the management of this inferior and subordinate character, was to remind the World who have eyes, that they have no *right* to expect in sightless men a degree of virtue and goodness to which they, in full possession of all their senses, can lay no claim – that it is a very easy thing for those who misuse every gift of Heaven to consider resignation and cheerfulness the duty of those whom it has deprived of some great blessing – that whereas we look upon a blind man who does wrong, as a kind of monster, we ought in Truth and Justice to remember that a man who has eyes and is a vicious wretch, is by his very abuse of the glorious faculty of sight, an immeasurably greater offender than his afflicted fellow. (Pilgrim, 2, pp. 336–7)

The Pilgrim editors describe this as a 'disingenuous' defence and add that Dickens's treatment of Stagg changes from this point in the novel, probably in response to the protest.

CHAPTER THE FORTY-SIXTH

1. *seven senses*: The senses are usually thought of as five – sight, hearing, touch, smell, taste – but were sometimes brought up to the more symbolic and mystical seven by adding speech and animation.
2. *Six guineas*: A guinea was worth £1 1 shilling (£1.05).

CHAPTER THE FORTY-SEVENTH

1. *the cage, the stocks, and the whipping-post*: Forms of punishment for vagrancy and other offences.
2. *fear and trembling*: A phrase that appears several times in the Bible, notably 2 Corinthians 7:15, Ephesians 6:5; Philippians 2:12.
3. *John Bull*: A typical Englishman, after Dr John Arbuthnot's *The History of John Bull* (1712).
4. *second of June*: Dickens has made a mistake here, as was pointed out to him by the Revd. G. W. Brameld (Pilgrim, 2, p. 401n). Barnaby and his mother were discovered by Stagg 'in June' and have been travelling for a week.
5. *Westminster Bridge*: The second masonry bridge over the Thames, opened in November 1750 and replaced in 1862.

CHAPTER THE FORTY-EIGHTH

1. *Middlesex to the Surrey shore*: From the north to the south banks of the Thames.
2. *Saint George's Fields*: Undrained tract of land on the south bank of the Thames, between Westminster and Blackfriars bridges.
3. *a roaring lion, going about and seeking whom he may devour*: 'your adversary the devil, as a roaring lion, walketh about, seeking whom he may devour' (1 Peter 5:8).

CHAPTER THE FORTY-NINTH

1. *a boy at a breaking-up*: A schoolboy at the end of term.

2. *The strangers' gallery*: Of the House of Commons, to which members of the public were admitted.

3. *General Conway*: Henry Seymour Conway (1721–95), nephew of Sir Robert Walpole, later a Field Marshal and Commander-in-Chief. He had a varied and distinguished military and political career and was at this point MP for Bury St Edmunds.

4. *Colonel Gordon*: Lord Adam Gordon (1726?–1801), son of Alexander, second Duke of Gordon. MP for Kincardineshire, later general and commander of forces in Scotland, and Lord George Gordon's uncle.

5. *The Riot Act*: (1715) made it illegal to remain in a particular area after one hour following the proclamation of the Riot Act by a magistrate. The law was difficult to enforce, and caused considerable confusion, and 'a great deal of damage was done in the statutory hour on many occasions during the 1780 riots, because the authorities believed themselves unable to interfere' (Hayter, *The Army and the Crowd in Mid-Georgian England*, p. 10).

CHAPTER THE FIFTIETH

1. *Duke Street ... and in Warwick Street Golden Square*: The chapel of St Anselm and St Cecilia, used by the Sardinian ambassador and a resort of Roman Catholic nobility and gentry, was in Duke Street, off Lincoln's Inn Fields. The chapel of the Bavarian ambassador was in Warwick Street, Golden Square, Soho.

CHAPTER THE FIFTY-FIRST

1. *Tower Stairs*: Landing-place at the foot of Tower Hill, leading down to the Thames.

CHAPTER THE FIFTY-SECOND

1. *Moorfields ... a rich chapel*: One of the poorest districts in London, just east of the slum quarter of St Giles, with a large Irish population. The chapel was in Ropemaker's Alley.

2. *pioneers upon a field-day*: Soldiers who prepare the ground and dig trenches for the main body of an army on the day of a military exercise or review.

CHAPTER THE FIFTY-THIRD

1. *the King's birth-day*: King George III's birthday was on 5 June (24 May, old style).

2. *demolishing those chapels on Saturday night*: A mistake. The chapels were demolished on Friday night. Dickens has already said 'All day, Saturday, they remained quiet' (ch. 52).

3. *East Smithfield*: Area east of the Tower of London.

CHAPTER THE FIFTY-FOURTH

1. *a monstrous carbuncle in a fairy tale*: It is not clear if Dickens is referring to a particular fairy-tale here. Carbuncles, which are precious stones of a red or fiery colour, appear in a number of tales, of which the best-known is probably 'The Fisherman and his Wife' collected by the Brothers Grimm. Nathaniel Hawthorne in 'The Great Carbuncle: A Mystery of the White Mountains' (*Twice Told Tales*, 1837) tells the story of a search for the great carbuncle, a 'wondrous gem' which 'gleams like a meteor'.

CHAPTER THE FIFTY-FIFTH

1. *the candles ... made long winding-sheets*: Solidified grease on the side of a candle, thought to resemble long folded sheets and to be an omen of death.

CHAPTER THE FIFTY-SIXTH

1. *Clare Market ... Sir George Saville's house in Leicester Fields*: Clare Market was established in the seventeenth century on land close to Lincoln's Inn Fields. Savile House stood on the west side of Leicester House, in Leicester Square (See also note 5 to ch. 40.)

CHAPTER THE FIFTY-SEVENTH

1. *whispering secrets to the earth and burying them*: Midas, the legendary king of Phrygia, had ass's ears bestowed upon him by Apollo, whom he had offended. He hid them with his head-dress, but his barber learned of them and found relief from the burden of the secret by whispering it into a hole in the ground. The reeds which grew over the hole whispered

the secret whenever the wind blew over them. The tale is told in Ovid's *Metamorphoses* 11, 153ff. In later editions, Dickens makes the reference more explicit, by adding the phrase 'Midas-like'.

CHAPTER THE FIFTY-EIGHTH

1. *Sir John Fielding*: Blind half-brother (1721–80) of Henry Fielding the novelist, whom he succeeded as Chief Magistrate at No. 4, Bow Street, his office and court, in 1754. He continued in office until his death and was responsible for a number of reforms in policing, including the creation of the original Bow Street Runners and the use of foot patrols on the main roads out of London.

2. *he built on sand*: Matthew 7:26.

CHAPTER THE SIXTIETH

1. *Farringdon Street*: Formed in 1737 when the Fleet River was covered over and a meat and vegetable market was established on the site with two rows of one-storey shops. It was cleared 1826–30.

CHAPTER THE SIXTY-FIRST

1. *Mile-end*: Area in the East End, one mile beyond the City of London boundary.

2. *Mansion House*: The official residence of the Lord Mayor of London, built in 1739–52. The Lord Mayor is chief magistrate of the City.

3. *Lord Mayor*: Alderman Brackley Kennet (died 1783), a former brothel-keeper, made little serious effort to contain the riots.

4. *Langdale*: Thomas Langdale (1714–90), a prominent Catholic distiller. His premises in Holborn were next to Barnard's Inn and contained 120,000 gallons of spirits. According to the *Public Advertiser* of 20 June 1780: 'For several days after the fire at Mr. Langdale's the Pump at Barnard's Inn yielded nothing but spirits' (de Castro, *The Gordon Riots*, p. 134). See also note 1 to ch. 73.

5. *thief-takers*: Sir John Fielding employed seven thief-takers, the original Bow Street Runners, who formed one of the first organized bodies to undertake the detection and arrest of criminals.

CHAPTER THE SIXTY-SECOND

1. *a man again*: *Macbeth* III.iv.107.

CHAPTER THE SIXTY-THIRD

1. *the Commander-in-Chief* Jeffrey, Baron Amherst (1717–97), former governor of Virginia and commander-in-chief, 1778–92.
2. *Houndsditch*: Poor area in the East End of London, with substantial Jewish population (as had Whitechapel).
3. *the Pope of Babylon*: Revelation 17. As Dennis Walder points out, Miggs 'cannot bring herself to use the word "Whore"' (*Dickens and Religion* (London: Allen and Unwin, 1981), p. 100).

CHAPTER THE SIXTY-FOURTH

1. *Mr Akerman*: Richard Akerman (1722–92), keeper of Newgate, 1754–92, and a friend of James Boswell.
2. *St Sepulchre's*: The Church of the Holy Sepulchre without Newgate was founded in 1137 and largely rebuilt after the Great Fire of London. At the junction of Snow Hill and Holborn, it stood opposite Newgate prison and its bell marked the time of impending executions. Death carts would stop outside St Sepulchre's while the prisoners were presented with a nosegay.

CHAPTER THE SIXTY-FIFTH

1. *a Lucifer among the devils*: Satan, the Devil. See Isaiah 14:12.
2. *the good old laws on the good old plan*: Cf. Dickens's song 'The Fine Old English Gentleman, to be said or sung at all Conservative Dinners': 'The good old laws were garnished well with gibbets, whips and chains, / With fine old English penalties and fine old English pains' (published in *Examiner*, 7 August 1841; John Forster, *Life of Charles Dickens*, ed. A. J. Hoppé (London: Dent, 1966), Vol. 1, pp. 163–5).
3. *Sessions House*: Built in 1534 beside Newgate prison and replaced in 1774, it was the main location for criminal trials in London.
4. *a face go by*: Dickens may have spoken to eyewitnesses of the riots. His paternal grandmother, for example, was in service with the Crewe family, whose London house from 1777 was at 18, Grosvenor Street (see note 2 to ch. 67), an area where, as Dickens points out, many houses were barricaded and had soldiers to defend them. Michael Allen,

'The Dickens/Crewe Connection', *Dickens Quarterly* 5:4 (December 1988), 175–86, explores this connection further.

CHAPTER THE SIXTY-SIXTH

1. *Secretary of State*: David Murray (1727–96), seventh Viscount Stormont, Secretary of State for the Southern Division who himself had been roughly handled by the mob and pelted with mud on 2 June.

2. *myrmidons of justice*: Originally the loyal followers of Achilles in Homer's *Iliad*; by this time it was a common phrase to mean agents or hired ruffians. Byron refers to 'Bow-street myrmidons' in *English Bards and Scotch Reviewers* (1809), and Dickens also uses the phrase in *Great Expectations*, ch. 12.

3. *took ... a large quantity of blood*: It was customary until well into the nineteenth century to 'bleed' certain categories of patients, removing blood either through cupping or with leeches.

4. *Lord Mansfield's house in Bloomsbury square*: William Murray (1705–93), first Earl of Mansfield, Lord Chief Justice, 1756–88, called by Macaulay 'the father of modern Toryism'. His house was on the east side of Bloomsbury Square, a fashionable location in West London, laid out in the early 1660s (it was destroyed in the Riots).

5. *Caen Wood*: Now known as Kenwood House; originally built *c.* 1616 but extensively remodelled by Robert Adam in 1764, it was Lord Mansfield's country house from 1754.

6. *canary birds*: This occurred at the house of Mr Malo, a merchant of Irish extraction in Moorfields. See Hibbert, *King Mob*, pp. 57–61 and de Castro, *The Gordon Riots*, p. 77.

7. *the New Jail at Clerkenwell*: Built in 1775 to relieve Newgate, the New Jail or House of Correction – more usually known as the New Prison – was rebuilt in 1845–6.

CHAPTER THE SIXTY-SEVENTH

1. *Lord President's in Piccadilly, at Lambeth Palace, at the Lord Chancellor's in Great Ormond Street, in the Royal Exchange, the Bank*: The Lord President of the Council was Henry, second Earl Bathurst (1714–94), and Piccadilly one of the most fashionable addresses in London. Lambeth Palace was the official residence of the Archbishop of Canterbury, which the rioters surrounded but failed to enter. The Lord Chancellor was Edward, first Baron Thurlow (1731–1806), whose 'political principles were merely a high view of royal prerogative and an aversion to change' (*Concise Dictionary of National Biography* (Oxford: Oxford University Press, 1992), p. 2979). He lived at No. 45, Great

Ormond Street, the location of a number of fine late-seventeenth- and eighteenth-century houses (Lord Thurlow's house still stands). The Royal Exchange in Cornhill dates from 1567 and was rebuilt after the Great Fire and again in 1844; it was a trading centre and meeting-place for City merchants as well as the home of the insurance market Lloyds of London. The Bank of England was founded in 1694 and the first bank on the present site in Threadneedle Street was built in 1734; a detachment of the Brigade of Guards was sent to guard the Bank, a custom continued every night until 1973.

2. *Lord Rockingham's in Grosvenor Square*: Charles Watson-Wentworth (1730–82), second Marquis of Rockingham, prime minister 1765–6 and 1782. From 1768 to 1781, Leader of the Opposition in the House of Lords. His house was on the east side of Grosvenor Square, near Hyde Park and a fashionable and grand address.

3. *King's Bench and Fleet Prisons*: The King's Bench prison, medieval in origin, moved to St George's Fields in Southwark, south-east London in 1755–8. It was burned down during the Gordon Riots, rebuilt and finally demolished in 1880. Many debtors were imprisoned there, including Mr Micawber in *David Copperfield*. The Fleet prison was also medieval in origin and a notoriously squalid and violent place. It was burnt down in the Riots, rebuilt 1781–2 and closed in 1842. Mr Pickwick is imprisoned in the Fleet in *Pickwick Papers*.

4. *the Arsenal at Woolwich, and the Royal Palaces*: The Arsenal, Woolwich, south-east London, was the centre for the manufacture and storing of arms and military ordnance. St James's Palace, built by Henry VIII, was at this point the principal royal residence in London, and Buckingham House ('the queen's palace'), St James's Park, was the early-eighteenth-century predecessor of Buckingham Palace.

5. *the privy council*: Originally, the British sovereign's private council, but by this period a mainly formal body.

6. *the queen's palace*: Buckingham House was bought by George III in 1762. In 1775, its ownership was transferred to Queen Charlotte, in exchange for Somerset House, and so was known as the Queen's Palace.

7. *the Temple, and the other Inns*: The Inns of Court and the Inns of Chancery were medieval foundations whose main function has been to provide lodgings and training for lawyers. There are four Inns of Court: Lincoln's Inn, Gray's Inn, Inner Temple and Middle Temple. There were a number of Inns of Chancery close to Holborn and the Strand, including Barnard's Inn, Clement's Inn, Clifford's Inn and Furnival's Inn, similar in function to the Inns of Court but unable to call students to the Bar. They increasingly became social clubs for lawyers and declined rapidly in the nineteenth century.

8. *Lord Algernon Percy*: (1750–1830), second son of the second Duke of Northumberland and Commander of the Northumberland militia; his

men were praised for their refusal to be provoked by the mob. See
Hayter, *The Army and the Crowd in Mid-Georgian England*, p. 183.

9. *the different companies*: The City Livery Companies are craft guilds
of medieval origin, which are incorporated by Royal Charter, and
formerly controlled conditions of employment and trade, as well as
electing the Lord Mayor and sheriffs.

10. *the Borough Clink in Tooley-street*: Small prison in Southwark,
south London, burned down by the rioters and never rebuilt.

11. *St Mildred's church*: In Poultry, in the City of London, rebuilt by
Sir Christopher Wren following the Great Fire and demolished in 1872.

12. *Holborn Bridge*: One of the five bridges spanning the Fleet River.

13. *a charmed life*: *Macbeth* V.x.12.

CHAPTER THE SIXTY-EIGHTH

1. *Finchley*: Village in Middlesex, now a London suburb, which was a
retreat for the wealthy in the eighteenth century, but also a notorious
haunt of highwaymen.

2. *drank until they died*: Gager suggests that there is a parallel here
with Shakespeare's *Measure for Measure* I.ii.120–22 (*Shakespeare and
Dickens*, p. 333).

CHAPTER THE SEVENTIETH

1. *Wenis*: Venus, the Roman goddess of love.

2. *deaf as any adder*: 'They are as venomous as the poison of a serpent:
even like the deaf adder that stoppeth her ears' (Psalm 58:4).

3. *a convenient piece of water in its midst*: 'When the square was laid
out and paved in 1727, it had a central "basin" of water' (Hill).

CHAPTER THE SEVENTY-FIRST

1. *potter's wessel*: 'They shall dash them in pieces like a potter's vessel'
(Psalm 2:9).

2. *whitening and suppulchres*: 'Ye are like unto whited sepulchres, which
indeed appear beautiful outward, but are within full of dead men's
bones, and of all uncleanness' (Matthew 23:27).

3. *his legs ... crushed into shapeless ugliness*: Dickens may have been
influenced in his description of Sim's fate by a passage in Charles Lamb's
'A Complaint of the Decay of Beggars', in *Essays of Elia* (1823):

These dim eyes have in vain explored for some months past a well-known figure, or part of the figure, of a man, who used to glide his comely upper half over the pavements of London, wheeling along with most ingenious celerity upon a machine of wood; a spectacle to natives, to foreigners, and to children . . . Few but must have noticed him; for the accident, which brought him low, took place during the riots of 1780, and he has been a groundling so long.

See Grahame Smith, *Charles Dickens: A Literary Life* (London: Macmillan, 1996), pp. 68–9.

CHAPTER THE SEVENTY-SECOND

1. *the defence of the Savannah*: In the autumn of 1779, in the American War of Independence, British troops were unsuccessfully besieged by French and American troops at Savannah, Georgia.

CHAPTER THE SEVENTY-THIRD

1. *one hundred and twenty-five thousand pounds*: Probably an underestimate, as was pointed out to Dickens by the Revd. G. W. Brameld (see Pilgrim, 2, p. 401). The loss of Langdale's house and distillery was estimated at £50,000, and a further seventy houses and four prisons were also destroyed.
2. *Mr Herbert*: Henry Herbert (1741–1811), later first Earl of Carnarvon.
3. *Monday se'ennight*: Monday the week after: 19 June.
4. *one good deed in a murky life of guilt*: Cf. 'So shines a good deed in a naughty world' (*Merchant of Venice* V. i. 91).
5. *I will love and cherish*: 'To love, cherish, and to obey' from the Marriage Service in the *Book of Common Prayer*.
6. *death would have been his portion*: Dickens is here drawing on contemporary accounts of Kennet's words (Hibbert, *King Mob*, p. 129).

CHAPTER THE SEVENTY-FOURTH

1. *'I was formed for society'*: 'Man was formed for society', Sir William Blackstone, introduction to *Commentaries on the Laws of England* (1765–9).
2. *cut off in your flower*: 'Man that is born of woman is of few days, and full of trouble. He cometh forth like a flower, and is cut down' (Job 14:1–2).

CHAPTER THE SEVENTY-FIFTH

1. *Surgeons' Hall*: In the Old Bailey, where bodies of murderers were dissected after their execution.
2. *worldly wisdom*: 1 Corinthians 3:19.

CHAPTER THE SEVENTY-SEVENTH

1. *Service for the Dead*: From the *Book of Common Prayer*.

CHAPTER THE SEVENTY-NINTH

1. *gall and wormwood*: 'Remembering mine affliction and my misery, the wormwood and the gall' (Lamentations 3:19).
2. *Prince of Wales*: Prince George (1762–1830), later King George IV.

CHAPTER THE EIGHTIETH

1. *milk of human kindness*: 'Yet do I fear thy nature; / It is too full o' th' milk of human kindness' (*Macbeth* I.v.13–14).
2. *bank-note*: The smallest banknote current at this time was for £10. It is difficult to give a value in contemporary terms, but multiplication by a factor of 70 gives a rough approximation.

CHAPTER THE LAST

1. *Archbishop of Canterbury*: John Moore (1730–1805), Archbishop of Canterbury, 1783–1805, excommunicated Gordon from the Church of England in 1786 for refusing to appear in an Ecclesiastical court as a witness.
2. *Ten or a dozen years ago*: In fact, the death of Robert Watson, who claimed to be Gordon's secretary at the time of the Riots, was reported in *The Times* of 22 November 1838. According to *The Times*, Watson, aged 88, had committed suicide and nineteen wounds were discovered on the body. On Watson's relationship with Gordon, see de Castro, *The Gordon Riots*, pp. 225–9, and Pilgrim, 2, p. 295nn.
3. *Millbank*: The north bank of the Thames between Westminster and Chelsea. Dickens describes it in ch. 47 of *David Copperfield* as 'a melancholy waste'.

4. *moved or grew, or had its being*: 'For in him we live, and move, and have our being' (Acts 17:28).

5. *the vulgar tongue*: 'It is expedient that Baptism be ministered in the vulgar tongue', from the service for the Publick Baptism of Infants in the *Book of Common Prayer*.

PENGUIN (◊) CLASSICS

The Classics Publisher

'Penguin Classics, one of the world's greatest series' JOHN KEEGAN

'I have never been disappointed with the Penguin Classics. All I have read is a model of academic seriousness and provides the essential information to fully enjoy the master works that appear in its catalogue' MARIO VARGAS LLOSA

'Penguin and Classics are words that go together like horse and carriage or Mercedes and Benz. When I was a university teacher I always prescribed Penguin editions of classic novels for my courses: they have the best introductions, the most reliable notes, and the most carefully edited texts' DAVID LODGE

'Growing up in Bombay, expensive hardback books were beyond my means, but I could indulge my passion for reading at the roadside bookstalls that were well stocked with all the Penguin paperbacks ... Sometimes I would choose a book just because I was attracted by the cover, but so reliable was the Penguin imprimatur that I was never once disappointed by the contents.

Such access certainly broadened the scope of my reading, and perhaps it's no coincidence that so many Merchant Ivory films have been adapted from great novels, or that those novels are published by Penguin' ISMAIL MERCHANT

'You can't write, read, or live fully in the present without knowing the literature of the past. Penguin Classics opens the door to a treasure house of pure pleasure, books that have never been bettered, which are read again and again with increased delight' JOHN MORTIMER

CLICK ON A CLASSIC
www.penguinclassics.com
The world's greatest literature at your fingertips

Constantly updated information on over 1600 titles, from
Icelandic sagas to ancient Indian epics, Russian drama to
Italian romance, American greats to African masterpieces

●

The latest news on recent additions to the list, updated
editions and specially commissioned translations

●

Original scholarly essays by leading writers: Elaine Showalter
on Zola, Laurie R. King on Arthur Conan Doyle, Frank
Kermode on Shakespeare, Lisa Appignanesi on Tolstoy

●

A wealth of background material, including biographies
of every classic author from Aristotle to Zamyatin, plot
synopses, readers' and teachers' guides, useful web links

●

Online desk and examination copy assistance for academics

●

Trivia quizzes, competitions, giveaways, news on
forthcoming screen adaptations

●

eBooks available to download

READ MORE IN PENGUIN

In every corner of the world, on every subject under the sun, Penguin represents quality and variety – the very best in publishing today.

For complete information about books available from Penguin – including Puffins and Penguin Classics – and how to order them, write to us at the appropriate address below. Please note that for copyright reasons the selection of books varies from country to country.

In the United Kingdom: *Please write to* Dept EP, Penguin Books Ltd, Bath Road, Harmondsworth, West Drayton, Middlesex UB7 0DA

In the United States: *Please write to* Consumer Services, Penguin Putnam Inc., 405 Murray Hill Parkway, East Rutherford, New Jersey 07073-2136. *VISA and MasterCard holders call 1-800-631-8571 to order Penguin titles*

In Canada: *Please write to* Penguin Books Canada Ltd, 10 Alcorn Avenue, Suite 300, Toronto, Ontario M4V 3B2

In Australia: *Please write to* Penguin Books Australia Ltd, 487 Maroondah Highway, Ringwood, Victoria 3134

In New Zealand: *Please write to* Penguin Books (NZ) Ltd, Private Bag 102902, North Shore Mail Centre, Auckland 10

In India: *Please write to* Penguin Books India Pvt Ltd, 11, Community Centre, Panchsheel Park, New Delhi 110017

In the Netherlands: *Please write to* Penguin Books Netherlands bv, Postbus 3507, NL-1001 AH Amsterdam

In Germany: *Please write to* Penguin Books Deutschland GmbH, Metzlerstrasse 26, 60594 Frankfurt am Main

In Spain: *Please write to* Penguin Books S. A., Bravo Murillo 19, 1°B, 28015 Madrid

In Italy: *Please write to* Penguin Italia s.r.l., Via Vittoria Emanuele 45 1a, 20094 Corsico, Milano

In France: *Please write to* Penguin France, 12, Rue Prosper Ferradou, 31700 Blagnac

In Japan: *Please write to* Penguin Books Japan Ltd, Iidabashi KM-Bldg, 2-23-9 Koraku, Bunkyo-Ku, Tokyo 112-0004

In South Africa: *Please write to* Penguin Books South Africa (Pty) Ltd, P.O. Box 751093, Gardenview, 2047 Johannesburg

CHARLES DICKENS
Great Expectations

*'It was now too late and too far to go back, and
I went on. And the mists had all solemnly risen
now, and the world lay spread before me'*

A terrifying encounter with an escaped convict in a graveyard
on the wild Kent marshes; a summons to meet the bitter, decaying Miss Havisham and her beautiful, cold-hearted ward
Estella; the sudden generosity of a mysterious benefactor – these
form a series of events that changes the orphaned Pip's life forever, and he eagerly abandons his humble origins to begin a new
life as a gentleman. Dickens's haunting late novel depicts Pip's
education and development through adversity as he discovers
the true nature of his 'great expectations'.

This definitive edition uses the text from the first published
edition of 1861. It includes a map of Kent in the early nineteenth
century, and appendices on Dickens's original ending and his
working notes, giving readers an illuminating glimpse into the
mind of a great novelist at work.

Edited and with notes by CHARLOTTE MITCHELL
With an introduction by DAVID TROTTER

GEORGE ELIOT
Silas Marner

'God gave her to me because you turned your
back upon her, and He looks upon her as mine:
you've no right to her!'

Wrongly accused of theft and exiled from a religious community many years before, the embittered weaver Silas Marner
lives alone in Raveloe, living only for work and his precious
hoard of money. But when his money is stolen and an orphaned
child finds her way into his house, Silas is given the chance to
transform his life. His fate, and that of the little girl he adopts,
is entwined with Godfrey Cass, son of the village Squire, who,
like Silas, is trapped by his past. *Silas Marner*, George Eliot's
favourite of her novels, combines humour, rich symbolism
and pointed social criticism to create an unsentimental but
affectionate portrait of rural life.

The text uses the Cabinet edition, revised by George Eliot in
1878. David Carroll's introduction is accompanied by the
original Penguin Classics introduction by Q. D. Leavis.

Edited with an introduction by DAVID CARROLL

WILKIE COLLINS
The Woman in White

'In one moment, every drop of blood in my body was brought to a stop ... There, as if it had that moment sprung out of the earth ... stood the figure of a solitary Woman, dressed from head to foot in white'

The Woman in White famously opens with Walter Hartright's eerie encounter on a moonlit London road. Engaged as a drawing master to the beautiful Laura Fairlie, Walter is drawn into the sinister intrigues of Sir Percival Glyde and his 'charming' friend Count Fosco, who has a taste for white mice, vanilla bonbons and poison. Pursuing questions of identity and insanity along the paths and corridors of English country houses and the madhouse, *The Woman in White* is the first and most influential of the Victorian genre that combined Gothic horror with psychological realism.

Matthew Sweet's introduction explores the phenomenon of Victorian 'sensation' fiction, and discusses Wilkie Collins's biographical and societal influences. Included in this edition are appendices on theatrical adaptations of the novel and its serialization history.

Edited with an introduction and notes by MATTHEW SWEET

ANTHONY TROLLOPE

Phineas Redux

'He had given up everything in the world
with the view of getting into office; and now
that the opportunity had come ... the prize
was to elude his grasp!'

Phineas Finn is living quietly in Dublin, resigned to the fact that his political career is over and coming to terms with the death of his wife, when he receives an unexpected invitation to return to Parliament. He jumps at the chance and old romances and rivalries are revived. When his adversary Mr Bonteen is murdered suspicion immediately falls on Finn, and even the friends and lovers who formerly advanced him seem only to add to his shame. The fourth novel in the Palliser series, *Phineas Redux* stands alone as a compelling work of political intrigue, personal crisis and romantic jealousy.

In his introduction, Gregg A. Hecimovich relates the political and historical background of the time to the Phineas novels. This edition also contains a detailed chronology, further reading and notes.

'We have come to believe that his style of writing was certainly the best (and probably the only) way of constructing a political novel' ROY HATTERSLEY, *Guardian*

Edited with an introduction and notes by
GREGG A. HECIMOVICH

ELIZABETH GASKELL

North and South

*'How am I to dress up in my finery, and go off
and away to smart parties, after the sorrow I
have seen today?'*

When her father leaves the Church in a crisis of conscience, Margaret Hale is uprooted from her comfortable home in Hampshire to move with her family to the north of England. Initially repulsed by the ugliness of her new surroundings in the industrial town of Milton, Margaret becomes aware of the poverty and suffering of the local mill-workers and develops a passionate sense of social justice. This is intensified by her tempestuous relationship with the mill-owner and self-made man John Thornton, as their fierce opposition over his treatment of his employees masks a deeper attraction. In *North and South*, Elizabeth Gaskell skillfully fused individual feeling with social concern, and in Margaret Hale created one of the most original heroines of Victorian literature.

In her introduction, Patricia Ingham examines geographical, economic and class differences, and male and female roles in *North and South*. This edition also includes a list for further reading, notes and a glossary.

'[An] admirable story ... full of character and power'
CHARLES DICKENS

Edited with an introduction by PATRICIA INGHAM